A TAPESTRY OF BRONZE NOVEL

Titles in the Tapestry of Bronze series:

JOCASTA:
THE MOTHER-WIFE OF OEDIPUS

NIOBE AND PELOPS:
CHILDREN OF TANTALUS

NIOBE AND AMPHION:
THE ROAD TO THEBES

NIOBE AND CHLORIS:
ARROWS OF ARTEMIS

ANTIGONE AND CREON:
GUARDIANS OF THEBES

CLYTEMNESTRA:
THE MOTHER'S BLADE

Learn more about the Tapestry of Bronze series at

www.tapestryofbronze.com

NIOBE AND CHLORIS:
ARROWS OF ARTEMIS

VICTORIA GROSSACK
AND
ALICE UNDERWOOD

This book is a work of fiction. Names, characters, places, and incidents either are the product of the authors' imagination or are used fictitiously. Any resemblance to actual events or locales or persons, living or dead, is entirely coincidental.

NIOBE AND CHLORIS: ARROWS OF ARTEMIS

MAPS

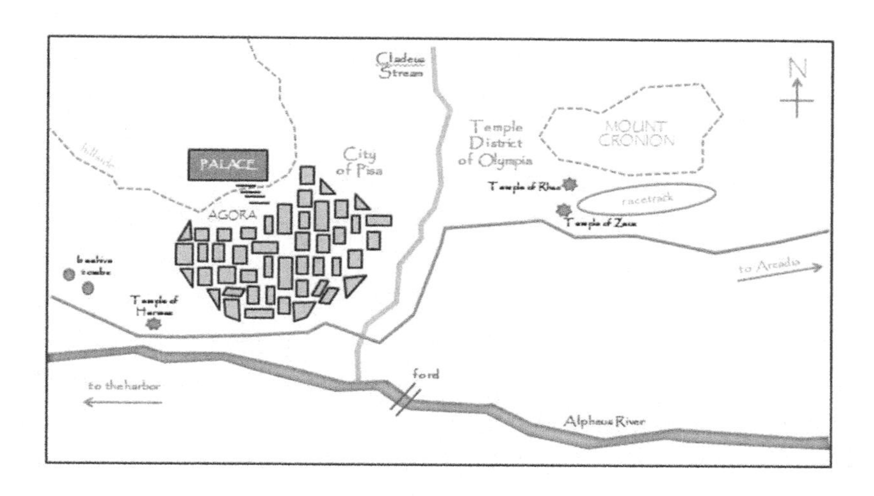
Cladeus
Stream
N
Temple
District
of Olympia
MOUNT
CRONION
PALACE
City
of Pisa
racetrack
AGORA
to Arcadia
ford
to the harbor
Alphaus River

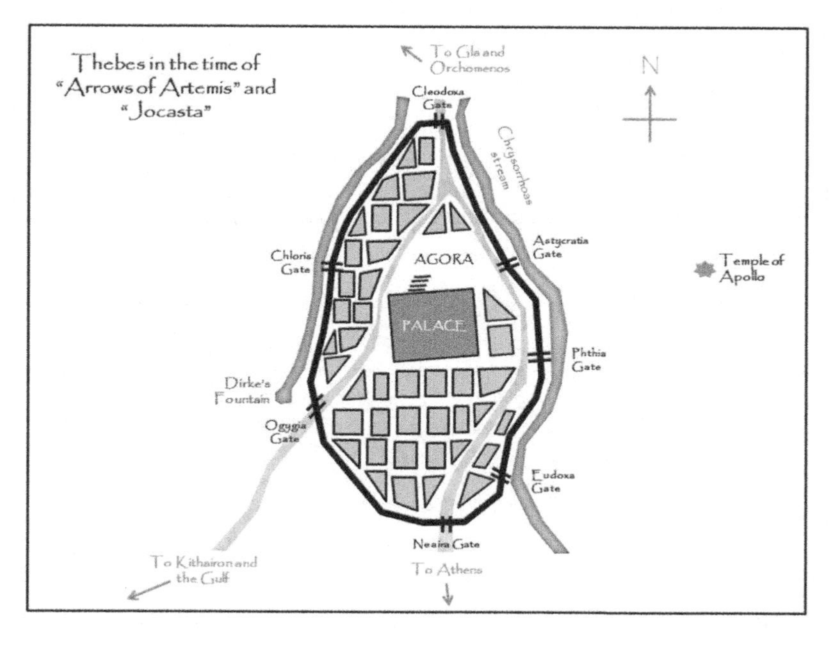
Thebes in the time of
"Arrows of Artemis" and
"Jocasta"
To Gla and
Orchomenos
N
Cleodoxa
Gate
Chrysorrhoas
stream
Astycratia
Gate
Temple of
Apollo
Chloris
Gate
AGORA
PALACE
Phthia
Gate
Dirke's
Fountain
Ogygia
Gate
Eudoxa
Gate
Neaira Gate
To Kithairon and
the Gulf
To Athens

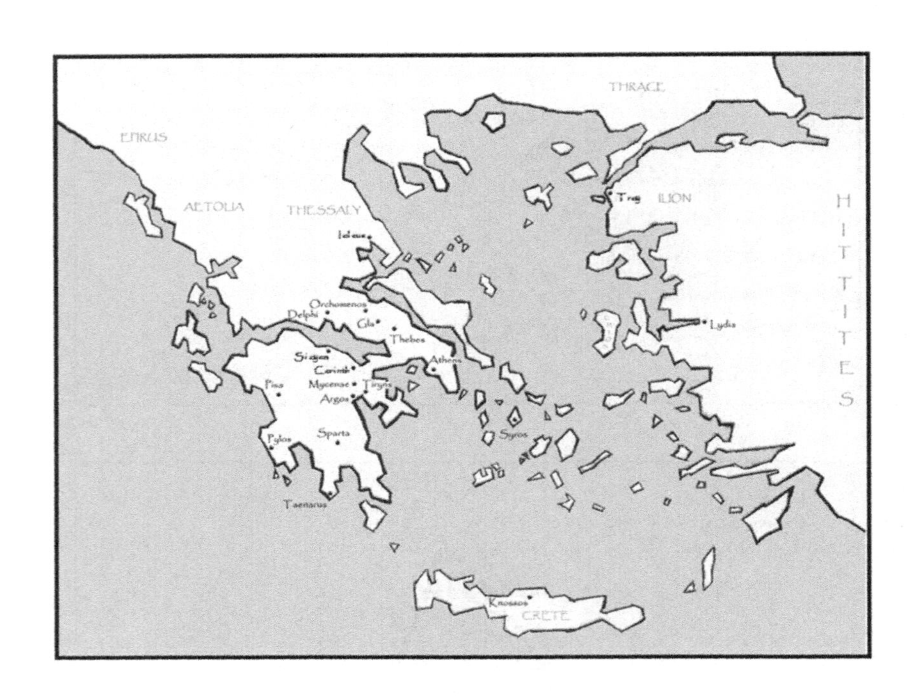
THRACE
EPIRUS
AETOLIA
THESSALY
Iolcus
Troy
ILION
HITTITES
Orchomenos
Delphi
Gla
Thebes
Sicyon
Corinth
Athens
Pisa
Mycenae
Tiryns
Argos
Lydia
Pylos
Sparta
Syros
Taenarus
Knossos
CRETE

ONE: MORTAL THREADS

§ 1.01

Chloris ran down the hallway, her bare feet slapping against the stone floor-tiles. Dodging a servant polishing the bronze wall-sconces, she turned into the corridor and darted up the stairs to the weaving room.

The door stood open; inside, well-born ladies gossiped as they worked the tall looms, their voices raised to carry over the rhythmic clatter of the warp-weights. In one corner, maidservants carded wool; nearby, Chloris' grandmother and aunt sewed golden spangles onto the flounces of a new skirt.

The queen looked up from her seat by the wide window. "Chloris! Where have you been?"

"In the kitchen, Mama," she said, staring at her mother's chest. Unfortunately Mama dressed in the style of her faraway Eastern homeland: she always kept her breasts covered – unlike most ladies, who made a great display of rouging or gilding their nipples. It was impossible for Chloris to tell which of her mother's breasts was larger. The chief cook and her helpers said if a pregnant woman's right breast was bigger that meant she was carrying a boy, while a larger left breast meant a girl. But Chloris couldn't tell any difference, at least not through the fabric. They both just looked, well, *big*.

"So I see," said her mother. "You have crumbs on your chin."

The cook had given her a pastry with a sweet fig filling. Chloris brushed the back of her hand across her lips to remove the telltale remnants.

"Go wash your hands," her mother said, "and take up your spindle."

Sighing, Chloris slouched over to the basin that stood on a table by the door. Her mother was very particular when it came to wool-work: everyone's hands had to be perfectly clean. She rinsed her fingers in the jasmine-scented water and dried them on a cloth offered by one of the serving women. Then Chloris went over to the empty stool beside the queen. Her wool-basket, distaff, and spindle were waiting for her. She settled the long wooden shaft of the distaff under her left arm; as she fixed a clump of carded wool about its tip, she peered once more at her mother's swollen belly and breasts. She still couldn't see any difference between right and left – no more than she could tell whether the baby was resting high or low in the womb. That was how the washer-women said you could tell a boy from a girl.

Her mother the queen preferred loom-work to spinning, but when her belly was large it hurt her back to stand at the loom. That meant spinning instead – which meant Chloris had to do the same. And spinning was dull. At least with weaving there were stories to think about as she helped her mother put shapes and patterns into the cloth: stories about the gods, and about the city of Thebes. But spinning was just – spinning.

The thread she was making snapped, and her ivory spindle dropped to the floor with a sharp clack. Chloris bent to retrieve it. She licked her fingers and mated the two frayed ends of thread together, rolling and pinching them tight so that the fibers would stick together. But when she set the thread spinning it broke again.

"You're letting it get too thin," her mother said, catching up her own spindle and reaching over for the one in Chloris' hand. "See?" Deftly the queen mended the break in the thread, and drew out a new twist of wool. "Keep it even, dear." She handed the spindle back to Chloris. "Your thread was better yesterday. Is something bothering you this morning?"

Chloris looked into her mother's dark eyes. "I want a sister, Mama," she said. "Can't you give me a sister this time?"

The queen lifted an eyebrow. "Why do you want a sister?"

"I'm tired of being the only girl." She rested her distaff across her knees. "Alphenor says that boys are better. Boys are stronger – they get to drive chariots and fight with swords."

A few of the ladies, including her grandmother and her aunt, giggled or exchanged indulgent looks. Chloris frowned at them, and they pretended to grow serious, but she could see that their eyes were still filled with mirth. Deciding to ignore them, Chloris continued: "I want to show him that girls are just as good, but it's hard with five brothers and no sisters."

"Isn't your father teaching you archery alongside your brothers?" asked her mother, putting her own spindle in motion once more. The thread drew out behind it, slender and straight. "And you've already gone on several hunts – didn't you shoot a hare last month?"

That was true; she *was* learning to handle a bow. But still—

"My dear, Philomela needs more brown thread. Take that skein over to her."

Embarrassed, Chloris realized she had not noticed the gestures of the woman working the largest loom. Philomela was always kind; for example, *she* had not raised her eyebrows at Chloris' mention of chariot racing and sword fights. Maybe that was why she hadn't seen the movement of Philomela's hand – because she was too irritated by the laughter of the other women. Chloris set down her own work and carried the skein of brown wool to her mother's friend.

Philomela touched Chloris' cheek in thanks. Philomela could not speak, and always wore a veil covering her nose and mouth, but Chloris didn't know why. She had asked, but Mama had said she would explain when Chloris was older.

As Philomela began wrapping the thread around her empty shuttle, Chloris returned to her mother's side. "I still want a sister."

The queen shook her head. "Child, that's not up to me."

Was Mama telling the truth? Her mother was the queen, Queen Niobe of Thebes, and Father always said that she was the most capable woman alive. So surely she could make the baby a girl if she chose.

"Father says *you* can do anything," Chloris ventured.

This time all the women laughed – and then Mama stopped, rubbing her belly as if it ached. "Why don't you go ask your father just how I should go about that task? You're too fidgety for wool-work today anyway."

Chloris jumped up. "Is Father at the new temple?"

The queen gave a little shrug. "I expect so."

Chloris' father the king was building a temple to Apollo. Everyone said that Father played the lyre and sang like the god Apollo himself. Well, almost everyone: Mama said that she'd never heard Apollo sing, so she couldn't make the comparison – but still Mama agreed that Father's music was the most beautiful she had ever heard. "That's why I first fell in love with him," she would say, and then her eyes would go dreamy, as if she had stopped seeing what was around her.

Relieved to be released from her chores in the weaving room, especially on such a sunny autumn day, Chloris kissed her mother's cheek in parting.

"Don't run inside the palace, dear," her mother called as she headed out.

Chloris walked primly to the end of the corridor, then held herself to a moderate lope after rounding the corner. She headed first to her own room to find her nursemaid; the palace guards would not let her wander outside by herself.

Her nursemaid made her put on sandals, even though Chloris preferred going barefoot in warm weather. But because she wanted the woman to accompany her without too much grumbling, Chloris slipped her feet into the sandals and tied the thongs around her ankles.

At the front door of the palace, she asked the guards the whereabouts of her father. "The king's down at the cattle-pens on the southwest side of the city," said one of the men, pointing with his spear.

Chloris thanked the soldier, then went down the palace stairway and across the agora at a pace slow enough for her nursemaid to keep up. Even though it was an easy walk – the road sloped downhill, after all – her servant complained about the steep climb they would have to make on their return.

Her father was easy to spot from a distance; he was so tall, and the golden circle of his crown caught the sunlight. Uncle Zethos was by the pens too, of course – he was Master of the Herds – but so were several other noblemen and a whole crowd of servants. The visitor who had arrived the night before was also there, with all his foreign soldiers in their blue cloaks and kilts. As Chloris drew nearer, she saw her brothers standing off to the side – and she noticed that her father and uncle looked distinctly unhappy. This was *not* the time to ask Father about Mama giving her a sister.

Leaving her nursemaid, Chloris slipped through the crowd until she reached her eldest brother, Alphenor. "What's happening?" she whispered.

"Shh," was the hissed answer. Chloris made a face at him, then looked over at the knot of blue cloaks.

"I'm following the king's express orders," said the leader of the foreigners.

Her father frowned at that. She whispered to Alphenor: "But *our* father's the king!"

"Another king. King Pelops of Pisa."

"Pisa – where they hold the Olympic Games?"

The Olympic Games, which happened every four years, attracted the best athletes from all across Hellas. The next games were to take place in another two years and Chloris desperately wanted to go – as did Alphenor and their younger brothers.

"Yes. Now be quiet."

Obviously, Chloris thought, Alphenor didn't know what was happening either. She would just have to listen and figure it out for herself.

She shifted from one foot to the other, watching the men's faces. King Pelops of Pisa was one of her mother's brothers. What could King Pelops' messenger be saying to make her father, King Amphion of Thebes, so unhappy?

§ 1.02

With an effort, Amphion kept his tone civil. "What do you mean, it's not enough?" He felt the support of the Theban nobility just behind him, sensed the restive movements of his brother Zethos at his shoulder. "Count it for yourself! Twenty oxen, four dozen jars of olive oil and two dozen amphorae of wine. Six wagon-loads of wheat and barley. And—"

"The king expects more," said the envoy from Pisa.

"*Amphion* is king here," bristled Zethos, stepping forwards with fists clenched. Veins stood out along the thick muscles of his arms. "You will not interrupt him."

"Are you threatening me?" The slender Pisatan would certainly lose to Zethos in any sort of physical contest, but he did not shrink back. Instead he made a casual gesture towards his escort. It was normal enough for King Pelops to send a dozen soldiers to retrieve the tribute, since it was necessary to protect the goods in transit against thieves; but Amphion had been quick to note that each man wore a helmet tiled with precious boar's-tusks, and their shields were cut in a new style, rounded at the top but with a curve at the bottom to permit a spear-thrust from underneath. He had no doubt that his brother-in-law Pelops meant to remind Thebes of his superior fighting force, which he had used to extend the boundaries of his kingdom. Most recently Pisa had suffered a surprise attack by soldiers from the island Zakynthos, but Pelops had rallied his men and won such a resounding victory that the king of Zakynthos was now sending tribute to Pisa.

"Let's be calm," Amphion said in a level voice. He knew that Pelops, despite the new source of revenue from Zakynthos, had recently lost a wealthy benefactor; his brother-in-law had to be feeling pinched. Amphion had a solution – a short-term solution.

Zethos' eyes narrowed. "But—"

Amphion put a hand on his twin brother's arm. "Calm," he repeated. He turned back to the envoy, and let his hand drop to his belt. "King Pelops will have to be satisfied with this."

There was a chorus of agreement from the Theban nobles. Red-haired Menoeceus, who was responsible for the inventory, held up his wax-coated wooden tablet. "It's significantly more than Thebes sent last year!"

The envoy, Okyllus, spread his hands. "Your contributions support the games, and the building of new temples. Would you stint the gods?"

"We prefer to worship the gods *here*," interjected Menoeceus.

The other noblemen echoed this sentiment. "At Apollo's new temple," one of them said with a lift of his chin. Inwardly Amphion flinched. Though the new Temple of Apollo was the project dearest to his heart, he thought it unwise of his subjects to remind the visitor of its ongoing construction – and its precious marble floor-tiles.

The envoy stroked his neatly trimmed beard. "Ah, yes. So I heard over dinner last night. But Thebes already has a shrine to Apollo. Why go to such expense?"

Tact was not working with this man. "Thebes' resources belong to Thebes," Amphion said, raising his voice. "You – and *your* king – would do well to remember this." He pulled Okyllus aside.

Okyllus' voice was low but forceful. "You, my lord king, would do well to remember that you would never have gained the throne of Thebes without King Pelops' support."

"My brother-in-law's support is always appreciated," said Amphion smoothly, grabbing Okyllus' forearm. "But he's demanding too much from his only sister."

The envoy's eyebrows went up as he felt the small bag of jewels that Amphion had surreptitiously pressed into his hand. He gave a slight nod of comprehension, and clutched his hand into a fist to hide the jewels. "Hmph," he grunted. "King Pelops will expect better next year!" As he led his men away, Amphion heard him mutter: "Marble. What hubris!"

King Amphion bit back the retort he longed to make. Of course he was making Apollo's new temple as magnificent as possible – the old shrine was not the thing of beauty that Apollo deserved.

Since assuming the throne Amphion had done much for Thebes: widening and smoothing the roads, paving the agora and the city's main streets with cobblestones, clearing new fields for cultivation, improving the management of the herds and granaries. But, though these changes made the lives of his subjects easier, they did not lift his Thebans' hearts or fill visitors with awe. Apollo's new temple would change that. It would remind everyone that Thebes was the city where the Tiresias – the most powerful seer in all Hellas – was chosen. It would honor Apollo, the god of music, with its grace and elegance. And it perhaps most importantly, it would encourage the people of Thebes to prefer the serene peace and wisdom of Apollo to the divine madness of Dionysus and his Maenad cult. Naturally Amphion would never openly campaign against the Maenads – not only because his mother and sister-in-law were ardent followers, but because defying Dionysus had proven hazardous for Theban kings in the past. But Amphion could set a better example for his people.

At least Amphion's wife Niobe was no Maenad; she joked that so many young children left her no strength for dancing through the night. She had a keen eye for beauty, and supported most of Amphion's goals; even so, she had warned him that the new temple could attract unwelcome attention from her brother Pelops.

But no king could make decisions that always pleased everyone. A wise ruler had to seek balance, and conduct patient diplomacy. Amphion summoned his self-control as he watched the Pisatan force make their way back up to the palace. His resentment over the tribute to Pisa would remain concealed; he must not begrudge the lavish meal he would serve in the palace's central megaron that evening. The jewels, though – he had hoped to use those to hire a sculptor for Apollo's temple, and he hated to relinquish them. But, unlike sending an even greater portion of the harvest, it was a way of pacifying Pelops that need not attract the attention of Thebes' leading citizens.

Zethos approached him, muttering, "Those oxen are the best our herds have to offer. They should stay in Thebes. Your wife's brother demands too much."

Amphion took a deep breath. The truth was that offending Pisa was potentially dangerous, and he was not ready to take that step. "Thebes' herds and fields are more productive than ever. We can afford to be generous."

"Costly generosity, my lord king," said Menoeceus. He held up his note-tablet. "Almost all our surplus goes to Pisa."

"Other Theban kings have married *Theban* women," said another.

Amphion turned to see which nobleman had spoken, but he could not be sure. "Other Theban kings have cost the city far more than a few oxen," he said, addressing the group as a whole. "And Queen Niobe does plenty for Thebes." His tone with his subjects was neither sharp nor conciliatory: he was simply reminding them of the facts. He did not want to silence the occasional grumble. The autocratic manner of his brother-in-law Pelops meant that Pisatan nobles feared to voice their opinions – and that in turn meant that Pelops did not receive all the information he needed to choose the best course of action. Amphion would rather hear the murmuring against his wife than have it remain unknown to him.

He saw some of his children standing at the edge of the crowd, and waved at them. "Chloris, my dear! Did you come with your brothers to see the animals?"

The eleven-year-old girl ran up to him. "I came to ask you a question, Father."

The presence of his daughter lifted Amphion's spirits. Though she looked more like him than her mother, she had Niobe's inquisitive mind and daring nature. As Amphion's brother Zethos walked the royal princes around the cattle-pen, pointing out the excellent features of the oxen to be sent to Pisa, Amphion set a hand on Chloris' shoulder and entertained her questions. He laughed when she demanded a sister, and explained that all anyone could do was make offerings to the goddesses who protected women in childbirth.

The afternoon with his children was, as always, enjoyable, and when the time came for the evening meal Amphion entered the megaron in a cheerful mood. Niobe was already seated on her throne, looking especially radiant; a smile lit her eyes as she rested her hands on her rounded belly. When Amphion bent to kiss her cheek, she whispered, "The child will be here soon." In response he gently squeezed her soft, plump fingers before taking his seat.

Amphion's good spirits lasted through the meal; but after the tables were cleared and the wine poured around, the Pisatan envoy Okyllus lifted his cup and called out: "Give us a song, Amphion!" There was no deference in the man's tone, no respect for his host: he spoke as though addressing an itinerant bard.

Summoning a smile to hide his anger, Amphion beckoned a servant to bring his lyre. Perhaps because the Maenads were celebrating tonight in a field north of the city, he had already chosen his verses. He checked the tuning-pegs quickly, fixed his gaze on the Pisatan envoy, and slammed his hand across the seven strings to bring forth the first dire chord of the lament for Pentheus.

In time past, when gods walked openly among men, King Pentheus ruled in Thebes. Filled with pride and envy, the mortal Pentheus forbade the worship of his divine cousin Dionysus. But the young vine-god could not be denied; the cult of his Maenad followers grew and grew, until even Pentheus' own mother joined. The jealous king spied on the new god's secret rites – and the Maenad mob discovered him and tore him to bloody pieces. Thus was the power of Dionysus made manifest, and all future kings warned that they should never curtail the honor rightly due to the deathless ones.

Amphion let the last chord linger, scanning the pensive faces of the leading citizens of Thebes. He hoped that the song served to remind his subjects that neither a king of Cadmus' line nor a queen of Theban blood was a guarantee of sound rule: that needed reverence for the gods, and devotion to the city. And he hoped that Okyllus would carry the message of the song to his master Pelops: no king could deny the gods their due, including Apollo's new temple in Thebes.

Compensating for his previous lapse in courtesy, Okyllus offered words of praise. Amphion nodded and set his lyre aside. His wife Niobe reached over and touched his arm. "Beautifully sung, Husband," she said. "Your mother will be sorry to have missed it."

He shrugged. "She's heard me sing many times."

"I've often thought that subject—" She suddenly stopped speaking, her mouth still open, her fingers grasping his wrist.

Noting the familiar expression, Amphion covered her hand with his own. "Is it time?"

She nodded. "I must go to the birthing-room." She beckoned her chief maidservant and instructed the woman to go ahead and make sure that all was ready.

Amphion stood, and assisted his wife down from her throne. "Excuse us, friends," he said, pulling her arm through his. The dinner-guests rose, wishing them a good night; many offered prayers for the health of the queen and her child.

Niobe's steps were slow and awkward, but soon enough they reached the shadows of the corridor and a measure of privacy. As they shuffled towards the birthing-room Amphion kissed the top of Niobe's head, thanking the gods – as he did so often – for blessing him with such a remarkable woman. How could a man be more fortunate? Niobe's advice was better than the best of his other counselors. She appreciated the deepest nuances of his music; she livened his days with her clever wit and his nights with her ardent lovemaking. In their thirteen years of marriage, she had given him a beautiful daughter and five healthy sons. And tonight another child would be born.

His subjects might be right to complain that so far his marriage had not brought a profitable alliance for Thebes. But Niobe had relatives other than just King Pelops of Pisa.

§ 1.03

Niobe entered the birthing chamber to discover that the servants had already fetched her friend Philomela. Niobe clasped Philomela's hands, and saw the concern in the Athenian woman's blue eyes.

"Everything's fine, so far," said Niobe, answering the unspoken question.

Philomela nodded, then pointed at the birthing chair.

"Not yet," said Niobe. "Philomela, do you think it's wise for Amphion to sing about mobs tearing apart their kings?"

Philomela shrugged.

Niobe was hit by another contraction; she leaned on Philomela while it passed. When it was finished, she continued her thought. "At least he only sang it to the nobles."

Philomela pointed to her ears and, from the way the corners of her eyes crinkled, Niobe could tell the mute woman was smiling beneath her veil.

"True, Amphion sings beautifully," said Niobe, interpreting Philomela's thoughts, as she so often did. Philomela, a princess of Athens, had suffered terrible abuse as a young woman: a cruel captor had raped and beaten her, disfiguring her once-beautiful face. He had cut out her tongue so that she could not tell what he had done to her, but she had managed to make the truth known nonetheless. One reason she preferred Thebes to her native city was so that she could avoid the stares of the pitying and the curious – but Niobe suspected that Amphion's music was another strong motivation.

The door opened, and the young midwife Theora entered with her assistants. "How are you, my lady queen?" she asked while the assistants spread fresh straw on the floor.

"Ready," Niobe said, as birth-water seeped out between her legs. "I should remove these clothes."

"Of course, my lady queen." The midwife helped Niobe out of the formal gown and sodden undergarment and handed these to her assistants; then she drew a robe of undyed linen across Niobe's shoulders and tied it loosely over her swollen breasts and belly.

Niobe's womb clenched, harder this time. She leaned against the back of the chair, feeling fresh fluid drip down her legs, drawing a deep breath and letting it out slowly, slowly, as the child within her demanded. Once the intensity of sensation subsided, she realized Theora had been speaking to her.

"...would you like to sit, my lady queen?"

"Not yet. I'll walk for a while." Supported by Theora's strong arm, she made her way around the room, wondering if the child were a boy or a girl. Probably a boy; after Chloris, Amphion seemed to sire only sons, and this pregnancy felt much like the last.

The next pain came. Niobe surrendered herself to its grip, aware of nothing but her breath and the movement inside her. As the moment passed, and thought returned, she found herself considering the term "birth-pains" – she used those words herself, though she no longer found the sensation precisely painful. Intense, yes, sometimes overwhelming, but it was not the same as the pain of injury or illness. Certainly childbirth could be an ordeal of agony, and cost many women their lives. But Niobe had not feared the birthing-room since bringing her firstborn, Alphenor, into the world. Alphenor had taught her that her body knew what to do, if she would simply let it, and listen to the child within. Oh, even for her, birthing was work – hard work. But Niobe had never been afraid of hard work.

"Some water, my lady queen?" Theora asked, as the birth-pain ended and Niobe relaxed.

"Yes." She drank a few sips; her stomach would not tolerate much until she was finished.

"You've made this birthing chamber very pretty, my lady queen," the midwife said as they paced once more around the room. "I like the new frescoes."

"Yes," said Niobe, breathlessly, as another pain came upon her, and she distracted herself by counting the painted songbirds swooping low over red and white blossoms. She had redone the old, stained stucco floor, and polished bronze basins rested on the work table beside a stack of sun-bleached towels. Whenever the weather was good, the window-shutters were latched open to admit the breeze so that the room always smelled fresh. Though she spent little time here compared to many other rooms in the palace, in an important way this room was the center of her life.

Niobe walked several more circuits of the room, until finally she was ready to push. Theora helped her into the birthing-chair, where Philomela wiped the sweat from her brow with a damp cloth. And then the heavy wooden door creaked open, admitting Amphion's mother Antiope and Zethos' wife Thebe. Their makeup was smeared, their hair in disarray; both women were crowned with wreaths of ivy. Each also carried a thyrsus staff with a large pinecone lashed to one end.

"My dear, my dear!" trilled the older woman, a little too loudly. "Why didn't you *tell* us your time was coming? We'd never have gone to the ceremony!"

"I didn't know for sure," said Niobe, panting.

"What, with all your experience, you couldn't tell?" Antiope walked over to Niobe and kissed her cheek. The smell of wine on her breath sickened Niobe; she swallowed back nausea. Antiope patted Niobe's shoulder and turned to the other women. "This is the best daughter-in-law any woman could have. So many grandchildren, and another on the way! Isn't she a marvel?"

Niobe's mouth twisted. She had hoped to avoid this distraction, but there was no help for it. She could hardly ban her mother-in-law from the birthing chamber – besides, Antiope meant well. Another contraction started, and Niobe escaped for a moment by closing her eyes and letting out a hissing breath.

"There, there, my lady queen," said the midwife, edging in past Antiope, and holding Niobe's hand while she pushed.

When the contraction was finished, Niobe opened her eyes and saw that her sister-in-law Thebe still stood before the door. "I trust it's going well, Niobe?" asked the copper-haired woman.

"Yes," Niobe gasped, panting. She saw that Thebe's gaze focused not on her face but on her heavy belly. Thebe had wed Amphion's brother Zethos only days after Niobe and Amphion married – but in those same thirteen years Thebe had never carried a child to term. Now Thebe, aging and desperate, participated in every possible fertility ritual. The thyrsus staff was the image of an erect phallus; Niobe wondered what exactly the Maenads did with them. Whatever the rituals, Thebe remained barren. Niobe would have spared Thebe from coming to the births of her children, but her sister-in-law was expected to attend and Thebe was too proud to stay away.

Antiope patted Niobe's cheek. "Of course it is! Your pregnancies always go well, dear!" Hiccupping, she sent a maidservant to fetch a pitcher of wine. When the door swung open Niobe heard music beyond: Amphion's voice, his skilled hands on the lyre. He was out there in the colonnade, singing her favorite songs, even though she could only catch snatches of melody.

Not for the first time, she wished Amphion could be in here with her, instead of waiting outside. She would far prefer his calm strength to Antiope's tipsy cheer and Thebe's silent bitterness. But the Theban women insisted it was unlucky for a man to enter the birthing chamber. Niobe had once objected to Theora that this stricture made no sense: surely peasant women sometimes gave birth before their husbands had a chance to send for the midwife, and many of them lived in one-room huts. Theora only folded her strong arms across her chest and shook her head. "You're hardly a peasant woman, my lady queen. And even if you don't fear the ill omen, the people of Thebes certainly would." With an inward sigh Niobe had yielded. She did not want her children thought ill-omened.

The contractions were steady; the baby was moving down. Theora knelt between Niobe's knees; after a while she looked up, smiling. "I can see the top of the baby's head, my lady queen." She called an assistant for a flask of olive oil, and guided a stream of the fragrant liquid over Niobe's flesh to ease the child's passage. The urge to push grew overwhelming; and then Niobe felt the child's head slip from her body. Gasping, squeezing Philomela's fingers hard, she summoned her strength and pushed again.

"There he is, my lady queen!" cried Theora. "A boy!"

An assistant brought a lamp close, and the midwife held up the child for Niobe to see; the bloody birth-string stretched over the midwife's arm, pulsing rhythmically. The babe opened his mouth and let out an indignant cry.

"A boy!" exclaimed Antiope, clapping her hands. "Another grandson!"

A boy – Chloris would be disappointed. But Niobe wanted to weep with happiness. Covered in blood and creamy vernix, dark damp hair plastered to his tiny head, the baby was nonetheless perfect.

"Not quite finished, my lady queen," said the midwife; but Niobe did not need to be told. Her womb contracted again, and soon the afterbirth fell to the straw between her feet with a wet thud. One apprentice held the baby while the midwife cut the birth-string and tied a knot at the child's belly; the other assistant brought over a basin of warm, thyme-infused water, untied the laces of Niobe's gown, and sponged the sweat and blood from her body. Niobe breathed in the familiar scent, soothed as much by the fragrance as by the warmth of the water. She heard Antiope and Thebe cooing over the baby as Theora washed him. Then Philomela and Thebe assisted Niobe to the cot and propped her up on pillows stuffed with wool; they drew a linen sheet up over her hips.

"Let me hold him," Niobe said, stretching out her arms. The midwife nestled the small, warm bundle into the sunken pocket of Niobe's belly; his head rested in the valley between her breasts. Niobe stroked his narrow back, feeling an overpowering tide of love.

"I should present him to Amphion," Antiope said.

"Not just yet." Niobe was not ready to relinquish the newborn, whose tiny mouth was opening and closing like a baby bird's. Niobe fitted her nipple to his mouth and felt the unique euphoria of the first thin, watery milk being drawn into her newest son's mouth.

"Well, I'll go tell him at least," Antiope said, making her unsteady way out of the room.

Niobe let the babe suckle his fill. Then glanced over at Thebe, and judged she was sufficiently sober. "Would you carry him out to Amphion?" she said quietly. "Antiope's in no condition..."

Her sister-in-law nodded; gently she lifted the baby from Niobe's arms and went to present the child to his father. Niobe heard her husband's exclamation of delight: "There you are, my little son!"

Thebe returned soon with the child; Amphion knew that Niobe did not like to be separated from her newborns for long. Pressing the boundaries of tradition, he stood at the threshold of the open door and called to her. "Get some rest, my love. When morning comes I'll tell the children they have a new brother."

Niobe settled the infant against her bare skin, comforted by his small warm body and by the sound of her husband's voice. Before long she slept.

She woke in her own bed, the sun high in the sky, and heard her maidservants chatting in the antechamber as they went about their duties. Amphion sat in a chair beside the bed, the sleeping baby cradled in his arms. "He's a handsome one," Amphion told her, his gray eyes shining.

Niobe smiled. "Takes after his father, then!" She pushed herself to a more upright position.

Her husband settled the baby into the crook of her arm, then stroked Niobe's hair. "You're the most beautiful woman I've ever seen."

She looked up at her husband. From anyone else, the comment would have been absurd flattery – if not outright mockery. She was past thirty, and even as a young maid had been no beauty. Seven pregnancies had ruined whatever charms her short, stocky figure might once have possessed. And just now her face must be pillow-creased and puffy-eyed.

But Amphion was a man who looked beyond the surface. She knew he spoke from the heart when he said that he found her beautiful, and tears sprang to her eyes.

He stretched out a finger to brush away her tears, then handed her a cup of fresh goat's milk. Niobe drank gratefully, glad for the distraction as much as the sustenance. Her emotions were always undependable after giving birth, and she did not want to trouble her husband by dissolving into sobs.

When she had finished the milk, Amphion set aside the empty cup. "Niobe, I'd like to talk about his name."

"Yes?" She inspected the soft hand of the child sleeping at her breast. He had long fingers, like his father. Perhaps this boy would also play the lyre.

"I want to name him Tantalus."

She looked up. "After my father?"

Amphion nodded.

Niobe wrinkled her brow. "But he's—"

"A powerful king."

She leaned forward, hissing: "He tried to kill my brother!"

Her sudden movement woke the baby, who blinked and began to fuss.

"Niobe, your brother demanded even more tribute this year – Thebes can't afford to continue like this. Besides, your father's kingdom lies across the Great Sea. There's no reason to fear his drunken rages here. And he could be a useful ally. The whole world respects the wealth and power of King Tantalus of Lydia."

Niobe could not contradict this last statement; and with a child crying in her arms, she did not want to. She stroked the baby's hair, then shifted him so that his pink lips lay against her nipple. His mouth closed over her skin eagerly, his ill humor forgotten.

"Should we name you Tantalus?" she asked the nursing infant. "But we don't want you to turn out like your grandfather, do we?"

Amphion touched her cheek. "My love, I'm thinking of this little one and the rest of our children. Good relations between Thebes and Lydia could help secure their futures."

Closing her eyes as she nourished her newborn, Niobe considered this. Her brother Pelops would not like it, not at all. But this was her sixth son, not the heir to the throne; and the name Tantalus would remind people of her powerful family. She might even convince Pelops that a warming of relations between Thebes and Lydia could work to his benefit as well. Pelops and Tantalus could never be on good terms: son and father each felt gravely wronged by the other. But if Thebes and Lydia had an alliance – and a trading relationship – that could provide Pelops with access to the resources he needed for his perpetual building projects. And *that* could ease the strain that Pelops imposed on Thebes.

Niobe opened her eyes and kissed the top of the baby's head. "Ah, little one – your father's a wise man. Perhaps we should call you Tantalus after all."

She only hoped that Pelops would not be too upset.

§ 1.04

King Pelops of Pisa walked across the muddy clearing behind his main storerooms, inspecting the line of ox-carts just arrived from Thebes. Six were packed with tall storage jars filled with wheat and barley; two held jars of olive oil, cushioned with straw; the last two carried amphorae of wine, stacked on their sides, covered over with tanned hides, and lashed tight to the wagon-bed. There were baskets of raisins and dried beef and of course the sturdy Theban oxen pulling the carts. Still—

"Only ten carts?"

Pelops looked over into the shadows of the nearby trees, frowning at the ghost whose mocking voice interrupted his thoughts. In the privacy of his own rooms, he might have snapped a sharp retort; but he had long since realized that no one else could see the charioteer's insubstantial form or hear his annoying comments. He kept his mouth firmly shut, for he wanted no rumors that the king of Pisa was a madman – or worse, cursed.

And yet Myrtilus had a point. Pelops' payment for a shipload of eastern cedar was months overdue – let alone what he owed the gold-merchants and that team of Cretan fresco-painters. This delivery would barely make a dent in his debts. The next set of games was less than two years away, and there was still so much to be accomplished by then – things that could not be finished without additional resources.

If only his friend Aeolius had not left to explore the southern oceans! Aeolius had supplied him with so much over the years, from his best horses to the new altars near the chariot racetrack. But when the sea captain departed last spring, he had made it clear he was not planning to return.

"You should have paraded your son Chrysippus in front of him," said Myrtilus. "That might have kept Aeolius' interest—"

Shut up, Pelops said silently, automatically, to the ghost. Scratching his beard, he asked his envoy: "Is this all?"

Okyllus shook his head, and spoke softly. "Not quite, my lord king."

"What else is there?"

"This, my lord king," said the envoy, stepping closer and handing him a small leather pouch.

Pelops opened the pouch and shook its contents into his left palm. It was a brilliant mixture of small jewels: chalcedony, amber, and precious amethyst. But there were only seven stones. He handed them back to Okyllus. "No more?"

The envoy glanced uneasily over his shoulder at the soldiers who had gone with him to Thebes and back, then at the servants tending the oxen. "My lord king, King Amphion insisted Thebes could not afford more. He said this was more than they sent last year."

Pelops turned to his steward. "Is that true?"

Exarchos was a short, round man who had recently been promoted from herald to steward. He cleared his throat and consulted his wax-covered wooden note tablet. "Yes, my lord king. Last year King Amphion sent eight carts."

Even with two cartloads more than the previous year, it was not enough to pay for the cedar rafters spanning the extensions to Hera's temple. "Amphion could have sent more," Pelops said, pacing a circle around the nearest wagon. "Thebes had a particularly good harvest this year. The gods will not be pleased by such stinginess."

"My lord king, the Thebans are building a new temple to Apollo," Okyllus ventured. "The floors will be tiled with marble."

Pelops' eyes narrowed. He had been creating a complex full of temples to the gods – he called it Olympia to encourage them to look upon it as a second home – and he wanted his to be the finest in all Hellas. Pelops did not welcome competition from his brother-in-law. "Marble, you say?" That did not sound like his sister Niobe, who preferred practicality to extravagance.

"There's a small quarry near Thebes, my lord king. And of course King Amphion is devoted to Apollo."

Pelops glanced up at the sun, which was finally making an appearance this afternoon after three days of rain. Apollo – yes, the god of music and light certainly favored Amphion.

"If Apollo already favors him, then Amphion doesn't need to build the god a fancy temple, does he?" said Myrtilus' ghost, moving closer.

Pelops shook his head and stepped away from the ghost.

But Myrtilus continued: "If Laius was king of Thebes, do you think he'd build a new temple?"

"No," Pelops said aloud, regretting it even as the word left his lips. Okyllus and the soldiers looked confused: how could anyone deny that Amphion was devoted to Apollo? To cover his slip, he said, "No, I don't want any of the Theban marble, Okyllus. The quality isn't as good as what we're already getting." Ducking beneath a low-hanging branch, he walked over to the next wagon to give himself a moment to think.

Prince Laius had relinquished his claim to the Theban throne long ago – and, no matter what Myrtilus hinted, Pelops did not want him ruling Thebes. Laius was a handsome young man, good company and an excellent wrestler, but he was ill-suited for real responsibility. He would never govern Thebes more efficiently than Niobe, even if her husband wanted a new temple. The only pity was that Niobe was not here in Pisa giving Pelops her valuable counsel.

Pelops adjusted the ivory-tiled armor that covered his shoulder, a piece he had worn ever since an injury in his youth. Then he looked back to his soldiers. "Okyllus, what news of my sister?"

The man shrugged. "I scarcely saw her, my lord king. While we were there she gave birth to a son. They said both mother and child were doing well."

Another nephew! Niobe was making up for the time she had lost by marrying late – this must be her sixth son. Or was it her fifth – or her seventh? He had lost count. Well, Pelops too had plenty of children, both sons and daughters. "What did they name him?"

"We left Thebes before the child's name-day, my lord king."

Pelops grunted acknowledgement, his mind returning to the problem of his outstanding debts. Finally he walked back to his steward. "See all this safely stored away," he told the man. "Make sure that none of it has started to rot in this damp. Then get the best deal you can with the gold merchants and those Cretan artists. We'll have to find some other way to cover the costs of the cedar when that ship sails back into port."

Exarchos bowed and bustled off, snapping his fingers at the ox-drivers. Pelops headed back towards the main palace, passing the stables without stopping to check on his horses. They were perceptive beasts who would sense his troubled mood – and he had no desire to put up with the snide comments the ghost would make if the horses did not respond well to his hand. Having been a charioteer himself, Myrtilus was particularly cutting about such matters.

"Pelops, how can you think such a thing?" the dead charioteer said, affecting a wounded tone. "Don't you value my equine expertise?"

By Zeus, the ghost was irritating today! If only there were some way to get rid of him!

"It's your fault, Pelops! You should have let me sleep with your wife, and given me half the kingdom, as I was promised! But instead you murdered me."

Pelops quickened his pace, though he knew it would do him little good. He had tried many strategies to rid himself of the ghost: sacrifices, ritual purification, dedicated games, special hymns – and consultation with the Tiresias, the most powerful seer in Hellas. Occasionally, rarely, the ghost vanished for a while, but so far he had always come back.

"If you won't leave me in peace," Pelops muttered, his mind reverting to his more pressing concerns, "then give me some useful advice. How can I pay for that cedar shipment?"

"Pelops, I was a charioteer, not a merchant. You should ask my father Hermes."

Pelops had always doubted that the divine Hermes really sired Myrtilus, who had been an ill-favored commoner in life. Nevertheless, the ghost's suggestion was reasonable. After all, Hermes was the god of merchants – as well as tricksters, travelers, messengers, and thieves, and the escort of deceased souls on their way to the Underworld. Pelops had given Hermes a magnificent temple and many other rich gifts over the years. If the god would not compel his son Myrtilus to remain in the Underworld, at least he could help with matters of trade. "Hermes," Pelops whispered, "help me: show me how to satisfy this debt!" Focusing on his plea, Pelops ignored his door-guards' salute and walked into the walled exercise-ground.

"Father! What's troubling you?"

The question came from Pelops' son Chrysippus, whose boyish voice was had recently begun to change. The thirteen-year-old and his two older brothers had stripped to their loincloths for afternoon exercise; patches of wet sand clung to their bodies where they had taken falls. Atreus and Thyestes were swarthy, muscular youths, dark stubble just starting to shadow their chins; golden-haired Chrysippus was like the sun shining between two storm clouds.

He walked over to his boys, all standing near the water-urn; Chrysippus held out the dipper to Pelops. He drank, then fitted the dipper's curved bronze handle back into place on the lip of the urn. "What makes you think I'm troubled, Son?"

Atreus, the eldest, said, "You were frowning, Father."

"That could have been just the sun in my eyes," Pelops said, challenging him. By the gods, Atreus was growing! He was only sixteen, but would soon be as tall as Pelops himself. Unfortunately, his broad face was marred with oily blemishes.

"That wasn't it," Chrysippus said, brushing sand from his forearms. "It was the way you were walking. Very fast, looking down at the ground instead of all around you."

"He's right, Father – you were doing that." Thyestes lifted his wooden practice-sword in a mock salute to his younger brother. "But you might just have been in a hurry. Now if you'd been pacing, we'd know for sure."

Pelops folded his arms across his chest. He was pleased that his sons were learning to read men – an important skill of kingcraft – but unwilling to show his approval too easily. "All right, if you boys are so clever, here's a question for you: how can we increase Pisa's wealth? My old friend Aeolius was always a great contributor to the games, but he has sailed away."

The ghost made a snorting sound in Pelops' ear. "You're asking *children* for advice?"

Be quiet, Pelops retorted mentally. *I'm testing my sons' ability.*

Thyestes waved his wooden sword dismissively. "You're the king, Father! Just tell the peasants to produce more."

Pelops shook his head. "It's not that simple, Son." The handsome boy sounded like his mother Hippodamia, who had yet to learn that jewels were not strewn along Pisa's roads for the peasants to gather at his command. "Our fields and herds will only produce so much."

"The peasants could get by with less," suggested Atreus.

"Perhaps. But hungry subjects don't work as hard for their king as ones that are well-fed. And we couldn't raise enough by such means anyway."

Chrysippus drew his fair eyebrows together. "Our teacher says Mycenae is the wealthiest city in Hellas, now that Athens' power is fading. How did Mycenae become so rich in gold, Father?"

"The city's founders brought great wealth with them from the north," Pelops said. "And the ruling line has kept close ties with their kin; they get good terms on Thracian gold and amber."

"Mother has relatives in Mycenae," said Thyestes. "We could ask them to send us gold."

Atreus laughed, and punched his brother's shoulder. "Stupid, they won't just *send* it to us. We'd have to take it." He spat on the ground, and then turned back to Pelops. "That's what we should do. Father, our soldiers are the best. You saw how well we did against Zakynthos."

"Zakynthos was a weakly defended island," Chrysippus objected. "Mycenae has huge walls."

Lifting his square chin, Atreus said: "The greater the challenge, the greater the victory!"

"Atreus," Pelops said dryly, "have you forgotten that Mycenae is an ally? Thyestes just mentioned your mother's relatives there."

Chrysippus' hazel eyes lit up. "Maybe we could trade them something for the gold."

"We don't have anything they want," Thyestes said. "If we did, Father would have already thought of it."

Yawning, Myrtilus said, "They won't come up with anything you haven't already considered. How could they? They're your sons... well, except for Atreus."

Pelops swatted a biting fly that had landed on his leg, trying to crush his doubts at the same time. His wife Hippodamia vowed, always, that the boy was his. And years ago Pelops had promised to treat Atreus as his own as long as she treated Chrysippus as *her* own.

"Is there a way to strengthen our alliance, Father?" Chrysippus asked. "To get better trading terms?"

That was an interesting thought. "A marriage is often the best approach."

"Send Chrysippus, then!" snickered Thyestes. "He's the prettiest!"

Chrysippus picked up his training-sword. "You mean the fastest," he said, swinging the weapon around so that the flat of its wooden blade caught Thyestes on the flank with a ringing smack.

"Ow!" yelled Thyestes, lifting his weapon.

Atreus grabbed his arm. "Stop it. Father's thinking."

Thyestes wrenched his arm loose from his brother's grip. Then a figure on the other side of the exercise yard caught his attention. "Hello, Laius!" he shouted. "Are you going to show us that wrestling hold this afternoon?"

Pelops turned and acknowledged the Theban prince with a lift of his hand. Laius grinned, quickening his pace; his two hunting-dogs barked loudly and bounded over to Chrysippus, wagging their tails. As propriety demanded, Laius bowed to Pelops before addressing Chrysippus. "See, you should have come today! These two missed you. We took four hares, but we'd have done better with you along. I swear they think they're your dogs and not mine."

"I had sword practice," the boy said, scratching the ears of one dog, then patting the other's rump. "Next time?"

"Next time," agreed Laius, calling his dogs to heel. "Thyestes, hand me that dipper. I'm parched."

The handsome youth dunked the ladle into the water-jar and passed it over, saying, "We were just talking about whether anyone in Mycenae would give us a good bride-price for Chrysippus."

Laius tossed down the water, then wiped his mouth with the back of his hand. "For this one? He's not full-grown yet. Best you'd get is half price." He winked at Chrysippus and gave him the dipper, then met Pelops' eye. "To be serious, my lord king, your eldest daughter may be rather young – but King Electryon's wife died three days ago."

Pelops stared. "How do you know this?"

"Learned it crossing the agora a moment ago. A Corinthian pottery-merchant's just arrived, and his customers are spending more time talking about his news than his wares." Laius shifted the leather game-bag slung across his shoulder. "Seems it was nothing more serious than a bee sting, but the poor woman swelled up like a pomegranate and dropped dead on the spot."

Pelops glared at the ghost of Myrtilus. *Why do you never tell me these things? Didn't you know she was dead?*

The ghost waggled an insubstantial finger at him. "Pelops, if I told you that would spoil the surprise! What fun would that be?"

"...that can't be true," Thyestes was saying. "Who dies from a bee sting?"

"The queen of Mycenae, apparently," Laius said, shrugging.

Pelops set a hand on Laius' arm. "Useful news."

"Thank you, my lord king."

If Pelops was to take advantage of this, he needed to act quickly. Every city in Hellas with a marriageable daughter would be pushing her at King Electryon – especially since the man had no sons.

"Where's your mother?" he asked the boys.

"In her chambers," answered Atreus.

"Or with Grandmother," ventured Thyestes. Hippodamia's mother was ill and confined to her sickroom.

Chrysippus shrugged and smiled. "Somewhere in the palace," he said.

"I'll go find her." Pelops departed, the ghost following close behind.

§ 1.05

Queen Hippodamia of Pisa sat up on her couch and waved her maidservants out of earshot. "She's so young!" she gasped. Sixteen was the customary age for brides, although girls occasionally wed as young as fourteen. But Eurydike was only twelve.

Her husband Pelops sat down beside her. "She's reached womanhood. And she's met Electryon and many other Mycenaean relatives at the games. She wouldn't be among strangers." He rested his hand on her knee; even through her skirts she could feel the hardness of his palm, calloused from many years of chariot racing. "Hippodamia, our daughter could be queen of Mycenae. Think what that would mean for Pisa. For us. For *her*."

Hippodamia bit her lip. Her daughter was lovely, nearly as beautiful as she herself had been at that age, though Eurydike's breasts and hips had not yet rounded out. The girl did not lack for suitors, but so far all offers had been deferred for later consideration. Hippodamia wanted to be sure that her daughter would have the best possible husband – and her husband was determined for the match to bring the greatest possible political advantage.

King Electryon could offer just such a match. He was a good man, and Mycenae was wealthy and powerful. But Eurydike had been a woman less than a year – was she ready to wed so soon? Her daughter seemed younger than Hippodamia had been at that age; certainly, she was far more sheltered.

"If we seal the betrothal, the marriage itself could wait a year or two," Hippodamia suggested. "Until she's a little older."

Pelops shook his head. "Engagements can be broken."

Hippodamia looked down at her skirts, fingering the golden rondels that trimmed the uppermost flounce. Her cousin Electryon was at least twenty years older than Eurydike, but he could adorn her with gold and jewels. She would have the best of everything. There was no better marriage for her.

"You're right," she sighed, knowing it was so – though she hated to think of her daughter leaving home.

Pelops kissed her cheek. "I'm glad you see that," he said. "I need your help to make sure Electryon selects her for his bride. You must send a personal message with the courier who leaves in the morning with our formal condolences." He paused. "Your mother's ill, but perhaps she could add a few words? I could speak with her, if you like, or send a scribe—"

"No!" Hippodamia broke in hurriedly. She wanted no visitors to her mother's sickroom, *especially* not a scribe. "No, I'll prepare the message for Electryon. Mother has one foot in the Styx already; she hasn't spoken sensibly in days."

"I'm sorry to hear that," Pelops said, patting her hand. "But I'm sure you'll be persuasive, my dear. And you need to explain the situation to Eurydike, too. It seems a time for motherly advice. I want her to be happy and excited about this – I want her to look forward to her wedding."

Hippodamia looked into her husband's dark eyes. Even though she knew what he really meant – that he wanted her to ensure that Eurydike would make a good impression on her future husband – she still felt the pull of his charm. How desperate she had been to marry him, all those years ago! Of course, there had been many reasons for that. But her desire for Pelops had been about much more than escaping her father's brutality. None of her other suitors had been a man like Pelops. Though their passion had faded away – and at times, over the years, been replaced with open hostility – her husband was always a man to reckon with. A *king*.

She nodded. "I'll speak with her."

"Good." His squeezed her fingers. "I'm glad we agree."

She was not entirely sure that they did, but she let his statement pass. Releasing his hand in order to reach for a goblet of honeyed barley-water on the table beside her couch, she said, "I hear the tribute has arrived from Thebes."

"That's right."

From his short response, she gathered that the tribute was not all that her husband wished. Well, what could he expect, putting that cowherd Amphion on the Theban throne? The fact that Pelops' sister Niobe had taken a fancy to the man did not make him a leader. But Hippodamia kept these thoughts to herself; she was glad that Niobe and her meddlesome ways were far from Pisa. Especially now that her mother was facing the journey to the Underworld, and might feel the need to settle accounts in the land of the living before she departed.

"I trust your sister is well?" she asked, carefully keeping her tone neutral.

Pelops nodded. "She's just given birth to a son."

"Another one?" Hippodamia asked, more sharply than she intended.

Her husband rose to his feet. "That's right. Her sixth, so she hasn't passed you yet."

His tone implied an insult; Hippodamia's eyes narrowed. "What's that supposed to mean?"

"No more than I said," he answered, heading for the door. "Hippodamia, I know you're distressed about your mother. I only came to speak with you about Eurydike because the messenger must leave at dawn. I won't trouble you again today."

Hippodamia watched her husband's tall form as he left the room. He was nearly as trim as he had been the day they married – while her own waist, even with the tightest laces, was unmistakably that of a middle-aged matron.

Lifting her drink, she shifted her thoughts from herself to her daughter. *Would* Eurydike be happy with this marriage? Given her youth, she could not be deeply attached yet to any suitor; and surely the prospect of becoming queen of Mycenae would excite her. Hippodamia imagined her lovely young daughter bedecked with gold, and was comforted by the thought that the girl would go into her marriage with her innocence intact. More than anything else, Hippodamia prided herself in the care and protection she had bestowed on her children – unlike what her own mother had given her.

A serving-woman approached. "My lady queen, the healer wishes to speak with you."

Finally! She had been expecting to hear from the man all day. "Send him in," she ordered. In a moment the bald, gray-bearded servant of Apollo was before her. He bowed, but waited for her to speak.

"Well?" Hippodamia asked abruptly. "Is she dead yet?"

"No, my lady queen," he answered. "Your mother still lives."

Hippodamia set her cup down; its silver base met the inlaid tabletop with a sharp clack. "You said she'd be dead by now!" At once she realized she had spoken too harshly. "I don't like watching her suffer," she added, softening her tone.

The healer spread his hands. "My lady queen, it will certainly be soon." He hesitated, dropping his arms awkwardly to his sides. "She's awake, my lady queen. She's asked to see you. And the rest of her family."

"Is that so?" Hippodamia pushed herself to her feet. She had no desire to visit her mother, but she had to keep others away from the dying woman. "Then I must go to her at once." She shook the tiers of her skirt to be sure they hung properly, then walked out of the room, the healer following at a respectful distance.

Dusk was coming earlier as the seasons changed, but the lamp-lighters had not yet reached these corridors. How gloomy the wall-paintings seemed with all their colors gone to murk in twilight! Hippodamia was reminded of her father's palace, where grime and soot had soiled the frescoes and the unpolished bronze wall-sconces turned a sickly green. Cobwebs had covered the corners, and the doors had creaked on unoiled hinges. Even though that edifice had burned long ago, for an eerie moment she thought she heard her father's drunken bellow down the hall…

She shivered, and thrust away the memory. Lifting her chin, she acknowledged the salute of the soldiers standing guard outside her mother's chamber, noting with satisfaction that when the healer opened the oaken door it swung smoothly and silently.

A young acolyte of Apollo sat by the sickbed while an elderly servant woman tended the brazier; the curtains were already closed against the night's coming chill, and several lamps burned brightly. Thank Hera, no one else had arrived.

Snapping her fingers at the young man seated beside her mother's bed, she said, "Wait outside." She waved the servant woman out as well, then turned to the gray-bearded healer. "You too. I must speak with my mother privately. You will not permit anyone else to enter until I give you leave."

"But, my lady queen—"

"No one, do you hear me?" she said, letting menace color her voice.

"Ah," stammered the healer, "yes, my lady queen. Of course, my lady queen." He hurried out, shutting the door behind him.

Hippodamia crossed the room and took a seat on the stool the acolyte had occupied. Her mother Evarete was propped up on a cushion, and even that slight elevation seemed to weary the old woman. Her once-plump face had grown thin; the seamed, fragile-looking skin of her cheeks hung in deep folds. She squinted at Hippodamia with rheumy eyes; her cracked lips gaped slackly, revealing the few scattered teeth left to her.

"Mother," said Hippodamia, wrinkling her nose at the smell of sickness that clung to the dying woman. It was revolting to think that this creature had given her birth.

"I – I want to see my grandchildren," Evarete whispered.

Hippodamia did not care what the old woman wanted. She would not let her mother make any deathbed confessions: Evarete's inability to hold her tongue had already cost Hippodamia far too much. But she forced a smile to her face and shook her head gently, as though the invalid's well-being were her only concern. "Mother, they're so noisy! They would exhaust you. You need rest."

"Rest!" Evarete coughed, and Hippodamia jerked back to avoid a spray of spittle. The cough continued for a moment and subsided into wheezing. After a moment she gasped, "I'm *dying*. No need to save strength."

"You mustn't give up hope, Mother." Hippodamia leaned forward. "The healer tells me the medicine he's given you will work if you let it – but you must get more sleep."

"He – he told me I was dying."

"You heard wrong, Mother," Hippodamia said, feeling no guilt over the falsehood. "He must have said you *would* die if you don't take care of yourself." She took her mother's cold, frail hand in both of her own. "But we won't let that happen. I'll make sure you get some sleep tonight, and a hot porridge in the morning, and you'll be up and about soon."

Evarete closed her blue-veined eyelids as if yielding to her daughter's words. Perhaps, thought Hippodamia, the old woman was too feeble-minded to realize that a healer was more likely to give his patient hope of recovery – and convey the harsh truth to the relatives – than to do the reverse; or perhaps she was just too weak to fight her daughter's will.

Hippodamia set the old woman's hand down on the coverlet. "Relax, Mother," she said soothingly. "There's nothing to worry about – nothing at all."

She talked as she might to her younger children, hoping to lull her mother into slumber. The old woman's eyes remained shut, and her labored breathing slowed and grew more regular.

As she continued murmuring words of comfort, Hippodamia recalled a summer fever she had once had as a child. Her mother the queen had not come to her, because she was pregnant and feared taking ill herself. Hippodamia had endured the nightmares and the fever-haze with only a lowborn nursemaid for company. Evarete had never been there when Hippodamia needed her, *never.* Always too afraid – too fearful to do a mother's foremost duty and protect her daughter. And yet Hippodamia was here at *her* side. How strangely the Fates twisted the life-threads they spun!

Was the old woman finally asleep? Hippodamia let her voice grow softer, softer, and then fell silent.

But Evarete's eyes opened. "I want to see them," she whispered. "The boys – the girls – Pelops…"

"Mother, don't agitate yourself – give the healer's medicine a chance to work!" Hippodamia rearranged the cushions so that her mother was lying flat. Then she went over to a table on which the healer's kit rested. Among the various herbs and vials was a neatly tied bunch of dried marjoram; its aroma would help ease her mother to sleep. She returned to the bed and bound the marjoram to the bed post near her mother's head, as herb-women did to help insomniacs. "There, isn't that a pleasant, restful scent?"

But Evarete jerked her head away.

By Ares' bloodstained spear! Hippodamia cursed silently. How much longer would this take? Perhaps she should let the old woman overtire herself; death might come quicker. And if Evarete preferred suffering to passing peacefully – well, that would be her own doing!

Suddenly the old woman grew still, turning her head slightly as if she heard something. Then Hippodamia heard it too: an argument outside the door.

"You're not allowed entry," came the healer's muffled voice.

"We're going in." Hippodamia recognized the confident tones of her son Atreus.

One of the guards spoke. "But, my lord prince, the queen says—"

"She's our *grandmother,*" said Thyestes.

"Are you going to raise your weapons against us?" challenged a third boy. Hippodamia's heart leapt with anger when she realized who had spoken. "If not – and you'd better not – you'll let us through."

"Now," Atreus barked. Hippodamia heard a scuffle, then the door swung open. Three boys – Atreus, Thyestes, and Chrysippus – pushed their way inside.

Hippodamia jumped to her feet. "What are you doing here?"

"We're here to see Grandmother," Atreus said, folding his muscular arms across his chest. The sight filled Hippodamia with pride – what a king he would make some day! But this was not the time for him to assert his leadership.

"To comfort her," Thyestes added.

The third boy, Chrysippus, went towards the bed. "You want to see us, don't you, Grandmother?"

"Out," hissed Hippodamia. "All three of you, get out of here *now*! She's tired, and I won't let you bother her!"

Atreus' broad shoulders sagged, and Thyestes took a step back, but Evarete herself whispered: "Let them stay … please…"

"See, Mother?" said Chrysippus with irritating smugness. "I knew she wanted us."

Hippodamia realized she had lost the first battle; she would have to tolerate their presence for a short while, and ensure that her mother said nothing untoward. "Very well," she said, looking at Atreus rather than Chrysippus. "But only for a moment. She's exhausted."

She watched the boys move to the old woman's bedside. Each of them offered a respectful greeting. Sixteen-year-old Atreus gave his grandmother a soldier's nod and crossed his thick arms in a way that reminded Hippodamia of her own father; she wondered whether Evarete noticed the resemblance. Thyestes, just a year younger, was a hand-span shorter than his older brother, but at fifteen he was still growing quickly. He bent his handsome head, and muttered his wishes for his grandmother's health. Golden-haired Chrysippus sat on a stool beside the bed, and clasped the old woman's wizened hand.

"You came," the invalid said, her voice faint.

"Of course we did, Grandmother," Chrysippus said, stroking her fingers.

Hippodamia frowned. Why *had* the boys come? Strange, that three active youths wanted to spend time with a sick old woman. Her younger children had shown no inclination to pay their last respects.

"My darling boys," Evarete said, her eyes filling with moisture. "I must – I must tell you—"

"Mother!" Hippodamia interrupted, and Evarete started to cough. Hippodamia grabbed Chrysippus' arm and hauled him to his feet. "I told you that you'd tire her!" she said. "That's enough. Your visit's over." She herded the three youths toward the door, not stopping until they were on the other side of it. The healer and his apprentice, and the two serving women, edged further back into the shadows, looking uneasy; the door guards stared straight ahead, feigning deafness.

"We have to stay, Mother," objected Atreus.

"You can't. Your grandmother needs peace." Hippodamia closed the door behind her. "She's dying."

"That's why," Thyestes said.

"Laius said we wouldn't be real men until we've seen death," Atreus continued.

Thyestes added, snickering: "And until we've gotten a girl pregnant."

"*Laius*?" Hippodamia exclaimed, glaring at each of the boys in turn. "*Laius* is no expert on what it means to be a man!" She needed to limit the time that Laius spent with her sons. He was too old to be with them, really; the fact that he liked their company was proof of his own immaturity. She would not allow Laius to taint Atreus and Thyestes with his irresponsible ways. "How *dare* you upset your dying grandmother because of something *Laius* said!"

Hippodamia watched them lower their heads in shame; she then changed the subject. "Atreus, Thyestes: go find your sister Eurydike and tell her I want to speak to her. Not you, Chrysippus; you stay here." After her two eldest sons were out of sight she gripped the fair-haired boy's shoulder, hard. "You will never, ever countermand one of my orders again, do you understand? *Never.*"

He looked up at her, but the angle was slight; he would soon be as tall as she was. At least he seemed startled by the strength of her anger.

"Yes, Mother," he finally said.

"Very well," she said, releasing him; he rubbed his shoulder, looking more surprised than resentful. "You may leave."

"Yes, Mother." He turned and loped down the shadowy corridor. A burst of laughter told her that Atreus and Thyestes had been waiting for him just around the corner.

Hippodamia gritted her teeth. How could her boys be so blind? Why did they *like* their bastard half-brother so much? They must realize how their father doted on him. Didn't they understand he was a threat?

As she opened the door to the sickroom, she shook her head. Their age could no longer be an excuse for such foolishness. She herself had understood the harsh nature of political realities at a much earlier age. But, then, she had needed to.

It was time, Hippodamia realized, to stop shielding Atreus and Thyestes. Time to teach them what they must know if they were to be kings.

She walked back to her mother's bedside; the invalid did not stir, and at first Hippodamia thought she had finally gone to sleep. But then she saw that the old woman's eyes were open, and the wheezing breath had stopped.

Evarete was dead.

Suddenly queasy and lightheaded, Hippodamia stepped away from the corpse. She fell heavily into a cushioned chair.

Her mother was dead. She had been waiting for this so long – and now that it had happened she did not know how to feel. No tears came to her eyes, but her breath was shaky, and a strange tightness gripped her chest. Part of her felt intense relief: her mother's ill-timed words and foolish revelations could no longer harm her or her children. And yet in the constriction of her throat there was – guilt? Anger? Regret?

She remembered how she had felt when her father died: elated, jubilant, desperately relieved – and horrified, knowing that her father the king was really dead, and she had helped to make it happen.

Now – now her emotions were not so strong; there had been so many more years to wear away at the sharp edges of her resentment of Evarete. She despised her mother's weakness; she feared her age-loosened tongue. But what kind of daughter rejoiced at her mother's death?

Well, the people of Pisa must not be allowed to speculate about that. Hippodamia drew a deep breath and got to her feet, brushing a hand across her skirts. She forced herself to walk back to the bedside. No, she would not have the people of Pisa say that she had left her mother to die alone. That was not what had happened. She had come back into the sickroom to find her mother wearied by the boys' visit, but happy to have seen her grandchildren. She had died peacefully, with Hippodamia at her side.

Hippodamia reached out and pressed the dead woman's eyelids closed. Then she shifted the corpse slightly, bringing the withered arms into a restful position.

Her mother's last words... what had they been?

Something about Atreus: that would be useful. Might she have said that she could die happy, knowing that Pisa had such a fine heir to the throne? No, that wasn't right. Evarete's mind had never worked that way.

Then the door opened. Hippodamia turned around abruptly – fearing, illogically, the return of Chrysippus, but it was only Eurydike. The slender girl, her hair falling over her shoulders in graceful ringlets, stepped into the room. "You wanted to see me, Mother?" Then she stopped, her mouth falling slack. "Grandmother?" she whispered? "Oh, no!"

Hippodamia nodded gravely. "Yes, my dear. She died just a few moments ago. Her last words..." Suddenly Hippodamia knew what Evarete's last words should be. "Her last words, darling, were about *you*."

"About *me*?" asked Eurydike, her eyes going round. "What did she say?"

"She told me how happy she was about your wedding plans."

"My wedding plans?" The girl took a hesitant step closer. "Who—?"

Hippodamia reached out and took her daughter's hand. "It's not yet certain, darling, but your father is negotiating for you to marry King Electryon of Mycenae."

Eurydike's fine dark brows drew together. "But I thought he was married already."

"His wife died, my dear." Hippodamia put her arm around her daughter's waist, and pulled her away from the deathbed. "Death comes to all mortals; it can't be escaped, and we should not grieve overmuch for those who have gone to the Underworld." She glanced at her mother's corpse. "Your grandmother had a long life, and our staying in this sickroom won't help her now." She guided her daughter out into the shadowy corridor, telling the healer to prepare the body for burial and ordering a guard to inform King Pelops that his mother-in-law had died.

Then she touched her daughter's face. "We must speak of happier things, Eurydike. Let's go back to my rooms – we've a wedding to plan."

§ 1.06

"Aha!" cried Laius when he saw how the knucklebones fell. Triumphantly he removed his last pebble from the senet board.

"My friend, you play a good game," said the Corinthian trader. He leaned backwards, his bald pate shining in the torchlight. "But I've still got fight in me! Shall we make the next round more interesting with a wager?" He gestured to Laius' belt. "Your dagger against mine?"

But Laius was distracted by a slim figure entering the courtyard; he shook his head. "Some other time."

The visitor accepted this gracefully and rose to his feet. "Of course, my lord. Until then."

"Until then." Laius scarcely looked at the departing merchant; when Chrysippus was present, Laius had eyes for nothing else. Chrysippus had always been a beautiful boy, but now that he was entering adolescence – by Eros, no words could describe him. The golden hair against his tanned skin, the taut curves of his youthful muscles, the brilliance of his eyes: he glowed like a flame. He was like Ganymede, the youth so handsome that Zeus himself had kidnapped him. Even when, as now, he looked troubled—

"What's wrong, Chrysippus?" Laius asked, gesturing to the empty stool. He tossed the lees from the merchant's wine-cup into the shrubbery, wiped the rim on his kilt, and filled it for the fair-haired lad.

"Grandmother's dead," Chrysippus said, accepting the cup.

"Ah," Laius said. "And did you witness the death?"

The youth's eyebrows – just a shade darker than his hair, like bronze against the gold – drew downward. "We weren't allowed. Mother made us leave."

"Atreus and Thyestes too?"

Chrysippus nodded. "But she – she wasn't really angry with them. With me...." He let his words trail off, and took a sip of his watered wine.

Laius sighed. The queen was not kind to her third son – her *adopted* son, gotten by King Pelops on a servant woman, as all Pisa knew, though no one ever mentioned it in public. Laius considered comforting the youth, but did not want to offend his pride by offering pity.

Chrysippus set aside his cup. "Didn't you promise to visit Nerissa today?" he asked in a sudden change of subject.

Laius frowned; Nerissa was the last person on his mind. "I don't think I promised, exactly. Besides, it's dark, and it's a long walk to the temple."

"But she's the mother of your child," Chrysippus said. "Your son. Don't you want to see him?" His voice did not waver, but his eyes shone with moisture.

Laius studied the youth. Was this really about Nerissa and their small son? Nerissa was also Chrysippus' aunt, the much younger sister of his dead mother, and her mother was the boy's natural grandmother. Laius suspected that after Evarete's death and Hippodamia's nastiness, Chrysippus wanted to be with his blood kin. The king usually discouraged Chrysippus from spending time with his true mother's relatives; but if Laius was going to see his mistress, the youth's visit would be less conspicuous.

"You're right," Laius said, gathering the knucklebones and putting them in a pouch at his waist. He wiped his hands on his kilt and stood. "I should go see my son. Will you join me?"

Chrysippus smiled – and that alone was worth any annoyance that might result from this visit.

"All right, then," said Laius, pulling his cloak over his shoulders. "Let's go to the Temple of Rhea!"

As they left the palace, Laius grabbed a torch to light their way. In the agora, people discussed the news of Evarete's death in hushed tones while the last straggling merchants packed up their wares. Lamplight glowed in the upper windows of the houses of well-to-do Pisatans, and the aroma of roasting meat wafted from the palace kitchens, making Laius' mouth water. Well, perhaps Nerissa and her mother would feed them.

As they approached the Cladeus stream, Laius held the torch higher. Chrysippus said little, but he kept close beside Laius as they crossed the bridge. By the gods, the youth even *smelled* good – not with the perfumer's art, but a healthy scent that somehow reminded Laius of the king's best horses after a swift race. He held out his hand to help Chrysippus across a muddy patch on the far side of the river; when he let go, his fingers tingled with warmth that spread through his body.

"When were you here last?" asked Chrysippus.

"What?" Laius asked, startled out of his reverie. "Um, earlier this month."

They neared the Temple of Rhea where Nerissa's mother, Polyxo, served as chief priestess; Nerissa was also in the goddess' service. The temple was a dark silhouette against the starry sky; the altar-fire within was warm and welcoming. A young, white-robed acolyte started when they crossed the threshold, then bent her head and curtseyed. "My – my lord Prince Chrysippus," she stammered. "Lord Laius. I'll fetch Nerissa at once." She hurried out, headed for the cottage a little distance away.

Chrysippus went straight to the temple's back wall, where the image of the goddess was painted: a youthful, beautiful Rhea with golden hair and hazel eyes, an amethyst necklace around her elegant throat, standing in a chariot pulled by two lions. Everyone knew that she had been painted in the likeness of Chrysippus' true mother.

"You look like her," Laius said.

"I do, don't I?" asked the youth, gazing at it.

The resemblance, even given the stylized nature of the fresco, was clear: the shape of Rhea's neck, her chin, her sun-colored hair, even her graceful posture somehow reminded Laius of Chrysippus – and of Nerissa.

Laius put his torch in a bracket, noting that the pedestal for Rhea's mastiff – a golden icon in the shape of a dog, with rubies for eyes – was empty. Often Pelops kept the mastiff in the palace rather than on display, for he prayed to it frequently.

A woman's clear voice broke the silence: "Lord Laius."

He turned to see the mother of his son: garbed in the red of Mother Rhea's priestesses, a color which set off her shining blonde hair and the vivid green of her eyes. Her small, round breasts were firm, the nipples rouged; the belted jacket and flounced skirts emphasized her slim waist.

She was stunning. Laius wondered at himself: why *did* he visit so seldom?

Nerissa bent her knee ever so slightly, then turned back. "Come, Polydorus. Your father's here to see you."

The boy hesitated, a finger in his mouth. Laius knelt and held out his arms. "By Zeus, you've grown! Come here, Son – say hello to your papa!"

The two-year-old came forward on plump little legs, gaining speed as he came closer. "Papa!" he announced proudly.

"That's right, your Papa's here," Laius said. He ruffled the boy's pale curls, then pulled out the knucklebones he had been using in the senet game. "See if you can make a lucky throw, my boy." He dropped them onto the painted stucco floor just before the boy's feet.

Fascinated by the knucklebones, Polydorus gathered them up and then tossed them back to the floor, giggling.

Nerissa stepped over and crouched down beside her son. "He's so happy to see you," she told Laius.

"You're beautiful tonight," Laius said, pitching his voice low.

Flushing at the compliment, she reached over to take a knucklebone out of their son's mouth.

"I mean it," he said, catching her hand in his. "You've never looked lovelier."

"Oh, Laius," she whispered, her green eyes shining. "Why don't you come more often?" They both glanced back in the direction of Chrysippus, but the youth was still entranced by the image of his mother, tracing her shape with his forefinger.

"Stay tonight," Nerissa urged quietly. "Once the baby's asleep—"

"Who has come to pray to Mother Rhea?" called a voice from the doorway.

The gray-haired chief priestess walked into the temple; her fleshy arms held a bundle of pine branches. When she glared at Laius, he remembered exactly why he visited so seldom.

"Laius!" She began to arrange the pine boughs around the base of the inner altar, her back stiff with disapproval. "What business do you have with Rhea?"

"Mother," said Nerissa, "Lord Laius is here to visit his son. You want Polydorus to know his father, don't you?"

"Why, so he can learn how to drink and gamble?" snapped Polyxo, gesturing at the knucklebones.

"Mother!"

"What? I should show this one more respect? He might be the son of a king, but that king's been dead many years. And this Laius thinks he's still too fine to marry you."

Laius felt his face go hot. "It's not my idea – King Pelops…"

"You're not the son of King Pelops, are you?" challenged Polyxo.

"But I am," called out Chrysippus, still standing by the fresco. "Please, Priestess, little Polydorus needs his father."

At once the old woman's expression changed; a smile dimpled her plump face. "Prince Chrysippus!" she exclaimed, hurrying over to kiss the prince on both cheeks. "What a joy to see you!"

"I trust you're well, Priestess," he answered, looking serious.

"Well enough – though I need more herbs nowadays to find relief for my old bones." Releasing the boy from her embrace, she rubbed her hands against one another. "Pardon these hands, Prince Chrysippus. The goddess loves the scent of pine, but the resin is so sticky! So, tell me what made you come to visit."

"Grandmother Evarete died today," Chrysippus said solemnly. "I thank Lady Rhea for *your* health, Priestess."

The old woman sighed. "Evarete – well, I've been expecting that news for days. Poor thing, her health was wretched for years. I'll pour a libation for her shade tonight."

"Thank you, Priestess."

"We're all of us mortal, Prince Chrysippus. The gods granted the queen's mother a long life." She patted the young man's arm. "And you – you're getting so tall!"

The youth's blush was just visible in the firelight. "Father says I may be ready to race a chariot in the next games."

"That's all right, I suppose – but remember your royal duties, my boy. Don't follow the example of this one," the old woman said, jerking her chin toward Laius. "Too many games and not enough responsibility!"

Laius was tiring of this. He gathered his knucklebones and put them back in his pouch. "We've stayed long enough, Chrysippus. Your father will expect us back at the palace."

Nerissa stepped closer. "But, Laius—"

He shook his head. "Time for us to go." He walked over to the altar and took a pinch of incense from the golden bowl that rested on a tripod nearby, then scattered the incense over the flames as an offering to Mother Rhea. Chrysippus did the same. Laius retrieved his torch and soon they were back outside and away from the old woman's scolding tongue.

They walked along a while in silence, pulling their cloaks tighter against the night's chill air. Then, sounding hesitant, Chrysippus asked, "Laius, do you ever want to return to Thebes?"

"I left when I was so young, I don't even remember it," Laius said as they crossed the wooden bridge. This was not exactly true: Laius did have memories, unpleasant ones filled with screams and blood. Yet it would be unmanly to admit his terror and revulsion. "What would I do there, anyway? King Pelops' sister is queen of Thebes now."

"I suppose you're right," Chrysippus answered slowly.

"Besides," Laius went on, "to be king – by the gods, don't you see how hard your father works? Sorting out conflicting advice from his counselors, dealing with his builders falling behind schedule, having to settle arguments among the peasants – would *you* want to be king?"

"Me?" Chrysippus blinked. "I'm the third son! And not even…" he trailed off, not mentioning the matter of his bastard birth.

The torchlight revealed the firm line of Chrysippus' jaw, the graceful curve of his neck. By Eros, how glorious he was! His beauty far surpassed Nerissa's.

"Your father loves you," Laius said wistfully. "He may choose you to rule after him."

"I don't know about that," said Chrysippus. "But he'll find a place for me."

"That he will," agreed Laius. "He's found places for all his relatives." Pelops had arranged for his sister's husband to become king of Thebes. One of Hippodamia's younger brothers now ruled in Sicyon, and another was creating a city on the coast, strengthening Pelops' access to the sea. And an advantageous marriage had been made for Hippodamia's young sister. "But me – I'm no relation." His voice turned bitter for a moment, as he remembered what Polyxo had pointed out: he, Laius, was not one of Pelops' many sons or brothers-in-law.

"Father's fond of you," Chrysippus assured Laius. "He'll arrange something for you."

"I hope you're right," said Laius. But he could not imagine wanting to be in any place other than where he was that moment, with Chrysippus at his side.

TWO: FOREIGN RELATIONS

§ 2.01

Pelops' daughter stood beside him in his gilded chariot, a wreath of marjoram on her head; they followed the wedding procession eastward up the broad thoroughfare, towards the citadel of Mycenae. Lifting one hand, he waved in response to the cheers of the peasants lining the roadway. He wished he could simply bask in their adulation – but the ghost of Myrtilus, sitting backward on one of the chariot-horses, kept distracting him.

"Perseus is buried there, you know," the ghost said, pointing an insubstantial finger at the grave circle to the right of the road, a short distance outside the city walls. Pelops did know, for he had visited Mycenae before, but Myrtilus continued his commentary. "Now *there* was a man favored by the gods! My father Hermes lent him winged sandals to assure his victory."

Long ago Perseus had come from the east, like Pelops himself; he had slain a monster, married a princess, and founded this magnificent city. But had Pelops done so much less? He had defeated and killed Hippodamia's father, an evil man; and under Pelops' rule, the kingdom of Pisa had become a power respected in Hellas.

Yet Pisa's resources were still stretched too thin. The bride-price paid for Eurydike was not as large as Pelops had wanted, for King Electryon had been approached by many ambitious fathers, and he parlayed each option against the others. It finally occurred to Pelops to promise Electryon seats of honor at all future Olympic Games – something only *he* could offer – and that sealed the deal at last. Unfortunately, Pelops had yet to find means for hosting the next spectacle in little more than a year, and the extensions to Hera's temple remained unfinished.

"Such a costly wedding," Myrtilus observed. "So much finery!"

The reins resting lightly in his hand, Pelops silently agreed with the ghost. At least Eurydike looked lovely: in the noonday sun her long curling hair gleamed like polished obsidian, and the golden spangles sewn to her stiff flounced skirts shimmered with the movements of the chariot. How her mother had fussed over her this morning before they set out from Argos!

Hippodamia was at the front of the procession, reclining in a cushioned litter. "Her bearers must be exhausted," commented the ghost. Pelops snorted, for it was true – over the years his wife had become a heavy burden.

The two younger princesses walked after their mother's litter, accompanied by their well-born attendants. Nikippe would soon match her elder sister's beauty, and even stocky Astydamia looked graceful with her armful of white lilies and purple larkspur. Behind the girls, Pelops' three eldest sons followed in royal chariots, each drawn by two of Pisa's best horses. Pelops noted proudly that Chrysippus handled his team well. After that came a mule-cart in which Pelops' younger sons rode, with two stern nursemaids to make sure they behaved. Pelops himself, with the bride-to-be, concluded the column, and a contingent of Pisatan soldiers, their blue cloaks rippling in the breeze, surrounded the procession on all sides.

"A shame I can't change *my* clothes," complained the ghost.

Pelops glanced at Myrtilus: as always, the charioteer wore the tattered, bloodstained tunic in which he had died.

"I hope all this expense is worth it," said Myrtilus.

It will be, Pelops answered silently, but within he wondered.

They were approaching the city gate; above its massive lintel, two carved stone lionesses faced outwards, challenging any foolish enough to dare Mycenae's defenses. The road within the gate was cobbled with smooth stones; onlookers crowded onto the flat roofs of houses in the lower town and filled the narrow side streets. When the procession reached the agora, Pelops stepped down from his chariot and reached out a hand to help his daughter descend. After his sons dismounted, several of Pelops' soldiers led the horses away towards the palace stables; with pleasure Pelops overheard people admiring his steeds. Hippodamia left her litter and came to stand at Eurydike's other side, while the bride's brothers and sisters took their places behind. A wooden altar decked with roses stood at the center of the agora; beyond, at the top of the grand palace stairway, waited the Mycenaean royal family. Electryon and his younger brother wore torques and wrist cuffs of gold; their cloaks and tunics were dipped in purple. Electryon's crown, set with clusters of emeralds and pearls, had to weigh as much as a newborn child.

"Now *that's* wealth," sighed Myrtilus, and Pelops silently agreed.

They stepped into the agora; Eurydike gave her parents a nervous smile and then led her sisters towards the altar. The crowd, held back by Mycenaean soldiers cloaked in saffron trimmed with purple braid, fell silent – making it all the more grating when Myrtilus exclaimed: "She's even prettier than Hippodamia used to be!"

The ghost moved towards the girl, lowering his head to inspect her firm young breasts with their gilded nipples. "Are you sure you don't want to keep her for yourself, as Oenomaus kept her mother?"

Clenching his fingers into a fist, Pelops nearly missed his cue; Hippodamia jabbed an elbow into his side and nudged him forward. Refocusing his attention on the ceremony, he affirmed that he, Pelops, king of Pisa, offered his daughter in marriage to King Electryon of Mycenae.

The priest poured a libation of oil over the altar flames, and King Electryon kissed his bride. Then Eurydike, as she had been taught, turned and waved to greet her new people. The assembled Mycenaeans acclaimed their king and their young queen; the delegation from Pisa added their jubilant voices. Hippodamia clutched Pelops' hand, smiling and laughing despite the tears flowing down her cheeks.

Pelops lifted his chin, feeling a grin spread across his face. His daughter was now queen of Mycenae! What more could a father want?

The newly joined couple led the way up the great staircase into the palace. The interior was magnificent: brilliant, elaborate frescoes covered the walls, and the bronze fixtures were brightly polished. Lyre-players filled the hall with music, and servants offered each guest a goblet of wine as they entered the room. Hippodamia embraced her Mycenaean cousins, and then she and the younger girls were swept away by a group of chattering women. His sons mingled with other relatives, while Pelops received congratulations and compliments on the beauty of his daughter.

"The very likeness of Aphrodite!" cried a Mycenaean noble. There were bawdy shouts of agreement, and men called out the usual ribald jokes. "Why are you waiting, Electryon?" shouted King Electryon's younger brother. "Get her to bed now, while there's plenty of light to see beneath her skirts!"

Eurydike's cheeks went bright pink, but she giggled; Electryon swept her into his arms and carried her out of the room.

Pelops saw pride mingled with loss in his wife's expression as she watched the couple head for the king's bedchamber. He walked over to Hippodamia and touched his wine-cup to hers. "We'll be grandparents soon."

"Too soon," said Hippodamia ruefully. She sipped from the cup and then set it down, her shoulders sagging.

Did Hippodamia still think Eurydike was too young for marriage? At any rate, the matter was now settled – or, at least, Electryon was in the process of settling it, and the bloodstains on the nuptial sheets would soon be displayed as proof.

"You've missed the point," Myrtilus explained. "It's not Eurydike's girlhood she's mourning. It's her own."

Pelops adjusted his ivory shoulder-piece, sticky with sweat, while he considered the ghost's observation. From a distance – to the Mycenaean peasants who watched the wedding ceremony, say – Hippodamia might still present an image of queenly beauty. Up close, though, the deep creases in her forehead were plainly evident. Her hair was still abundant, but strands of silver sparkled beneath the dark henna dye; her breasts drooped above the tightly tied laces that firmed her thickened waist. Since Copreus' birth four years ago she had had two miscarriages. Pelops doubted she would bring another child to term, and felt no more duty to visit her bedchamber. Her ability to entice him was long gone; he summoned various serving women to sate his desires.

"It's our turn," Pelops said. "We're the older generation now." The fact that he was nearing forty did not trouble him; he was in better shape than Electryon, for example, who was several years younger. "After all, both your parents are dead."

Hippodamia frowned. "We're not that old. And your parents are still alive, aren't they?"

"As far as I know," he snapped. His father, King Tantalus of Lydia, had once attempted to kill him, destroying Pelops' filial loyalty – while Tantalus was furious that Pelops had taken the golden mastiff of Rhea when he left to seek his fortune in the west. Though there was no official contact between their kingdoms, Pelops always listened to the news brought by traders sailing the Great Sea. If either of his parents had died, he would have heard.

The lyre music stopped, and a herald announced a troupe of acrobats. Space was cleared before the empty thrones, and a group of lithe young men in loincloths began performing. Hippodamia joined hands with her younger daughters and led them forward for a better view of the performance.

Pelops had no interest in the show. He surveyed the crowd, searching for a likely source of information, and his gaze lit on the balding head of Prince Butes of Athens. Butes was the high priest to Poseidon in the busy port city; he would know the latest. Pelops made his way through the crowd to the Athenian.

"Your parents are in good health," replied Butes, turning away from the acrobats' cartwheels with reluctance. "Not long ago Lydia had another dispute with its northern neighbor – you know how it is with those Trojans! But your father and your brother Broteas won the battle. However much it may pain you to admit it, King Pelops, your father's a clever man."

Pelops ignored the jab and took another sip of wine, considering both the news and Butes' appraisal. Despite the Trojans to the north and the powerful Hittite Empire on his eastern border, King Tantalus had maintained Lydia's independence, and had developed profitable trading relationships with the empires of Egypt and Babylon as well. Lydia was wealthy – far wealthier than any of the Hellene kingdoms, even Mycenae.

"I know what you're thinking," Myrtilus said, yawning. "But you can't get your hands on any of that shiny Lydian gold. Tantalus will never reconcile with you – not unless you return the mastiff."

The ghost was right. Years ago Pelops had tried to establish diplomatic relations between Pisa and Lydia. Via the prior king of Sicyon, a neutral third party, Pelops sent a messenger bearing a pair of jeweled slippers as a gift and a request for a formal truce. Tantalus had flown into a rage, thrown the slippers into the fire, and – in clear violation of the duty owed from host to guest – ejected the envoy from his palace just as a thunderstorm was about to break. They later heard that Tantalus boasted the thunderstorm was the doing of his father Zeus, showing that even the gods spat on Pelops' effort. But since the man returned safely to Sicyon to tell the tale, Pelops thought it likelier that the storm was Zeus' way of rebuking the Lydian king's inhospitality.

"Do you have any news of Aeolius?" asked Pelops.

"Since he sailed away last year?" asked Butes. "No. He said that he was going to sail around the Encircling Ocean. I don't think we'll see him again, my lord king."

"He left a large part of his wealth with your family." Pelops tried not to sound resentful, but it was impossible not to think of it: Aeolius' vast treasure in the care of Athens. It galled him to see the enormous topaz glittering on Butes' thumb.

"He left it to the Temple of Poseidon," the Athenian corrected. "He left large gifts to many of Poseidon's temples."

"So I heard," muttered Pelops. Olympia had no temple dedicated to Poseidon – only the altar near the chariot track, honoring the god's creation of the horse. On that altar was a painting of the god, in Aeolius' likeness – but perhaps it was not enough. However, Pisa was not a sea-faring city – there were other deities to honor first.

"And I understand he's given quite a bit to you, my lord king, over the years—" Butes broke off, his head swiveling. "By the trident, that boy's beautiful!"

Pelops followed Butes' gaze. "Prince Chrysippus," he remarked, making no effort to conceal the pride in his voice. "One of my sons."

"So fair," observed Butes. "Your other boys are so dark."

"Yes," Pelops said. He decided it was best to change the subject once more. "Have you had any news from your sister Philomela recently?"

Butes nodded slightly. "As always, my lord king, my family is grateful to your sister, Queen Niobe, for her kindness to my unfortunate sister. The last messenger from Thebes informed us that your sister and her family were well, and that the new Temple of Apollo is almost ready."

"I see," said Pelops, struggling to hide his irritation; he should have heard such news from his sister, not this Athenian. "When is the dedication?"

"A month after the solstice," replied Butes. "I understand that the Tiresias herself will lead it."

"That's no surprise," said Pelops. The prophetess was handmaid to both Apollo and Athena; she generally participated in any important events celebrating those deities.

"She may even cease her wandering and take up permanent residence there," Butes continued, and a sly smile lifted the corners of his mouth.

Pelops scowled. He had not been especially concerned about the new Theban temple; Amphion was devoted to the god of music, and all cities needed shrines for their healers. But Apollo was also the god of prophecy, and the Tiresias – an itinerant prophetess who had been born in Thebes – gave voice to his words. If she decided to remain in Thebes permanently, it could change the balance of power in Hellas. Visitors seeking her wisdom would journey to Thebes, just as they now made pilgrimages to the Oracle at Delphi.

Had Amphion influenced the prophetess in this matter? Was he seeking to displace Pelops' favored status in the eyes of the gods? By Zeus, Niobe should have *told* him about this!

"The Tiresias adores music," Myrtilus whispered, his voice softly insinuating. "You may give her exotic incense, Pelops, but you can never give her Amphion's music."

"Of course, the Tiresias is not as young as she was," added Butes. "It would be understandable if she chose to stay in one place."

"She's not so old yet," Pelops snapped. He had to make sure that the Tiresias – and the gods who spoke through her – preferred Pisa and its king to any other city.

A commotion at the entrance to the megaron put an end to their conversation. King Electryon had returned with his disheveled, pink-cheeked bride. Several Mycenaean matrons followed them to the head table; once the pair stood before their thrones, the groom's old mother unfurled the nuptial sheets, displaying the requisite red stain. The room erupted with cheers and a fresh round of bawdy jokes; Electryon puffed out his chest and called for more wine, and Hippodamia rushed over to embrace her daughter. Even Pelops felt an unexpected shock at the thought that his daughter was now a wife.

"There was no blood-stained linen the night you first had Hippodamia," Myrtilus whispered in his ear, "just my blood on the rocks. There was no one to hail the consummation of your marriage – only my last words, cursing you and your descendants for all time."

My daughter is now the queen of Mycenae! Pelops retorted silently. *How well is your curse working?*

Electryon raised his golden wine-goblet, and the shouts and joking hushed. "I have an announcement," he said. "I am making a special gift to my new bride and my new father-in-law!"

Pelops grinned. This was what he had been waiting for. At last, Electryon would share some of his kingdom's wealth with Pisa!

"Mycenae will honor the custom started at Pisa," King Electryon continued, "and build herms at every major crossroads in the kingdom!"

Years ago Pelops had introduced the herm pillars which served as markers for travelers, and paid tribute to the god Hermes. Eurydike clapped excitedly, beaming at her new husband, and the rest of the guests applauded the king's gesture of respect to his new father-in-law.

"Excellent!" said the ghost. "My father will be pleased."

But herms in Mycenae would do nothing to pay down debts in Pisa. Masking his disappointment, Pelops stepped across the room to embrace his son-in-law and kiss his daughter's forehead. The musicians began a new tune, and servants led the honored guests to their banquet seats.

"My dear," Pelops said quietly, putting an arm around Eurydike's shoulder, "come, let's talk a little."

She came willingly. "What is it, Father?" she asked.

He found them a bit of space in the corner, partially hidden by a tall tripod lamp. "Eurydike, you have bewitched your new husband with your beauty. Soon he'll do whatever you ask."

She dimpled. "I hope so, Father."

"You must persuade him to make a large donation for the upcoming games in Pisa."

"But, Father ..." Eurydike glanced awkwardly around her, and lowered her voice. "How can I do that?"

"Remind him it's for the glory of the Olympian gods."

"But—"

"And then smile, plead, pout – whatever it takes. You're a clever girl – you persuaded your mother and me to find you all these pretty new clothes and jewels!"

Eurydike chewed her lip and frowned.

He grasped her right hand, held it up. "Jewels like this one." Deftly he twisted the ring on her middle finger and slipped it loose. It was gold set with lapis lazuli, the dark blue of the gem flecked with yet more precious gold. Pelops and Hippodamia had given it to Eurydike when her woman's blood first flowed. Stepping between his daughter and the wedding guests, he held the ring up for her to see. "You're fond of this ring, aren't you?"

"Of course, Father," she said. "You gave it to me."

He closed his fist around it. "I'll return it when you've persuaded your new husband to make a donation for the games."

"But Father!" she gasped, shock plain on her face.

"She's going to cry, and everyone will see what a cruel father you are," Myrtilus whispered. "Even *I* wouldn't steal from my daughter on her wedding day."

Ignoring this reproach, Pelops focused on Eurydike. "My dear, don't look so upset. It will be easy. You'll soon be with child; then your husband will do *anything* for you." He touched her soft cheek. "All brides ask their husbands for gifts. Trust me: your mother never hesitated to ask."

She nodded uncertainly; her lower lip trembled.

"I know you want to love your husband, but your first loyalty should be to your father. Now, you're not going to cry, are you? You shouldn't, not in front of all these people."

Blinking back the tears, she tried to smile. "No, Father."

"See there? You're a good daughter – you'll be a good wife and a beautiful queen. You'll earn your ring back very soon, I'm sure." He put his arm around her, and then escorted her back to her husband.

Myrtilus looked skeptical. "She won't be much help."

She will, Pelops retorted automatically, but he feared that Myrtilus was right. Like her mother, Eurydike seemed to think that wishing for clothes and jewels was enough to make them appear. If only his daughters had taken after their practical Aunt Niobe! *She* had never been overly attached to gems or glittering gold.

"But even Thebes isn't providing all it could," Myrtilus reminded Pelops. "And if your sister didn't tell you about the Tiresias' visit – can you still trust her?"

All through the evening Pelops worried about this question, scarcely tasting his food and paying even less attention to the jugglers and dancers who performed once the meal was done. Finally he settled on a course of action. After Electryon and Eurydike departed for the royal chambers, Pelops summoned the rest of his family to join him. He led them out of the raucous banquet hall, seeking someplace quiet where they might talk; a servant directed them up to the roof garden.

Upstairs, the sound of the wedding celebration was muted; as Pelops had hoped, the garden itself was deserted. A warm breeze stirred the leaves of the potted laurel trees, and stars shone bright in the ebony sky overhead.

Hippodamia took a seat beneath an ivy-twined trellis and drew her youngest son into her lap. "What is it, Pelops? The little ones should be in bed."

"I've decided I won't accompany you back to Pisa. I'll take half the soldiers and continue on to Thebes. It's been too long since I saw my sister."

"To Thebes?" Hippodamia sat up straighter. "How long will you be gone?"

"At least two months," he said. "Perhaps longer. I may visit some other cities."

His wife narrowed her eyes. "You can't leave Laius in charge that long. I assume you'll give authority to Atreus until you return?"

Pelops looked at his sons. "Atreus, I'm putting you in charge of the army, and Thyestes will be responsible for matters of trade. Chrysippus, you'll resolve any disputes among the people of Pisa. The three of you will form a ruling council while I'm away."

Atreus took a step forward, his disbelief plain to see even by starlight. "But, Father! I'm the eldest!"

Pelops set a hand on his son's broad shoulder. "That's why you'll be in charge of the army. But your brothers must also learn responsibility. They will listen to your advice – and you will listen to theirs." Atreus was too hotheaded; Pelops would not give him sole power. Chrysippus' intelligence would temper his elder brother's impetuous nature, and if Pelops put Chrysippus on this council, he had to include the handsome but less talented Thyestes.

The tension in Atreus' muscles did not lessen. "But—"

"I also expect you to seek advice from your mother and Laius," Pelops continued, speaking over the boy's objection. "All decisions will be made by the three of you, as the ruling council; but wise rulers consider the opinions of others."

"Yes, Father," Atreus said. Obviously he was disappointed; but Pelops found the fact that he mastered his temper encouraging.

Nodding, Pelops released the young man's shoulder. "Over the next two days I want each of you to think about how you will handle your new responsibilities. We'll speak again before I leave for Thebes."

Thus dismissed, the three boys headed back down the stairs, talking excitedly. "I'm going to try that new battle-drill!" Atreus said, his deep voice carrying.

Hippodamia handed the drowsing little boy in her lap to Nikippe and stood. Grasping Pelops' elbow so tight that her nails dug into his flesh, she pulled him to the far end of the roof garden. "I won't allow you to make Chrysippus the king of Pisa!" she hissed.

"Don't be a fool, woman!" said Pelops. "Thyestes and Atreus – *your* sons – will be two-thirds of this council."

She sniffed angrily. "I'll make sure they remember that." Whirling away, she went to rouse the younger children and shepherd them down the stairs.

Pelops rested his hand on the balustrade while looking up at the stars. The constellation of the Lyre was overhead – perhaps that would bring harmony, help to cool Hippodamia's temper overnight. Surely she could see that Atreus could not run Pisa by himself. Once he had settled matters with her he would speak with the boys, individually and together – and he would speak with the captain of his guard as well. He also needed to write out instructions for Laius; he could give his soldiers a clay tablet, sheathed in a sealed leather envelope, to convey to him.

And then, on to Thebes. He had to see what was happening there.

§ 2.02

Chloris stood on a stool in the middle of the room, trying not to fidget while the seamstress tugged the folds of her new skirt into place. The garment, with its four flounces, was unpleasantly heavy, and the waistband itched. But any time she shifted her weight or tried to scratch, she was pricked by one of the bronze pins the seamstress had inserted.

"Please be still, my lady princess," said the seamstress. "We're almost finished."

Chloris forced herself to stop moving. "Mother, why do I have to wear this tomorrow?"

"You know why," said her mother from her seat by the dressing-table. "The dedication of Apollo's temple is an important ceremony. You're not a little girl any more, and the people need to see you looking like a princess." Glancing down at the maidservant who was gilding her toenails, she added: "Although I admit it's hard to see what gold-tipped toes have to do with running a city."

Encouraged by that comment, Chloris pushed her argument. "The goddess Artemis wears a tunic, and she's more important than a princess, even."

The seamstress pinned another fold of cloth. "Just wait till the Maidens of Artemis come to Thebes next time, my lady princess," she said through teeth clenched to hold several pins. "You can wear a tunic to *that* ceremony."

"But if I can wear a tunic for Artemis, why can't—"

"Enough!" said the queen.

Hearing the annoyance in her mother's voice, Chloris ceased complaining; but she still disliked the new skirt. Its many layers of cloth would make her sweat, especially in this summer weather – though, she mused, the alternating colors of yellow and blue *were* pretty.

Lying in his bed near the queen's dressing table, Chloris' nine-month-old brother began to fuss; Mother reached over to rock the cradle. "Hush, Tantalus."

Three-year-old Sipylus glanced up from the floor, where he was playing with a toy wooden dog that Uncle Zethos had carved for him. "Ta-na not sleeping?"

"No," Mother said in a soothing voice, "your brother Tantalus is awake now."

Sipylus got to his feet and walked over to the cradle. "Ta-na," he said.

"Tan-ta-lus," Mother said, slowly and clearly; then she looked back down at the baby. "Hello, little Tantalus! Did we give you a good name?"

"Tan-lus," said Sipylus. He walked around the cradle, moving his toy dog along the wooden rim; the baby giggled. "Tan-lus, Tan-lus."

"What's wrong with the name, Mother?" Chloris asked.

"It's my father's name."

"How can that be bad?"

"I don't want him to be like my father."

Chloris twisted to stare; the seamstress gave an irritated click of the tongue and jerked her back into position. "Don't you *like* your father?" Chloris asked, confused. Mother usually had good reasons for what she said and did – but how could anyone not like their father?

Mother did not answer immediately; she first peered down at the gilding on the toenails of her right foot, nodded, and then stretched out her left foot for her maidservant. At last she said, "Father – my father is very capable. And very fortunate." She looked up to meet Chloris' sidelong gaze. "So perhaps it *is* a good name for your brother. Anyway, we can't change it now."

That was right, Chloris thought; after all, everyone in Thebes knew the name of the youngest prince. And once you told something to the whole city, you couldn't change it, could you? She recalled the baby's naming ceremony: dressed in their best clothing and sparkling with gold and gems, Father and Mother had gone out onto the terrace atop the main palace staircase. The crowd filling the agora below hushed to an expectant silence and then Father took the eight-day-old infant from Mother's arms and held him high for everyone to see. "Thebes, greet your new prince," he announced: "my son Tantalus!" Then everyone had shouted and clapped. But the best parts of that day were the abundant hazelnut cakes and Father's singing.

"How did you choose my name, Mother?" Chloris asked.

"Your name means fresh, like springtime. And that's when you were born, Daughter, in the spring."

"Tan-lus!" shouted Sipylus suddenly, banging his toy dog on the side of the cradle.

Chloris jumped at the noise, and the seamstress' needle jabbed into her back. "Ow!" she yelled. The flustered seamstress apologized as the baby began to wail. Sipylus' nursemaid rushed over to pull away the toddler, and Mother reached into the cradle to soothe the baby.

"Here, my lady princess," said the seamstress, "let's get you out of this, we don't want blood on the cloth—" She loosed the laces and slipped the skirts off.

"Let me see," said Mother. The baby in her arms, she inspected the wound. "It's already stopped bleeding. But perhaps you've had enough for now. Can you finish without her?"

"Yes, my lady queen, everything's pinned in place," said the seamstress.

"You mean I can go, Mother?"

"Yes," said the queen. "But don't get dirty, or you'll have to bathe before the banquet tonight."

At last, *at last*, Chloris changed back into her comfortable tunic. She kissed her mother and little brothers, then ran out into the corridor.

She started in the direction of the kitchens – with the preparations for a banquet underway, honeycakes might be available for filching – but as she rounded a corner she nearly collided with a woman holding a wooden staff.

"By Apollo!" The woman held her staff horizontally, blocking Chloris' forward progress. "Watch where you're going, child!"

Chloris stared at the unfamiliar woman and her stocky bald servant. The woman was very short: about the same height as Mother, but much thinner. She was dressed in drab gray robes; her long hair, likewise gray, was tied back with a simple leather thong. Her face was lined and sun-weathered like a peasant woman's. But the most unusual thing about her was the strip of black linen covering her eyes.

"Are you – are you the Tiresias?" Chloris blurted out.

The blindfolded woman smiled slightly, but it was a smile that spread chill instead of warmth. Feeling awkward, Chloris stepped backwards until she stood against the wall, but still she could not help staring.

"I am," said the gray-haired woman.

Chloris shivered: the Tiresias, although blind, was supposed to be the most powerful prophetess in all of Hellas – in the whole world. What if she had run into the woman and knocked her down? The gods might have cursed her!

"I'm – I'm sorry I was careless, prophetess," Chloris stammered.

The woman's colorless lips twisted wryly. "Next time you will take more care." She turned her staff and rested its tip on the floor. "And who are you, young maiden? A daughter of King Amphion and Queen Niobe?"

"Their only daughter, prophetess. I'm Chloris – Princess Chloris."

"I see," said the Tiresias, nodding.

The words struck Chloris as odd – the prophetess was blind, after all. And yet people called her a seer, so perhaps she *could* see, somehow. Chloris wanted to ask, but decided it would be rude – especially after she had almost run into the woman. The Tiresias was a guest in Thebes, and Chloris was a princess, so she was supposed to be polite. She should ask something else. "Are you here for the dedication of Father's temple?"

"The temple belongs to Apollo, not your father," corrected the woman. "But yes, that's why I'm here."

It occurred to Chloris that she could ask the Tiresias about her brother's name. If anyone could soothe Mother's worries, surely it would be the world's most gifted prophetess. "Tiresias, my mother is worried about the name she and Father gave my youngest brother. Will he grow up to be like my grandfather Tantalus?"

The Tiresias shook her head slightly. "You don't need to worry about that."

The words should have been reassuring, but somehow they did not make Chloris feel better.

"Come here, child," said the prophetess, tapping her staff lightly on the floor.

Chloris hesitated. For some reason she remembered the time her brother Phaedimus had found a poisonous scorpion beneath a rock and called her over to look: she had been both fascinated and frightened. But the Tiresias was a holy woman, wasn't she? And though her servant had said nothing – in fact Chloris was beginning to wonder if he *could* speak – the expression on his face was kind. Surely there was nothing to fear.

She stepped closer.

"Kneel," said the Tiresias, indicating a spot on the floor with her staff.

Chloris knelt on the floor; the tiles were hard and cool against her bare knees. She noticed the whitish dust on the hem of the Tiresias' garment and the marks of wear on her leather sandals.

The Tiresias reached out and touched her face. Chloris closed her eyes, trembling now with real fear; she had to resist the urge to shrink away. She felt utterly exposed, as though she was kneeling not in the familiar palace corridor but at the windy top of Mount Kithairon; for a moment she thought she heard something – a distant murmuring…

"Chloris of Thebes," said the Tiresias, her voice sounding far away. "You–"

"What are you doing?"

Mother's voice, sharp with anger, pulled Chloris back into the here and now. She opened her eyes and twisted around to see her mother rushing toward her. In an instant Mother was beside her, yanking Chloris to her feet.

"Ah, Queen Niobe," said the Tiresias, inclining her head. "I thought you must be close by."

Mother was breathing hard – Chloris did not think she had ever seen her mother run before. She gripped Chloris' shoulder tightly, and when she spoke Chloris could tell that she was struggling to keep her temper. "Tiresias, I would prefer that you make no prophecies regarding my daughter!"

"Do you fear so much what I might say, my lady queen?"

Mother's hand squeezed even tighter, then relaxed its grip; she patted Chloris on the shoulder. "She's too young for your pronouncements."

The Tiresias turned to Chloris. "Then, my lady princess, we will have to wait until you are older." Without any of the usual words of deference, she swept past Mother and continued along the corridor, tapping ahead with her staff. "Come, Dolichus," she called.

The servant bowed hastily to Chloris and her mother, then followed his mistress down the hallway.

Mother set her hand between Chloris' shoulder blades. "Come with me, Chloris," she said, heading in the opposite direction, towards the kitchens.

Though Mother said nothing further, Chloris could tell that she was furious. And there was more to her mother's anger than the prophetess' arrogant manner: Mother, she realized, *hated* the Tiresias.

More than ever, Chloris wondered what the Tiresias had been about to tell her.

§ 2.03

Her jaw taut, her heart beating hard, Niobe propelled her daughter away down the corridor.

"Mother, what's wrong?"

"That woman—" Niobe began, then stopped herself. The excuse she had given the Tiresias was at least partly true: Chloris *was* too young to hear whatever venomous nonsense the blind woman might spout – but by the same token she was not old enough to hear the entire truth of how Niobe felt. The girl might let slip a careless word, which would not do when so many people all across Hellas – her beloved Amphion included – revered the Tiresias.

Niobe took a calming breath and slowed her steps. "The Tiresias is a powerful prophetess," she told her daughter. "She is called the Voice of Apollo, and is said to sometimes speak the words of the god. Her words are not to be taken lightly. They can be dangerous."

Chloris walked along for a moment in silence, then ventured: "Like the holy serpents at Ares' shrine?"

It was a good analogy. "Yes, that's right," agreed Niobe. "Now, come along. I need to check on the kitchens – you can help." They reached the end of the hall and started down the stairway.

"Why?" asked Chloris, leaping down the steps two at a time. "Can't the servants handle it themselves?"

Yes, thought Niobe, the staff was competent; but still her sister-in-law Thebe should have confirmed that everything was ready. Since Thebe had neglected her duty, it was – as usual – left to Niobe to take up the slack. Aloud she said: "You can't count on things being done right unless you actually check." Niobe's own mother had said something similar to her when she was young; Niobe hoped Chloris would likewise take the lesson to heart.

Chloris stopped at the foot of the stairwell to wait for her. "But don't they mind?" she asked. "Doesn't it seem as if we don't trust them?"

An unusual question, thought Niobe. Most princesses gave no thought to the feelings of those who served them. "Well, you *can't* always trust your servants. At least not all of them."

"But what about the ones you *can* trust?" Chloris persisted, as they crossed the kitchen garden, filled with herbs and vegetables flourishing in the sunshine.

"They appreciate me noticing their work," Niobe said, detecting the aroma of roasting beef. She added, partly to remind herself: "Praise is important, too."

The cheerful noise of the servants' conversation filled the kitchen. Over the great fire-pit, the carcass of a calf roasted on a thick bronze spit; a husky woman turned the handle at one end, occasionally pausing to wipe perspiration from her forehead. Another woman scooped freshly cooked honeycakes from the long earthenware griddle while a third set out uncooked rounds of dough for the next batch. The head cook and her assistant worked at a wooden table, chopping mint and young onions.

The woman at the spit looked up with a start. "Oh – my lady queen! Princess Chloris!"

Niobe told the cooks to continue their tasks, and soon ascertained that all was in order. The meat would be ready in time; the pears were stewed to the right consistency, and the staff was adding the chopped mint and onion to a large pot of simmering chickpeas. Niobe allowed her daughter to eat a freshly baked honeycake while she reviewed the menus for the next few days with the head cook. Fortunately Chloris' fondness for honeycakes was offset by how quickly she was growing – like a bean shoot, that girl. And the way she ran everywhere – what was it like, to have so much energy? Niobe sighed, and absent-mindedly rubbed her belly. She felt so exhausted lately that she wondered if she were pregnant again. By Aphrodite, it sometimes seemed Amphion had only to *look* at her to get her with child.

And there was so much work to do! Niobe wondered how she would ever manage to survive the next few days. As they left the kitchens, she remembered what it had been like to supervise the arrangements for the first of her brother's great festivals in Pisa. That had been *far* more work than this event, and she had handled it with ease. But, then again, she had been much younger – and in those days she had not juggled the duties of wife, mother and queen. Well, Chloris was old enough to help. "We have to dress for the banquet," Niobe told her daughter, as they moved out of the hot kitchens into the cooler air. "And I want *you* to make sure that your brothers are ready."

Chloris wrinkled her nose. "I wish it were a ceremony for Artemis," she said. "Then I wouldn't have to wear those long skirts."

"Don't let your father hear that; he's devoted to Apollo." They re-entered the palace and started up the stairs. "You don't need to wear the skirts tonight; your best tunic will do." Entering her rooms, she paused a moment on the threshold: her mother-in-law and sister-in-law, both elegantly dressed, had arrived during her absence.

"Niobe!" cried Antiope. "There you are!"

"Yes, here I am," said Niobe. Her voice was sharper than she had intended – but she *was* annoyed to find her sister-in-law here, sitting on the room's most comfortable couch, instead of attending to her share of the work. Thebe, before she married Zethos and became the king's sister-in-law, had been a mere servant, and Niobe suspected that she resisted anything that reminded her of her former low status. Niobe, who felt that she toiled harder than anyone, had little patience for this attitude.

But she saw Philomela's blue eyes widen above her veil; the mute woman's gesture silently asked Niobe not to be angry.

Antiope seemed not to notice Niobe's mood: she went on breathlessly, "Thebe has the most wonderful news!"

"What is it?" Niobe asked.

Thebe looked up form her seat on the couch; her eyes were reddened and her full lips swollen. "I'm – I think I'm pregnant," she whispered.

"Ah," Niobe said, reluctant to sound too encouraging. Thebe had mistakenly thought herself to be with child many times before.

Thebe's pale face flushed, nearly matching the red of her hair; tears welled up in her eyes. "I know I've been wrong before, Niobe, but this time I feel different. Something's changed. I'm *sure* that Hera has blessed me at last."

Niobe groped for words. "I hope you're right."

"Such wonderful news!" Antiope said. "It's about time my Zethos had a son!"

Though the older woman seemed genuinely happy, Niobe watched Thebe cringe at their mother-in-law's words. For all her voluptuous beauty – and for all that Zethos doted on her – Thebe's barrenness marked her a failure. The pain of her situation was only exacerbated by the fertility of her closest female relatives. Niobe, Thebe's sister-in-law, was now the mother of seven while Thebe's twin sister, who had married a wealthy merchant and moved away to an island, had a grown son who was rising to power there. The pressure Thebe felt had to be enormous.

But kindhearted Philomela – unmarried, without living children, whose past was far more tragic than any other woman's in the room – sat down beside Thebe. She wrapped an arm around the copper-haired woman's shoulders; her sympathetic touch brought a wan smile to Thebe's face.

Antiope dropped into a nearby chair. "Let's have some wine!" she cried.

"Some wine to celebrate!"

As a servant prepared a cup for Antiope, Niobe sent her daughter Chloris off to dress and to check on the progress of her brothers. She then subjected herself to the ministrations of her own maid. The woman draped her in a loose gown of purple-dyed linen, fastening the shoulders with pins of silver and amethyst. Unlike Thebe and Antiope, Niobe had never been beautiful, except to Amphion's fond eyes. Still, she did her best to appear regal, to be worthy of her glorious husband. Her skin was good and her hair, though straight, was thick and dark. With a touch of kohl around her eyes and a crown on her head, her appearance was queenly enough.

Chloris returned, attired in a lapis-blue tunic and clean sandals; little Sipylus clutched her hand with his chubby fist.

"Are the other boys dressed?" Niobe asked.

"Yes, Mother. They're waiting for us in the side courtyard."

"Good," said Niobe. Her maidservant dabbed perfume on her wrists and behind her ears; Niobe breathed in the familiar scent of sandalwood and jasmine. She turned to her sister-in-law. "Thebe, would you prefer to lie down?"

"No, I'll come," she answered, rising.

Antiope put down her cup and got to her feet. "Of course you will, my dear!"

With the exception of Philomela, who rarely attended public events, the women left the queen's rooms. They met Niobe's sons in the courtyard; in the fading light of sunset, she inspected their attire. A tug of the belt here, a straightened cloak-fold there, and they were ready to enter the megaron. Her eldest son Alphenor – already a full head taller than Niobe herself – led the way into the crowded room, with Niobe on his arm; the other women and younger children followed. In one corner, a youth plucked chords on a tortoiseshell lyre; servants circulated with goblets of wine and trays of stuffed olives. Well-born Thebans chatted brightly, inclining their heads in deference as Niobe passed them. Antiope and Thebe stopped to speak with some of the women; but Niobe, fatigued, went straight to her throne.

Amphion and several nobles were in conversation with the Tiresias; he looked up and smiled, then took his leave and came over to Niobe. "You look radiant, my dear," he told her, "and your arrangements for this evening are as always, excellent."

But Niobe could not help staring at the prophetess. Standing near red-headed Menoeceus and his lovely young wife, the Tiresias gave a slow nod of her blindfolded head. Her haughty manner irritated Niobe. "Does *she* have to be here?" Niobe kept her voice as low as possible, for the Tiresias had keen hearing.

"We've had this discussion before," Amphion said smoothly. "Let's not repeat it now."

"Very well," Niobe said, gripping the arm of her throne tightly, "but I want her to stay away from our children. They're too young for her prophecies." Long ago in Athens, years before Niobe and Amphion wed, the Tiresias had threatened that Niobe's future children would suffer if she did not sufficiently respect the gods. Like so many of the Tiresias' prophecies, it was vague and subject to multiple interpretations. While Niobe did not believe the woman could see the future, most of Hellas did – and therein lay the Tiresias' true power.

"I know her words frightened you once," said Amphion, reaching up to push a few stray hairs back under her crown. "But look how well everything has turned out! We mortals can never completely know the minds of the gods. Prophecies which seem dreadful turn out well; those which seem wonderful sometimes hide an awful fate. It does no good to worry about it. Besides, look how pleased the Spartoi are to have her here!"

As usual, her husband spoke sense; a number of Thebes' leading men – called "Spartoi" or "Sown Men" because their ancestors had sprung from the soil of the city – clustered near the Tiresias, each hoping for a word with the prophetess. For these men, reverence for the gods was paramount; Amphion's construction of the new temple to Apollo, and the favor he enjoyed with the Tiresias, enhanced his legitimacy in their eyes.

But Niobe remained wary. "And what were *you* discussing with her?"

"Her travels," Amphion whispered. "The Tiresias was recently in Athens – and afterwards she visited *Delphi*." He grinned triumphantly.

Niobe could not resist her husband's delight in this coincidence; he had just composed a song to celebrate Delphi, a place sacred to all the gods, but particularly to Apollo. But before she could do more than smile back, there was a great stir at the entrance: Amphion's brother Zethos had arrived. "I'm looking for the most beautiful woman in Thebes!" he bellowed. "Thebe, my heart, where are you?"

Thebe and the women around her giggled; several of them eyed Zethos' muscular frame suggestively, but Zethos paid attention to no one but his wife. He pulled her into the circle of his arm, making the buxom Thebe look delicate beside his broad frame, and demanded a goblet of sweetened barley-water. Food was served after that, and Niobe was satisfied that even the Tiresias seemed pleased by the cumin-flavored beef.

Once the guests had eaten their fill, and even Zethos' enormous appetite was sated, the blind prophetess said: "King Amphion, it would be a pleasure to listen to your music."

"And it is my privilege to play for you, Prophetess," he said.

All conversation in the megaron ended as Amphion retrieved his seven-stringed lyre from its table. Standing in the space before the thrones, he called the children to take their places beside him. Chloris and the three oldest boys had parts in the new composition; they were all musically talented, taking after their father rather than their mother in this – for which Niobe was deeply grateful. As she pulled sleepy young Sipylus onto her lap, she watched her husband's long, elegant fingers as he adjusted the tuning-pegs. By the gods, how handsome he was!

Amphion nodded to the children, and sounded the opening chord. Many years ago, he sang, the Great Flood covered the world; and when the waters slipped away, strange new creatures crept forth from the mud. Among them were sheep and cattle and all the wild beasts – and a terrible serpent called Python. This serpent lived at Delphi, guarding a crack in the ground through which the Earth Mother, Gaia, whispered her secrets.

The lyre's chords shifted, and Chloris and her brothers sang the refrain, praising Mother Gaia.

Resuming the lyric, Amphion told how Hera, queen of Heaven, called the serpent to her. "Python," she commanded, "chase down the goddess Leto. She is with child by my husband and must be punished."

Python coiled and hissed. "I will follow her everywhere the sun shines, Queen of Heaven."

Heavy with child, Leto fled relentless Python, but she could find no rest: for what spot on Earth was untouched by the light of the sun? Then Poseidon, god of the seas, took pity on the pregnant goddess and led her to Delos. There he struck his trident and raised waves so tall and fierce that they hid the island from the sun. And there Leto at last gave birth to the twin gods she carried: Artemis and Apollo.

The sweet chords of the refrain rang out again: Chloris and her brothers praised the glorious young gods, shining Artemis and radiant Apollo.

Brother and sister were brilliant archers; so Hephaestus, god of the forge, crafted divine arrows of gold and silver to fill their quivers. Young Apollo – his part voiced by Alphenor – pursued the serpent that had tormented his mother. With a hundred golden arrows he killed it and thus conquered Delphi. He threw Python's carcass into the crack in the earth; this strengthened Mother Gaia, and she whispered louder.

As her eldest son sang, his boy's voice clearer than a nightingale's, Niobe realized that every woman and girl in the room was gazing at him. Even the Tiresias seemed enchanted.

Amphion concluded the song. Apollo chose a priestess to serve at Delphi and called her the Pythia; since that time mortals made pilgrimages to Apollo's oracle to hear the Pythia's advice.

Applause rang out; Sipylus, now awake, tried to clap too, moving his hands awkwardly together; Niobe laughed and bent over to help him. Thus engaged, Niobe did not notice the herald until he stood beside her throne.

"My lady queen," he said, "I have been sent to inform you that your brother has arrived."

"My brother!" exclaimed Niobe. There had been no word that Pelops was on his way to Thebes! She glanced over at Amphion, surrounded by a group of well-born men and women praising his performance. She turned back to the herald. "Quick; show him in!"

But the man who appeared at the entrance to the megaron was not Pelops. This fellow was short, thick-set, and balding, with a streak of gray in his long, curling beard. His tunic and cloak were edged with a costly border of purple and thread-of-gold, and his boots turned up at the toes in the Eastern style.

"Greetings, Niobe!" the newcomer shouted, throwing his arms wide. "How are you, little sister?" He began crossing the painted floor. All conversation fell silent; everyone turned to stare.

"Broteas?" gasped Niobe. She had not seen her oldest brother in nearly twenty years – and their last meeting had nearly ended in her own death. "What are you doing here?"

Amphion stepped over to her throne and covered her hand with his. "I invited him."

§ 2.04

"Welcome to Thebes, Prince Broteas," Amphion said. He smiled, then continued: "I fear Niobe's surprise has left her without words."

Amphion had seen Broteas only once, long ago at a festival in Athens. Since that time the Lydian prince had lost much of his hair, but his beard was longer as if to compensate. The beard covered most of the pockmarks left by the plague the prince had survived as a child, but Broteas was still far from handsome. His large dark eyes were dominated by heavy brows, and a great slab of a nose jutted harshly from his face. However, the man seemed energetic and vigorous, and his clothing and jewelry proclaimed his great wealth. And it was *extremely* promising that he had come in person.

A grin split Broteas' face. "My sister, speechless? She must be *very* surprised then!" He winked, and then continued in a formal tone: "My father King Tantalus of Lydia is pleased that his daughter has finally remembered him with the name you have given your new son. He has sent gifts to honor the boy. So that I could reach the palace tonight, I left the harbor before the unloading was finished, but Captain Naucles should arrive with the shipment tomorrow."

Niobe's lips parted as if she meant to speak; Amphion squeezed her hand sharply to discourage this and said, "We are grateful for King Tantalus' generosity – and to you, Prince Broteas, for traveling so far to deliver your father's gifts. But first let us offer you the hospitality of our palace. No doubt you'd like a hot bath and a good night's sleep after your long journey. I can have your meal sent to your rooms." Though Amphion eagerly anticipated private negotiations with the Lydian prince, just now his concern was making sure Niobe said nothing to sour this promising start.

Broteas glanced down at his dusty boots. "I suppose," he said, with a rueful look that reminded Amphion of Niobe. "Your herald said that you're in the middle of a formal celebration."

"Yes, we're dedicating a new temple to Apollo in the morning," Amphion explained. "I hope you'll attend the ceremony." He ordered a servant to take Broteas and his escort to guest rooms suitable for honored visitors. Broteas departed with a nod, following the man out of the megaron.

Reading the omens in his wife's expression, Amphion commanded the flute-players to take up a new song; he chose a lively tune, one that would soon have people clapping along with the rhythm.

When he turned back to face her, Niobe hissed: "You invited *him*? You know how I feel about Broteas!"

Sitting on her lap, little Sipylus tugged at her dress. "Mama?" he asked worriedly. Niobe ignored the child, which told Amphion that her mood was even worse than he had guessed.

"I extended a general invitation to members of your family," he explained. "I didn't know Broteas would come, but it seems a very good sign that he's here." He patted his wife's hand. "Why do you dislike him so?"

Niobe snatched her hand away. "You saw what he did to Pelops in Athens!"

"Yes: he accused Pelops of stealing Rhea's golden mastiff. But, as I recall, Pelops *did* steal Rhea's golden mastiff."

"That's beside the point," she retorted. "Pelops was completely humiliated!"

Amphion moved to stand directly before his wife's throne, hiding her angry expression from their guests. "My dear, that was so long ago—"

She shook her head, setting the tiny golden leaves and flowers of her crown into motion. "Broteas tried to *kidnap* me – I would have drowned, if Naucles hadn't rescued me!"

Remembering what both Niobe and the sea-trader Naucles had told him of this episode, Amphion selected his words carefully. "It was wrong of Broteas to try to force you to leave with him. But he did not try to drown you. You went into the water of your own accord."

Niobe reproached softly: "The Tiresias – and Broteas. In my own home!"

"You've been polite to emissaries you like less," he cajoled. "And you don't have to spend much time with either of them. We can make excuses."

She said nothing, but he sensed that she was yielding.

"My love, we have seven children already, and may have more." He reached out to stroke his small son's head, and Niobe looked down at the child on her knee. "It's our duty to them to secure resources and alliances to make their future more secure," Amphion continued. "Lydia is rich and powerful – why not let them help us?"

"Very well," she said, wrinkling her nose – a signal that she would do what he asked even though her heart was not in it.

The flute-players' piece ended; someone called for another song. Amphion gave them the ballad of Zeus' war with the giants. He followed this with a pair of rustic cattle-herding songs demanded by Zethos. After the third tune his wife told the servants to put all the children to bed; yawning, she followed them.

Niobe's departure prompted other guests to take their leave; Amphion set his lyre aside and went to speak with the Tiresias before she departed. "Won't you stay in the palace, prophetess?"

She shook her head. "Thank you, my lord king, but my sister expects me – it has been many years since I visited her. You and I both have family members to please," she added, indicating that she was well aware of Niobe's antipathy. Then her faded lips curved into a genuine smile. "But I will always remember this evening in the palace – such beautiful music! Your songs, your new temple: you are a gifted king, Amphion. I know you will do other great things for Thebes in the years to come."

Amphion wished that his wife could have heard *those* words from the prophetess. Assisted by her servant, the Tiresias departed; most of the guests followed. Only those very fond of their after-dinner wine remained. "Amphion, dear," his mother Antiope said a little too loudly, "why can't we have a temple to Dionysus too? After all, the wine-god is *from* Thebes."

Yes, thought Amphion: but the drunken orgies of Dionysus' devotees were often destructive, and had led to the deaths of two Theban kings. Not wanting to start a conversation on this topic, he responded mildly: "Dionysus and his Maenads already have a sanctuary north of the city. Besides, Mother, the Maenads prefer the open fields. You've told me so yourself."

Leaning back against her third husband, one-armed Phokos, Antiope frowned. "Yes, well..."

Zethos tossed back the last of the wine in his cup and beckoned the servants for a refill. "But, still, the Maenads might like a better place. What do you think, Thebe?"

"I think it's late," Thebe said. "The dedication ceremonies start very early in the morning. We should all get some sleep."

Agreeing with this sentiment, Amphion took his leave, ambling off down the torch-lit hallway. *Other great things for Thebes in years to come...* what did the Tiresias foresee? Perhaps an alliance with Lydia was what his city needed.

Amphion went to the guest wing. Outside Prince Broteas' room, both a Lydian and a Theban soldier stood guard. Amphion saw yellow light glowing through the crack beneath the door. He tapped on the door; from within, a deep voice invited him to enter.

Broteas, wearing a night tunic, his hair and beard damp, stood by the window. "King Amphion!" he exclaimed. "I didn't expect you at this hour."

For a moment Amphion looked past the other man, out at the many houses of Thebes, their tiled roofs lit by the waxing moon. His people, out there: all depending on him. He focused on his guest. "I trust you're comfortable, Prince Broteas?"

"I am. You are to be congratulated for the skill of your bath-attendants and your cooks, King Amphion."

Amphion smiled. "We're brothers-in-law; shall we dispense with formality?"

"Gladly," said Broteas. "But *you're* the sovereign here – I couldn't be the one to suggest it!"

Amphion took a seat. "I'm honored that you came to Thebes yourself."

"I wanted to see my sister and her family." Broteas patted his beard with a cloth. "My son's named Tantalus, too, you know. He's nineteen years old. And now you and Niobe have a babe named Tantalus." He sat down on the other couch; the lamp on the low table between them illuminated his homely face. The light did not flatter him – and yet somehow the wry twist of the man's mouth was engaging. "But Pelops has no son by that name, eh?"

"No, he doesn't."

"Our father is pleased by Niobe's long-overdue acknowledgement. And I'm sure you'll be pleased by the gifts." Broteas put his towel down on his knees. "Amphion, I'll be blunt. We want you to stop supporting Pelops."

So *this* was the reason Broteas had come in person. Amphion considered this, absently running his thumb across his callused fingertips. Finally he said:

"King Pelops has been building a group of temples. Our gifts to Pisa support this effort, and thus honor the gods."

"Amphion, I know my sister: she wants to keep Pelops happy. He was always her favorite brother." Broteas leaned forward. "*You* know what he stole from Lydia."

Amphion nodded. "I was there in Athens all those years ago, when you arrived to denounce him." He could not help smiling: that was the night he had fallen in love with Niobe. When Broteas' announcement threw Pelops into disfavor with the Athenian king, Amphion had been concerned for Niobe's welfare. As impetuously as any man ever pierced by Eros' arrow, Amphion had gone to the exotic eastern princess to offer his assistance. Though then a man of no standing, only a court musician, he had dared a kiss, which Niobe had returned – but then she had declined his help. That young musician would never have believed that years later he would be Niobe's husband, and the king of Thebes.

"The look on Pelops' face *was* amusing that night," Broteas said, misinterpreting Amphion's expression. "But his impiety is no laughing matter." A moth fluttered by; Broteas snatched at it, trapping it in his hand. "He's earned the gods' wrath."

"I don't know," said Amphion slowly. "The gods seemed to have treated Pelops fairly well. And Rhea's golden mastiff has a place of honor in her temple at Pisa."

Broteas frowned, but said nothing.

"Interpreting the gods' will is always difficult," Amphion added. "But they seem to favor Pelops."

Broteas opened his fist; the moth flew away. "We want your help in getting the mastiff back. You'll find Lydia a much more generous friend than Pisa."

It could hardly be otherwise, thought Amphion, remembering the ten cartloads of goods he had last sent to Pisa. But Broteas and his father asked a high price for their friendship. Amphion leaned back, waiting to hear what his guest would say.

"You have open access to Pelops' city," the Lydian prince continued. "I don't. He'll be holding those games again next summer; all you have to do is take the mastiff and bring it back to me. You'd be returning it to its rightful owner. A pious act."

Amphion was not convinced of this. Zeus, king of the gods, demanded honor between host and guest; and given Pelops' good fortune it was far from clear that the gods wanted the mastiff returned to Lydia. Yet it seemed unwise to refuse Broteas explicitly.

As he pondered this, a new thought occurred to him. King Tantalus was known for his utter ruthlessness – and Pelops certainly bent rules when it suited his purposes. How far was Broteas willing to go to achieve his aim?

"If the icon is so important to you," he probed, "why not take it by force?"

"That's a costly strategy," said Broteas. "And a chancy one."

These were sentiments Amphion could appreciate. Transporting an army from Lydia all the way to Pisa would be an expensive undertaking – and Pelops could slip away with mastiff despite everything.

Broteas spoke again. "The goddess will bless Lydia if it is returned. And anyone who assists in bringing the icon back to its proper home will prosper. Lydia will see to that."

"I'll consider it," Amphion said cautiously. "But perhaps you should find some other way to honor Rhea."

"*Another* way?" asked Broteas, lifting his thick eyebrows. "There's no way to replace the mastiff – it was made by Hephaestus himself!"

Amphion shrugged.

Broteas continued. "Rhea and Zeus have sumptuous temples. We make generous offerings to them both. But they want the mastiff returned."

Amphion lifted his hands in a placating gesture. "I meant no offense, Broteas. But surely you see this puts Thebes in a very difficult position. I'll have to give the matter some thought." The gods' will was obscure; furthermore, Amphion wondered if there was some reason for Broteas' sudden urgency after so many years. He needed to discuss this with Niobe.

"Of course," muttered Broteas.

Amphion got to his feet. "And what can we do to make your stay in Thebes more enjoyable?"

The Lydian scratched his beard. "It's always interesting to hunt in a new place. I hear there's good game around Thebes."

"Of course," Amphion said. "We have plenty of deer and boar in our forests. I can pair you with an expert tracker – my stepfather Phokos. And if you don't mind a bit more company, my elder children would love to join you; they're always eager for the chase."

"I look forward to it."

Amphion stepped towards the door. "Thank you for your candor, Broteas. But we should both get some sleep. The ceremony for Apollo starts before daybreak."

He left the room, hoping that the god of light and prophecy would help him make the right decision about how to deal with his wife's two powerful brothers.

§ 2.05

The first glow appeared in the eastern sky; around Broteas, the crowd fell silent. From their place at the top of the temple's marble steps, the white-robed priests of Apollo began to chant. The song was soft at first, but quickly gained volume and intensity. Just as the golden rays of dawn burst forth, King Amphion emerged from the temple's shadowy interior: he held aloft a burning torch and sang out a clear, joyous note.

Even though Broteas did not know the exact significance of this act, he sensed its power; a chill ran down his back, while the tall redheaded man standing beside him inhaled sharply. Broteas felt the shining presence of Apollo in the beams of sunlight striking the white tiles of the portico, in the harmony the king's voice made with the voices of the priests, in the hushed anticipation of the gathered worshippers – including his sister Niobe, standing with her children on the opposite side of the terrace.

Singing praise to the god of music and light, King Amphion slowly descended the temple stairs. He held the torch higher as if to share the new day's sunlight, and walked around the large altar that stood before the temple. Then, still singing, he turned and climbed the steps once more. The hymn was one Broteas had never heard – but it was glorious, magnificent, filled with rich harmonies. Amphion was said to be the greatest musician in all Hellas; swept up in the song, Broteas was certain no better bard could be found in Lydia – not even in the powerful Hittite Empire, or the wealthy lands of Egypt or Babylon.

As the day grew brighter Broteas could see the smaller altar within the temple; a blindfolded woman holding a staff stood beside it. Amphion's song finished with his final step towards the inner altar, and for a moment he stood motionless.

Broteas realized that he was holding his breath.

Then Amphion thrust the torch into the tinder on the altar; it flared up brightly, and the people cheered, shouting for joy.

The small woman, garbed in gray, lifted her staff high. "Apollo is here!" she cried, her voice surprisingly strong. "Praise be to Apollo!"

The priests began another hymn; there was a commotion at the back of the crowd as people shifted to make way for the sacrificial ram, its horns gilded, its head decorated with a garland of flowers. At the same time, Amphion descended the steps; an acolyte approached him and offered a gleaming bronze knife, which Amphion used to slit the ram's throat. Soon the god's portion burned on the outside altar; the scent of roasting meat filled the air. Broteas' stomach rumbled so loudly that the redheaded man beside him turned and stared.

"Excuse me," said Broteas.

"The ceremony proper is over – I doubt the god will be offended," the fellow said, though his tone implied the opposite.

An awkward beginning, but nonetheless an opening for conversation; Broteas fell into step beside the man as the crowd started down the hill, heading west towards town, and introduced himself. Rather reluctantly, the Theban gave his name as Menoeceus.

"Menoeceus," Broteas repeated with a polite nod. "I'm curious – religious traditions differ from one city to the next. What was the significance of the torch?"

"Its flame was lit at the altar of Apollo's old temple. Apollo's flame must never be allowed to die."

"Ah." Interesting: leaving aside the incomparable music, Thebes seemed a rustic place in many ways – but this was a civilized tradition. "And the priestess – why was she blindfolded?"

"That is the Tiresias," the Theban said, reverence in his voice. "She serves both Apollo and Athena."

"But why the blindfold? Shouldn't one who serves Apollo see his light?"

"Each man or woman who serves as Tiresias must be blind, Prince Broteas. But the Tiresias sees more than you or I: the sight of the eyes is only a distraction from the second sight granted by Apollo." Menoeceus raised an eyebrow. "Our current Tiresias is the most powerful in living memory. She put out her eyes with her own hand."

At this image – self-inflicted pain and blood followed by darkness – Broteas suppressed a shudder. But the Theban was clearly impressed. "A holy woman indeed," Broteas said, hoping to win Menoeceus' good-will. "It is a great honor to be assigned a difficult task by the gods."

"Yes," Menoeceus agreed, his manner warming slightly.

Their conversation continued all the way back to the palace; Broteas found his companion to be a laudably pious man and an avid student of Thebes' history. During the morning feast, he encouraged Menoeceus to speak of his city's traditions, hoping to learn something useful – something that would help convince Amphion to side with him against Pelops, and recover the Rhea's mastiff for Lydia.

He had known, of course, that Thebes' wealth lay in its prodigious herds of cattle; but the plain in which the city lay also yielded barley, wheat, and olives, and the vineyards produced a passable vintage. In speaking with the red-haired Theban, Broteas began to suspect that the city supplied even more to Pelops' kingdom than he had realized. This could be good news – the local people might be eager to rid themselves of such a burden – but Pelops would surely fight tooth and nail to safeguard such a resource. Perhaps, Broteas mused, it would be best if he did not encourage an open break with Pelops; Niobe would resist that anyway. But a Lydian alliance that helped refill the storerooms of Thebes might be valued. And once that friendship was established, perhaps he could convince Amphion to assist in covertly retrieving the mastiff.

As the sun neared its zenith and the morning banquet-tables were being cleared, Broteas' man Geranor and the captain of their ship arrived with the royal gifts. The timing was auspicious; it enabled Broteas to display the wealth and generosity of Lydia before a large audience. Two royal chalices adorned with golden bead-work drew appreciative exclamations from the Theban nobles; sumptuously patterned cloth – intended to make garments for the king, the queen, and their seven children – also garnered admiration. The most spectacular piece of fabric was the smallest: dyed in Tyrian purple and covered with glittering sequins, it was meant for little Tantalus. Broteas also delivered bags of myrrh and precious frankincense, and finally a carved ivory box filled with cylinder-seals of lapis lazuli that could be reworked into jewelry or ring-seals. Amphion's gratitude seemed genuine, but Niobe remained cool.

It would take time, Broteas knew, to win her over; he should plan to stay for several days. Because the king and queen were busy with events connected with the dedication of the new temple, he arranged to go hunting on the morrow.

The party that joined him early the next morning was rather odd. Phokos, the so-called expert tracker, proved to be an aging fellow with only one arm; the princes, Alphenor and Phaedimus, were smooth-cheeked boys. There were four servants, none of whom looked particularly impressive. And then there was Princess Chloris. Of course, some women sought to emulate holy Artemis, and called themselves huntresses – but Broteas had never met a woman who possessed with any real skill, and Chloris was only a child! Suppressing his disappointment, Broteas reminded himself that pleasure was not the point of today's outing; he was here to become acquainted with his nephews and his niece.

In the cool of the morning, Phokos led the hunting party north of the city. And, despite his unpromising companions, Broteas' mood quickly improved. The sky was cloudless, a wash of pink spreading over the eastern horizon. Crimson poppies bloomed between the road and the marshy lake to their right, bright as drops of blood in the sun's first slanting rays. Phokos' dogs were well trained: not bounding too far ahead, but keeping their noses active, seeking the scent of prey. There *was* nothing like the hunt – even if they came back empty-handed, which seemed more than likely, it could be an enjoyable day.

They followed King Amphion's broad roadway until the sun was well risen. Broteas was impressed by the quick pace the princes and princess maintained; Alphenor and Chloris, both tall for their ages, obviously had strength and endurance to move even faster, but they held back out of consideration for their younger brother Phaedimus and old Phokos. As they walked, Alphenor pointed out the sights: orchards of olives and pomegranates; the sanctuary of Dionysus where the Maenads held their revels; and a pair of mountains further to the north that formed a narrow passage, an ideal spot for brigands to mount an ambush. "My father killed most of them," Alphenor reported, pride in his voice, "and chased off the rest. His soldiers patrol there all the time. It's been safe for travelers for years."

"Commendable," said Broteas, impressed that King Amphion was a soldier as well as a musician.

Some distance ahead the dogs stopped, rigid with attention. The hunters quickened their steps to catch up, and Phokos gestured northwest with his single arm. "This way."

Broteas nodded, noticing a few faint hoof-prints in the hard earth. They left Amphion's well-maintained road and entered the wilderness. In the forest, Princess Chloris' mettle became clear. She was a better tracker than her brothers, spotting traces even one-armed Phokos failed to see: the broken twig, the spoor hidden in shadow, the bushes and patches of grass where the deer had grazed. When they spotted their quarry and had to give chase, Chloris proved fleet-footed and fearless: outpacing all but the swiftest of the hunting dogs, she leapt easily over fallen logs and pushed on through brambles and stinging nettles. Broteas found himself more mesmerized by the girl-child than the pursuit itself: it was as if his favorite goddess had taken mortal form to run before him. In the end, once the stag had fallen and the dogs led them to its bleeding carcass, he found Chloris' arrow, fletched with yellow-dyed feathers, buried deep in the beast's right eye.

Kneeling beside the stag, he looked up at her. "Your arrow alone might have felled it, Princess. We should award this kill to you."

"I told you!" she crowed, grinning, and slapped her older brother Alphenor on the arm. "I told you I could take a stag myself!"

The prince knelt to adjust his sandals. "Still, you'd better not go out hunting without your brothers, Chloris. Pretty soon every boy in Thebes will be running after you."

She stuck out her tongue. "Of course they'll run *after* me. I already run faster than Phaedimus. Even you have a hard time keeping up with me."

Broteas freed the arrow, wiped it on the stag's pelt, and returned it to Chloris. "You're certainly favored by Artemis, Princess."

She took the arrow with dirt-smudged hands. "Do you think so?"

"Yes," he said, shifting his quiver-strap back into place. "The gods sometimes decide to bless particular mortals with gifts; Lady Artemis seems to have chosen you." Though it seemed impious, he could not help thinking that this girl had something of the goddess about her. No statue or painting of a goddess had ever inspired him so: she was beauty, grace and ability incarnate.

Well, be that as it may, there was work to be done. Broteas pulled out his obsidian-bladed knife and assisted Phokos in field-dressing the stag. Its entrails, thankfully, looked normal; Broteas hoped that meant his likening of Chloris to the Divine Huntress had not offended the goddess. The servants lashed the dead beast's legs together and then hoisted the carcass on a shoulder-pole for the walk back to Thebes.

Before they had gone far, the younger prince touched his arm. "Uncle Broteas!" he whispered excitedly, pointing, "I think those are hare tracks!"

"Well spotted," said Broteas, patting the boy's shoulder. "But we've taken our quarry for the day."

During the long walk back to town Broteas turned the conversation to the games that Pelops would hold next summer, and found the children enthusiastic on the topic. Chloris and Phaedimus listed all of the athletic contests that would be held, and named the previous winners of each; they emphasized the wrestling triumphs of Zethos, their father's brother. Alphenor and Phaedimus said they planned to enter the youth archery competition and the boys' footraces; Chloris seemed annoyed that as a girl she could not compete. Broteas asked how the athletic fields were laid out, and where the temples were located. Alphenor, the only one of the children who had been to Pisa, answered this question somewhat vaguely – but he did mention visiting the temples of Zeus and Rhea. Broteas probed, asking the boy whether he recalled a golden icon in the shape of dog.

"About this big?" asked Alphenor, gesturing with his hands. "With red eyes?"

The eyes of the sacred mastiff were blood-red rubies; Broteas' heart leapt. "Yes – where was it kept?"

Alphenor frowned, and admitted that he could not recall exactly. "One of the temples."

"No matter," Broteas said, not wanting to pursue the matter so intently that it would be reported back to Amphion and Niobe. Changing the subject, he told the children about their grandfather's riches and the battles Lydia had won against Troy; this entertained them until they reached the palace.

The following day Niobe finally received him – in the queen's audience room, as if his only connection to her was that of a foreign dignitary. She sat stiffly on a cushioned chair near the central hearth. The frescoed walls depicted a procession of young maidens taking gifts to an altar, all wearing expressions far more cheerful than Niobe's.

Broteas took a seat and sought to improve his sister's mood by praising her children. It was easy to do: they were clever, attractive and strong. "It must be your husband's devotion to Apollo, Sister," he said. "The god of medicine has blessed your children with beauty and good health."

Niobe picked a bit of lint from her skirts. "Perhaps," she said, sounding indifferent.

With a rueful thought about his own homely countenance, Broteas sought another approach. "Our own family was less fortunate." A plague had struck the royal house of Lydia before Pelops and Niobe were born, carrying off Broteas' other brothers and sisters and leaving him with scarred and pitted skin. "Do you think in his devotion to Zeus, Father offended Apollo?"

His sister glanced towards the eastern wall. "Father offended in many ways."

Clearly *that* was not the right path to take. "Ah, yes, well, I only meant that – that it would have meant so much to Mother to see all her children as healthy as yours, Niobe."

Niobe's expression softened. "How is Mother?"

"She misses you. She speaks of you often, Niobe. She regrets the misunderstanding that made you leave Lydia."

"If she hadn't tried to make me marry that horrible old priest—"

"Niobe," Broteas snapped, "my *wife* is the daughter of that 'horrible' old priest!" He took a deep breath and continued. "Besides, that was years ago – and the man's been dead nearly as long. Can't you forgive Mother?"

"I don't know," she said slowly. "Maybe."

"Let's heal the breach between us, Sister, for her sake. And for your children's sake. Lydia is wealthy – you of all people know that. An alliance between our cities will benefit your family."

"Will it? It would certainly cause problems with Pelops."

"Pelops," Broteas repeated slowly. This was the core issue that divided them. "Why are you so devoted to him? I'm every bit as much your brother. Just because he's handsome and I'm ugly—"

"Don't be ridiculous," she interrupted – but from the way her face reddened, Broteas was sure that his words held some truth. "Pelops helped me when I wanted to leave Lydia," Niobe continued in a defensive voice. "You tried to kidnap me and force me to go back!"

"That's true. But later *Pelops* tried to force you to wed the king of Athens. He even locked you up, said he wouldn't let you out until you agreed – you had to run away again."

"How do you know that?" she asked hoarsely.

"Captain Naucles told me. Don't be angry with him for speaking the truth." He extended a hand in entreaty. "And, Sister, the truth is that Pelops does not merit your loyalty."

"Pelops' support made it possible for my husband to hold the Theban throne. He's a powerful man in Hellas," Niobe said. "He's accomplished a great deal. Pisa was nothing before he became its king, and now his influence is felt throughout the southern peninsula. His games and his temples are talked about from Crete to Thrace."

"In Lydia as well." Broteas leaned forward, resting his elbows on his knees. "And tribute is what pays for all of that: tribute from places like Thebes. How much more do you want to send to him? Those resources should be going towards your children's future!"

She did not answer him directly, which convinced Broteas that some of his arguments were reaching her. "I won't help you steal the mastiff."

"How can you call it stealing," Broteas asked, "when Pelops stole it in the first place?"

She twisted a ring that she wore on her thumb. "Why do you want it back, after all these years?"

"Father's always wanted it back."

"Did he make trouble for you when you failed to retrieve it – and me?"

"Some." Broteas preferred not to describe Tantalus' enraged reaction; only success in the battles against Troy had restored him to his father's favor. "But then he decided that Zeus would help him regain the mastiff when the time was right. Now, he says, the time has come."

Niobe's keen eyes seemed to read his thoughts as if they were chiseled on his forehead. "Is Father threatening you?"

"Niobe!" he exclaimed, avoiding the question. "I just think he would be – ah – more relaxed if the icon returned to Lydia. That's its rightful place, after all." He paused. "But you say you won't help."

She hesitated, but only for an instant. "I never go to Pisa anyway. I'm with child so much of the time."

"Of course," said Broteas. Clearly he would have to find some other way. "Niobe, promise me this much: neither you nor your husband will tell Pelops of Lydia's interest in the mastiff."

Again she hesitated. "It... it wouldn't be proper to mention that," she said at last. "You're our guest. We wouldn't violate the bond between guest and host."

Broteas nodded, grateful for her agreement but also hearing the unspoken message: as guests in Pisa, Niobe's family would not violate that bond either.

Niobe shifted in her chair. "I'd like to write Mother a letter, if you'll carry it back to Lydia."

"Of course," said Broteas. He turned the conversation to other matters.

The next day Broteas returned to Apollo's temple, hoping the god would grant him wisdom. It was a pretty place – nothing spectacular by Lydian standards, but the building was harmonious and its hilltop setting peaceful. The wooden columns were painted saffron-yellow, their round stone bases and capitals covered in gold leaf; the warm glow enlivened the white marble of the tiles.

Inclining his head to the priests, Broteas entered the temple. Just behind the inner altar stood a painted wooden image of the god on a pedestal, half life-size. The god held an ivory lyre with real strings; his head was crowned with a wreath of fragrant laurel leaves.

Broteas loosed a small leather bag from his belt. *Apollo,* he prayed silently, *enlighten me. Show me what I must do next.* Then he upended the bag into his right palm and sprinkled the precious incense into the altar flames.

"What a lovely scent!"

Broteas turned to see who had spoken. "Tiresias?" The god was answering his prayer – and so quickly! He could scarcely believe his good fortune. He dusted off his hands, and slipped the pouch back into his belt.

The small, gray-haired woman stepped forward. She did not use her staff to feel ahead in her path, as the blind often did – she did not even use it as a walking-stick, but held the wooden shaft as a king might a scepter. "Your gift to the god is pleasing."

"I am his servant," Broteas answered. "And I am honored by your presence, Tiresias."

"All Thebes talks of your visit, Prince Broteas. The brother of Queen Niobe and King Pelops – and of course the son of the magnificent King Tantalus."

She had known who he was without asking – she *was* a powerful seer! His excitement building, he exhaled slowly. "Prophetess," he asked, "how can I fulfill the task my father Tantalus has given me?"

She set the tip of her staff against the polished marble floor. For a moment she was silent; the black cloth that covered her eyes rendered her expression obscure.

"You wish to take Rhea's mastiff."

Again Broteas was amazed – he wondered for a moment if Amphion had revealed his intentions to her. But he did not believe Amphion would do this; besides, given what he had heard, Amphion and the Tiresias had not met privately since Broteas' arrival in Thebes.

"The mastiff belongs to Lydia," he admitted. "My father wants it returned."

"And King Pelops wants it to stay in Pisa."

Of course, thought Broteas – but then he wondered how to interpret her words. He had asked the god for guidance: was the prophetess saying the gods meant the icon to stay with Pelops?

And yet… Broteas remembered how readily his father-in-law, the high priest of Zeus, had yielded to King Tantalus. Was the Tiresias speaking for the gods, or for his charismatic brother?

"What should I do, Tiresias?" Broteas asked.

"You cannot expect me to advise you against King Pelops," said the Tiresias. "Not when I have enjoyed his hospitality so often." She summoned her manservant and turned to go.

Pelops was brilliant, Broteas thought bitterly. His games incurred guest-debt from the most powerful people in Hellas. Had his temples incurred guest-debt even with the gods?

That night after dinner, Broteas invited his man Geranor to share some of Amphion's wine in his guest chamber. Geranor was blunt: "Will your sister and her husband agree to retrieve the mastiff, my lord prince?"

Broteas shook his head. "Niobe won't do it. Amphion – well, he listened, at least. He knows his ties to Pelops are draining his kingdom, while alliance with Lydia would enrich him."

"No commitments, then, my lord prince."

"Not yet." Broteas set down his wine-cup and walked over to the window. Compared to the starry sky above, the lights of Thebes were insignificant. Yet – insignificant town or no – his sister was queen here; and his brother Pelops was king of Pisa, with a reputation that spanned the Great Sea. Yet he, Broteas, was the eldest; by birthright he should be the most successful.

He turned back to face his companion. "We'll have to arrange a party to fetch the mastiff." He would tell his father that his visit to Thebes had yielded information that would prove useful in this endeavor. "Pelops' games would be the best opportunity."

"I'd like to see those games myself," said Geranor.

"So would I," Broteas admitted, although he did not see how he could go without being recognized. "So would I."

§ 2.06

Pelops' visits to Sicyon, Corinth, and Athens proved worthwhile. Sicyon's king, one of Hippodamia's younger brothers, owed his recently acquired throne to Pelops; he yielded readily when Pelops demanded a greater tribute of dried fish and worked leather goods to be delivered in the fall. Pelops could not demand tribute from Corinth – the wealthy trading center was too powerful – but he leveraged the king's piety and self-importance. "Corinth has its famous Temple of Aphrodite, where men can take their pleasure," Pelops said, "but don't you think Corinth should do something to support marriage as well?" So the Corinthian king agreed to donate a statue of Hera, goddess of marriage, to grace her temple in Pisa. Then in Athens, after King Erechtheus was well into his cups, Pelops described – with some exaggeration – the statue promised by Corinth. Pelops followed this with praise of Athens' riches, saying that the ships of Corinth were nothing to the Athenian fleet, but that no one would know it unless Athens made a more generous donation to show up its rival. When the Athenian king agreed, his brother Butes was hard-pressed to disguise his scorn at his brother's gullibility. The morning Pelops left for Thebes, Butes congratulated him on his deviousness – and warned that if Butes ever inherited the throne from his brother, Pelops would have a harder time procuring Athenian silver.

Still, Pelops needed more resources for next year's festival. And now, as his chariot neared Thebes, Pelops was unsure what to expect – from a city where he should have had no doubts. By Zeus, Niobe was his sister! Amphion had been a common musician when they first met! How could his position here have weakened? Squinting against the morning sun, Pelops brushed sweat from his forehead and shifted his left shoulder beneath its ivory-tiled armor; his skin clung to the perspiration-soaked leather straps holding the piece in place.

When they passed the herm marking the boundary of Theban territory, Pelops sent a runner ahead to inform the palace of his arrival.

"If you arrived unannounced you might learn more," Myrtilus' shade whispered.

The ghost had a point, but it was more important that he arrive in a manner that befitted the king of Pisa – especially if his influence here had lessened.

The crowd turning out to cheer his arrival was as large as could be expected given the short notice. Youths ran alongside his column, admiring his horses and praising the Olympic games – but Pelops heard one shrill-voiced woman exclaim about the gold leaf on his chariot, and wonder whether her husband's labor had purchased it. Pelops craned his neck to identify the speaker, but the street was too packed for him to find her. Making his way into the agora, he saw that his sister and her husband waited for him on the palace steps.

"King Pelops – Brother! We are honored by your visit!" Amphion called out, descending the stairs with his arms wide in welcome.

Pelops jumped down from his chariot and accepted the embrace, noting that Amphion remained trim and fit. But his brother-in-law had aged in other ways: his face was lined, and the hair on his head and chest was scattered with gray – whereas Pelops' hair was still dark.

"It's so good to see you!" cried Niobe.

Pelops hugged his little sister, who had not made her way down the steps as quickly as her husband. "Niobe, you look wonderful!" he exclaimed, with some astonishment. Niobe had never been a beauty – not like Hippodamia – but in comparison to his wife, his sister glowed with health in a way that Hippodamia's cosmetician could not replicate.

"We heard you were traveling, and hoped you might come to see us," said Amphion.

"We'll have a formal banquet tomorrow," Niobe said, taking Pelops' arm, "when you've had a chance to recover from your journey. In the meantime, come inside and relax."

Pelops told his men to take care of the chariots and the horses; only one pair of guards followed him up the stairs and into the palace. Amphion led the group into a central courtyard, where a trellis covered with a flowering vine offered shade, and servants stood ready with broad wicker fans. Pelops took a seat on a wooden bench beneath the trellis. A maidservant knelt at his feet to unbuckle his sandals, while a second girl brought a basin of water scented with mint. Pelops allowed himself to enjoy the sensation of having his feet washed by two pretty girls, and drank a cup of watered wine to quench his thirst. The servants' fans created a comfortable breeze.

"Don't get too relaxed," said Myrtilus' ghost, wandering around the courtyard. "You can't let your guard down with these two."

The girls toweled his feet dry and offered him a pair of house-slippers. He watched them depart with the foot-basin, enjoying the gentle sway of their hips – but he did not allow himself to get distracted. He was here for a specific reason. "I heard you have a new temple," he said.

"Yes—" Amphion's face reddened beneath his tan. "Ah, well, of course it's nothing compared with *your* temples, Pelops. But Apollo deserved better than the old shrine."

"Thebes' population has been growing," added Niobe. "We needed more healers, and our healers needed more space."

Amphion's and Niobe's explanations seemed entirely reasonable and rational. Their tone suggested embarrassment at the expenditure, perhaps – but they did not seem like people plotting against him.

Myrtilus crossed his arms and stood straight as a herm. "What about the Tiresias?" he asked, staring at Amphion.

A point worth pursuing. "I understand the Tiresias attended the dedication. Is she still here?"

"No," said Amphion. "She left Thebes a few days after the ceremony."

"I heard that she quarreled with her sister," Niobe added, her lips twitching. "I suppose having such a powerful prophetess in a small house might be – awkward."

Or maybe it was impossible for two women to find peace under a single roof, Pelops thought, remembering the hostility that had existed between Niobe and Hippodamia. But at any rate, he was relieved to hear that the Tiresias had not taken up permanent residence in Thebes. So what if she spent a few days visiting the new temple? That was part of her duty as Apollo's handmaiden.

"Still," Myrtilus objected, "Thebes should have sent you more tribute!"

They sent two carts more than the previous year, Pelops retorted silently.

"Tell me about Eurydike's marriage," said Niobe. "Is she happy?"

Pelops laughed. "Only *you* would ask that question! Of course she's happy – she's the queen of Mycenae!" Throwing his good arm over the back of the bench, he related a few details of the ceremony. Then an idea occurred to him – something that would forestall any estrangement between Thebes and Pisa. "Your daughter will soon be of an age to marry. We should link our houses by wedding her to one of my sons."

"An excellent proposal," commended the ghost, as Amphion and Niobe looked at each other. "This will test their loyalty."

"She's not a woman yet," Niobe protested.

Pelops shrugged. "I'm sure she will be soon," he said smoothly.

This time Niobe was slower to respond; she looked upset. "Only – only if Chloris agrees."

"Niobe, I thought being a mother and a queen would cure you of the notion that young girls should choose their own husbands." He shook his head. "Amphion, what do you say?"

Amphion spoke quietly but firmly. "I would never compel Chloris to marry. My mother was forced into a marriage against her will. It did not turn out well."

Pelops frowned. Amphion should be grateful for the chance to marry his daughter to one of Pelops' sons! On the other hand, Amphion's mother *had* cuckolded her first husband and then run away from him. And, of course, Niobe herself had fled Lydia to escape a marriage she did not want.

He glanced at the ghost; Myrtilus was bending over to peer at Amphion's worn footwear, and did not look up. Evidently he had nothing to add.

When he finally spoke, Pelops' voice was cool. "Three of my sons are a little older than Chloris. They're all promising young men. I'm sure at least one of them would satisfy her."

Amphion scratched his beard. "Chloris has been begging to attend the games next summer. If I bring her along she can meet your sons, and then we can discuss a betrothal."

"It's such a long trip!" Niobe objected.

"Hypocrite," Amphion teased. "You were only a couple years older when you traveled all the way across the Great Sea."

Niobe's lips twitched. "Mother certainly didn't give me permission."

"And I'm grateful you were such a willful girl." Amphion squeezed her hand, then looked up at Pelops, his gray eyes sincere beneath the graying brows. "I'm also grateful to you, Pelops, for supporting her in her mad adventure!" He smiled. "Let's have the children brought here, so that you can meet your nephews – and Chloris."

The horde of children that soon poured into the courtyard surprised Pelops. Alphenor had grown from a lanky boy into a tall, good-looking youth with Amphion's easy smile and Niobe's straight black hair. Princess Chloris was a startlingly beautiful girl, with huge gray eyes and full lips, her long arms and legs moving with uncommon grace. Then there were all the younger princes – each one healthy and handsome and well-mannered, even down to the baby that a nursemaid placed into Niobe's arms.

Pelops' attention returned to Chloris. The girl kissed her father's cheek, and then bowed as she was formally introduced. What a wife she would make for one of his sons! He pondered this, turning his goblet between his fingers. Chrysippus, it had to be Chrysippus – he was the only one worthy of her.

"Too bad you're stuck with Hippodamia," Myrtilus said, eyeing the girl. "Otherwise you could save her for yourself."

Niobe concluded the introductions, saying: "...and the baby's name is Tantalus."

Pelops could not believe his ears. "What?" he asked, his voice full of fury. He slammed down his cup. "Did you say *Tantalus*?"

Everyone, including the children, fell silent – except for the baby, who began to cry. Pelops realized he needed to restrain his anger, especially if he wanted Chloris to marry one of his sons. He took a deep breath, trying to calm himself, while Myrtilus stared slack-jawed at little Tantalus. Niobe bent over the baby, murmuring reassurance, and he stopped fussing.

Finally Amphion said, "The name was my suggestion, Pelops. I wanted to remind the people of Thebes of the queen's powerful family connections."

"I see," said Pelops. A muscle twitched in his neck.

"There's more," continued Amphion.

"What?" asked Pelops.

"Your brother Broteas was here recently."

Handing the infant to the nursemaid, Niobe broke in: "He just brought a few gifts, in acknowledgement of the baby. And I sent a message to Mother back with him – just a personal message to give her my love, and to tell her about my children. He didn't stay long; he left a few days after the dedication of the temple."

Pelops stared at her, but could not tell what she was thinking.

"I told you they were hiding something," Myrtilus said triumphantly. "I'll wager there's more to this!"

The ghost was probably right, Pelops thought, frowning. But what would be the quickest, surest way to discover the truth of the situation?

"The children, of course," Myrtilus said, gesturing at Alphenor and Chloris. "Those two are old enough to wander everywhere – but not old enough to know when to hold their tongues."

Pelops stood. "I'd like to see your new temple," he said. "Amphion, I'm sure you're busy – why don't Alphenor and Chloris escort me there?"

Amphion and Niobe exchanged a look Pelops could not fathom, which increased his suspicions. Finally Amphion said, "I don't see why not."

"Could we ride in your chariot, Uncle Pelops?" asked Alphenor.

"Tomorrow, perhaps: this afternoon my horses need rest." He glanced at Niobe, then back at his nephew. "I brought my favorite stallions with me, Wind and Wave – your mother named them a long time ago. Is the temple far from here?"

"It's not far at all," Chloris said.

"Then let's walk."

As they walked down through the city, Pelops' two guards trailing behind, the two children chatted freely, full of energy despite the oppressive midday heat. They were curious about Pisa and the Olympic Games and his plans for the next set. Pelops answered their questions, keeping them talking. If he let them get comfortable with him, he might learn something interesting.

He told them the story of how Niobe named his horses, and then said: "So, your Uncle Broteas just visited. What did he do while he was here?"

"He took us hunting," Alphenor said.

Chloris announced: "I shot a stag!"

"Really?" asked Pelops, surprised.

"She did," Alphenor confirmed proudly. "Chloris is an amazing shot."

"A fascinating maiden," Myrtilus said, leering at her. "Look at those long legs!"

"You must get your talent from your father," said Pelops. "My sister – your mother – never showed any aptitude for archery."

"Father's skilled with strings," said Chloris. "The bow... the lyre..."

"True," said Pelops. "Tell me more about your time with Broteas. I haven't seen my brother in years."

The children mostly spoke about the stag hunt, but they did confirm what their parents had said: Broteas had brought some valuable gifts from Lydia, and had remained only a few days.

"Is there anything else?" Pelops pressed. "Did my brother ask for anything?"

Alphenor and Chloris shrugged and shook their heads.

"Did your parents ask Broteas for anything?"

Alphenor frowned. "Mother asked Uncle Broteas to take a message back to Lydia, like she said. It was written on a clay tablet."

"A private message?"

"No," said Alphenor. "She let me read it, because she wanted me to practice the Hittite script. She told her mother about us – my brothers and sister."

"And she told Grandmother Dione that she often thought of her," said Chloris. "I read it too."

Interesting: Niobe had taught her children to read the script of the Hittites. But it did seem that the clay tablet was nothing more than Niobe had said – a sentimental message from a daughter to her mother.

"Niobe's not a fool," Myrtilus said. "Negotiations would not take place in front of her children."

"You're probably right." To his regret, Pelops realized that he had spoken aloud.

"Right about what, Uncle?" Alphenor asked politely.

"About everything." He pointed up the road, squinting in the noonday sun. "Is that the temple?"

It was not built to the same scale as Pelops' construction projects in Olympia, so from a distance it did not look as impressive. But the pale marble and the yellow color of the columns were attractive, and appropriately evocative of the God of Light. Pelops was reassured to see that it was not too large. Pretty, respectable, practical – but not so magnificent that people would journey a great distance just to see it.

As they reached the temple he turned the conversation to the Tiresias. Again, Chloris and Alphenor confirmed their parents' version of events: the Tiresias had been in Thebes only a few days. The prophetess did not sleep even a single night in the palace; this heartened Pelops. If Amphion had a scheme to gain greater access to the gods through the Tiresias, it was not working.

"Still," Myrtilus said, "why does he need special favors from the Tiresias? Obviously he's made an alliance with Broteas and Tantalus. Besides, the gods love Amphion. Just look at these children! They're cleverer and more beautiful than any of yours. Well, except Chrysippus. But Hippodamia will never let him inherit."

Pelops halted to glare at the ghost; the children went a few steps on ahead, then waited for him to catch up. "Stop it," he muttered under his breath. He was fatigued and thirsty; he did not need this annoyance just now.

Despite this plea, Myrtilus continued to goad him. "She'll make you give the kingdom to Atreus, whether you want to or not. And you don't even know if he's really your son!"

Pelops lifted clenched fists, wishing that the ghost were again a man of flesh and blood so that he could kill him a second time. "Shut *up,*" he hissed.

"We didn't say anything," said Alphenor defensively.

Myrtilus shrieked with laughter that grew louder and louder. "You don't know! You can never know!"

"Stop it!" Pelops shouted, covering his ears with his hands – which did not lower the sound of the ghost's cackling.

Chloris stared at him. "What's wrong with you?" she asked bluntly.

"Nothing's wrong with me, you little fool!" he yelled, shaking his fist.

The girl shrank back; Alphenor pulled her away from Pelops and stepped before her. "Don't you hit her!"

Pelops' guards jogged up. "My lord king?" the senior man asked nervously.

"Poor Pelops," Myrtilus said in a mocking, childlike voice. "Now you've terrified your niece. Do you think she'll come willingly to Pisa to live? She won't marry any of your sons now!" He laughed. "Remember, I've cursed your descendants, for all time!"

With a tremendous effort of will Pelops turned away from the charioteer's shade. He forced his hands to relax and turned to look at the children. They stared back at him, round-eyed.

"I'm sorry," he said, catching his breath. "The heat makes me short-tempered sometimes – I must have gotten too much sun. I didn't mean to frighten you." He noticed that a pair of priests had come forward on the temple steps; almighty Zeus, must they witness this as well?

"I'm not frightened," Alphenor said, squaring his shoulders much as Pelops had seen Amphion do when challenged.

"Neither am I," said Chloris firmly. Her tone was like Niobe's: Pelops remembered the day years ago when he had first confessed to his sister that the ghost of Myrtilus tormented him. Niobe declared that she was not afraid of Myrtilus – or of him.

"She's as brave as her mother," observed the ghost. "And far prettier."

§ 2.07

Niobe learned from her children what had happened at the Temple of Apollo. She told Alphenor and Chloris not to worry, but over the next few days she kept a watchful eye on her brother. She detected nothing unusual when Pelops proudly displayed his chariot and horses to a large group of excited Thebans. And at the official welcome banquet – cubed veal simmered with mint and figs – her brother remained perfectly composed as he interacted with the local nobles. He responded graciously when Captain Naucles praised him as the most natural sailor he had ever seen. Pelops told Amphion's brother Zethos that he looked forward to watching him wrestle at the next set of games; Thebe batted her eyelashes at him when he kissed her hand. He even flirted with Antiope, declaring that she remained the loveliest woman in Hellas. Niobe had to cough to cover her reaction to this exaggeration – yes, Antiope was still a handsome woman, but she was well into her fifties.

"I can see that your granddaughter has inherited your beauty," Pelops continued. "I hope I can persuade her to take an interest in one of my sons. I think Chrysippus might be worthy of her."

Niobe glanced at Chloris; blushing, the girl slipped behind her brother Alphenor.

"Tell us, my lord king, what it takes to organize the games," said Antiope's husband, one-armed Phokos.

That subject caught the attention of the entire megaron, and Niobe was gratified when Pelops credited her with helping to plan and manage the first set of games. "Without Niobe they would never have happened," he said, lifting his cup in salute.

The Thebans looked at her with new respect; her children gaped at this bit of history. Seated on his throne beside her, Amphion laughed. "Why are you surprised, children? I've always told you that your mother is the most talented of women!"

Niobe sought to turn attention back to Pelops. "Of course, the Olympic Games have grown tremendously since that time."

She leaned back on her cushioned throne while Pelops continued describing the work his festival required. "For the feasts we need many flocks of sheep for mutton – not to mention cartloads of fish, and hundreds of amphorae of wine and olive oil. Then there's the preparation of the campgrounds: we have to clear away the brush and nettles so that people can pitch their tents." The stepped wooden benches beside the chariot-track, which seated noble visitors, had to be reassembled and repainted; ground nearby and on the opposite side had to be cleared for the peasants to sit. Guest quarters must be found for the athletes and their trainers, and facilities for them to exercise must be maintained. Then there were the games themselves. He described how his men carted sand from the shore to prepare the wrestling pit and the chariot track. Judges for each competition had to be selected and trained; the wreaths of olive leaves to crown the victors had to be fashioned. "And of course my stable-hands must inspect all the horses brought for the chariot race. One year someone brought a mare in heat, to distract all the stallions." The Thebans burst into laughter; Pelops continued, "It *was* funny – at least, once the horses were back under control. But it could have meant death to one or more drivers in the race if my men hadn't been attentive."

"It must take a lot of resources to do all this," Prince Alphenor said.

"Yes, it does," Pelops agreed. "That's why Thebes' support is so important."

Amphion rested his hand on Niobe's. "He's good," he murmured. "He's winning some of them over."

That could be helpful in reducing complaints about tribute to Pisa – but Niobe knew they could not afford more than they were currently sending. Thebes' oil and grain were needed to keep their *own* people fed next winter. And if the Thebans' reaction encouraged Pelops, he would be bound to ask for more.

"How is Prince Laius?" asked red-headed Menoeceus.

Niobe frowned at this; but it was natural – if inconvenient – for Thebans to be curious about the prince who had resigned his claim to Thebes' throne.

"He's the most dedicated drinker and gambler in Pisa," Pelops answered.

During the ensuing laughter, Niobe's gaze darted back to Amphion. Surely he could see that Pelops *was* on their side. Her brother's demands might be unreasonable, but it was only by being unreasonable that he achieved so much.

Conversation turned to other matters; Amphion played his newest song. Niobe continued to observe Pelops – and as the evening wore on, every now and then she caught him frowning or shaking his head at some spot in the room where no one stood. That spot shifted around the megaron, but to her eyes, it was always empty.

She sighed. Pelops was still haunted.

The next morning, Niobe had her maidservant wake her early so that she could have a moment alone with her brother. Once she was dressed, she retrieved a small leather pouch from the place where she had tucked it away, and proceeded to Pelops' room. The Pisatan guards outside the door admitted her with a gesture of respect, and she found her brother sitting on the edge of the bed, dressed only in a linen kilt. The old scars on his left shoulder had faded; once an angry red, now they were white, lumpish tracks across the pale skin of his misshapen shoulder. The distinct line where his suntan ended showed where the ivory-tiled armor covered part of his chest and upper arm as well as his shoulder.

He looked up in surprise. "Niobe!"

"We've had no chance to talk," she said. "Why don't we sit on the balcony while the air's still cool?"

"I'll be right there. Let me put on my shoulder-piece."

Out on the balcony, they could speak without being overheard. How long was it, Niobe wondered, since just the two of them had been together like this? Years and years, she realized as she took her seat and her brother leaned against the balustrade. Even when she had lived in Pisa, Hippodamia had done what she could to prevent Niobe from being alone with her brother.

"Pelops," she said quietly, "how are you, really?"

"Fine, of course." His expression was quizzical. "Why? Don't I look well?"

"You look marvelous!" Privately she thought he resembled their father Tantalus – an undeniably handsome man – but she was sure that Pelops did not want to hear *that*. "I was afraid that you might be lonely, since Aeolius sailed away."

"Aeolius." Pelops turned from her, squinting in the direction of the rising sun. "Of course I miss his visits – not that he came to Pisa often recently, anyway. But there's nothing as lonely as a throne."

Niobe thought she would agree with her brother, if she were married to someone like Hippodamia. She leaned forward and said even more softly: "But you're never *really* alone, are you?"

He whirled around. For a moment anger flashed in his dark eyes; then his shoulders – one muscular and sun-browned, one encased in polished ivory – sagged. "No."

"How bad is it?"

He slumped forward. Closing his eyes, he rubbed his temples with both hands. When his eyelids lifted, he was staring at the empty chair beside Niobe.

"He's here now, isn't he?" she asked.

"Yes."

Niobe folded her arms, clutching her elbows hard to keep from shaking. She resisted a sidelong glance at the vacant – or was it? – chair.

"He's almost always with me," Pelops continued. "Sometimes it's not so bad – he even gives me a good idea once in a while. Other times he tries to trick me into saying and doing things I shouldn't." He hesitated. "Does it make you afraid of me, Niobe?"

"Of course not," Niobe said, though her heart was thumping hard. She wasn't afraid, she told herself – at least, she would not let Pelops or that cursed ghost see that she was afraid. "What can the ghost do to me? I can't even see him. You're my brother, Pelops: I love you."

Pelops paced the length of the balcony and back again. "Have you ever told anyone?" he asked. "Did you tell Amphion?"

"No," she said. Then, seeing Pelops' doubting look, she repeated firmly: "*No*. There's never been a reason to – and I won't tell him now."

He stared at her for a moment, and finally nodded as if to say he believed her. "All right. Now tell me, what was Broteas doing here?"

"Exactly what Amphion and I said. He brought gifts from Lydia. He took back a message to Mother."

"Did he want anything in particular?"

Niobe frowned. There was the mastiff, of course, but she wasn't about to mention that. "Such as?"

"I don't know." Pelops walked to the corner of the balcony again and stopped, looking at the leaves of the potted laurel tree. No – he was looking *past* the laurel tree.

"What does the ghost think?" she asked.

Pelops sighed and rubbed his temples again. After a short silence he said: "He doesn't have any suggestions. He's just suspicious." He walked a few steps toward her. "Niobe, it's torture, living with someone who is always so suspicious!"

"You handle it very well," Niobe comforted him, and was glad to see that her words reassured him. "If you can't be rid of him, all you can do is deal with the situation." She changed the subject to what was no doubt the main reason for her brother's visit. "But with Aeolius gone, can you afford the games?"

"It's difficult." Pelops began to pace again. "I was expecting more from Mycenae, now that my daughter's queen there – but Electryon's turned out to be a tight-fisted bastard. Next summer's going to be hard. I don't have nearly as much in the storehouses as I should have at this point." He paused and gave her a hopeful grin. "So, my darling sister, what can I count on from Thebes?"

Niobe struggled to resist his charm. Somehow, when he asked for her help, she *wanted* to give him more; but Amphion would hate that – and so would her subjects, come winter. If she could stay firm, and settle the matter this morning, it would prevent bad feelings between Pelops and Amphion. "Pelops, we sent you *ten* cartloads last fall. We'll try to match that this year, if the gods are willing. But Thebes has its own to care for."

Pelops was persistent. "What about the gifts that you received from Lydia?"

"We accepted them in a public audience," Niobe said. "It would look strange if we were to give them to you less than a month later." She held out the leather pouch she had brought: it was filled with large, perfect pearls. "Aeolius sent me these as a remembrance before he left. I'm sure he'd want you to have them now." Her husband would not like what she was doing; but then *he* had slipped Pelops' envoy a bag of gems last fall.

Her brother's face lit up when he saw what the pouch contained. "They're beautiful, Niobe! Thank you – they'll make a big difference."

"I hope so. But, Pelops, Thebes *can't* keep giving more. You've got to find what you need some other way."

The sun was rising higher; the chair where the ghost might have been a moment ago was now in the morning light. Pelops shifted it to face her, and took a seat. "I know," he said, his voice serious. "Every four years people expect a spectacle greater than the last. And I have to deliver on that. I can't afford to disappoint – people would wonder if my power is slipping. What do you suggest?"

"Tell me what you've done so far."

He related his dealings with Sicyon, Corinth, and Athens; he explained how Electryon's bride-gift had been only of symbolic value. Listening to her brother, Niobe felt that she had been transported back to her girlhood, plotting with Pelops to achieve the impossible. Their flight from Lydia, the sea crossing, their attempt to make a place for themselves in Athens – and then, later, the chariot race that won Hippodamia's hand and the kingdom of Pisa for her brother: it had all seemed mad, completely impractical – yet they had managed it, somehow. Closing her eyes, Niobe saw her brother in the flush of youth, standing in his racing chariot, the reins in his right hand and the goad in his left. His horses Wind and Wave – names she had suggested – gray as the stormy sea, tossing their heads with spirited impatience. Such glorious steeds!

Her eyes flew open. "Pelops – your horses!"

"My horses?"

"You're famous for your champion horses, Pelops. Other kingdoms would trade handsomely for horses like that."

He scratched his beard. "It's a good idea, Niobe, but it still doesn't help me in time for next year. I can enlarge my breeding program, but I don't have a big enough herd now to—"

"Then lend Wind and Wave out to stud," she said matter-of-factly.

He grinned at her: a broad, delighted, genuine smile, and for the first time since his arrival she was sure that he was not being tormented. "An excellent suggestion! I'll do that on the way home – and then start breeding in earnest when I return." After a pause, he continued: "I wish you were still in Pisa. If *you* were helping me run things, instead of Hippodamia, I wouldn't go through this agony every four years."

"If it weren't for Hippodamia you wouldn't be king of Pisa."

"True," he said, with a small laugh. "Niobe, why not come with your family to the games next year?"

"I don't know," said Niobe. She was sure that she was pregnant again, but she did not want to tell Pelops – not yet.

"You could meet my son Chrysippus. He'd make Chloris a fine husband, Niobe. You'll be amazed at him."

Niobe's heart wrenched at the idea of Chloris leaving to marry, but she kept the hurt to herself. The eager happiness on Pelops' face offered a welcome change of subject.

"Tell me about Chrysippus, Brother."

THREE: STEEDS OF GOLD

§ 3.01

Hippodamia peered into the polished bronze mirror and frowned at what she saw. "More color on my cheeks," she ordered her maidservant.

Looking doubtful, the girl pursed her lips. "Are you sure, my lady queen?"

"Yes, I'm sure!" Hippodamia snapped. How dare this girl question her? She snatched the mirror out of the maid's hand and held it closer.

By Aphrodite, when had she turned into the image of her mother? So many new lines in her face; gray hairs popping up more quickly than she could dye them. And now she was demanding too much make-up, hoping it would hide what could not be hidden.

She slapped the mirror down on her dressing table and waved away the girl with the rouge-pot. "Never mind," she said, getting to her feet. "I'm late already – I'll have to go as I am." The maidservant bowed and backed away.

Hippodamia *was* late: it was well past noon. She left her chambers and headed towards the reception room. It was Pelops' private audience chamber, actually, but since he was away and she was forced to tend to matters that should have been his concern, she felt justified in appropriating it for her own use. As she walked along the outer colonnade, overlooking the vineyards to the east, she saw some of the peasants picking grapes while others tended to those already laid out in the sun. The scent of the fruit hung sweetly in the air; another ten days or so, and they would start making wine. They were well into the harvest season. Pelops had already been away from the city nearly three months, and had sent word that he could be gone longer than that.

And who could know? He might never come back.

There could be storms at sea, or a pirate attack; he might meet bandits on the road. He could fall suddenly dead, struck by one of Apollo's invisible arrows. Or, like his old friend Aeolius, he could embark on some insane adventure – a journey to the Garden of the Hesperides at the world's western edge, or a descent into Tartarus. With such a husband, any fool thing was possible.

Re-entering the interior of the palace, Hippodamia reflected that she did not actually *miss* him – but the uncertainty surrounding his absence was another matter.

Exarchos the steward was waiting for her in the reception room. The plump little man bowed with a flourishing movement of one hand. "My lady queen, the artist working on the new statue for Hera's temple desires an audience."

"Tell him I'm not available," Hippodamia said. She took her seat, slightly winded by the walk from her chambers. That incompetent maidservant had tied her skirt-laces too tight again.

The statue of Hera had been Hippodamia's favorite topic when the sculptor arrived, along with a cart full of precious cargo from the king of Corinth and an encouraging message from Pelops. It was intended to dazzle all those who came to attend next summer's games at Olympia: the size of a mortal woman, it would be carved in wood and then overlaid with ivory to represent Hera's milky skin, with precious stones for the eyes and jewelry. The hair and clothing were to be covered with never-tarnishing gold, symbolizing Hera's divine immortality. The combination of materials was known as chryselephantine, explained the artist. He begged Hippodamia's permission to make the image in her own likeness, for he had never been so inspired by the beauty of any woman. Naturally, Hippodamia granted this permission. At last Pisa would have something in *her* image. The Temple of Rhea, with its fresco of Pelops' dead mistress, always galled her – and a gilded statue would be far more impressive than a wall-painting.

Lately, however, the artist brought her nothing but complaints. Since completing the wooden carving, his progress had been slight. There was little ivory in the palace storerooms to begin with, and some of the pieces had proved unusable. He did not have the precious stones he wanted. And instead of resolving these difficulties on his own, he came whining to her.

"Yes, my lady queen," Exarchos said. "He gave me a message to convey to you, my lady queen, if you were not available to speak with him. Would you care to hear the message?"

"No," Hippodamia snapped. But as soon as the word left her lips, she wondered what the message might be. Perhaps it was good news, for a change. "Oh, all right," she said, realizing that she sounded as capricious and unreasonable as her husband or her father had ever done. Well, it was Exarchos' job to deal with unreasonable rulers. "What's the message?"

"The artist does not have as much gold as he needs to gild the statue of Hera. The gold trader refuses to deliver until he receives payment."

More complaints! How was *she* supposed to find the payment for the trader? Pelops should have taken care of it months ago!

"Tell the artist he shall incur my *severe* displeasure if he brings up such problems again." Hippodamia narrowed her eyes. "You're the steward, Exarchos. You should make sure that he has what he needs."

"I understand, my lady queen. But, unlike Zeus, I cannot simply pull what we need from a hollow goat's-horn."

"Isn't there anything left from what the king of Corinth sent? He shouldn't have sent a sculptor without sufficient supplies to create the statue."

"As you know, my lady queen, some of the Corinthian treasure was used to pay for the cedar used to build the extension to the temple," Exarchos responded. "It has all been gone for more than a month."

That was Pelops' fault, for not bringing in enough resources to pay for everything. Hippodamia glanced up at the swirling patterns painted on the ceiling. *Hera,* she asked silently, *don't you want your statue to be magnificent?*

"What about the granaries?" she asked.

"My lady queen, we already took from them to pay for the improvements to the race track. And before that, to trade for the indigo dye for the soldiers' uniforms."

"Bring Atreus and Thyestes to me," she said. Perhaps they would think of something.

"They are holding court just now, my lady queen."

Hippodamia tugged at the skirt laces, which were chafing her skin. She had been queen of Pisa for nearly twenty years, yet sometimes she felt as powerless as a bleating lamb. Whatever she wanted done never seemed possible when she wanted it.

Nevertheless, she would not take her sons away from their royal duty; that would make them look weak. And although Exarchos had the tact not to mention Chrysippus – her antipathy towards her stepson was well-known, at least in the palace – no doubt the boy was part of the court.

She pushed herself to her feet. "Are they in the megaron, or out in the agora?" When the weather was good, local matters were heard out-of-doors, so that the peasants could attend and witness justice being done. Trade negotiations and other diplomatic matters, if they were not too delicate, were discussed in the megaron.

"Outside, my lady queen."

Hippodamia grimaced. By her husband's orders, Chrysippus was not just part of the council on domestic matters: he was in *charge* of it. "Very well. I will go and observe."

The guards snapped to respectful attention as she approached the palace door; the royal herald announced Hippodamia when she stepped out into the afternoon sun. From the top of the staircase she smiled and lifted a hand to her people, and they acclaimed her with shouts and applause. Then she gestured down to the foot of the stairway. There, where the broad space of the lowest tread formed a sort of dais, three chairs had been set up for the boys. Laius stood off to one side. Five peasants in dirty rough-spun tunics stood before the bottom step; palace guards, their spears held horizontally to form a barrier, kept back the rest of the crowd.

"Pisatans," Hippodamia said loudly, "do not allow the presence of your queen to interrupt these proceedings. I have only come, as have you, to watch the princes mete out justice."

Golden-haired Chrysippus, seated in the center, turned and nodded. Thyestes smiled at her while Atreus called for a chair to be brought for her.

After Hippodamia had made her way down the stairs and had taken her seat close to where Laius stood, Chrysippus addressed the delegation of peasants. "Continue."

The front-most man glanced uneasily at Hippodamia before speaking. The barley rations doled out from the last harvest, he said, were too meager. It wasn't right, toiling and sweating in the grain fields and then not getting enough to keep the flesh on their bones. If they starved to death over the winter, who would work the fields next year? They were doing their best – their children and wives were out foraging for acorns, food usually left for pigs – but if the rations were not increased they would starve.

The three young men listened impassively; they had agreed never to pass judgment before discussing the case among themselves. Once the peasants had finished their statement, Chrysippus nodded. "Very good. Step back, while I confer with my brothers."

The peasants backed away several paces, and Atreus and Thyestes turned their chairs to face Chrysippus. Laius edged closer and Hippodamia, getting to her feet, followed.

"I was afraid of this," Chrysippus said quietly. "The rations have been reduced too low."

Thyestes shrugged. "If the peasants weren't so lazy, they would have produced more. Then we wouldn't be in this mess."

Hippodamia silently concurred with Thyestes. What a good-looking boy he was! If it wasn't for Chrysippus' fair hair, everyone would call Thyestes the handsomest.

"It's not laziness," said Chrysippus. "The rains came at the wrong time – after *we'd* emptied the granaries for other things."

"If we had fewer peasants, we could feed them easily," said Atreus. "Maybe we should banish some of them."

Chrysippus looked puzzled. "Banish them where? Besides, you'd have fewer men for the army."

"Then let's use the army to take food from another city," said Atreus. "That's what it's there for!"

"Father would be angry if we attacked our neighbors without good reason," said Chrysippus.

"Especially with the games just next summer," said Laius.

Thyestes, an unenthusiastic soldier, supported Chrysippus and Laius in this; Hippodamia was silently relieved. She did not want to lose any of her sons in battle.

"We can increase the grain ration a little." Chrysippus rested his elbows on his knees and leaned his chin on his fists. "But not much, because the granaries are so low. We'll have to find other sources of food. Cull the flocks, and dry the meat; Laius, you could talk to the shepherds about that. And we should arrange more hunting parties – you'd be good at that, Atreus. Thyestes, can you see if there's some way to improve the fishermen's hauls?"

Thyestes and Atreus both nodded. Hippodamia was irritated to see them yield to Chrysippus so readily.

"Maybe," she said, "the gods sent the rains at the wrong time because they *want* the peasants to go hungry."

Chrysippus stared at her with his golden-brown eyes. His expression remained blank, but Hippodamia was sure he realized how much she hated him.

"You may be right, my lady queen," he said after a moment. "We should appeal to the gods."

Rising from his chair, he nodded to Atreus and Thyestes. They too got to their feet; Laius went back to the far side of the stairway, and Hippodamia had no choice but to follow.

"Pisatans," Chrysippus said in a clear, ringing voice, "we have heard your concerns. Your ration-shares of barley will be increased. And my brothers and I will arrange hunting and fishing parties to make sure that you all have enough to eat."

A ripple of satisfaction passed through the crowd; but the peasants' spokesman said, "That's a start, my lord prince. But what if the huntsmen and fishermen come back empty-handed?"

"We're cursed because the king is away!" shouted someone from the thick of the crowd. "We never starved when King Pelops was here!"

"What if he's dead?" cried another. "It'll be like the old days! Who'll take care of us?"

Hippodamia felt the eyes of the crowd upon her and she wondered whether they blamed her, the old king's daughter, for his long years of misrule that had brought Pisa to the brink of ruin. And yet *she* was the one who had ended her father's terror and made Pelops' rule possible.

"My father will return soon," Chrysippus answered. "But until then, my brothers and I will protect you! In return we ask only for your hard work, and your prayers. Pray that the gods shower their blessings on Pisa once more! Pray that my father, King Pelops, will safely return!"

Chrysippus lifted his arms to the sky; the posture emphasized the narrowness of his waist and kilt-clad hips, the growing breadth of his shoulders. His lithe, tanned form was youth and beauty personified; he made Hippodamia all too aware of her aging bulk and the thick layer of cosmetics on her face.

"Let us ask the gods' blessing!" cried Chrysippus.

Powerful cheers arose. "May the king return soon!" cried out one. "May the gods bless us!" called another. "Blessings of Zeus upon the king's sons!" called a third. A chant started: "Atreus – Thyestes – Chrysippus!" But some in the crowd shouted only Chrysippus' name, over and over.

The bastard was too popular – he overshadowed her own sons!

There was a commotion at the edge of the agora; the soldiers lifted their spears to allow a man through. He wore a blue cloak and kilt, the colors of Pisa: when he drew off his tall-crested helmet Hippodamia recognized Okyllus, a Pisatan nobleman and one of Pelops' most trusted men. As he bowed she experienced a moment of unease: did he bear good news or bad? But when he lifted his face to her, she saw that he was smiling.

"Okyllus," she said, stepping down from the stairway. She was not going to permit Chrysippus to receive the messenger as if he were in charge of the kingdom. "You bring news from my husband?"

"Yes, my lady queen!" He paused, sounding out of breath, and then continued: "King Pelops will return to Pisa within the month. He's bringing with him many carts full of barley and amphorae of oil."

Chrysippus, his hair lit by the afternoon sun, grabbed each of his older brothers by the arm. "You see?" he shouted, "Our prayers have been answered already! Our father is returning with plentiful food! There will be no more hunger!"

The people shouted and clapped in relief; she heard some begin the chant of Chrysippus' name again.

"Long live King Pelops!" Chrysippus shouted.

While the Pisatans cheered their king, Atreus and Thyestes smiled and waved to the crowd, as though they did not realize that they were being pushed aside. Then they linked arms with the bastard Chrysippus and headed up the palace stairs. Sensing that the moment was over, with no way to salvage it for her sons, Hippodamia followed them back into the palace, leaving Laius to deal with Okyllus.

The brothers were still smiling and laughing as the tall bronze-bound doors swung shut behind them, dampening the sound of jubilation from the agora. But Thyestes caught Hippodamia's frown. "It's good news, isn't it, Mother?" he asked. "There's going to be plenty!"

"And Father will be home soon!" said Atreus. "I can show him the new maneuvers I've practiced with the soldiers."

"I want to speak with you," she told Atreus and Thyestes.

"Do you want me to come too?" Chrysippus asked.

Hippodamia wanted to say no, but she bit back the word. "Why not, since you're so clever?" As she led them towards her rooms, she explained about the gold needed for Hera's statue, and how Pisa had insufficient resources to pay for it.

Atreus and Thyestes were slow to respond. "We could use the resources that Father is sending us," Thyestes said finally.

"And risk a riot? After we've just promised them barley?" asked Atreus. He rubbed his broad jaw. "I could take soldiers and confiscate the gold."

Thyestes rolled his eyes. "No one would ever deliver gold to Pisa again. Besides, the trader is a friend of Father's."

Chrysippus had remained silent, irritating Hippodamia further. If he was determined to attend, he could at least contribute something. "What are your ideas, Chrysippus?" she demanded.

He hesitated, then said: "Instead of gilding the goddess' robes, you could dress the statue in some of your clothing. That would hide the wood, and you'd only need enough gold for her hair and jewelry."

"That's a good idea!" said Atreus, and Thyestes nodded; but Hippodamia was annoyed.

"That wouldn't honor the goddess appropriately – remember, she's the queen of Heaven."

"It's more than any other goddess is honored in Pisa," Chrysippus answered, and Hippodamia knew he was thinking of Rhea's temple. When she did not respond, the boy added: "But if you feel that's insufficient, you could ask Lady Hera to provide."

"True," said Thyestes. "Look what just happened after Chrysippus' prayers!"

"I saw what happened." Hippodamia folded her arms beneath her breasts. "Chrysippus, you have interesting ideas, as always. Now, leave us. I want to talk with my sons." She snapped her fingers to dismiss all the servants as well.

The heavy oaken door swung shut behind them. Hippodamia went to the side of the room and took a seat on one of the low couches. There was a pitcher of barley-water on the table; she poured herself a cup, considering how to begin. She decided to be blunt.

"If you boys don't do something, Chrysippus will usurp your place. He'll be the next king of Pisa."

"What?" asked Atreus, his nostrils flaring. "He's not the oldest!"

Thyestes sat down beside her. "He's not even *your* son, Mother. And Father is only king because he married you! How can he make Chrysippus king?"

Hippodamia was relieved to see that they both hated the idea. She reached over to push a lock of curling hair back from Thyestes' brow. "Thyestes, kings do things that they should not do all the time. And Chrysippus is very popular."

To Atreus she said: "Remember, your father is a younger son himself. He may not believe the eldest son is always the best heir." And to Thyestes she added: "Your father rules in Pisa though he is not of Pisatan blood. He may not believe my family line is critical, any more." She sipped from her cup and then continued, more to herself than to her sons: "And he believes that as king, whatever he does is by definition right."

Her sons exchanged a look; then Atreus spoke for them both. "What should we do?"

Hippodamia tried to swallow, and found her mouth inexplicably dry. Even after taking a sip from her cup, it was difficult to utter the words. "Dispose of Chrysippus."

Atreus and Thyestes stared at her as if she were speaking Babylonian.

After a long silence, Atreus said: "You mean *kill* him?"

She lifted her cup again; annoyed to find her hand shaking, she steadied it with both hands to swallow and set it down carefully. "Yes," she said, relieved to find her voice growing firmer. "Atreus, you're skilled with weapons. You could manage it."

"Chrysippus is a good fighter, too," he objected.

"And he's our *brother,*" said Thyestes. "You think we should kill our brother?"

She found it difficult to meet their eyes. "He's not your full brother, you know. He was born to a peasant – a palace servant!"

"But Father loves him," whispered Atreus. "If we did anything to Chrysippus, Father would be furious."

Hippodamia turned the empty cup in her hand, running a finger around the moistened edge. "You may be right," she said grudgingly. If Pelops suspected either of them in the death of his golden son, he might very well kill them in anger. "Forget the idea," she said. "You will not speak of this to anyone."

She swore them to silence, then told them to leave. They departed slowly, as if considering things that had never occurred to them before.

When they had gone, Hippodamia shouted for Exarchos, and told him to fetch the artist working on Hera's statue; she would give him Chrysippus' suggestion.

Her sons were still too inexperienced and naive to perceive the threat that Chrysippus posed to their futures. That meant *she* would have to find a way to rid the kingdom of the youth – something that implicated neither her sons nor herself.

But how?

Walking over to the window, she looked down to the courtyard below. Chrysippus was speaking with Laius, the fellow who encouraged her sons to spend their time drinking and gambling. Hippodamia could not make out the young men's words, but she could tell the two were laughing together.

Then Laius reached out to stroke Chrysippus' beardless cheek, and Hippodamia caught her breath.

§ 3.02

Laius delivered the messenger into the capable hands of a senior bath attendant. Okyllus' estate was some distance south of the city, and the princes and their mother would want to question him at length over dinner – so, Laius explained, there was no point in heading home just yet; he might as well enjoy the services of the palace after his journey.

Okyllus brought welcome news, Laius thought, whistling as he walked down the corridor. Very welcome!

The shadows were growing longer; servants were going about their tasks, refilling the lamps with oil and trimming the wicks. But light enough remained in the courtyard, Laius thought, and the warm air of late afternoon was sweet. He spotted Chrysippus heading into the courtyard. "My lord prince!" he called out. "A game of senet before dinner?"

The youth started, as if his spirit had been wandering elsewhere. "Laius!" Chrysippus turned and clasped his hands behind his back. The motion flexed the muscles of his chest and shoulders. "May I ask you something?"

Laius stepped closer. "Of course."

"What did you think of the court, earlier? Did I perform well?"

"Well?" Laius repeated, and then laughed, and stopped when he saw Chrysippus' earnest, uncertain expression, and realized the youth's real need for reassurance. "I'm sorry, my lord prince, but you performed far better than just *well* – you were magnificent! The people love you."

Chrysippus smiled wryly, and then glanced up past Laius' shoulder. "Not all of them."

Laius followed his gaze – the queen's chambers were in the upper story. She was probably not there at this time of day, but the young man's meaning was clear.

"She wants me to fail at the task my father set me," the youth said in a low voice. "She even wants me to fail at tasks *she herself* sets me." He explained the queen's dilemma with respect to the statue of Hera, and the solution that he had proposed.

"Clever!" Laius exclaimed, and the boy brightened at the praise; but the expression did not last. "I take it she didn't thank you for your help."

Chrysippus shook his head. "You'd think she'd be happy that I found a way to complete her precious statue. But it just made her angrier." He scuffed at the gravel path with his sandal. "She hates me."

Laius' throat tightened in empathy. He swallowed hard, and said quietly: "I know how you feel. When I was a boy in Thebes, the regent's wife always treated me as if she wished the earth would open up and swallow me. That's one reason I've been happier here."

"I wish there was somewhere I could go. I don't want to face her at dinner tonight."

Laius reached out to stroke the youth's cheek. Chrysippus did not draw back; he seemed to welcome the gesture. Feeling as if he had stumbled upon a cache full of treasure, Laius said: "Then don't. Let's have dinner brought to my rooms. We'll send word that you're not feeling well – and while Okyllus is being questioned in the megaron, I can tell you all the details myself." His words echoed distantly in his ears, as if they were being spoken by someone else.

Chrysippus looked up at him with eyes that shone in the fading sunlight. "I'd like that."

Laius could hardly believe his good fortune; with hesitance, he slipped an arm around the youth's warm shoulders. Again, Chrysippus did not pull away, and Laius felt privileged to be allowed to touch such beauty.

As they walked back towards the residence wing, Chrysippus said: "I was lucky that Okyllus arrived with that news when he did. How did my father obtain so much oil and grain?"

"What?" Laius asked, for his thoughts were already in his chamber. "Oh – your father's been managing many things, but the latest is that he put Wind and Wave up to stud."

"Really?" The fair-haired prince was surprised. "He never wanted to share their bloodlines before."

"Maybe he didn't realize how much others would be willing to trade for them." They had reached the narrow staircase; reluctantly Laius let his arm fall from the boy's shoulders. But it gave him the chance to better appreciate the graceful taper of Chrysippus' tanned back towards his slim, belted waist, and to watch his calf muscles tighten as he ascended.

"It's a good deal for the stallions, that's sure," joked the youth. "What a way to fill Pisa's storerooms!"

Laius' chamber was not as luxurious as the royal family's; his room was smaller, the furniture older. A cobweb clung to one corner, and a wine-stained tunic lay crumpled on the top of his clothes chest. His belongings were scattered about: a goad that King Pelops had given him, an old set of knucklebones, and a faded olive wreath from his victory in a wrestling match. At least the servants had emptied the chamber pot.

Laius called out to a servant and gave instructions regarding the evening meal. Then he pulled back the curtains and opened the balcony door to admit the last of the day's light. He and Chrysippus stepped out onto the tiny terrace that faced the setting sun; the air was fresh but the sun's slanting rays were warm and dazzlingly bright.

The red-gold light of sunset played over Chrysippus' thick, waving hair like flame. His tall frame was slender, but – as Laius knew from the gymnasium and the chariot-track – there was strength in those supple limbs, and the curving lines of his muscles would soon swell into their full adult power.

"What are you thinking, Laius?"

Laius realized that he had been caught staring. "You – you're like the sunset. The sunset is the moment between day and night, and you're at that time between youth and manhood. And both you and the sunset shine with beauty."

Chrysippus' lips parted slightly. "Do you say that to the women you bring up here? No wonder you're so popular!"

"Never," said Laius. "And I've never seen a woman as glorious as you."

Chrysippus turned his face towards the west; the great red disc was slipping down beyond the horizon. "I'd rather be like the dawn than the sunset."

"You've the fire of sunset," said Laius, "and all the promise of dawn."

Chrysippus' look promised other things, kindling heat in Laius' loins, but just then the door opened. A pair of servants brought in trays of food, setting them down on the low table. The fare was simple: bean stew flavored with mutton, onions, celery and salt; hard cheese and soft warm bread; and a bowl of apples, grapes and berries. Laius poured two cups of wine, and Chrysippus sat beside him on the room's single couch. As they ate, Laius relayed the details he had gleaned from Okyllus about Pelops' visits to the various cities of Hellas, and how much he had persuaded various kings and nobles to donate in support of the games. The conversation flowed naturally to games themselves, what preparations Laius was making, and which contests he and Chrysippus would enter.

After the meal was done, and Laius was wondering if he should reach for the youth's hand, Chrysippus slid him a long, questioning look from beneath his thick lashes. "This afternoon you mentioned the regent's wife who hated you – she's been dead a long time, hasn't she? You could return to Thebes."

Despite the warmth he felt from Chrysippus' proximity, Laius shivered. "I don't want to go back to Thebes."

"Why not?"

"Because I'd have to leave you," he said lightly, not wanting to explain.

But the youth was too perceptive. With slender fingers he grasped Laius' wrist, and a warm tingle spread through Laius' body. "That's not all," Chrysippus insisted. "There's some other reason you don't want to go back – even though you should have been king."

"I relinquished that right a long time ago. I even swore an oath."

Chrysippus' eyes shone in the lamplight. "Why?"

"Thebans don't respect their kings the way Pisatans do," Laius said quietly. "Did you never hear what happened to my father?"

The youth shook his golden head.

"I was only five years old. There was supposed to be a sacrifice, but something went wrong – one beast escaped, and the fire wouldn't light for the other. The crowd went mad. They started shouting curses at my father, throwing stones." Laius closed his eyes for a moment, remembering. When he was able to continue, he said: "They tore him to pieces. In my nightmares I still hear him screaming – and I hear them laughing. They *laughed* as they killed him."

"I'm sorry. I didn't know."

"I haven't talked about it in years," Laius admitted. "I don't want to seem…" *Cowardly,* was the word he could not say.

Chrysippus' eyes flared as if he heard Laius' silent self-accusation, and meant to deny it. He squeezed Laius' hand. "Of course you were frightened – you were only a child!"

Laius did not want to describe the fear that still gripped him at the mention of Thebes.

"I know you can't go back to Thebes," Chrysippus said. "It's just that, if you were king somewhere else… I could come with you."

"You want to leave Pisa?" He touched the youth's bright hair. "Chrysippus, your father is the greatest leader in Hellas – and he loves you. Don't worry about the queen; King Pelops will do well by you. And the people here – the Pisatans – they revere you. They were cheering the king – and *you.*"

"Were they?" asked Chrysippus, leaning closer.

"They adore you," said Laius, and then, even softer: "*I* adore you."

"Do you?" asked the youth, in a voice that was scarcely louder than a whisper.

Laius nodded. He stroked the smooth cheek, then moved closer; Chrysippus did not pull away. His mouth tasted of honeyed wine, and the hard young muscles of his back, his waist, his thigh were warm beneath Laius' caress.

§ 3.03

Chloris stood at the head of a line of girls, all dressed in saffron-colored tunics and thick sandals. Dusk was falling, and the air of early autumn was sweet; a warm breeze ruffled her hair. This was an important night: the Maidens of Artemis had finally come to Thebes.

Two young women garbed in deerskin crossed the agora, carrying torches held high. They bowed to the king and queen and the noblemen and women who stood behind them, parents of Chloris' companions. One of the Maidens of Artemis went with her torch to the last of the girls; the other came to stand before Chloris. "We will leave now," she said.

Chloris and the other girls, aged seven to fourteen, followed the servant of the goddess through the mostly empty streets of Thebes and out into the forest. No one spoke. The front of the procession felt like a hunting party, for the acolyte leading the way walked across the dead leaves and fallen acorns even more softly than Chloris herself, ducking overhanging branches and stepping over rocks with practiced grace – but the girls behind Chloris would have scared off any game with their giggles and the noise they made stepping on dry twigs.

Just as Chloris was starting to worry that their long walk would tire the younger girls, she saw the glow of a bonfire. They emerged into a broad clearing; the fire, ringed by soot-blackened stones, burned bright at its center. The glade somehow reminded Chloris of the palace megaron – but instead of red-painted columns there were trees all around, and the starry sky, embellished by the rising crescent moon, made the ceiling overhead. Grass and dirt took the place of the painted floor, and the hearth at the center of the glade belonged to Lady Artemis instead of the goddess Hestia.

The acolytes led their charges towards the warm glow of the bonfire; they directed the girls to form a circle around the fire and join hands. Artemis' two servants sang a hymn to the Huntress while the girls performed the slow circle-dance they had been taught in preparation for the ritual.

The song came to an abrupt end – and then the acolytes tossed their torches into the fire and disappeared. A few girls gasped nervously; even Chloris shivered, wondering what would come next. An owl hooted in the distance.

A cloaked figure stepped into the circle of light. Chloris jumped, startled, and then recognized gray-haired Melissa, Artemis' chief priestess. Following behind her, several acolytes dragged something heavy over the grass. As they came closer, Chloris saw that it was the field-dressed carcass of a stag, resting on a leather blanket; ropes were tied to each corner of the blanket so that the young women could pull their burden forward.

Melissa's cloak was a wolf-skin; her deerskin tunic was streaked with what looked like dark, dried blood. She spoke: "Artemis, Lady of Animals, Mistress of the Hunt, loves the wilderness and shuns the streets of the city. We come to honor her here, in her forest. Tonight we offer her the fat and thigh-bones of this stag; its flesh is her gift to us, and we will feast upon this gift tonight." She beckoned the girls forward, and they bunched around the carcass. Chloris saw that the animal's skin had already been peeled back from the uppermost rear haunch.

"Each of you," Melissa continued, "must slice a piece of meat from the carcass and put it on a stick to roast; then I will prepare the goddess' portion." The priestess held up a knife whose blade was blacker than the sky overhead; it gleamed in the firelight, revealing strange ripples in its surface.

"Cut with *that*?" asked one of Theban girls. "It looks like a stone!"

"Obsidian from the island of Melos," Chloris said. "My Uncle Broteas has a knife like that."

"Does he?" asked the priestess, with what seemed like real interest. She turned the knife in her hand and offered it hilt-first to Chloris. "You first, Princess."

The knife's hilt was bone, dark with old blood and the passage of countless years; a leather thong wrapped tight around the join where the tang of the blade fitted in, keeping the bone from splitting. It was surprisingly light, as if lifted by Artemis' own fingers.

Chloris knelt before the carcass, the leather blanket stiff beneath her knees: the small hairs on her arms prickled at the holiness of the moment, and she felt as though the goddess stood just behind her. *Lady Artemis, guide my hands*, she prayed, and sliced out a chunk of venison for herself. Holding the piece of meat, she rose and passed the knife to the next girl; then she went over to the acolyte who stood nearby, a blonde girl just a little older than herself who held a fistful of long slender sticks with sharpened ends.

"You've done that before," whispered the blonde girl, handing her a skewer.

"Once or twice," Chloris whispered back, as she shoved the point of the stick through the slippery piece of venison.

"Watch the others," said the acolyte.

The next girl struggled with the knife, slicing out a meager, odd-shaped piece for herself; the third cut a gash in her own thumb. Despite these mishaps, the young Theban girls each soon had a portion. The Maidens of Artemis made quick work of skinning the rest of the carcass, then removed the stag's long thigh bones and coated them in bloody fat. Melissa led the girls in a prayer to the goddess and then tossed the offering into the flames. The fat sizzled and spat, the smoke went heavenwards; Chloris' stomach rumbled.

The servants of the goddess guided them close to the fire to roast their pieces of venison. Chloris noticed how different the girls looked from their everyday selves – their hands streaked with blood, dark smudges on their cheeks, their eyes wide at the strangeness of it all – and supposed that she looked much the same. And yet she had never felt more alive.

When the meat was finally ready to eat, Chloris was so hungry that no honeycake had ever tasted better, though the venison was charred on the outside and bloody within. One of the Maidens of Artemis handed out plain wooden cups, and a second followed with a skin of mead mixed with water; another passed around a basket of apples.

"Sit down, girls," said Melissa, and the girls settled down on the ground near the fire. The priestess herself sat on a tall stump; in the moonlight her graying hair gleamed like silver. "I will tell you the story of Artemis and the huntsman Actaeon."

Actaeon, she said, was a man clever with spear and bow. One day he and his dogs tracked a wide-antlered stag deep into the forests of Mount Kithairon. The stag was fleet, and ran far, so that the chase continued even after the sun had set and the constellations appeared. Actaeon continued through the moonlit forest, outpacing his exhausted hounds. In the deepest part of the forest, he heard an unexpected sound: maidens' voices, singing and laughter! He crept towards the edge of a glade; hiding behind a tree, he spied a spring-fed pool glistening in the silvery light of the moon. A group of nymphs laughed and splashed as they bathed in its waters; their leader was the most beautiful woman Actaeon had ever seen. She was tall and slender, her arms and legs shapely, her movements more graceful than a doe's. Unable to resist, Actaeon stepped forward – and then a maiden cried out in alarm: *Lady Artemis, a man is here!* Startled, the goddess turned to see him. Her maids tried to shield her nude body from the hunter's sight; but the goddess only scooped up a handful of water and flung it into Actaeon's face, saying: *Go and boast to other men what you have seen – if you can.* Terrified, Actaeon turned to flee, but it was too late: he had looked upon the goddess' form, seen what no man dare see. As he ran crashing through the forest, he felt antlers sprout from his head; his feet changed to hooves, and soon he was bounding forwards on four legs. The goddess had changed him into a stag. Then Actaeon heard the barks and growls of hounds – his own hounds, which no longer recognized him, but saw only their quarry. Their sharp teeth dug into his stag's-flesh, tore out his throat, and took his life. Thus was Artemis avenged against the man who dared to violate her privacy.

"This is why we eat the meat of a stag tonight," Melissa concluded. "To remind us that the virgin goddess has mysteries forbidden to men."

Licking her fingers, Chloris wondered if she and the other girls were more like the nymphs who had bathed with their mistress – or the dogs who had eaten their master. *Lady Artemis,* she prayed silently, sleepily, *show me the way.*

One of the Theban girls screamed and pointed. "A bear!" she shrieked.

Chloris jumped, trying to twist away from the girl beside her, who was clutching her arm. A bear *was* lumbering towards them! But bears were scarce near Thebes – in all her hunting trips she had never seen one. And what wild animal would approach a blazing fire? Then she saw the human feet beneath the furry pelt.

She laughed, though her heart still thudded crazily in her chest. "It's not a bear!" she yelled. "There's a woman beneath that bearskin!"

The Maidens of Artemis joined her laughter, as an acolyte appeared from beneath the bearskin and bundled it in her arms, its attached head lolling emptily back. The Theban girls stopped shrieking, though they still clutched each other and giggled nervously; now they were all wide awake.

"Each of you will take your turn in the bear dance," said Melissa. "We do this in honor of Calisto, one of Artemis' closest friends. Princess Chloris, you'll be first. When you wear the bear-skin, you must become a bear. Move like a bear, growl like a bear: that is the bear dance!"

Several of the Maidens began to sing, clapping in time to their song; the bear-acolyte helped Chloris into the bearskin. "You're tall, my lady princess," she said. "That will help – but still, be careful not to trip."

The pelt was heavy, with a powerful musky scent. Chloris settled the bear's head atop her own head, as the acolyte showed her; again she felt as if the goddess were with her. Closing her eyes, she summoned up what she had been told of bears: they were ferocious, perhaps even more dangerous than lions, and the she-bear was the most dangerous of all. She opened her eyes slowly, imagining that she was a bear summoned here by Artemis. A growl escaped her throat and she lunged at the nearest girls, who shrieked and laughed and darted away.

Chloris lurched around the fire, feeling as if she had doubled in size to fill the bearskin, far more powerful than a mere girl. Was that what it meant to serve Artemis, to be given the strength of the goddess? If she remained with her parents, and then married as a princess was supposed to, she would be expected to spend most of her time indoors. She would have to wear long skirts in which she could not run; she would bear a baby every year, making it impossible to hunt. Out here in the wilderness, with the followers of Artemis, she *could* be a bear – or whatever she pleased. She could run, she could hunt, she could laugh; the only rules were those of the goddess. She roared, feeling as free as a bear on the mountainside.

In turn each of the other girls played the bear; and then, when they were done, one of the acolytes offered a basket of cakes made from barley and hazelnuts, while another carried around a waterskin. The girls seated themselves around the fire, munching their barley-cakes as they listened to the priestess' next words.

"Artemis is the goddess of young virgins," Melissa said, sitting back down on the tree-stump. "When you are betrothed, you will dedicate your short tunics, along with your dolls and other childhood toys, to Lady Artemis. Do not be afraid: once you yield your virginity to your husband, Artemis will still protect you. Remember, on her first day in the world she helped her mother Leto give birth to her twin brother Apollo; that is why her priestesses serve as midwives. Artemis will watch over you in pregnancy and childbirth, and if you worship her as you ought, she will fight like a mother bear to protect your babies against disease and other perils. But once your virginity is lost, you can no longer dance the bear dance around the fire."

She stood, throwing her wolf-skin cloak over her shoulders. "Come, it's time to return to the city and your parents."

Leaving two acolytes to tend the fire and to finish butchering the stag, the girls followed the priestess and the other Maidens of Artemis back through the forest. Many of the girls were yawning; a few stumbled in their fatigue, and had to be helped by the servants of the goddess. But Chloris felt more awake than she had ever been, filled with restless energy.

She found herself walking beside Melissa. "So, child, what did you think?" asked the priestess.

"I've never had such a night," Chloris said, struggling to put her emotions into words. "I – I'm sorry it was over so soon. I wanted to stay back there, beside the fire."

Melissa nodded. "I thought so. I believe the goddess has called you, Princess."

"Will you – will you talk to my parents?" Chloris asked. "And tell them?"

The priestess shook her head. "That is something you must do yourself, Princess."

Chloris' shoulders sagged. She knew her mother would not understand.

"And, Princess, those who join us must be women already; we need maidens old enough to take care of themselves. Has your monthly blood started yet?"

She blushed at the question. "Not yet, Priestess."

"You'll be old enough soon, my lady princess. We spend most of our time in Arcadia. Seek us there."

These words were encouraging, like the glimmer of light just peeking above the eastern hills. "But... my parents..."

"If you can't face your parents – who love you – then how can you face the dangers of the wild?" Melissa smiled. "Ask Lady Artemis for guidance, Princess. She will help you."

§ 3.04

Broteas and his party had left the harbor fog well behind; the imposing bulk of Mount Sipylus loomed ahead, growing larger with each turn of the chariot's wheels. He held his horses to a walk, so that his foot soldiers had no trouble keeping pace – and so that he might enjoy for just a short while longer the freedom he had outside the walls of his father's city.

"It's good to be home, isn't it, my lord prince?" asked Geranor, who stood beside him in the chariot.

"If you say so." Broteas had postponed his return as long as he could, sailing the long way home along the coast instead of taking the shorter route through the islands. He explained to his men it was important for Lydia's presence to be felt, and so they had stopped to visit all the most important kingdoms: Athens and Euboea, Iolcus and Thrace. He had even made an appearance at the Trojan court, since their nations were not currently at war.

"Ah, do you regret leaving the waters of Lemnos, my lord prince?"

Broteas lifted an eyebrow: Geranor was certainly perceptive. Their visit to Lemnos was many days in the past, but it had been Broteas' favorite part of the journey. As an avid hunter, he was devoted to Artemis; but he also felt a special affinity for Hephaestus, a god who was ugly like himself. When Zeus first saw his son's ill-favored countenance, he threw Hephaestus from the heights of Mount Olympus; Lemnos was where the young god landed, crippled by his fall. But Hephaestus made the best of the situation: there, within the island's smoldering volcano, he built his first forge and began to create things of beauty. Lemnos was the holiest sanctuary of the cult of the smith-god, and there pilgrims could bathe in the steaming waters warmed by the god's forge.

"A sacred place," said Broteas. "And I did enjoy the waters."

They were drawing closer to the city; he decided it was time to send a messenger ahead to announce his arrival. He could have given this task to Geranor, who was a capable runner, but Broteas preferred to send another and keep the familiar guardsman at his side until they reached the palace. Geranor had a knack for finding the right thing to say, and avoiding uncomfortable topics. And though he could not compete with Broteas in his ugliness, at least Geranor was not a man of great beauty. In fact, he was neither handsome nor plain, neither tall nor short, neither fat nor thin, but as nondescript a fellow as any that Broteas had ever known. His only distinctive features were his long narrow face, and a mouth full of large and crooked teeth.

Soon enough they had passed through the city's main gate. Broteas paid little heed to the crowds who had gathered to cheer his return; he was thinking ahead to the audience with his father, and feeling at least as tense as when he passed through the streets of Troy. But he had survived that situation, even achieving some useful agreements with the Trojan king – he would manage this one too.

The palace guards greeted him with respect; he dismissed his own men and proceeded to the throne room. There he found his father in conversation with a man who wore a long colorful robe wrapped so as to leave one shoulder bare, and sandals decorated with polished agates: a Babylonian envoy, no doubt. Knowing that his father refused to be interrupted – even by his son – Broteas stood to one side of the crowded room.

As he waited to be announced Broteas turned the message-tablet he carried in his hands, pondering how little he resembled his father. King Tantalus was a tall, well-built man, still powerfully muscled despite his years; his waving hair and beard had the color and luster of silver, and his face and hands had been sprinkled lightly with gold-dust. His robe, dyed in the precious purple of crushed sea-snails, was sewn all over with pearls; beneath the golden circlet-crown of Lydia he wore a pointed cap, likewise dipped in purple and adorned with both pearls and rubies. Twenty years ago, King Tantalus had claimed to be the son of Zeus Thunderer, and the people of Lydia now accepted this as a fact.

Queen Dione occupied the smaller throne beside her husband. The milk-white border of her indigo gown echoed the color of her hair, carefully arranged beneath her polished gold crown. A necklace of sapphires circled her fleshy neck, and jeweled rings adorned her short, plump fingers. Broteas tried to catch her eye, but she did not acknowledge him – which was no great surprise, since her eyesight had been weakening for years.

Eventually the Babylonian was dismissed and the herald announced: "My lord king – your son, Prince Broteas!"

Broteas came forward and bowed deeply before the king's throne. "Father," he said, pitching his voice to carry over the crowd. "I rejoice to be in your presence once more." His head still bent, he watched his father's hand: waiting, as everyone must – even the king's eldest son – for permission to lift his head. Finally the hand moved; in the light streaming through the high windows, the gilded mastiff of the king's lapis signet-ring flashed as if to accuse Broteas of failure.

Broteas closed his fist around his own signet-ring, the one his father had given him so many years ago, feeling his guard go up as if he were driving a chariot into battle.

"Broteas, my son," King Tantalus said in his ringing voice. "We expected you back a month ago."

"I stopped at many ports, my lord king and father, to represent the interests of your kingdom. During the last month we had to contend with unfavorable winds."

A murmur started at the far side of the room, but not in response to Broteas' words: his wife Euryanassa and their son, he saw, had just arrived.

"And?" snapped the king. "Tell us the news of your journey."

Broteas turned his attention back to his father. "My lord king and father, what would you learn first?"

"How is my new namesake in Thebes?"

"Very healthy, Father," Broteas answered. "All of Niobe's children are thriving."

Queen Dione clasped her hands together. "Oh, that's so good to hear!"

Broteas held out the clay tablet he had brought, sheathed in its leather carrying-case. "Mother, I have a message for you from Niobe."

The queen took the message tablet, her fingers running over it as though it were more precious than diamonds. "How wonderful – Broteas, thank you!"

"She has six sons and one daughter, I understand?" asked King Tantalus. "And all you've got is Young Tantalus!"

Glancing at his wife and son, Broteas said, "That is what the gods have seen fit to give me, Father. But I could ask for no better son."

"Hmph," the king grunted. "Thebes is prosperous, then?"

"It's not Lydia, Father, but as those western kingdoms go it's fairly wealthy. They have great herds of cattle, and rich farmland. And, Niobe and her husband

Amphion would like to open trading relations with Lydia."

King Tantalus stood, and descended from his throne. "Walk with me." He snapped his fingers at the musicians who stood to one side of the throne; they began a song, so that the sound of their flutes and sistra might shield the king's conversation from being overheard. Broteas fell into step beside his father, looking up at him in an unsuccessful effort to assess his mood. Without speaking, the king led him towards the windows; they passed by Euryanassa and Young Tantalus, but as the king did not stop Broteas could not offer even a word of greeting.

When they reached the windows, King Tantalus set his hands, shining with gold dust, on the wooden sill. He did not look at Broteas; he directed his gaze outwards, over the city. "Did you retrieve the mastiff?" he asked.

"You sent me to Thebes, Father. The mastiff is in Pisa."

"I know that!" The king whirled around to face him. "But did Niobe and her husband pledge to retrieve it?"

"No, Father. They—"

"No?" interrupted Tantalus. "Why not?"

Broteas took a deep breath before speaking; he needed to choose his words carefully. At last he said, "Because King Amphion is unwilling to violate the sacred obligations between guest and host."

Tantalus glared down at him angrily; Broteas could see his father's face redden beneath its dusting of gold. Then, suddenly, he sighed and nodded. "My father Zeus reminds me that this is a law he established; if Amphion will not break it, that shows his piety."

Thankful that the king made this argument himself, Broteas breathed a little easier.

Then the king pointed a long finger at Broteas' nose. "This does not release you from your task! You *will* find a way to bring the icon back to Lydia. You should have done so twenty years ago. But you came back from Athens as empty-handed as now!" His mouth twisted in an expression of disgust. "Were he in your place, your brother Pelops would have thought of something years ago. He was always a clever one. And he *looked* like a prince." He laughed shortly. "Unlike you. It'd take half the gold-dust in Lydia to hide the pockmarks on your cheeks."

Pelops stole from you, Broteas fumed silently, *while I have been a loyal son.* And Pelops had only been able to steal the relic because King Tantalus had removed it – inappropriately, the priests had complained – from Zeus' sanctuary. Why should it be *his* responsibility to retrieve the golden mastiff when his brother and father were the ones at fault?

Still, Broteas knew such thoughts accomplished nothing. It always came down to the same set of facts: his father was the king, and Broteas had to do his bidding if he wanted to inherit the throne. Tantalus had been furious, all those years ago, when he failed to retrieve the mastiff; but soon after Broteas' return from the west problems with the Trojans absorbed the king's attention, and the matter was not mentioned for years. Apparently the message from Thebes had reminded Tantalus of the matter – or had something else renewed his interest in the subject?

"Well," said the king, "don't you have anything to say for yourself?"

Not sure what sort of answer his father wanted, Broteas ventured: "I can't help my appearance, Father. I am as the gods have made me."

Tantalus rolled his eyes. "I meant about the mastiff! What do you propose to do?"

"The most direct approach would be for me to go, with your support, to Pisa and take it back myself. But it is kept in a temple, Father, and to violate the sacred precinct by force of arms would be sacrilege. In addition, Pelops has been diligent about making alliances in the west; his games have assured that. Attacking Pisa would harm Lydia's relations with many other kingdoms."

"I'm still waiting to hear a solution," said Tantalus, folding his arms.

Broteas shifted uneasily. "I didn't know what to do, my lord king. So I stopped at the island of Lemnos."

"Lemnos? Why?"

"The god Hephaestus created Rhea's mastiff. I went to ask his advice on how to get it back."

"Ah." King Tantalus scratched his chin for a moment, as if turning this over in his mind. "Well, then, what did the god tell you?"

"I climbed up the burning mountain Mosychlos, where the god built his first forge. Though there were no flames or smoke from the volcano that day, it smelled of metal and sulphur." Broteas recalled the sweat pouring down his face after the steep climb, the sun's fierce heat, the warmth of the ground underfoot. "There at the high shrine I sacrificed a dog, and asked Hephaestus for guidance."

"Go on," said the king.

"I waited, Father, hoping for a sign. There was still no smoke from the god's forge; but these words came to me: *I am a craftsman.*" Broteas heard a tremor in his voice: the experience had felt holy, there in the blazing sun, but afterward he was not sure whether the god had truly spoken to him. He might have imagined it.

"What does *that* mean?"

"I consulted with the priest," Broteas said. "His interpretation was that craftsmen take time to do their work. He said Hephaestus was counseling patience, my lord king."

"Patience?" asked King Tantalus. "Patience!" he repeated, roaring so loudly that he startled one of the flute-players into sounding a discordant note; everyone in the throne room turned to stare. Broteas' wife and son looked worried and even Queen Dione held up a hand to silence the scribe who was reading Niobe's tablet to her.

The king glared at the musicians, and they continued their song; the onlookers turned away, as if there had been no outburst.

"I know it's not very satisfactory, my lord king," Broteas said.

"No," said King Tantalus. "It's not." He turned away, resting his hands on the windowsill once more; Broteas saw his back move as he took several long breaths, and wondered what punishment his father was devising.

"Still," said the king, "if that's what the lame god told you…"

"It is," averred Broteas, taken aback by his father's relatively restrained reaction.

The king turned back to him. "Very well. We will speak of this again later. For now you are dismissed."

Puzzled, Broteas watched his father walk back to the throne. Well, the king always managed to surprise him. Broteas only hoped that Hephaestus *had* counseled patience, up on that mountaintop.

His wife and son approached him; Broteas embraced the young man, thumping him affectionately between the shoulder blades, and then took his wife's hands. "You're looking well," he told her. Her dark, curling hair was artfully arranged; her complexion remained lovely, with only a few lines at the corners of her eyes and just a delicate touch of makeup to enhance the natural rosiness of her lips and cheeks. Her figure remained shapely, if not quite as spectacular as it had been when they first wed.

"Thank you, Husband," she said correctly, formally. "I give thanks for your safe return. I've arranged for a hot bath; Young Tantalus will join us later for a meal in our chambers."

As Broteas and his wife left the throne room, he recognized the signs that she would dutifully allow him to touch her that night – not that her passive submission was anything to anticipate with much eagerness. Once her beauty had enchanted him; but her indifference to lovemaking had sapped his desire over the years. Still, she was his wife, and had always shown loyalty. So, as they walked down the colonnade that led to the royal living quarters, he asked quietly: "Do you know why my father is so eager these days to retrieve the mastiff?"

Euryanassa shook her head.

"Your father was the high priest of Zeus," Broteas persisted. "Did he ever speak of any special omen related to the mastiff?"

"Not that I know of," she said.

"Well, your cousin is now in charge of Zeus' temple; perhaps you can learn something from him. If he knows any special prophecies about the mastiff – or if you can learn why my father is now intent on retrieving it, after so many years – you must tell me."

"Of course, Husband."

The two soldiers who guarded the domestic wing bowed and opened the doors for them to pass. Beyond, the shadowed hallway was familiar and yet oppressive; after so many days spent on the deck of a ship, the ceiling seemed too low, the indoor light too dim. Soon winter would be upon them, which meant spending even more time within doors – a dispiriting thought.

As they approached the suite he and his wife occupied, Broteas pondered his disheartened mood. Perhaps it was nothing more than the transition from the excitement and variety of travel – the wide open spaces and fresh air – to the confines of domesticity. But he suspected it had just as much to do with the fact that Lydia was not *his* kingdom. Surely his younger brother Pelops, a king in his own right, felt far different when he returned to the palace where he ruled.

§ 3.05

Pelops strode into his megaron, accepting with pleasure the greetings of his subjects. It was good to be back in Pisa—especially with so many cartloads of provisions for his people and items for trade.

"Husband!" Hippodamia exclaimed, coming forwards to take his hands. "Welcome home!" She kissed his cheeks, the scent of her musk-and-honey perfume so thick it threatened to bring on a sneezing fit; Pelops drew back, rubbing his nose to forestall this indignity, and turned to greet his children.

"You've all grown, every one of you," he said, surveying the youngsters. His youngest son, Copreus, looked a whole hand taller; the girls were quickly becoming pretty maids, and there was a shadow along Thyestes' upper lip. Atreus' shoulders looked even broader than before, and Chrysippus seemed to have gone in just these short months from a beautiful boy to a strikingly handsome young man.

"They have," said Hippodamia, looking pleased with herself. "And there's good news from Mycenae – Eurydike is with child!"

"Wonderful!" Pelops exclaimed. Surely *now* his daughter would be able to convince her stingy husband to cough up some of Mycenae's gold.

"I wouldn't count on it," said Myrtilus, the perpetual pessimist. He went over to Pelops' throne and inspected it. "Do you think anyone's sat up here while you were gone?"

Pelops ignored the ghost and turned to the crowd of well-born men and women who filled the room. "Pisatans, I thank you for your greeting – but I will not hear official business until tomorrow. This afternoon and evening I wish to spend time with my family." He set his hand on Chrysippus' shoulder – by the gods, did the boy gain all that muscle in the past three months? "Let's go to the courtyard," he said, starting that direction. Summoning Atreus and Thyestes to walk alongside, he asked what had happened during his absence.

"All's well, Father," Atreus reported. He related some of the past months' events as they walked down the hallway, emphasizing his drills with the army but also touching upon the preparations for the games and the management of local affairs. As they entered the sunny courtyard, Atreus said: "The peasants were worried having enough to eat this winter – but then Okyllus arrived with news that your ship's hold was filled with sacks of barley and jars of olive oil."

"It was like a message from the gods," said Chrysippus. "We had just prayed to them for assistance!"

While Hippodamia ordered servants to bring refreshments, Pelops seated himself beneath a fig tree, laden with the green and purple fruit of late autumn. "The peasants have no cause for concern." With pleasure he detailed what, besides oil and barley, he had brought: incense, worked agate, bronze ingots, and – from the island of Zakynthos – baskets of seashells and tortoise shells. He concluded, "We'll have enough for next summer's games even without contributions of my friend Aeolius."

"We heard about your putting Wind and Wave out to stud," said Thyestes.

"A brilliant idea, Father!" exclaimed Chrysippus.

Basking in the admiration of his sons, Pelops reached up for a ripe fig and bit into its sweet flesh.

"You didn't really do it by yourself," observed Myrtilus, who had moved behind Pelops and stood in the shade. "Wind and Wave were a gift from Aeolius, long ago. And if it weren't for Niobe, you never would have thought of breeding them to others' mares."

Pelops frowned at this.

"Is the fig bad, Husband?" asked Hippodamia. "Here, have some wine to wash away the taste."

There was nothing wrong with the fruit, but Pelops accepted a cup of wine to hide his inappropriate expression.

Still standing over him, Hippodamia set her hands on her ample hips. "If you brought home such wealth, then we ought to be able to finish the statue of Hera properly. As the sculptor originally intended."

"What are you talking about?" Pelops asked.

He learned that the artist had run out of gold and that Chrysippus had suggested that they dress the statue in Hippodamia's clothes to hide the lack.

"Very clever, Son!" Pelops said.

Hippodamia sniffed. "But of course now that's not necessary. We can obtain more gold for the sculptor. That way we won't offend Hera—"

"No," Pelops broke in. "Chrysippus' suggestion is a good one. With real gowns, the goddess will look even more lifelike – and she can wear different garb according to the occasion. I'm sure she'll like that better." He met Hippodamia's gaze, speaking firmly. "You know how much you would dislike it, my dear, to wear the same outfit each day."

Then Pelops looked over at his son Chrysippus – the son who would strengthen his hold over Thebes. Even if his sister and her husband were so foolish as to allow their daughter to choose her own husband, Princess Chloris could not possibly reject Chrysippus.

§ 3.06

The sculptor wiped his hands on his leather apron. "Does it please you, my lady queen?"

The artist's workroom was drafty; Hippodamia pulled her winter cloak closer as she walked a circle around the nearly-finished statue. "It does," she admitted.

"If I may say so, my lady queen, the resemblance to you is striking."

"Do you think so?" He had made Hera's waist far trimmer than hers: more like the waist she had possessed ten years and five children earlier. But she was content to be flattered. Her mortal beauty might not last, but it would be preserved for all time in this statue.

"Absolutely, my lady queen." He bowed, then made a sweeping gesture towards the work. "And such a brilliant idea to garb the goddess in beautiful clothing to hide the missing gold. I understand it was the young prince who—"

"You will not speak of this," she said coldly. "Let people believe that it is entirely covered with gold."

She saw the knot in the sculptor's throat bob as he swallowed. "Of course, my lady queen. Of course."

Pelops had been determined to do things as Chrysippus suggested – but she had found a way to press sweet oil from sour olives. Instead of donating one of her own outfits, she ordered the royal seamstresses to make identical copies of her three favorite ensembles for Hera. That way, the visitors coming to the games in a few months could not fail to see the similarities between herself and the queen of the gods. And the goddess would have pristine garments instead of used ones; that would certainly put Hippodamia in better stead with the gods than the bastard, Chrysippus. Of course, divine Hera had no great love for bastards either: the philandering of her husband Zeus had always infuriated her.

Hippodamia waved the sculptor away. "Go. I wish to commune privately with the goddess."

The man backed out, closing the door behind him. Hippodamia gazed into the agate eyes of the goddess, then bowed her head.

Lady Hera, she prayed silently, *queen of Heaven – you know the pain of a husband who rejects your child while showering favor on the get of lesser goddesses and even mortals! Help me, goddess. Show me what to do.*

Since Pelops' return six months before, it had become increasingly obvious that her husband preferred Chrysippus to her sons. He barely acknowledged the food brought in by Atreus' hunting parties and Thyestes' fishermen, yet lavished praise on the bastard for his management of the grain-stores. Then he put Chrysippus in charge of the new horse-breeding program – the endeavor he saw as the future of the kingdom! When Hippodamia protested he said only, "Thyestes is helping Laius with the games, and Atreus is in charge of the soldiers: they both have important roles."

Then, at the winter solstice, Chrysippus had attracted far too much attention. The seasonal celebration of the Cronia marked the one day of the year that Zeus allowed his child-swallowing father Cronus freedom from his imprisonment in Tartarus: the year's shortest day. The Cronia was a merry festival of music, outrageous disguises and silly contests; and Chrysippus had outshone her sons with his lithe dancing, his riddle-telling and even his throws of the dice. Hippodamia heard many onlookers – well born and commoners both – observe that Almighty Zeus was a third son who bested his two elder brothers and rose to rule Mount Olympus. Some even dared compare golden-haired Chrysippus to the god Zeus.

If this went on, the bastard would soon supplant her own sons! There was only one solution.

At first she hoped that the admiration of Chrysippus at the winter solstice festival would prompt her sons to reconsider, but when she raised the subject they repeated their objections. And finding another to do the deed was difficult: Chrysippus was simply too popular.

The women of the palace staff – even those most loyal to Hippodamia – were apt to flutter their eyelashes at the fair prince; the younger ones fantasized about being the first woman to share his bed, and the older ones laughed and joked and offered advice on how to catch his eye. Finally, in a fit of temper,

Hippodamia raged at her maidservants that she would brook no more such talk in her presence – but she knew that none of them could be trusted to kill the youth.

Some of the palace guard, she suspected, might be prepared to violate their oath of loyalty to Pelops for the right amount of gold – or the right pressure. But Hippodamia had no gold to offer, and she did not know the men well enough to divine what pressure would persuade them. Years ago Pelops had started the custom of rotating the men who guarded her, leaving no opportunity for rapport to develop.

She would have to get rid of the bastard herself; the only question was how.

Poison would be easiest, but Pisa's expert on herbs was the priestess Polyxo, who also happened to be Chrysippus' doting grandmother. Hippodamia could not go to her. Overcoming the youth by force seemed impossible: he was a young, supple athlete, well-trained at arms, whereas she was a middle-aged matron. Perhaps, were she a skilled archer, she could have shot him – but Hippodamia had no such ability.

What should I do, Lady Hera? Hippodamia implored the goddess. *What sacrifice will make you hear me?*

If only the goddess would take care of Chrysippus through divine intervention! A scorpion bite, a lightning strike, a bite of food that choked him… but Hera gave no sign that she would bring about such a convenient event. To Hippodamia's frustration, she heard only her own plea echoing through her mind.

Could the goddess be trying to tell her something by repeating back the question? Hippodamia pondered this – and in her own words she discovered a glimmer of an idea.

Since the Temple of Hera was first dedicated, Hippodamia had served as chief priestess. But in all those years, not liking to stain her hands or spatter her garments with blood, she had never conducted an animal sacrifice herself, instead delegating this task to the priestess who managed the day-to-day affairs of the temple. But the new chryselephantine statue offered an excuse to conduct the sacrifice herself. And if she could kill an animal, she could kill her husband's bastard son.

The next day, a rainy one, she sent for the priestess and explained that she wanted to learn. "How is it done?"

The middle-aged woman was flattered to be invited to the palace for a private audience with the queen. Over a cup of watered wine and a plate of savory cheese-and-barley bread, she described this aspect of her duties. "The animals receive an infusion of herbs beforehand," she explained. "That makes them easier to manage."

"What sort of herbs?" Hippodamia realized that this woman could be a source other than Polyxo. "What's their effect?"

"They make the animals docile, my lady queen, so that the sacrifice goes smoothly. We only give them a small amount, or else they would fall asleep in their pens."

"I understand," Hippodamia said. "Bring me a supply of these herbs, and the infusion, so that I can be familiar with their appearance and scent."

Swallowing a bite of cheese-flecked bread, the priestess nodded. "Certainly, my lady queen."

"What else must I know to perform the ceremony?"

"When the acolytes lead the beasts to the altar, my lady queen, draw your hand down the victim's forehead to its nose, like this," she said, gesturing. "That encourages them to nod, so the people may see they assent to the sacrifice."

Clever, thought Hippodamia. She had not known this trick. "And the knife-cut itself?"

"May I see your dagger, my lady queen?"

Hippodamia drew her blade from its jeweled leather sheath and offered it to the priestess.

"Thank you, my lady queen. You must grasp the forelock and pull the beast's head back, exposing the neck. Then make a quick, decisive cut across the throat." She demonstrated by pulling back the head of an imaginary animal and slashing the blade through the air. "It takes a bit of force – think of slicing through a very tough piece of meat at the table, and cut even more firmly than that. The blade must go deep to open the windpipe."

"Why is slitting the throat best?"

"The animal can no longer cry out, my lady queen – of course any bleating would be a bad omen. And with a deep throat cut the beast bleeds to death rapidly: it's the most merciful way."

"I see."

The priestess ran her finger along the dagger's edge. "This could use sharpening. Shall I arrange it, my lady queen?"

"Yes," said Hippodamia, leaning back against her cushioned chair. When the gray-haired priestess was gone, she considered the woman's advice. A firm slash across the throat. That did seem wise. She was indifferent to Chrysippus' suffering, but she wanted his death to be quick – with no chance for him to cry out.

Her newly sharpened dagger and a supply of herbs were soon delivered. Now that Hippodamia knew what to do, and had the means to do it, she needed only to find the right time. That required circumstances under which neither she nor her sons would be suspected; better still to implicate someone else. And the obvious candidate was Laius of Thebes.

As Chrysippus' lover, no one would question how he got close to the youth. Besides, Hippodamia would be glad to be rid of him. He was a bad influence on her sons, and Pelops showed the young man too much preference: he had given Laius much of the responsibility for planning the upcoming games, when that prestigious assignment should have rested with her sons.

One morning, as Pelops was getting out of his bath, she had raised this issue; but he responded: "Why should I change anything? Laius is doing well. Atreus is occupied with the soldiers, and Thyestes, although he's assisting, is not ready to be in charge. The other boys are too young."

"Why do you favor Laius?" she objected. "He's never done anything for you!"

Pelops held up his arms so that the bath attendant could towel off his torso; his bad arm, of course, he could only lift part way. "Didn't we just agree that he manages the games?"

Hippodamia suspected her husband of harboring a fondness for the Theban prince because the two of them had fathered their bastards upon a pair of sisters: Nerissa, the mother of Laius' brat, was also Chrysippus' aunt. But she dared not fling this fact at Pelops. Instead she said, "Haven't you heard how he's been 'managing' Chrysippus? Everyone is talking about the way he carries on with the boy."

Pelops turned so that the servant could dry his back. "So? Why shouldn't they enjoy each other's company?"

While her husband dressed, Hippodamia remembered the rumors about Pelops and his old friend and benefactor, the sea captain Aeolius: perhaps that gossip had been true after all. At any rate, Pelops clearly had no intention of removing Laius from his position.

Implicating Laius in Chrysippus' death would remove two problems at once. And it could easily be explained – a lovers' quarrel, passions inflamed by wine and jealousy. She simply had to find an opportunity. And the time must come soon; she wanted *her* sons to be the only Pisatan princes at the summer games.

The best opportunity, she decided, was the festival of new wine. Each year, just as the first spring flowers began to scent the air, a celebration was held under the full moon. During the day, the townspeople opened the pithoi, the huge earthenware jars in which the wine had been fermenting since the previous fall. At sundown there was always a drinking contest – a contest in which Laius was sure to participate.

When the festival day finally came, it was clear and warm. That afternoon Hippodamia and her daughters joined the women of Pisa, laughing and clapping their hands as Pelops, the princes, and the other well-born men rode horse-drawn carts through the streets of the town. The carts of merrymakers went to fetch the wine jars, and then brought them back into the agora to cheers and applause. Children followed behind them, wearing flower garlands and dragging toy wagons filled with special festival cups. When the sun touched the western horizon, Pelops shouted for the palace servants to bring out the great mixing-bowls; the new wine was poured and mixed with water, and all the citizens of Pisa filled their cups. Hippodamia, feigning giddiness, encouraged her maidservants and her daughters to drink deeply – that way they would not notice her absence later in the evening.

Torches were lit, and in the fading light of dusk Exarchos – who had served as herald before assuming the duties of steward – called for entrants in the drinking contest. Laius, of course, stepped forward first with his capacious festival cup. Atreus and Thyestes also volunteered, as did several Pisatan noblemen – and a handful of common soldiers and peasants, for during this festival distinctions of birth were forgotten. Chrysippus, Hippodamia noted, did not join the game, but stood with the spectators.

"You all know the rules," Exarchos bellowed, and the noise of the rowdy throng diminished slightly. "Each of you has a vessel of the same size—"

"How do you know how big my vessel is?" bawled one of the soldiers, clutching his crotch. The crowd roared with laughter.

Exarchos put a hand to his plump cheek in a farcical gesture. "Well, now that you mention it – from what I've heard, Laius of Thebes has the biggest one!"

Laius winked at Chrysippus, and raised his cup to the steward; the crowd laughed and cheered. Pelops, standing beside Exarchos, joined in the merriment. Hippodamia breathed slowly, drawing strength in her resolve. Her right hand slipped down to the vial hidden in her belt, filled with the infusion that calmed sacrificial animals. Laius would surely be drunk before long; she needed to make sure he slept soundly.

Exarchos continued, "When the horn is blown—"

"I'll get my horn blown tonight, for sure!" shouted some wag in the crowd.

"—each of you must drain his cup. The first man to finish will receive—"

"A FULL SKIN OF WINE!" yelled the crowd in unison, as Pelops held the promised wineskin aloft.

Exarchos motioned his assistant forward; the young man put the ram's horn to his lips and sounded the note. Immediately each contestant lifted his cup and began guzzling down his wine. As expected, Laius held his empty cup up first.

"Laius! Laius! Laius!" shouted the crowd.

The losing contestants lifted their cups in salute to the victor; realizing that this was her moment, Hippodamia moved forwards to kiss a surprised Laius on both cheeks. "Congratulations to the winner!" she cried brightly. "Let me refill your cup!" While everyone was distracted by Pelops presenting the prize wineskin to Laius, Hippodamia took Laius' cup, dipped it in the great mixing-bowl, and with trembling fingers emptied the vial into the cup before returning it to him.

The night wore on. Atreus, Thyestes and Chrysippus challenged their father to a second drinking-contest, which Atreus won. Flute-girls moved through the crowd, and peasants started a line-dance snaking through the agora. Normally Hippodamia would have departed before some goatherd attempted to paw her; instead this evening she borrowed a plain cloak from a tipsy maidservant and sent all of her attendants back to the palace with her daughters and younger sons. Then she ducked into the shadows, discarded her crown of flowers and pulled the old, plain cloak around her shoulders. Hidden in darkness, she moved to the edge of the festival crowd. There she remained, watching until she spotted Laius and Chrysippus leaving the celebration. Laius' steps were starting to weave; he yawned like a lion, and his arm draped across the youth's shoulders.

They were heading away from the crush of the mob, northeast towards the trees lining the Cladeus stream. Hippodamia followed them, her heart pounding hard. She tried to be stealthy but knew she was not – her footsteps sounded overly loud, and what with the full moon, the night offered little cover. But Laius was drunk with spring wine and herbs, and the youth had downed many cups himself. They did not notice her.

Laughing together at Laius' stumbles, the lovers selected a spot and spread their cloaks on the ground. Panting with exertion, Hippodamia hid herself behind a nearby tree. Laius kicked off his sandals and fumbled with his belt; with an inviting smile Chrysippus helped him undo the buckle and unwrap his kilt. Hippodamia saw that Exarchos' jest had been well-founded; Laius *was* impressively endowed, though his erection seemed dampened by the night's excesses. Still, he reached eagerly for Chrysippus as the boy shed his own kilt.

Hippodamia shrank back behind the tree, afraid that she would be seen as the pair moved around. What if they saw her?

This is my chance, Hippodamia told herself. *This is my chance to fight for my sons*. Cautiously she peered around the trunk.

The two were exchanging a kiss, and Laius' hands wandered clumsily over the youth's thighs. Chrysippus returned the caresses, but after a few moments he pulled back from the embrace, saying: "Laius, you're too drunk."

"Never too drunk for you, golden one," he mumbled.

Chrysippus stroked his lover's face, then nestled into the curve of his arm. "You should sleep it off."

"Just a little while," Laius said, his eyes already closing. "Just a little…"

Soon he was snoring. Chrysippus pulled one edge of the cloak up to cover him and rested his blond head on his lover's shoulder. The youth seemed to nod off quickly, but Hippodamia waited and watched until she was sure both were sound asleep. Once Chrysippus stirred, and she feared he would awaken – but then she saw it was a dream-movement, and heard the heavy sound of his breath. This was her moment. She slipped from behind the tree and looked down at the sleeping pair.

Laius' kilt had been carelessly tossed aside – and with it the dagger in a sheath attached to his belt. What a piece of good fortune: Laius' own dagger! Much better than using hers. She bent down and pulled the blade from its sheath. She touched its edge; it was sharp enough.

But Laius' arm still draped across his beloved, blocking access to the youth's neck. Should she try to move it? That seemed risky – either of them could wake. Laius was a champion wrestler, and Chrysippus an athlete: it was simply too dangerous. She would have to forego the recommended slash across the throat. How could she be sure to deal a fatal blow? Gut wounds, she was sure, were nearly always mortal. Chrysippus' lean stomach was exposed; she would try that.

She squatted beside the boy, but that was awkward; she changed her position and knelt instead. Yes, that was better.

For a long breath she held Laius' dagger aloft in both hands, watching the youth's chest rise and fall.

Do it, she told herself. *Do it now!*

She struck with all her strength, feeling the bronze bite into the boy's flesh. At once three things happened: a rush of blood welled up; she released the blade and pulled back, hoping to avoid any telltale spatters; and the boy's eyes flew open.

Chrysippus gasped, clutching at the wound; the dark blood coated his hands, and he screamed – a sound full of pain, terror, and disbelief.

Hippodamia got to her feet, ready to flee; but the shock in the boy's gaze transfixed her.

"What—" he cried, choking. "Mother? Mother!"

Hippodamia turned and ran, the boy's screams of pain following her like winged Furies. "Help me," he cried. "Mother! Laius – Laius, help me!"

She had wanted to be far away before anyone else arrived – but she was not fleet of foot, and other pairs of lovers had sought privacy nearby. She heard approaching footfalls, and feared that if she hid and was found people would realize she had wielded the knife. She would have to pretend she had come to help, in response to the boy's screams.

"What's going on?" a man's voice called through the darkness.

Someone was coming with a torch. "Hurry!" Hippodamia shouted, and ran towards the light.

"He's been stabbed!" shrieked a woman.

Hippodamia and the torchbearer arrived to find a disheveled couple leaning over Laius and Chrysippus. The man with the torch held it high, asking, "What's happened?"

"Prince Chrysippus has been attacked!" Hippodamia shrieked, feigning surprise and horror. "Look – that's Laius' dagger!"

Chrysippus was moaning; Hippodamia hoped that he was in too much pain to say anything coherent. His blood pooled darkly on the fabric beneath him and covered his belly and thighs; thank the gods, his agonized movements had smeared Laius as well. There was so much blood – surely he would die soon.

"No!" wailed the woman kneeling at Chrysippus' side; she burst into tears. "Not the golden prince!"

"Gods help us!" cried her lover.

Despite all the noise, and the writhing of the wounded boy beside him, Laius still snored. Was there any hope that, with all the wine he had drunk, the herbs might kill him? Hippodamia chewed her lip, hoping the Theban would die in his sleep.

Other revelers were gathering; their horrified expressions made a sharp contrast with their festival garb and tattered garlands. "You," said the man with the torch, pointing at one of those newly arrived, "fetch a healer! And you, find the king!"

Hippodamia stood there while Chrysippus whimpered like a wounded dog, clutching the knife in his belly – and Laius slept on.

§ 3.07

"Oho!" cried Pelops, lifting his festival cup. "This one's good!"

The peasant gyrated wildly, his arms wheeling, but his feet remained atop the greased, air-inflated wineskin. The crowd chanted the count. "Ten! Eleven! Twelve!"

"He may make it to twenty!" Pelops said. "What do you think, Exarchos?"

"Perhaps—"

"Sixteen!" shouted the onlookers – but before the count of seventeen was finished, the fellow slipped off, his rump hitting the trampled grass.

"A count of sixteen!" boomed Exarchos. The rowdy throng cheered and whistled as a soldier helped the peasant to his feet; those holding torches waved them back and forth against the starlit sky. "That's the longest yet," called out the steward. "Can anyone beat it? Who wants to try?"

"I'll beat it," Atreus said, staggering forward. He handed his drinking-cup to a friend and approached the air-filled bag.

The ghost of Myrtilus moved out of the shadows, shaking his head like a dismayed old woman. "Drinks as much as Hippodamia's father," he said. "But doesn't hold his wine well."

Shut up, Pelops told the ghost silently. But Myrtilus was right; Atreus had barely gotten his second foot on the wineskin when he slipped off, landing on his knees.

"That didn't count!" Atreus said.

"It did so!" shouted Thyestes, his arm around a giggling flute girl.

"Did not," Atreus insisted. "The count hadn't started!"

Thyestes rolled his eyes. "You won't make it to three."

Atreus wiped fragments of grass from his knees, and clambered back atop the wineskin. "One!" shouted the crowd. Atreus' feet slipped; his arms flapped as if he were trying to fly. "Two!" Then the wineskin burst, flattening.

The people laughed, and Thyestes said, "See? I told you."

"I'm still standing," Atreus pointed out. "I'm even still *on* the wineskin!"

"But you broke it!" Thyestes argued, and the men in the crowd started arguing about the interpretation of the rules in this situation; Atreus told Exarchos to keep on counting.

Pelops grinned, and even the ghost seemed to be enjoying the spectacle.

"My lord king!" a voice shouted. At the edge of the crowd there was a disturbance. "Make way, I must speak to the king!"

People moved back, and soon Okyllus had pushed his way through the throng.

"What is it?" asked Pelops, unnerved by the terror on the man's face.

"Your son," said Okyllus, breathing hard. "Chrysippus – injured!"

"Injured?" Pelops repeated. "What happened?"

"Stabbed, my lord king."

There were gasps in the crowd. Stabbed! Who would dare to harm the king's beloved son? Was Pisa under attack?

Cold fear clenched Pelops' heart. "Is he dead?"

"They've sent for healers, my lord king."

Pelops grasped Okyllus' arm. "Take me to him."

Okyllus nodded and led the way, accelerating to a run as soon as they reached the edge of the crowd; Pelops sprinted alongside, and though many from the festival crowd followed, all but the fastest runners soon fell behind. They had started on the western edge of the city; Okyllus brought Pelops back through the agora towards the north and east, heading for the river Cladeus. Soon Pelops saw the glow of torches in the distance, past a screen of trees: a crowd had gathered. As they drew near Pelops saw the priestess Polyxo, her daughter Nerissa, and three white-robed healers among the group. Even Hippodamia had somehow made her way to this spot.

Pelops scarcely noticed as the people parted to let him through. In the center of the gathering, two men lay on a blood-smeared cloak: Laius and Chrysippus, both nude. Laius was snoring. A healer knelt at Chrysippus' side; he was binding the youth's abdomen with a linen bandage, but even in the torchlight Pelops could see that Chrysippus' face was gray as ash.

Panting, Pelops dropped to his knees. "What happened?"

"Here's the dagger, my lord king," said the healer.

Pelops accepted the blade; it had been wiped down, but traces of blood – Chrysippus' precious blood – remained in the crevices of the gold-worked hilt.

It was Laius' knife. Pelops had given it to the Theban himself.

"Almighty Zeus!" Pelops bellowed, his fists clenching in anger. "I took this Theban into my home! I raised him like one of my own sons! How could he do this to me?"

Myrtilus whispered into his ear: "He should pay."

"He *will* pay, by the gods!" Pelops cried. "By all that is holy!" With his left hand he grabbed Laius' curling hair and jerked back his head, baring the Theban's neck, and lifted the knife to strike.

"No!" shrieked a woman. Nerissa threw herself between Pelops and Laius. "No, my lord king!"

"Out of my way, woman!" cried Pelops.

Thyestes dragged her away; from behind Pelops, Hippodamia said: "Justice must be done."

"This is not justice, my lord king!" Nerissa shouted. "Please, no!"

Pelops hesitated; in Nerissa's voice he heard the echo of her sister, Chrysippus' mother. Pelops remembered how, once, she had pleaded for a man's life, and he had denied her plea.

"Look at his hands, my lord king! Look at Laius' hands! There's no blood on them!"

That gave Pelops pause; glancing down, there was no obvious trace of blood. But Laius could have wiped his hands.

"He loved Chrysippus, my lord king," Nerissa was saying. "I know he did. Laius would never hurt him. And why does he sleep? It makes no sense!"

Pelops looked up at Nerissa; her eyes were wide with terror.

"Laius is the father of her son," Myrtilus said, squatting beside the Theban. "No doubt she would lie for him. It *is* Laius' knife."

The ghost was right, thought Pelops. He should slit Laius' throat.

"Father," said Chrysippus. The word came out as a sigh.

Dropping the blade, Pelops released Laius' hair and turned to his son. He caressed the boy's ashen face; there was little warmth in his flesh. "Chrysippus, I'm here. I'm here."

"Father," the boy said, his eyes fluttering open. "I… hurt…"

"I know. Stay with me, son – stay with me."

"Father," the boy, said, and coughed. Bright blood spilled from his lips.

His heart aching, Pelops took his son's hand; it was cold and sticky with blood. Blood already soaked the bandage around his abdomen. Pelops had seen battlefield wounds; he knew that his son could not possibly live.

He gripped the hand hard, then brought it to his lips and kissed it, tasting the salt of his son's lifeblood. "Laius will die for doing this to you," he said firmly. "Your death will not go unpunished."

"No…" said Chrysippus, "not Laius. Mother."

"What?" Pelops asked, wondering if the spirit of his beloved Danais had come to accompany their son to the Underworld. He looked around, but the only ghost he saw was Myrtilus. "Do you see your mother?"

"No," whispered Chrysippus. "The… queen. *She* did this. The queen."

Chrysippus' voice was faint – but in the silence of the night it was loud enough. The onlookers murmured uneasily, and stared at their queen.

"Hippodamia did this to you?" asked Pelops. "*Hippodamia*?"

"Never!" cried Hippodamia.

"Quiet!" Pelops barked harshly. "Okyllus, hold her."

Chrysippus coughed, and Pelops turned the boy's head to the side to keep him from choking on his blood. "Yes," the boy gasped. "Her, not… not Laius."

Pelops embraced the boy. "My son," he said. "My dearest son—"

"Cold," Chrysippus whispered. "So cold." The boy shuddered and then went limp in his arms.

"No," said Pelops softly. He caressed his son's cheek, but the spark of life had left his eyes. They stared upward without seeing, empty. Pelops clutched him tight against his chest. "NO!" he screamed to the moonlit, pitiless sky.

Chrysippus was gone.

Pelops groaned and then, gently, he lay the limp body of his son back down on the bloodstained cloak. He closed Chrysippus' eyelids with the edge of his hand and held his fingers there for a moment, as his grief was overwhelmed by fury. Then he climbed to his feet.

"Wake him," he told the healer, pointing at Laius.

The man pressed his lips together, then said, "We've tried, my lord king, but we can't. He has taken a powerful sleeping potion."

"Husband," Hippodamia began again. "Laius *must* have—"

"Silence!" Pelops lifted his fist; she cringed away. Everyone – Atreus and Thyestes among the onlookers – watched him, but no one spoke.

He turned again to survey the scene. The truth shimmered before him, but it was so terrible that he could scarcely believe it.

The shade of Myrtilus sidled up to him. "You know she did it. Chrysippus told you so himself."

Pelops inspected at the sleeping Theban. There was dried blood on his legs, his torso – as though Chrysippus had brushed against him after being wounded.

"She never wanted him," Myrtilus continued. "She hated his mother. She was jealous for her sons' sake."

Pelops squatted beside Laius. He lifted the Theban's right hand and inspected it. There was no trace of blood. Even if he had wiped his hands clean, some blood would have remained under the nails, in the folds of the skin. There was none.

"Why would Laius harm Chrysippus? Just as Nerissa said, he adored the boy!"

There was no blood on Laius' left hand, either.

"And then fall asleep so deeply that he does not wake, with all these people around? A likely tale!"

Pelops picked up the fallen dagger.

Myrtilus kept whispering, insistent. "If a man had done it, he would have done the job right: Chrysippus would have died at once."

Pelops got to his feet and turned to look at his wife. "You killed him," he growled, stepping closer.

Color rose on her cheeks. "No!" she said, but she stepped backwards. "He was delirious, Pelops! I – I never—"

With his left hand he gripped her arm, his fingers sinking deep into her soft flesh. "You lie! You've always lied!"

Her dark eyes went wide. "Pelops – *Husband*—"

The lines of kohl circling her eyes showed no trace of tears. She had shown no pity for Chrysippus; Pelops had none for her.

He set the blade against her throat.

"Father, no!" cried Thyestes.

"Father – stop!" said Atreus, grasping Pelops' wrist and pulling it back.

"Get away!" Pelops barked, shaking it off, but then he saw that Atreus' plain face was streaked with tears.

Hippodamia spoke. "Pelops, believe me, this is not my doing. You – *we* – have lost a precious child, a beautiful son. But, Pelops, when the Fates cut a life-thread there is nothing we can do about it." She swallowed again. "Pelops, it wasn't me! I'll swear any oath you like!"

Pelops hesitated.

She set a hand on his chest. "Please, Husband, calm yourself—"

And in the torchlight he saw blood on the edge of her cloak. It was not even her cloak, but a plain one, one that she must have taken from a servant in order to disguise herself.

"She's lying," Myrtilus repeated in a soft sing-song voice. "She's always lied."

"Would you add oath-breaking to the crime of murder?" Pelops shouted. "Take her away!" he told Okyllus. "Keep her under guard. And you, Atreus, Thyestes – find the priests."

He covered the body of his beloved son with his own cloak, sank down beside it and wept.

Hippodamia shrieked as the men pulled her away; Polyxo sobbed in her daughter's arms. The other onlookers were silent; they edged back to give the king space to mourn. Only Myrtilus dared speak, his voice gloating.

"I told you that I cursed you and your children."

FOUR: GIFTS TO GODDESSES

§ 4.01

Laius walked down the slope towards the river Alpheus, where he had been told he could find Nerissa. His dog kept bounding ahead, then stopping to wait, wagging its tail – but Laius did not increase his pace. The sun was warm on his shoulders; the rushing of the river announced spring and new beginnings. Neither suited Laius' mood. The last few days' weather, gray and rainy, had allowed him to sit by the fire with a jug of wine, remembering what he had lost – what they had all lost.

Today's sunshine mocked his grief. But Nerissa would understand.

He spotted her some distance upstream; slowly he made his way along the bank, ignoring the cheerful yips of his dog, urging him to walk faster. Nerissa stood knee-deep in the flowing water, the skirt of her gown pulled up and wrapped around her narrow waist. On the riverbank, various articles of clothing were draped over the lower tree branches, or spread over large stones to dry; beside a large fallen log lay an empty wicker basket and a pair of sandals.

Nerissa glanced up as he approached, then looked back down at the garment she was rinsing.

"Where's Polydorus?" Laius asked, looking around for their small son.

"With Mother," she said, rubbing a spot on the wet fabric. "I wouldn't take him here; he could fall in the water and drown."

The sharpness in her voice reproached him for not realizing that a river was a poor place to bring an active toddler. Laius looked down at the smooth-rounded stones beneath his feet, knowing he had earned the rebuke. He did not deserve a son like Polydorus – and obviously he was not fit to be responsible for the boy's safety. If Nerissa despised him now, well, she had every right to.

He looked back at her but she pointedly ignored him, working with grim determination on some stain, then dunking the garment back into the water.

This was a mistake, thought Laius, scratching his bearded jaw. He should not have come.

He turned away, snapping his fingers to summon the dog, which was busy sniffing Nerissa's sandals. He had already gone a few steps when Nerissa called out: "How's the king?"

Laius turned back. "Not well." Walking slowly towards her, he continued: "You saw him at the funeral."

He swallowed hard, fighting back the tears that threatened whenever he remembered the sight of Chrysippus on the funeral bier. King Pelops had led the prayers for Chrysippus' shade, but the fury in his voice would better have suited a battle-cry than a eulogy. When the tomb's door swung shut, sealing Chrysippus into the darkness, Laius felt that his own soul and that of the king had been entombed as well.

"The king's spending all his time in the armory. He had an artist paint a likeness of the queen on a plank, and he's been throwing knives at it. He hardly speaks to anyone. The games are less than four months away, and I can't imagine how he'll be fit to preside. I've been working with Atreus, Thyestes and Exarchos to make all the arrangements, but it's going to be a gloomy festival."

Nerissa pulled the garment from the river and inspected it; Laius realized that it was a child's tunic. "What's he doing about the queen?" she asked, dipping the tunic back into the water.

Laius seated himself on the log, near the laundry basket. "She was banished this morning. King Pelops won't say where, but she'll be kept under guard for the rest of her life."

Shaking her head, Nerissa pulled the dripping cloth from the water again. She frowned at the spot that offended her.

"I know." Laius picked up a stick and threw it some distance along the bank; his dog raced after it. "I hate it, that he's letting her live. But she's his best claim to the throne of Pisa. And she has powerful relatives in Mycenae and Argos." The dog returned to him with the stick and he threw it again, further this time. "Besides, I'm not sure what her children would do if Pelops executed her."

Apparently satisfied with the eradication of the spot, Nerissa started wringing water from the little tunic. "Perhaps banishment is the greater punishment for her," she finally said. "Isolation. Loneliness."

Laius looked down at his feet. "She deserves worse." He blinked back tears of anger and loss.

"How are *you*?" Nerissa asked as she waded towards the riverbank.

"I did nothing to save him." His voice grew rough. "He warned me that Hippodamia hated him; he wanted to leave Pisa. He was murdered at my side, and I did *nothing*. Nothing!"

She shook out the wet tunic. Drops landed on Laius' arms and neck like icy tears; he did not brush them away. Nerissa walked past him and draped the tunic over a branch, safely out of the dog's reach. Then she gathered the items that had been spread out over the rocks, and hung them out of reach as well.

"Laius, listen to me." She unwrapped her skirt from around her waist, letting the cloth fall to cover her legs, then slipped her feet into her sandals. "My mother thinks you were given some sleeping potion. And the amount you must have had – if you weren't such a big man, it could have killed you."

For a moment the cloud blocked the sun; Laius looked up at the sky, blinking. "You think Hippodamia wanted *me* dead, too?"

"She used *your* dagger to kill him. If she'd had her way, you'd have been executed for murder before you woke." Nerissa came to sit beside him. "And that's exactly what would have happened, if Chrysippus hadn't managed to tell King Pelops who really attacked him."

Laius buried his face in his hands. "He saved me. He saved my life – when I didn't protect him—" His sorrow burst forth in great, aching sobs.

Her slender arm reached around his back. "Let your tears flow," she said softly, rocking him as she rocked their young son. "We're all grieving for him."

Laius wept, his shoulders shaking with emotion. Over the sound of the river he heard a dove's trill – a mournful sound as if it, too, shared his loss – and somehow Laius was comforted. He drew a shaky breath and said: "He – he was the most beautiful creature I ever saw."

"I know," Nerissa said simply, quietly. "He was like a young god."

Laius used the corner of his cloak to wipe his wet face, and looked at the woman beside him. How much she resembled her nephew Chrysippus! The same oval face, the same straight nose and full lips, the same golden hair. But her eyes were different: leaf-green rather than golden brown. They shimmered with unshed tears.

"He told me that I should visit Polydorus more often," he said. "And you."

Laius felt Nerissa's back stiffen; she looked away, up at the cloud-dotted sky, and he could not begin to guess what she was thinking. That was the problem with women: no matter how much pleasure one took in their soft beauty, they remained strange creatures with unfathomable ways.

Finally, still not looking at him, she said: "He was very perceptive. He understood responsibility."

Laius heard another unspoken reproach: that he himself was not responsible – at least not with things that did not interest him, like baby-tending.

"What do *you* want, Laius?" she asked, turning back to him.

"I want Chrysippus back."

She was silent a moment. "I don't think that's possible."

Laius pressed his lips together. There *were* stories of heroes who went down to the Underworld to fetch their loved ones – but in the end the dead were never rescued, and frequently the hero lost his life.

"No," he finally said. "I suppose not." The dog came closer and nudged his knee with its head; without thinking he reached down to scratch its ears.

"But as long as we remember him," Nerissa said, "a part of him is with us." The dove trilled again in the tree above them and then took wing, heading west. "Look," said Nerissa, pointing. "Maybe that bird is carrying our message to Chrysippus and will tell him that we're thinking of him – that we love him."

This thought lightened Laius' heart; he looked into Nerissa's shining eyes. "You're too good for me," he said, reaching out to stroke her golden hair. It was a strange thing to say, for – no matter that she and her mother served in the Temple of Rhea – she was of low birth, and he was the son of a king. Yet Nerissa was always wise and patient, and always forgiving despite his periods of neglect.

"Yes," she said.

"I don't know why you love me," he said, and gently kissed her. She melted into his embrace, and her answering kiss told him that she *did* love him – that she would always be there for him, despite everything.

Her reply was so faint that Laius almost did not hear it. "Perhaps for the same reason Chrysippus loved you."

As Laius spread his cloak on the ground, he wondered what that reason was. But then she was in his arms again, soft and yielding and offering comfort, and there was no more need for thought.

§ 4.02

"Mother, I need to talk to you," Chloris said.

"Just a moment, Chloris," Niobe answered impatiently. Ilioneus had deliberately tripped his younger brother Sipylus, and now the smaller boy's knee was scraped and bleeding. Niobe sent Ilioneus to a corner of the courtyard and told him to stand there, facing the wall, until she gave him permission to turn around. Then she knelt to comfort Sipylus, using her handkerchief to wipe the tears from his cheeks and blot his knee. She suggested he go play with the dogs – and as soon as the one with russet splotches licked his face, the boy giggled, his hurts forgotten.

The baby within her kicked, hard; Niobe grimaced as she struggled to rise. It was a beautiful spring day after many rainy ones, and the family had come out to enjoy the afternoon in the palace courtyard. The gardens were bright with narcissi, and butterflies fluttered from bloom to bloom. Phaedimus and Damasichthon were arm-wrestling while Alphenor and Zethos cheered them on; a nursemaid bounced little Tantalus on her knee, and Amphion sat with his lyre on the bench beneath the trellis, working on some new composition.

Chloris helped her to her feet. "Are you all right, Mother?"

"I'm fine," Niobe said, gasping a little. She glanced discreetly at Thebe, who was seated beneath the apple tree with Philomela, spinning woolen thread. Last year Thebe had been so certain that she was finally pregnant – and then so desperately depressed when that hope evaporated. It must have been very hard for her to learn that Niobe was with child *again*. Though Niobe did not want to complain in front of her sister-in-law, who would be grateful for any pregnancy, carrying this child was especially exhausting. Her belly had grown huge so quickly, and the babe inside her never seemed to stop kicking.

With her daughter's help, Niobe took her seat on a cushioned chair. "All right, my dear. What is it?"

"It's about the Maidens of Artemis—"

Niobe waved a fly away from her face. "We've had this conversation before." They had, in fact, had it many times. Chloris had brought up the idea the day after her outing with the Maidens of Artemis: she wanted to join the cult of the virgin goddess. Niobe told her daughter that she was too young to make such a commitment, and the priestess of Artemis agreed. And yet Chloris persisted, wheedling for a promise that she would be allowed to join the Maidens as soon as her monthly blood started. Niobe insisted that it was too early to determine the matter, but her daughter came back to the subject every few days: citing her devotion to the goddess, her love of the wilderness, her skill at the hunt – and the fact that Niobe herself had left home at a young age.

Reaching for a honeycake – she was always hungry, though she could never manage a large meal – Niobe repeated the same response she always gave. "We'll decide when the time comes."

"It's come, Mother," Chloris said quietly.

It took a moment for the significance of her daughter's words to sink in. Niobe lowered the honeycake and looked up at her daughter. "You mean—"

Chloris nodded. "Yes, Mother. My blood started yesterday."

"Oh! Oh, Chloris!" Niobe struggled to her feet and hugged her daughter. "My little girl! Why didn't you tell me yesterday?"

"I wasn't sure at first," Chloris said. "There wasn't much blood yesterday. But now I'm sure. I'm using the rags you gave me."

Philomela and Thebe came over to learn the reason for the commotion; Niobe explained, and Chloris accepted a congratulatory embrace from each woman. Her hand lingering on the girl's cheek, Thebe asked: "Are you feeling all right? Would you like some lettuce?"

Besides its use in enhancing fertility – some said the goddess Hera had become pregnant with her son Hephaestus simply by touching a lettuce leaf – lettuce was the standard remedy for women's monthly cramps. Niobe felt a spasm of guilt for not suggesting this herself.

"Thank you, Aunt Thebe, but I feel fine." There was determination in Chloris' gray eyes when she continued: "Well, Mother? May I join the Maidens of Artemis now?"

"Oh, Chloris!" Niobe dropped back into her chair and looked up at her daughter. "*Why* do such a thing? Why not marry and have children?"

"There's no one I want to marry."

"You haven't even considered any suitors," Niobe objected. She picked up the honeycake and took a bite. "Your Uncle Pelops wants you to meet his sons, remember?"

"But what if I meet them and I *still* want to join the Maidens of Artemis?"

"But, Chloris," said Thebe, "don't you want children?" Her voice was wistful.

Tightening a tuning-peg, Amphion interjected: "The oath isn't for life, Thebe. If Chloris joined the Maidens, she could marry after her service is done."

Niobe swallowed the last of the pastry and took her daughter's hand. "I don't want to lose you," she confessed. "I don't want you to go away. You're my only daughter."

"Hard to argue with that," said Amphion. He drew his fingers across the lyre-strings; the chord was still slightly off, and he twisted the tuning-peg again.

"But if I married one of King Pelops' sons, I'd have to move away then too!"

"Maybe," Niobe said, hearing an echo of her own mother's voice. Queen Dione of Lydia had not wanted her only daughter to leave Lydia – but Niobe had rejected her mother's wishes, and sailed away. How her mother's heart must have ached all these years! "I'm sorry, Chloris. I don't know what to say."

Amphion strummed the chord again; this time it rang true. He rose, lyre in hand, and came over to kiss Niobe's cheek. "If it's the will of the goddess, Artemis will show us. We don't need to decide this afternoon." He rested his long-fingered hand on his daughter's shoulder. "Forgive your old parents, Chloris; it's hard for us to realize that you're all grown up."

Niobe saw that – though the girl was still not satisfied – Chloris could not help but answer Amphion's smile with one of her own.

"Now," Amphion said, "let's rehearse my new song." He turned to look at the arm-wrestling match. "Boys!" he called. "Come on: you, too Sipylus – and Ilioneus, I release you from your corner!" The younger boys ran over excitedly; this was their first time for their father to ask them to sing a new piece with him.

Everyone, even those who would not sing, gathered closer. Niobe massaged her belly and watched her husband and children.

"This song is about the Muses," Amphion explained. "When Apollo first led them in song, mortal men had never heard anything so beautiful. Some of them could not stop listening – they were so enchanted by the music that they forgot to eat and to drink and to sleep."

"They forgot to *eat*?" asked Damasichthon incredulously. "Weren't they hungry?"

"The music was so beautiful that they didn't notice their hunger."

Phaedimus looked puzzled. "But if they forgot to eat, wouldn't they die?"

"You're right, Son. Without food or sleep, the music-loving mortals became so weak that they were close to death. They'd shriveled up so much that they no longer looked like men. When the Muses noticed this, they didn't want their listeners to suffer – so they turned them into grasshoppers."

"Why grasshoppers?" asked Alphenor.

Amphion grinned. "Well, I'm not exactly sure – and it's not always wise to question the gods." He shot a glance at Niobe. "But I'd guess it's because grasshoppers make a sort of music, too. Now I want Alphenor, Ilioneus and Sipylus to sing the part of grasshoppers. The rest of you will be the Muses."

Amphion demonstrated the grasshoppers' part, a simple "Bzzz – bzzz" sound in a syncopated pattern. Soon Ilioneus and Sipylus were imitating the rhythm. Amphion asked Alphenor to help them practice while he taught Chloris, Phaedimus and Damasichthon the parts of the Muses. The composition was not lengthy; the older children quickly had the tune, and Amphion led all of them through the complete song together. Niobe, Zethos, Thebe and Philomela applauded when it was finished.

"Do you like it, Mother?" asked Ilioneus, running over to her.

"Very much," she said, laughing. "It's clever of you, Amphion, to create a song that our youngest boys can enjoy!" Then the baby kicked again – she winced, pressing her hand to her belly.

Amphion set down his lyre and came over to caress the swollen curve of her abdomen. "I create only songs – you create life. And this will be the biggest boy yet!"

"I know," Niobe groaned. "I'm enormous!"

"He must take after Zethos," said Amphion.

Zethos laughed. "He's not mine, Brother, I promise!"

The palace herald stepped into the courtyard and bowed. "My lord king, my lady queen – Captain Naucles has arrived."

"Excellent!" said Amphion. "Bring him here." Soon the seaman, freshly returned from his first sailing trip of the season, joined them.

"Naucles," said Niobe, "It's good to see you again."

The sailor shook his head; his bearded face was somber. "You'll change your mind, my lady queen, when you hear the news I bring."

Despite the sunshine, Niobe shivered. "Why? What's wrong, Naucles?"

Standing by an olive tree in bloom, Naucles told them that King Pelops' beloved son, Chrysippus was dead: murdered by Queen Hippodamia.

Niobe was so horrified she found it hard to breathe – how could Hippodamia have done something so terrible? Murdering a child! What kind of monster had her brother married?

"Pelops allowed her to live?" Zethos asked.

Naucles rubbed his bearded chin. "Well, my lord, she's the mother of his sons. His other sons, I mean."

"And Pelops' marriage to Hippodamia set him on the throne of Pisa," observed Amphion.

Niobe closed her eyes, pressing her hands to her face. She recalled how Pelops lit up when he spoke of his son Chrysippus: the only child of his beloved Danais, who had been Niobe's maidservant – and her friend. In fact it had been Danais who made it possible for Niobe to come to Thebes and wed Amphion. Niobe had never met Chrysippus, but she imagined the boy in Danais' image. Pelops had been so sure he would be a good match for Chloris – and now Chloris would never marry him, would never even meet him.

"Pelops must be devastated," she whispered.

"He is, my lady queen," Naucles said. "I only saw him briefly, but he looked like a ghost. They say he doesn't sleep."

"Will he still hold the games?" asked Amphion.

"Yes, my lord king," answered the sailor. "He believes the games are his sacred duty – he dares not offend the gods. Every four years; that's what they expect."

Zethos and the older boys received this news with relief; all had been training hard for the games in Pisa. But Niobe, imagining her brother's despair, was barely aware of them.

She felt Amphion's fingers wipe a tear from her cheeks; then he kissed her forehead. "I know it's sad, my love, but what can we do?"

Niobe did not think her husband expected an answer, but still his words echoed in her ears. What *could* they do to help Pelops in his grief? She and Pelops had once been so close – but now she and her favorite brother were separated as much by their royal responsibilities as by the six-day journey from Pisa to Thebes. They met only rarely, when Pelops came to visit; her nephew Chrysippus had lived and died without her ever setting eyes on him!

A sharp pain gripped her belly; Niobe gasped, and felt moisture between her legs.

"Niobe?" There was concern in Amphion's voice. "Are you all right?"

The pain did not slacken; she gritted her teeth against it, drawing in a hissing breath. Then the trickle of moisture became a gush, and she realized that her water had broken.

"The baby's coming," she gasped when the contraction abated.

Amphion grasped her arm; Chloris came to her other side to help her up. "Let me," Chloris said to both Philomela and Thebe. "I'm a woman now."

"I'll fetch the midwife," Zethos said. He shouted for a servant to bring him his cloak.

"I'll come with you," offered Naucles, and the two men hurried out.

Amphion wrapped a strong arm around Niobe's shoulders. "Alphenor," he said, "go tell my mother – she's probably in her house." As their son sprinted out, Amphion spoke directly to Niobe. "Let's get you to the birthing room."

Thebe said she would watch the boys, and Philomela signaled that she was going ahead to prepare the room. Niobe leaned against Chloris and her husband as they made their way into the palace. "I'll be all right. I'm an old hand at this now."

"I'll help you, Mother," said Chloris as the three of them reached the corridor.

"But, Chloris—"

"Mother, don't say I'm too young. I'm a woman now – and Artemis helped her mother deliver Apollo just as soon as she was born!"

"Chloris, you're not Artemis," said Amphion, sharper than usual. "And if you want to help your mother, remember that she knows what she's doing."

"You can come," said Niobe. It was time for Chloris to start learning about childbirth – and if she saw what a miracle it was to bring a new baby into the world, perhaps she would relinquish her idea of taking virgin's vows.

The three of them made their awkward way to the birthing chamber; Philomela was already inside. Chloris entered immediately, but Niobe paused on the threshold as another pain seized her. Amphion supported her until it had passed, then said: "My love, I'll make an offering to the gods for you and the child."

She nodded, smiling – but as soon as the door shut behind her she was flooded with sudden, unaccustomed fear.

Philomela peered at her closely. *What's wrong?* she asked with her gestures.

Now that the bustle of getting to the birthing room was past, Niobe realized how unlike all her other births this felt. The very familiarity of the room made her aware of the strange sensations in her body. "It feels different this time," she whispered, not wanting Chloris to hear. "Always, before, I could tell when the birth was approaching. Today was a surprise."

Philomela swept her hands in a broad curve to indicate how very large Niobe's belly had grown.

Niobe laughed shakily. "Yes, I suppose – he's too big to stay inside any longer."

Philomela helped her over to stand beside the birthing chair. One maidservant was scattering fresh straw on the marble floor, while another lit the lamps. Chloris, under her mother's direction, told a third serving woman to set out the linens and sponges, and to fetch water.

"Anything else, Mother?" asked Chloris.

"Only Theora," said Niobe.

"Uncle Zethos will bring her soon," said Chloris.

Chloris removed the golden circlet from Niobe's head and set it on the work table; Philomela undid the jeweled pins that fastened her gown at the shoulders and removed the gown and undergarment, both drenched with birth-water. Then she helped Niobe into a loose linen shift that tied down the front.

A breeze wafted through the open window; Niobe took a deep breath, trying to calm herself. She looked around at the familiar wall paintings, the doves perched in the branches of the painted garden. "It seems that I'm always in this room," she said, trying to sound cheerful. But inside her a frightened voice seemed to whisper that this time was different.

Philomela covered Niobe's hand with her own – and Niobe realized she had clenched her hands into fists. Gently the Athenian princess smoothed her hand open and stroked it, then kissed Niobe's cheek.

The woman who had been scattering straw spoke up; the birthing chamber was a room that brought women of all rank together. "My lady queen, there's never been a woman like you for birthing babies. This one will be here before you know it, and healthy as all the others!"

"Maybe it'll be a girl this time!" said Chloris.

Niobe shook her head, then paused as a new contraction gripped her. When she was able to speak, she said: "No, Chloris. It's too large to be a girl. Besides, no girl would kick so hard – or so often." She turned to Philomela. "Here, help me walk a bit."

Round and round the room she went, the fresh straw crunching beneath her feet; the afternoon shadows grew longer and longer, and then dusk fell. She paced and rested and paced again, supported by Philomela, then by the serving women, then even by Chloris. The pains came and went – but without the sense that the baby was ready to be born. Completing another circuit of the room, Niobe realized that the sky outside was wholly dark. "Where's Theora?" she gasped.

"I'll go ask, my lady queen," said a maidservant, and departed.

With Chloris' help, Niobe eased herself onto the birthing-chair and sat there panting hard. Philomela dipped a sponge into water scented with fenugreek and wiped the sweat from Niobe's brow.

"Mother," asked Chloris, "if it *is* a girl, will you let me become a priestess of Artemis?"

Philomela set her finger before her veil and gave Chloris a stern look.

"It's all right, Philomela," said Niobe, "it's something to think about besides when Theora will arrive."

Chloris fetched a second sponge and dabbed Niobe's arms with cool, fragrant water. "Well, Mother?"

"Lady Artemis helps women with childbirth," said one of the servants.

"Yes, my lady queen," said another. "Surely the goddess would be pleased if Princess Chloris became her priestess!"

Exhausted, Niobe glanced up at Philomela. The mute woman inclined her head thoughtfully, then handed Chloris the basin and sponges and gestured for her to take them back to the work table. In that brief moment of not-quite-privacy, Philomela pressed her hand to her forehead as one did when making reverence to the gods, then indicated Chloris with a quick motion of her chin.

"Yes," Niobe said quietly. "Very pious."

Philomela ran her hands over Niobe's swollen belly; a contraction started then, and her friend's gentle touch helped to soothe the spasm. When the contraction was finished Philomela pressed her hand to her own forehead once more, a silent plea in her eyes – asking Niobe to seek the help of the goddess. Chloris returned and Philomela moved behind the girl, setting both hands on her shoulders. The mute woman tilted her head to one side, beseeching Niobe to accept Chloris' dedication to Artemis.

Niobe was too exhausted to argue. Besides, the last five children had been boys – and the baby she was carrying was too large to be a girl. "Very well," she sighed.

"Really?" asked Chloris, bouncing a little in her excitement. "You'll let me join?"

"*Only* if it's a girl," Niobe said sharply, already regretting her agreement. "And I want your vows to be temporary, like your father suggested."

"That's all right," said Chloris, standing taller, buoyed by happiness despite the fatigue that weighed on everyone else. "Do you want to walk some more, Mother? Artemis will help you now, I'm sure of it."

Niobe chewed her lips and remained silent. Perhaps Artemis *would* do something for her. She had made her monthly pilgrimages to the shrine; she and Philomela had woven a brilliant tapestry to give to the goddess as a thanks-offering once the child had come. And now she had even agreed to give her daughter, if it was the goddess' will. What more could Artemis want?

Leaning on Chloris' arm, she resumed her pacing. But the pains continued, and the baby did not come. The night air grew chill; the maidservants lit a brazier, pulled the shutters closed, and drew the leather curtains to keep the room warm. Thebe arrived, reporting that Niobe's sons were finally in bed and that Antiope was with the Maenads and would be out all night. Niobe walked till her feet ached and then rested, panting; she endured the contractions with clenched fists and gritted teeth, and drank a little water when she could – and still the baby did not come.

"You've never had it so difficult," said Thebe, taking her turn to wipe Niobe's brow.

"No," Niobe said shortly.

Some weary time later, through a haze of pain and fatigue, Niobe heard her daughter's worried prayers: "Please, Lady Artemis, help my mother as you helped your own mother Leto!"

Suddenly Philomela clapped her hands together, drawing Niobe's attention. The Athenian princess pointed to her ear, then towards the door.

"Theora's coming?" Niobe asked, feeling a flicker of hope. "You can hear her?"

Philomela nodded. After a moment Niobe could hear men's voices out in the corridor, and the sound of hurrying feet. Then the door swung open and Theora entered, accompanied by one of her apprentices.

"What took you so long?" Niobe gasped.

Theora removed her cloak and handed it to her apprentice. "I was attending a difficult birth, my lady queen. I left for the palace as soon as lord Zethos found me."

Chloris asked: "The other birth – is everything all right?"

"I hope it will be, my lady princess," said Theora, washing her hands. "I left an apprentice to manage the delivery. When the queen is in labor, my place is here."

Another pain clutched Niobe's belly; she moaned in frustration until it passed. "Theora," she managed to gasp, "what's wrong? Why won't the baby come?"

Calmly, Theora said: "Lean back against the chair, my lady queen. Rest as much as you can between the pains." She touched Niobe's belly, her cold fingers like ice against the overheated skin. The midwife's hands moved here and there, pressing hard, and she frowned. Then she turned back to her apprentice. "Bring the oil flask."

The younger woman drew the stopper from an alabaster flask and poured green-gold olive oil over Theora's slender hands. Niobe saw her daughter's eyes go wide as Theora reached up between Niobe's legs – and then the pain of Theora's probing hand shut out all else, and it was all Niobe could do to breathe, breathe, breathe, and try not to resist, not to clench down.

"Here's a foot," said Theora, "and here's another – yes, and another—"

"It's a monster!" shrieked one of the servants.

"Don't be a fool!" snapped the midwife. "The queen's carrying twins!"

Niobe gritted her teeth, feeling Theora start to reposition the unborn child – children! – within her. Twins! That explained her huge size and the constant kicking— "But why aren't they here yet?" she gasped.

"Philomela, hold her shoulders," said the midwife. "My lady queen, once the first is out, the second will come easily. I just need to get the first into position—"

The hours that followed were the most difficult and painful that Niobe had ever experienced. Her world narrowed down to the sensation of Philomela's strong hands gripping her shoulders and the battle Theora was waging with the recalcitrant babes. She could not tell how much time had passed; it seemed she was slipping in and out of awareness, hearing the sound of her own screams, and her daughter's prayers, from a great distance. The golden thread of Theora's voice wove through it all, like the long-ago thread that had guided Theseus from the labyrinth: "My lady queen, we're making progress." "Just a little more, my lady queen." Through the dizzying nightmare Niobe tried to follow that thread of voice, clutching at it for guidance. "Almost there, my lady queen." At some point she realized that morning had come: someone had thrown back the curtains and opened the shutters to admit more light. Dust specks floated in the sunbeam, swimming slowly, like tiny fishes.

"Now, my lady queen!" cried Theora. "Push now, with all your might!"

Too tired to scream, Niobe pushed and pushed and pushed – and felt the child break free at last in a gush of warm fluid.

"You did it, Mother!" cried Chloris as the servants cheered and clapped their hands together.

"It's a girl, my lady queen," said Theora. "A beautiful little girl."

"Congratulations," said Thebe.

Blinking, Niobe looked down to see the new child, small and glistening red. She heard its thin cry: thank the gods, it had survived the birth.

"A girl, Mother, a girl!" said Chloris. "Artemis has helped you deliver a girl!"

Theora cut the birth-string and handed the babe to her apprentice. "Your work's almost done, my lady queen."

"You can do it, Mother," said Chloris, taking her hand. "The goddess is with you."

Niobe gripped her eldest daughter's hand; drawing strength from the reassuring touch, she bore down once more – and the second child slipped from her like a bean pinched from its pod.

"Another girl, my lady queen," announced the midwife, as a tiny wail confirmed her statement. "Twin girls!"

The words echoed around her as the afterbirth slipped from her body. She closed her eyes, exhausted, weak, grateful that it was over. Chloris wiped her sweat-dampened brow with a cloth and then kissed her cheek. "Father's right," she said. "You're the strongest woman in the world."

Able hands helped Niobe over to the bed in the corner. As she lay down she heard Theora sending for a wet nurse.

"You think I'm going to die," Niobe whispered.

"Of course not, my lady queen!" Theora's tone had a cheerful brightness that alarmed Niobe further. "But two babies drink twice as much milk. You'll need help."

"You won't die, Mother," said Chloris, handing her a cup of wine mixed with honey. Her voice was filled with certainty. "The goddess is with you. Not just one girl, but two!"

Niobe drank as much as she could and fell back among the pillows, feeling that she could sleep for a year. She closed her eyes, dozing while the apprentice midwife bathed her with a sponge and set a pad of soft linen between her thighs.

She slept again, to wake later in her own room. She glanced around: the midwife and Amphion were both there at her bedside. "Husband…" she began, the word rasping past her parched throat and dry lips.

His gray eyes glistened. "You're awake." She heard the relief in his voice, saw the dark circles beneath his eyes, and knew he had feared she would never wake again.

From the other side of the bed Theora said: "She'll be fine, my lord king. She's just a little more tired than usual." She held a cup to Niobe's lips. Niobe took a swallow of the warm medicinal tea, bitter and yet oddly soothing. Then she sank back against the pillows.

"The babies?" she asked, hoarsely. "Are they—"

"They're fine," Theora said, patting her hand. "They're suckling strongly. Two healthy, lovely little girls."

Amphion stroked her cheek. "No wonder you're tired, my love. *Two* daughters!"

"The babies," she asked. "Where are they?"

"With the wet nurse," said Theora. "You'll need help with them, my lady queen. And you must get plenty of rest." The midwife paused. "She needs a rest after this birthing, my lord king – do you understand me?"

Amphion nodded wryly. "I understand."

"I want to see my babies," said Niobe, her full breasts aching.

"I'll fetch them," said Theora. She rose and left the room.

"Two girls," said Niobe, finding it hard to recall the experience of the birth in any detail. Two girls! "Amphion, I… I promised Chloris that if I had a girl…"

He smiled. "Yes, she's already told me."

"I wish I hadn't," Niobe said, tears welling up in her eyes. "I don't want her to go!"

"I'm glad you did, my love." He kissed her forehead. "Artemis saved your life. And the will of the goddess is clear: not just one but *two* girls!"

Theora and the wet nurse arrived, each carrying a newborn. Niobe saw that the wet nurse was a plump, rosy-cheeked young woman, robust and healthy.

"Do you feel strong enough to hold one now, my lady queen?" asked the midwife.

"Yes," said Niobe, stretching out her arms.

Theora gave the child she was holding to Amphion while the wet nurse nestled the other infant against Niobe's breast; quickly the child began to suckle, the sensation easing Niobe's heart. Both babies were a healthy-looking pink, with fine dark hair on their heads and blue eyes fringed with dark lashes. They were as alike as a pair of barley corns.

"They're beautiful," said Amphion. "You've outdone yourself, dear wife. My mother is very impressed."

They *were* beautiful. But they could not make up for the fact that Chloris would leave her. One child did not replace another. Still, as the flow of milk relaxed her, Niobe reminded herself that Chloris would not leave home immediately, and she would visit from time to time – her daughter was becoming a priestess, not leaving for the Underworld.

That thought led to another: her brother Pelops and the death of his beloved son Chrysippus. She did not know if there was anyone in Pisa that Pelops trusted, now. Was there anyone at all to comfort him?

"I have an idea, my love," Amphion said. "We should heed Theora's advice and avoid getting you with child again too soon. Why don't we distract ourselves by journeying to Pisa this summer for your brother's games?"

Niobe rested her cheek on the top of her daughter's tiny head and looked at her husband, marveling at how he sometimes seemed to read her thoughts. "But if we both go, who will take care of Thebes?"

"Zethos. He'll want to go to the games, but I'm sure I can persuade him." He looked down at the child in his arms, and then back to Niobe. "I think it would comfort your brother to see you, my love."

"Yes," Niobe said. She yawned, feeling sleepy once more. "If I'm strong enough, I want to go. Pelops needs me."

"I know," Amphion said.

§ 4.03

Broteas stood with his son at the foot of the palace stairway. Though the sun had already risen over the eastern hills, the king remained inside. The others ordered to participate in the procession – a priestess, a few nobles, a small contingent of the palace guard, and the bearers who would carry the king's sedan chair – waited with resigned expressions on their faces. One never knew when King Tantalus of Lydia would decide to begin any ceremony – early, late, or not at all.

Patience, thought Broteas, recalling what the priest on Lemnos had said. Though he still was not completely convinced the god Hephaestus had spoken to him, he did his best to follow the advice.

Shading his eyes, he spotted Geranor among the soldiers and beckoned the man forward. Geranor approached him and bowed slightly; Broteas led him off to one side, a few paces away from his son and the others.

"So," Broteas began, "all is in order? You leave for Pisa tomorrow?"

"Yes, my lord prince. I've arranged the first leg of my passage with a Chian merchant. We'll set sail as soon as I reach the harbor."

"Any final questions about your task?"

"No, my lord prince," said Geranor. "As ordered, I'll attend King Pelops' games and explore the area; I'll determine where Rhea's mastiff is kept. If I can take it and bring it back to Lydia, I'll do so. If not, I'll return with a report on the local conditions to support future action. And during all this I will make sure that I accept none of Pelops' hospitality, so that I incur no guest-debt."

"Very good," said Broteas, pleased by the man's thorough understanding of his assignment. "Take this in token of my appreciation." He slipped a ring loose from his left forefinger: made in Egypt, tiny gold beads encrusted the jewel of polished agate.

Geranor took the ring and held it to catch the sunlight; his dark eyes gleamed.

"If you retrieve Lydia's mastiff," said Broteas, "you'll earn a much greater treasure."

"Yes, my lord prince," said Geranor, closing his fist over the ring. "I'll do my best, my lord prince."

"The king approaches!" cried the herald, stepping through the doors.

The soldiers snapped to rigid attention; a ripple of motion passed through the rest of the assembly. Some, like Broteas and Geranor, hurried to their places while others tugged at their tunics or adjusted their belts. Broteas was pleased to see that his handsome son, Young Tantalus, was impeccably garbed and held himself straight and tall. Surely King Tantalus would find no fault with his grandson.

There was a sound of cymbals, and then the king emerged from the palace. He paused at the top of the stairway while the herald announced: "Thrice-Blessed Tantalus: son of Zeus Thunderer, king of Lydia, and favorite of all the gods!"

Those assembled below cheered, and the cymbals crashed once more. Then

Tantalus began a stately descent of the stairs. His ivory-colored robes were bordered with golden spangles, sewn to form a shining swath more than a handspan wide; with the powdered gold dusted over the skin of his hands and face, he glittered in the sun.

When the king stepped down from the final stair-tread, Broteas approached and bowed. "My lord king and father," he said, following the words of the ritual: "May we join you in the ascent to the shrine?"

"Yes," said the king. He went over and took his seat; the bearers lifted the poles of the sedan-chair to their shoulders. "I want to speak with you, Broteas," he said in clipped tones. Then he signaled his bearers to start.

Broteas hurried to his father's side, but the procession continued without King Tantalus uttering a word. With each passing moment Broteas' unease grew. What was it that his father wanted to discuss – and why didn't he begin the conversation? They passed the edge of the city and started up the narrow path that led to Rhea's shrine on the slopes of Mount Sipylus, and still Broteas had no answer.

When Broteas made this pilgrimage on his own he preferred a more leisurely pace – especially at this time of year, when the wild tulips painted the rocky slopes with bright colors and birds twittered in the pines overhead. But this morning he had no choice other than to match the strides of the powerful men who carried the king's sedan chair, and wait for whatever it was his father wanted to say.

They had gone more than halfway to the shrine when the king told his bearers to lower the chair. "You and I will walk ahead," he said to Broteas.

The rest of the procession took this cue, pausing to let the king and his son move ahead. King Tantalus proceeded at quick pace; when they were out of earshot of the others, he turned to Broteas and said: "Your plan to retrieve the mastiff is insufficient."

"Insufficient, Father?" Broteas panted. He regretted that his voice betrayed the exertion of the climb, for his father would not respect this.

"Entirely." The king slapped a low pine branch out of his way. "You should go yourself."

Broteas ducked to avoid the branch's recoil. "I can't, Father. I'd be discovered."

"Pelops hasn't seen you in years," the king said with a dismissive wave of his shimmering hand. "How could he guess that you would grow so bald?"

Ignoring the insult, Broteas said: "Even if Pelops failed to recognize me, Amphion of Thebes would. Or one of the Athenians."

"A task this important should not be delegated."

Hurrying to follow his father around a bend where the path hugged the curving mountainside, Broteas failed to contain his frustration. "Then why don't *you* go, Father?"

They were at the narrowest part of the path; King Tantalus stopped and turned to face him, fury in his eyes. Seeing the king's cheeks redden beneath the dusting of gold, Broteas experienced a tremor of fear – it was most unwise to challenge the king as he had just done.

"You dare to question me?" Tantalus hissed. He took a step towards Broteas, his right fist lifted.

Acutely aware of the steep drop-off behind him, Broteas lifted his arms to ward off a possible blow and sought to brace his boots against the rocks – but if his father meant to push him off the cliff, Broteas would not be able to stop him.

"Of course not, Father," Broteas gasped. "If it's your will that I go to Pisa…"

Just then the escort came around the bend. Broteas heard their footsteps come to an abrupt halt, but he dared not take his eyes from his father.

"Is something wrong, Grandfather?" asked Young Tantalus.

The king glanced past Broteas' shoulder; then he dropped his hand and let out a short, derisive breath. "You should not stand so close to the edge, Broteas." With that comment he turned and continued upwards, towards the shrine.

Broteas lowered his arms and followed a few paces behind, his heart racing not from exertion but from the sense that his father had nearly sent him to his death. He recalled Niobe's concern from the summer before, asking if their father was threatening him. He told himself that his father had not in fact tried to push him over the precipice; the king had only been angry, and rightfully so, at a son who had given offense. Yet he could not shake off the conviction that something more lay beneath his father's fury.

He kept reviewing the incident even after they reached Rhea's shrine and the priestess began the ceremony. Now that Broteas' son was a man, the king had another heir – an heir who carried his name. He no longer needed Broteas.

As the king offered his sacrifice to the goddess, Broteas closed his eyes and sought her guidance. Mother Rhea knew well that fathers could be dangerous to their children: her own husband Cronus, warned that his offspring would overthrow him, had swallowed his children as soon as they were born – her efforts to protect them failed until finally she was able to smuggle the youngest, Zeus, away to safety. While Rhea's priestess sprinkled incense on the altar, Broteas decided to consult his own mother when he returned to the palace.

He found Queen Dione in her weaving room, in the company of her maids and Euryanassa, his wife. Though the afternoon light was good, the queen was not at her loom; she did not have the strength to stand for long periods of time. The colorful fabrics she had sent to Niobe were the last finished products of her loom – and though she claimed the work as her own, in reality it had been woven mostly by other hands. Now the queen sat before the window, and in her lap she held the tablet Broteas had brought back from Thebes. She often called a scribe to read it aloud to her – and she had developed a habit in idle moments of simply holding it, running her fingers over the wedge-shaped impressions in the hardened clay.

Would his mother ever cling to something of his in such a fashion? Standing in the doorway, Broteas doubted it. His parents seemed to value only the children who abandoned them.

He cleared his throat. "Mother," he said. "I trust the day finds you well."

Queen Dione looked up. "Broteas! How nice of you to visit me."

"Husband," Euryanassa acknowledged, turning from where she worked at one of the tall looms.

He went to her. "My dear," he said, "I must speak with my mother alone. Go to our chambers and wait for me – and tell the servants to pack my traveling-bag."

"As you wish," said Euryanassa, nodding. She hung the wool-wrapped shuttle on a peg projecting from one of the loom's support-posts, and then ushered the servants out.

"Did the ceremony go well?" asked the queen.

Broteas realized he had been too distracted to pay attention to the details. "The priestess seemed to think so," he said, seating himself on a stool beside his mother's chair.

"That's good." Dione sighed. "So, my son, what do you wish to discuss with me?"

"Father wants me to go to Pisa."

Dione tilted her head to one side. "I see."

"He's – he seems very troubled about Rhea's mastiff."

"Ah," said his mother, nodding.

"Why *now*, Mother? It's been gone from Lydia for twenty years! We've fared well in our clashes with the Trojans. The harvests are good; trade is flowing. I see no evidence that Rhea is angry with the kingdom. Why is *he* so concerned?" He leaned forward. "Or does he just want me to leave Lydia?"

The old woman's eyes narrowed. "Your father does not confide in me, Broteas."

Broteas smiled. "Perhaps not. But little in this palace escapes you, Mother." The queen's network of female informants – noblewomen, servants, slaves, even several of the king's concubines – reached nearly every corner of the palace.

"I don't know everything." She held up the tablet as if to remind him of how Niobe had defied her and run away.

"Even if Father has said nothing, you still know his mind. You've been married to him for more than forty years."

His mother leaned back in her chair. "You know that your father used to sleep in the Temple of Zeus every tenth night, to commune with his divine father and hear what the god would tell him."

"Used to?" Broteas frowned. "When did he stop?"

"After last year's summer solstice."

Broteas drummed his fingers on his knees, thinking. That was when his father had sent him west to Thebes. "What happened?"

"His dreams. Messages from Zeus. For years Tantalus had pleasing dreams, or none at all… but more and more, these last few years, the dreams that came troubled him. Last summer he was given a dream more terrible than any before – letting him know that Zeus and Rhea are angry with him."

"Because of the mastiff?"

She shrugged; Broteas noticed how the afternoon sun shone through her thinning white hair to the pink scalp below. "In part. When your father-in-law was high priest of Zeus, he told the king not to remove the mastiff from the Temple of Zeus. But that wasn't the only warning. When Tantalus drank the gods' holy nectar – and shared it with others – he offended the gods."

Broteas nodded, remembering.

Her voice lower than before, the queen continued: "And what he did to your brother Pelops – he said he was offering the boy as a sacrifice, giving them the best he had. But perhaps the gods believe he had other motives." She pressed her lips together for a moment, gripping the clay tablet in both hands; she looked to be fighting back tears. "At least Pelops survived, even if he is scarred forever."

"Do you know what Father saw in the dream last summer?" Broteas prompted.

She nodded. "I know the wife of the priest. But if I tell you this, Son, you must swear not to reveal it to anyone."

"I promise, Mother."

She whispered: "In your father's dream Zeus appeared wreathed in lightning, his angry voice loud as thunder. He told Tantalus what he must do to make amends for his crimes: he must bring the mastiff back to Lydia. Or else – or else he will suffer terribly in the Underworld, for eternity…"

The back of Broteas' neck prickled: this explained the situation perfectly. His father feared no mortal man – but he would certainly fear a threat from Zeus himself. And to be tormented in the Underworld, for all time – there could be no worse fate.

Queen Dione leaned forward and set a hand on Broteas' arm. "And Zeus told him that the ugly son – forgive me, Broteas – the ugly son would be the one to make amends."

Broteas sat up straight. He was not offended by the word; he *was* ugly, and besides, the message was a favorable one. "*I* will be the one to make amends?"

"So it seems."

Broteas squeezed his mother's plump hand. If her report was right, his father had reason to want him alive. That incident on the mountain path – his father *had* simply been angry with him. If he could help his father now – and save him from eternal agony – then, *then* surely King Tantalus would value him at last.

He leaned over to kiss her cheek. "Thank you, Mother. May the gods watch over you. I'm leaving tonight."

Her snowy eyebrows drew together. "Where are you going?"

"To visit your *handsome* son – and see the Games in Olympia."

§ 4.04

Pelops walked around the statue of Hera. It was well made, and dressed in Hippodamia's best skirts, jacket, and cloak; it even wore the jewels and crown that had been hers for so many years.

It looked entirely too much like her.

"Does the statue please my lord king?" asked the sculptor, his voice tremulous. He had returned from Corinth to supervise its installation into Hera's temple before the Games – and to claim the work as his when the crowds came. With Hippodamia's newfound infamy, everyone would want to see her likeness; the Temple of Hera would be a prime attraction. But looking at the statue made Pelops' stomach churn.

The ghost of Myrtilus caressed the statue's face. "You could have it destroyed," he said. "But that might offend the Goddess Hera."

"Your work is adequate," Pelops said to the sculptor, then walked away. He had no patience for the man's effusive gratitude.

As Pelops left the temple, Laius, Atreus and Thyestes fell in step just behind him; as always, the absence of Chrysippus was a wrenching agony. He tried not to think of it – but that was as hopeless as trying not to breathe.

The three young men seemed relieved that Pelops had approved the statue, but none of them mentioned it. Instead they spoke of preparations at the other temples: the Temple of Zeus had been adorned with a gleaming lightning bolt of polished bronze; the golden mastiff had been put on display at the Temple of Rhea; and at Hermes' temple, the first one to be seen by most visitors, the tall herm pillar with the face and phallus of the god had been freshly painted. Pelops barely listened, watching instead as Myrtilus' ghost went on ahead, his form faint in the afternoon's harsh sunlight.

Would it give him comfort, Pelops wondered, to glimpse the shade of Chrysippus? Of course he had given the boy a proper burial, and made lavish sacrifices at the funeral – so there was no reason for his ghost to wander the earth. But he longed to see the boy's face, hear his voice.

Beside him, Thyestes tripped over a loose stone; he did not fall, but the jerky movement recalled Pelops to his surroundings. He forced himself to talk to his companions.

"How are the preparations going for the games?" he asked, the only question that came to mind.

Laius glanced at the younger princes. "All in order, my lord king," he said.

"Good," Pelops said, meeting Laius' brown eyes and seeing the sadness there. It was Laius who best understood Pelops' grief, Laius who – like him – had placed Chrysippus above all others in his heart. Sometimes Laius was the only person that Pelops could bear to have near him. Thyestes was his son, but he reminded Pelops too much of Hippodamia. And Atreus… Pelops still did not know if he was Atreus' father.

"I've ordered more sand for the race course," Laius was saying. "And the wooden viewing stand is almost complete. We'll have games worthy of the Olympians, my lord king. They're sure to be pleased."

Myrtilus' ghost stopped his forward movement and turned to face Pelops. "Even Hera? You just banished her chief priestess…"

Myrtilus was irksome, but sometimes he made good points. Pelops interrupted Laius' report about the readiness of the archery targets with a single word: "Hera."

Laius fell silent; all three young men stared at him. Finally Atreus asked, "What about her, Father?"

"The goddess may be upset by recent events. If she disapproves of what the queen did, she may be angry about the statue being made in her likeness. If not, she may be angry about the queen's banishment."

The three young men looked confused. Thyestes asked: "You mean, we don't know whether or not what we're doing is pleasing the goddess?"

"That's exactly what I mean." That was always the challenge, to please the gods. They could be as capricious as his father Tantalus.

"The statue has a lot of gold," said Atreus. "Surely that will please her."

"We need to honor her in some other way," Pelops said. "But how?"

But the faces of the three young men stayed blank. If only Chrysippus were here! *He* would think of something.

"We'll work on it, my lord king," Laius finally offered.

"See that you do." Pelops strode away, unable to bear even Laius' company any longer.

"Hera's punishing you already," whispered Myrtilus. "How much have you slept lately? If you don't find some way to appease her things will be worse."

How could they be worse? Chrysippus was dead.

"You don't know yet," Myrtilus said. "Even I don't know yet."

"I thought you wanted to curse me," Pelops muttered. "So why are you warning me?"

That baffled Myrtilus enough to silence him – which was no comfort, because without the ghostly voice Pelops was left with his own terrible emptiness. He felt as if he were groping in the void of chaos: more oppressive, more stifling than darkness. Darkness only made men blind; but Pelops felt choked off from all his senses. He scarcely heard the voices of those around him, and took no pleasure in food or wine. The perfume of budding flowers did not reach him; the warmth of his bath did not ease the cold of his bones. He felt less and less substantial each day – as though he were becoming a ghost without dying first.

And yet the meaningless days continued to lengthen; the sun grew warmer without warming him, and visitors began to fill his palace with conversations he could not bring himself to hear. The guests brought rich gifts that Pelops barely looked at, and pledges of friendship that brought him no joy. Instead his losses increased: a few days before the solstice, Wave stumbled and broke a leg. Pelops slit the stallion's throat himself, the last favor he could give his old friend, and marveled that he did not weep as the horse's blood covered his hands and sank into the earth. The following morning, Wind was found dead in his stall; the grooms could give no reason, saying he must have died of grief.

Pelops did not know how he could survive his own sorrow – and yet every morning he woke to face another bleak day. Whenever he entered the megaron, where a dark cloth shrouded Hippodamia's throne, he was reminded of his wife's crime and how she had silenced Chrysippus' bright laughter. While Hippodamia lived, Pelops could not remarry; but Pelops gave little thought to the matter. He had no interest in women. Strangely, Myrtilus did not mock him for this lack of virility – but Myrtilus said less these days.

Fortunately the routine of the festival was well-established enough that Pelops was not needed to supervise details. Laius, assisted by Atreus and

Thyestes, took care of registering the athletes and organizing the competitions; the steward Exarchos managed everything else. Seeking to avoid the feigned sympathy of people who had neither known nor cared about Chrysippus, Pelops spent more and more of his time in the shadows of the armory, throwing knives at Hippodamia's image.

His last blade buried itself in the wooden panel; Pelops trudged over to the wall and wrenched free the knives he had cast, one after another. Gripping them tightly, he walked back to throw again.

Myrtilus, perched on a heap of old chariot wheels awaiting salvage, let out a sigh.

Alone with the ghost, Pelops spoke aloud. "You're quiet lately."

The ghost shrugged. "You're unworthy of my insults. Do you plan to hide in here the rest of your life? You might as well just descend to the Underworld."

"Perhaps I should," Pelops retorted, letting a knife fly. It struck the target just where Hippodamia's mouth was painted. "All those I've loved best are gone." Chrysippus. Danais. Wind, and Wave. The sea captain Aeolius.

"I'm bored with your target practice," said the ghostly charioteer. "You're as useless as these old wheels."

Ignoring this comment, Pelops hurled a second knife; the blade embedded itself, quivering, in the throat of Hippodamia's likeness.

"The Tiresias should arrive soon," Myrtilus offered. "She may even reach Pisa today."

But that prospect only reminded Pelops how far his fortunes had fallen. Once he had believed himself a man favored by the gods: he served them well, and they blessed him in return. That was the bargain he had made with the deathless ones, the bargain the Tiresias had witnessed so many years ago. But the gods must have found his offerings lacking. That was the only explanation for why they had turned on him. He had done everything he could, and yet it was not enough.

"It doesn't matter. She'll tell me nothing I don't already know: I've failed in the eyes of the gods." Pelops shook his head. "I might as well die tomorrow."

The door swung open; he turned to look, but against the light streaming in from outside he was not entirely sure who had come. One portly silhouette certainly belonged to Exarchos, but beside him was another plump figure, even shorter than the steward.

"I told you to leave me alone," Pelops said, squinting. He turned away from the dazzling light.

"My lord king, the party from Thebes has arrived," the steward said.

"So?" Chrysippus was no longer alive to marry Chloris, and Pelops could not bear to be around Amphion and his brood of handsome, healthy sons. "I'll see them later." He threw the third knife; his aim was wide, and the blade caught just the edge of the target before clattering to the stone floor.

"How about seeing me now, Brother?" asked the woman standing at the door.

The familiar voice caught Pelops wholly off guard; he twisted back towards the light.

"Niobe?" he asked.

§ 4.05

"Yes, Pelops," Niobe said, trying to sound reassuring. "It's me."

Wonder spread across her brother's features, softening the deep furrows in his brow. Niobe walked across the shadowed room, pained to see that Pelops looked as worn and haggard as everyone said. Exarchos told her some feared that Chrysippus' death had driven him mad: but there was recognition in her brother's dark eyes.

"Niobe," he repeated. "I never thought you'd come…"

She gripped his calloused hands. "When I heard what happened—" she hesitated, swallowing back a sudden tightness in her throat, "—when I heard, I had to come."

Though she had not uttered Chrysippus' name, grief welled up in Pelops' eyes. Niobe waved Exarchos away; the steward left, closing the door behind him, and Niobe led her brother to a bench. She pulled him down to sit beside her, cradled his head against her shoulder as if he were one of her sons; he broke down and wept. As she smoothed his hair and patted his back, she noticed how thin he had become since his visit to Thebes the previous summer.

After a time his sobs stopped, his breathing grew more even. "I thought I'd lost everything," he managed to say. "Everything…"

Not since their father's blade brought Pelops near to death had she seen him so vulnerable. "No," she said, squeezing his hand. "Not everything."

"I should have known you'd come to help me. You've always been there for me, Niobe."

She wiped the tears from his face. "Come with me, now, Pelops. The sun is shining. We don't need to stay in the dark."

Pelops rubbed at his beard, unkempt and in need of cutting. "No room was dark when Chrysippus was in it," he said. "But he hated to stay indoors on a sunny day."

"Then let's go out and enjoy the sunshine for him." She stood and tugged him up from the bench; holding her hand, he followed as readily as one of her children. The steward, who had been waiting outside, opened his mouth as if to ask a question, but Niobe shook her head. In a low voice, she said: "I'm taking the king to his rooms."

Exarchos nodded and rushed on ahead. Niobe nodded to the guards they passed – some, she noticed, recognized her, while others would have been toddlers when she was last in Pisa. When they reached Pelops' rooms she told the servants to bring food and drink, then told Exarchos to fetch the king's bath-attendants and his barber. She got a cup of well-watered wine and a bit of bread into her brother before the bath was drawn; then she left Pelops to his servants and retreated to the antechamber, where Exarchos supervised lesser servants in setting out a proper midday meal.

"Ah, my lady princess, it's good to have you here again!" he exclaimed. "Excuse me, I mean, my lady queen…"

Niobe smiled. "That's all right." His use of the title that had been hers when she lived in Pisa was a natural slip.

"I've brought you minted barley water and olives stuffed with goat cheese. And you must try the cherries – they're excellent this year."

"That's kind of you, Exarchos." Niobe seated herself and accepted a goblet from a serving-woman.

"It's the least I could do, my lady queen." He lowered his voice. "If you can dispel the king's dark mood, all of Pisa will be grateful."

Niobe turned the goblet in her hands, studying its red-and-white glazed surface. "It's a terrible thing, to lose a child." She took a long sip, then set the cup down. "But he can't keep on grieving. His kingdom needs him."

"He'll listen to you, my lady queen," said the steward. "I'm sure of it." With a respectful bow, he left to attend to other duties; Niobe remained seated, pondering the best course of action. Finally she decided that dwelling on Pelops' loss just now would only drag him back towards the abyss: instead she should remind him of his duties as king, and help him focus on the present.

So when the muffled sounds from the inner room indicated that Pelops had left the bath chamber, she called out cheerfully: "You have so many guests this year, Pelops! I heard the choice camping spots have been occupied for days, and we saw tents pitched all along the roadside as we came up from the harbor. They start long before the Temple of Hermes!"

"They multiply like maggots," he called back, but there was good humor in his remark.

"Amphion told me how the festival had grown, but I had to see it with my own eyes to understand how much. Everyone is so excited to be here!"

The door swung open and Pelops entered the antechamber, looking like a different man. His hair and beard had been trimmed; he was dressed in a fresh linen kilt and his jeweled ivory shoulder-piece.

As he took a seat, Niobe gestured to the armor that covered her brother's bad shoulder – she had helped to design it before they left Lydia. "The ivory's yellowed a bit, but it seems to be holding up."

"I have to replace the leather laces, of course. And I broke one of the tiles in the battle with Zakynthos." He pointed to a replacement that was lighter in hue. "But it serves me well. The Pisatans call it my gift from Demeter."

Niobe reached for a handful of cherries. "Demeter has given you other gifts as well."

"The harvests have been good lately," he agreed, taking a seat across from her. "Thank the gods, with all the mouths to feed at festival time!" A servant poured him a cup of barley water; he took a swallow and then popped a stuffed olive into his mouth.

Pleased to see her brother eating, Niobe drew him out on the subject of agriculture: Pisa's domain had enlarged over the years, as Pelops' influence grew. New lands had come under cultivation, and old fields were better managed. The flocks and herds prospered – "though now and then we do lose a few to lions and wolves."

"You've handled far worse than a wolf or two," Niobe said drily.

A grin spread across Pelops' face. "I suppose you're right." He set his cup aside and stood; reaching for her hand, he pulled her to her feet. "Ah, Sister, you make me feel young again. What adventures we've had!"

"And still have – I'm looking forward to these magnificent games! Shall we go to the megaron and greet your guests?"

"Yes, why not," he said, crooking his arm for her to hold. She let him lead her down the hall; as they walked, she encouraged him to talk of the various guests who were likely to be in attendance, hoping that the focus on relations with other kingdoms would help bring him more fully to himself, help him forget his grief. And it seemed to her that his manner grew easier, his posture straighter, with each step.

The megaron was jammed with people – and all fell silent when Niobe and Pelops entered, staring as the two of them crossed the painted stucco floor. Niobe knew that, although some might be curious about the unfamiliar woman, this rapt attention was not for her: according to Exarchos, Pelops had not yet made an appearance during the festival.

Her brother maintained an aura of confidence, nodding to each guest they walked by and offering a brief word of greeting to one and another of them. Only when they reached the front of the room did he hesitate, stiffening as they neared Hippodamia's shrouded throne. Then the moment passed and he released Niobe's arm to take a seat on the king's throne.

The room remained silent. "People of Pisa and honored guests," Pelops said, "I present my sister, Queen Niobe of Thebes!" There was a soft murmur of appreciation; Niobe smiled, while wishing ruefully that she had changed out of her traveling dress. Then Pelops clapped his hands and ordered a chair for her; two servants hurried to comply.

It was strange and yet familiar to be once more seated in her old place, near her brother's throne. She scanned the crowded megaron for her husband and children, but could not locate them. Perhaps they were out exploring the festival grounds.

Pelops presented his own children to Niobe; though she knew how many years had passed since she left Pisa, it was startling to see how much they had grown. Atreus' face and physique reminded Niobe of his maternal grandfather – she only hoped that he had not inherited his grandfather's vicious temper. Thyestes was now a slender and handsome youth rather than the chubby toddler Niobe remembered; he had Pelops' square jaw, but she saw Hippodamia in the curve of his lower lip and his dark, almond-shaped eyes. Next Pelops introduced two daughters: Astydamia had the bad luck to share the large-boned frame of her brother Atreus, while Nikippe showed more promise of beauty. Then there were several young boys, whose names Niobe had trouble keeping straight.

"You must all be gracious to your Aunt Niobe," Pelops said. "She saved my life, you know."

Her nephews and her nieces gaped at her. "Really?" gasped the stocky girl. "How, Father?"

"That's a story for another time, Astydamia."

"But, Father—"

"I *said* that's a story for another time." A harsh edge entered Pelops' voice, and his brows drew together.

Astydamia faltered backwards; Thyestes and Atreus exchanged nervous glances. What a terrible time these children had been through! Their half-brother murdered, their mother banished for the crime, their father consumed with rage and despair. They must be desperate for words of kindness. And she was only here for a few days; it was not enough.

"Why don't they come stand by my chair?" Niobe suggested. "The servants could bring cushions for the little ones to sit at my feet."

Pelops grunted. "As long as they don't fidget."

"We won't, Father," promised Nikippe, pulling her sister over to stand by Niobe.

"You'd better not," Pelops said in a low voice, his look thunderously dark. Their elder brothers edged towards Niobe cautiously; only once Pelops looked away did the servants come forward with floor cushions for the smaller boys. Concerned, Niobe watched her brother: could he handle this occasion in the megaron, or had she encouraged him to appear before he was ready? She seemed to have a calming influence on him, but she was not sure how long would it last.

The Pisatan herald cleared his throat; after Pelops motioned permission to speak, the man asked: "May I present your guests, my lord king?"

Pelops sighed and looked at Niobe; she gave him what she hoped was an encouraging smile. "Very well," Pelops agreed.

Niobe observed her brother carefully as the herald began with King Electryon of Mycenae, who had recently married Pelops' daughter Eurydike; the young queen herself was not in attendance because – as Electryon related proudly – she was with child. The kings of Argos, Sparta and Corinth were presented next; all were carefully polite, and Niobe remembered that Pelops' banished wife had relatives in each of these cities as well as in Mycenae. The youthful king of Sicyon – one of Hippodamia's younger brothers – was a little friendlier: Pelops had done much for him. King Neleus of Pylos was next to offer his greetings; Niobe was pleased to renew the acquaintance with her former student, and noted that the awkward boy had grown into a thoughtful, confident man. She shared another moment of recognition with Aeacus, the nephew of her sister-in-law Thebe; he had become king of Aegina upon his father's death a few years ago. Soon the parade of visiting rulers and dignitaries began to blur – and though the megaron already seemed filled to capacity, more people kept arriving.

Then Niobe's breath caught in her throat. A woman with graying hair, her eyes covered by a black blindfold, was making her way to the front of the room on the arm of her servant.

"The Tiresias," Niobe muttered in dismay – and quickly regretted it. The prophetess' hearing was as keen as Amphion's.

"Of course," said Pelops. "She attends all my festivals."

Could she never escape this woman? But Niobe fixed a polite smile on her face for her brother's sake.

The blind woman moved closer to Pelops' throne than any of the previous guests had done – near enough, in fact, that if she stretched out her hand she would have touched him. "King Pelops," she said, and her voice was gentler than Niobe had ever heard it. "I offer my condolences on the loss of your son."

The megaron turned silent as a tomb. Through the dozens of formal greetings that had been exchanged, not one person risked alluding to Chrysippus. But the Tiresias was said to speak with the voice of the gods. She had the authority – even, the divine duty – to say that which no one else dared to utter.

Pelops' visage froze into a mask of tight control; his knuckles whitened as he gripped the arms of his throne. Finally he spoke, his voice a hoarse whisper. "Why did the gods take him from me?"

Hippodamia killed him, Niobe thought with a flash of anger. *Don't blame it on the gods!*

The Tiresias pursed her pale lips. "The gods – the gods are not always in agreement. The preference of one cannot always protect a mortal from the vengeance of another."

Niobe struggled to contain her temper. Why was the Tiresias bringing up this painful subject now – in front of all the distinguished guests! – when she had just coaxed Pelops into behaving normally? Pelops was so fragile; it would be disastrous for him to lose control now.

Niobe leaned forward. "Perhaps this conversation could be continued later," she said softly. "In private."

Pelops blinked, and met her eyes; then he nodded. He turned back to the seer. "Yes, prophetess, perhaps later…"

The blind woman shrugged. "Perhaps." Her head inclined towards Niobe. "Or perhaps another will reveal the will of the gods." Her acid tone made clear what she thought of Niobe's interruption.

Niobe disliked drawing the Tiresias' attention – but at least the prophetess had not cursed her! She returned to scanning those crowding the megaron, and saw that Amphion and the four children who had accompanied them to the games had squeezed into the room. "Brother," she said, relieved to change the subject, "My husband and children are here. May they come forward?"

"Of course!" Pelops said. His cheerful tone was forced – but at least he was making an effort. "My children should meet their cousins."

Bestowing a mark of honor, Pelops descended from his throne and kissed his brother-in-law on both cheeks. The two men were the same height, a head taller than most men present, and it was hard to say which of them was handsomer.

I am the sister of one great man, and the wife of another, Niobe thought with pride – exulting, too, in the beauty of her children. The Tiresias might be a powerful seer, but she was also a barren and aging woman.

"Chloris, my dear," Pelops was saying, "let me introduce you to your cousins Atreus and Thyestes."

Pelops still wanted a marriage match, Niobe realized, even though

Chrysippus was dead. Of course, Niobe had promised Chloris that she could join the Maidens of Artemis. But that was a promise made by Niobe to her daughter, not by Chloris to the goddess. If Chloris preferred to wed one of her cousins, she did not need to join the cult – but such a marriage would take Chloris away from Thebes permanently!

I've turned into my mother, Niobe thought sourly, realizing she had lost the thread of the conversation. Amphion was speaking to Pelops: "My daughter would make a request of you."

"Is that so?" asked Pelops. He leaned forward. "Tell me, my lovely niece, what can we do to make your visit more enjoyable?"

Chloris clasped her hands behind her back. "Uncle," she said, "why are there no games for women?"

Pelops gaped, then guffawed. "Games for *women*?"

Many in the room laughed too, but Chloris held her ground. "Why not, Uncle?" she said. "Artemis is a huntress; Athena is a warrior. Iris is a messenger goddess, and Nike herself is the goddess of victory." Her clear, melodic voice filled Niobe with pride. As Chloris spoke, the ripple of laughter ceased, and Niobe heard murmurs of agreement.

Pelops tilted his head. "Of course, but—"

"Father," said Atreus, "you were looking for another way to honor Hera."

"That's right!" agreed Thyestes. He flashed a grin at Chloris.

Niobe decided to add her own voice in support of her daughter's cause. "Why *shouldn't* there be contests for girls?" she asked. She remembered how, when only a little older than Chloris, she herself had adored swimming.

Scratching his beard, Pelops turned to the side of the room where the blind prophetess stood with her servant. "Tiresias," he asked, "would games for women please the queen of the gods?"

The Tiresias inclined her blindfolded head. "I believe they would."

Niobe was surprised that she and the seer should be in agreement. At any rate, this matter was diverting her brother from his depression.

Then a broad-shouldered young man pushed forward through the crowd. "My lord king," he said, sounding doubtful, "there's no time to arrange anything. And the women have not come prepared for competition."

"That's true, Laius," said Pelops. "But still…"

Laius? thought Niobe, peering closely. Could this handsome fellow be the forlorn little boy she had once coaxed from his hiding place in a grain-storage jar?

"What about a footrace?" asked Chloris. "No one needs special equipment to run a footrace."

Pelops nodded. "A footrace – yes, why not? If we can find young women to participate—"

"I'll run, Father!" exclaimed Astydamia.

"So will I," called Nikippe.

"Lady Hera is the patron goddess of my city," said the king of Argos. "I will be honored to contribute a prize for the winner."

"Very well," said Pelops. "Laius, organize it."

Niobe thought that Laius looked as if he still found the idea of young women racing absurd, but he bowed. "As you wish, my lord king."

§ 4.06

Broteas woke before daylight, opening his eyes to darkness within the tent. Patience, Hephaestus had counseled. On the other hand, Zeus Thunderer had sent a dream to Broteas' father that the ugly son would restore Rhea's glory to Lydia. And Zeus was the greatest god of them all.

He sat up and scratched his chest, wishing he had been able to accompany Geranor into the Pisatan palace yesterday – but it would have been too risky. Geranor reported that Niobe, of all people, had appeared in Pelops' megaron; Geranor quickly took his leave before she could recognize him as one of Broteas' men. But if Niobe was in Pisa, so was her husband, Amphion – and either would recognize Broteas immediately.

Yawning, he rubbed his eyes and then glanced at the man snoring softly on the other side of the tent. Geranor had not seen the mastiff in any of the public areas of the palace, which he had toured with other visitors, so the question remained: where was it? Geranor was competent, but to succeed in their mission they needed good luck.

Broteas retrieved his kilt from the foot of his pallet. Crouching in the low space of the tent, he belted it around his waist, then shook Geranor's shoulder. "Wake up."

"Wha – yes, my lord prince?"

"We need the gods' help; that means we should make an offering. And *that* means we're going hunting." Grabbing a skin of watered wine and the loaf of bread he had purchased in the market the day before – he was careful not to touch any of the festival food offered by Pelops – Broteas pushed aside the tent-flap and moved out into the morning air. The sky was growing light in the east, but the sickle moon was still visible overhead. Broteas poured out a libation for Artemis. "Be with me, Lady Huntress," he murmured, then took a swig of the tepid wine.

In the tents near their campsite, few others stirred; perhaps Broteas had a chance to find game if they moved quickly. He downed a few mouthfuls of dry bread as his companion moved around in the tent, gathering what they needed for the hunt. Geranor emerged, holding Broteas' sandals in one hand and their bows in the other. Two quivers were slung over his shoulder. "Here you are, my lord prince," he said, holding out the bronze-studded sandals.

To buckle them on, Broteas sat on the stump of a tree; then he stood and shouldered his quiver and bow. In order to discourage thieves while they were gone, he pulled an amulet from around his neck and tied it to the thongs that closed the tent-flaps: anyone thinking of robbing them would see the eye made of agate, and realize that if they stole anything the all-seeing gods would curse them.

Not, Broteas reflected as they made their way through the patchwork of campsites, that his tent looked particularly wealthy – but the wealthiest encampments had teams of servants, with people to guard them at all times. Nor was his tent the shabbiest; that would not suit, not when he was posing as a Trojan prince, even a disgraced one. He and Geranor had taken pains to ensure that their clothing and equipment were consistent with their adopted identities: a minor son of the Trojan house who had offended his father, and the loyal retainer who had accompanied him into exile.

Gradually, as they neared the edge of the woods, the space between the tents grew wider. Broteas led his companion in a northeasterly direction, away from settled areas. As the sun crept higher in the sky, he began to fear that the woods had been hunted out already – the only deer droppings they saw were old and dried, and there were no fresh tracks. Then they came to the edge of a grassy clearing at the base of a hill; Geranor touched his elbow and pointed. A hare was bounding down the slope.

Quickly Broteas drew an arrow, pulled back and let fly; Geranor's own arrow was only a breath behind, but Broteas' missile found the mark. It struck hard enough to propel the animal backward through the air; when the hare fell, it lay still.

"What a shot, my lord prince!" exclaimed Geranor. "Only you could hit a moving hare so cleanly!"

Broteas grinned, pleased with himself, and moved toward the downed animal. "It's not much," he said, "but it will let us offer something to the gods this morning."

"And give us fresh meat for breakfast!" Geranor agreed.

But before they could reach it, a gray-and-black dog wearing a red collar streaked down the slope. It went straight for the hare.

"Hey!" shouted Geranor – but the dog had already run off with the limp hare in its jaws.

Annoyed, Broteas started up the hill after the hound; fleet-footed Geranor ran ahead. Naturally, the dog reached the top of the hill before either of them – and at the top of the hill stood two strangers. The dog dropped its prize at the foot of one of the men, who bent to scratch the hound's ears.

"That's *our* quarry!" Geranor cried, pointing. "That's the arrow of my lord prince!"

The man nearest the dog knelt down by the hare and wrenched free the fatal arrow. No doubt of it, thought Broteas: that was his own arrow, fletched with feathers of white and black. But the man cast it aside without acknowledgement. "It's my dog that fetched it," he said, staring at Geranor. "So it's mine now."

The second man, dark but freckled, took a step nearer. "You'd best listen to my lord king," he said. His right hand gripped the hilt of the dagger belted at his waist.

"Hear, now—" Geranor began, but Broteas grasped his arm to silence him.

Broteas studied the man who had claimed his kill. He appeared to be in his mid-twenties, with a thick beard and black eyebrows that met above the bridge of his nose. His kilt and sandals did not proclaim any particular wealth, but the ribbon binding his hair had gold in the weave, and he wore a gold signet-ring on his right hand. The only other jewelry Broteas noticed was a necklace of wolf's teeth strung on a leather cord.

"King of what land?" Broteas asked.

The man folded his arms across his chest. "Arcadia. I am Stymphalus of Arcadia."

Arcadia was an inland kingdom bordering on Pisa: not a wealthy place, from what Broteas had heard. But the king of Arcadia might be a useful source of information, perhaps even an ally. After all, Broteas had made a libation to Artemis at dawn, and asked for her help – and this was where the hunt had led him.

Broteas inclined his head. "That's some dog you have there, King Stymphalus. Quick and clever."

Stymphalus seemed to relax. "Stormcloud's the best. She flushed that hare to begin with."

Squeezing Geranor's arm, Broteas said: "So the hare is clearly yours, my lord king." He would make some other offering to the gods. He had a bag of incense in his pack, back at the tent.

Stymphalus grunted assent, and knelt to gut the hare; his companion remained watchful. "And who would you be, stranger?" asked the Arcadian king. "Some relative of Pelops? You've got his eastern accent."

Broteas laughed, hoping his heartiness did not sound forced. "Oh no, not I. My name's Alexandros; my man Geranor and I hail from the great city of Troy. It's well north of Lydia – but the accent's similar."

"Well, you don't look much like Pelops," observed the Arcadian king, tossing the hare's heart and liver to his dog; the animal snapped up its reward, tail wagging. "Did I hear your man call you 'prince'?"

"I'm of the royal family," Broteas said with a shrug. "But I've many brothers – and every one of them my father prefers to me. So I'm not needed in Troy."

"You're here for the games, Prince Alexandros?" asked the other Arcadian.

"Yes, of course! Even Trojans have heard of the Olympic Games."

Stymphalus wiped his bloody hands on the grass, which was moist with dew. "It's a great spectacle," he said, straightening. "The best in all Hellas."

"I'm looking forward to it," Broteas said amiably. He gestured to the bow slung over the fellow's shoulder. "Are you entering the archery competition, my lord king?"

The younger man nodded. "Yes."

Broteas wanted to prolong their conversation. "I have a little skill in the sport myself," he said. "Care to take a few practice shots? The glade below would offer us a good space, and I'm always eager to learn from other archers."

King Stymphalus frowned a little – Broteas had already proven his ability – but he nevertheless agreed. Geranor retrieved the arrow cast aside by the Arcadian king; then the four men and the dog made their way down the slope. Stymphalus chose a gnarled tree on the clearing's northern edge as his target, and walked to the other end of the glade; Broteas and the other men positioned themselves behind him.

"See that knot, there?" Stymphalus asked. "The one that looks like a face?"

Shading his eyes against the sun, Broteas nodded.

The Arcadian took an arrow from his quiver, pulled taut the bowstring, sighted and let fly; his red-fletched arrow struck the tree just above the knot and embedded itself, quivering. Broteas offered a word of praise, but Stymphalus ignored him and instead fired off a second arrow that landed scarcely a hand's-breadth from the first. His third arrow landed just below the twisted lump of bark, forming a neat, tight triangle.

"Can you beat that, now, Trojan?" he asked Broteas, pride in his voice. His dog barked as if joining in the challenge.

Broteas lifted an eyebrow. "A difficult task, my lord king." He selected an arrow of his own and drew back the string, feeling the tension in his bow as he closed first one eye, then the other, sighting carefully. He released the string – and his arrow landed in the center of the triangle defined by Stymphalus' missiles.

"Oh ho!" cried the second Arcadian. "Here's an archer near as good as you, King Stymphalus!"

The shabbily dressed king frowned at his retainer, then turned to Broteas. "So, Alexandros of Troy, you plan to enter the archers' competition?"

Broteas realized that rising to Stymphalus' challenge had been a mistake; the young king was touchy in his pride. And of course he dared not risk recognition by entering any of the contests.

"Ah, my lord king," Broteas said, shaking his head, "years ago I would have. But my aim's not reliable these days. A back injury. I've had good luck this morning, though."

"Your back injury – is it from Troy's war with Lydia?" asked the freckled Arcadian.

Broteas was inventing his story on the spot; he glanced at Geranor, who had been mostly silent, letting Broteas guide the interaction. Geranor nodded slightly.

"Yes, it is," Broteas admitted. "And, well, King Pelops is a son of King Tantalus of Lydia, and Troy and Lydia – we don't get along."

"You can see why Prince Alexandros would not wish to call attention to himself," offered Geranor.

"Just here to see the sights," Broteas agreed. "What should we expect?"

"The games are magnificent," Stymphalus said, seeming relieved that Broteas would not enter the contest. "Come with me, Prince Alexandros, and we'll roast up the hare."

Broteas and Geranor accompanied King Stymphalus and his retainer to his camp. Geranor skinned the hare while the darkly freckled retainer stoked the fire. Another Arcadian brought out other food: some hard cheese made from sheep's milk, bread, onions and raisins, and a wine that was still bitter despite being mixed with a generous quantity of water. The hare, when shared among them, only gave them each a few bites, but Stymphalus said that it was all right – Pelops would provide plenty of roast meat later. The dog made sounds of pleasure as it gnawed on the hare's bones.

Since Broteas could not partake of Pelops' feasts, he might have wished for a larger portion – but with a little flattery and earnest interest, he sated his curiosity about many subjects. Pelops, he learned, was suffering from terrible depression since the murder of one of his sons a few months ago. Broteas also learned how the games had steadily increased every four years: Pelops added new temples and festivities each time, and pressed the neighboring kingdoms for contributions and support.

"Does King Pelops demand a lot?" he asked, curious about his brother's relationship with his neighbors.

Stymphalus' expression was enigmatic. "He demands what he can – as any other king would."

"Could you tell us about King Pelops' temples, my lord king?" interjected Geranor. "Which ones are most worth visiting?"

While Stymphalus detailed Pelops' many construction projects, Broteas listened carefully for any clue to the whereabouts of Rhea's mastiff. The two most likely candidates were the Temple of Zeus and the Temple of Rhea. But King Stymphalus was most interested in the Temple of Hera and its chryselephantine statue, made in the likeness of the banished queen.

"We'll have to take a look at that," said Broteas, a little curious about his bloodthirsty sister-in-law; Geranor nodded agreement.

"My lord king, we'd better get moving if we want to get good spots," said an Arcadian.

"You're right," said King Stymphalus, brushing his hands on his kilt and standing up. "I wonder if they'll hold the girls' footrace today?"

"A footrace for *girls*?" asked Broteas, surprised. He had never heard of such a thing. "That was Pelops' idea?"

"Actually," Stymphalus said, "a niece of his suggested it."

"Really?" Broteas asked, struggling to keep his voice even. "Which niece?"

Her name was Chloris, the Arcadians told him. Princess Chloris of Thebes.

§ 4.07

All her life, Chloris had heard people talk about the fabulous Olympic Games – and now she was here, in the middle of it all, and it was more marvelous than even her father's songs had conveyed.

Even now, when no competition was underway, the festival bubbled over with exciting new things: jugglers at one corner of the agora tossed large knives into the air and caught them to the gasps of the crowd; in the center of the square a team of acrobats in spangled loincloths tumbled and spun like dry leaves in the wind. Musicians rattled sistra and played rustic Pan-pipes; poets sang of love and war, monsters and gods. Crowded into another section of the agora were merchants offering wares she had never before seen: rings carved from a single piece of rock crystal, lamps and figurines of blue Egyptian faience, and linen sheer as a wisp of cloud.

"Here, now, Princess, you need a hat!" called one old woman as Chloris walked by her stall. "Don't let your pretty skin get brown and freckled!"

Glancing at the woman's wares, Chloris fingered the pouch of beads her father had given her to trade with, should she want something from the market;

but she already had a hat – she had just forgotten it in the guest-room she shared with her mother's maids. Chloris smiled at the woman, but shook her head and walked on; her chaperone trailed after her.

The ceremonies had begun with the contest of heralds. Each man shouted out his name and city; the fellow from Mycenae was judged by the blind prophet Tiresias to have the loudest and most resonant voice. He was assigned the honor of announcing the most important competitions. The first day's athletic events were the javelin, the discus, the axe-throw, and wrestling; from late morning until mid-afternoon Chloris watched the young men of Hellas demonstrate their skill. She cheered loudest of all when her brother Damasichthon won the discus competition for boys and was crowned with an olive wreath.

Once the contests were done, Chloris' parents gave her leave to explore under the supervision of one of her mother's serving-women. She kept her eyes open for any sign of the Maidens of Artemis – but upon inquiring, she learned that they never attended the games. That was disappointing, but it made her even more determined to enjoy this occasion fully. As daylight faded, the merriment moved to the palace and the encampments along the riverbank, where there were feasts and drinking contests. Chloris rejoined her family in the megaron for the evening meal: platters of delicious-smelling food covered the long tables, and servants bustled around between the benches.

Her mother explained that Chloris was to be seated between her cousins, Atreus and Thyestes – young men she should consider as potential husbands. Dismayed, Chloris hissed, "But I don't want to marry *anyone*."

"I know," said her mother. "But you will still be polite and talk to them. You can't turn them down without even speaking to them!"

Atreus seemed to feel just as awkward as she did about the whole thing; he ignored her completely, although he did pass the mutton with figs when she asked. Thyestes was more personable, and certainly better looking. He smiled at her often, and made a point of offering her a large portion of candied walnuts when dessert came around. But she could not imagine him as her *husband* – especially since his only topic of conversation seemed to be himself.

As soon as the meal was done her mother sent her and her two younger brothers off to bed; Alphenor, being older, was allowed to stay. Chloris made no objection – she was glad to escape her cousins' company, and she really *was* tired. The next day she rose early to find her chaperones still snoring – despite her mother's instructions, Chloris guessed they had slipped out to partake of the festival wine. Chloris dressed herself quietly and made her way to the room where her brothers were sleeping. She knocked softly at the door.

"Go away," she heard Alphenor moan – but Phaedimus opened the door.

"Look at him," said Phaedimus. "He's lucky the footrace isn't today."

"Let's go out without him, then," Chloris said. "What about Damasichthon?"

"He's asleep, of course," snorted Phaedimus. Damasichthon was a notoriously late sleeper.

Phaedimus belted his kilt over his loincloth and slipped on his sandals. "Where do you want to go?" he asked Chloris, shutting the door softly behind them.

"To the Temple of Hera," Chloris said promptly. "The girls' race is in Hera's honor; I want to make an offering."

Phaedimus nodded and followed her out of the palace and into the agora. They wandered the aisles of stalls where early-rising merchants hawked items of every description: pots, daggers, and baskets; cloth and leather goods; fruits and vegetables – but none of these things seemed right as a gift to Hera, the queen of Heaven and Earth. Beneath one awning, two broad-shouldered slaves guarded precious jewelry; nearby another merchant offered elegant cups of gold and silver. These things were fit for the goddess, but too costly for the beads in Chloris' pouch.

Then she saw an old woman selling bright garlands of flowers: wreaths of deep purple larkspur, spiky aster flowers, golden-yellow mullein blooms, sweet-smelling lavender, and bright red poppies. They were meant for festival wear, but surely their beauty and fragrance would please the goddess – and it was an offering she could afford. Chloris spent a few moments choosing, and on the merchant's advice she selected a garland of brilliant poppies twined with snow-white ribbons. The flower-seller accepted a small silver bead in payment, then explained how to reach the Temple of Hera.

In the meantime, Phaedimus had bartered for a packet of honeycakes wrapped in a broad fig leaf; he gave two cakes to Chloris in exchange for a bead of carved agate that he could trade with later. The air was fresh and cool as they walked through the potters' quarter, heading southwest towards the river Alpheus. Neither said much; Phaedimus was wholly occupied with his breakfast, and Chloris was considering what prayer she should make to the goddess. By the time she had brushed the last of the cake-crumbs from her fingers, she had decided what to say.

Both of them paused to stare when they neared Hera's temple, not far from the riverbank: the structure was far larger and more magnificent than the Temple of Apollo in Thebes. Its front columns were painted peacock blue; when Chloris and her brother stepped inside they saw that the frescoes depicted Hera's favorite birds, their many-eyed tail feathers spread out in brilliant fans, and they walked through an orchard full of trees laden with golden apples and bushes covered with red pomegranates. In the middle of the temple stood a life-sized statue of the goddess herself, all ivory and gold. A priestess was carefully arranging the robes worn by the statue; she looked over as Chloris and Phaedimus approached.

"Good morning, children," she said.

Chloris held up the garland. "May I give this to the goddess?"

The middle-aged woman nodded. Chloris came closer and knelt before the statue, placing the wreath of flowers on the floor. "Divine Hera," she said nervously, "I lay these flowers at your feet today, in the hope that my feet may show you honor tomorrow." She looked up at the goddess' pale, regal face, seeking some sign of approval.

"A lovely offering, my child," the priestess said. "May Hera's blessing be with you."

Chloris rose and backed respectfully away from Hera's image to where her brother waited.

"They say Queen Hippodamia was the model for the statue," Phaedimus whispered as they stepped away the temple.

"King Pelops' wife? The one who killed Prince Chrysippus?" The words made her stomach lurch. She looked back at the serene features of the statue. "I wonder if she really looks like that."

"Very much," answered a man's voice.

Startled, Chloris turned to see two men standing close by. One she recognized as the man in charge of the games; he was *very* good looking, but his dark hair was unkempt and his eyes were bleary and red. The other man was a little shorter, with a thin face, lank sandy hair, and protruding ears. His eyes were clear, and met Chloris' gaze with kindness.

"At least from what I remember," he continued. "It's been four years since I last saw her."

The dark-haired man scowled. "The artist flattered her," he said, bitterness in his voice. "Her waist was much thicker. And her face was full of lines."

The sandy-haired man answered in a mild tone: "Of course. The statue represents the goddess, not the queen."

"You're right, Neleus." He pushed his hair out of his eyes. "Well, now that the queen is banished, she'll have to do without her flatterers."

"Theban, go bathe! Soaking your head in water will do you good."

"You're right again," said the man with the bloodshot eyes. He clapped his companion on the back and staggered off.

"He's from Thebes?" asked Chloris, puzzled.

Phaedimus added: "*We're* from Thebes. And I've never seen him before."

The man called Neleus raised an eyebrow. "You don't know? Laius was heir to the kingdom. But he relinquished his claim when he was a boy. He's lived in Pisa ever since."

"Why?" asked Phaedimus.

"Being a king isn't everything," Neleus said. His voice had the quiet assurance of experience.

Finally Chloris remembered who Neleus was. "*You* are a king," she said. "The king of Pylos."

"Yes," he agreed. "And *you* are the bold princess who wants to run a race. May Hera smile on you!" With a nod and a wave, he took his leave; Chloris and Phaedimus made their way back towards the palace.

The next two days sped past in a blur: Phaedimus took the olive wreath in the boys' archery, and Alphenor won his footrace. Then, at last, on the morning of the third day, the time for the girls' race arrived. When the herald called out Chloris' name she stepped forward, wearing a short tunic tied with a cloth belt, her hair pulled back with a leather thong so that it would stay out of her face as she ran. She took her position at the starting line with about a dozen other young women – the drawing of lots had given her the outside position, nearest the crowd. This worried her a little: had her offering to Hera been insufficient?

Well, she would just have to work harder to win the goddess' favor. She felt the sand beneath her bare toes as she surveyed the racetrack. They were to run a single lap, out to the white marble turning-post, around and back. Chloris then glanced at her competitors, assessing their strengths and weaknesses. She was among the tallest of the girls, so the length of her stride would be an advantage. Though she was used to running, and guessed that the other girls might not be – only a few of them had the lean muscles of practiced runners – but given the course's short length, endurance mattered little. Someone like Princess Astydamia – not as tall as Chloris, but sturdily built – might summon speed from sheer strength.

"Contestants, make ready!" cried the herald, lifting his wooden starting-paddles.

Chloris and the other girls leaned forward, each with the toes of one foot just touching the line drawn in the sand.

The herald brought his paddles together with a sharp crack; the girls propelled themselves into motion.

Chloris pushed herself hard, arms and legs pumping; soon the slower girls had fallen back. Astydamia, though, was close beside her, and she heard the girl from Sparta just behind – and a long-legged girl from Corinth was pulling ahead of all of them.

They sped past the wooden viewing-stands where the favored guests had seats; other spectators stood, thickly clustered along the track. All were shouting, whistling, clapping, calling out encouragement – and then Chloris heard one voice rise above all the others, a deep voice with an accent from the east.

"Run, Chloris! Run!"

The familiar voice surprised her so much that she turned her head and nearly stumbled. Astydamia pulled in front of her before they reached the turning-post, and the Spartan girl's footfalls drew nearer.

She forced her attention back to the course, willing her legs faster, pushing to lengthen her stride even as she rounded the turn. *Lady Artemis,* she prayed silently, *give me strength! Let me do you honor, as well as Hera!*

Now she was gaining speed, and she could tell that the others were beginning to tire, but Astydamia and the Corinthian were blocking the inside of the track. To pass them she had to run wide. Narrowing her focus so that she saw nothing but the track ahead, heard nothing but the thudding of her bare feet in the sand and the panting of her own breath, she summoned all her strength and speed – and then she was past them and the course before her was empty. Chloris sped beyond the finish line and gradually came to a stop. She leaned forward, hands on knees, her breath coming in great heaving gasps; bit by bit her field of vision widened, and she saw the last girls staggering in, holding their sides.

"Congratulations!" someone said.

Chloris looked up to see the man called Laius standing before her. He looked far more presentable than he had yesterday morning, dressed in a fresh kilt and with his hair and beard combed. "An excellent race, Princess Chloris." He made a notation in his wax-covered wooden tablet, and gestured to the herald.

"Princess Chloris of Thebes is the winner of the girls' footrace!" shouted the herald.

Her uncle Pelops came forward from his seat of honor; he set a wreath of olive branches on her head and handed her the winner's ribbon of blue-dyed wool. Her mother and father embraced her, both smiling broadly; her brothers each kissed her cheek, and Phaedimus whispered, "I knew you'd win."

Others offered congratulations: the king of Argos gave her the victor's prize, a delicate two-handled goblet with bright pomegranates painted in the bowl. And King Neleus of Pylos said, "You run like the goddess of the hunt!"

Chloris beamed; no other words could have pleased her more.

"If only my wife could have seen you!" he continued. "She liked to hunt, before we married."

"You're married?" Chloris blurted out, and then was embarrassed by her outburst. Of course he was married; he was a king! And why should it matter to her? He wasn't even particularly handsome – his ears were too large, his face too thin. And soon she would be a Maiden of Artemis.

Yet when he answered her question with a gentle smile – one that reminded Chloris of her father, somehow – she felt her face flush even redder. "Yes," Neleus said. "My wife remained in Pylos – she's not well enough to travel. But I'll be sure to tell her of the race."

Chloris thanked him and turned away before she could make a greater fool of herself. One person after another praised her fleetness of foot – and yet there was no sign of the spectator she had heard cheering her on.

She scanned the crowd, wondering where Uncle Broteas was. She was *sure* she had heard his voice. Why didn't he come to congratulate her?

Her father's hand tapped her shoulder. "You look troubled, Chloris – is something wrong?"

"I—" She looked around again, fruitlessly, then said: "During the race, I heard Uncle Broteas cheering for me. But now I don't see him."

Grasping her upper arm, her father pulled her aside. "Daughter, can you tell me where you heard him?"

Chloris frowned, trying to remember exactly where she had been. She had already run past the stands, and gone perhaps half the remaining distance to the turning-post... "There," she said, gesturing; she stared, but no one in the milling crowds looked like Uncle Broteas.

Her father remained still for a moment, but his motionless stance was filled with pent energy, like a hunting-dog awaiting the command to flush the quarry.

"You must have been mistaken," he said, releasing her arm. "It's very unlikely that he would come here. Your uncle Broteas and your uncle Pelops are not on good terms with each other."

"But they're brothers," she said, puzzled.

"Even so. Brothers don't always get along." He hesitated, and then repeated: "I'm sure that Broteas is not here."

He began walking back to where they had been standing before, but Chloris saw the way his narrowed eyes continued to search the gathering – and she realized that, despite his words, he thought she was right: Uncle Broteas *was* in Pisa.

Which meant that her father, who always told the truth, was lying to her.

§ 4.08

Amphion frowned. He knew, from years of teaching music to his children, that Chloris had inherited his own keen hearing. She would recognize Broteas' voice if she heard it.

There was only one reason for Broteas to come to Pisa. He was here to retrieve the sacred mastiff that Pelops had stolen from Lydia twenty years before. And the mastiff, Amphion knew, was on display at the Temple of Rhea – not an impossible target.

Still, Amphion saw no sign of the Lydian: not in the crowds along the racetrack, not in the mass of festival-goers that filled the agora, and certainly not among the most favored of the noble guests, those invited to dine in the megaron with the king of Pisa.

If he told Niobe of Chloris' suspicions, she would go straight to Pelops; Amphion knew where his wife's loyalties lay. But Amphion held no ill will against Broteas: indeed, he sought to improve ties between Thebes and Lydia. Broteas had been a perfectly congenial guest, and the initial negotiations were promising. But now Amphion himself was the guest of *Pelops*: he owed his host a sacred obligation. Suspecting a threat, he could not remain silent – and yet he did not want to jeopardize relations with Lydia.

It was difficult to find a moment alone with Pelops, especially apart from Niobe. But in the afternoon Damasichthon twisted his ankle, and Niobe went to look after him; during the twilight banquet in the courtyard, Amphion had the chance to pull Pelops aside before she arrived. People were noisier and a little dirtier after three days of festival; the meal was less formal than the repasts of previous nights, and Pelops was circulating among his guests.

King Pelops spoke first. "What magnificent children you have – every one of them with a victor's wreath!"

"You provided a magnificent opportunity for them," Amphion said. "Games worthy of the Olympians themselves. The chariot race at the end was the best yet!"

Before Amphion could change the subject, Pelops continued his compliments. "Your daughter's a beauty."

"I've always thought so," Amphion admitted, forced to raise his voice above the hum of the crowd. "But I'm biased."

"As you should be!" Pelops grinned. "So: which of my sons does she prefer?"

Amphion feared that even the din of dozens of guests and the clatter of crockery all around would not provide sufficient privacy for such a delicate topic – but now that it had been broached, the subject must be resolved.

"Pelops," he said, "both Atreus and Thyestes are impressive young men. But Chloris wants to join the Maidens of Artemis. She has pledged herself to the goddess. After the Games, we'll take her to join the cult."

Pelops frowned, and muttered something under his breath that even Amphion's hearing could not discern.

"I beg your pardon?"

"Nothing," snapped Pelops. Then his expression changed, growing wistful. "Look, I know that Atreus and Thyestes aren't..."

With an upwelling of pity, Amphion realized that his brother-in-law was thinking of his murdered son. "Give them time to grow up," he said gently. "They're still very young. And, as you know, I now have two more daughters at home."

Pelops' dark eyes flashed. "Can you guarantee that *they* will marry my sons? Or are you going to let them choose husbands for themselves too?"

Amphion knew that Pelops thought he was foolish, permitting his daughter to have a say about her future – and he also knew that his wife would never allow anything else. "Pelops, your sister—"

"At least a dozen years will pass before your twin girls are old enough to wed. That will give you plenty of time to persuade your wife," Pelops said, his voice hard. "My influence is growing, Amphion. A marriage alliance would be the best thing for Thebes."

Amphion did not like his brother-in-law's tone. He had approached Pelops in good faith, intending to warn him about a threat – and now the man was threatening him. Part of him wanted to leave with the danger to the mastiff unspoken, but that would not be healthy for relations between Thebes and Pisa.

"I'll remember that, Pelops. But I wanted to discuss another topic." He chose his words carefully, seeking to master his emotions and to balance competing responsibilities. "I'm concerned about the wealth displayed in your temples. With the festival drawing to a close, perhaps you should increase security."

Pelops looked even more offended. "Are you saying that one of my guests would steal from the temples? Who would dare such sacrilege?"

"Not every man has your piety, Pelops."

"But to violate the obligations of guest and host – and to steal from the gods!"

Spreading his hands, Amphion said, "Some men just can't resist gold."

Pelops said nothing for a moment, frowning in the direction of a nearby fig tree. Then he turned back, impatiently waving an insect away from his face. "Don't be stupid. The gods would never permit it. What other king has honored them so well?"

Beneath the bluster, Amphion detected worry and insecurity; a distended vein pulsed in Pelops' forehead. Though Amphion was hearing this song for the first time, he understood its arrangement at once: the Pisatan king, long blessed by the gods, now feared that he had fallen from their favor. His beloved son had been murdered – and by his wife of twenty years. Threats lurked in every corner – even the innocent intentions of his young niece menaced him. He had probably established a secret watch on the temples already. The requisite change of key was clear: only Pelops' sister had been able to persuade him to leave the darkness.

"As you say, Pelops," he answered, inclining his head. In a conciliatory tone he continued: "May I make a request of you?"

"What is it?" Pelops snapped, his eyes narrowing.

"While my sons and I take Chloris to join the Maidens of Artemis, could Niobe stay here in Pisa?" Continuing, Amphion explained that it should not take more than a month to track down the devotees of the goddess as they journeyed across the southern peninsula: and with each word he spoke, he saw Pelops relax further, his hostility melting. Niobe would be annoyed by the suggestion – she would wish to cling to Chloris until the very last moment – but the journey *would* be difficult for her, and she herself had told him how much her brother needed her.

"Of course," Pelops said, somewhat mollified. "It would be good for my children, now that their mother…"

It was a sentence best left unfinished; when Laius approached, both men welcomed the interruption. Amphion watched his brother-in-law walk away – and, though he knew he had done the right thing, his own mood had soured. He did not want to give up his wife's company.

Sighing, he scanned the dinner guests seated at various tables in the courtyard, looking to see whether Niobe had arrived. A prickle went up his back when he saw the Tiresias facing his direction – but then she turned away to speak with another guest, and Amphion decided he was imagining things. Catching Chloris' eye, he felt a pang of guilt: he had misled her this afternoon. After they left Pisa he would speak with her and make things right. But just now he had to talk to Niobe; and for that conversation they needed true privacy.

She stood beside a laurel tree, chatting with the palace steward; he drew her away, took their leave for the evening, and led her up to their room. As soon as the lamps were lit he dismissed the servants, and helped Niobe out of her festival finery himself. Once clad in a lightweight linen robe, she took a seat on the dressing-stool; his fingers sought the hairpins holding her braids in place and began to work them loose.

"What is it, Husband?" she asked, catching his eye in the reflection of the polished silver mirror on its stand.

Best, with Niobe, to be direct. "I asked Pelops if you could stay in Pisa while the boys and I take Chloris to join the Maidens."

She stilled for a moment beneath his fingers. "*You* asked for this?"

Amphion removed the last hairpin and began to unravel the braids. "Yes. I did."

"But – Chloris – I'll never see her again!"

"Of course you will," Amphion argued. "We've already discussed this. You'll certainly see her more often than if she married Atreus or Thyestes. And, my love, you know the journey to Arcadia could be too much for you. It's mountainous country."

She was silent. Amphion knew she agreed with his logic, but hated being parted from her daughter.

"I admit I have concerns," Amphion continued. "Pelops wants your help in ruling Pisa." An edge entered his voice despite his efforts to remain calm. "If you stay here, he won't want to let you go."

"I'll leave when I want to," she said tartly. "He won't keep me from you – or from my babies. I'll climb out a window, if need be."

Amphion ran a hand over her thick hair, crimped into rippling waves by the braids. "I know you would." In her youth, Niobe had escaped from three different palaces. But she was no longer a girl – she was the mother of nine, and climbing out of windows and sneaking through the night could prove more difficult. Still, she was obviously a calming influence on her brother. If Pelops had more time to steady himself and recover from his son's murder, that would be best for everyone.

"Just a month or two," he said, stroking her hair. "Besides finding the Maidens of Artemis I'd like to visit Pylos and Mycenae, and make an offering at my father's grave in Sicyon. Then I'll return to Pisa so that we can all journey together back to Thebes." And make sure that Pelops did not try to keep Niobe with him – but this thought he did not voice.

His wife nodded; then she rose from the stool, and circled him with her arms. Her flesh was warm, her familiar curves enticing against his chest. "No more than a couple of months," she said, her voice low. "I couldn't bear to be away from you any longer."

He ran his fingertips across her soft cheek, breathing in the jasmine and sandalwood of her perfume. He still had not told Niobe of Chloris' suspicion regarding her other brother, Broteas, but he had already warned Pelops, and what more could Niobe do?

"Nor could I," Amphion said, and bent to taste her lips.

§ 4.09

Laius held out his wine-cup. "Pour me another!" he told the Corinthian prince who was hosting the drinking-party. Now that the competitions were over, he could drink as much as he pleased; there was no morning event to manage, no roll of entrants to verify. "And don't mix so much water in the next krater!"

The Corinthian – Laius had forgotten his name; there were so many new visitors this year – laughed. "Laius, this is already three parts wine to one of water!"

"Then make the next one four parts wine!" Other men at the campfire raised their cups and shouted agreement.

Lifting the cup to his lips, Laius knocked back a healthy swig. By all gods high and low, the festival had been a success. *His* success, as much as anyone's! Now if only he had good fortune with the knucklebones…

Prince Thyestes cast the bones, and had a lucky throw; the others groaned. Once bets were settled, the curly-haired man from Argos sitting beside Laius elbowed him in the ribs. "Laius!" he said, louder than was necessary, "do you know what's wrong with this festival?"

Laius set down his cup abruptly on the folding camp-table, sloshing wine over his hand. "Nothing's wrong with this festival!"

The Argive held up a placating hand. "Oh, the games and the food have been magnificent. Take no offense, my friend. But this place doesn't have enough *women*."

"Ah," said Laius, nodding.

"A few pretty maids running in the race," the man continued. "But mostly princesses well-guarded by their fathers. Some lovely wives among the spectators – none of them venturing far from their husbands. Laius, there must be ten times as many men as maids here."

"Come to Corinth!" said the host. "We've got the most beautiful women in Hellas. A whole temple full of them!"

"So why didn't you bring them with you?" someone shouted, to general laughter.

"I'll wager *you've* got a woman, Laius," said the Argive, grinning slyly.

"He does," Thyestes volunteered. "Nerissa's her name – and she's more beautiful than any Corinthian temple girl!"

The Corinthian raised his eyebrows. "Is that true, Laius?"

Laius flushed with pride. "She's like a wood nymph: eyes as green as spring leaves, and golden hair."

The Argive laughed and slapped Laius on the back. "You're a poet, Laius! I had no idea!"

"All right then," said the Corinthian, "let's go have a look at her."

"No," Laius said, and swallowed the last of his wine. "She wouldn't like that." He reached for the knucklebones, but his neighbor was quicker and scooped them up first.

"Why not?" asked the Argive. "We don't mean any harm."

"Right," said the Corinthian. "We won't touch her, Laius. I just want to see if you and Prince Thyestes are telling the truth. A jug of my best wine says the Corinthian girls are prettier. The Argive here can be the judge – he's been to Aphrodite's temple at the top of the Akrocorinth."

"Many times," the fellow agreed, leering.

"But—"

"Come on, Laius," needled Thyestes. "Don't tell me you'd let your woman decide whether your friends see her or not!"

Shrugging, Laius agreed; weaving only a little, he led the three men through the night to the cottage Nerissa shared with her mother Polyxo. It was small but well-made, its thick stone walls coated in whitewashed plaster. No light showed around the edges of the tightly closed window shutters.

Laius pounded on the door. "Nerissa – I have some people here who want to meet you." There was no answer; he knocked harder. "Nerissa!"

Her voice was muffled by the closed door. "Go away, Laius."

"I want my friends to see how beautiful you are," Laius called.

"Ha!" said the Corinthian. "If she won't show herself, I win the wager."

"You'd win anyway," said the Argive. "She can't possibly be more beautiful than the Corinthian girls."

"Did you hear that, Nerissa?" called Laius. "Come on out and prove me right!"

"Go away, Laius." From within came a child's high-pitched wail. "Listen to that – you woke the baby. You should be ashamed of yourself."

Realizing she was not going to come out – and he didn't really want her to, now, not with a screaming child to contend with – Laius turned back to the others. "All right. Let's go."

"Hey," the Argive objected. "I still want to see her!"

Laius felt less drunk than before; the walk had cleared his head. "Let's go, man. At Rhea's temple, just down the path, there's a wall-painting of her sister – that'll show you what a Pisatan beauty looks like."

"A painting?" complained the Argive, but Laius managed to pull him away from the cottage, towards the Temple of Rhea.

The altar-flame at the center of the temple cast a yellow glow from between the columns that framed its entrance; as they neared, the Argive was still grumbling, and the Corinthian continued to crow that he had won the bet. A high-pitched shriek interrupted the men's conversation, and all four of them froze.

Laius stared: in the fire-lit temple, two men were moving about. Despite the summer night's warmth, both wore hooded cloaks. A shorter, plump figure – Polyxo? – rushed forward to pummel one of them with her fists.

"What's going on?" yelled Laius. He drew his dagger and ran towards the temple. "You there – stop!"

"How dare you!" shrieked the priestess, struggling with one of the cloaked men. He pushed her roughly away; she reeled backwards and landed on the altar. She screamed and twisted in the fire, scattering a shower of glowing embers. "Help!" she shouted as she threw herself to the ground, rolling to extinguish the flames licking at the back of her gown. "Rhea, help me!"

"They've violated the temple!" shouted Thyestes from behind Laius. "Polyxo – we've got to help her!"

The two cloaked men in the temple hesitated. "Let's get out of here!" said one, his voice betraying an eastern accent. They sprinted out into the night.

One moved too swiftly for Laius to reach him, but from the corner of his eye he saw the Argive go chasing after. Laius went for the other man, a thick-set fellow. His first blow failed to connect, but then he caught the man's cloak in his left hand. The criminal tripped and fell, dropping a cloth-wrapped bundle that landed on the ground with a solid thud. Laius, still clutching the man's cloak, went down with him. Laius scrambled awkwardly across the ground, slashing out with his knife; he felt it connect, and the man yelped. Then his adversary kicked out, striking a glancing blow to Laius' jaw. Stunned, Laius lost his hold on the cloak. When his eyes refocused, the man was getting to his feet. The stranger looked back at the bundle he had dropped – Laius glanced over and saw a flash of metal in the moonlight. Instinctively he rolled towards the bundle; grasping it, he felt the weight of precious gold.

"Thyestes!" Laius shouted. "Catch him!" But the man had already stumbled away into the brush.

Breathing hard, Laius got to his feet. The Argive was some distance down the path, doubled over and panting hard. "Couldn't catch him," he gasped, shaking his head.

Laius scanned the surroundings, hoping for some sign of where the thieves had gone – but they had vanished into the darkness.

Then a wail from inside the temple caught his attention. The heavy bundle tucked in the crook of his arm, Laius headed that way; the Argive staggered behind him. In the shadows of the temple, Thyestes and the Corinthian were bent over Polyxo's fallen form. The coals of the scattered altar fire glowed with a baleful ruddy light; the priestess' moans prickled the hairs on the back of Laius' neck.

Thyestes looked up, his eyes so wide with fear that the whites showed all around. "Did you get it back?"

Laius unwrapped the bundle he held to reveal Rhea's golden mastiff.

"Praise Zeus!" said Thyestes. "If they had escaped with it, Father would slit our throats himself."

"How could anyone violate the sanctuary?" Laius asked, shaken. Rhea's hearth fire had been desecrated; her priestess had been attacked. He kicked aside smoldering embers and then knelt beside the old woman. "Polyxo?"

"Laius? Laius—" she gasped. "The fire…"

In the poor light he could not tell how badly she had been hurt, but he could smell the burnt cloth and singed hair. She needed a healer.

Laius got to his feet and handed the mastiff to Prince Thyestes. "Wrap that back up. We'll take it to Polyxo's cottage. I don't want it out of our sight. Corinthian—" he still could not recall the fellow's name, "—you fetch a healer. And you," he said, turning to the Argive, who had finally returned to the temple, "find King Pelops and tell him what's happened." As gently as he could, he scooped up the moaning woman and draped her over his shoulder, careful not to touch her scorched back. She lost consciousness before he reached the cottage.

"Nerissa!" he shouted, kicking the door, "let me in! Now!"

He could hear the child fussing inside. "Laius," Nerissa said through the closed door, "I *told* you to go away!"

"Open up, Nerissa! Your mother's hurt!"

"Mother?" He heard her slide loose the bar holding the door shut. "What's happened?" she asked as the door swung open – and then she saw the limp burden he carried. "Mother! Oh, no—"

Laius carried the injured woman inside; Thyestes followed, and barred the door once more. Laius lay Polyxo face-down on her bed in the corner, wondering what he should do next, but Nerissa had already brought a lamp so that she could examine the extent of her mother's wounds. "Burns," she said, speaking purposefully although her voice shook. "Damp compresses, then a poultice of ground mallow and mullein leaves. That's right, isn't it, Mother?" She moved about the cottage, seeking what she needed to treat the blistering flesh.

The toddler Polydorus, frightened, started to wail; Laius picked up the child. He knew nothing of herbs, but he could at least keep the boy out of Nerissa's way. The child clung to Laius' neck, and his cries subsided.

"There, now, my son," Laius said soothingly. "It'll be all right," he assured the boy, though he was far from sure that was so.

Still holding the cloth-wrapped mastiff, Thyestes stepped close. "You're a hero, Laius."

"What, me?" He shook his head. He had only done what any man would do.

But, he reflected as he patted his son's small back, maybe he *had* done something useful after all. He could never make up for having slept through the murder of Chrysippus – but perhaps he was not a complete failure as a man.

FIVE: FLAMES AND SACRILEGE

§ 5.01

"An outstanding festival, Pelops!" King Electryon of Mycenae clapped Pelops on the back, sending a jolt of pain through his bad shoulder; Pelops tried not to flinch.

"The best yet," agreed King Neleus of Pylos.

The young king from Aegina – Aeacus was his name – walked around the campfire to join them. "The footrace for girls: what an inspiration!"

Electryon sighed in appreciation. "Such grace. Like young does in the forest."

"Let's drink to Chloris of Thebes!" Atreus said, far too loudly. All the men who had gathered at Electryon's campsite shouted their agreement, and filled their cups.

"To the princess with the gray eyes of Athena, and the swift feet of Artemis!" one man shouted.

Another called: "Don't forget her legs!"

The reminder of Chloris' shapely legs led to several bawdy comments which Pelops thought better to cut short. "To my *niece*, Princess Chloris!" he said, raising his cup and then draining it.

More wine was poured around. Toasts were offered to the host Electryon, who had won the javelin contest, and to the victors of the men's footrace and the discus throw, who had also joined the drinking party. One man after another, in various stages of sobriety, praised Pelops for the magnificence of his festival, the generosity of his table, and the beauty of his palace and temples. Their words were like food and drink for his soul. Pelops' fear that these games would be cursed was unfounded, though Hippodamia's crime had dealt him a wound that would never heal.

The unending ache of Chrysippus' absence swelled in his heart. How his boy would have enjoyed these games!

"You haven't even drunk to his memory," said the ghost of Myrtilus, his voice clearly audible despite all the revelers' noise and laughter. "A fine father you are."

"I will," Pelops muttered. "I will drink to him." He told a servant to fill the cups anew. "I offer another toast: to the memory of my beloved son, Chrysippus!"

Despite the general inebriation, most conversation stopped – and those who continued talking were shushed hastily by others. King Electryon solemnly raised his cup and said: "To Chrysippus!"

In silence they drank, and to Pelops' shame he felt tears well up. He swallowed hard, determined not to weep like a woman. A glimmer of light appeared behind the eastern hills; to distract himself, he stared at the jagged line between earth and sky, until he realized that a man was running towards Electryon's encampment.

"King Pelops!" the fellow shouted, breathless and urgent. "King Pelops!"

Pelops blinked back the threatening tears. "Yes?" he said. "What is it?"

"My lord king," gasped the runner, whom Pelops recognized as a young noble from Argos, "there's been an attack at the Temple of Rhea! Thieves tried to steal the sacred mastiff!"

As he dropped his empty cup and got to his feet, Pelops recalled that his brother-in-law had warned him that something like this might happen. How had Amphion known?

§ 5.02

Niobe accompanied her family down to the harbor to bid them farewell. The exodus of festival-goers clogged the road with every type of conveyance: from chariots drawn by elegant horses, and gilded sedan chairs carried on the shoulders of slaves, to the mule-carts and plodding ox-carts of less privileged folk – and of course there was plenty of foot traffic. The Temple of Hermes, where travelers stopped to ask the god's protection, was jammed with people, and a huge pile of offering-stones had accumulated at the base of the massive pillar in the temple's forecourt. Dotting the roadside between temple and harbor were makeshift stalls where locals offered ready-made food for barter: barley cakes, cheese, dried fish, and savory bean paste spread on unleavened bread. At one point, Niobe sent her maidservant to fetch a snack for the family – ordinary fare compared to the palace feasts of the last several days, but plentiful and filling.

Most of the talk around them was about the attack at the Temple of Rhea during the night, but Niobe focused on her daughter. "Are you *sure* that you want to do this, Chloris?" she asked, even though she had asked many times before. "You'll be so far away."

"I'm not *dying*, Mother," Chloris said, reminding Niobe that her brother was still suffering from the loss of his son. "I'm sure I'll visit Thebes before too long."

And later, after Niobe repeated her concerns, Chloris added testily: "I see why *you* didn't warn *your* mother before *you* left."

The jab found its mark; Niobe drew a deep breath and resolved to stop nagging. Instead she reviewed with Chloris what she had packed: sturdy sandals, a lightweight cloak and a heavy one, tunics and a leather belt, a good sharp knife and her bow and arrows. This subject was better tolerated as they made their slow way towards the sea.

Just as the road reached the harbor the crush of travelers worsened; a group of Pisatan soldiers blocked the access to the shore. Hot, scarcely able to breathe, Niobe clung to Amphion's arm until they reached the front of the crowd. There she found her nephew Atreus in charge of soldiers who were questioning each set of travelers before allowing them to pass. Atreus explained that they were in search of the men who had attacked Rhea's temple the night before. And he turned specifically to Amphion.

"Uncle Amphion," he said, "my father says you told him last night that thieves might attack. Did you see anything – something that made you warn him?"

Surprised, Niobe looked at her husband: Amphion had not mentioned this.

"No, Prince Atreus, I saw nothing." Amphion shook his head. "But the situation had to be tempting for thieves: so much magnificence, and so many people to hide among."

Atreus nodded. "True enough."

"I understand nothing was actually taken?" Amphion asked.

"No. We stopped them from stealing any treasure – but the criminals themselves escaped."

"I wish you luck finding them," said Amphion. "May we continue?"

"Go ahead," said Atreus, waving them past the soldiers.

Amphion led Niobe and their children beyond the checkpoint, where they joined Captain Naucles. Niobe breathed more easily now that they were out of the worst of the crowd, but the harbor was still a busy place; several ships were being loaded, and they had to avoid the dozens of sweating stevedores carrying chests, amphorae, baskets, and other burdens.

As they walked toward his ship, Naucles said: "I heard it was a couple of men from Troy that violated the temple."

"*Troy*?" Amphion's thick gray eyebrows lifted. "Why would *Troy* want Lydia's mastiff?"

"Troy and Lydia have been rivals for years," Niobe said. "The Trojans might think that possession of the mastiff would give them an advantage."

Her husband frowned, and Niobe wondered if he *did* know something more.

Captain Naucles shrugged. "It's made of gold, right?"

Niobe's son Alphenor, also listening intently, interjected: "Everyone wants gold."

"You never know what people will do," Naucles said. Then he winked at Chloris. "But to change the subject – I hear you ran quite a race, Princess! All the men are talking about the beautiful maid from Thebes who's swifter than a swallow."

Chloris' cheeks turned pink, making her even prettier – she *was* developing into a lovely young woman, Niobe thought with a mixture of envy and pride. She herself had never been beautiful; no one had spoken of her in such admiring tones. But, then, Chloris was *her* flesh and blood – she deserved credit for bringing such beauty into the world!

"Chloris wasn't the only victor," said Amphion, setting a hand on Damasichthon's shoulder. "My sons won olive wreaths in their events, too."

Naucles congratulated the boys as they approached the small boat waiting to convey passengers to his ship, which was anchored out in deeper water; then he stepped over to speak with the harbormaster. Niobe removed her hat so that the breeze off the water could dry the sweat in her hair.

Her eldest son Alphenor bent down to hug her goodbye – how he had grown! "We'll be back for you soon, Mother," he said, and kissed her cheek. Niobe hugged young Phaedimus and Damasichthon and clung to Chloris.

"Be well, Daughter," she said. "Be safe."

"I will, Mother." She spoke with the confidence of a person too young to know all the calamities that the Fates had at their disposal. Then she slipped from Niobe's embrace and clambered after her brothers into the dinghy.

Amphion was next. Holding him close, she whispered: "Protect them, Husband."

He stroked her back. "I'll do my best, my love."

Pulling back a little, she asked: "What *do* you know about that attack on the Temple of Rhea?"

"Nothing," he assured her.

"But you suspect something."

"I thought Lydia might have sent men to take back the mastiff. But if there's evidence that it was Trojans instead... It's none of our business, Niobe, and we should stay out of it." He brushed her cheek with his fingertips. "You do what you can here with Pelops and his children. We'll return soon." He gave her one last kiss and then stepped easily into the dinghy, not even wetting his sandals; one of Naucles' sailors started to row. Niobe watched the little vessel cross the blue, blue water; a man aboard the ship tossed a rope ladder over the side and Amphion and the children climbed aboard. The rower turned the small boat and headed back for the shore.

His conversation with the harbormaster done, Naucles came to her side; Niobe looked up at the sea-captain's tanned visage. "Take care of them, will you?"

"My lady queen, you can depend on me," he answered, bowing over her hand.

"You've never failed me." Yet she felt abandoned as he climbed into the dinghy and pushed off; in all too short a time Naucles was aboard the ship, the anchor stone lifted, and the sail lowered to fill with wind. The ship grew smaller in the distance until it disappeared behind a jutting spit of land. Niobe thought of how it must have been for her own mother, watching her and Pelops sail away from Lydia, with no plans to return. But Niobe's children *did* plan to return to her – even Chloris.

Still, it was hard to see them go: the world contained so many dangers. Despite the heat, Niobe shivered.

"My lady queen?" Her maidservant's inquiry interrupted Niobe's thoughts. "My lady queen, are you all right? The sun's so hot today, my lady—"

Niobe realized she was standing there bare-headed. "I'm fine," she said, settling her hat back in place. "Let's return to the palace."

Atreus, still busy questioning travelers, ordered a soldier to take Niobe and her maid back in a chariot; she gladly accepted the courtesy. The crowds were thinning, and the remaining travelers made way for the chariot; they made good time, but the sun was low in the sky by the time Niobe returned to the city.

The rooms that had been hers years ago now belonged to her nieces Astydamia and Nikippe, so Pelops had given her the chambers recently occupied by Hippodamia. Niobe refreshed herself after the long, dusty day with a tepid bath. While she soaked, sipping a goblet of honeyed barley-water, a servant brought word that the king wished to consult with her in his study.

She arrived to find the lamps lit and Laius and Thyestes already there, with

Exarchos making notes on a wax-coated wooden tablet. On a low table was a large platter of food; although Niobe was hungry, the smell was unappetizing. She wrinkled her nose.

Pelops looked up to greet her. "Niobe! There you are! Did everyone get off safely?"

"Yes. They're on their way."

"Sit down," he said, gesturing to the couch. "Have some pickled octopus. It's a gift from King Aeacus."

Niobe looked at the slimy tentacles and grimaced. "Brother, you know I *loathe* octopus."

He blinked, as if he had forgotten, but then he grinned. "Of course! Sorry." He turned to a servant. "Roast mutton for my sister," he ordered. "In the meantime, Niobe, there's bread and cheese and wine."

"Yes," she said, taking a seat. "Thank you."

Atreus entered the room while Niobe helped herself to some bread, hoping it would settle her stomach. Was it just the smell of the octopus making her sick – or her discomfort at remaining in Pisa without her family?

Or – on her fingers she counted the days since her last month's blood. Was she pregnant again?

Niobe's thoughts distracted her from the men's discussion; it was only after she had filled her uneasy stomach with bread and cheese that she started to pay attention. Pelops and his advisors were discussing what had gone well – and what had not – with respect to the games. A sensible procedure, she thought, conducting this review while the events of the festival were fresh in everyone's minds.

"The wrestling pit needs more sand next time," Atreus was saying. "And a judge who's not half-blind!"

Laius rolled his eyes. "The judge was fine."

"You only say that because you won, Laius," Atreus argued. "And you only won because Zethos of Thebes wasn't here."

"Oh, Atreus," Thyestes interposed, "don't turn wine into vinegar just because *you* didn't win an olive wreath."

Atreus' ears turned red at his brother's remark – he had finished second in the javelin throw, but second place was not victory.

Exarchos cleared his throat. "My lord king, my lady queen, my lord princes: now that we have discussed each of the competitions, I would bring your attention to other items." He tapped his stylus against the tablet. "We did not have enough benches for all the royal spectators. As to provisions, we ran out of figs and fennel. And some of the barley fields were trampled."

Pelops frowned. "You never bring good news, do you, Exarchos?"

"My lord king, all these are symptoms of your success," countered the steward. "More people attended the festival than ever before. But that puts a strain on Pisa. Next time, we need to be ready for larger crowds."

"And a training facility for the athletes," added Laius. "*They* are what the people come to see. Many of them told me that they want to come to Pisa earlier to be well rested for the games, but they need someplace to continue their training. If we want the games to be even more magnificent next time, a place for the athletes to train is important."

"That would be costly, my lord." Exarchos shook his head. "These games were already superb. Why must the next set of games be *more* magnificent?"

Niobe pushed her damp hair back over her shoulder, feeling that she had had the same conversation with her brother and Exarchos' predecessor sixteen years ago. Pelops had *always* overextended Pisa's resources. No doubt he would ask her for more contributions. She resolved to be firm: Thebes could *not* afford to send more.

Pelops rubbed his temples. "We may never hold the games again," he said, his voice hollow.

Silence descended abruptly. Niobe stared at her brother: had he plunged back into depression? "Pelops, would you really cancel the games?" she asked cautiously.

He pounded the table with his fist; the platters and goblets jumped. "The sanctuary of Rhea was violated! Thieves tried to steal the sacred mastiff!"

The younger men looked at one another, their eyes uneasy. At last Atreus said: "Father, that was only *two* men, out of thousands who attended."

Pelops sprang to his feet and began to pace. "They injured the priestess – they put out the altar flame. It's a terrible omen!"

"But they didn't *take* the mastiff," ventured Thyestes. He gestured to where the golden icon rested on a pedestal at the side of the room. "Laius and I stopped them."

"You didn't catch them." Pelops glared at Atreus. "Where did they go?"

The young man licked his lips. "I don't know, Father. They didn't leave by ship."

"Then they could still be here!" Pelops swept his arm in a broad arc. "But Thyestes and Laius haven't found them any more than you have. How can we restore confidence without bringing these criminals to justice? How can we satisfy the gods when such sacrilege goes unpunished?"

Again there was silence. Niobe glanced at Exarchos, who gave a tiny, almost imperceptible shrug; Laius, Thyestes, and Atreus all stared at the tiled floor.

Niobe, hoping she had more influence than the others, decided to speak. "Brother, calm yourself," she said softly.

"Calm myself!" he exploded. "*Calm* myself! What about your husband?"

"What about him?" she asked, her heart jumping.

"He warned me that thieves might attack. What did he know? What did he see?"

"Nothing," Niobe said defensively. "Pelops, Amphion's had to fight bandits around Thebes. He knows what's likely to tempt criminals. You had so much wealth on display, and there were so many people—"

"Why did the gods warn him instead of me?" demanded Pelops.

Niobe considered pointing out that Pelops *had* been warned – through Amphion – but decided this argument would not help. "Perhaps you should ask the gods..." she began, then let her words trail away. Pelops' face was as thunderously dark as their father Tantalus in the worst of his moods.

The door opened and an elderly manservant entered.

"Yes?" Pelops snapped.

"My lord king, the Tiresias is in the palace," the servant said. "She seeks an audience."

Watching Pelops' change in expression was like watching a raging fire subside. The flush of anger drained away, and he nodded curtly at the old man. "Bring her in," he said. Then he smiled at them all; it was like sunshine after a thunderstorm. "You're right, Niobe: I should ask the gods what to do. See, fellows, how clever my sister is?"

Niobe shifted uncomfortably in her seat as Laius, Exarchos and her nephews turned to stare at her as if she had conjured the Tiresias out of thin air. She had not considered her words particularly wise as she spoke them, and they seemed no more prophetic now. The Tiresias' arrival was only a lucky coincidence. She distracted herself with another bite of bread and a sip of watered wine.

The seer arrived shortly. Small and slender, she was dwarfed by her thickset manservant. In the close quarters, Niobe detected the signs of age on the blind woman's face – the hollows beneath her cheekbones and the thinning of her lips – more distinctly than she had done in the megaron a few days before.

"Welcome, Tiresias," said Pelops.

"My lord king," said the prophetess, stepping forward. She swept her hand around the room to encompass the others. "Queen Niobe; Prince Atreus; Prince Thyestes; Prince Laius of Thebes."

Niobe frowned, wondering why the Tiresias gave Laius this title when he had renounced his claim to the Theban throne years ago. What was she implying? But no one else seemed to notice, and Niobe decided she was being oversensitive. The blind woman was just trying to dazzle everyone with her powers of perception. Niobe refused to be impressed: the servant who had fetched the seer could have easily informed her who was present.

The Tiresias addressed Pelops. "I thank you, King Pelops, for your generous gift. Spikenard is rare and precious, and its scent delights the gods."

Pelops acknowledged her thanks, and then described the situation with the mastiff and his concerns about where he and Pisa stood in the gods' favor. While he spoke, Niobe rubbed the bridge of her nose, considering his gift to the Tiresias. Spikenard *was* extremely rare and precious, made from pink flowers that grew on mountainsides far to the east. Why did Pelops make such a costly gift when his treasuries were so low? Perhaps he believed he could buy the Tiresias' favor. It was true that the prophetess generally had words of good omen for Pelops – far better than her pronouncements about Niobe had ever been. Niobe had never made a point of giving the woman extravagant gifts – but then, the Tiresias spent little time in Thebes.

When Pelops finished speaking, the Tiresias pursed her lips. After a moment she said, "You must continue striving to please the gods."

Pelops set his hands on the back of an empty chair and leaned forward. "But how?"

"As you have always pleased them."

"Another temple?" Pelops hazarded.

The blindfolded woman inclined her head, and Niobe frowned. Pisa was in debt, and Exarchos had just been speaking of the costs to maintain the games; how could Pelops possibly afford another temple? Suddenly Niobe wondered whether the Tiresias could be in the pay of the architects and stonemasons, and others who profited from temple construction. But no, that was not likely. Besides, the Tiresias had not mentioned temples – that was Pelops' idea. The prophetess might have only been requesting more spikenard.

"A temple for which god?" persisted Pelops.

The Tiresias shook her head slightly. "My lord king, the gods have not yet revealed this to me."

Niobe's mouth twisted; she felt sourly pleased at this evidence that the Tiresias was *not,* in fact, all-knowing, but at the same time she was irritated. If the Tiresias knew the gods wanted a new temple, it only stood to reason she should know *which* of the gods wanted the temple. So she *didn't* really know that a temple was what would please the gods. Why, then, did she encourage Pelops in this costly endeavor?

"How do I find out?" Pelops asked.

"I am sure that they will make their desires known soon." The Tiresias tapped her staff lightly on the floor. "Perhaps it is a shy god… or goddess…"

"Hephaestus?" hazarded Atreus.

"Or Lady Artemis?" Thyestes suggested.

Pelops looked from one of his sons to the other, then back to the prophetess. "It could be either," he said. "How can I tell, Tiresias?"

The Tiresias' only answer was to shrug, which exasperated Niobe. "It's a simple question," she snapped impatiently. "If you're the handmaiden of the gods, why can't you answer it?"

The blind woman lifted her chin. "The answer will come when the gods have decided among themselves," she said. Though Pelops had not dismissed her, she turned and reached for her servant's arm. "Dolichus, let's go." She departed without another word.

"How rude!" Niobe muttered.

"Niobe!" Pelops reproached her, apparently unconcerned by the Tiresias' breach of propriety. Then her brother resumed his pacing, talking as much to himself as to anyone present. "We have to determine which god is the right one," he said. "And then show him such honor that no one can doubt the sanctity of the games. No one must dare such a violation ever again."

Niobe yawned; the day had been long and exhausting. She rose to her feet. "Brother, I'm tired. Will you excuse me?"

He nodded without pausing in his restless pacing. "Yes, of course. Good night."

She walked through the corridors, considering the situation. She did not see how a temple could be so magnificent that it would prevent all future sacrilege. In fact, a rich new temple might prove an even greater temptation. As she climbed the stairs, Niobe decided that it was best that Pelops did not know which god to honor next. As long as that information remained hidden to him, he could hardly start building. Perhaps the gods would show mercy and remain undecided.

Niobe stopped to check on her nieces and younger nephews, but they were all asleep, worn out from the excitement of the games. Then she went to her room, where her maidservant helped her undress. Soon she lay on the large, comfortable bed; her maidservant extinguished the lamps. And in the darkness, Niobe seemed to catch the scent of her sister-in-law's musk and honey perfume.

She had little sympathy for Hippodamia; not only was the woman a murderess, but Hippodamia had always treated her poorly – even though Niobe had protected her darkest secrets. Still, as she lay on the woman's bed, using her very pillow, Niobe could not help wondering about her. Where was Hippodamia, and how was she faring in her banishment?

§ 5.03

Hippodamia's cage was a narrow strip of land between the cliffs and the sea. Waves lapped against the rocky shore; wind stirred the patch of grass near the cliffs where a small herd of goats grazed. Gulls nested along the cliffs, fouling the stones with their droppings. She hated the birds. Each day they soared overhead, coming and going as they pleased, their screeching cries mocking her.

She slept in a cave. A *cave!*

She was queen of Pisa – daughter of one king and wife to another – and yet she slept on a hard, narrow cot, wrapped in a rough woolen blanket to keep away the damp and chill. Besides the festival clothes she had been wearing when she was seized, she had only a few coarse tunics fit for slaves, an ugly brown cloak, and a pair of thick-strapped peasant sandals. Pelops had also sent along the mirror from her dressing-table so that she could see how quickly captivity was destroying her beauty.

Her only companions were a pair of servants, a married couple in their thirties. Both of them looked older than their years. The man, Ekhinos, had a broad streak of gray in his thinning hair; his wife Iopa's face and hands were baked dark as old leather by years of working in the pitiless sun. Ekhinos fished and did the heavy work, and occasionally rowed the small boat to another part of the island – Zakynthos was its name – to obtain supplies. Iopa tended a small herd of goats and grew some vegetables in a little fenced plot. She also fetched water from the spring at the back of the cave, which meant she constantly intruded on Hippodamia's privacy. They came from Arcadia, not Pisa, and hence had no natural loyalty to her. Hippodamia had always heard that the peasants of Arcadia were the most uncouth in all Hellas – and this pair confirmed that assessment. Neither one had any comprehension of the service due a queen. She had to order them to bow when approaching her, and to address her with her proper title – and even then they managed it poorly.

In Pisa she would never have suffered such servants, but now they were all she had, and her only chance of escape. She could not scale the cliffs; she could not swim; she did not have the strength to manage the boat. And even if she reached the nearest settlement – wherever that was – what then? Alone, she had no hope.

As the days of spring crept past without any sign that Pelops would relent and recall her, she dropped hints on the subject; but Ekhinos and Iopa were too dim-witted to catch her meaning and respond. Finally she confronted them directly. One afternoon, when Iopa was helping her husband carry in the barley, oil, and firewood he had brought by boat, Hippodamia said bluntly: "This charade has gone on long enough. Tomorrow the three of us will leave this place. We must go to a town other than the one where you get supplies, Ekhinos, so as not to arouse suspicion. From there I will send word to my relatives in Mycenae."

The couple shook their heads. "My lady queen," said Ekhinos, "King Pelops made us swear we would not help you leave."

Squinting against the sun and trying to ignore the salt wind blowing her hair into her face, Hippodamia set her hands on her hips. "I don't care about that. I am of royal blood! I am descended from the god Ares! I *order* you—"

Iopa had the gall to interrupt her. "He said he'd kill us! He said he'd hunt us down and flay us alive!" she screeched. "And then in the Underworld, Zeus would punish us as oath-breakers forever and ever!" She looked uneasily at her husband, then back at Hippodamia, and bowed awkwardly. "My lady queen."

Though Hippodamia sought to reason away these fears, she had no success; and so she tried another strategy. Though it turned her stomach, she spoke to Ekhinos in soft, coy tones, lowering her lashes and touching her hair seductively. She did her best to arrange the undyed tunics becomingly, and moved her skirts in such a way as to give the peasant ample opportunity to glimpse her ankles and calves. In this uncivilized place, her looks might be fading, but the only other woman was Iopa – and Hippodamia was surely more attractive than *that.* Her beauty, after all, had once tempted many suitors to risk their lives.

But her efforts only caused the fisherman to leer at her more openly, while infuriating his wife. Iopa said nothing, but she showed her resentment through her actions: she spilled stew on Hippodamia's feet, let fleas get into her blanket, allowed the lamps go out, and – worst of all – she refused to empty the chamber pot. Hippodamia was forced to choose between emptying the chamber pot herself or passing water and waste out in the open. Only when she stopped complimenting Ekhinos on his strength and his fishing skills did the peasant woman resume her duties.

As the days grew longer and hotter, Hippodamia changed to another tactic: speaking of her relatives who ruled Mycenae and Argos, and reminding the servants that someday one of her sons would be king of Pisa. This did not convince the couple to break their oath and free Hippodamia from her banishment, but their attentions improved significantly. Ekhinos even obtained for her a pair of wool-stuffed cushions.

Each day Hippodamia brought her cushions to a shady spot near the mouth of the cave; she sat watching the waves lap against the shore and remembered what it was like to wear soft Egyptian linen, to have her feet bathed in cool, perfumed water and her toenails painted with henna, to sit on her throne and receive the admiring words of visiting princes and kings.

And, constantly, she prayed for Pelops' death, imagining him dying myriad different ways. Thrown from his chariot, like her father. Choking ignominiously on an olive-pit at a formal banquet. Being caught in a storm at sea, and drowning beneath the waves. Simply dropping dead without explanation, felled by one of Apollo's arrows.

If only she could stab him with her own hand! With him she would not hesitate, as she had with Chrysippus. How she regretted her cowardice! If she had done the job properly, that fool Laius would have been blamed for the youth's death, and she would still be in Pisa, spending her days in luxurious comfort – not sleeping in a dank cave, garbed like a slave, subsisting on fish and barley and olive oil from the third pressing.

One day, as she watched the sun-dazzle on the waves, she asked Ekhinos how much longer it would be until the summer solstice.

"The solstice?" he asked, scratching his head. "Oh, that's past already, my lady queen. A couple of days ago."

So by now Pelops' games were finished, and the whole world knew of her banishment.

Hippodamia felt that she should weep, but no tears came. The sun sank lower until its light reddened and seeped away, reminding her how her life was seeping away each day, empty as the broken shells that washed up on the shore.

But as long as her sons lived, there was hope. One day they would understand what she had done for them, how she had secured their position in the world.

One of them would come to rescue her, some day.

§ 5.04

The morning sun was warm on Laius' shoulders as he and Thyestes walked up to the whitewashed cottage; birds twittered in the trees, and, at a distance, the Temple of Rhea looked perfectly serene. Other than the fact that Thyestes was with him, the scene was entirely unlike two nights before.

After he knocked on the cottage door, Nerissa opened it halfway. "Laius – Prince Thyestes – what do you want?"

Thyestes answered: "To question your mother."

"We need a better description of the men who attacked her," Laius added.

Nerissa spoke softly. "She's asleep. She had a heavy dose of herbs last night."

"Papa!" shouted Polydorus. He pushed past Nerissa's knees and ran towards Laius, arms outstretched. Laius bent down and picked the child up, swinging him high into the air; the boy shrieked in delight.

"Not so loud, Son," said Nerissa, stepping outside. "Let's go sit under the pine trees. Mother should wake soon."

Laius lifted the boy up onto his shoulders and walked over to a bench near the cottage; Nerissa took a seat in the shade. Laius put Polydorus on the ground; he toddled over to Thyestes. Nerissa watched protectively as Thyestes ruffled the boy's blond curls, but Polydorus giggled and the two began a game of peeka-boo around the tree. Nerissa turned back to Laius. "You've not found the men who attacked Mother?"

He sat beside her on the bench. "No. They may still be in Pisa. Atreus is supervising the soldiers down at the harbor, searching everyone with an eastern accent, but so far he's had no luck." Laius explained that King Pelops was furious about the desecration of the temple; he was *determined* to apprehend those responsible. "I only saw them for a moment, in the dark – we're hoping your mother can tell us more. Has she said anything to you?"

"Just that they were Trojans. But you know that." Her green eyes brimmed with moisture. "Laius, I never thanked you properly for what you did that night. You saved Mother's life."

Laius scratched his chin, seeking the right words. "She was badly burned. She may not survive."

"I know," Nerissa admitted, a tear slipping down her cheek. "But if not, at least we've had a chance to say goodbye. And she knows the mastiff is safe."

Laius reached out and wiped away the tear; Nerissa took his hand. "It was the deed of a hero," she said, kissing his palm.

"I'm no hero," he said, taking back his hand.

"Of course you are! You chased off thieves; you defended the temple; you rescued my mother. What else is a hero?"

Laius picked up a pine cone and started shredding it. "I don't *feel* like a hero," he grumbled.

"I don't suppose the brave men of ancient times *felt* like heroes, either," Nerissa countered. "What mattered were their deeds."

"A hero should conquer cities, or slay monsters, or travel to distant places in search of treasure." Laius struggled to express what he felt. "They do these things knowing the dangers they may face. I just reacted on impulse."

"I think heroes become heroes because the bards sing about them," Thyestes called from behind the pine tree. "Shall I make some verses about you, Laius?"

Laius had to laugh – any song by Thyestes was sure to be bawdy. "Not just now, please." More seriously, he said: "What I did wasn't worth a song. We stopped the theft, yes; but the priestess was injured and the criminals escaped."

A moan from the cottage interrupted their conversation; even little Polydorus stopped to listen.

"Mother's awake," said Nerissa, rising to her feet. "Let me get her ready before you come inside."

After she disappeared into the dwelling, Thyestes said: "You *were* a hero, Laius! I'm sure Father will notice and reward you."

"He'll reward us both if we catch the men who did it," said Laius, picking up his son and bouncing him on his knee. When the boy tired of that, he lifted him in the crook of his arm and stood up. "Let's go talk to Polyxo."

Nerissa had opened the window-shutters, but the cottage was still dim and musty. She took Polydorus and placed him in his crib, then busied herself preparing some potion for her mother. Polyxo lay on her stomach; a sheet covered her from the hips down, but her back was bare – and covered with enormous blisters, some as big as Laius' palm. Surrounding the swollen, fluid-filled blisters the skin was the reddish color of undercooked meat, except where it was peeling away in pale flakes. An angry streak, deeper red in color, spread across her shoulder and down her right arm. That was a bad sign, Laius knew; he had seen that symptom before, in a soldier injured during the battle with Zakynthos. The healers at Apollo's temple explained it was an evil humor, which they tried to purge – but the man became delirious and died a few days later.

Though revolted by Polyxo's burns, Laius forced himself to approach her bedside. This also took courage, he told himself; Nerissa's kind of courage. "Polyxo," Laius said, sitting down on a stool beside the bed, "I need to know more about the men who attacked you."

The old woman's sunken eyes turned towards Laius. "Trojans. Came earlier that day."

He leaned closer. "Can you tell me anything more about them?"

"Offered incense… sandalwood. Then they left."

Every syllable obviously cost the injured woman great effort, but Laius persisted. "Could you describe them?"

"Ordinary," Polyxo said. "Only the accent…." She closed her eyes.

"I need more than that," Laius said. "The king wants them brought to justice."

Her eyelids flew open. "Justice!" she snapped with sudden energy, as if his comment had goaded her back to life. "Justice? Like he gave the murderess? Hippodamia still lives – he should have had her head! Vile creature!"

"Watch your mouth, old woman," Thyestes said, stepping closer.

Nerissa ran over. "Please, Prince Thyestes, take no offense! My mother's had strong herbs—"

"Not strong enough to stop me speaking the truth," Polyxo said. "I'm a healer – I know death's coming. Before Hermes takes me, I'll speak the truth about Hippodamia. It's all I can do for my grandson."

Thyestes reached for his dagger; Laius put his hand on the prince's arm. "We all mourn Chrysippus," he said, hoping to soften the old woman's mood.

"Yes," she said, her tone sorrowful. Then her anger returned. "And the woman who killed him is an abomination!"

The muscles of Thyestes' forearm tensed against Laius' grasp. "You will not speak of my mother that way!"

But Polyxo was not to be stopped. "She was cursed from the time she welcomed her father into her bed!"

Laius stared at the injured woman, more revolted now by her words than by the pus and stink oozing out of her flesh. Thyestes, too, seemed stunned.

Nerissa spoke: "Mother, you don't know what you're saying."

"Of course I do!" Polyxo snapped viciously. "Hippodamus and Alkippe, her youngest brother and sister – King Oenomaus' children, yes, but they sprang from *her* womb! The midwife was a friend of mine. She told me the truth. And Atreus—"

"Polyxo!" A shiver raced down Laius' back at the thought of such abomination. "Stop your lies!"

But Thyestes let his hand from his dagger and dropped to his knees by the sickbed. "What about Atreus?" His dark eyes glittered strangely.

"Who's *his* father?" The woman's plump hand twitched. "I don't... don't know. Doesn't look like Pelops. Looks like the old king. When he was born... who can say?" With each word, her voice grew softer. Her eyelids drifted shut, as if she had spent the last of her strength.

Gathering his composure, Laius moved closer to the injured woman and spoke firmly. "About the men who attacked you in Rhea's temple. Can you tell us anything further?"

She spoke so faintly that Laius could barely hear her: "No. No. I told you everything. Nerissa, more herbs. Now."

Laius continued questioning her, but learned nothing more. The old woman was only interested in relief from her pain. Nerissa gave her an infusion to drink, and soon Polyxo was unconscious again.

Stepping back into the sunlight and the fresh, pine-scented air was a relief, but Laius was frustrated by his lack of progress. Polyxo would die soon, and he knew nothing more about the men who had violated Rhea's sanctuary than he had known before visiting her. The king would not be pleased.

"Let's talk to the temple acolytes," he said. "If the Trojans came earlier in the day, maybe one of them will remember something." He set off towards the temple, but Thyestes caught his arm and slowed him down.

"Wait, Laius. Do you think it's true?"

"What?" Laius asked – although he was sure Thyestes meant the accusation of incest. Repellent! He just wanted to forget what the old woman had said. Why would Thyestes even want to *think* such a thing about his own mother?

"If Atreus is not my father's son, then *I* am his eldest," Thyestes said.

Laius stopped and stared at the younger man; Thyestes' face wore a sly, calculating expression that Laius had never seen before.

"Father must know already," Thyestes continued. "No wonder he always favored Chrysippus! He must have been disgusted by her, and that's tainted me in his eyes as well. But there's no question about *my* paternity – I was born nearly two years after King Oenomaus died."

Laius was sickened to hear Thyestes speak like this. "It could all be a lie," he warned. "Polyxo hates your mother."

Thyestes' eyes narrowed. "How can I find out? Who would know?" He paused. "Say, do you think *Atreus* has any idea?"

"I don't know."

"Well, the old woman's right about one thing – Atreus doesn't look at all like Father. But I do, don't I?"

Laius studied Thyestes, noting the younger man's long-legged frame and lean musculature, his large dark eyes, the shape of his face and chin, the curve of his lips. "Yes. But you also resemble your mother."

Thyestes twisted his mouth wryly. "That doesn't help. But, still, I'm *his* son." He poked Laius in the chest with his forefinger. "And Father likes *you* – so you must show me how to please him!"

Laius looked beyond his companion, towards Rhea's compact temple. He and Pelops were bound by their profound grief for Chrysippus, something Thyestes did not share. Thyestes had been shocked and saddened by the sudden death of his half-brother, but his sorrow had not run deep – only a few days after the funeral, he had been ready to carouse again.

Then there was the matter of Atreus. Thyestes and Atreus had their quarrels, as brothers often did; but Thyestes' willingness to ruin his brother for the sake of his own advancement was new. Thyestes was Laius' frequent companion – a handsome youth who shared his love of knucklebones, women and wine – but Atreus was also his friend. Laius had shared many hours with the elder prince on the wrestling-grounds, and Atreus could spot the finer points of a swordfight better than anyone.

If Thyestes pursued this matter, and Polyxo had spoken the truth, it could destroy Atreus – and if Polyxo were lying, it could destroy Thyestes. Either way, it meant more heartache for King Pelops. But there was no way to unsay words once spoken – and the incest, if it had taken place, was another done deed. There was nothing Laius could do about any of it.

He met Thyestes' gaze. "The best way to please your father," he said, "is to succeed in the task he's given you. Find the men who tried to steal the mastiff."

§ 5.05

On the second day of their flight, when the sun reached its zenith, Broteas and Geranor stopped beside a stream. After slaking his thirst, Broteas set aside the walking-stick he had fashioned from a branch and sat on a rock to inspect his wound. His injured calf was throbbing, and the skin felt hot to the touch.

Refilling a waterskin, Geranor said, "Your limp's worse, my lord prince."

Broteas grunted noncommittally. His companion was right, but Broteas did not want to acknowledge it. He had to go on, that was all.

Geranor straightened. "It would have been easier to go by ship."

"Even easier to be dead," Broteas said flatly. "And that's what we would be if we'd tried the harbor."

"But we'll never get back to Lydia if we keep going inland. We need to find another harbor, my lord prince."

Broteas shifted his leg, wincing at the sharp stab of pain. "We're not going back to Lydia. Not without the mastiff. My father—" Broteas paused, remembering his father's rage on the path to Rhea's mountainside shrine. Never mind the dream that said his ugly son was the one who could save him from eternal torment: Tantalus might not be able to control himself if Broteas returned empty-handed. "My father expects success."

He opened his traveling-pack and dug out a dried fig. They could not survive long on what they carried; they had not packed for a lengthy overland journey. They had planned to make off with the mastiff undetected, and to reach the harbor by morning.

"Then where are we going?" Geranor said. "I thought we were just going south to get out of Pisatan territory, so that we could head for the next harbor town. You can't go much further on foot—"

"I know," Broteas said testily. "Geranor, you must have faith. Lady

Artemis will guide us."

"But—"

"Look," said Broteas, gesturing, "there's a mulberry tree. Pick me some berries."

The man bit back whatever he had been about to say and nodded. "Yes, my lord prince."

As his companion gathered the fruit, Broteas composed his thoughts. Geranor was right; they needed a better plan. Yesterday had been a matter of putting distance between themselves and Pisa. But today he had no idea which way to go.

He took a handful of berries from Geranor, whose fingers were stained red with their juice. The small fruits were tart and sweet; Broteas murmured thanks to the tree-dryad for her gift. He looked around as he ate, taking in their surroundings. The stream, which likely fed into the Alpheus, coursed over a rocky bed; the hills were growing steeper, and the countryside was wild and untouched.

He closed his eyes, breathing long and deep, listening to the hum of insects. Then he rested his hand on the knife he wore on his right hip: not the workaday bronze dagger belted at his left, but his sacred knife of shining obsidian. "Lady Artemis," he prayed aloud, "you know all tracks and trails through the wilderness. Have mercy on me, your servant. Show me the way forward, and I will make you a rich offering as soon as I can."

Broteas repeated his prayer three times, then opened his eyes. Blinking against the bright sunlight, he saw upstream a doe with a white-spotted fawn beside her, both nose down to drink. He stared at them for a moment, then reached over and touched Geranor's shoulder.

"What—?"

"Quiet," Broteas hissed, and pointed.

Geranor looked in the direction of Broteas' outstretched finger. He whispered, "Do you think Lady Artemis…?"

Broteas nodded. "Yes."

The doe lifted her head and gazed at them with enormous brown eyes. Her ears twitched once and then she bounded away gracefully, her fawn scrambling after her.

"Oh." Geranor sounded disappointed. "It's gone."

"Of course it's gone." Broteas reached for his walking stick and struggled to his feet. His leg had stiffened while he was sitting; he resolved to ignore the pain. "Lady Artemis is showing us the way."

Geranor slung his own traveling pack over one shoulder, Broteas' bag over the other, and grasped both their bows in his left hand. "She is?"

"Yes." Leaning heavily on his stick, Broteas headed upstream as quickly as he could. "Do you expect the goddess herself to appear? She sent the deer to guide us."

Following the doe and her fawn was not easy, but both men were experienced trackers. The search for hoof prints, broken twigs, and trodden grass was a welcome distraction from their worries. Still, as they headed into thicker woods, Geranor occasionally whispered words of doubt: "Are you *sure* Artemis means for us to go this way?" Then, later: "What if she's tricking us, my lord prince? She didn't protect us when we tried to take the mastiff."

Broteas dealt with these anxieties as best he could, oddly grateful to Geranor for voicing them, because his own worries were similar. Reasoning with Geranor forced him to clearly articulate counter-arguments. "The deer appeared at just the right moment," he said. "There's no reason for Artemis to turn against me; I've been her devotee for many years." And then: "The gods have their own aims: there must be another reason they want the mastiff to stay in Pisa just now."

But when the sun was slipping low in the sky, they reached a stony path where no hoof prints showed. The doe might have gone in either direction along the path. A hunting dog could have sniffed out her trail, but the two men were helpless.

"We've lost it," said Geranor, dismay in his voice.

Broteas glanced around. "Perhaps this is where we are supposed to be."

"*Here,* my lord prince?" asked Geranor incredulously. His gesture took in the empty trail, the forbidding woods to left and right.

"Here." Now that they had stopped, Broteas felt too tired to go further. He sat down on the trunk of a fallen tree and rested the walking stick against its slanting surface. His calf ached, his stomach grumbled, and he was thirsty. "Give me the waterskin." His vision was blurring; he blinked in an effort to clear it.

Geranor dropped the two traveling packs and handed over the waterskin. "But why would Artemis bring us *here*?"

"I don't know." Broteas took a sip of warm, stale water. The liquid soothed his parched lips and tongue; still, he felt uncomfortably hot – and he dared not waste any of the water to cool his brow. Well, night would soon fall; it would be cooler then.

Geranor remained standing, looking one way, and then the other. "I hear something, my lord prince. Look, look there – down the road."

Broteas squinted into the distance. Geranor was right; a party was coming towards them.

"Should we hide ourselves, my lord prince?"

Broteas considered. These travelers were coming from the direction of Pisa; they could be searching for the men who had violated Rhea's temple. But Broteas was incapable of moving with haste – and if he were to die, he did not want to be hunted down in the forest like an animal.

"No," he said. "This is where the goddess led us."

"Let's hope she favors us, then," Geranor muttered, resting his hand on his dagger.

Whatever the Fates had in store for them was arriving quickly, so Broteas took a large swallow of water, then poured some into his hand and splashed his face and chest. It cooled him a little, but he realized the heat he felt was not from the afternoon sun – it was fever.

The approaching group consisted of a half dozen men, their luggage on a cart pulled by two mules; a gray-and-black hunting dog trotted along beside. As they came closer, the dog barked; the party's leader silenced it with a curt command. It was King Stymphalus of Arcadia.

Stymphalus brought his party to a halt a few paces away, then ventured nearer himself. "By Zeus!" he said, looking down at Broteas. "Prince Alexandros of Troy!"

Grasping his walking stick, Broteas hauled himself to his feet and bowed clumsily. "Good afternoon, my lord king."

The young king's eyes narrowed beneath his heavy conjoined brows. "You're injured."

"Yes, my lord king."

"They say two men were nearly caught trying to steal a golden icon from the Temple of Rhea, in Pisa, two nights ago. Seems one man took a knife wound to the leg before they escaped."

Despite his fever, Broteas felt a chill at the back of his neck. He appeared to be trapped; had he unknowingly offended Artemis? "Is that so?" he asked. He had trouble staying upright; the ground seemed to rock beneath his feet. He needed to ask the gods for help, but did not know what to pray for.

The young king cleared his throat and spat. "That's what I heard."

Broteas straightened as best he could and looked the younger man in the eye. "If those men had partaken of Pelops' hospitality, such an act would offend Almighty Zeus. But if they'd not eaten from his table…"

Stymphalus cocked his head to one side. "They wouldn't be under the obligation of guest to host. And you might find them hunting for their breakfast some morning."

Broteas breathed deeply. "Even so."

The Arcadian watched him with suspicion and calculation. "The priestess was burned. She may not live."

Broteas swayed slightly, struggling against the dizziness. "If someone sought to wound a servant of Rhea, that would be a crime against the goddess. But – but if it were an accident, my lord king, in pursuit of a – a righteous cause – well, then, amends should be made. Blood price paid. Some worthy sacrifice to propitiate the goddess."

Stymphalus remained silent for a long moment, scratching his scraggly beard. Finally he said, "That leg must hurt."

Broteas shrugged. Conversation took too much effort.

"Where are you headed?"

Broteas grasped his walking stick with both hands to remain upright. "Earlier today, my lord king, we – we asked Lady Artemis for guidance. A doe appeared. We followed her until we lost her trail – here, my lord king."

These words had a marked effect on Stymphalus' men; they shifted on their feet and exchanged glances. The Arcadian king repeated: "You followed a doe – one sent by the goddess Artemis?"

"Yes, my lord king." Broteas lost his balance; fortunately Geranor moved quickly and kept him from collapsing on the ground.

Stymphalus reached a decision. "Put him on the mule-cart," he ordered the nearest men. "And you," he said, gesturing with his thumb at a sunburned fellow, "find them some bread, cheese and water."

Broteas was assisted onto a cart; its creaking motion mingled with the general spinning of the world around him and soon, drowsing, he lost track of time. His impressions jumbled, and days and nights passed in an incoherent scatter of waking and sleeping. Occasionally Geranor helped him to eat and to drink. At last he found himself in an unfamiliar, windowless room, not completely sure how he had gotten there. He gradually became aware of a thin man who moved around in the shadows, changing bandages, wiping his face, helping him to drink bitter willow bark tea and to use the chamber pot.

Finally he managed the strength to speak. "Where am I?" he asked, his voice hoarse.

"In Tegea, at the healer's shrine," said the man, coming over with a bowl. He felt Broteas' forehead. "Praise Apollo! Your fever's broken."

"My leg?" Broteas asked, panic welling up inside him. He struggled to rise up onto his elbows so that he could see.

"Both still there!" said the healer, chuckling. With a firm hand he pressed Broteas' shoulders back down against the straw-stuffed mattress. "You're a lucky man: it didn't go putrid. You'll be walking when you get your strength back. Now, eat this."

Broteas let the man spoon-feed him, a thin gruel of barley flavored with salt. He was still eating when Geranor arrived.

"You're awake!" Geranor exclaimed, grinning, his large teeth gleaming in the lamplight.

"Yes," said Broteas, waving aside the healer with his bowl. "How long have I been here?"

"Ten days, my lord prince," said Geranor.

Ten days! Holy Artemis, ten days – though Arcadia was a remote and mountainous kingdom, it should have taken no more than a few days to reach the principal city of Tegea. He must have been lost in his fever-dreams for half a month. No wonder he felt so weak.

"King Stymphalus wants to see you."

Broteas struggled to sit up, but a wave of nausea and dizziness hit him. "I can't – I'm not well enough to stand," he said, collapsing back against the mattress.

"You're awake, and he said to tell him as soon as you woke, my lord prince. He'll send a litter." While Geranor went on this errand, Broteas allowed the healer to sponge him clean with herb-scented water and dress him in a fresh tunic from his traveling-pack.

The litter was made of unpainted wood and old leather straps, nothing like the elegant curtained conveyance used by his mother in Lydia. The men who carried him were strong but ill-matched; their varying heights made the ride bumpy, unsettling Broteas' weak stomach. Turning his head from side to side, he tried to see where they were going – the village appeared to lie behind them, and the forest on either side of the dirt road was growing thicker and thicker. Where was the palace? He could not imagine why Stymphalus would site his dwelling away from the town: every king lived in the midst of his citizens. And yet the bearers were taking him into the wilderness. Finally they turned down a side path; some distance in, they reached a clearing. At its center, on a pedestal formed by a waist-high tree stump, stood an image about as tall as the length of Broteas' arm, carved in white marble. The form was slender; its face had neither eyes nor mouth, only a high-bridged nose. Small breasts were indicated by two slight swellings on its chest above thin, folded arms, and a broad pubic triangle was carved below with shallow incisions in the marble. An altar of the same lustrous stone rested on the ground before its wooden pedestal.

The bearers lowered him from their shoulders, and rested the litter on a base formed by two folding wooden camp-stools. The four men stepped back, and Broteas looked up into the face of King Stymphalus.

"Greetings, Trojan," he said.

"My lord king," said Broteas, struggling to rise. He looked from Stymphalus' heavy-browed countenance to the altar beyond, remembering what he had heard of these barbaric Arcadians. Had they brought him here to become a sacrifice to some uncouth deity? He could not possibly run—

"No," said Stymphalus, resting a hand on Broteas' shoulder. "Don't get up – you're not ready. You look better, though."

"I'll accept your judgment on that, my lord king."

"Have some wine – it will strengthen you," said the king. He snapped his fingers and a man came over with a wineskin. The servant poured wine into a wooden cup and handed it to Broteas.

The wine was harsh and bitter; at first Broteas wondered whether it had been drugged – but if so the herbs were beneficial, for the liquid put strength into his veins. He looked around at the clearing once more, studying the marble goddess on her pedestal. "What is this place?"

"The sacred grove of Artemis, patron goddess of Arcadia." Stymphalus tilted his head toward the icon. "When you said that you were following a doe she had sent…"

"I see," said Broteas, his fear easing. Perhaps he was *not* out of favor with Artemis!

King Stymphalus bent close enough for Broteas to smell his breath. "Do you know what I'm wondering, Trojan? I'm wondering if *you're* the answer sent by Lady Artemis."

Broteas' eyes widened. It had never occurred to him that the goddess Artemis could use him to answer another man's prayers. Well, why not? And if he served her interests faithfully, then she might choose to answer *his* prayers, too.

"The answer to what?" he asked. "How can I help?"

Stymphalus frowned, fingering the wolf's-tooth necklace he wore at his throat. "Before I tell you, Trojan, you must answer a question for me. I remind you that you are my guest. I have given you food and shelter."

"And wine. And the services of your healer – without which I would have died, my lord king."

This expression of gratitude did not soften Stymphalus' stern expression.

"You're clever with words, Trojan, but I need to know you speak the truth. You will swear. Here in this sacred grove. Swear by Artemis and her almighty father Zeus."

Broteas feared what the Arcadian might ask – but he had no choice. He poured a libation from his wooden cup onto the soil. "I swear by chaste Artemis and Almighty Zeus that I will answer you truthfully." The oath was sacred; he did not dare profane it.

Stymphalus nodded. "Good. Now, are you truly a prince?"

Broteas looked directly into Stymphalus' deep-set eyes. "Yes, my lord king. I am a prince." He offered silent thanks to the gods that the man had not said 'a prince of Troy.'

"I thought so," Stymphalus said, "what with your manners and clever speech, and your skill with the bow. But I had to be sure."

"But, my lord king, I must caution that – as I intimated before – I am not welcome in Troy. Not for the time being." Of course, as a Lydian prince, he was *never* particularly welcome in Troy. But he had kept his oath: he had answered Stymphalus' question truthfully. Now he could say whatever he liked.

"I'd like your advice, Prince Alexandros," said the Arcadian king. "King Pelops…"

"What about King Pelops?" asked Broteas, staring up at Stymphalus.

The young king snapped his fingers, and a servant brought him a camp-stool. Taking a seat beside Broteas' litter, Stymphalus explained that since Pelops assumed the throne of Pisa some twenty years ago, he had expanded his power and extended his realm through many different schemes. His games and his new temples provided an excuse to demand donations – with the clear threat that those who did not contribute would offend the gods. Every four years the games increased in size and splendor, and Pelops insisted on greater and greater contributions – which, as Stymphalus' deceased father had pointed out, enriched Pelops' coffers as much as they honored the gods. Pelops promised the local lords who held the lands between the kingdoms proper that if they swore allegiance to him, their sons might retain control of their farms and flocks as Pelops' vassals rather than lose them in battle – and so, with the capitulation of one lord and the death of another, Pisa now bordered on Arcadia. One of Pelops' brothers-in-law had founded a city by the sea; another had become king of Sicyon by marriage. Pelops' eldest daughter was now queen of Mycenae, the greatest city in the region. Even the husband of Pelops' sister had managed to become king of Thebes, while the dethroned heir remained in Pisa. Pelops' army was powerful, and his soldiers had routed Zakynthos in battle; now that island nation also paid tribute.

"I see," said Broteas. "And you're concerned that he'll target your kingdom next."

Stymphalus nodded. "My kingdom's large, but not wealthy. We've no harbor, and our crops are meager. The mountain soil is full of stones, fit only for sheep and goats. We've been left alone for generations, time out of mind. But Pelops – he has plenty of sons, and too much ambition. He won't stop till he controls the whole world."

Beyond Stymphalus' shoulder, the marble countenance of the goddess remained impassive – yet even though it had no eyes, Broteas felt as if the image was watching him, waiting to hear what he might say, whether he would serve her holy purpose.

Finally he said: "What do you want from me, King Stymphalus?"

"You have the same learning as Pelops. You were born a prince, like him; raised in the East, like him. You know how he thinks. How he trains his men. How he'll fight." There was eagerness in Stymphalus' voice. "You, Alexandros, can show me how to defend my kingdom."

"An interesting proposition. And you, my lord king, you can help me regain my father's favor by bringing him the Lydian mastiff."

"A fair bargain," said Stymphalus. He got to his feet. "You must be tired. I'll have the men take you back to the healers of Apollo now. We can talk again tomorrow."

"Thank you, my lord king," said Broteas. The trip back seemed shorter than the way outward, but perhaps, Broteas thought, that was because he kept dozing off – only to be jolted awake by the bearers. Geranor was there in the sickroom, waiting for him with a worried expression; when Broteas had been settled back into bed he asked the healer to leave.

"Well, my lord prince?" he asked nervously. "What did King Stymphalus want?"

Struggling to keep his eyes open, Broteas explained the bargain he had made.

Geranor looked dismayed. "My lord prince, while you've been ill I've had the chance to poke around. It'll take years – *years* – to turn these Arcadians into any sort of fighting force."

"Then we'll be here for years," Broteas said lightly. Then, more seriously: "Geranor, if we return to Lydia without the mastiff, our lives are worthless."

The man gaped. "But, my lord prince – *years…*"

"This is where Artemis led us: this is where she wants us to be." Broteas closed his eyes, unutterably weary. "The Arcadians are her people. If we help them, then she will help us."

§ 5.06

As the skiff's oars rhythmically plied the waters of Sicyon's harbor, Amphion shielded his eyes to stare up at the city on the bluff.

"Your father was king here, wasn't he?" asked his son Damasichthon.

"Yes, he was."

"Then why aren't you king of Sicyon?"

"That title went to my older half-brother," Amphion explained. "He died many years ago, so now his daughter's husband rules." That husband was another brother-in-law of Pelops, and Sicyon was now little better than a vassal state to Pisa.

But it was Amphion's own actions that had given Pelops power over the seaside kingdom. Amphion had last entered Sicyon at the head of a raiding party, intent on rescuing his mother from imprisonment at the hands of her stepson Lamedon, Amphion's half-brother. During the raid, their invalid father had died and Lamedon had been left a one-legged cripple. Pelops, befriending Lamedon, arranged a marriage between Hippodamia's youngest brother and Lamedon's daughter; after Lamedon's death, Pelops guided and influenced his brother-in-law's rule.

In the month or so since leaving Pisa, Amphion had seen Pelops' influence nearly everywhere, though taking many different forms. Young King Neleus of Pylos demonstrated the independent bearing of an ally rather than subservience. In Argos, with its strong ties to powerful Mycenae, there was ill-concealed resentment that King Electryon of Mycenae had married one of Pelops' daughters rather than an Argive princess. Mycenae itself was imposing, its citadel protected by massive walls; its king spoke as though he had the upper hand in all dealings with Pelops – and yet, seeing how Electryon doted on his young wife, Amphion suspected that Pelops' power was greater than the Mycenaean realized.

After Mycenae, Amphion and his children went to Corinth; there Amphion took his eldest son to the famous Temple of Aphrodite. As Prince Alphenor stared raptly at the lavish display of female flesh, Amphion chose a priestess to guide his son in the sensual rites of the goddess. The next day the youth alternated between grinning vacantly and telling his younger brothers about his experience; Amphion decided not to linger lest Alphenor become overly fixated on Aphrodite's pleasures. He arranged with Captain Naucles to meet at a later date in Pisa, and hired a ship anchored on the west side of the isthmus to set sail for Sicyon.

Their skiff pulled ashore; Amphion stepped out and slung his lyre's carrying case over his shoulder. As seagulls called overhead, he and his children and servants began the long, steep walk to the city. Much seemed unchanged by the passage of years: the busy harbor, the olive groves, the hills in the distance. But, despite the afternoon's heat, Amphion shivered when they passed the path that led to the cave where he and his men had hidden themselves before the raid. So many lives had been lost in the clash between Thebes and Sicyon – and so many others had died in the years since.

"Father," Chloris asked, "do you think these people will know where to find the Maidens of Artemis?" In each city they visited, they had inquired about the whereabouts of the itinerant cult. Everyone knew of the priestesses, but none could say where to find them at the moment.

"We'll ask," said Amphion, squeezing her shoulder. "If not, we'll go to their shrine in Arcadia, as we discussed. The Maidens will return there eventually."

When they reached the top of the bluff, Amphion sent a runner to the palace to announce their arrival. Then he turned to his children. "First we'll visit your grandfather's tomb."

Leading their little procession across the agora, he heard whispers, saw fingers pointed at him by the merchants and their customers – but he ignored them. Whether they welcomed him or not, he would deal with the people of Sicyon after paying his respects to his father.

The royal tomb was on the far edge of the city; fragrant laurel trees, sacred to Apollo, had been planted around its tall beehive form. Amphion was pleased to note that the structure was well-tended: the zigzag patterns of the columns by the great oaken door were freshly painted, and the forecourt was swept clean. It was a peaceful place – a place where a king famous for his music, wisdom, and love of beauty might rest after a long and eventful life.

Amphion halted before the raised step at the front and beckoned forward the servant who carried a jar of wine. Taking the white-painted jar in his hands, he lifted it high and prayed in a loud voice: "King Epopeus, I am Amphion your son, who remembers you with reverence and love. Accept this offering in my name, and the names of your grandchildren Alphenor, Phaedimus, Damasichthon, and Chloris." He poured the dark wine onto the ground; it pooled like blood before seeping into the earth.

Wine was said to wake the spirits of the dead, for a little while. Amphion hoped that his father heard him, but Epopeus was not the only king whose bones rested within the tomb. His half-brother Lamedon might be listening as well. Facing the closed door, he said, not as loudly, "Lamedon, my brother, while you lived we had our quarrels. Let there be peace between us now."

He turned back to face his children; they stood solemnly, eyes wide in their young faces. "You know that your grandfather was celebrated for his music," he said. "The ballad that tells how Prometheus brought fire to mankind is one he composed. Let's sing it for him now." He drew his lyre out of its case and checked the tuning of the strings; then he closed his eyes, feeling Apollo's warmth on his shoulders. Silently he asked for the blessing of the god. He struck the first chord; it echoed bright and true.

In ages past, they sang, when the world was new, the titan Prometheus came before Zeus to plead for mankind.

"Almighty Zeus, lord of Heaven and Earth," he said, "take pity on mortal men! Sheep have thick fur and doves are warmed by their feathers, while humans shiver in their nakedness."

Zeus shrugged. "That is their lot."

"But, Lord Thunderer, that is not all!" Prometheus continued. "Lions and wolves have sharp claws and teeth and even scorpions have tails full of poison, but men are weak and defenseless!"

Zeus' brows lowered, and lightning flashed around his head. "As they should be! If we give them too much, they will grow proud and cease to worship us." And so the king of the gods turned his back on mankind's misery.

But kind-hearted Prometheus was determined to help the suffering people. He visited divine Athena at her loom, praising her clever fingers and bright eyes until she agreed to teach him to weave. Prometheus shared this skill with mortal women, and the humans clothed themselves against the cold of winter and night. Then Prometheus visited the forge of lame Hephaestus. He admired the smith-god's power over flame and metal – and when Hephaestus was not looking, Prometheus placed some glowing embers in a small urn. He smuggled away the precious fire and gave it to mankind; then he taught men to work copper and tin into bronze, and to make sharp knives and spears. The mortals flourished, and were successful in their hunts; in thanks they burned offerings to the gods, and the savory smell drifted up to Mount Olympus.

At first the aroma pleased Zeus – but his pleasure turned to rage when he realized that Prometheus had defied him. Zeus chained Prometheus to a rock, and sent his eagle to eat the titan's liver. As an immortal, Prometheus could not die – each night his liver grew back, and each new day Zeus' eagle returned to torment him. But Prometheus was comforted by the lights of hearth fires across the land, and the knowledge that his beloved mortals were warm and safe despite the darkness.

Amphion stilled his lyre and closed his eyes. *Accept this offering, Father*, he prayed.

"That was beautiful!" called a woman's voice.

Opening his eyes, Amphion turned around to see that a group had gathered while he and his children sang. In front, a richly dressed young woman was seated in a sedan chair, her hands resting on her pregnant belly; beside her stood the young king of Sicyon, a circlet of gold shining bright against his dark curls.

"King Amphion," he said, holding out his hand. "My wife, Zeuxippe, insisted that we come out to greet you."

Amphion clasped the man's hand. "I'm honored."

With the assistance of a handmaid, Queen Zeuxippe descended from the chair; she was small and fair, with eyes gray as Athena's. She came forward and stood on tiptoe to kiss Amphion's cheek. "Welcome, Uncle!" She smiled brightly at the children. "And, Cousins, welcome to Sicyon!"

"We have *more* cousins?" asked Damasichthon, who had been overwhelmed by those he had met in Pisa and Mycenae.

Amphion laughed, partly at his son's astonishment, but also because he was warmed by Zeuxippe's welcome. "Yes, son. But for a change, Queen Zeuxippe is *my* niece, instead of your mother's."

Zeuxippe patted the boy's cheek. "I'm so happy to meet you! I have no brothers or sisters, you see, and both my parents are dead. So you cousins must keep me company. Come, let's return the palace where we can receive you properly."

She returned to her red-painted sedan chair, and her bearers hoisted the poles up to their shoulders; her husband led the way and Amphion and his children followed, surrounded by a curious but apparently welcoming crowd. It seemed, Amphion thought, he had not needed to worry about his reception in Sicyon; the war with Thebes had occurred so many years ago that it was practically forgotten.

In the megaron, the king and queen called for servants to wash the guests' feet, and then Amphion and his children were all offered elegant new sandals: Sicyon was famous for its leatherwork. As the afternoon sun dropped lower in the sky, servants brought out platters of olives and raisins, fresh-baked bread and tart goat's cheese. Amphion's sons, especially the perpetually hungry Damasichthon, fell upon the food with gusto.

As they ate, Amphion turned the conversation to the city's tribute to Pisa. The young king described their annual shipments of wine and olive oil, raisins and figs, dried and pickled fish – as well as the worked leather belts, bags and sandals.

"We get much of our leather from Thebes, of course," he concluded. "Perhaps we could review our trade agreements tomorrow. If your people would like more of Sicyon's fish, my workmen could handle more leather. Pisa always wants more."

"Isn't the tribute hard on your people?" Amphion asked.

"Hard on my people?" He stared blankly, as if he had never considered this. "We have to support the games."

"It's our duty to the deathless ones," Queen Zeuxippe agreed. "The gods have always blessed our city. Remember, Prometheus brought the fire from heaven here first – here to Sicyon."

Amphion smiled at his niece, and then studied her husband. "That was, of course, in defiance of Zeus' command. Very daring." He watched this remark sink in, wondering whether the young king would ever dare to defy their mutual brother-in-law, Pelops.

Sicyon – the king had discarded his old name, Hippodamus, and taken the name of his new country when he assumed its throne, thus strengthening his claim – reached for a stuffed olive. "Daring, yes. But I wonder if he realized how great Zeus' anger would be."

"Do you think Zeus will ever forgive him?" Amphion's son Alphenor asked. "Prometheus has been punished so long already."

Queen Zeuxippe shook her head. "If Zeus' heart's still hard after all these eons, Cousin, he's not likely to change."

"Such a sacrifice," said Chloris.

"I wouldn't want that eagle pecking *my* liver!" agreed Phaedimus, defensively rubbing his tanned chest.

"So you'd best obey the laws of Zeus," said Sicyon.

Amphion pressed his fingertips together. There was nothing in Sicyon's manner that suggested he would risk defiance of Pelops – not unless Pelops' demands grew far worse.

"Still," said Damasichthon, "I like the song!"

"You all sang it so beautifully," sighed Zeuxippe. "And Chloris, your face is as lovely as your voice. You must have more suitors than there are stars in the sky."

Blushing, Chloris said, "I don't have any suitors, Cousin."

"No suitors?" asked Zeuxippe, nonplussed. "Why not?"

"I'm going to become a Maiden of Artemis."

"A Maiden of Artemis!" exclaimed Zeuxippe. "You want to run barefoot through the forests? To sleep out in the cold, and hunt your own food?"

Amphion covered his mouth with his hand to hide his smile. Chloris and Zeuxippe might be cousins, but the only resemblance he could detect was their gray eyes – eyes they had inherited from their mutual grandfather.

"The Maidens came through here several days ago," said Sicyon. "They were on their way to their shrine in Arcadia. Are you planning to travel there?"

"Yes," Amphion said.

"Arcadia's *very* wild," said Zeuxippe, shaking her head. "Not civilized at all."

"True," said her husband. "There's little cropland; that country's only fit for goats and sheep. But their king's a good archer, even if he didn't win the olive crown at the games."

Given his kingdom's poverty, King Stymphalus might be someone who *would* resist Pelops' ruinous levies, thought Amphion. He asked about the best route to the Maidens' shrine in Arcadia. Queen Zeuxippe had the most to say on this topic – and the more she talked about the rigors of life in the forest, the more difficulty Amphion's daughter had repressing her excitement.

While the servants poured the sweet after-dinner wine, Chloris leaned close. "So, Father – when do we leave for Arcadia?"

"In a few days," Amphion promised.

"Oh, Father!" Chloris grasped his hand in both of hers, with a smile of such beauty that his heart ached. How could he let his little girl go? But such was the demand of Lady Artemis.

§ 5.07

The sun had just set; overhead, the half moon shimmered. Smoke rose from the crackling campfire, and insects hummed in the surrounding grove. Chloris brought the required offering, a hare she had killed and gutted earlier that day; carrying the animal by its long ears she came forward to face Melissa, the high priestess of Artemis. Melissa stood on a tree stump; the other Maidens of Artemis gathered in a half-circle behind her. Each woman wore a sleeveless tunic of undyed linen; each had an obsidian dagger at her belt; each had her hair tied back from her face. The firelight revealed limbs tanned brown by living outside, with muscles made strong through the exertions of the hunt. Each woman – whether tall or short, slender or sturdy, young or approaching middle years – looked capable, assured, powerful.

Chloris squared her shoulders and prayed that they would find her worthy.

"You wish to enter the service of the Huntress?" asked Melissa. She set her hands on her waist, drawing attention to her leather belt, which was fastened with a gleaming silver buckle in the shape of a crescent. "Tell me your parentage."

The question was part of the ritual; Chloris answered it. "My parents are Amphion and Niobe, the king and queen of Thebes."

The priestess nodded. "And your father's parents?"

"My father's father was Epopeus, king of Sicyon," Chloris answered. "My father's mother is Antiope, once queen of Sicyon."

"And your mother's parents?"

"King Tantalus and Queen Dione of Lydia."

The priestess gave an approving nod. "Bring forth your offering."

Chloris stepped forward, holding out the large hare.

"This you slew with your own hands?" Melissa asked. "No one assisted you?"

"No one, Mistress," Chloris answered. "I shot it with my own bow, and cleaned it myself."

"Very good," said Melissa. "Selene, take the hare and prepare it."

A dark-haired woman came forward and took the carcass from Chloris' hands.

Melissa continued: "Only untouched virgins may serve the goddess of the hunt as one of our band. Are you untouched, Chloris?"

Chloris lifted her chin. "Yes, Mistress."

"Know now," Melissa said, her heavy eyebrows drawing together: "If you lie, Artemis will strike you down. Do you swear by all that is holy, by the blood of your mother and father and their mothers and fathers, that you have never had a man between your thighs?"

Feeling all the women staring at her, Chloris' face went hot. "By all that is holy," she said, "by the blood of my mother and father and their mothers and fathers, I so swear."

"If Artemis accepts you, Chloris, you must take an oath to remain a virgin throughout your years of service. Artemis tolerates no exceptions. To break that oath is to forfeit your life. Do you understand?"

"Yes," said Chloris, hearing a quaver in her voice. "I understand."

"Hand her the pebbles," commanded Melissa. "Position the divining branch."

A blonde acolyte gave her a double handful of small pebbles: they felt round and smooth against her palms. Another maiden placed a long, slender willow branch on the ground several paces away from Chloris and stepped back, so that the branch formed a line between them.

"Now we will see whether Artemis accepts you," said Melissa. "Cast the pebbles toward the branch. All of them at once."

Chloris swallowed, judging the distance in the dim light. She had been told of the need to bring an offering slain by her own hand; she had been told that only untouched maidens were accepted into service. No one had told her about this test. Was the goddess trying to judge the accuracy of her aim? But no one could hunt with such useless projectiles! And both handfuls at once? Perhaps that was part of the test, to manage an awkward throw with grace. Chloris glanced at the watching maidens, but read nothing in their faces.

Please, Lady Artemis, accept me, she prayed, her heart thudding loud in her chest. She took a deep breath, then pitched the double handful of stones at the willow branch. They pattered to the ground and she realized she had thrown too hard: many of the stones had landed beyond the branch. She stared in dismay, horrified by the thought that the goddess had found her unworthy.

The woman who had positioned the branch stepped closer. She bent over the fallen pebbles and counted aloud, touching each stone with her finger. "One, two, three…"

Chloris listened, her dread increasing with each new number. How badly had she failed?

The maiden stopped when she reached a count of thirteen. "Thirteen, Mistress," she said, straightening. "Thirteen landed beyond the branch."

Melissa nodded gravely. "Each pebble that landed on the far side of the branch is a year that you will serve Lady Artemis. Each pebble that landed short is a year that the goddess rejects. You will serve among us for thirteen years, Chloris."

Her dread evaporated, replaced by a surge of joy – she had not failed! And so *that* was how they determined the length of her service.

Melissa stepped down from the stump. "Bring Chloris' offering," she said.

The acolyte Selene brought a wooden bowl filled with chunks of fresh meat. Melissa plucked out a piece of flesh and smeared it on Chloris' forehead, leaving a sticky trail of blood. "Now you must swear, Chloris, to serve Artemis faithfully for the next thirteen years, keeping yourself virgin pure."

Chloris nodded. "I swear it."

The high priestess smiled; then she kissed Chloris on both cheeks. "Chloris of Thebes, you are now a Maiden of Artemis. So you shall remain, the goddess willing, for thirteen years to come."

The other maidens cheered, and crowded close to offer kisses of welcome. Someone draped a bearskin across her shoulders, explaining that she must wear it through the evening. It was heavy and hot, but Chloris welcomed the reminder of the bear dance in Thebes – the night she had *known* she was called to the service of the goddess.

With the formal part of the ceremony over, the intimidating panel of priestesses turned into a group of lively young women. Sitting cross-legged by the fire, they passed around wooden skewers and the bowl of meat from Chloris' kill; to this were added quartered onions, apples, and turnips, and soon each maiden had loaded up her skewer and set it roasting over the fire. The woman called Selene brought out a skin of watered wine, and the blonde girl who had given Chloris the pebbles carried out a basket of wooden cups. In the meantime, she started learning the names of some of the other maidens, and how many years they had to serve. Selene, a tall dark woman with snapping black eyes, had eighteen years remaining; Batia, the blonde, had sixteen years left, and a stocky girl called Anyte would serve another fourteen years. The others had far fewer.

"That smells delicious!" said a girl. "Chloris, that hare was enormous."

"Better than *your* first kill, Batia," another said to the girl passing out cups.

Batia made a face and tossed a cup at her; the maiden who had spoken snatched it out of the air, laughing.

"It's time for the stories," said Melissa, taking a seat on the tree stump where she had stood earlier. While the maidens shared out the wine and took their meal, Chloris listened to the high priestess. Here in the moonlight, dressed in the bearskin, even things Chloris already knew about the goddess seemed mysterious and wonderful. Melissa spoke of the invisible arrows of Artemis, silent and deadly, that felled those who offended the goddess. She told the story of Calisto, who Artemis punished for her unchastity by turning her into a bear and hunting her down. Her belly full, pleasantly drowsy and soothed by the lilting cadence of Melissa's voice, Chloris wrapped her arms around her knees and dozed off.

Later she was awakened by movement nearby. The blonde girl, Batia, spread a cloak on the ground and lay down.

"You'll have to say goodbye to your father and brothers tomorrow," the girl whispered.

"Yes." Chloris yawned and stretched, then lay on the ground likewise, wrapping the bearskin around her like a blanket.

"I saw them with you this afternoon," said Batia. "How many brothers do you have?"

"Six," said Chloris. "But only three are here in Arcadia."

"The tallest one's really handsome—"

"Hush, girls!" said Melissa, striding past.

That stopped Batia's whispering, which was fine with Chloris; she did not want to talk about her brothers. She wanted to listen to the cicadas in the distance, and think about the new life beginning for her tonight. For thirteen years she was bound to the service of Artemis, and that oath meant she was freer than she had ever been before: free to run and to hunt, to roam the hills, to learn the ways of the forest.

In the morning Batia and Selene brought her a tunic of undyed linen, such as the other maidens wore; they girded the waist with a leather belt, and gave her an obsidian dagger. Then Batia helped her with her hair, twisting it up and away from her face and fastening the dark thick locks with leather bands so that it was off her shoulders and out of her eyes. Chloris had never felt so light and free. "I could run all day," she said.

"That's the idea," said Melissa. "Now you must take your old tunic and girdle to your father, as a sign that you have left your old life behind. He's waiting for us at the palace. And no, Batia," she cut off the golden-haired girl before she could speak, "you may *not* come with us."

When they reached the town, Chloris felt people gazing upon her in a new and different way. Two days before, arriving in the principal city of Arcadia, she and her father and brothers had been gawked at as strangers. Now, garbed as a Maiden of Artemis, people greeted her with respect. Children waved at her, women smiled – and men followed her with their eyes. At first, the men's attention made her uncomfortable; but Melissa assured her: "No man will bother you, child. The punishment for that is death." And, indeed, none of the men approached them. By the time they had crossed the dusty agora Chloris no longer felt self-conscious.

The men standing guard outside the palace – not much of a palace, really, just a large one-story house with a roof of tile instead of thatch – gave Chloris and Melissa leave to enter. A servant guided them through the corridor, but Chloris could have found her way without him, for she heard the sound of her father's seven-stringed lyre. The music led to a small, weedy central courtyard; her father set his instrument aside when they approached. He smiled at her, but she saw sadness in his eyes.

Damasichthon gaped at her. "Chloris, you look so – so *strange!*"

"She's an acolyte now," said Phaedimus, sounding glum. "She's supposed to look strange."

Phaedimus was next to her in age, and his downcast look filled her with guilt in a way that neither her mother's resistance nor her father's reluctance had managed. She touched his elbow and then, as if she needed to justify her new status – or to make plain that there was no going back – she said, "I've taken the oath." But, instead of making her feel better, the words deepened her sense of separation. For the first time since joining the Maidens of Artemis she felt lonely.

Alphenor strode across the gravel path. "She'll come see us in Thebes," he said, and Chloris could tell he meant to comfort their younger brothers – *her* role before this day. "Won't you, Chloris?"

Chloris' throat went tight. "If it's allowed," she said, glancing at the high priestess.

"It is," Melissa assured them. "Artemis and her brother Apollo are good friends, after all! The goddess demands chastity of her maidens, but she values the bonds of family."

At this, Phaedimus brightened; Chloris' heart felt lighter.

"And you are welcome in Thebes, always," Father said. He stood, and the silver streaks in his hair gleamed in the morning sunshine. "Chloris, I want to speak with you in private. Come with me."

"What about?" asked Alphenor.

"In *private*," Father repeated. Alphenor frowned, but fell silent.

Chloris glanced at the senior priestess, who nodded. Leaving his lyre propped against the wooden bench, Father led her into the shadows of the colonnade. Chloris clasped her hands behind her back, wondering what Father did not want to say before her brothers.

"Chloris—" he began, and then stopped, looking down at his feet. A lizard darted across the stucco floor, pausing in a patch of sunlight between two columns to puff out its ruddy throat.

"Yes, Father?"

He met her eyes. "Daughter, I'm proud of you. You'll do Artemis great honor, I'm sure."

"Thank you, Father."

He set his hand on her shoulder. "Chloris, be careful," he said quietly.

She smiled, trying to reassure him. "I'm a good huntress, Father."

He shook his head. "That's not what I mean. No beast of the forest – not even a wild boar – is more dangerous than the beast that walks on two legs."

"I don't understand."

"For one thing, you're a beautiful young woman, Chloris."

She felt her cheeks flush hot. "Melissa says no man would dare to trouble a Maiden of Artemis."

He squeezed her shoulder. "No *sensible* man. But some men go mad, and others don't care if they offend the gods. Now, I want to talk to you about something else. You may not have noticed, but we were not particularly welcome here in Arcadia."

"Well…" She *had* noticed. "They don't get many travelers here."

"There's more to it than that. What, I don't know – yet. I'd hoped to make an ally of King Stymphalus, but he's kept me at arm's length." He dropped his hand from her shoulder. "Daughter, whatever it is, I don't want you involved in it. But I ask you to remember who you are."

"Who I am?"

"Princess Chloris of Thebes – the eldest daughter of Amphion and Niobe. Your oath is to Artemis – but remember what the priestess said: Artemis values the bonds of family. Your loyalty to your family must not change." He hesitated. "You're observant, Chloris – you may have been right about the voice you heard in Pisa."

Chloris started. "You mean—?"

"Yes," he said, cutting her off before she could mention her uncle Broteas. "Daughter, I want you to listen and learn – but don't get involved. Remember to put your family first."

Frowning, she said, "I don't understand."

"You will, as you grow older and more experienced. For now, I just need you to do as I ask."

His request did not seem at odds with her new vows. She nodded. "Yes, Father."

He hugged her, then brought her back to her brothers. All too soon the final farewells were said, the last message given for her mother; and then she was following Melissa through the palace halls and out into the agora. She watched the Arcadians with renewed attention, wondering what exactly had troubled her father. She could not guess – they seemed ordinary peasant folk – but she would do her best to fulfill his request.

The thought remained with her all the way back to the maidens' camp; there Melissa dispatched her and Batia, the two most junior acolytes, to fetch water from the nearest spring. Chloris took up the terracotta ewer and tried to balance it on her shoulder as the blonde girl did, then followed her down the packed-dirt path. The challenge of this task took her mind away from her talk with her father, and she thought only of the weight on her shoulder, the sound of the stream as they approached, and then the cool liquid flowing over her hands as she held the mouth of the jar to the spring.

"No, Chloris, look," Batia said. "Hold it this way. Have you never done this before?"

"No," Chloris admitted, struggling with the heavy, slippery jar. "The servants always did it."

Batia laughed. "Well, we're the servants here. The servants of Artemis. We do everything ourselves."

Chloris did not mind. It was interesting – pleasant, even: the weight of the water-filled ewer in her arms, the feel of the sun on her shoulders, birds fluttering in trees. After they passed a cluster of cottages she noticed a pair of chaffinches, the male with his bright blue head, the female drab but still distinctive.

A vaguely familiar man heading in the opposite direction passed them on the path; he nodded to Chloris and winked at Batia.

"Where's my walking stick?" called a man from inside one of the cottages. He spoke with an eastern accent.

Chloris froze. She knew that voice.

"What's wrong?" asked Batia, looking back.

Remembering her father's advice, Chloris said, "Sorry – my grip was slipping." She shifted the ewer to a different position and they continued in the direction of their campsite. When she judged they were out of earshot, she asked Batia: "What place was that?"

"Apollo's healing shrine," her companion answered. "When King Stymphalus returned from the games, he brought two strangers with him. One of them was injured, so they took him to the shrine. People thought at first that he would die, but they say he's better now; even walking again."

"Do you know their names?" Chloris asked, trying to sound nonchalant.

"No. But the one we passed back there – the injured man's friend – he's good-looking, don't you think?"

"Not particularly," Chloris said; the fellow had struck her as rather ordinary. "But, Batia, we're Maidens of Artemis. Should we be looking at men?"

"There's no harm in *looking*," Batia argued.

Chloris listened with only one ear as Batia continued speculating about the stranger who had winked at her. Of more interest to her was the man who had called out from inside the cottage – the man who had been wounded and was now recovering. She had heard only a few words, but the voice was distinctive…

Why was Uncle Broteas *here,* of all places?

Her father had told her to listen and to learn, but not to become involved. She readjusted the heavy jar on her shoulders and resolved, again, to do just that.

§ 5.08

Niobe followed her niece Nikippe into the megaron; Astydamia and the well-born girls and women of Pisa making up the rest of the procession came afterward. They were returning from the Temple of Rhea, where Nikippe had just been installed as the chief priestess. The ceremony had gone well; and then young Nikippe, crowned with a garland of purple asters and yellow mullein, accepted the people's gifts – baskets of apples and jars of honey from the common folk, lengths of cloth and beautifully painted pottery from the nobles – with grace.

The steward came over to Niobe, his eyes twinkling, and reported that all was in order for the feast. The volume of conversation rose as the guests began to take their places. Under the sound of the chattering crowd, Exarchos continued: "You've made such a difference, my lady queen. The king is truly himself again. And thanks to you, the treasuries aren't giving me anxious nights!"

Niobe smiled and whispered, "Don't tell my brother!" Of course they both knew that Pelops was perfectly aware of the healthy level of his treasuries.

"Installing the king's daughters as the chief priestesses, my lady queen – may I ask how that idea came to you?"

With Hippodamia's banishment and Polyxo's death, there had been vacancies at both the Temple of Hera and the Temple of Rhea. Niobe had suggested to her brother that his daughters Astydamia and Nikippe assume these roles. Her reasoning for this was simple: temples constantly received gifts of all sorts from the people, and the chief priestesses had authority to direct the use of these goods. At first Pelops demurred, but Niobe pointed out that using these donations to enable building other temples meant they would still go towards honoring the gods. Yes, the girls were young and inexperienced – but their positions need only be ceremonial. Once Pelops agreed to the idea, Niobe arranged for Polyxo's daughter Nerissa to continue supervising the daily duties at the Temple of Rhea; and after interviewing the women who served in Hera's temple she selected a sensible widow to manage the operations there. Then it was simply a matter of finding propitious days on which to formally install the princesses in their new positions.

"The Pharaohs of Egypt do something similar," she said. "And, of course, my own daughter must be an acolyte by now…" Niobe bit her lip, wishing that she had news of Chloris. She glanced back towards the doorway, wondering how much longer it would be until Amphion and the boys returned. With summer drawing to a close, her sons would be taller and even more suntanned, and no doubt bursting with stories of their adventures.

Unless, of course, misfortune had befallen them: an accident at sea, an attack by bandits along the road – even a scorpion sting could be deadly.

Stop it, she told herself. The pregnancy she had discovered after Amphion's departure was making her more emotional; she missed her husband's calming influence, and panicked at the prospect of doing without it forever. But there was no reason to think that anything had gone wrong; many harmless things could have delayed them. But as the days passed and they did not appear, Niobe found herself full of worry. The best remedy for that, she knew, was to keep busy.

She walked over to speak with her brother. His hand rested protectively on the golden mastiff, which was displayed on a pedestal beside the throne. Since the attack on the Temple of Rhea, the precious icon only left the king's private chambers on special occasions, and even then he did not let it out of his sight.

"She looks lovely, doesn't she?" Pelops asked, nodding to where his daughter Nikippe sat with her sister Astydamia, surrounded by the well-born ladies of Pisa.

"Yes," Niobe agreed. "She did very well today. She and her sister both seem to be taking to their new responsibilities."

"You've set them a wonderful example, Niobe." He rubbed his bearded jaw. "Now, what advice can you give me about my sons?"

Niobe looked over at the boys. The younger ones were busy with their food; nearby, Atreus was engaged in conversation with a nobleman who commanded a battalion of Pelops' foot-soldiers. Thyestes stood some distance away, his arms folded across his chest, an odd expression on his face as he stared at his older brother. Now that Niobe thought about it, the relationship between those two seemed strained. "Are there problems between Atreus and Thyestes?" she asked.

"No," Pelops said quickly, and then he hesitated. "At least, there never used to be. When Chrysippus was alive those three were always together, like the three heads of Kerberos. But now that Chrysippus is—" he paused as if he could not manage the word *dead*, then continued: "Now Atreus and Thyestes seem to have drifted apart."

Niobe said softly: "I'm sorry." She doubted that Pelops would ever truly recover from the loss of his son. Trying to distract him from his grief, she said: "Why do you ask about your sons? Is something troubling you?"

Pelops waved his hand as if trying to shoo away a moth – but nothing was there. "The usual," he said, and she realized the ghost must be bothering him. "How do I find enough resources for the next games? Which shy god is waiting to be honored? And how do I make sure that my temples are never violated again?"

Niobe attacked the issues in order. "We're doing what we can to fill the treasuries," she said. "I don't know which god to recommend – since nothing has been revealed to you, maybe the time is not yet right. With respect to thieves, you've instituted guards at the temples – and the last set of thieves did not succeed." She gestured to the golden mastiff.

Pelops stroked the dog's gleaming back. "You make many good points," he said. Then his head jerked to the side; he stared at the empty air to the right of his throne, and his frown deepened. In a low, urgent voice he said: "Niobe, are you *sure* Amphion didn't see anything?"

"Pelops, my husband's not a liar!" she snapped, exasperated. Struggling to speak calmly, she continued, "Amphion's had to fight off bandits before; he always has the Theban patrols looking out for them. And if he wasn't loyal to you, why would he warn you at all?"

"See?" murmured Pelops. "That's exactly what I said."

That cursed ghost! It was frustrating that she could not help her brother with *that* problem – but after all these years, he should not be bothered by it so. "I'm tired," she said abruptly. "Will you excuse me?"

"Of course," Pelops said, his voice so mild that Niobe felt ashamed of her outburst.

Since the princesses were occupied with their companions, Niobe slipped out without calling attention to her departure. Returning to the rooms that had belonged to Hippodamia – Niobe could never think of them as *her* rooms – she took a seat on a cushioned chair and allowed a maidservant to remove her sandals and rub her feet. Three months into this pregnancy, she *was* tired, and the noise in the megaron had been giving her a headache – but now she almost regretted departing, for there was nothing to distract her from worries about Amphion and their children. Why were their travels taking so long?

Before her mind could invent any new disasters, a servant informed her that Prince Thyestes was outside and wished to speak with her.

"Let him enter," she said.

Thyestes was accompanied by a servant carrying a tray laden with food: fresh bread, skewers of roast lamb, a baked apple stuffed with walnuts and cheese, pastries shining with drizzled honey. "Aunt Niobe, I saw you leave early – I didn't want you to miss out on the banquet entirely. The cooks have outdone themselves tonight."

"Thank you, Thyestes," she said, surprised by his thoughtfulness. The servant placed the tray on a table beside her.

"Are you too tired for some conversation?"

The glint in his dark eyes reminded her of Hippodamia when she was trying to be charming – but Niobe was grateful for both the food and the diversion from her own worries. "Not at all." She reached for the bread – it was still warm – and tore off a piece, dipping it in the small dish of olive oil before popping it into her mouth. It roused her hunger and she took up a skewer of meat, savoring its aroma as she bit into a plump morsel with plenty of fat.

Thyestes sat down across from her on a stiff chair; his posture reminded her of Pelops. "I'd like to speak privately, if that's all right."

Niobe dismissed the servants. Her nephew waited until they had all departed, then said: "It's about my mother."

She set the now-empty skewer on the tray and reached for a goblet. "Your father hasn't told me where she's being kept."

"That's not my question," said the young man, piquing Niobe's curiosity. He hesitated, as if searching for the right words. Finally he spoke in a low, urgent tone: "Aunt Niobe, who is the father of Atreus?"

Niobe choked on her drink. "By Hera," she managed eventually, "what a question!"

Thyestes rose to pat her back and then handed her a linen napkin. "It's a terrible thing to have to ask," he said. "But I must know the truth."

She wiped her lips. "Why should I know any more than you?"

"You were in Pisa when Mother and Father married," he insisted, sitting down beside her. "And you're very clever. If something – if something was going on back then, you surely knew about it."

"Whatever rumor you've heard, I—"

"I've heard that Mother slept with her own father," he interrupted her, his words pouring out in a rush. "That she had two children by him at least – and that Atreus might be the third."

Niobe met her nephew's gaze. "Who told you this?"

"The priestess Polyxo. Shortly before she died."

Niobe's thoughts raced. What had Polyxo known? She had been an herb woman before she became priestess of Rhea, and could have assisted the midwife – or simply been friends with her.

"I tried to locate the old midwife, but she died several years ago," Thyestes persisted. "Then I remembered that Grandmother wanted to tell me something, when she was dying – and Mother wouldn't let her."

Niobe had sworn not to speak of what she knew. "I suggest that you talk to your father."

The young man's dark eyes were intent. "It would explain why Father always favored Chrysippus."

"I never met Chrysippus; I couldn't say whether Pelops favored him," she said firmly. "Why aren't you discussing this with your father? This is none of my business. If you have questions, you need to speak with him."

Thyestes' handsome face went pale. "I – uh, I didn't want to bring this up with Father. It might upset him."

"If you won't bring it up, I will," Niobe said, getting to her feet. She was not about to give Pelops reason to wonder why she didn't come to him with this – especially since he had just asked her for advice about his sons.

Then she saw how nervous Thyestes looked. More gently, she said: "Come with me. We'll broach the subject with him together."

The servants admitted them to Pelops' private chambers, even though the king was still in the megaron. But they did not have long to wait; soon Pelops arrived, carrying the ruby-eyed mastiff of Rhea in his good arm.

"Thyestes – Niobe!" he exclaimed, obviously surprised to find them there. "Sister, I thought you had decided to retire early."

"I did, Pelops, but Thyestes came to see me. He has something to ask you. You'll want to dismiss the servants first."

Pelops set the mastiff on a table and waved the servants out of the room. "Very well, Son, what is it?"

"It's about Mother," Thyestes said.

Pelops tensed. "What about her?"

"I – I heard something, Father. But I wasn't sure if it was true." He bit his lip. "And, well, you see, I—"

"Thyestes was with Polyxo shortly before she died," Niobe interrupted, realizing that the young man would not manage the words on his own. "She told him that Atreus might not be your son."

Pelops frowned and shifted his shoulder piece as if it chafed him. "Very well. I suppose it's about time we had this conversation. Niobe, you don't need to be here for this. But tell the servants to fetch Atreus."

Relieved to be dismissed, Niobe left the room. She did not envy the position of any of the three men in the conversation that was about to take place – least of all Atreus.

§ 5.09

From across the lamp-lit room, Pelops looked at his son Thyestes. The large dark eyes, the oval face, the curve of his brows were all so much like Hippodamia; but the young man's physique and his square hands were the same as his own.

"*He* is yours, you know," Myrtilus said, walking over Thyestes.

Nodding, Pelops answered silently: *I know.*

The charioteer's ghost rested insubstantial hands on Thyestes' shoulders. "You always knew this might come up."

Without speaking, Pelops repeated: *I know.*

Thyestes shifted in his chair. Though he gave no sign of perceiving the ghost behind him, he looked uncomfortable. "Father, I just—"

"We'll discuss the matter when Atreus arrives," Pelops said, turning away. He paced the length of the room, ignoring Myrtilus' sporadic comments, until at last there was a knock at the door. "Come in," he said curtly.

Atreus entered. "You sent for me, Father?"

"Yes," Pelops said. "Close the door. Take a seat."

"He doesn't look like you at all," observed Myrtilus. With a sweep of his arm, the ghost indicated Atreus' thick arms and legs, his barrel-chested form, his round chin. "But the resemblance to Hippodamia's father is obvious."

For a third time Pelops told the ghost: *I know.*

Frowning, Atreus glanced at his brother and then went to sit on the couch. His posture remained stiff, his demeanor wary. "What is it, Father?"

Pelops exhaled, knowing there was no tactful way to begin. "Atreus, your brother came to me because he heard a rumor that you may not be my son."

"What—?" Atreus' face darkened, his fists clenched; he turned menacingly towards his younger brother. "Uranus' balls, Thyestes! Why would you repeat such filth?"

"Atreus," Pelops said loudly, commanding the young man's attention, "your mother was *not* a virgin when I married her."

"What?" Atreus repeated, then stared up at him.

The best thing, Pelops knew, was to be as thorough and dispassionate as possible. He continued, "Given the date of your birth, Atreus, I could not be certain that you were my son. But Hippodamia and I had an agreement. I would treat you as mine if she would treat Chrysippus as hers." He pressed his lips together. "Then she broke her word, and murdered Chrysippus."

"Father," Atreus sputtered, "how can you say this? How can—"

"Because it's the truth," Pelops interrupted. "Your mother gave birth to two children before you were born."

"Children?" asked Atreus. "What children?"

"Aunt Alkippe," Thyestes interjected. "And Hippodamus – now known as Sicyon."

Atreus' gaze darted from Thyestes to Pelops and back again. "Don't be ridiculous!" he said, but an uncertain quaver entered his voice. "They're our aunt and uncle! Mother's sister and brother!"

"Yes," Pelops agreed evenly. "They are also her children. Sired by her own father, King Oenomaus." He continued calmly, explaining the facts as he knew them. Before Pelops arrived in Pisa, Hippodamia had borne two children to her father – and there was no way to know for certain whether she had already been carrying a third when Pelops married her. As Pelops spoke, Thyestes' manner grew bolder; in a smug voice he added what he had learned from the priestess Polyxo. Understandably, Atreus grew even more bewildered and angry. And the ghost continued to gloat.

Finally Atreus said, "My lord king, I want to visit my mother – to ask her about this. May I have your permission?"

"No," Pelops said, shaking his head. "I will not reveal her whereabouts. In everything else, Atreus, you have my support. Your mother broke her bargain, but I will not."

Thyestes objected. "But, Father—"

Pelops folded his arms. "I keep my bargains. I have raised you both as my sons, and I won't change that now." He locked his gaze on Thyestes. "Be assured that I intend to live a long time. But if you are thinking of your future –

what I want to see is excellence." Addressing both of them, he said: "Show me what you're capable of. Serve me well; serve Pisa well. Do that, and neither of you will lack for opportunities."

Atreus and Thyestes glanced at each other, as if taking one another's measure. Then Atreus asked: "Father – may I still call you that?"

Pelops nodded.

"Have you asked the Tiresias about my paternity?"

Myrtilus moved closer. "That's interesting. Why *haven't* you asked her that question, old friend?"

Pelops studied the young man he had raised as his eldest son for the last eighteen years. Atreus could be hotheaded and impetuous – but he was strong and brave, a good friend to the soldiers.

"No, I haven't."

"Why not?" Atreus asked, his voice plaintive. "She might be able to tell you the truth."

Pelops replied softly: "And what if she says that you're not my son?"

Atreus gaped, as if that possibility had not occurred to him. After a moment's silence he stood. "May I be excused, my lord king?"

Pelops inclined his head and Atreus departed, leaving him alone with Thyestes – and Myrtilus.

"Father, if there's no question about me," Thyestes said, "shouldn't *I* be your heir?"

"Should you be?" Pelops snapped. "You had this information from Polyxo months ago, but you didn't come to me with it. Instead you went to your Aunt Niobe! Are you so afraid of me?"

Thyestes said nothing, but a bright red spot formed on each of his cheeks.

"You also have my permission to go!"

Abashed, Thyestes rose from his chair and left the room without another word.

Curse you, Hippodamia, Pelops thought. *Curse you for causing all this, by opening naked thighs to your own father! And curse you a thousand times over for taking Chrysippus from me!*

He knew he would be unable to sleep; as he paced restlessly, he considered taking a warm bath to relax his muscles – but he did not want to sit still, and could not abide the thought of servants hovering over him just now. The room itself, echoing with Myrtilus' taunts, felt too confining. A walk, that was what he needed. A walk, and perhaps a cup of wine – Laius might still be in the megaron. A man mercifully unrelated by either blood or marriage, Laius: a man who mourned Chrysippus as he did.

But the megaron was deserted, except for the servants working to put things in order. A pair of maidservants wiped down the empty tables, while a young boy swept the floor. And an old servant woman knelt by the great central hearth, brushing spent ashes into a terracotta bowl. Pelops strolled across the floor and paused by the fire, murmuring a brief prayer to Hestia, goddess of the hearth. Idly he watched the old woman work; the careful motions of her age-gnarled hands were somehow soothing. When she had swept up the ashes she used the short handle of her whisk-broom to poke at the glowing coals; then she laid a few branches on top, and the fire flickered to life once more.

Pelops blinked at the sudden brightness. *Of course!*

"What is it?" asked Myrtilus.

"A *shy* goddess," Pelops said aloud. There was no goddess more retiring, more self-effacing than Hestia. According to legend she had even relinquished her throne so that her nephew Dionysus could sit alongside the other Olympians, while Hestia herself sat quietly on a stool beside the divine hearth.

"My lord king?" asked the old servant woman, looking up at him.

"It's nothing," he said. "Keep up the good work." The old woman flushed at this mild praise; Pelops scarcely noticed. He had found the solution, he was certain.

Filled with renewed optimism and confidence, he went back to his chambers – where Rhea's mastiff awaited him, its ruby eyes glowing in the lamplight. The sacred flame in Rhea's temple had been extinguished during the attack: but a place sanctified especially for Hestia – an Olympic hearth, here in Pisa – would ensure that the holy flames were protected.

Laius had suggested a facility where athletes could train. What if that were combined with the hearth for Hestia? That would make Pisa a sort of second home for the athletes, binding them closer to him.

"Not bad," admitted the ghost. "Not bad at all."

And Niobe could serve as priestess. That was perfect! It kept the office, once again, in the family; and Niobe's organizational skills would be invaluable in making arrangements for the next games—

"*Niobe*?" Myrtilus gave a quick snort of laughter. "That's pushing things too far. Your daughters were one thing. But the Pisatans won't want their Olympian Hearth to be the responsibility of the queen of Thebes!"

"Amphion is already overdue," Pelops muttered. "If anything has happened to him, she might stay..."

"I'm glad you realize that she loves Amphion more than she loves you," said the ghost. "And what about her children? She loves her children *far* more than she loves yours." The ghost seated himself on Pelops' bed. "And why shouldn't she? Chloris caught the eye of every man at the festival – did they notice your girls? *Niobe's* sons won their competitions; yours didn't."

"Niobe's sons won in contests for boys, not men," Pelops retorted.

"They'll win when they're men, too," countered Myrtilus. "Look, old friend, your idea to honor Hestia is a good one – but Niobe as the priestess? Never!"

"We'll see," Pelops muttered. He thought about having his sister brought to him then and there, just so he could prove Myrtilus wrong – but Niobe was surely asleep. Rousing her would only irritate her.

Having stayed up so late into the night, it was midmorning when Pelops woke. He rose and stretched; one servant filled the basin for him to wash his face, and another inquired as to his preference for breakfast.

After splashing his face with cool water, Pelops felt more alert. He told the man to bring cheese and bread, and some of last night's roast mutton if any was left. “Oh, and have Queen Niobe brought to me. I wish to speak with her.”

The man blinked. “Yes, my lord king – but she’ll not be back for some time, my lord king.”

“Back?” Pelops said, rubbing his face with the towel. “Where has she gone?”

“Down toward the harbor, my lord king. A messenger brought word early this morning: her husband, King Amphion of Thebes, has arrived.”

SIX: CREATORS

§ 6.01

Niobe woke, relieved to find herself in her own bed, in her own rooms once more. Her husband snored peacefully beside her; the fresh breeze of a morning on the cusp between summer and autumn stirred the curtains. She looked up at the familiar patterns of the painted ceiling beams. Almost, it was as though the last four months had never taken place: as though she had never left Thebes.

Almost.

Though Chloris' absence made Niobe's heart ache, yesterday's homecoming had been joyful. She felt sheer delight at embracing her younger boys – and when Philomela and the wet nurse brought out the baby girls, she could only gasp, "They've grown so big!"

"But I still can't tell them apart," Amphion admitted.

"This is Cleodoxa," Niobe said. "Her face is fuller." She turned to the baby held by Philomela. "And here's Eudoxa – she smiles more." She kissed the top of Eudoxa's head, breathing in the scent of her wispy hair. How quickly the years had passed since Chloris was this size!

Niobe saw a bird land on the windowsill, hopping along as it pecked at insects. It reminded her of how Chloris liked to scatter bread crumbs on the balustrade to coax the sparrows close.

Amphion yawned and rolled over to face her. "You look thoughtful. What's on your mind?"

"Chloris." She took his hand in hers. "It's hard to believe she's gone."

"I know. But it's what she wants, love. And it's the will of the goddess." He kissed her forehead. "You yourself told me you're happier for her to join the Maidens of Artemis than to marry Atreus or Thyestes."

"True." She closed her eyes briefly. "But I wish she'd stayed to serve in the shrine here in Thebes instead. Then I could see her this morning when I make my offering."

In Thebes, pregnant women made monthly offerings at the shrine of Artemis, situated in the forest a short distance outside the city proper. Once Niobe had breakfasted and dressed, she left the palace with Philomela. As they walked, Niobe described the events of the games, her stay in Pisa, and the journey home; her friend responded with the occasional nod, or a smile that Niobe detected from the crinkling at the corners of Philomela's eyes above her veil. Sometimes the Athenian conveyed a question with gestures. By the time they reached the shrine, the sun was well risen and the air was warm.

"My lady queen!" exclaimed the midwife Theora. "So good to see you again!" She took Niobe's hands, and then looked at Niobe's belly. "May I?" Niobe smiled and nodded; Theora set her practiced hands on Niobe's swelling abdomen. "Just over three months?"

"That's right."

"You've recovered well from birthing the twins," Theora said. "Your next birth should be as easy as spitting out a pomegranate seed!"

Niobe doubted *that*, but she turned to the shrine. It was a simple wooden building with three walls, its front open to the sacred glade. Inside, an image of Artemis, hunting bow in hand, was painted on the rear wall; the side walls depicted deer and ibex. A stone altar used for burnt offerings stood before of the shrine; stepped shelves on either side of the altar were filled with other gifts – wooden carvings, brightly patterned ribbons, a few wilting flowers.

Niobe knelt and placed her offering – a terracotta figurine of a woman with upraised arms – on a shelf beside the altar. "Accept this gift, Lady Artemis; bless me and my unborn child." Her words were perfunctory; over the years, she had been here so often.

When she got to her feet in order to go, Niobe saw another woman approaching with a group of companions. As the sun caught the woman's coppery curls, Niobe recognized Thebe, her sister-in-law. Thebe had missed last night's banquet; Zethos had explained she was feeling poorly. Now, a basket on her arm, she was apparently coming to make an offering. Niobe felt embarrassed for her sister-in-law; of course women came to beg Artemis for the blessing of conception as well as to ask for a healthy birth, but after so many years of disappointment Niobe thought Thebe should accept her barrenness.

And yet, as she approached the shrine, Thebe did not seem downcast. She wore skirts dyed crimson and purple, and trimmed lavishly in gold; beads of polished agate adorned her neck, and golden ribbons wove through her shining hair.

Niobe walked forward to greet her. "Good morning, Thebe," she said, summoning a smile. She nodded to the other women, recognizing them as followers of the Maenad cult.

"Good morning, Niobe." Thebe swept past and knelt before the altar. From the basket she drew out sprays of hyssop and larkspur and arranged them on the altar; then she sprinkled them with incense. At her gesture one of the Maenads led forward a young black-and-white goat.

Niobe remained with Philomela a few paces away from the shrine. It would be rude to leave, but she did not wish to intrude on Thebe's communion with the goddess. As the goat was slain and more prayers offered, Niobe worried that Thebe's extravagance made her own gift seem paltry in comparison. Then again, perhaps it simply made Thebe look desperate. At any rate she was certainly taking her time. Niobe soon regretted her decision to wait: her back ached from standing in one place, and she kept thinking of all the tasks that had piled up for her in the palace after her long absence.

At last the ceremony was complete, the goat's fat-coated thigh bones roasting on the altar; Thebe rose to her feet and stepped away from the shrine. Niobe looked up at her sister-in-law, who was a full head taller. "Well, that should certainly get Artemis' attention."

"I need her help, Niobe," Thebe said quietly. "I don't want to lose this baby."

Niobe's gaze went down to Thebe's belly. "You're pregnant?" she said, trying not to sound incredulous.

Thebe rested her hands on her abdomen. "Yes."

"You're *sure*?" Yet as soon as the words left her lips, Niobe realized that Thebe *was* different. Her full breasts were rounder than usual, the gilded nipples larger. Her face was plumper, with a ruddy glow to her cheeks that had nothing to do with cosmetics. Niobe glanced at Philomela, who nodded in confirmation.

"Congratulations," Niobe said, feeling foolish. She noticed that some of the Maenads who accompanied Thebe were smirking, enjoying her discomfort. "How far along are you?"

"A little more than three months," said Thebe.

The midwife came over. "My ladies, you could be sharing the birthing chamber! May the blessings of Artemis be with both of you."

As they returned to the city and passed through the agora, many well-wishers offered their prayers; but to Niobe it seemed that there were more words of congratulations for Thebe than for Thebes' queen. As the next days passed, she noticed this again and again. "Lady Thebe is producing a child for Thebes!" she heard. "A blessing on Thebes!" And: "The gods made her wait so long – they must have something special in store for her child." Reminding Niobe that her people still saw her as the *foreign* queen, one man went so far as to say, "We rejoice that at last a Theban woman – the woman for whom our city is named – is adding to the royal nursery!"

"Now I'm to be snubbed for producing *too* many children," Niobe grumbled to her husband one evening. They were sitting in his study; Amphion plucked the strings of his lyre, humming a new tune as he worked out the refrain. Outside the rain came down hard; gusts of wind blew drops against the closed window-shutters. "I've given them nine so far – this child will make ten! Yet they make much more fuss over her!"

But Amphion shook his head. "Niobe, let her have her moment. Think how left out she's felt all these years – and look how happy my brother is!"

"She acts like she's the queen," Niobe warned. "You saw how she smiled when Chaerilis made that remark about Thebes being named for her, instead of the other way around! I've heard others say that lately, and she never corrects them."

"She's enjoying her time in the sun, Niobe. It would be petty to take that from her."

Niobe persisted. "You know there are some who resent me. And Pelops' influence, and the tribute we pay to Pisa. What if they decide to make Zethos king in your place? They say he did a fine job while we were gone."

Amphion laughed. "We both know that Zethos doesn't want that! He hated being stuck in the palace during the summer – he wants to be out with his herds."

"What he wants may not matter. Amphion, you should consider our position. We must do something to strengthen it."

He stilled the lyre-strings. "On that, my dear, I agree with you," he said, his gray eyes serious. "And I have something in mind."

§ 6.02

Dressed in his oldest kilt and a pair of sturdy walking sandals, Amphion stepped out onto the landing and blinked against the bright sunlight. With a nod he acknowledged the salutes of the soldiers guarding the palace doors and started down the steps.

He set his hand on the small belt-bag beside his dagger, and considered which direction to take. Best to head north, and then around to the west, so as to keep the sun out of his eyes. He strode across the agora, hailing various merchants and tradesmen as he went. Along the way he encountered his three eldest sons together with Damasichthon's friend Pelorus, a boy of noble birth whose father had died of apoplexy the previous year. The youths were throwing stones at a cracked urn set on a tree stump.

Alphenor turned toward him. "Father, where are you going?"

"Are you going hunting?" asked Phaedimus. "Can we go with you?"

"I'm just walking around Thebes," Amphion said, his words as literal as could be. "Would you find that interesting?"

The boys shrugged. "Why not?" said Alphenor.

"Better than trying to hit that stupid old urn," Damasichthon agreed.

"Then come along." Amphion led them north along the road that led towards Orchomenos and Gla. As soon as they had left the main cluster of houses he turned southwest, paralleling the course of Dirke's stream. The water was low, at most ankle-deep in spots, after the heat of summer. Amphion stopped every twenty paces and withdrew a bright scrap of ribbon from his belt-pouch to tie to a bush or tree.

"My lord king," asked young Pelorus, "what are you doing with those ribbons?"

Amphion grinned. "See if you can figure it out."

This set the boys wondering and guessing as they continued along. When a spot contained no suitable branch, he made the boys rearrange stones to mark their route. Still curious about his motive, the youths were willing and helpful – until he led them through a clump of stinging nettles.

"We'll just have to clear a path," he said. "Each of you find a stick, and we'll beat the plants down."

Phaedimus asked, "Why can't we go around?"

"Because we have to go this way," said Amphion.

"Ow!" cried Damasichthon, leaping backwards and sucking his fingers.

"I told you, Son, get a stick! If you beat down the nettles, you can crush them beneath your sandals." He picked up a fallen branch near the streambed. "What sort of warriors will you make, afraid of a few leaves? Old women gather them for medicine and food!" This goaded the boys on and soon they had cut and trampled a path – though even Amphion winced when the stinging leaves brushed the side of his calf.

"Father," asked Phaedimus, "why *are* you tying those ribbons?"

"And why must we go this exact way?" asked Alphenor, stamping on the hairy nettle-stalks at the edge of the patch.

Amphion stuck the branch he had been using into the ground and tied a ribbon around it. "It's a riddle for you, like the Maenads tell. Try to solve it."

"Is it something to do with the Maenads, my lord king?" asked Pelorus. "Are you telling them to stay out of Thebes?"

"No," said Amphion, leading them onward.

Soon they encountered a pair of peasant women tending their pigs as the animals foraged for acorns beneath the oaks.

"Look," gasped one of the women, "it's the king!"

"The king!" snorted her companion, not bothering to look up. "Don't be an ass!"

Damasichthon giggled; Amphion shushed him and turned to the peasants. "Good day!"

"Good – good day, m'lord!" stammered the first woman. "I mean, my lord king!"

The second woman gaped at him. "You ain't really the king?"

"I assure you, I am," he answered. Ignoring their astonished gaze he climbed onto a boulder and studied the slope of the hill. The youths took this opportunity to rinse their nettle-stung hands in the shallow stream. Then Amphion leapt down, staying well clear of the nearest pigs, and tied a ribbon to a tree branch.

Soon they were out of view of the curious women; but Amphion could still hear them.

"What was *he* doing *here?*" asked one. "With us and the pigs!"

"He's mad, sure."

"Or showing his upbringing. He was raised as a cowherd, don't you know?"

"There ain't no cows here," retorted the other woman, her voice full of scorn.

Amphion frowned.

"They're forgetting, my lord king," said Pelorus, "that Cadmus himself followed a cow to find Thebes!"

"That's true," said Amphion, impressed by the youth's reasoning.

"I know what you're doing, Father," Alphenor announced. "You want to build walls around Thebes, don't you?"

"Yes," said Amphion, proud of his eldest for solving the puzzle. "That's what I'm considering. But you will not speak of it until I do."

The boys all swore themselves to silence, and became even more interested in what Amphion was doing. They accompanied him through the rest of that day and the next, until they had completed their circuit of Thebes. And on the third day, a sunny morning just before the equinox, Amphion called a meeting of the Spartoi in the megaron.

Seated in his throne and garbed in his best, the golden crown of Cadmus on his head, he announced: "It is time to build walls for our city."

Beside him on her own throne, Niobe remained impassive. Of course he had discussed his plans with her; comprehending the massive scope of such a building project, she had expressed doubts, but she agreed not to voice them in public.

Several men folded their arms – never a good sign – while others pulled at their beards.

"What sort of walls, my lord king?" asked Chaerilis, his eyes narrowing.

"Stout walls, built of stone from Mount Kithairon," Amphion answered.

Menoeceus shook his head. "My lord king, why is this necessary?"

"Thebes is a great city; and no great city can escape attack forever," Amphion answered. "We need to build the walls *before* that time comes. For the sake of our children, our children's children, and their children."

"We haven't had war for years!" objected one of the Sown Men, a fellow whose paunch hung over the front of his kilt.

"Athens and Thebes were at war in the time of Labdacus," offered young Pelorus.

"Labdacus was a fool," Zethos muttered darkly. He had suffered as a foot soldier in Labdacus' army.

"We had war with Sicyon, in Lycus' day," said another man. A murmur of conversation started to swell, as more skirmishes and threats were remembered.

"We may be at peace now," Amphion said, cutting off this talk. "But Thebes is richer than it once was, and more populous – a greater temptation for those seeking booty and slaves." The world was also more dangerous, he thought, but that he did not say.

"If Thebes was supposed to have walls," said red-haired Menoeceus, "Cadmus would have built them."

"Things can always be bettered," said Amphion. "Aren't you glad to have wider roads? Don't you like the new Temple of Apollo, and the improvements at Dirke's spring? Don't the new cattle pens make things easier?" These were just a few of his accomplishments.

"The new cattle pens sure made a difference," said Zethos; and several heads nodded in agreement, despite Menoeceus' implication that nothing should ever be changed.

Niobe spoke up. "The greatest cities have walls. Mycenae. Troy. Tiryns."

Amphion smiled at his wife, grateful for her words.

Then Thebe added, "And *Thebes* should be the greatest city in the world!"

Amphion saw his wife purse her lips, but he was happy to accept their sister-in-law's support – she might be the one to tip the balance.

"Thebes!" cried Chaerilis. "The greatest city in the world!"

"Long live King Amphion!" shouted another – and the megaron erupted into cheers.

§ 6.03

The Maidens of Artemis spent the rest of the summer and autumn wandering through the forests of Hellas' southern peninsula; they made camp in one spot for a few days, hunted, then moved on. Sometimes they stopped near cities Chloris had visited with her father and brothers – Sicyon, Corinth, Mycenae – but the maidens never slept within doors. They camped beneath the stars, often in sacred groves; when it rained they pitched tents, or took refuge in caves. At local shrines they conducted ceremonies to celebrate Artemis; they accepted offerings of meat from men and boys who wanted successful hunts, and woven cloth from women who wanted Artemis' protection in childbirth. They traded herbs with the midwives, and shared stories about recent difficult births. And, on clear nights, they sang and danced by the light of the moon.

Following no road, their route led through the thickest forests. At first Chloris was amazed that the high priestess Melissa could find her way; her tracking skills and sense of direction surpassed even those of Uncle Broteas or old one-armed Phokos. But, as the days and months passed, Chloris learned to recognize the signs that marked their path: arrangements of rocks and notches carved in the tree-bark, meant only for Artemis' followers.

In late autumn they reached the land's western edge, in the kingdom of Pylos. They made camp on a patch of high ground overlooking the city and the ocean beyond, sheltered from the wind by several large boulders. As the sun dipped toward the sea, Chloris and Batia gathered wood from the nearby forest for the campfire while the rest of the maidens went about other tasks.

Recently Chloris' hands and feet had been cold in the evenings; she was eager to start the fire. While she arranged the wood, Batia retrieved the terracotta vessel in which the coals from the previous night's fire were kept. Batia set the small urn on the ground and used bronze tongs to lift out a glowing orange ember. She placed it beneath the stacked firewood, and Chloris covered it with dry straw; this tinder lit quickly, and the girls fed small dry twigs into the flames.

Batia rubbed her arms briskly. "Winter's almost upon us. Melissa should take us to the sacred cave soon."

Chloris never would have thought that she would look forward to spending winter in a cave, but after the last chilly night, huddled with Batia beneath a blanket for warmth, the prospect was inviting. "How far is it from here?"

"It's—" Batia began, but abruptly stopped speaking. Chloris followed her companion's gaze to see the king of Pylos arriving with an escort.

The Maidens of Artemis had not ventured into the city of Pylos, but Chloris recognized King Neleus from the games in Pisa and her visit to Pylos with her family during the summer. He was a pleasant-looking man of medium height, with straight brown hair and prominent ears.

Chloris straightened from her crouch; she and Batia edged backward into the group of maidens as the king and his men approached. Two Pylians carried the carcass of a stag, its hooves bound to a pole resting on the men's shoulders.

"Look at those antlers," whispered a priestess behind Melissa.

Batia nudged Chloris. "Even better, look at the biceps on the bearer in front."

Chloris looked deliberately in another direction.

"Maidens of Artemis," said King Neleus, "we bring this offering in honor of your mistress."

Melissa stepped forward and inclined her head. "I thank you in the name of Lady Artemis. The goddess will surely bless you and your hunters."

As the men lowered the carcass to the ground, the king spoke: "Priestess, I have come to ask for more than the goddess' help in the hunt. My wife is heavy with child. I seek Artemis' protection for them both. Will you stay in Pylos until her time comes, and assist at the birth?"

Melissa nodded. "As you wish, my lord king."

"Thank you," said King Neleus. He turned to go, and then stopped. "Princess Chloris?" he asked. "Chloris of Thebes?"

Chloris had not expected him to recognize her now that she was dressed in the garb of a Maiden of Artemis, her hair tied back and her face browned by the sun. But he surprised her. "My lord king," she acknowledged, stepping forward.

"When did you join the Maidens of Artemis?" asked the king.

"A few months ago, my lord king."

"May you serve the goddess well," Neleus said, his voice solemn. Then he turned back to Melissa. "I thank you for your help, Priestess. I'll send a runner to you when my wife's labor starts." He paused, and Chloris saw a twinkle in the man's eye. "Though I don't have any runners as swift as your Princess Chloris!" With that the Pylians took their leave.

When they were out of sight, Melissa said: "Chloris, Batia – skin and carve that carcass. We'll eat well tonight!"

Enthusiasm swelled among the maidens; the last few days' travel had left little time for hunting, and they had subsisted on dried meat, nuts, and raisins. The thought of roast venison made Chloris' mouth water. She and Batia squatted beside the carcass and drew their obsidian knives. Batia was more experienced than Chloris in dressing out a kill, but – taking seriously her duties of teaching the cult's newest member – she nodded to Chloris. "Start here," she said, pointing.

Chloris grasped the edge of the stag's hide along the belly-cut where the hunters had previously removed the organs. She turned the knife blade sideways to sever the connection between the hide and muscle and then peeled back the skin, working the knife to loosen the connective tissue as she went. There was a certain satisfaction in the act, though Chloris knew she worked slower than the other maidens. And as the sun sank below the western horizon, they grew restless.

"Hurry up – I'm hungry!" chided Anyte, a stocky girl.

"You've done enough for now, Chloris," Melissa said. "Let Batia and Anyte finish."

Only when she stood up did Chloris notice how stiff her shoulders were; she wiped her hands on a rag while the others finished skinning and butchering the carcass. As the first bright stars glittered in the east, hunks of meat roasted on skewers over the fire; by the time the sky was fully dark, the maidens were well into their feast. The first waterskin was soon emptied, and one of the priestesses fetched another.

King Neleus' messenger arrived while Chloris was eating a second skewer of charred venison. "Where is the priestess Melissa?" he called loudly, holding a torch aloft.

Melissa rose to her feet. "I am she."

The man bowed. "Priestess, you are summoned to the palace. The queen is in labor."

"Already? The king just mentioned—"

"Yes, Priestess. Her pains began at sundown."

Melissa nodded briskly, and glanced around. "Selene – and you, Chloris – come with me to assist."

Chloris handed her skewer of meat to Anyte and followed the two elder priestesses. Being second to Melissa in experience, Selene was a logical choice; but Chloris suspected that Melissa had chosen her only because King Neleus had spoken to her.

Melissa and Selene gathered several bundles; then they followed the man, their way lit by his torch. Chloris could see the lights of Pylos down below, clustered thick around the harbor like a constellation of stars. Neleus' man urged them to move quickly; in his voice Chloris heard real concern for the queen's health.

They passed through the quiet streets of the city and up the palace steps; the guards admitted them at once, and they were guided immediately to the birthing chamber. It was smaller than the one in Thebes, and its rose-colored walls were decorated only with a band of white spirals at waist height – but braziers in each corner lit it well, the floor was strewn with fresh straw, and the birthing-chair looked sturdy. On a table were bronze basins and several ewers of water, as well as a stack of folded linen cloths. The queen herself lay on a couch, wrapped in a linen robe that strained to cover her swollen belly; beside her stood an old woman in plain garb and a richly dressed woman of middle years.

The old woman introduced herself as Nossis, the local midwife. "The queen, the king's mother and I are grateful to you for coming," she said. "I've done my best, Melissa, but we need Artemis' help."

Sweat dampened the queen's curling hair. "Please," she said. "My last child was stillborn, but I can feel this one moving. This one must live! I must give my husband a son!"

"We'll do what we can," Melissa answered.

Chloris leaned against the wall while Melissa and Selene gathered information from the local women. The queen's first pregnancy, years ago, had ended in miscarriage; next she gave birth to a son who was born healthy – but soon his skin and his eyes turned a sickly yellow color, and he died before his name-day. The next child, a girl, was born dead.

Melissa nodded solemnly. "I have heard of such things."

"Priestess, my husband needs a son – a son who *lives!*" The queen gripped Melissa's hand. "If I can't give him one, he'll put me aside!"

King Neleus' mother folded her arms beneath her breasts; gold earrings flashed as she shook her head. "He won't, child. Even if it were politically sensible. He's a loyal husband."

The queen gasped; her hands went to her belly and she groaned through gritted teeth as the contraction passed. It left her panting like a runner at the finish line, but her ordeal was just beginning.

"Please, priestess," the queen whispered. "Help me."

"Yes, my lady queen," Melissa said, her voice gentle. "Can you stand?

Walking may help."

The queen was not strong enough to walk around the room, but they persuaded her to move to the birthing chair. The contractions came and went, and as the night wore on they occurred more frequently. Melissa opened the queen's robe and felt her belly, then declared that it was time for the queen to push. She knelt between the queen's knees while Selene and Chloris grasped the queen's shoulders. Nossis, the old Pylian midwife, held a lamp for Melissa.

The next contraction ripped a wail from the queen's throat, and liquid dripped onto the straw between her feet. "My baby," she gasped. "Does he live?"

"Yes, he lives," said Melissa, her ear against the queen's abdomen. "But unless you keep pushing he will surely die."

The queen nodded, and cried out again; Chloris held her sweat-damp shoulder tightly. She could smell the woman's fear.

"The head has crowned," Melissa said. "Push with the next contraction, my lady queen. Push hard!"

Moaning in agony, the queen strained against Chloris and Selene – and then Chloris heard a cry of triumph from the old midwife. She set aside the lamp and brought over a knife to cut the birth-string. There was a thin squeak from the infant, and relief washed over Chloris: the child lived.

"A girl," said the queen's mother-in-law, clearly disappointed. "But she's a fat little thing."

"Yes," Melissa agreed – yet there was worry in her voice.

Selene left the queen's shoulder and took the child from Melissa; Chloris saw that she, too, looked concerned. "Come," she said, beckoning to Chloris. "Help me wash the child."

Chloris filled a basin with water that had warmed over one of the braziers, and mixed in enough cool water to bring the bath to blood temperature. But when she looked at the child, fear touched her heart. Beneath the coating of waxy, blood-smeared vernix the baby's skin was pale, so pale – as white as the linen washcloths. And she was not so much fat as, well, *swollen.* Her breath was labored, and her tiny plump fingers strained open and then clutched tight into fists, as though she were fighting to stay alive.

"There, there, little one," Chloris crooned softly, as Selene lowered the baby into the basin.

The night was just ending as the queen delivered the afterbirth; the old midwife scooped it and the bloodstained straw into a basket, then opened the window-shutters to admit the new day's light.

"Morning's come," murmured the queen. "I'll call her Eos, for the dawn."

King Neleus' mother made a sign against the evil eye with her right hand. "No, child! It's bad luck to choose a name before her naming day!"

Selene lifted the child from the bath, then set her ear against the babe's swollen abdomen. "Oh, no," she murmured, dismay in her eyes.

Chloris saw the baby trembling, heard its wheezing breath. "What's wrong?" she whispered.

Selene spoke sharply. "Melissa!"

The senior priestess rushed over.

"My baby?" called the queen, panic in her voice. She struggled to rise from the birthing-chair.

Melissa looked at Selene and shook her head.

Her voice rising in volume and pitch, the queen ordered, "Bring me my baby!"

Chloris watched Selene and Melissa exchange a troubled glance. "Go ahead," Melissa said. "The babe will die soon." Selene nodded. She wrapped the child in a cloth and took her over to the queen.

Horror tightened Chloris' throat. "Why?" she asked, grasping Melissa's arm. "Why must she die?"

"Quiet," said Melissa. Chloris forced herself to swallow her questions, and released the arm of the high priestess. Melissa went over to the queen; Chloris remained several steps behind.

The baby struggled to breathe; her tiny body trembled with each breath. King Neleus' mother looked away, pressing her lips tight together. The old midwife stood nearby, praying; Chloris heard defeat in her old voice.

"Help my daughter!" begged the queen, her face wet with tears.

Melissa met her gaze steadily. "I'm sorry, my lady queen. There's nothing my skill can do."

"Then pray to the gods! Ask your mistress Artemis for mercy!"

"The gods have already decided to take the child," Melissa answered.

"If you won't pray," sobbed the queen, "then I will!" Her voice choked with tears, she joined the chant of the Pylian midwife; but even so little Eos' breath stopped. As the daylight in the room grew stronger, Chloris saw that the tiny lips and ears were tinged with blue – and then the infant shuddered and was still.

"She's dead, my lady queen," Melissa said.

Chloris put her fist against her mouth and tried not to weep.

The queen's mother-in-law blew her nose. "You shouldn't have given her a name."

"No!" wailed the queen.

"I'm sorry, my lady queen," said Melissa.

The king's mother left the room; she returned with King Neleus, who went to comfort his wife. Feeling useless, Chloris retreated to the shadows along the wall.

"Husband," the queen moaned, clutching her dead child, "I've failed again."

Neleus helped her out of the birthing-chair and half-carried her over to the cot. "Hush, my dear, hush." He sat beside her on the cot, rocking her gently while she held the child's body to her chest. "You did all you could," he told her. "I know you did."

Despite Chloris' efforts, tears slipped down her cheeks – but the eyes of Melissa and Selene remained dry.

Neleus looked over his wife's shoulder, and beckoned Melissa close.

"Is my wife in danger?" he whispered.

"No, my lord king," Melissa answered softly. "But she should sleep." She gestured to Selene, who began preparing a sleeping potion. The old midwife brought over a cup of wine, and when the mixture was ready Selene took the medicine to the royal couple. The queen drank and lay back on the cot, closing her eyes, still holding her dead daughter.

Neleus set one hand on his wife's shoulder, and wiped his face with his other hand. His voice hoarse, he told the old midwife: "The child – see to the child's body." Nossis took the infant from the arms of its sleeping mother and left to dispose of the tiny corpse.

The king's mother sighed. "Will she *ever* give my son a child that lives?"

Melissa and Selene exchanged a long glance, then Melissa cleared her throat. "My lady, there are some women whose children die shortly after birth. No secret of the midwife's art can alter this; the gods decide it so. But sometimes the deathless ones change their minds, and permit a child to live."

"Then we must seek the gods' help," said Neleus, his voice strained, "through prayers and sacrifice."

"Yes," Melissa agreed. Bowing to the king and his mother, she said: "Would you excuse us, my lord king – my lady? The night has been long for all of us."

"Yes," said the king. "I thank you, Priestess, for your efforts."

Melissa nodded gravely, then led the way through the corridors of the palace. Outside, clouds obscured the early morning sun, threatening rain; gusts of wind tossed dead leaves across the deserted agora. It seemed the entire world had been drained of life. Chloris stared at the sky, wondering why the gods had so little pity. That poor woman – and her helpless baby—

"Chloris, you should not weep," Melissa chastised her.

Surprised by the rebuke, Chloris wiped the tears from her face, but they were soon replaced by others. "The baby—the queen—"

Melissa shook her head and started down the palace stairs. "It's not our place to question the gods."

"But – for a child to die as soon as it is born—"

"Better then, than when the child is older," said Selene.

Chloris wondered if that were true. "Still—"

"We represent the goddess," Melissa said, her voice stern. "Do you think *she* would weep?"

Chloris swallowed hard. Did Artemis really have so little pity? But then, did Artemis grieve for a stag brought down in a hunt? Yet – though this might not be the way of the goddess, Chloris sorrowed for the child and its grieving mother.

"Would you mind," she asked, hoping her voice would not break, "if I went for a run? That might help me..."

Skepticism flickered in the senior priestess' eyes, as if she guessed that Chloris planned to weep in private. Nonetheless, she nodded permission. "Be at our campsite by midday; we'll leave Pylos then. Do you know your way?"

"Yes, Melissa." Chloris loped away through the agora; she made her way around the city's outer edge, and then eventually headed down towards the harbor. Along the broad beach men tended the ships, which had been pulled up onto the sand for the winter. Some scraped barnacles from the wood; others used odorous black pitch to coat the hulls of boats already scrubbed clean. Chloris stayed away from the bustle by running close to where the wind-twisted pines met the sand. Usually running raised her spirits, but today her heart remained as heavy as the boulders ahead. Nevertheless, she continued, and the beach began to narrow; the coast turned rocky, and cypress trees marked the end of the beach. Breathing hard, she sat down on a large smooth stone near the sea.

The baby had never had a chance! It seemed so cruel of Melissa and Selene, their refusal to weep. Yet their words about the goddess made sense. Countless mortals, young and old, died every day. The gods could not stop to mourn each one.

Still, *she* could mourn.

Her arms wrapped around her shins, Chloris rested her chin on her knees. Tears trickled down her face.

And then a shadow blocked the light.

"Princess Chloris?"

Though she could not make out his features, she recognized the man's voice. "My lord king," she said, sliding down from the boulder to greet him with a proper bow.

"You're crying," he said. "For the child?"

Chloris rubbed her nose. "Yes."

"You've a kind heart, Chloris." His voice quavered as he spoke her name, and he stared out at the sea. "I come here when my heart aches. I suppose you came for the same reason."

She stood there, awkwardly. She was upset by the baby's death – but he had lost a daughter. What could she possibly say to that? The silence lengthened, filled only by the sound of the surf against the shore. Finally she asked, "How's the queen?"

"She's asleep. Poor thing – she'll be desperate when she wakes. I must be strong for her then. I must leave my grief here." His voice cracked.

Chloris, trembling, felt as if she was observing a forbidden mystery: the sorrow of a king. It seemed a sacrilege, like Actaeon watching Artemis at her bath. "My lord king, I should go."

"You're shivering," he said. "You've been awake all night, and the wind off the water is cold." He slipped his cloak from his shoulders and draped it around her, his fingers brushing her. "Here, take this."

The cloak held the warmth of his body, and smelled of cedar and old leather; its weight was comforting. She had not realized how chilled she was, nor how fatigued. She closed her eyes, enjoying the warmth. And when she opened them and looked up at Neleus he reminded her of – no, not her father – she did not know *what* he reminded her of, but she had a powerful urge to step even closer to him and rest her head against his chest.

The impulse terrified her. "I must go," she gasped. Letting his cloak drop to the ground, she darted away.

She would not have guessed she still had the strength to run so swiftly – but horror propelled her onward. She was *attracted* to Neleus! How awful of her –

not only the urge itself, contrary to her vow of chastity, but – blessed Artemis, he was a married man! A man whose baby daughter had just died! A man whose wife desperately needed his strength and support!

"Artemis, forgive me," she whispered, as she ran. "Help me, goddess, please!"

When she reached the camp the other maidens were preparing to depart. Chloris ate a few pieces of venison from last night's feast to give herself strength, then helped the others gather their things and clean up the site. All the rest of that day, and the days that followed, she kept as busy as possible – it was better than thinking about King Neleus. A Maiden of Artemis was not supposed to have such feelings! Of course, some of them did – Batia made lascivious comments often enough. Perhaps the goddess tolerated it as long as the thoughts were not acted upon. But, even if it was no violation of her vow, what woman looked with lust upon a man who had just lost a daughter? And what if Melissa or Selene suspected? The senior priestesses were very perceptive.

Fortunately, during the journey to the sacred cave, the other priestesses seemed to attribute Chloris' distraction to her sorrow at the death of the baby. Late one evening, as Chloris stared into the fire, Melissa slipped an arm around her shoulders. "It's hard, I know. But, Chloris, childbirth is difficult and dangerous. That's why women seek protection from Artemis – and help from us. We must be strong for them."

In Melissa's words, Chloris heard the echo of King Neleus' voice. "I must be strong for her," he had said. He was kind, and wise, and firm.

And he loved his wife.

And *she* was a Maiden of Artemis! Chloris thanked the senior priestess for her understanding and resolved to banish Neleus from her mind.

Once they reached the cave, life settled into a different rhythm, and it was easier to stop thinking about Pylos. There were hazelnuts, acorns and chestnuts to gather, animals to hunt and to trap, carcasses to clean and to skin. Chloris learned the smelly process of curing leather; she learned to make tools of antler, wood, bone, and stone. She helped Selene prepare mixtures of herbs, and learned from Melissa how to read omens in the entrails of an animal. She worked with the other maidens to transform the gifts of cloth, received from pregnant women in the cities they had visited, into clothing and bedding and tents. Each day the cave – a tall fissure in the limestone with a floor of packed earth, which started from a broad open room and branched back into dark fingers reaching into the depths – had to be swept, and as the most junior this was Chloris' responsibility. Meals were cooked over the fire: roasted meat or big pots of stew. Wine, heavy to transport so far, was saved for special ceremonies, but the fresh cold water from the nearby spring was plentiful. During the long evenings, the maidens swapped stories and riddles, and they sang. Chloris was in high demand, for her voice was clear and true, and her father had taught her many songs.

And as the winter wore on Chloris realized that although the Maidens of Artemis were virgins in respect of men, they were not ignorant of love. Sometimes in the darkness she heard groans of ecstasy from a side chamber, and she knew that Melissa and Selene, or one of the other pairs, were taking pleasure in each other. In time Chloris found comfort in Batia's touch, in the warmth of her body at night – and learned to offer pleasure in return.

When the snow was piled high before the cave, the maidens decorated their dwelling with fragrant evergreen boughs and then, when the branches dried, fed them into the hearth fire. After the midwinter feast, the days gradually began to lengthen. Cold rains pelted the bushes outside the cave, and in the mornings the ground was a frosty mud; but in time Apollo's sun chariot brought more warmth, and leaf-buds appeared on the tree branches. While tracking a hare through the forest, Chloris saw a crocus pushing its purple head through a layer of fallen pine needles. She plucked it and brought it back to Melissa.

The senior priestess nodded. "It's time. Tomorrow we leave for the grove north of Tegea."

The journey to Tegea, the principal city of Arcadia, took three days; during this time Batia told Chloris about the spring rituals of cleaning and renewal. At the center of the sacred cypress grove there was a deep, spring-fed pool, where the maidens could wash their clothing and bedding, and bathe. Some spent as little time as they could in the chilly water – but Chloris found it utterly refreshing, after so many months, to wash herself thoroughly. One sunny afternoon shortly after their arrival she stood hip-deep in the water while Batia sluiced her with a bath-jug.

"Your hair's impossible," complained Batia. "There are knots in it."

"Then you didn't comb it well enough! Did I leave knots in your hair?" Chloris teased.

There was a long whistle, and then a male voice rang out. "Alexandros, would you look at that! Nymphs in the water!"

Chloris and Batia stopped and turned; a young man had pushed his way through the brush. Chloris darted from the water, heading to where she had left her tunic, belt, and knife, while Batia's hands dropped to cover her groin.

"What is it, Geranor?"

Unclothed, knife in hand, Chloris whirled at the familiar voice.

Another man – older, balding, with gray in his beard – limped through the brush to join his companion. "Ah!" he said, "Maidens of Artemis." He spread his hands in apology. "Forgive us, Maidens, for intruding—" He stopped, squinting. "Chloris?"

Chloris lowered her knife. "Uncle?" she whispered.

§ 6.04

Broteas needed a moment to gather his wits. Even faced with such a startling situation – first encountering two nude young women in the forest, and then realizing that one of them was his niece – he should not have said anything that could reveal his identity.

"Why do you call me Uncle?" he asked awkwardly. He should have been prepared for this meeting: he had learned last summer that Princess Chloris had joined the Maidens of Artemis. Of course, he had not realized that the cult had returned from its winter refuge.

"I—" Chloris glanced at her companion in the water. "You sounded like an uncle of mine. But now that I see you, I realize I'm mistaken."

He did not understand why, but she was maintaining his cover. As she slipped on her tunic, he saw that she had blossomed since the games last summer. Her breasts and hips were filling out, but her waist remained trim; her arms and legs were long, slender, and shapely.

Her fair-haired companion emerged dripping from the pool. She grabbed a garment from a stone and held it before her with one hand, then picked up her knife. "Who *are* you, then?" she asked, her cheeks as pink as her nipples. "How do you know my friend's name? And by what right do you venture into Artemis' grove?"

"I am Prince Alexandros of Troy, a guest of King Stymphalus," Broteas said, words coming more easily to him. "Any man who had the privilege of watching Princess Chloris win the race of the maidens last summer will never forget her. And as for our intrusion, please forgive us. We were out hunting, and did not know this place was sacred to Artemis." Gesturing at the two hares Geranor carried, Broteas realized the younger man was grinning at the young women with unabashed lust. "Geranor, these are Maidens of Artemis. We should not disturb them." He took his companion's arm and pulled him away.

Geranor allowed Broteas to lead him back in the direction from which they had come, but he kept twisting to look back over his shoulder. "That – that's the most glorious vision I've ever seen."

"They are dedicated to Artemis," Broteas said sternly. "To touch them is death."

"Who said anything about touching them?" Geranor asked indignantly. "I was only looking – *admiring*. Like admiring a fresco, or a carving."

"If you say so."

"Besides, I'm not the one endangering us," said Geranor. "Princess Chloris recognized *you*!"

"I know," said Broteas. He ducked beneath an overhanging branch. "But she pretended not to."

Geranor followed, lifting the branch out of the way; it snapped back when he released it, sending a bird fluttering. "Why?"

"I don't know," said Broteas. Why *had* she gone along with his story? They had formed a bond while hunting, back in Thebes – was she protecting him from Pelops? It seemed unlikely.

"You'll have to find out," Geranor continued. "And you'll have to persuade the other one to keep her mouth shut, too."

Broteas kept walking, turning over the situation in his mind. "You're right. I need to speak with Princess Chloris."

"Let me arrange it, my lord prince," Geranor volunteered. "I've seen the blonde before. *With* her clothes on. I know where she set out traps for small game last fall."

"Very well," Broteas said. "Let's head back to the palace. Stymphalus wants to talk to us." He was not looking forward to his conversation with the king of Arcadia, but he hoped that a gift of two freshly-killed hares would make that meeting easier.

The palace cook put the hares' meat into a stew with beans and fennel, which King Stymphalus seemed to enjoy. When his bowl was empty, he said to Broteas: "Tomorrow the soldiers report for this month's training."

Broteas nodded. "Yes, my lord king."

Stymphalus leaned close. "Tell me," he said, his eyes narrowing, "how are they really doing? I want the truth, Trojan."

Broteas glanced down at his wine-cup, a thick piece of pottery decorated with a wolf crudely outlined in red. The wolf was the emblem of Arcadia – the royal family even claimed to be descended from wolves.

Broteas took a deep breath. "My lord king, they're good men. Brave. Fierce." He met Stymphalus' gaze. "But they're few in number. Their equipment is not the best. And they still lack discipline."

Stymphalus rubbed the place above his nose where his eyebrows met. "You mean I'll have to keep sending tribute to Pisa?"

"It wouldn't be wise to challenge Pelops directly," Broteas said, setting down his cup. "Arcadia isn't ready."

Geranor added: "And King Pelops' allies surround us: Sicyon – Mycenae – Argos."

Stymphalus pounded his fist on the table. "I'm sick of sending the best of my flocks to him. My people go hungry while he decorates statues with gold!"

Broteas pressed his palms together. "We have another idea," he said quietly. "One your men *are* suited for. One I think you'll like." As he and Geranor explained his plan, Stymphalus' fists unclenched; by the time Broteas had finished, a wide grin split the man's homely face.

"You're as sly as Hermes himself!" said Stymphalus, fingering the wolf tooth at his throat. "If this works—"

"It will," said Broteas. "Once the men are trained."

"You'll still send animals to Pisa," said Geranor. "But it won't cost you anything."

"If this works I'll – I'll do what I can to help you get the mastiff," said Stymphalus.

The promise warmed Broteas' soul, but he replied cautiously. "My lord king, I don't see how this will help us do that."

"We'll find a way," said Stymphalus. "We'll keep thinking about it. And if we're as clever about that as we are about this plan to, ah, increase our flocks – then we'll find a way."

Broteas glanced at Geranor; they both realized that the Arcadian king had just claimed their plan as his own. Broteas shrugged. "I hope so, my lord king."

"The divine Hermes was born in Arcadia, you know," said Stymphalus. "On Mount Kyllini. And he was raised by one of my ancestors."

"Let's hope he smiles upon us," said Broteas.

The next morning Broteas and Geranor started selecting men. They had to be fit, able to run while carrying a heavy load. They needed excellent hunting skills, especially stealth. And, most of all, they needed the ability to keep their mouths shut. After two days of tests and interviews they had a total of thirteen men, making up a squad they would train.

"We'll go up Mount Kyllini tomorrow," Stymphalus said as they headed back towards town. "We'll sacrifice to Hermes and ask his blessing. I'll go arrange it."

At the prospect of such a climb, Broteas' bad leg throbbed with pain; but he nodded briskly. "Excellent idea, my lord king."

King Stymphalus strode on ahead with the men; Geranor stayed back, matching Broteas' slow pace. When the Arcadians rounded a bend along the wooded path, Geranor said softly: "My lord prince, I've arranged for you to speak with Princess Chloris."

Broteas stopped. "When? Where?"

"Now," said Geranor. "Follow me." He led Broteas away from the main path; before long they reached a twisted pine, with three main branches that formed a shape like a trident. Chloris and her blonde companion emerged from the shadows of the brush as they approached.

"Prince Alexandros," she said. "I'm Princess Chloris."

She *was* sharp-witted; she even remembered his assumed name. Broteas glanced at the fair-haired girl, and at Geranor. "I'd like to exchange a few words in private."

"Very well," Chloris said, and the two of them walked a distance away from the others.

Broteas could still see Geranor and the blonde girl standing by the crooked pine; the two were speaking, but he could not hear them, so he assumed that he and his niece could not be overheard either. "Chloris, I ask you not to suggest to anyone – anyone at all – that I could be someone other than Prince Alexandros of Troy."

She shrugged. "If you choose the name Alexandros, that's what I'll call you."

That was not exactly the response he had expected. "You're not asking why?" he asked, studying her limpid gray eyes.

"Father told me to stay out of politics. Besides, it's not suitable for a Maiden of Artemis."

"Your father's a wise man," said Broteas. Could his secret be safe for such a simple, straightforward reason? Surely that meant the gods *were* with him! When a deathless one offered a gift, a mortal should not question it – so he changed the subject. "Chloris, I'm proud of you for entering the service of Artemis."

She smiled up at him, her expression beautiful as the dawn. "Thank you, Prince Alexandros. I was inspired by your own devotion."

Chloris turned and started back towards their companions; Broteas limped behind. Despite the pain in his leg, his heart was light: he felt certain that both Hermes and his beloved Artemis were smiling on his endeavors at last.

§ 6.05

Niobe's birth-pains began at dawn on a clear spring day. As Theora had predicted, this birth was easy; by late morning she had delivered a healthy baby girl, and by noon she was back in the royal suite. Amphion sat with her a while, praising the beauty of his newest daughter in the cradle beside the bed; then, telling Niobe that she should rest, he went off to address the day's business.

Weary, content, Niobe drowsed while the maids went about their chores and Philomela spun wool into thread nearby. She had only just drifted off when a commotion of excited feminine voices woke her.

The baby began to cry. From the angle of light streaming in from the balcony, Niobe judged it was mid-afternoon. She pushed herself up to sit, her breasts full and tender. Philomela dropped her distaff and spindle and stepped over to help.

"Where are the maidservants?" Niobe asked, irritated, after Philomela had rearranged the pillows and handed her the baby. "You shouldn't be doing their work!"

The mute woman raised her hand beside her face and with a twirling downward motion of her forefinger indicated the flame-red curls of Niobe's sister-in-law. Then she moved her hands in a curving motion as if smoothing them over a pregnant belly.

"Thebe's baby is coming," Niobe interpreted, and Philomela nodded. That explained why Antiope, usually the most doting of grandmothers, was not here cooing over the infant. Niobe continued: "Well, Theora did say the children would be born close together. I hope she's ready to attend a second birth. Could you find my maid, please, Philomela? I want a cup of goat's-milk, and something to eat."

While Philomela left the room, Niobe suckled her new daughter. This being Thebe's first occasion to sit on the birthing-chair, it would surely be many hours before that child drew breath. And the labor might be difficult, with Thebe past thirty.

It occurred to her, as it had more than once these past months, that Thebe might not survive – and that this might make matters easier for Niobe and Amphion. As always she pushed the idea guiltily away. Yes, Thebe had put on airs lately, but that was no cause for such thoughts. Thebe had waited so many years for a child – surely, Niobe chided herself, she could be magnanimous enough to wish her sister-in-law well.

And. yet as the afternoon wore on, and no women visited her other than her maid and Philomela, Niobe's spirit of magnanimity slipped away. Before sunset, her maidservant reported that a crowd had gathered in the agora, hoping for word of the birth.

Niobe could not stop herself from asking: "Was there a crowd for me, this morning?"

"No, my lady queen," said the maidservant. "But you were so quick about it, there was no time for people to gather."

Niobe stroked the cheek of her sleeping child. "You deserve their attention too, little one," she murmured – though she knew it was for her own sake that she felt slighted.

Philomela set a hand on Niobe's arm; she gestured to the newborn, then put up one finger, and then another, and another, until all ten fingers were outstretched.

"That's right!" Niobe answered. "I've given them ten royal children. Ten! Doesn't that deserve their respect?"

Philomela response was a kindly smile, and Niobe fought to quash her irritability.

The crowds, Amphion reported when he came to bed, still remained outside the palace. "It's like a festival day," he said with a chuckle.

Niobe found it hard to sleep; and of course she rose several times during the night to feed the baby. Dawn found her weary, hungry, and thirsty – but before she could call for a servant there was a great cry from outside.

Amphion stirred beside her; the cheering went on and on. "The child must have been born," he said groggily.

"Your brother announces this to the people of Thebes, before he announces it to the king?" Niobe was truly angry now. "As if *he* were king himself!"

"Brother!" came a booming yell. Without sending in a servant to announce him, without waiting for any permission at all, Zethos burst into the royal bedchamber. "It's a boy, Amphion! A big, strapping, healthy boy!" He crossed to the bed in three long strides and took Amphion by the shoulders, practically lifting him from the mattress. "I have a son!"

This noisy entry woke the baby, which began to wail. Niobe sat up and swung her legs over the side of the bed, wincing at the pain in her nether regions, and picked up the child. "And his cousin is trying to sleep!"

Zethos' huge hands fell from Amphion's shoulders; he looked briefly abashed, but then the enormous grin returned. "A son, Amphion!" Though he tried hard not to shout, his voice filled the room. "And you have a new daughter. Maybe they'll make a match of it!"

Amphion rose from the bed and put an arm around his brother's wide shoulders. "Congratulations, Brother," he said. "I know you've prayed for this for years. But my wife needs her rest."

"Of course," Zethos said, and he finally did look guilty. He and Amphion headed towards the door. "I've been thinking about names. I'd like to name him for our father Idmon…"

"Idmon wasn't their father," Niobe whispered to her youngest daughter, remembering her husband's foster-father, who had died several years before. "Your real grandfather was King Epopeus of Sicyon."

The child found her breast, and with Zethos and Amphion gone Niobe could hear the sounds from outside once more. The crowd was still noisy as a festival gathering. She could imagine what the people were saying: Thebe has borne a son – while Niobe only gave birth to a daughter!

I've already had six sons, Niobe thought. And she told the baby: "You're as precious to me as any boy."

Niobe ordered a servant to bring breakfast, and by the time it had arrived, Amphion was back. He kissed her and then took the baby his arms. "Zethos is so happy," he said. Guessing the nature of her thoughts, he added: "Let them have this moment."

She drank a cup of goat's milk, feeling small and mean and selfish, but there was still something she had to say. "Listen to the crowds outside," she said. "Listen to that. What if *all* the moments from now on belong to Zethos and Thebe?"

"No one is fortunate every moment, love – you know that. Clotho's spindle is always turning, and all our fates turn with it." Jiggling the baby, he said, "Just think of everything that we've been through."

"Your brother's wife was only a servant before you took the throne," she said, "and now she's claiming the city was named for her! I can hear the peasants already: they'll say that a son of Thebe is a son of Thebes. How can we fight that?"

"I have a few ideas," he said, a twinkle in his eye. "We'll start by calling this one Ogygia."

"Ogygia," repeated Niobe. "After King Ogyges?"

"Yes," said Amphion.

Cadmus was hailed as the city's founder, but before he arrived, people already lived in the region – and Ogyges had been one of their rulers. Naming their daughter Ogygia would remind Thebans that there was an alternative to the line of Cadmus.

"It's a start," Niobe conceded. "What else?"

"The walls," her husband said.

The walls: Amphion was obsessed with the walls! The project still seemed impossible to her. But, then, she once would have thought it just as unlikely that she would ever be a mother; yet here she was, with her tenth. Her husband was a clever and capable man: if he was determined to fortify the city, Thebes would get its walls.

§ 6.06

The summer sun blazed down mercilessly; the men's shoulders and backs glistened with sweat. Their faces showed exhaustion, and against the weight of the massive stones some were beginning to falter. Amphion called for a halt, and suggested a break in the shade near Dirke's spring. The workers wearily wiped dust from their faces and trudged off towards the water.

"We're not making any progress."

Amphion looked to see who had spoken. Chaerilis, of course; the fellow was a perpetual malcontent. Menoeceus, uncharacteristically grimy, his red hair matted with perspiration, walked beside him.

"How can you say that, Chaerilis?" objected Amphion, lengthening his stride to catch up. "We've cleared the path for the wall, and tamped down the earth."

"And the first tier of stones for this section is almost finished!" said Pelorus. The fatherless youth dogged Amphion's steps like a puppy, as devoted as any of his own sons.

Zethos was already at the spring; he dipped his cup into the water and drank, then wiped his mouth with the back of his hand. "But what about the second row? And the third? And bringing stones from the quarry?"

Amphion shrugged. "We'll build the ramps to carry them up once the first course is complete. And we'll improve the roads to the quarry." Their progress *was* too slow, but as the king he had to show confidence even when he did not feel it.

"Husband!" called a woman. Zethos' wife led a group of women towards the spring, carrying baskets of food for their midday meal. Thebe was dressed, as so often these days, magnificently; a thick necklace circled her neck, and her maidservant walked alongside with a sunshade. Thebe's only burden was the infant in her arms.

Zethos dropped his cup and went over to meet his wife; heedless of the sweat and dust that caked his arms he embraced her and tousled four-month-old Idmon's chestnut curls.

Amphion sat on a large stone near the spring as the loaves of bread and hunks of cheese were passed around. He observed how the workmen's eyes followed Thebe: not as a man would watch a beautiful woman – though Thebe was that, and her gown displayed her lush curves to full advantage – but with reverence, as if they were in the presence of some holy priestess.

Or of the queen.

The true queen of Thebes remained in the palace. Niobe was once more with child, and in the early days of pregnancy she tired easily. Thebe, in contrast, seemed to be everywhere these days. Amphion sighed, suddenly aware of his own fatigue. Though he was not doing the heaviest work, his back ached and his feet were sore.

"My lord king?"

Menoeceus stood before him; Amphion gestured to a large rock nearby. "You may sit."

"Thank you, my lord king," said the man, but he remained standing. His tone crisp and precise despite his unkempt appearance, he spoke loudly enough for all to hear: "My lord king, my calculations show that the walls will take more than forty years to finish." He gestured towards the youths – Alphenor, Phaedimus, Damasichthon and Pelorus – who sat on the ground nearby, devouring bread and cheese. "At this rate it will be *their* children who complete the task."

Needing time to formulate his answer, Amphion dipped his cup into the water. Yes, the task was formidable; and he was all too aware that he was not getting any younger. But after drinking the water he summoned his most cheerful mien. "Remember how slow the progress was when we first cleared the land? But with practice, we moved much more quickly."

The men who were closest paused in their chewing to stare at him; then their gaze wandered over to the massive blocks of stone waiting to be hauled into position. Amphion knew he had not convinced them – no more than he had convinced himself.

"He's right!" chirped Thebe. "We're Thebans – we'll find a way!" She patted her husband's arm. "My Zethos is the strongest man alive!"

Zethos grinned and flexed a bicep; the men laughed, and a few clapped.

"And if it takes forty years – which I'm sure it won't," Thebe continued, "little Idmon here will complete it!"

At this the men cheered outright, and went back to their meal with more energy than Amphion had seen in several days. Amphion chewed a piece of bread, considering this. He was pleased that Thebe had heartened the men, but he heard the underlying challenge: she implied that his brother Zethos would be a better leader, and that *her* son would take over. This, when three of his own sons labored on the walls!

Niobe was right. Thebe was ambitious.

Thebe held her son high; the infant laughed. She swung him down and lifted him again, smiling. "Zethos," she said, "why not have a competition?"

"A competition?" Zethos asked.

"Like the contests they hold in Pisa." Thebe turned to Amphion. "Who can build a section of wall faster: you, my lord king, or your brother Zethos?"

"A contest!" Zethos repeated. "That's a good idea!" But the tone of his voice was strained, and he looked away.

Amphion realized that Zethos and Thebe had planned this in advance. It had to be Thebe's doing, for his brother *never* challenged him. But here it was. Declining the challenge would make him appear weak – in front of his sons as well as his subjects. "Very well," Amphion agreed, looking straight at the couple. "Let's pick teams and set up the rules."

Though Zethos was unwilling to meet his gaze, Thebe had no such problem. Her blue eyes sparked with defiance. "What will be the prize?"

Amphion guessed that she wanted the very kingship to be at stake. But before anyone could suggest this, he said: "In Olympia the contestants vie for honor. Their only other prize is the olive wreath."

Thebe's coppery brows drew together. "But for *such* an effort…"

The men and women muttered, while Amphion's mind raced. But – either because his body was fatigued from the morning's labor or because his spirit felt betrayed by this challenge from his brother – his mind found nothing.

Then young Pelorus said: "How about the privilege of naming the gates?"

The muttering stopped; Pelorus' cheeks reddened as the crowd stared at him.

"That would be a real honor," ventured Alphenor.

"And an *earned* one." This came from Menoeceus, who – well-versed in Theban history – ridiculed those who claimed their city was named for Zethos' wife.

The right to name the gates – Amphion did not want to put that at risk! He looked from Thebe to Zethos and back again, but he was unable to find any reasonable objection. Why was he so slow this afternoon?

He nodded reluctantly.

Over the next few days they decided the rules for the competition and formed their teams. Zethos seemed to attract the strongest men – many herdsmen joined him, and several of the soldiers, including Chaerilis and his nephew Chabrias. But Amphion's team included many of the soldiers as well, and a larger proportion of tradesmen and merchants – including the sea captain Naucles, who was in town with his partner Euxenos. Menoeceus, who disliked hard labor and was not particularly good at it, declined to participate at all; he asserted that some of the Spartoi needed to remain outside the competition in order to judge it. He was joined by old Phokos, whose missing arm prevented him from being much use to either of his stepsons.

Two building sites were selected, on opposite sides of Thebes. Zethos' team had an eastern section, while Amphion chose a location on the western side of town. "It's half a day's walk from one site to the other," Menoeceus explained. "That will reduce any temptation to mischief."

"What mischief?" Zethos' roar echoed across the megaron. "This is just a friendly competition between brothers."

From her throne beside Amphion's, Niobe spoke: "Remember, the walls will protect *all* of Thebes."

Thebe's eyes glittered. "Of course."

"No matter what happens, I'll be proud of both my sons," said Amphion's mother, who had both Idmon and Ogygia on her lap.

Several days into the contest, after many long hours of toil, Amphion and his men climbed back up the hill to the city. The sun had already set behind them, and the sky was quickly growing dark. Dirty, hungry, exhausted, most went straight to their homes, but several accompanied Amphion to the palace, where Zethos and part of his team were already in the megaron. As had become the custom, Zethos' men clustered on the eastern side of the room; Amphion's team sat towards the west, while the servants brought basins to wash the men's grimy hands and feet.

"A long day, my love," Niobe said softly as Amphion took his seat on the throne.

He nodded. "We had trouble shifting the last stone into place." Glancing across the room, Amphion saw that his brother's team also looked weary – but they were not as worn out as his own.

By Apollo, he had never thought that *Zethos* would turn on him! If he lost this contest, it would diminish his standing. Already he had heard whispers that since he and Zethos were twins, Zethos had as much right to rule Thebes as he.

A servant girl arrived carrying a basin filled with lavender-scented water; Amphion rinsed his hands and dried them on the proffered towel, then wiped his face while the servant settled the basin at his feet and unbuckled his sandals. He eased his feet into the cool, soothing water.

"How about some music, Brother?" shouted Zethos.

Amphion shook his head. "Not tonight."

"He's too tired," snickered Chabrias. Amphion frowned, and Zethos hushed the younger man. But Amphion noticed Thebe's smirk.

The girl patted his feet dry and slipped them into soft house-shoes; another servant handed him a goblet of watered wine. He had not realized just how thirsty he was until his first sip – he quickly drained the goblet and held it out to be refilled. The scent of the meal being served made Amphion's mouth water. Roast beef, fresh-baked bread, barley boiled with garlic, onions and spices – his stomach growled so loudly that even Niobe raised an eyebrow.

As the servants filled everyone's plates, the herald announced Phokos, Menoeceus, and Menoeceus' young son Creon. The small boy had his father's features but not his coloring; Kreon was dark-haired like his dead mother. Imitating his father, the child bowed to both Amphion and Zethos, and he repeated the ceremonial words of greeting in a high-pitched lisp.

Then Menoeceus lifted his wax-covered writing tablet. "Would my lord king care to hear the day's tally?"

Amphion swallowed his mouthful of bread. "Yes, of course."

"Seven stones moved by Lord Zethos' team; three by yours, my lord king."

A cheer rose from Zethos and his men; those on the western side of the megaron groaned. Phokos went first to congratulate Zethos, and then over to join his wife Antiope, who poured a cup of wine for him.

"You can't keep this up," Niobe said softly, when people had stopped looking at them. "Zethos' team is stronger, so you'll have to be smarter."

Amphion speared a bite of meat on his knife. "I'd be glad for a suggestion."

Niobe frowned, tapped a finger against her lips, then motioned to the sea captain and his partner. "Naucles, Euxenos – we would speak with you."

The two men, who had worked alongside Amphion all day, pushed aside their plates and came to stand before the royal table.

"You've traveled in Egypt," Niobe said.

"Of course, my lady queen," answered sandy-haired Euxenos, who was married to an Egyptian woman that he had brought with him to Thebes. Their small daughter was a stunning child with skin the color of amber.

"Then you've seen the pyramids," Niobe continued.

Both men nodded. "They're amazing, my lady queen," said Naucles.

"Enormous," Euxenos added. "The size of mountains!"

Amphion set down his knife. "How were they built?"

Naucles looked at his partner, but Euxenos shook his head. "They're ancient, my lord king. They've been there for thousands of years. No one knows how they were built."

"The Pharaohs claim to be divine," Naucles added. "Perhaps their gods helped them."

"That's possible," said Euxenos. "Just as the Cyclopes built the walls of Mycenae, Athens and Tiryns."

This was not helpful, as Amphion had no one-eyed giants on his team. "Egypt is a crowded country, isn't it?"

Yes, my lord king," said Naucles. "The people are numerous as the grains of sand on a beach."

Euxenos nodded. "Next to the cities of Egypt, Thebes is a village. Thebes is to Egypt like a torch is to the fire of the sun—" The man broke off suddenly, and glanced nervously from Amphion to Niobe, as if he feared he had offended his king and his queen.

But Amphion only shrugged. "So the Pharaohs may have used thousands of men to build these pyramids," he said to Niobe. "And who knows how long they took to complete?" He turned back to the merchants. "Thank you. You may return to your meal."

Fatigued and frustrated, Amphion ended the evening early. He and Niobe retired to their chambers; kicking off his house-shoes, he stretched out on the bed. "I almost wish I'd never started these walls."

Sitting on her dressing-stool while her maid let down her hair, Niobe said: "Giving up would be worse than never starting."

Amphion stared up at the ceiling. "And Thebes *needs* walls."

For a time they remained silent, while Niobe's maid combed out the queen's long hair. Closing his eyes, Amphion pictured the massive walls of Tiryns, Mycenae, and Athens. If only he could summon a group of Cyclopes to do the labor here in Thebes! But he had no giants at his disposal, one-eyed or otherwise. Nor could he call upon hordes of Egyptian workmen. If he were of divine birth, like the Pharaohs, he could ask the gods…

Wait. Why *couldn't* he ask the gods for help?

When the project was begun, he had sacrificed a bull, asking the gods – especially his patron god, Apollo – to bless the endeavor. He had sprinkled the bull's blood, mixed with wine and olive oil, along the route where the walls were to be built. But he had never asked the gods for advice. It was time to change that.

He sat up and called to his manservant. "Bring me my walking sandals."

"Where are you going at this hour?" Niobe asked, twisting around so suddenly that her maidservant dropped the ivory comb.

"The Temple of Apollo," he said as the servant fastened the sandals on his feet.

"In the dark? When you're so tired?"

"I'll sleep there tonight," he said, getting to his feet. "I'll ask Apollo to send me an answer in a dream." He kissed Niobe on the forehead and picked up the jug of wine that stood on the side table.

As he strode out of the room he heard her mutter, "Husbands!" with both exasperation and fondness.

Amphion grabbed a torch from a wall-sconce in the corridor and started out into the night, heading east towards the Temple of Apollo. His feet traced the familiar path: down from the agora, across the summer-shrunken stream of Chrysorrhoas, and then up the slope of the neighboring hill. Cicadas buzzed in the trees; at one point he heard an owl, and whispered a prayer to Athena, asking the goddess for wisdom. At the top of the rise, the temple's white walls gleamed in the moonlight.

Reaching the summit, Amphion stopped before the marble forecourt. He poured a libation of wine onto the ground, then raised his hands and spoke: "Lords of Olympus, accept my gift; hear my prayer. Show me how to build these walls. Almighty Zeus, give us strength. Athena, grant me wisdom – and Hermes, lend me your cleverness. Dionysus, help me protect Thebes, which is so dear to you. Apollo, master of music: if my songs have ever pleased you, I ask you now to light my way."

Amphion then crossed the broad portico, passing the outer altar where burnt offerings were made. A white-robed acolyte was inside the temple, sitting beside the fire beneath Apollo's wooden image. The man had obviously heard his king's prayer, and nodded with understanding when Amphion explained that he had come to seek a dream from the god. The acolyte took Amphion's torch, fitted it into a wall bracket and then opened a painted cedar chest to retrieve a pallet and a blanket. These he spread on the tiled floor of the sanctuary, between the small inner altar and the image of the god.

"May Apollo Light-bringer send you the answer you need, my lord king," said the acolyte. He went outside, leaving Amphion alone with the god.

Amphion settled down on the wool-stuffed pallet and covered himself with the blanket, staring up at the god's painted face. In the light of the altar-fire Apollo's expression seemed to shift from moment to moment, as though the image were imbued with the god's presence.

Feeling the weight of what he was doing – Amphion had never before sought the god's assistance so directly – at first he feared sleep would elude him. But eventually his exhaustion returned. With the warmth of the altar-fire at his back and the god watching over him, he soon slept.

The sound of a broom brushing across the floor-tiles woke him; then he heard the song of a lark outside the temple. He stretched and sat up, feeling the stiffness in his arms and back from the previous day's labor.

The senior priest approached, bowing. "My lord king! May Apollo bless you! Did the god send you the answer that you sought?"

Amphion searched his thoughts, trying to recall his dreams... and found nothing.

No dreams at all.

It seemed that the gods were indifferent to the construction of the city walls. Or indifferent to the city's king. They were willing to sweep him aside, even as the acolyte swept away pebbles with his broom.

Amphion's heart felt as heavy as stone.

"My lord king?" the priest repeated, concern coloring his voice.

Amphion forced himself to smile, and with an effort he climbed to his feet. He accepted a piece of bread and a cup of water from the priest, then did the only thing he could do: he walked out to face the day. His men would soon be gathering at the western building site; he owed them the courtesy of a timely arrival.

Puddles on the ground indicated that it had rained overnight, yet Amphion remembered the storm no better than he remembered any dream. It was as though those hours had vanished for him.

Though he was not looking forward to the day, Amphion kept his pace swift. When he reached the spot where the path crossed the Chrysorrhoas he found an elderly couple whose mule cart was mired in the mud. The woman lashed at the beast with a goad, and the old man strained to push, but the cart's wheels did not budge.

"Hello, citizens!" Amphion said.

Startled, the old man slipped and fell on his rump, while the gray-haired woman gaped at him, her goad held high. The mule swished its tail indifferently.

Amphion suppressed the impulse to laugh at the scene before him. "Here," Amphion said, "let me help you free your cart."

The old man climbed back to his feet, brushing at the mud on his rear. "My lord king, d'you really think you – I – I mean, you shouldn't waste your time on the likes of us!"

Amphion heard doubt in the peasant's first aborted sentence; surely the man thought Zethos' strength would be better help in this instance. But in his youth Amphion had wrangled many carts over the roads surrounding Thebes.

"No, no, we can do it. Just wait a moment." He stepped over to the trees that lined the streambed, searching for a pair of sturdy branches among the deadfall; soon he found what he needed. He kept the shorter branch for himself and handed the other to the old man. "We can pry the wheels loose with these," he said. He went to the right rear wheel, which had sunk deep into the mud. Examining more closely, Amphion saw it was also blocked by stones; he had to wedge his branch between the stones to get at the wheel. The old man's access to the left wheel was much clearer.

When they were both in position, Amphion told the woman, "We'll pry it loose on the count of three. Give the beast the goad then." She nodded, and Amphion turned to the old man. "Ready? One … two … three!"

The woman shouted at the mule and struck it with her goad; Amphion and the old man leaned down on their branches. The left wheel moved only a little, but Amphion's own branch, wedged against the rock, achieved better traction. In a moment the wheel popped free of the mud, and the cart rolled forward.

"Aha!" cried the old woman, clapping her hands together. "You did it, my lord king! Sent by the gods, you were!"

Amphion studied the branch in his hands. In his youth he had often used a lever to free a cart-wheel, or to pry a large stone out of the ground when his foster-mother wanted to expand her garden. Could this be the answer to another problem?

Casting his stick aside, the old peasant stepped nearer. With muddy hands he pulled off his straw hat. "She's right, my lord king. The gods took pity on us and sent you to help."

Amphion grinned. "No. It's *you* who were sent by the gods." He bid them good day and walked on. Perhaps, he thought after he had gone some distance – perhaps the old peasant couple were gods in disguise. The deathless ones were known to appear to mortals in this way.

And he had feared that Apollo had abandoned him!

He was singing by the time he reached the worksite. Not all of the men had arrived, and those who were seemed almost as tired as they had last night. Alphenor, standing on the earthen ramp that led to the top of the first tier of stones, stared at him. "Father? Is everything all right?"

Amphion stopped his song and laughed. "Never better, my son! The god has shown me the answer to our problem. If we can't make our men stronger, we'll make the stones lighter!"

Looking puzzled, his sons and the others came nearer; Amphion explained what he had in mind. He sent Alphenor and his brothers to fell the trees they would need and prepare the wood; he sent Naucles to his villa to fetch several coils of rope. Amphion worked with Pelorus and a few others to create the structure they needed, while others placed log rollers beneath the next stone to be moved into place. All this took half the morning, during which time a few doubters complained that they were losing valuable time.

But once the apparatus was ready, even these men stopped grumbling. Amphion had two men position the stone on the shorter end of the lever and tie it into place. Then others heaved on the long end of the lever. The stone went up easily; by rotating the long end of the lever they guided the block into position on the wall.

Pelorus whooped with triumph. "By Apollo, that was quick!" The men and boys all cheered and slapped each other on the back.

Amphion let them enjoy the moment, and then said: "Let's try it again – and consider how we can make it better."

They moved the fulcrum of the lever and positioned another stone on the short end; with the experience they had gained, the second stone was raised more easily than the first. And then a third, and a fourth. By the time the sun reached its zenith they had finished the second row of stones, and over the midday meal they discussed ways to improve the system further. Phaedimus observed that they needed to extend the lever in order to reach the third row of stones; Naucles suggested using ropes on the long end of the lever so that more men could haul.

"And if we have posts on either side of the fulcrum," Alphenor suggested, "the lever won't slip." With this innovation the men could pivot the apparatus more easily, with less fear that the stone would come crashing down below.

Halfway through the afternoon they finished the third row of stones in the wall.

As they began work on the fourth row, the men found it difficult to pull the rope far enough down to position the stone properly. "We need something to keep the ropes in place," said Damasichthon, looking at his red-chafed hands.

"I have an idea," said Naucles. He positioned another log behind the fulcrum, raised just a hand's-breadth above the ground by stones at either end, and weighted down by two building blocks to keep it in place. Then he threaded beneath this log the ropes used to pull down the high end of the lever – and the men pulling these ropes had an easier time of it.

And so the fourth row of stones was lifted into place.

The cleverness with which they had come up with ways to move these stones assured Amphion that somehow they would find ways to overcome other challenges – cutting and moving stones from the quarries, constructing massive gates, and strengthening the foundation where the ground was uneven. And although his team of men and youths toiled with all their strength, their pride in their achievements gave them stamina.

As the sun dipped toward the western horizon, Amphion called a halt to work and ordered them to disassemble the equipment and hide it in the woods. "Menoeceus will be here soon, and we don't want to give away our secrets just yet!"

When Menoeceus arrived for the inspection, Amphion was especially glad to have hidden the equipment: the red-haired man was accompanied by Zethos and part of his team. Zethos stopped in his tracks and laughed. "You were worn out last night, Brother – I came to see if you needed help!" He laughed again, and at his brother's obvious good will Amphion felt the shadow between them disappear. Zethos continued: "I see I should have asked *you* for help instead!"

His pale eyebrows raised high, Menoeceus said, "*Most* impressive, my lord king. How did you accomplish this?"

The youth Pelorus said: "King Amphion sang, and the stones flew into place at the sound of his voice!"

Amphion's team burst into laughter. When they quieted, Amphion said, "The boy exaggerates." He winked at Pelorus, then turned back to Menoeceus. "I didn't make the stones fly. I just made them lighter."

§ 6.07

The priest's knife slit the throat of the flower-garlanded bull; its lifeblood gushed out. The animal dropped to its knees, autumn sunlight gleaming on its black pelt as it breathed its last. A young acolyte held a bronze basin beneath the beast's throat to catch the crimson stream.

The jeweled crown of Pisa on his head, Pelops sat on a chair which had been placed in the portico of Zeus' temple, facing down the broad marble stairway. His daughters, dressed in their official garb as priestesses of Hera and Rhea, sat at his left hand; the golden mastiff of Rhea rested on a pedestal to his right, while trusted guards armed with spears stood behind him. Today was the ceremony of oath-taking, held every four years at harvest time in the year following the Olympic Games. All subjects who had come to manhood in the previous four years gathered to swear their oath of loyalty to the king.

Myrtilus, lounging on the stairway, scratched his chin. "What if he doesn't take the oath?"

Pelops, unwilling to dignify this question with even an unspoken answer, looked steadfastly away; but he knew that the ghost was referring to Atreus. Ever since learning Pelops' doubts about Atreus' paternity, the relationship between the two had been strained.

"He's too friendly with the soldiers," said Myrtilus.

That's because he works with them, Pelops retorted mentally, and then thought, in addition: *Which is what I assigned him to do.*

The high priest of Zeus came forward, his acolyte walking behind with the basin of fresh blood. The young men who would take the oath formed a line with Atreus at its head and Thyestes just behind. Atreus stood stiffly at attention. He wore a kilt and cloak of ocean blue, the borders worked in thread-of-gold with a pattern that looked like bronze arrowheads.

"The army's loyalty is a king's most valuable possession," said Myrtilus, leaning on an insubstantial elbow. "What if Atreus turns it against you?"

He has no cause for that, Pelops responded silently. *I've always treated him well.* Turning away from the ghost, he gestured to the priest. The white-robed man led Atreus up the stairs. Atreus drew his sword; kneeling, he placed the weapon on the marble at Pelops' feet. Pelops could not help reflecting on how much Atreus looked like a young version of Hippodamia's father, King

Oenomaus: his broad shoulders and thick chest, his dark hair and beard, his heavy brow. His face was clouded, as if opposing emotions struggled within him.

The priest moved to stand beside Rhea's mastiff. "Do you, Atreus son of Pelops, swear by Zeus Thunderer to remain a faithful servant of King Pelops – your sword, and your very life, at his disposal?"

Myrtilus wagged a finger. "If he isn't your son, then he's not 'Atreus son of Pelops.' Is his oath still valid?"

I've always treated him as my son, thought Pelops, staring down at the young man.

Atreus met Pelops' gaze. Without hesitation, he declared: "I swear by Zeus Thunderer: I, Atreus son of Pelops, place my sword and my life under King Pelops' command, today and all days to come."

"I declare you my loyal subject," Pelops pronounced.

The priest dipped his thumb into the bowl of bull's blood and smeared a glistening line down Atreus' forehead.

At Pelops' gesture, Atreus re-sheathed his sword. He rose from his knees and bowed deeply. "I thank you, my lord king." He descended the stairway; when he reached the final tread, Laius – who had sworn his own loyalty oath eight years earlier – patted his muscular shoulder.

Out of the corner of his eye, Pelops saw the Tiresias join the group of spectators. The gray-haired prophetess had no role in this ceremony, but Pelops was glad she had come, for her presence always seemed to dampen the power of the ghost. Myrtilus faded from view, and Pelops relaxed.

Thyestes, dressed in a brilliant red kilt and tunic that set off his tanned good looks, climbed the stairs. Hiding the resentment that he surely felt at having to follow Atreus, he knelt and placed his own gleaming sword on the floor-tiles. He spoke the ritual words of the oath even louder than Atreus had done, and received Pelops' answer with a smile that seemed genuine.

Pelops watched Thyestes make his way down the stairs until he stood beside Atreus: both now men of Pisa. His throat tightened. If only Chrysippus could be here today!

The pain of Chrysippus' absence would never leave him. But its sharpness had lessened, like the pain of his old shoulder wound. Actually, today, his shoulder ached more than usual – a sign that, despite the blue skies, rain was coming. Pelops shifted in his chair, seeking a more comfortable position, as the next man knelt before him. Dysponteus, one of Hippodamia's brothers, was among the oldest of the group today; he had missed the last opportunity due to an injury. The noble Evenus, husband of Hippodamia's youngest sister Alkippe, was the next oath-taker. These brothers-in-law were followed by a succession of young noblemen, talented athletes, junior soldiers, farmers' sons, youthful herdsmen, apprentices to merchants and tradesmen. The younger generation, all swearing their loyalty to him, despite some having close ties to Hippodamia. Pelops' influence was growing.

When all the oaths were sworn, the acolytes of Zeus set the god's portion of the sacrificial bull on the altar in the temple forecourt. The fat sizzled, and a plume of smoke rose skyward: Zeus Thunderer had accepted the oaths. The crowd cheered, and the temple servants quickly finished butchering the carcass of the bull and set the meat to roast over the cooking-pit behind the temple. While the meat cooked, palace servants circulated with baskets of bread; others poured wine and water into a mixing-krater the size of a bathtub, and Pisatans lined up with the cups they had brought to receive their portion.

Pelops stood and discreetly adjusted his shoulder-piece, then descended the stairs to congratulate the young men. Then he spotted Atreus in conversation with the Tiresias. He headed towards them, and Atreus' expression seemed to turn to stone as he joined them.

"Greetings, Tiresias. Has my son come to you for advice?" Pelops asked, not mincing words.

"That is precisely his question, my lord king," the seer answered. "Has your *son* come to me? But at this time, I cannot answer."

"Why not?" Atreus demanded, his voice gaining in volume.

"Atreus!" Pelops snapped. "You will address the Handmaiden of Apollo with respect!"

The Tiresias turned her blindfolded face towards Atreus. "The gods grant me knowledge of many things, Prince Atreus. But they have not made me all-knowing."

Atreus clenched his fists, and the Tiresias' stocky manservant moved forward protectively.

"Enough," Pelops said. "Leave now. I wish to speak with the Tiresias."

Atreus took a deep breath, nodded curtly and stalked off to speak to a soldier nearby.

"Tiresias, your visit honors us," Pelops said, seeking to smooth over the awkwardness. "We're pleased that our plan for the Temple of Hestia meets with your approval."

The colorless lips curved. "The gods will feel at home if they have a hearth where they can gather." She gestured with her cornel-wood staff, a broad sweep that encompassed the Temple of Zeus and several other shrines. "Ah, King Pelops! Not yet forty, and look how much you've achieved."

Standing taller at her praise, nonetheless he was aware of how much remained to be done. "It's nothing compared to Lydia."

"Your father started with a realm that was already wealthy," she said, stepping closer. "When you arrived here, the kingdom was descending into chaos. Now it's prosperous and powerful. Your games are spoken of throughout Hellas, and beyond. You have built many temples and offered generous gifts to the gods."

"And what may we give the Voice of Apollo?" he asked, lowering his voice. "We've received a shipment of spices and incense from the east..."

"Such generosity!" Her wry expression suggested that she detected more than magnanimity in this gesture. "I look forward to enjoying their fragrance. But just now you have other business." She nodded her head to Pelops' right.

Pelops turned and saw the palace steward approaching with a slender, redheaded man he recognized as a Theban envoy. "Menoeceus," he said.

The Theban was extremely correct, bowing formally to Pelops and acknowledging the Tiresias with reverence. He then conveyed a lengthy greeting from Thebes' ruling couple that sounded little like Amphion and nothing at all like Niobe. And instead of simply handing over the inventory of tribute goods for Pelops' review, he proceeded to read the list aloud.

"...thirty hides of the best quality; thirty pairs of horns; sixteen amphorae of first-press wine; and ten amphorae of late-season wine." At long last Menoeceus folded his tablet.

"Very good," Pelops said quickly. "How are my sister and her husband?"

"Both in good health, my lord king," said the Theban. "Queen Niobe gave birth to her tenth child, a daughter called Ogygia, last spring; she is expecting again."

"May Artemis watch over her," Pelops said automatically; his words prompted another thought. "When you return to Thebes, tell them that their daughter Chloris is also well. She visited Pisa with the Maidens of Artemis during the summer."

Menoeceus inclined his head. "Certainly, my lord king."

"What other news from Thebes?"

"King Amphion and his brother Zethos are building walls around the city," Menoeceus reported.

Atreus, still close by, edged nearer at this information.

"An enormous task," said Pelops, rubbing his chin. "That could take years. Decades."

"Yes, my lord king." Disapproval tinged the Theban's voice. "Of course, Cadmus never considered walls necessary."

"Maybe he didn't have the means," Atreus said. "Walls give a city strength. We could build walls, here, too, Father."

"That's not our strategy," Pelops said. "Our building efforts are dedicated to honoring the gods." He nodded to the Tiresias.

"It is always wise to honor the gods, my lord king," said the red-haired Theban.

"True," Pelops said. "As does Thebes, Menoeceus, with its gifts."

Menoeceus' face went carefully neutral; he handed the inventory tablet to Exarchos. "As you say, my lord king." He bowed and then turned to the Tiresias. "Prophetess, may I consult with you?"

The seer took her leave of Pelops and departed with the Theban; she apparently had patience for Menoeceus' officious manner.

"Perhaps his piety impresses her," said Myrtilus, joining him now that the prophetess was gone.

Or she wants to learn more about Thebes, Pelops retorted silently. *She has family there, you know.*

"My lord king," said Atreus.

"What?" snapped Pelops.

Atreus glanced around, as if making sure that none could overhear. In a low voice, he said: "Father, I've taken the oath. I've sworn my loyalty before all of Pisa and the king of the gods. *Now* may I visit my mother?"

"No," Pelops said firmly. "And do not ask again."

"Father," he whispered, "I must know the truth!"

Annoyed, Pelops said: "What you must do, Atreus, is to serve me, and obey me, in accordance with your oath. That is what I ask of you – what you have sworn to me."

Atreus remained silent for a moment, then pulled back his broad shoulders. "All right, Father. I believe it's in the interests of the kingdom to build walls around the city. Like Mycenae – or Athens. Give me this task."

Pelops shook his head. "Mycenae and Athens – even Thebes – these are all cities at the top of hills; they benefit from walls. Whatever small advantage Pisa might gain would not be worth the drain on our resources."

"But what if we're attacked?"

"Atreus, think," Pelops said. "Thanks to the games, nearly every king in Hellas owes us the duty of a guest. The gods would curse any who dared to violate that sacred trust."

"Not every man has your piety, Father—"

"Then we can depend on our army, which you've helped train."

"But—"

"Since you want responsibility," Pelops interrupted, his patience exhausted, "I've another task for you. There were too many wolf attacks on our flocks this summer. We lost a lot of sheep and one of the shepherds. That must stop. Take some men and thin the wolf population. Organize better protection for the herdsmen."

Atreus' jaw dropped. "You're sending me to guard *shepherds*?"

"Do you want mutton for the table?" Pelops asked, his own voice rising. "Do you want blankets and cloaks for winter? Where do you think these things come from? The soldiers protect the peasants from danger. That's what you will do. Gather a squad and leave tomorrow."

Atreus' face was dark with anger, but he executed a proper bow. "Yes, my lord king." He turned on his heel.

Seeing that Thyestes was grinning smugly, Pelops roared: "Don't look so pleased with yourself. *You* never caught the thieves from Rhea's temple!"

As if unnerved by his outburst, the Pisatans fell silent, edging away from him. Only the ghost dared approach him. "That was a nice spectacle!" said Myrtilus. He gestured at Atreus and then Thyestes. "I don't care whether they've sworn their loyalty or not: those two are going to make trouble."

SEVEN: BECOMING BEASTS

§ 7.01

Hippodamia sat on a rock, trailing her right foot in the cool water of the sea. She had twisted her ankle the day before – or was it two days before? She did not remember, but it didn't matter. Days were irrelevant. Months were irrelevant. Her banishment had long since been reckoned in years, and even of those she had lost count. She was aware, vaguely, that another winter had given way to spring.

Her aging body reminded her, though, of the years' passage. Her skin had coarsened, and brown spots appeared on her hands. She had lost several teeth; the ache in her jaw and the slight motion she felt with her probing tongue told her that she would soon lose another. Her hair was completely gray. Her monthly blood had ceased long ago. That, at first, she had mourned – and then she came to see its absence as a blessing: one less event tethering her to the passing months, one less inconvenience to deal with. Twice she had fallen so ill that she believed she would die – trembling with fever in her damp cave, with only her two miserable servant-guards in attendance – but both times she recovered.

Sometimes she wondered if she really had died, and this lonely cove beneath the cliffs was really the Underworld. But surely the dead did not suffer from toothache.

A gull screeched overhead. Hippodamia glanced up at the white bird; it wheeled in the salt breeze and then swooped low over the water. Something in the distance caught her attention: she shaded her eyes from the sun and peered intently. Was that a boat? It couldn't be – Ekhinos was here in the cove. She glanced over at the patch of sand. Yes, there was his boat. He was not due to fetch supplies for several days.

But – *was* that a boat, out on the waves?

Hippodamia shook her head and lowered her hand. She must be imagining it – after all, her eyesight was not as good as it used to be. Or some cruel god might be sending a false vision to mock her. So often she had prayed for a boat to come, to take her away from this place…

But – she looked again – it *was* a boat! A small boat, rowed by two men with a third standing at the bow. As it neared, the man waved, and Hippodamia stared in disbelief.

It was her father.

How could her father possibly be here? He had been dead so many years! But it *was* him – the broad shoulders and thick chest, the dark beard, the richly dyed cloak and kingly bearing – as the boat drew nearer, she recognized his features clearly.

So she *had* died. She was dead, and her father was coming with Charon the ferryman to take her across the Styx.

The man waved again. "Hello!" he shouted. "Is Queen Hippodamia here?"

She gasped. That was not her father's voice.

And – and – yes, this man was younger than her father had been when he died – sweet merciful gods, could it possibly be…

"Atreus?" she asked of the air, then licked her dry lips and called, louder: "Atreus?"

The man shaded his eyes with his hand. "Mother? Is that you?"

She scrambled to her feet; a stab of pain reminded her of her injured ankle. Shifting her weight, she waved frantically, screaming: "Atreus!"

The man waved again. "Mother!" he shouted.

Her heart pounding with excitement, Hippodamia realized that the boat could not land where she was standing; it was too rocky. With frantic gestures she indicated the little stretch of sand. "Over there!" she shouted. "That way!" Atreus nodded vigorously, and the rowers changed direction.

"My lady queen?"

She turned to see the servant couple who guarded her staring nervously at the boat. "Who's that, my lady queen?"

"It's my son! My son, Atreus!"

She leaned on Iopa for support as she limped hurriedly towards the beach. "Your son has come, my lady queen?" repeated the peasant woman, her voice full of fear.

"Of course, you fool!" Hippodamia snapped. "Hurry up!"

Now that the boat was closer, Hippodamia could see how much Atreus had changed from the youth she had left behind. His once-scraggly beard had grown thick and full; his arms and legs – always strong – were even more powerfully muscled. Dark hair covered his chest, shins, and forearms. He resembled her father, but he was plainly Atreus, her son.

One of the rowers leapt into the water and pulled the boat up onto the sand. Then Atreus climbed out, his crimson cloak and kilt rippling in the wind.

"Atreus!" Hippodamia flung herself at him, sobbing.

He embraced her; blessed Hera, he *was* real. She felt the warmth and strength of his arms, and heard his beating heart. Then, after a moment, he gently but firmly pulled away. "Mother," he said, looking down at her. His dark eyes gleamed with moisture.

A sudden surge of anger filled Hippodamia. "What's taken you so long? Where have you been all these years, you ungrateful child?"

He pushed her back, holding her shoulders at arm's length. "Please, Mother—"

She struggled to control herself. "I'm sorry, Atreus. It's just – it's been so long." She took a deep breath. "You can explain everything later. Let's go."

But he prevented her from going to the boat. "Mother, my men have rowed a great distance. They must rest."

"But—" Hippodamia glanced at the two men, standing a few paces away. She wanted to curse them, but these were the men on who her life depended. She had waited years; she could wait a few more hours. She nodded. "Very well. Of course."

The two rowers stared at her, as Ekhinos and Iopa stared at Atreus; even the goats wandered closer, as if they too were curious. To gain a measure of privacy, Hippodamia pulled Atreus aside.

Her son looked back. "Go over there," he ordered his men, pointing to the far side of the cove. "And you," he said, pointing to Ekhinos and Iopa, "get these goats away." His voice was commanding; the rowers and the peasant couple obeyed immediately.

She clung to his arm. "Atreus," she breathed. "I can hardly believe it..."

"Here, Mother," he said, leading her over to a rocky ledge. "Let's sit down." He unpinned his cloak and folded it for her to sit on. It was thick and soft, the beautifully dyed wool a reminder of civilized life. Hippodamia felt it between her fingers and fought the urge to weep.

Questions began to occur to her: was Pelops dead? Was Atreus now king?

She studied him. He wore no crown, but the sword at his waist had a hilt worked with gold and jewels. His kilt was dyed the same brilliant crimson as the cloak on which she sat, and his sandals had gilded clasps. She had lost track of the years, but he had to be at least thirty – perhaps more than thirty.

"Here, Mother," he said, opening a pouch belted at his waist and withdrawing a package of oiled cloth. "I brought you some cakes. I thought you might like something sweet."

"Oh, yes!" she said, snatching it from his hand. She unwrapped the small parcel, then took a bite, savoring the honey and raisins on her tongue. Nothing so delectable had passed her lips since her banishment to this miserable cove. The first honeycake disappeared quickly; not wanting to seem like a starving beast, she folded the cloth back over the others and put down the package. "Atreus, tell me: why did you leave me here so long?"

He squatted down, picking up a shell from the sand and turning it over in his hands. "I didn't know where you were. And Father – King Pelops would not tell me."

So Pelops was *not* dead. Hippodamia felt a swell of disappointment – but, she realized, this meant her children had not abandoned her by choice. "How did you persuade him?"

"I didn't. He doesn't know I'm here." He dropped the shell and straightened, then sat down beside her. "He ordered me to stop asking him – and I could see he would never relent. But I was sure he hadn't had you killed – he wouldn't want trouble with your relatives in Mycenae and Argos."

"Besides," she said bitterly, "marriage to me gave him the throne of Pisa."

Atreus nodded. "I realized I'd have to discover your whereabouts on my own. But none of the palace guards knew anything. He must have killed the men who first brought you here, or sent them to live somewhere far away." He ran a hand through his dark, curling hair. "I kept asking, searching for a clue... but for years I found nothing. And all the while I did everything the king asked of me; I patrolled the borders with Arcadia, I protected his cursed herds of sheep and goats – and still he would not trust me. I followed false leads to Pylos in the south and Thebes in the east. Then, once, after a wolf hunt along the Arcadian border, I heard talk of a local couple who had gone to work for King Pelops. That seemed strange to me – why would Father hire a pair of Arcadian peasants for any job of responsibility?"

"Ekhinos and Iopa," Hippodamia whispered.

"It took a long time to uncover the truth," Atreus continued. "The peasants who told me of this in the first place seemed to think their neighbors had gone somewhere to the west – somewhere along the coast. So I listened to the talk of all the merchants working the western routes. Because the king had assigned me to protect the Arcadian border and look for the man-wolves that the people there are so afraid of, it was natural enough for me to ask about people from the region. Eventually I heard of a childless Arcadian couple who lived like hermits on the island of Zakynthos. The husband, they said, rowed into town twice a month for supplies – the expenses were covered by a merchant who handled a lot of trade for Pisa. I realized I was near to discovering your place of exile – so I set out to search the coasts of this island."

"And now you're here," she breathed, grasping his hands. "Fine, if Pelops is still in power you'll take me somewhere else. Kill those two peasants – that way they can't talk—"

"Mother," he interrupted, "I have not come to take you away."

She coughed; her throat was dry from eating the cake without wine or water, and she struggled to draw breath. Finally she managed to say: "Why not? Don't be afraid of Pelops—"

"Pelops is my king," he said, his voice firm. "As a man of Pisa, I've sworn loyalty to him." Atreus leaned forward, his eyes narrowing. "He's also my father, isn't he? A son must obey his father."

"And care for his mother! Especially when—" She stopped, for his heavy eyebrows had lowered.

His dark eyes watched her with the intensity of a hawk preparing to swoop down on a mouse. "Finish your sentence, Mother. Were you going to say that he is *not* my father?"

Hippodamia felt her face flush. "What? No, of course I wasn't going to say that." She strove to sound calm, but her heart pounded hard; her voice sounded high and squeaky in her ears. "What do you mean? Is someone spreading lies about me?"

Atreus folded his arms across his chest. In a cold, hard voice he told her that the herb-woman Polyxo, on her deathbed, claimed that Hippodamia had borne children to her own father. That Thyestes had learned this and claimed he was truly Pelops' eldest son. Pelops neither confirmed nor denied it, but had sent Atreus off to the hills to guard the sheep and goats.

Hippodamia listened, wondering what she should say. What *could* she say?

At least Polyxo, grandmother to the bastard Chrysippus, was dead, long dead. That bit of news was satisfying.

Atreus finished reciting his suspicions, and then reached back into his belt-pouch. He withdrew a small bronze figurine and held it out to her. It was delicately made, perhaps of Cretan manufacture: Zeus, wielding a thunderbolt. He pressed it into her hand.

"I need the truth, Mother," Atreus said. "Swear now, before Zeus, Lord of Heaven and Earth. Swear by the lives of all your children that King Pelops is my father."

She looked from the polished bronze figurine in her palm up to her son's dark eyes.

"Swear it, Mother!" Atreus barked harshly.

Feeling dizzy, Hippodamia clutched the figure of Zeus tight in her hand. The clouds above seemed to swirl in the sky, as if Zeus were stirring them.

To swear by the lives of her children – *all* her children – not just Atreus and Thyestes, but lovely Eurydike, brave Astydamia...

"Well, Mother?"

Nikippe, Pittheus, Letreus, Alcathous, Copreus... and the other two, the two she could not claim...

Hippodamia closed her eyes. "No," she whispered. "I can't take that oath."

Atreus leapt to his feet, thundering: "You mean that old bitch told the truth, and I was sired by your father Oenomaus?"

She shook her head, not daring to look up at him. "I'm not saying that."

He grabbed her chin and jerked her face upward. "Then what *are* you saying? By Zeus, woman, was there *another* man?"

"No! Atreus, I – I'm saying – I don't *know.*"

His hand dropped from her face. "*What*?"

"I don't know," she repeated dully. "My father took me shortly before I married King Pelops. You could be the son of either man."

Atreus bared his teeth, and then – it happened so fast that she did not see it coming – he slammed his fist into her jaw. The pain crashed through her like Zeus' own lightning. She fell backwards, screaming as he struck her again and again. Raising her arms in a feeble defense, she screamed: "Stop! Atreus, stop! I am your mother!"

To her surprise, the beating stopped. Breathing hard, Atreus stepped away from her.

Hippodamia spat a mouthful of blood onto the pebbles; her loose tooth went with it. "I did not ask for this, Atreus!" she wept. "I was only a girl – how could I stop him? I never wanted it!"

His face, contorted with rage, looked more than ever like her father's. She thought back to her childhood: when King Oenomaus' temper seized him, defiance only further infuriated him; contrition was the only approach.

"Atreus," she pleaded, "have mercy! Think – I could have taken that oath and forfeited the lives of my children to Zeus. But I didn't! All my life, I've done everything I could for my children. I'm only here, banished, because I did what was necessary to protect *your* inheritance. Don't you see that?"

His expression softened, just slightly. Her words were reaching him.

"All these years I've been here for what I did to protect you. All these years... how many is it, now?"

"Twelve years," he muttered.

"Twelve years! *Twelve years*! Please, Atreus, *please* – take me with you!"

He looked away. "I won't break my oath to my king."

"There must be a way to get around it – tell someone else where I am, and that person can fetch me. How about King Electryon? The king of Mycenae would have no qualms about defying Pelops—"

"Forget it," Atreus said flatly. "Electryon would never go against him – they're closer than ever. Nikippe even married Electryon's brother."

There was so much that she did not know. "Tell me," she said, reaching out in entreaty. "Tell me everything."

Atreus let out a deep breath. "What do you want to know?"

In response to countless questions, she learned that Eurydike had borne a daughter to Electryon, and that Nikippe had married Electryon's brother. Atreus, Thyestes, and her other sons by Pelops remained unmarried. Pelops had not officially named an heir, but he relied on Atreus for most serious work – though he had never yet found any of the mysterious wolf-monsters said to be responsible for taking sheep and killing shepherds along the Arcadian border. Meanwhile Thyestes bred horses and chased skirts, and Laius of Thebes handled the arrangements for the games.

Hungry for information, Hippodamia asked even about people and things she disliked; Pelops' sister Niobe and her cowherd husband still ruled Thebes, and had produced, in total, fourteen children: seven sons and seven daughters. Pelops continued with his Olympic Games, and would hold another this summer. In the meantime he had completed a facility for visiting athletes dedicated to the goddess Hestia, several smaller altars to other gods, and was now working on a large public bath for guests.

A whole building, just for bathing! It had been so many years since she had soaked in warm water scented with lavender oil…

"I must go now, Mother," he said. He touched her bruised face. "I'm sorry I struck you."

"It doesn't matter," she said. "Atreus, will you come back for me? Or send someone else?"

He got to his feet. "I – I'll try."

"Please – Son, please—" She clung to him but he pushed her firmly away. She begged, pleaded, shrieking, but he walked away and did not turn back. Soon his rowers had his boat underway.

Clutching the figurine of Zeus and the cloak her son had left behind, Hippodamia fell to her knees and wept.

§ 7.02

"A long time ago," Niobe said as Philomela pointed to the first scene depicted on her tapestry, "there lived a girl named Arachne. She was so clever and industrious that she caught Athena's attention, and the goddess decided to teach her to weave."

It was a lovely day, white clouds scudding across the bright blue sky – perfect for the spring festival honoring Hephaestus and Athena. The agora was crammed with the shining works of bronze and colorful tapestries proudly displayed by Theban smiths and weavers.

Niobe scanned the faces of the children who had crowded close to listen. Her own younger children were there, of course, as well as Thebe's son Idmon; she saw her midwife's daughter Rhodia, Menoeceus' children Creon and

Jocasta, Naucles' daughter Chrysippe, and golden-skinned Melanthe, the daughter of Naucles' trading partner. The storytelling had been a tradition at the festival for several years now, and Niobe enjoyed it as much as the children. Each year Philomela brought a different story to life on her loom, then Niobe spoke the words that the Athenian princess was unable to utter. It was one of the few occasions that Philomela ever appeared in public, and although a veil covered her face, her eyes conveyed her joy as Niobe shared the tapestry's story with the children of Thebes.

"Arachne was a brilliant pupil," Niobe continued. "When she left Athena, she taught many others, and her fame increased." Beside her, Philomela gestured to a scene in which Arachne was surrounded by admirers. "But Arachne grew proud, and failed to acknowledge Athena. She took all the credit and glory for herself." A gust of wind struck Niobe; she shivered and pulled her short cloak closer. "This angered the goddess Athena. She changed herself into an old woman and went to visit her former pupil in disguise." Philomela indicated the next scene, a crone depicted on the cloth. "She said to Arachne: 'You have boasted that you are the best weaver in the world. I challenge you to a weaving contest.'

"Arachne looked at the old woman's gnarled hands and laughed. 'You think *you* can best *me?*'

"Athena answered: 'I do. Are you afraid of competition?'

"Arachne's hubris compelled her to accept. Two looms were set up in the agora; Arachne and the old woman agreed to start weaving at dawn, and continue until the sun set in the west." Philomela pointed to the section of the tapestry that depicted the sun rising behind Athena in her old-woman guise. "When the first light glimmered in the east, Arachne laughed again: the old woman was so stooped that she could not even reach the top of the loom!" At these words Philomela bent over, imitating the crooked crone, and the children giggled.

Niobe went on: "But then the old woman flung off her tattered cloak. She straightened up and stood tall – taller than any mortal woman – and all those who had gathered to watch the contest knew that this was the goddess Athena. 'Foolish mortal,' she said, 'do you still wish to challenge me?' Arachne should have made amends for her disrespect, but she was too filled with pride. 'I do,' she said defiantly. And so the contest began: each of them fastened the warp threads to the loom and attached the weights; each of them passed the wool-wrapped shuttles back and forth."

Philomela had divided this horizontal section of the tapestry into two pieces; the one on the left depicted the work of the goddess, while the one on the right depicted Arachne's weaving. "Athena's tapestry showed how she won the loyalty of the Athenians by giving them the olive tree. But Arachne wove scenes of the gods wooing mortal women: she showed Zeus turning himself into a bull to seduce Europa, Apollo pursuing the huntress Cyrene, and Poseidon lying with Aethra. She wanted her scenes to show that mortal women were as good as goddesses – at least in the lustful eyes of the gods."

As Niobe finished these words, Philomela made a sudden violent gesture, as if to tear her tapestry from the frame on which it hung. Niobe explained: "When twilight fell, the goddess saw what her competitor had done. Although Arachne's tapestry was perfectly made, Athena could not permit such insolence. She ripped Arachne's tapestry apart, and then turned her anger on its weaver. Arachne's form began to change: her body shrank, and her arms and legs grew long and thin. Athena had turned her into a spider." Niobe pointed to the spider depicted at the bottom of the tapestry, clinging to a web that sparkled with silver thread. "Arachne could still weave, but she could never again be disrespectful towards the gods."

The young audience applauded, and then Niobe moved away from the tapestry so that they could come closer. Many praised Philomela's skill – but they were careful to honor the goddess Athena, too. Niobe had a secret sympathy for Arachne; the goddess' jealous action seemed overly harsh. But she pressed her lips together and kept this thought to herself.

"I like how you tell stories, Mother," said Ogygia, appearing at Niobe's side.

"Thank you, sweetheart," said Niobe. "But I've heard you share tales of gods and heroes with your brothers and sisters. You're a good storyteller too!"

The eleven-year-old girl glowed at her mother's praise.

Idmon pushed his way through the crowd. "Gigi," he said, calling Ogygia by his pet name for her, "come here! You have to see this helmet!" The cousins, inseparable, ran off together.

Niobe pressed her hands against the small of her back; after standing for so long, it often ached. But she still had much to do. With Amphion and Zethos away working on the walls – even though it was a festival day and their crews were at leisure, the brothers insisted on using the break to take new measurements and inspect the progress – Niobe and her sister-in-law Thebe were left to manage the festival just as they managed the everyday affairs of the city.

The wind picked up again, and Niobe's teeth chattered. She must simply be tired – it was not that chilly. Wishing she could just go inside and take a hot bath, Niobe ordered one servant to bring her a chair, and told another to fetch a cup of chamomile tea. Her queenly duty required that she preside over the celebration at least until dusk.

After Niobe finished her tea, she spied Captain Naucles with his wife and daughter, and beckoned to him. Naucles left his family to continue admiring the tapestries and approached Niobe's chair. After making a polished bow he said: "My lady queen – an excellent festival, as always."

"Thank you, Naucles." She smiled, remembering him as the uncouth young sailor she had first met so many years before. Now wealthy and successful, he carried himself like a well-born man; in his finely made linen tunic and blue woolen cape, fastened with a golden pin, anyone making his acquaintance would think him born to a leading family. "How were your travels?"

The sea captain had just finished his first trip of the sailing season; Lydia had been among his destinations. "Fair weather, praise Poseidon. Your parents are in good health for their age, my lady queen, and your mother sends her love.

They sent gifts for their grandchildren – Euxenos is bringing those into town by ox-cart, but I came ahead." He paused, scratching his light brown beard. "Your parents wanted me to ask a question of you, my lady queen: do you know anything regarding the whereabouts of your eldest brother, Prince Broteas?"

Niobe blinked. "Broteas? Why? I thought he was dead." Years ago a message had come from Lydia that her brother Broteas had never returned from a voyage, and was presumed lost at sea.

"Your father rarely reveals information, my lady queen." Naucles said. "But afterward I spoke with Prince Broteas' wife. She said that King Tantalus recently had a dream about him."

"Well..." Niobe did not want to say anything negative about her father in public. "He's getting older. We're *all* getting older."

"All except you, my lady queen," was Naucles' gallant response. Then he peered closely at her. "Are you feeling well, my lady queen?"

"I'm fine," Niobe lied.

Naucles lowered his voice. "Are you expecting again?"

"At my age? I hope not," Niobe said with a laugh. She did feel peculiar – but her symptoms did not suggest pregnancy. "No, I'm not. I would know."

Thebe sauntered over, sunlight gleaming from the henna-red of her hair. Her heavy skirts clanked with golden spangles. "Niobe, have you seen the way my Idmon can run? He should go to the games in Pisa this summer. They have a race for boys as well as for men, don't they, Captain Naucles?"

"They do indeed, my lady Thebe," said Naucles, bowing low.

"Then he must enter." Thebe threw back her shoulders so that her large round breasts jutted out. "I'm sure he'll win."

"He just might," said the sea captain.

Idmon *was* tall for his age, Niobe thought, frowning. If he won, thought Niobe, his mother would be even more insufferable.

"What?" said Thebe. "What's wrong, Niobe?"

Naucles also looked at Niobe with concern. "The queen's not feeling well."

"Oh?" Thebe squinted down at her. "Maybe it's the change."

"Maybe," said Niobe, shrugging. Thebe had entered menopause the year before, but Niobe's flows – although shorter and lighter than in the past – still came and went with the moon. Still, she would not mind if the change of life had come to her. She had given her husband fourteen children; and for women past forty, childbirth was often hazardous.

Thebe turned away. "Look! Here come our husbands!"

Naucles took his leave and headed back to his wife, and Thebe bustled off to greet Zethos. Still feeling achy and tired, Niobe remained in her chair and waited for her husband to come to her. She watched Amphion pause to take two skewers of meat from a servant's tray; then he continued towards her with his uneven gait. Two years ago – just after his mother's funeral – a stone had landed on his left foot, crushing the two smallest toes, which the healers had been forced to remove. This left him with a limp, but that did not slow him down. He came over and kissed her, then offered her a skewer of veal.

Niobe shook her head; she was not hungry. "How are the walls?" She posed the same question every evening.

"Nearly finished!" He took a bite and chewed hungrily.

"You've said that every day for two years!"

"And every day my answer becomes even more true!" He grinned down at her, creasing the deep lines that radiated from the outer corners of his eyes. "My love, believe me: we're nearly finished. I predict we'll be done before the year is out."

It *was* an enormous project, and they *had* made tremendous progress. "I'm glad," she said. "You must be weary of it."

He took another bite, considering this. "I suppose I am. But it's a blessing to be able to do something important for Thebes, something that will outlast my songs." He peered at her. "Are you feeling all right, my love?"

Everyone was asking her this! "I'm tired," she admitted. "I'd like to go inside and lie down."

He waggled a finger at her. "You can't, not yet."

"Why not?" she asked crossly.

"Because Chloris is here."

Niobe clutched her husband's wrist. "Is she really?" The Maidens of Artemis traveled considerably – but they seldom ventured as far north as Thebes.

"Really. Zethos and I were on top of the west curve of the wall when we saw the huntress band coming. We accompanied them into town. See?" He pointed. "There's our fleet-footed daughter!"

A tall, slender woman dressed in a short tunic was making her way through the teeming agora. Her arms were bare and browned, her curling hair bound up in leather bands, her eyes lively and her lips full and pink. Niobe sprang from her chair and ran towards her daughter. "Chloris!"

"Mother!" Chloris pushed through the crowd to reach Niobe, and bent down and hugged her.

Amphion caught up with them. "For *you*, your mother leaves her chair."

"Oh, Chloris," Niobe said, holding her daughter close. She felt strength in the young woman's embrace. "It's been so long!"

"Four years," said Chloris. "I meant to come sooner, but – oh, Mother, you're crying!"

"I am not!" Niobe protested, pulling back – and then Chloris reached out to wipe away a tear and Niobe had to concede that she was. "Are you the chief priestess yet?"

"No, Selene is – and I probably never will be: I've only one year left in my service to the goddess. Ah, Philomela! Hello, Alphenor! And Phaedimus! Cleodoxa – Eudoxa – you've both grown so tall!"

Reluctantly Niobe yielded her place so that Philomela and Chloris' siblings could greet their sister. Pelorus stood nearby, admiration plain on his face; exotic-looking Melanthe, toying with her Egyptian-style braids, also stared at the tall, confident princess. In fact, the whole agora seemed spellbound.

At last Niobe had the chance to ask: "Can you stay in the palace, Chloris?" The Maidens of Artemis usually set up their own encampment outside the city.

"Selene already granted me permission," answered her daughter, laughing. "Can the Maidens join us for dinner?"

With Chloris' arrival, the evening banquet in the megaron was even more festive than anticipated. Chloris and the others maidens recounted their adventures to an enthralled audience, and Amphion played a song in honor of Artemis. Niobe had little appetite – at first she thought it was only the excitement of seeing her daughter again, but then she started shivering again and had to send a servant for a warmer cloak. She told the nursemaids to take away the youngest children: her son Ismenus wailed in protest, but Neaira and Phthia were already asleep. Niobe longed to join them. Her back and shoulders ached, but she could not retire while Chloris was speaking; Amphion was consulting her about likely marriage matches for her brothers and sisters. The names swirled past Niobe like sea-mist, insubstantial and dizzying.

"What about Pelops' sons?" Amphion was asking. "They're still unmarried, aren't they?"

"As far as I know," Chloris said, helping herself to a hazelnut pastry. "And so is King Neleus of Pylos. His wife died last fall."

"King Neleus is a good man," Amphion said, stroking his white beard. "Your mother always said so. Right, Niobe?"

Niobe struggled to answer.

"Mother, what's wrong?" asked Alphenor.

"I—" Niobe was unable to form the words.

"Your mother's ill." Amphion's voice sounded both sharp and far away. "Alphenor, carry her to the bedroom. Phaedimus, run and fetch the chief healer from Apollo's temple."

Niobe attempted to argue, to explain that she was simply tired, but they ignored her mumbles. The strong arms of her firstborn lifted her, then everything went dark: when she reopened her eyes, she lay in her bed.

Chloris' hand was cool on her forehead. "Father, she's fevered."

Again Niobe struggled to speak.

Chloris knelt by the bed. "What is it, Mother?"

"Leave me," she gasped. "Amphion – keep the children – away." She did not want this illness to spread to them. But Chloris insisted on nursing her, assisted by another Maiden of Artemis with blonde hair. Philomela also remained beside Niobe's bed, wiping her brow with soothing damp cloths.

The days and nights merged into an indeterminate gray haze where dreams and reality blended. Was Chloris truly here? No, that was impossible: she was with the Maidens of Artemis, down south in Arcadia. Chloris could be no more real than the sound of Philomela's voice – and yet Niobe was sure she heard Philomela speaking, her voice sweet as a nightingale. Once Naucles appeared to her, a wiry, beardless boy once more, with Captain Aeolius behind him. "Princess Niobe?" Naucles said, sounding worried. "Princess Niobe, please, wake up: we're almost there – we're about to make dock in Athens!" But Niobe knew this was a fever dream.

Amphion holding her hand – that was real. That had to be real. Oh, dear gods, he was so handsome. Those serene gray eyes, that silver hair… how had *she* ever won the heart of such a man? If her time to die had come, at least she had known deep and abiding love. She had given him children, many children; they would take care of him when she was gone.

Then she found herself dressed in her best clothes, seated on her throne in the megaron. People filled the large room, milling about the broad central hearth. She saw her children, various of the Spartoi and other citizens of Thebes – even the Tiresias. It was an ordinary scene. And yet she was filled with dread.

She had seen this before: years ago, this dream had come to her in Lydia.

Something terrible was about to happen.

She had to stop it. But she could not stop it – she could not move at all. Her right hand clutched the arm of her throne; she could not raise it. Desperately she tried to call out, "No! Stop!" but her tongue was leaden in her mouth, and her lips felt as if they had been sewn shut. A man shouted: "Niobe, no!" That voice – was it Broteas?

"Darling. Darling! It's all right, my love. I'm here."

She struggled to open her eyes. Though her vision was blurry, she saw Amphion sitting by her bed, felt him holding her hand. She parted her lips and tried to speak, but her tongue felt thick and her mouth parched.

Amphion helped her to sit up; Niobe realized she was bathed in sweat. Philomela held a cup to her lips, and with effort she drank a sip of water, then another. The cool liquid coursed down her throat.

Chloris approached the bed. "How do you feel, Mother?"

"Terrible," she said, hoarsely.

Chloris put her hand on Niobe's forehead. "The fever's broken. You may not feel well yet, Mother, but you should live."

The dream of danger was already fading. It had seemed so real – familiar, even. Perhaps it had recurred several times during her illness. But she was safe; she was healing.

"Praise Apollo," whispered Amphion, stroking her cheek. "I was afraid I was going to lose you, Niobe."

"I thought so too," she said. "I even thought I heard Broteas calling me from the Underworld."

"Uncle Broteas?" asked Chloris. "But—"

"But what?" asked Amphion.

Chloris looked confused.

"Broteas has been missing – presumed dead – for years," said Amphion. "Now suddenly his parents and his wife want to know where he is. Chloris, do *you* know anything about this?"

Weakly, Niobe looked from her husband to her daughter, watched them stare at each other – and with bewilderment realized that Amphion was right: Chloris *did* know something.

Chloris took a deep breath and exhaled slowly. "Uncle Broteas is alive and in Arcadia. Or at least he was last fall."

"What?" asked Niobe, and started to cough. Philomela patted her on the back, and then held another drink to her lips, this time warm chamomile tea with honey.

"If you've seen him, why didn't you ever say anything?" asked Amphion.

"He asked me not to," Chloris said mildly. "I don't think he wants King Tantalus to know he's alive. He's been calling himself Alexandros of Troy."

Amphion's thick white eyebrows came down, and he said, "We'll talk more of this later. I can see that Philomela wants to put your mother into a different gown."

Niobe was too exhausted to ask any questions while Philomela and Chloris changed her bedding and her gown. She sank with relief back onto the soft mattress. Broteas was in Arcadia? Then why had he been warning her?

Closing her eyes, she remembered: Broteas had not been warning her about anything. It had only been a fever dream.

§ 7.03

The rising moon washed silvery light over the grove of ash trees where thirteen men had gathered. Standing beside Broteas and Geranor, the king of Arcadia touched his wolf's-tooth necklace. "This will be a good night, Prince Alexandros," he said. "I can feel it."

Broteas nodded. "I'm sure of it, my lord king."

King Stymphalus stepped forward and turned to face the others. "Men of Arcadia!" he began, commanding their attention. "Tonight we remember Lykaon, our first king. In the days of his reign, the gods sometimes demanded human sacrifice; but Lykaon dared to eat of this sacrifice himself. For this terrible crime, all-powerful Zeus transformed him into a wolf."

"This we remember," chorused Broteas and the others.

"Since the days of Lykaon, other men of Arcadia have from time to time been changed into wolves. If they dare to eat human flesh, they must remain wolves the rest of their lives. But if they spend nine years in wolf form without tasting human blood, they may resume human shape."

"This we remember," Broteas chanted again, feeling the power of the moment building. Inspired by Arcadian tradition, he had suggested to Stymphalus many years ago that they hunt among Pelops' flocks in the guise of wolves; but the ritual now felt like a religious mystery he had discovered rather than something he had invented. And, after all, why shouldn't that be so? The gods often worked their will through the deeds of mortal men.

Stymphalus beckoned, and Geranor carried forward the wineskin. Stymphalus unsealed it and sent a stream of wine arcing through the air to splash upon the ground. "We offer this libation to the shade of Lykaon," he said. "And if Zeus grants us success tonight, we will burn the lamb-fat and thigh bones upon his altar!" He took a swig of wine and handed the skin back to Geranor, who swallowed a mouthful and then carried the skin to each of the other seven men. Broteas was last; he savored the rich, musty taste and offered a silent prayer to Zeus, and then one to Artemis, his patron goddess.

Then all of the men removed their tunics and slipped out of their sandals. Clad only in gray loincloths, they opened their packs and began the elaborate process of dressing: tying pieces of wolf-fur about the shins like greaves, and additional pieces to cover each thigh. A sword belt went around the waist, with a wolf's tail fastened at the back so that it hung down over the buttocks.

Geranor came over to tie the fur around Broteas' forearms and upper arms; then Broteas returned the favor, though Geranor complicated the task with restless shifting. "Be still," Broteas said. "You want this knot to hold, don't you?"

"Sorry," Geranor muttered.

"What's wrong with you tonight?" Broteas asked. "You're not usually nervous before a raid."

Geranor shrugged. "It's a warm night for fur."

Broteas snorted. "If it were winter, you'd complain about the cold." Geranor had a talent for complaining. During the first couple of years in Arcadia, Geranor had frequently mentioned how much he wanted to return to Lydia. But, as their status in Arcadia grew – King Stymphalus appreciated their efforts – Geranor's complaints switched to other topics.

Mumbling thanks, Geranor squatted down to tie on his paws. The special sandals were Broteas' own invention: wolf's paws were fastened beneath the ball of the foot, and the men's tough, calloused heels were left bare. The patterns they left in the dirt looked like tracks of neither wolves nor men – but a great deal like tracks of the man-wolves that the Pisatan shepherds so greatly feared.

Broteas fastened his own paw-sandals and then settled his helmet into place. The wolf's head rested atop his skull, its long snout casting his face into shadow. He buckled the strap beneath his chin, pulling flaps of fur down to cover his cheeks, ears, and neck. Then he opened the container of ashes he had brought and smeared them over his face and chest, making his skin gray. When he was done, Stymphalus and he inspected the men.

"You," King Stymphalus said, pointing, "your head's not on straight."

Broteas went over and adjusted the man's helmet so that his human ears were no longer visible.

When King Stymphalus was satisfied, he raised his arm. "You know what to do. May Hermes guide you – may he guide us all!" Stymphalus lowered his arm, and then he and Broteas headed away. Following the plan, Geranor and the others padded off in another direction.

"This will be a profitable raid, my Trojan friend," Stymphalus said softly. "One of the largest flocks yet to come so near the border."

Broteas agreed. "With our attacks concentrated in the north lately, they think this valley is safe."

"You're clever, Alexandros. Each season you have a different tactic."

It gave Broteas great satisfaction to consider how the strategy had evolved over the years, growing ever more ambitious. At first they had taken only a lone sheep here or a goat there, leaving paw-prints and bits of fleece, skin and gore to make it seem the work of wolves. From time to time they raided other nearby kingdoms, to divert suspicion that only Pelops' flocks were under attack; they even stole from a few Arcadian flocks.

The shepherds set traps for wolves, but of course Broteas and his men were not tempted by haunches of rotting mutton. Stymphalus' spies reported that the

Pisatans tried leaving out carcasses laced with poison; this killed a few scavengers, wolves among them, but it did not stop Broteas' raids.

Shepherds occasionally glimpsed Broteas' men in the darkness. As the seasons passed, the peasants spoke fearfully of the man-wolves – and with each retelling, the monsters grew more terrifying. The man-wolves hunted in packs; their bites could transform humans into monsters. They could devour a sheep quicker than a man could count to twenty. They had the strength of ten men, and claws as sharp as knives.

Learning of these fears, Broteas grew bolder. By showing themselves from a distance, howling at the moon, he and his men frightened many young shepherds into abandoning their flocks completely – which were then claimed for Stymphalus. Rarely, a shepherd stayed to defend his animals – in these cases the man's death was made to look like the work of savage man-wolves. And the anxiety among the Pisatan peasants swelled.

The Arcadians heard that Pelops had sent Prince Atreus to deal with the situation; Stymphalus' spies reported on his movements, and so the men never attacked when he was nearby. They dared not risk capture.

Tonight, Broteas and King Stymphalus had a special role to play in the raid. Broteas' men had observed this flock for several days; they had assessed the terrain, and formulated a strategy. The previous night they left man-wolf tracks along a dirt road used by the farmers and shepherds; with luck these had been noticed, and the young men guarding the sheep would be anxious. Tonight the moon was full.

They reached the selected spot, just below the crest of a ridge; the other men needed time to get into position. Broteas and the Arcadian king stretched out on the grass, watching the moon and stars wheel slowly overhead. Insects' song filled the silence; off in the distance, an owl called.

"We're near Zeus' birthplace, you know," Stymphalus remarked.

Broteas had always heard that Zeus was born in a cave on the island of Crete, but he was not going to contradict his friend and host. Many places and people claimed a special relationship to Zeus. Even Broteas' own father, King Tantalus, claimed to be Zeus' son – first making that assertion the night he shared the gods' sacred nectar with Pelops. Later that night he attacked Pelops with a sword, saying that the gods had asked him for this sacrifice; Pelops survived, though his shoulder was permanently injured. Perhaps that was Pelops' punishment for daring to consume the holy nectar, but Tantalus had never really been punished. Perhaps he truly was the son of Zeus, and thus entitled to partake of the divine food. Or, Broteas thought, perhaps losing the golden mastiff *was* Tantalus' punishment.

Broteas dared not return to Lydia without the mastiff; but since that night in Pisa years ago, there had been no good opportunity to take it. Sometimes he felt that the gods did not want the mastiff to return to Lydia. Besides, he had found contentment as Prince Alexandros. In the wilds of Arcadia he was close to the goddess Artemis, who he had always revered. The mountains were beautiful, the game plentiful. Stymphalus was good company, and life was comfortable. He was able to annoy his brother Pelops, and thwart his ambitions in some small measure; this gave him satisfaction. Perhaps *this* was the fate the gods had chosen for him.

Looking up, Broteas realized that the constellation of the Lyre was in position. He pointed at the sky and said: "It's time, my lord king."

The two men got to their feet; Broteas' bad leg had stiffened, making him wince as they climbed to the ridge-top. Their silhouettes against the moonlit, star-filled sky would be plainly seen by the shepherds in the valley below. Stymphalus threw back his shoulders and howled. The sound, eerie and mournful, echoed over the hills.

There was shouting down by the shepherds' camp-fire. From this distance Broteas could not make out the words, but the sound of panic was clear.

Stymphalus howled again.

The herd-dogs barked furiously; the sheep bleated, probably frightened as much by their guardians' terror as by Stymphalus' wolf call. One shepherd took off at a run, heading in the direction of the nearest village; the other snatched up a spear and shouted something after his fleeing companion.

Broteas saw the shadowy forms of Geranor and the other man-wolves emerging from the forest. Even knowing their secret, dressed as a man-wolf himself, their hybrid beast-man form was menacing. No doubt the other young shepherd would soon take to his heels.

"That's enough," said Broteas, gesturing down below. "They're moving in."

Stymphalus stopped howling. "All right. Let's head for the meeting place."

They reached the grove of ash trees, where they removed their wolf garb and cleaned their skin with oil and strigils; then, dressed once more as men, they started a small fire from coals brought in an earthenware vessel. Broteas dug a parcel of bread and cheese from his pack; the king poured wine into two wooden cups. They waited, while the stars in the east began to fade.

"They should be here by now," Stymphalus said.

Broteas sprinkled a few drops of his wine on the ground, praying first to the trickster god Hermes and then to his beloved Artemis. Then, just as the red rim of the sun glowed above the eastern horizon, they heard the sound of bleating sheep. Geranor and two other men came running into the grove.

"There you are!" said Stymphalus, relief plain on his face. "Is everything all right?"

"Yes, my lord king." Geranor bowed, which looked odd in his guise as man-wolf; his pelt was spattered with blood. "We got the entire herd."

"Well done!" exclaimed Stymphalus, breaking out into a grin.

The three other men bowed to their king and then started stripping off their helmets, paws, and fur; they would lead the flock into the next valley, inside Arcadian territory. One of them added, "Should be about six dozen animals, including twenty or so lambs, my lord king."

"Excellent! Bring a lamb here, for our thanks-offering to Zeus. And take food with you for the journey."

"Yes, my lord king," said the men, pulling on their tunics and sandals.

"Once you've got the flock settled," Stymphalus continued, "take a ewe without offspring to the Maidens of Artemis. We owe that goddess our thanks as well."

Acknowledging this order, the men headed back to the flock to assist their colleagues. Soon the other man-wolves arrived, one of them driving an injured ewe and her lamb along with a stick. Broteas went over to supervise the animals while the other men removed their disguises and cleansed the ash from their limbs. Then, after a prayer to Zeus, King Stymphalus slit the throat of the lamb. The Arcadians made quick work of skinning and jointing the carcass; they tossed the thigh bones and the fat onto the flames as an offering to Zeus and then spitted pieces of meat to roast for their own meal.

"That smells good," said Geranor, scrubbing at his ash-smeared face with a cloth. "I'm starving." He grabbed a hunk of bread and a wooden cup of wine, and sat beside Broteas.

"How was it?" Broteas asked.

"Not bad," said the younger man, dipping the end of his bread into his wine. "The first shepherd panicked as soon as he heard the wolf-cry!" Geranor laughed, then ate his bread. "The coward ran off towards town, screaming, 'They'll turn us into monsters!' The other one, he had a bit more fight in him. He had his dogs gather the flock closer together – but that just made it easier."

A man brought King Stymphalus a serving of lamb, then offered portions to Broteas and to Geranor. His mouth watering, Broteas accepted a skewer. "Did he see you?"

"Well, yes. But—" Geranor paused to take a bite of meat. "Doesn't matter. He's dead now. Him and those cursed dogs." With a jerk of his chin he indicated one of the other men, who was wrapping a wine-soaked bandage around a wound in his calf. "They were more trouble than the shepherd."

Broteas frowned. "You didn't leave any visible knife wounds, did you—"

"Of course not," Geranor interrupted, sounding irritable. "It'll look just like wolves done it." He pulled the last chunk of meat from the skewer with his teeth.

"I don't doubt you," Broteas said. "It was a good night's work. You've enriched Arcadia."

"Yes," Geranor said impatiently. He set aside his now-bare skewer. In a low voice, he said: "My lord prince, could we talk privately? I have something to discuss."

So *now* he would find out what troubled the man. "Very well," Broteas said, rising to his feet. "Let's take a walk."

They excused themselves from the king and headed into the woods. A blackbird warbled his morning song; dew sparkled on the leaves and stones. Geranor led the way, moving so quickly that Broteas, with his bad leg, had trouble keeping pace. Finally Geranor stopped near a large oak.

"All right," said Broteas, rubbing his aching leg. "Speak your mind."

"My lord prince, you said that we've enriched Arcadia. True enough. But do you mean for us to spend the rest of our lives this way?"

Broteas' eyes narrowed. "What are you getting at?"

Geranor folded his arms across his chest. "You've made no attempt to recover the mastiff in years."

"There's been no opportunity," Broteas objected.

"You haven't *made* an opportunity," countered Geranor.

The two of them had attended the games in Arcadian guise over the years, but they found the temple too well guarded. They had sought, through middlemen, to bribe the temple staff – but their approaches were rebuffed and they had again barely escaped with their lives. Still, Broteas knew he could have tried harder. The truth was he did not have the same ambition that drove his brother and his father.

"We could try again this year," Broteas said, for the next Olympic Games were only a few months away. "But I don't see what more we can do. Perhaps this is where Lady Artemis wants us to be."

Geranor shook his head; his voice rose in frustration. "Even if we can't get the mastiff, my lord prince, your father's an old man! He couldn't threaten you now. If we return to Lydia, you could become king any day!"

Broteas stared at the younger man. "Why are you saying this now?"

"Because I want to leave," Geranor said firmly. He turned and called out: "Come join us, my dear!"

A woman emerged from the shadows of the forest. She wore an undyed tunic that bared strong-looking arms and legs. She was full-breasted and tanned, and her golden hair was piled atop her head.

Geranor reached out to her; she came to his side and clasped his hand.

"Batia and I want to leave," Geranor said. "Together."

Broteas blinked, for he recognized the woman. "But you're a Maiden of Artemis!"

The woman shook her head. "No, my lord prince, my time with the Maidens is finished. Geranor has asked me to marry him, and travel east to his homeland."

"Of course," said Broteas, his wits returning. The Maidens of Artemis took only temporary vows of virginity; when their service was over, they could wed. But Broteas had not thought his friend was the marrying type. More than once, Geranor had passed up the opportunity to wed the daughter of an Arcadian merchant or artisan; Broteas assumed he had a woman – or several – among the local peasants.

Broteas considered, then spoke: "You may be right, Geranor: perhaps it's time to return home. There's an Argive trader in Tegea just now; we can speak to him about transport. He has a ship headed east next month."

Geranor and Batia exchanged a glance. Geranor said, "We'd rather leave now, my lord prince."

Broteas frowned. "Why hurry?"

"There she is!" called out a woman.

Three Maidens of Artemis emerged from the forest: when Batia saw them, she dropped Geranor's hand and sprinted away. Geranor looked wildly from her fleeing form to the approaching maidens, and then ran in a different direction.

"Quick," yelled a stocky woman, "catch her!" This was not a maiden that Broteas recognized – but one of the other two was his niece Chloris. She ran past him, her arms and legs pumping; the other two women followed. Batia had a head start, but Chloris was a champion runner; the distance between them quickly shrank. The blonde woman glanced over her shoulder, her eyes huge with fear; she stumbled slightly, giving Chloris a chance to get within arm's-length. Chloris lunged. Batia dodged and Chloris lost her balance, but caught at the other's ankle as she fell. Batia went sprawling; before she could get back to her feet, the thick-set woman had caught up and pinned her to the ground.

Batia struggled, but the other woman was stronger. "Geranor," she shrieked, "Geranor, help me!" But Geranor was gone.

Chloris stood, brushing dirt from her long legs. The other two women pulled Batia to her feet. Her right knee was scraped from the fall; crimson blood trickled down her shin. While the stocky woman bound Batia's arms behind her back with a leather thong, the third of the pursuers – Broteas did not recall her name, but the crescent-shaped silver buckle on her belt indicated she was the chief priestess – drew her obsidian knife. As Broteas stared, dumbfounded, the priestess grasped the neck of Batia's tunic, slit it all the way to the hem, and ripped it from her body. Chloris bent over to pick up the fallen garment, and then the three grim women led their captive, pleading for mercy, back the way they had come.

As they passed him, Broteas reached out to touch Chloris' elbow. "What's going on?" he asked.

Chloris stopped, her gray eyes flashing with anger. "Batia has broken her vow to Artemis," she said curtly. "She's with child."

"What?" gasped Broteas, shocked by this sacrilege. He glanced over at Batia's naked form; her buttocks jiggled as the other two dragged her away. "By my man Geranor?"

"I expect so," said Chloris.

Broteas swallowed. This appalling offense against Artemis could bring the goddess' curse upon Arcadia. Even if Artemis showed mercy to the kingdom, Stymphalus would be justifiably furious – and might blame Broteas for what had happened.

"What will happen to her?" Broteas asked.

Chloris' only answer was a shake of her head. She darted forward to join her companions and soon the four women were out of sight, leaving Broteas alone in the forest.

§ 7.04

Batia struggled and wept, but Anyte and Selene kept a firm grip on her bound arms. Chloris followed, ready to seize the woman who had been her companion for so many years in case she managed to twist free.

Anyte shouted over Batia's shrieks. "What about the man? We can't let him get away!"

Selene, chief priestess since Melissa's retirement three years earlier, shook her head. "With his head start, he'll be hard to catch. He looked like a fast runner. And, until the others return, there's only the three of us."

Anyte lowered her graying brows and told her captive: "See? If we hadn't found you, the others would have. You never had a chance of getting away. Why should he?" She shook Batia's arm. "Who is he? Tell us who he is!"

"Let me go!" screamed Batia.

Selene spoke sternly. "That man violated the sanctity of Artemis. He must be punished."

"That man violated *you*," added Anyte. "And look at him – he's run off, without you! He only wants to save his own skin! Why should you protect him?"

Chloris took a deep breath. "I know who the man is."

Selene and Anyte halted and turned to look at her. "Well?" asked Selene.

"Chloris, no!" begged Batia.

"His name is Geranor. He's originally from the east, but he's been a guest of King Stymphalus for many years."

"How do *you* know this?" Anyte asked, her eyes narrowing, as if she suspected Chloris of also dallying with a man.

Chloris felt her face redden, but she also knew that she had done nothing wrong. Lifting her chin, she said: "The man who was with Geranor is an old friend of my parents." Chloris rarely called attention to the fact that her father was king of Thebes, but this seemed like a good moment to remind the other Maidens of her lineage.

"He's even less attractive than Geranor," observed Selene. "I don't see him tempting our princess to break her vows."

"Of course not," Chloris said, her voice filled with scorn.

"Hmph," grunted Anyte. "Maybe not."

"Come on," said Selene, pulling Batia forward once more.

They soon reached the encampment. None of the other Maidens had returned; their packs and bedrolls remained in a neat circle around the banked campfire, and the bundles containing food hung from high tree branches, out of reach of foraging animals. Chloris went to check the coals; they were still glowing beneath the ash, and she added some fuel to rekindle the flames. While Anyte kept a firm grip on the weeping captive, Selene retrieved a length of rope and tied one end around Batia's neck, the other to the trunk of a sturdy tree just above a branch at shoulder height. As she worked, she said, "We should tell King Stymphalus about the man." She glanced over at Chloris. "You said his name was Geranor?"

Chloris nodded.

Selene pulled the final knot tight and stepped away from the captive. "His crime could bring Artemis' anger on Arcadia," she said. "We must inform the king at once. Anyte, you'll come with me."

"But what about this one?" Anyte kicked Batia, who squealed in pain.

"Chloris can guard her. Chloris, when the others return, tell them that Batia will be dealt with shortly."

"Can we trust her?" asked Anyte, pointing at Chloris. "They're good friends."

"You can trust me," Chloris snapped.

"Of course," Selene said, but Chloris knew Selene meant this to be a demonstration of her trust – to dispense with any question about Chloris' dedication to her vows because of her friend's failing. "We'll be back soon."

"We'll both be here," Chloris assured her.

As Selene and Anyte departed, Batia sank down against the tree trunk; the rope was just long enough to allow her to sit. She huddled into a ball, hiding her nakedness; Chloris guessed that if her hands had not been tied behind her back she would have wrapped her arms around her shins. The wound on her knee had crusted into a scab, and the streak of blood on her leg was brown and flaking. She wiped her running nose awkwardly against her shoulder, and looked at Chloris with eyes swollen from crying.

"Chloris, please – untie me."

Chloris turned away. "No," she said, not looking back.

Batia's voice trembled. "Remember when you first joined the Maidens? I'm the one who taught you how to tend the fire. I showed you how to clean and skin a deer. Chloris, we shared our *bed* when the nights were cold! How can you forget that?"

Chloris resolutely said nothing.

"Remember bathing together in the pool? And gathering herbs and firewood? And – and – just last month, I helped you nurse your mother when she was sick."

"I know," Chloris said. So many years of friendship – she swallowed hard, pushing away the memories. When she was sure she would not weep, she turned to look at her friend. "Batia, why did you do it?"

Batia looked up. "I was weak. I'm twenty-seven, and I had three more years of service left. I – I just couldn't wait any longer!"

Chloris rose and paced a circle around the fire. "Artemis is not merciful, Batia."

"But I was faithful for fourteen years!" Batia wailed. "And in all that time, for one moment of weakness – the penalty's too harsh, Chloris! You know they'll kill me!"

Chloris took a step towards her friend. If Batia were freed, could she possibly escape? Death did seem a cruel and disproportionate punishment.

But *had* it been only one moment of weakness? Batia had always had an eye for men. Chloris remembered how Batia had maintained, years ago, that it was all right to *look* at them. And, actually, that first time she spoke with her uncle Broteas here in Arcadia, not long after joining the Maidens, *Geranor* had arranged the meeting through Batia. The story had been that he approached Batia near one of her rabbit-snares and said that his master needed to speak with Chloris… but was that *really* the way it happened? Batia had always been eager, over the years, to return to Arcadia – and then reluctant to leave.

"You're lying," she said. "It wasn't just once. You've been meeting him secretly for years!"

"Chloris—"

"And look at your belly – you must have known that you were pregnant at least a month ago! Why didn't you leave as soon as you realized it?" Not only had her friend done wrong, she had behaved stupidly – and now Chloris would have to help the Maidens of Artemis kill her.

"I—" Batia tossed her head, trying unsuccessfully to shake a stray lock away from her eyes. "We met right after the Maidens came down from the cave to the spring. It had been so long – all winter – that I couldn't resist, even though I knew the time was wrong." A fresh tear slipped down her cheek. "I realized I was with child when we were in Thebes. Then after we got back, for a while I – I couldn't find the courage to tell him... but finally I did, and he was going to take me away!" She shrieked: "I love him! And he loves me! Why must the goddess punish love?"

"So filled with love that he ran like a hare!" Chloris stomped her foot. "Where is he now?"

Batia wailed, "I don't know! He wouldn't just leave me like that…"

A chill darted down Chloris' back, and her hand went to her dagger. *Would* Geranor try to rescue Batia? If so, she was in serious danger. She drew her blade and scanned the area warily.

"What are you doing?" asked Batia.

Chloris did not answer. Moving silently, she circled the perimeter of the encampment. The brush seemed undisturbed; a dove cooed in a tree.

"Chloris, what made Selene suspicious?"

Still looking for a desperate lover that might be prowling through the woods, Chloris said: "Anyte noticed that you've been vomiting in the mornings. So Selene decided we should follow you."

There was a noise in the brush; Chloris whirled around, knife at the ready. But it was only two other Maidens of Artemis, a pair of Corinthian sisters who had joined the cult three years earlier.

"You found her!" exclaimed the younger girl.

"Where's Selene?" asked her sister.

"She and Anyte went to speak with the king," Chloris said, lowering her dagger.

The younger sister peered at the naked prisoner. "By the crescent moon – Anyte was right! This *porni is* with child!"

"You've disgraced us all," said the other Corinthian. She slapped Batia across the face.

Chloris grabbed the girl's arm before she could strike again. "She'll be punished soon enough." She told the sisters to string their bows and keep watch for potential rescue attempts. But Geranor did not appear, and by mid-afternoon Selene and Anyte and all the other Maidens of Artemis had returned. Selene declared that the time for justice had arrived.

The high priestess bade the Maidens prepare their bows and arrows and then form a circle around Batia. Stepping into the circle, she pointed at the captive woman. "This creature, once called Batia, vowed virginity to Lady Artemis. She has broken that vow and must pay the price."

The women, each holding her bow, nodded solemnly.

Selene continued: "Just as Actaeon, who looked with lust upon the goddess, was transformed into a deer and torn to pieces by his own hounds – as Callisto, who broke her vow of chastity, was changed into a bear and hunted down – so is this creature now nothing more than a beast to be hunted and killed."

Chloris shivered. The punishment was fitting, but merciless.

"Please," begged the creature who had been Batia, "please, Selene—"

Ignoring this entreaty, Selene drew her obsidian knife and held it aloft. "I will release the quarry by cutting the rope that binds it to the tree. I will then count out the years this creature once pledged to Artemis, a full seven times. Then we will hunt down the quarry. It is the duty of every Maiden here to shoot to kill. Only that will cleanse us of this curse." She severed the rope that fastened Batia's neck to the tree, and then freed her hands. "Now!" she cried, shoving Batia's shoulder. She began to count: "One... two..."

Batia ran off, her full breasts bouncing as she darted through the trees in the grove.

Chloris' tension grew as Selene cycled through the numbers. It did not take very long.

"To the hunt, Maidens!" commanded the priestess, taking up her bow.

Chloris and the other Maidens sprang into pursuit, fanning out through the forest. Chloris knew they would soon spot their quarry. It would be best, she realized, to do this quickly – that way Batia would suffer less.

She darted through the brush, following the southward path that Batia had taken. She could no longer hear the sounds of movement – had Batia changed course? Perhaps she was hiding somewhere, hoping her pursuers would pass her by. Chloris slowed to scan the ground for signs. Soon she noticed a snapped twig and a faint heel print: she was on the right track.

The trees thinned out – and then Chloris spied the naked woman hurrying down a steep hill. The area was exposed, dangerous, but several goat-herding families had cottages nearby – there Batia might be able to hide until nightfall, steal some clothing, and escape under cover of darkness.

Chloris could not give her that chance. She pulled an arrow from her quiver, drew back the string, and took aim.

There was a crunching footfall in the gravel behind her; Chloris started in surprise just as she let her arrow fly. It shot past Batia's left shoulder, missing her by a hand's-breadth. Batia whirled, her mouth gaping in terror – then she scrambled faster down the slope.

Anyte, breathing hard, stopped beside Chloris. "I knew you'd never shoot your friend!" she said, her voice full of scorn.

"You startled me," objected Chloris, grabbing another arrow from her quiver.

Anyte grunted as she pushed forward and positioned an arrow on her bow. Her aim was not the best, and it was a long shot to make: would her arrow find its mark? Chloris held her breath, knowing that if Anyte missed she would have to take aim next.

Anyte's arrow left the bow with a sharp twang. It was the best shot Chloris had ever seen the woman make, and it pierced Batia through the back. Screaming, Batia staggered and fell; she rolled to the foot of the hill.

"The quarry's down!" Anyte shouted triumphantly.

Selene and several other Maidens came running up. Anyte pointed to the crumpled form at the bottom of the slope. "Well done," she said. "Your shot, Chloris?"

"No," Chloris said quietly. "It was Anyte."

"Really?" exclaimed two Maidens simultaneously.

Selene patted the stocky woman's shoulder. "Well done, Anyte! Lady Artemis must be pleased."

The other Maidens gathered around, pushing Chloris aside in their eagerness to congratulate Anyte. Chloris listened, but could not join in. After a moment she decided, despite the disapproval she might incur, to go to the fallen woman. Her quiver slapping against her back, she jogged down the hill.

She hoped that Batia was already dead – but as she came nearer, she could see the faint rise and fall of her chest. She lay sprawled on the rocky ground, one foot twisted at an unnatural angle: the ankle must have broken in her fall. The arrow's point did not penetrate her chest, but a broad pool of crimson was spreading from the wound in her back.

Chloris crouched beside her. She knew that, by the traditions of Artemis, the woman who had been her friend was now only a beast to be slain... and yet...

"Batia," she whispered.

Batia squinted up at Chloris, unable to shade her eyes from the afternoon sun. "Chloris," she moaned. "It hurts..." New tears traced pale, glistening tracks down her dirt-covered face.

Tears welled up in Chloris' own eyes – tears that she knew were unwarranted, unseemly. Blinking them back, she put her hand on Batia's shoulder as she had learned to do for women about to die in childbirth. When there was no way to ease the pain of the dying, a comforting touch eased the spirit as it was forced out of a broken body to make its journey to the Underworld.

"Chloris," Batia sighed, blood trickling from her mouth. Her body trembled violently, and then she was still.

Chloris murmured a prayer for her journey. When she was sure that Batia's life was gone she straightened and climbed slowly back up the slope. The silence of the maidens watching her was a clearer rebuke than words.

Anyte snorted. "Is it dead?"

"Yes," said Chloris. She turned to Selene. "What should we do with the body?"

"Leave it for carrion," said Anyte.

Chloris' stomach lurched at the idea of crows feeding on Batia's flesh. "Lady Artemis showed mercy after Callisto's death," she said. "The gods hung her image in the sky."

Selene stared at Chloris; Chloris stared back. "We will burn the body," the high priestess finally said. "The smoke will reach the goddess and she will know that we avenged her honor."

So the maidens gathered wood for a funeral pyre; just as the sun was setting, they lit the fire. Soon the stars of late spring sparkled overhead, Callisto's bear constellation among them, and Batia's corpse was reduced to seared bone and ash.

Chloris pulled her blanket around her and lay down alone, hiding her tear-stained face from the others. For the first time since joining the Maidens of Artemis, she wished her service were finished.

§ 7.05

"Your turn, Father!"

Laius drained his wine-cup, leaving only the thick sediment of lees at the bottom. Then he sized up the target, a shallow dish floating in a tub of water. It took skill to toss the lees from one's cup so that they landed on the dish. Most failed attempts splashed some liquid into the dish, giving the next player a better chance of sinking the target. But, of course, the real point of the game was the drinking.

"Remember," said Thyestes, "before you throw, you must say which beauty you admire most."

With his son Polydorus joining the drinking-party for the first time, Laius decided to name the boy's mother. "Nerissa," he said loudly, lifting his cup. He winked at his son; the boy grinned with pride.

Laius flicked his wrist, tossing the cup's contents – but he put too much force into it, and most of the lees fell into the water beyond the dish. The men laughed, and Thyestes called for a servant to refill Laius' cup.

"My turn," said Atreus, stepping forward and lifting his cup. "This for the glorious Princess Chloris!" A finger looped through one of the two handles of his cup, he flung the dark lees out – they plopped directly onto the target, and the little dish sank.

The men, mostly athletes arrived early to train for the Games next month, cheered loudly; a discus thrower shouted that it was a sign that Chloris would wed Atreus when her service to Artemis was done. A servant fished the target from the bottom of the tub, while another refilled the drinkers' cups. It was a warm night in late spring; flaming torches lit Hestia's courtyard. As the men continued their game, one kept count of all the different beauties Thyestes named, from serving women to the wives of visiting dignitaries, and each new name was greeted with raucous laughter. As the evening went on, and more wine went down, a wrestler named Polydorus as the object of his desire; the youth's cheeks flushed, which only made him more attractive. Laius clapped his son on the shoulder, proud of his good looks.

Thyestes took the next toss, and missed; the turn passed to Polydorus, and then to another man and another. After the target sank once more, Thyestes suggested they call for flute-players; another man suggested acrobats instead.

"Why not trained monkeys?" The voice from the side entrance was filled with contempt.

"Stand up straight," Laius hissed at his son. "It's the king!"

As Laius snapped to attention the other men followed his lead, but several were unsteady on their feet. One man hiccupped.

Pelops strode into the courtyard, strands of gray in his hair and beard shining like silver in the torchlight. "Monkeys would be too dignified for you,"

Pelops snapped. "Look at you – the three wastrel princes. Wine, women, and song." He looked from Atreus to Thyestes and then Laius. "Did you know that an entire flock has been taken? One of the shepherds killed, all the animals gone!"

"An entire flock?" gasped Atreus. "Where? How? I had patrols out..."

"They must have been in the wrong place. And you – and these other two – are *here*. Your drinking and your negligence are costing me a fortune. When do you ever do anything *useful?*"

"But Father," objected Thyestes, "we're—"

Laius squeezed Thyestes' arm. "You're right, my lord king, it's late. Time to turn in."

Pelops' eyes narrowed. "Past time." He turned to go, but Laius heard his snort and the mutter that followed: "Three good-for-nothing princes and a good-for-nothing bastard!" He stalked out.

The athletes hastily retired to their chambers adjoining the courtyard, leaving Laius with Atreus, Thyestes and Polydorus. Atreus sank heavily down onto a bench. "A whole flock," he muttered. "I don't believe it!"

"Why can't you catch a few stupid wolves?" asked Thyestes.

Atreus' voice echoed in the now-empty courtyard. "They're not wolves. Last month I saw one, lit up by the moon: neither man nor wolf, but something in between." He rubbed his temples. "Some god must have taken the form of a wolf and seduced a tree-dryad. That's the only way such creatures could have been whelped. What man can slay monsters sired by a god?"

A chill ran down Laius' back. Atreus had spoken of the peasants' fear of man-wolves before, describing the remains of sheep – and sometimes men – found with their throats ripped open. But his friend had never before claimed to have seen one of the monsters himself. Laius' son edged closer as if he, too, were unnerved at the thought.

"Obviously *you* can't," Thyestes said.

Atreus clenched his fists. "I'd like to see either of you do better."

"I've served King Pelops well," Laius said, still smarting from the king's words. "I've managed three sets of Olympic Games, with the fourth just to come. I supervised the building of this temple for Hestia, and the practice grounds, even though sometimes the treasuries were nearly bare." This was a swipe at both Thyestes and Atreus, for both demanded the finest clothing, the best horses, and the most excellent of the bronze-smiths' art. Thyestes was best known for his extravagant presents to pretty women, and Atreus for his drinking parties. "What have you done for Pisa?"

"Well," Thyestes said defensively, "I manage the horses."

Atreus gave a snort of derision. "You make sure that the stallions cover the mares – they'd do that *without* your encouragement. The king hasn't sent you out to watch the flocks because he doesn't want you buggering the sheep!"

Thyestes shrugged and stroked his well-trimmed beard. "Who do you think he was calling a bastard?" he asked, glancing at Atreus.

Laius guessed Pelops had meant his son; the boy looked anxious. Not wanting Polydorus to serve as a game-piece in the ongoing conflict between

Atreus and Thyestes, Laius put an arm around his son's shoulders. "Let's go, Polydorus. The king told us to call it a night, and your mother will be wondering where you are." The boy did not protest as Laius led him out through the corridor, past the frescoes that showed the goddess of the hearth at work: kindling the flames, feeding the fire, sweeping up ashes. Taking a torch from a wall-sconce, he led his son down the side stairway and out across the field.

It *was* late, Laius realized, looking at the position of the stars. Nerissa would scold him for keeping Polydorus out too long. On the other hand, she often complained that he didn't spend enough time with his son – she couldn't have it both ways.

"Did you enjoy yourself?" he asked.

"Mostly," the boy said. "But King Pelops was very angry."

Polydorus was right: the king's temper had been short lately. Laius was unsure if this was only because Pelops was growing older, or if something particular was bothering him. But he said: "You'd be angry, too, if a flock of sheep had been stolen from you."

Polydorus walked several steps in silence, then asked: "Do Atreus and Thyestes always fight like that?"

"Usually. It's like putting two bulls in the same pen. They can't help charging each other."

"But they're men, not bulls." The boy kicked at a fallen pinecone. It skipped ahead, out of the circle of torchlight into the darkness. "What are they fighting for?"

"They both want to be king after Pelops. But he hasn't named either of them his heir."

"What about you?" asked Polydorus. "King Pelops likes you."

Laius laughed. "My boy, even if the king disowned both Atreus and Thyestes he's got plenty of other sons." He held no illusion that Pelops meant to join him to the Pisatan royal house. In all the years Laius had lived in Pisa, the king had never suggested that Laius wed one of his daughters. Instead he arranged a match between Astydamia and the king of Tiryns, and strengthened his alliance with wealthy Mycenae by marrying Nikippe to King Electryon's younger brother.

"But you *are* the son of a king, aren't you, Father?"

Laius took a turn at kicking the pinecone; it bounced off the path. "Yes; Labdacus of Thebes was my father."

"Then why aren't *you* king of Thebes?"

"I gave it up. It's not much of a kingdom, anyway. More cows than people."

Polydorus seemed to accept this; for a while he remained silent. Then, after they had crossed the Cladeus stream, he said: "King Pelops wasn't born here. He won Pisa in a contest."

"You're right, he did," said Laius, yawning. "Queen Hippodamia's father offered the kingdom and his daughter to the man who could beat him in a chariot race."

Polydorus rubbed the side of his nose, obviously thinking. "Are there any princesses I could win?"

"The Spartan throne always passes from mother to daughter – the man who marries the king's daughter becomes the next king. But Sparta's princess is a little girl, and I haven't heard of any kingdoms to be had for a chariot-race lately. It might be simpler to start a new city, like our ancestor Cadmus." Laius continued along the path, not wanting to mention the obvious: before Pelops succeeding in winning Hippodamia's hand, thirteen men had lost their lives trying. But who could say whether those men had made the wrong choice? Perhaps life without power and glory was not worth living – at least not for them.

As they passed the Temple of Zeus and approached Rhea's temple, Laius saw that the sky was no longer so black in the east. He began mentally rehearsing his excuses he would have to make to Nerissa: already he could hear her saying how worried she had been; how he should be a more responsible father, now that they had *two* sons together. Laius decided to remind her how important it was for Polydorus to get to know the princes, if he were to become an important man in Pisa...

"Father, look!" Polydorus whispered, clutching Laius' arm.

Stopping abruptly, Laius looked in the direction his son pointed; a man stood before Rhea's shrine. A chill gripped Laius: he was reminded of that night, so many years ago, when the Trojans had tried to steal Rhea's golden mastiff – and dealt Polyxo a fatal injury.

Laius shook his head at his fear. Rhea's mastiff was no longer displayed in the temple, except on special occasions; the shrine contained nothing worth stealing now. Still, it was odd to see someone standing here at this hour, when no sunrise ceremony was planned.

As his son was beside him, Laius decided to set a good example. "What brings you here so early, stranger?" he asked, his voice more challenging than friendly.

The man started at the sound; turning, he lifted his hands in a placating gesture. "Excuse me," he said. "I'm not from these parts." His accent was odd – rather like that of the Arcadian hill-folk, but with another element Laius could not immediately identify.

"And what are you doing here?" As soon as he had spoken the words, Laius regretted the question: it was rude to ask a traveler his business before offering hospitality.

"Admiring this temple," the stranger said. "I've heard great things about the temples of Pisa – I've always wanted to see them."

Laius stepped closer, lifting his torch – though in the growing light it was not really necessary. The man did not seem threatening. His sandals were dirty and well-worn, and his shins were scratched. His kilt, belt, and cloak were nondescript; there were smudges on his face, and dust in his beard. He carried nothing, not even a waterskin.

"You travel light," Laius observed.

"I was robbed," the man said. "I was lucky to escape with my life."

"Bandits? Where?" asked Laius. Then he stopped himself. "I'm sorry. You must be hungry and thirsty. Come with us – I'll make sure you get something to eat." It was his duty to help a traveler in distress – and the presence of this man might forestall any complaints from Nerissa about Polydorus' late night.

"I'd be most grateful," said the stranger.

Laius and his son led the man down the path to Nerissa's cottage. The shutters were open, so Laius guessed that Nerissa was awake and the door unbarred. He was correct on both counts; as he opened the door, Nerissa called out: "There you are! I was so worried – you've been gone *all night*!"

Extinguishing his torch, Laius told the stranger to wait outside. The man nodded and folded his arms; Laius and Polydorus stepped into the cottage. A pot of barley porridge hung over the hearth-fire. Nerissa sat on a bench by the table with their new son on her lap; she was feeding him with a small wooden spoon. "I couldn't sleep, and of course Gogos kept fussing. Finally I decided to get up and make breakfast." There was reproach in her eyes. "Laius, why did you keep Polydorus out so late?"

Because of the man waiting outside, Laius kept his voice low. "It was a party! Of course we were out late."

"A growing boy needs his sleep!"

"Mother," Polydorus said, rolling his eyes, "I'm *fifteen,* not a baby!"

"Nerissa," Laius interrupted, "I've brought a guest."

Nerissa set the small wooden spoon into the bowl on the table. "A guest? *Now?*" she whispered angrily. "Who is it – Thyestes? Atreus? Or some other drunk?"

"No, a stranger we met on the way home. He was set upon by bandits – doesn't seem hurt, but he has nothing."

"He's just outside," added Polydorus.

"And he's hungry," said Laius. "Starving, by the looks of it."

"So am I," said Polydorus.

Nerissa's expression softened. "Very well. Give me a moment; I'm not fit to be seen."

"Nonsense," said Laius. "You're as lovely as ever."

"You know, Mother, during one of the drinking games each of us had to name the most beautiful creature we'd ever seen," Polydorus said. "Father picked you."

This elicited a grudging smile from Nerissa. "Go back outside, the two of you," she said. "I'll let you know when you can come in." She stood, lifting the child in her arms. "Polydorus, since you're so fond of drinking, you take some water to our guest."

Laius went back outside and bade the stranger take a seat beneath the pine tree; Polydorus followed, carrying a pitcher of water and three wooden cups. Just as the foreigner was finishing his second cup of water, Nerissa opened the door and invited them inside. The cottage – always tidy – was freshly swept. Nerissa had combed back her long blonde hair and fastened it with a green ribbon; it matched the gown she had put on, and emphasized the color of her eyes. She moved with grace as she served them bowls of barley porridge and then set out a plate of raisins and dried figs. The stranger ate greedily, but his eyes followed Nerissa as she tended the hearth and then carried over a fig to little Gogos, lying in his crib.

Laius felt a surge of pride in his woman. She *was* beautiful – everyone said so. Nerissa might not be the most fertile of women; between Polydorus and young Gogos there were many years. But what did he need with a horde of sons?

The stranger finished the pitcher of water and downed two bowls of porridge; finally he belched loudly. "Excuse me."

"You shouldn't eat so fast," Nerissa remarked.

His smile displayed large, slightly crooked teeth. "You're right, mistress."

Laius pushed back his own empty bowl. "Feeling better?"

"Yes," said the stranger, wiping his mouth. "I've eaten almost nothing for the last two days. May Zeus, Lord of Heaven and Earth, bless you and your family for taking care of a traveler." There was sadness in his voice – understandable, when he had lost all his belongings.

"Will you tell me your name and your business in Pisa?" Laius asked.

The man seemed to consider, then shrugged. "Why not? My name's Geranor. I'm from Lydia, originally – but I haven't been there for many years."

"Like King Pelops," said Polydorus, his eyes wide.

Laius nodded slowly. *That* was what he heard beneath the Arcadian accent – this Geranor pronounced some words the same way King Pelops did.

Geranor smiled weakly. "Like your king, I sailed west to seek my fortune. But unlike him, I've had no success." He fell silent for a moment, looking down at his dusty feet. When he continued, his voice was hoarse and low. "And now – now...." He pressed his hands to his face; his lank brown hair fell forward, and his shoulders shook as he choked back sobs.

Nerissa rose and leaned over the table. "I'll rinse these," she said gently, taking Geranor's bowl, "and then bring you a basin so you can wash your face."

"I thank you, kind mistress," said Geranor, wiping his eyes. "You're as generous as you are beautiful."

Nerissa took the bowls and the empty pitcher; with a word to Polydorus to watch his brother, she went to fetch more water from her cistern. Once more the stranger's gaze followed her.

"You're fortunate to have such a woman," said Geranor. "Mine..." His words trailed off.

"The bandits?" Laius asked.

"You could say that," said Geranor, his voice suddenly harsh. "She's dead now. So there's no reason for me to remain in these parts. I might as well go home – see if anyone remembers me after all these years. I've got a mother and sister, back in Lydia. Or at least I did when I left."

Laius rested his chin on his fist, peering at the man they had encountered outside Rhea's temple. A Lydian. A Lydian who had spent time in Arcadia.

A *Lydian* accent – not a Trojan one. That could explain everything.

Nerissa returned with the pitcher; she placed a basin on the table before

Geranor and filled it with water, then gave him a towel. "I thank you," muttered the man, dipping his hands into the water and splashing his face and beard.

"You must be exhausted," Laius said.

Polydorus gave a huge yawn. "I know I am."

"Go into the back room and sleep, Son," said Nerissa.

"No, I want him to stay up a little longer," Laius countered. Nerissa frowned at this, but because of the stranger, she said nothing. Polydorus yawned again and leaned against the wall.

Laius, however, felt as alert as a hawk as he watched Geranor wash his face. Polyxo had told them the thieves who attacked Rhea's temple were from Troy. But what if they had lied to her? The rival nations were neighbors; Lydians sounded much like Trojans. What if the thieves had been from Lydia? And didn't *Lydia* have more motive than Troy to seek the mastiff? After all, it was the icon of Lydia!

The man dried his face, then stood and stretched. He was about the height of one of the Trojan thieves. A little heavier, true, but men's forms often thickened with time.

Laius' hand fell casually to his dagger. "What brought you to the temple?"

Geranor dropped the towel on the table. "The Temple of Rhea?"

"Yes," said Laius, leaping from his seat as he drew his blade. With his left hand he grasped Geranor's wrist and twisted his arm back into a wrestling hold, then pressed the dagger to the man's throat. "You bastard!" he hissed.

Gogos shrieked, and Polydorus asked: "Father?"

"Laius, what are you doing?" cried Nerissa, springing to her feet.

Laius ground out: "This is one of the Trojan thieves." He pressed the bronze against the man's neck. "He tried to steal Rhea's mastiff."

"I don't know what you're talking about," Geranor gasped.

"If you're a stranger to Pisa, how did you know that was the Temple of Rhea?"

"I—"

"It was still dark!" Laius shouted. "You said you'd never been to Pisa before!"

"What if I have?" sputtered Geranor. "That's no crime!"

"It *was* a crime!" Laius wrenched the man's arm further back. "You violated the temple!"

"You beast!" screamed Nerissa. "You killed my mother!" She kicked his shin; Geranor yelped.

"Are you going to kill him, Father?" Polydorus asked, sounding eager.

"Laius—" Geranor's voice took on a pleading note. "I'm your guest. I've eaten at your table. Zeus will curse you if you harm me."

Laius' heart thudded hard. Nerissa and Polydorus expected him to kill the man. All he had to do was slit his throat. And yet...

As if sensing his reluctance, Geranor continued: "Besides, I have information for you. Valuable information!"

Laius eased the blade back a hair's breadth, but he did not slacken his grip. "What information?"

"I know who's raiding King Pelops' flocks."

This was unexpected. "You know about the monsters?"

"Yes." Geranor breathed deeply. "I know everything about them. Everything! If I tell you, will you let me go? And let me leave Pisa without harming me?"

Laius considered this. "If your answer satisfies me, I will."

"Laius!" objected Nerissa. "He killed my mother!"

"That was an accident, beautiful mistress. An accident!"

"We can't bring your mother back," said Laius, his mind working rapidly, "but if we can stop the raids on Pisa's flocks, think what that will mean to the king! And what *that* will mean for me – and our sons!"

Nerissa made a frustrated, wordless noise, but she did not argue.

"Start talking," Laius growled.

Geranor trembled. "Do you swear by Zeus not to harm me?"

"I swear by Zeus, Lord of Heaven and Earth, that I will not harm you – *if* your words are satisfactory," said Laius. "Now, speak."

§ 7.06

"What!" raged Pelops, slashing the racing goad he held against the frame-post of the nearest stall. The dappled mare within it whinnied in alarm, stepping protectively in front of her young foal. "Those dung-eating Arcadians have been raiding my flocks all along?"

Laius flinched, his arm lifting as if to ward off a blow; Atreus and Thyestes edged backwards, and even Myrtilus slid out of reach.

"My – my lord king—" stammered Laius, "I thought you would – would want to know…"

Myrtilus said: "And we do want to know, don't we, old friend?"

Pelops took a deep breath, struggling to calm himself. He glanced at Thyestes, who had brought him and Atreus to see the young horse – then at Atreus, who *should* have brought him this information about the flocks. Then he turned back to Laius. "And just how do *you* know all this?"

"My lord king, a man came to Nerissa's cottage begging for food and drink. He's been living in Arcadia, where he learned the man-wolves' secret. He told me."

"Why?" Pelops demanded. "Why did he tell you this?"

"He had some falling-out with the Arcadians."

Pelops twisted the goad with his hands. "All right. Where's this man now? I want to speak with him."

"I – I don't know, my lord king."

"You. Don't. Know," Pelops ground out. "*Why* don't you know, Laius?"

Laius licked his lips. "He's gone, my lord king. He left Pisa."

"You let him *go?*" The willow-wand snapped in his hands; Pelops cast the two halves aside and closed on Laius, standing so near that their noses almost touched. "If this man knew all about how Stymphalus has been tricking the peasants with stories of monsters, he must have been one of the thieves! Yet you let him go!"

Dropping to his knees, Laius admitted: "I did, my lord king. I gave my word, my lord king."

Pelops could not believe his ears. *"Your word?* How dare you give your word!"

"He – he was my guest, my lord king," Laius said, his brown eyes widening, his tone pleading. "To harm him would have angered Zeus."

"Your guest! How can a man be a guest anywhere in Pisa when he has stolen from me?" Pelops spat and whirled away, unable to bear the sight of Laius an instant longer.

Myrtilus' ghost sidled closer. "Stymphalus has been making a fool of you. For years."

You're right, thought Pelops. He reached out to stroke the neck of the stallion Foam, a son of his beloved chariot-horse Wave. The feel of the steed's strong muscles, its well-groomed coat, helped to calm him. The stallion nuzzled his hand, and Pelops noticed a bluish cast to the horse's eye: even Wave's sons were growing old.

Turning back towards Laius, still kneeling in the dirt, Pelops said: "You have no right to give your word, do you understand?" Extending his index finger, he pointed at Laius, Thyestes, and then Atreus. "Any of you! You've already given your word to your king – all authority belongs to me." He paced down the line of stalls and back again, obscurely satisfied and yet at the same time disgusted to see that none of the three princes had moved. "Should any of you ever become a king – which I *seriously* doubt – you will understand."

Laius gazed at Pelops' feet; Atreus and Thyestes studied the ground as well.

"They fear you," Myrtilus said. "That's good."

None of them deserves the title of prince, let alone king, Pelops fumed silently.

"Then disown them," Myrtilus said. "Or kill them. That's what old King Oenomaus would have done. And your father Tantalus would never tolerate incompetence." He tapped a ghostly finger against his lips. "Of course, he did try to kill *you...*"

Pelops strode over to the man who might or might not be his eldest son. "Atreus," he barked.

Atreus threw back his shoulders and stood straighter. "Yes, my lord king?"

Their relationship had worsened ever since Atreus had disobeyed Pelops to visit his mother on Zakynthos. To his credit, Atreus had confessed the deed immediately after committing it – and Pelops had received a report from Hippodamia's guards that Atreus had not attempted to rescue her, but had only spoken with her. Pelops had considered executing Atreus – but how could he kill a son for visiting his mother?

"It was your task to find the culprits," Pelops said. "You failed completely."

Atreus flushed, his pockmarked face turning an ugly red.

He can't be my son, thought Pelops. *I could never have sired anything so hideous.*

"Well?" Pelops prompted. "What do you have to say for yourself?"

"I—" Atreus began hoarsely, then stopped to clear his throat. "I believed they were monsters, my lord king. We saw them only from a distance – wolf-headed creatures with tails and fur. Their tracks were not the footprints of men."

"You're an incompetent fool," Pelops said.

"Forgive me, my lord king." Like Laius, he fell to his knees. "I have failed you."

"Two useless cowards," observed the ghost, going to stand between Laius and Atreus. "Two tempting necks."

Disgusted, Pelops looked away – to see Thyestes still standing, a smirk on his handsome face.

"Why are you grinning?" Pelops snapped.

Thyestes' mouth moved to a more neutral position, but his lips still twitched.

"Pretty boy, isn't he?" said Myrtilus. "Looks just like his mother. And he's been just as useless to you."

Pelops walked over and shoved Thyestes' shoulder. "Think you're better than those two? Think you've made no mistakes?" Pelops shoved him again; his son staggered backwards. "That's because you've *done* nothing!"

Thyestes gaped. "I – Father—" He swept his hand around at the stables. "But the horses…"

"Oh, yes, the horses. And the parties you've thrown, and the women you've bedded!" Pelops snorted. "At your age, I'd been king of Pisa for more than ten years!"

Slowly, gracefully, Thyestes brought one knee to the ground. "You're right, Father. I'm nothing compared to you. No one is." He stretched out a hand in a gesture of entreaty. "It's my good fortune to call you king and Father. It's my duty to bring glory to your name. I swear to you, Father, I'll do better."

"Humph," grunted Pelops. "Such a honeyed tongue. No wonder so many women lift their skirts for you." He knew better than to let the flattery soothe him – and yet it reminded him of the real target of his anger. Folding his arms across his chest, he said: "What glory can I claim, when a hill-king can steal from me? A man whose 'kingdom' consists of scrub-covered rocks? This Stymphalus must be punished!"

The three young men glanced at each other, but none of them ventured a word.

"How could a peasant king could be so clever?" said Myrtilus.

"Oh, get off your knees," Pelops said.

Warily they rose to their feet; Laius was the first to speak. "You're right, my lord king. This is intolerable."

Pelops paced the length of the stable; the grooms and other servants stirred from shadowed corners like rabbits after an eagle had passed over. Finally he said: "We'll teach Stymphalus a lesson. Muster the army and march on Arcadia."

"My lord king," Laius said, "the Games are about—"

"How can we hold games when we're being attacked?" Pelops interrupted. He turned to Atreus. "We have better soldiers, more of them. And the best chariots! We'll crush them."

Atreus combed his fingers through his beard. "We have superior soldiers. But the terrain…"

"You've been running around their terrain for more than ten years."

"Father," Thyestes interjected, "Our chariots will be useless in those mountains. They only give us an advantage on a level battlefield."

Myrtilus laughed. "You've been preparing for one war while Arcadia has waged another."

"The Arcadians would melt back into the hills," Atreus said.

"Then we follow them," Pelops said. "We smoke them out, like wasps from the nest."

Atreus shook his head. "Too costly, my lord king," he said. "Each man we killed would mean two Pisatan lives lost. Maybe three."

"Afraid, Atreus?" Pelops asked. "All those years in charge of the army, and you're still a coward."

This time Atreus' face did not redden. "If I were a coward, Father, I would not risk your anger by pointing out the difficulties."

His head throbbing, Pelops stared into the younger man's eyes. When, after a long moment, Atreus still did not flinch, he felt a grudging respect. The last twelve years had been hard on this possible son of his, and though Atreus was not handsome or well-spoken, he was a devoted soldier. And what he said about Arcadia's hills was true.

Laius cleared his throat. "My lord king, maybe there's another way to go about this. Arcadia has been raiding flocks from other kingdoms, too. Kingdoms with which you have close ties. Mycenae – Pylos – even Sicyon."

"Go on," said Pelops.

"They'll be outraged as well. They could help us settle the dispute."

"Dispute?" Pelops yelled. "There's no dispute! Stymphalus is raiding my flocks!"

Thyestes lifted a hand. "Laius may not have chosen his words well, Father, but I think I know what he means. Most of the kings will soon be here for the games. Speak to your allies then, Father. By joining with them, we can force Stymphalus to pay back what he has stolen – and more."

Pelops nodded slowly. His Olympic Games would start in less than a month. He had worked so hard, for so many years, to make them events of peace – he should not mar this festival with a battle. With his allies' help, he would find another way to punish Stymphalus.

"If they really are your allies," said the ghost, insinuating himself between Pelops and Thyestes. "Maybe they were conspiring with Stymphalus. Pisa has lost more sheep than any other kingdom to the man-wolves. They might have given Stymphalus those few sheep that were allegedly taken, in exchange for the humiliation he was heaping on you."

Pelops closed his eyes and rubbed his temples, trying to ease the pain.

"You've been taking tribute for years," the ghost continued. "Some kings must resent that."

Myrtilus was right. Though they should be happy to support his games – to honor the gods with splendid temples – some of the other kings probably resented his success. But which? He needed to find out.

§ 7.07

To Amphion, it seemed that the conversations at that year's Olympic Games were as much about marriage as about sport. When King Pelops greeted the group from Thebes he first asked about Niobe's health, since she had not made the long journey – but his next question was not about which contests Amphion's sons would enter, but whether his twin daughters were betrothed.

"They'll make perfect brides for Atreus and Thyestes," said Pelops. "Those two are rivals in everything – but if they marry twin sisters, there'd be no arguments." He smiled at the girls and beckoned them forward; they complied, smiling shyly, but clearly won over by their handsome uncle in his gleaming ivory armor and golden crown.

He's aging better than Zethos and I, Amphion thought ruefully. Pelops' hair was only gray at the temples, while Amphion's had gone completely silver and Zethos, standing beside Amphion, was almost totally bald. Pelops' right shoulder and chest were bare, displaying a tanned and muscular physique; but for the lines in his face, he could pass for a man of thirty-five instead of one nearing fifty.

"How old are you, Cleodoxa?" Pelops asked.

"I'm Eudoxa, my lord king," said the girl Pelops had addressed. "We're twelve."

"A good age for betrothal! And as pretty as a pair of pearls." Pelops turned to his sons. "Well, boys? What do you think of your cousins?" The men – Atreus had to be about thirty, with Thyestes only a year younger – looked the girls up and down.

"Pelops, I must protest," said Amphion.

"What? This has to be done sometime. Our, ah, wives—" Pelops hesitated over the word, reminding Amphion of the long-absent Hippodamia, "our wives are not here to remind us to be delicate. Make me an offer. Tell me what dowries the girls would bring, and promise that you'll let me have both of them for my sons." He stopped, peering at Amphion. "You're not still letting your daughters choose for themselves, are you?"

Amphion spread his hands. "You know that your sister will insist."

"Then my sister should have come with you," Pelops said.

"She's recovering, as I said, but the illness left her weak." Amphion did not want to reveal that, about a month after her fever ended, Niobe had lost most of her hair and now refused to appear in public.

Pelops' eyes narrowed, as if he suspected that Amphion was not telling him everything. Then he addressed Atreus and Thyestes: "You two, treat your cousins well, understand?" He turned to welcome the next set of guests.

That night at the Theban campsite, while young Tantalus strummed his lyre, Thebe broached the subject of marriage again. "King Pelops thinks it's time you betrothed the twins. Well, I think it's time we betrothed Ogygia to Idmon."

"They'll make a good couple," Zethos agreed, gesturing to the far side of the campfire, where Idmon and Ogygia sat with most of the other children, listening to Tantalus' song. "They're always together anyway."

Amphion spluttered his mouthful of wine. "They're only eleven!"

Thebe frowned. "Are you saying you don't want them to marry?" Her voice assumed that fierce mother-bear tone that emerged whenever anyone said anything that could be interpreted as a slight against her beloved boy.

"I'm saying – I'm just saying they're only eleven."

"Nonsense." Zethos reached for Thebe's hand. "Idmon's like me. He knew the woman for him from the moment he saw her."

Her cheeks dimpling, Thebe rewarded Zethos with a kiss; Amphion looked away, considering. Niobe *did* want to give her daughters a say in choosing their husbands – and they all knew that Ogygia would pick Idmon, if asked. "This needs to be decided in Thebes," Amphion said firmly. "Niobe must take part."

Thebe rested her head against her Zethos' broad shoulder. "Idmon and Ogygia could even be the next king and queen of Thebes!" she whispered – softly, but loud enough for Amphion's sharp hearing.

Amphion glanced around to see if any of the children had overheard; but Alphenor and Phaedimus were playing knucklebones, and the others were listening to Tantalus' music. Amphion confronted his sister-in-law. "Alphenor's my heir," he said, his voice low but firm. "He'll succeed me."

Thebe bristled, but Zethos held up his hand. "Brother, think about it. It might be best to choose a younger heir."

"How so?" asked Amphion, quelling his anger. Before shooting down this idea, he needed to understand what his brother and sister-in-law were thinking.

Thebe took over the argument. "Amphion, you and Zethos are both healthy and strong. You could easily live another twenty years. Thirty, even! What's Alphenor supposed to do during all that time? A young man with his talents should be running a kingdom."

"You mean running a kingdom other than Thebes," said Amphion, nettled. Obviously, Thebe was making this suggestion because she had ambitions for her own son – and, just as obviously, she had won Zethos over to her scheme. It pained him that his twin would turn against him; but, then, sons were dearer to the heart even than brothers.

And *his* son mattered more than *his* brother. Amphion emptied the lees from his wine-cup onto the ground. "Forget it," he said. "Alphenor will be king after me."

"Is that what Alphenor wants?" Thebe asked.

"Of course it is," Amphion snapped, and then realized he had never put that question to his eldest son. He frowned at his empty cup.

"Thebe," said Zethos, "this is just idle talk. As my brother said, Idmon and Ogygia are only eleven."

"And right now what's important for Thebes is finishing the walls," Amphion said.

"Of course," Thebe said cheerfully. "Do you still think they'll be done this summer?"

"Yes," said Amphion. "They'd be finished already, but for the Games."

To his relief, the conversation turned to the next day's contests. Zethos had finally decided he was too old to enter the wrestling; four years ago, he had lost to a younger man. But the next generation of Thebans planned to enter many competitions – and as the festival continued, they distinguished themselves impressively. Phaedimus easily took the prize for archery, and Alphenor won the javelin-cast after Atreus' throw went wide; Damasichthon wrestled Pelops' son Letreus to finish first in the men's wrestling contest, while Idmon placed first in the short-distance footrace for boys. In the girls' race, Eudoxa and Cleodoxa crossed the finish line with only a finger's-breadth between them. The twins refused to say who had won, and the judges could not tell them apart, so they were given a single olive crown to share. They seemed content with this: one twin wore it in the mornings; the other in the afternoons.

Thebes' many victories brought much attention, and Amphion found himself conversing again and again about betrothals for his children. The king of Corinth had two eligible daughters, and Sparta's king mentioned that he had a young daughter as well. This item Amphion found particularly intriguing, for the man who married the princess would become Sparta's next king. With so many sons, this was an excellent opportunity – but the Spartan princess was still very young.

On the second afternoon of the festival, King Neleus of Pylos approached him. They ducked into the shade of an awning to avoid the blazing sun and then, after the usual pleasantries, Neleus mentioned that his wife had died two years ago. She had given him a son several years before, but he wanted to marry again.

"My daughters are rather young," Amphion said, scratching his chin, for it seemed that he had practically promised off Cleodoxa, Eudoxa and Ogygia, and the others were even younger.

Neleus smiled. "Not all of them. What about Princess Chloris?"

"She has a year remaining in her service to Artemis."

"I know. But I already have a son; I can afford to wait. And Chloris is worth waiting for." Neleus waved off a fly. "The Maidens of Artemis visit Pylos nearly every year, but I haven't discussed this with Chloris. I didn't think it would be appropriate, while she's still among the Maidens. But I wanted to know whether the idea would meet with your approval – and Queen Niobe's."

Amphion wiped sweat from his brow. "My wife always liked you, Neleus. And I'd be honored to call you son-in-law. But Chloris is a grown woman, used to her independence. She'll have to make the decision herself, and she may choose not to marry at all."

Neleus grinned at him. "Of course. And if not Chloris, I'd be happy to wed another of your daughters. I would be honored to be connected with your family."

Of more concern was Pelops' offer for the twins. Amphion discussed the matter seriously with the girls, both together and individually, but Cleodoxa and Eudoxa did not know what they wanted. They liked the idea of not being separated from each other, but they did not want to live so far from Thebes. And they were unsure about Atreus and Thyestes.

At sundown on the last day of the games, Amphion went to the Temple of Hera to seek guidance from that goddess, patroness of marriage. He scattered a handful of incense on her altar-flame; as the fragrance filled the shrine, he knelt before the chryselephantine image. Concerned that Hera's priestess could report anything she heard – even words of prayer – to Pelops, Amphion formed his question for the goddess in his mind: would Atreus and Thyestes make good husbands for his daughters?

He focused his thoughts on this question, and sought the goddess with all his heart; yet, though he knelt on the marble floor until his knees ached, Hera gave him no sign. She stared down at him, her beautiful face reminding Amphion of Pisa's banished queen, but the agate eyes revealed nothing.

Concluding that the goddess would offer no wisdom to him this evening, Amphion got to his feet and limped down the temple stairs, feeling stiff and old and wishing that Niobe had come to Pisa with him. He sighed, waiting for his eyes to adjust to the darkness. The sky overhead was black and scattered with stars, but the waning moon gave enough light to recognize the familiar figure passing by: a tiny, aged woman clutching a staff and accompanied by a muscular manservant.

"Tiresias," Amphion said, breathing thanks to Hera for sending him someone who could guide him.

The blindfolded woman stopped. "King Amphion of Thebes."

"May I ask your advice, Prophetess?"

She shrugged. "Not everyone likes my advice, Amphion."

She sounded cross. Had he offended her in some way? But he could not imagine how.

A twinge of pain went through his right knee, prompting a more likely explanation: the Tiresias was an old woman now – well into her sixties, Amphion judged – and the festival had been long and arduous. Her bones probably ached more than his.

"I value your words, Tiresias. You are the Voice of Apollo."

"When the god chooses to speak through me."

There was no point in dragging this out. "Should I marry my twin daughters to Atreus and Thyestes?" he asked.

The seer grunted. "I wouldn't worry about that."

"I don't understand," he said, frowning. "Do you mean they'd be good husbands for the girls? Or that I should oppose the match?"

"I meant what I said," she snapped. "Now, let's go to the palace. Pelops is expecting you."

Clearly she did not want to be questioned further. Amphion accompanied her in silence, trying to puzzle out the meaning of her frustratingly vague pronouncement. It could mean anything – or nothing. Perhaps it only meant that the Tiresias had more important things on her mind.

When they arrived at the palace, the megaron was filled with hard-drinking men enjoying the last night of banqueting and wine. A servant pressed a red-striped goblet into his hand and Amphion moved through the crowd, exchanging greetings with various acquaintances. He looked for Atreus and Thyestes, hoping that when he saw the princes, the Tiresias' opaque words would take on meaning; but before he spotted them he encountered Pelops, confronting a group of men wearing necklaces made of wolf's teeth.

"I know what you've been doing, Stymphalus," Pelops was saying, his voice overloud. "Afraid to show your face until now, eh? I might be drunk, but I'm not drunk enough to let that insult go!"

At the back of the group, a man with eyebrows that formed a single horizontal line folded his arms. "I don't know what you're talking about."

"Yes, you do, Arcadian. Your host-gift: those were sheep that you and your men stole from me!"

At these words, the crowded room fell silent. Every guest, every servant, turned to stare at the king of Pisa and the guest he was accusing of theft. For one king to charge another with such an offense could mean war. And Amphion knew that Pelops had complained about raids on his flocks for years.

Stymphalus laughed. "He's mistaken," he said, elbowing the nearest of his companions. Looking uncertain, the man slowly joined in his king's laughter – but without conviction.

"The shepherd identified them!" shouted Pelops. "Shepherds know their flocks. You've been stealing from my herds for the last twelve years!"

Amphion watched Stymphalus' face; he could see the man trying to think up a plausible tale, and failing. Finally Stymphalus said: "You're right. But no more than you've stolen from every other kingdom in Hellas, Pelops!"

This accusation prompted muttering around the room, and Amphion realized he was not the only man there who resented Pelops' dunning for tribute.

"Exactly!" Stymphalus continued, gesturing at the crowded megaron. "The rest of you know what I mean! How much of the food we've had tonight, how much of the wine, actually came from *your* kingdom? Pelops parades his armies in front of us, shows off his fancy horses and chariots hoping he'll strike fear into our hearts." He turned to face Pelops again. "You and your threats, your demands for tribute and gifts!" The discontented murmurs were growing louder; Stymphalus raised his voice to be heard. "You and your Hittite chariots, your Thracian horses, your Lydian education – you think you're so smart!" He snorted. "Acting as if you were *so* much cleverer than the rest of us!" Stymphalus lifted his cup, laughing. "Well, *I've* fooled you, Pelops. I've fooled you for more—"

He stopped abruptly, his eyes bulging. His wine-cup dropped to the floor and shattered, while his hands clutched at the jeweled knife-hilt protruding from his throat.

The crowd fell silent. Pelops shouted: "Who's the fool now, Stymphalus?" Only then did Amphion realize that Pelops himself had thrown the knife, with lethal accuracy.

Stymphalus crumpled to the floor.

Pelops drew his sword and held it aloft, the bronze flashing in the torchlight. "Who's next? Who will challenge me next? I know you're plotting against me!" He swung in a slow circle; men scrambled back, pushing to get as far as possible from Pelops' blade. "You've accepted my hospitality for years –

and all the while you've been assisting this thieving dog! Admit it!"

Many guests spoke at the same time, each hastily denying any conspiracy. Some headed for the exits, while others warned that Pelops would take flight as evidence of guilt, and his soldiers would cut them down as they left.

Amid the tumult, Atreus pushed his way forward. "Father," he said, holding out his hand, "my lord king – please, sheathe your sword."

Pelops stared at him, wild-eyed. "You're part of this! That's why you never caught them!" He leveled the blade at Atreus. "Your mother killed Chrysippus to secure your inheritance – I should kill you now, to even the scales!"

His face paling beneath his beard, Atreus dropped his hand; but he did not step back.

Though Amphion had no special fondness for Atreus, he admired the man's courage. "Pelops," he said, "listen to your son. Put away your sword."

Pelops whirled left to face Amphion. "You! You ungrateful cowherd! You're in league with them!"

He's mad, Amphion thought. Keeping his voice calm, he said: "Pelops, Thebes is too far away for us to be stealing your sheep."

"But you keep my sister from me!" countered Pelops, lunging forward.

The crowd gasped, and a woman screamed; Amphion dodged the thrust and then Atreus tackled Pelops from the side, knocking him to the floor. He landed on his left shoulder, his ivory armor clattering against the floor. Pelops lost his grip on the sword; a Pisatan youth ran forward and picked it up.

"Pelops!" The crowd parted to make way for the Tiresias. Pointing the end of her cornel-wood staff at Pelops, she continued: "Killing a guest is an offense against the gods!"

Pelops struggled against Atreus' grip, but the younger man held firm. "Stymphalus was stealing from me," Pelops shouted, "inciting others against me!"

The old woman shook her head slowly. "That does not allow you to break the law of Zeus. Nor does it excuse your attack on Amphion."

"He's holding my sister prisoner!"

"No, Pelops, it was you who once did that," she contradicted him, still not using his royal title. "Queen Niobe is no captive now. Her recent illness left her too weak to travel. And besides, she has small children."

"But—"

"Enough!" snapped the seer. "Pelops, your deeds anger the gods."

Pelops closed his eyes and let out a long, shuddering breath; he ceased to struggle against his son's hold. When he opened his eyes once more, there was some semblance of self-control in his expression. "Amphion, I regret my action. Accept my apology."

Amphion, still breathing hard, had no idea how to respond to this. Before he could say anything, the Tiresias spoke once more. "What amends will you make to Stymphalus? He was your guest, and you murdered him in your home." She rapped her staff three times on the tiled floor. With each echo of sound she seemed to stand straighter, taller: Amphion realized that the gods now possessed her. She spoke as the voice of Apollo, and as Athena's chosen one: "Pelops, you are cursed."

Silence descended. Atreus released his hold on his father and moved away from him, as if he might be tainted.

Pelops blinked once, twice, like a man stunned by a blow to the head. He pushed himself up onto his good arm and awkwardly climbed to his feet.

"Tiresias," he said, his voice subdued, "what must I do to rid myself of this curse?"

The holy presence had left the seer; she seemed to shrink back into her mortal form. An old, blind woman once more, she shrugged. "You will have to ask the gods."

Amphion backed away. If Pelops was cursed, what did that mean about Atreus and Thyestes? Was that why the Tiresias had refused to answer his question – because the curse would be passed to his sons? If Pelops was cursed, Amphion thought, then Pelops would no longer be the rising power in Hellas – and *another* could lead.

People began to move. Pelops seated himself on his throne and ordered the servants to pour a round of drinks. The Tiresias, clinging to her servant's elbow, departed the megaron; men and women stepped aside to make way for the prophetess. Citizens of Arcadia knelt by their dead king. His voice hoarse, Pelops summoned a pair of litter bearers to take the corpse to the Arcadian camp.

Amphion's eldest son came to his side. "Father," he said, his voice low and urgent, "are you all right?"

"Yes, Alphenor, I am," said Amphion, feeling as if a burden had slipped off his shoulders. "Gather your brothers and your sisters and let's go."

EIGHT: ORACLE ANSWERS

§ 8.01

After their lovemaking was done, Laius stared into the darkest corner of the room. Nerissa finally whispered, "What's bothering you, Laius?"

He rolled over in the bed and circled her in his arms. "It's my fault that the king is cursed. I shouldn't have let that man go."

Resting her head on his chest, she spoke: "At the time I was angry with you. I wanted you to kill him for what he did to Mother. But you were right. If you'd done that, *we* would be cursed now."

"Maybe." He stroked her soft hair, wondering what would have happened if he had turned in Geranor. "But if our king is cursed... you heard what people were saying as they left the festival. It couldn't have been any worse if a plague had broken out. King Pelops may never hold the games again."

"Then what will you do?"

"Me?" Laius shifted on the pillow.

"The games have been your main responsibility. Without them, you'll have nothing to do here. And if the king is cursed, do we really want to stay in Pisa? There *could* be plague. Or famine. And we have two boys to think about!"

Frowning, Laius said, "But where would we go?"

Nerissa sat up, crossing her legs; the lamplight played over her body's curves. "What about Thebes? Everyone was impressed by King Amphion – and his children seemed so capable."

"Nerissa, be serious. King Amphion would not welcome me."

"But you've renounced the throne—"

"Even so. He knows I'm King Pelops' friend – and Pelops tried to kill him, not ten days ago."

"All right," she said, "perhaps not Thebes. But you know what it takes to put on a magnificent festival – aren't the Olympic Games the envy of every other king? Another ruler would value your knowledge and experience."

Laius considered this. "It's an interesting idea. Mycenae has the wealth for it... and there's always Athens." He looked up at her. "You'd come with me? Leave the Temple of Rhea?"

"Rhea has other priestesses," Nerissa said. "And she'll hear my prayers in Mycenae, or Athens, or wherever we go. You're the father of my children, Laius. Of course we'll come with you."

He reached over and squeezed her knee. "Let's wait and see what happens after King Pelops visits Delphi – we may not need to go anywhere. The Oracle may be able to cleanse him of the curse."

§ 8.02

The road to Delphi was steep: difficult and tiring for a traveler with a bad leg. As he negotiated the dusty path, leaning heavily on his walking stick, Broteas hoped his persistence despite the pain would win the clemency of some god.

Once he had believed himself favored by Artemis, but the events of the last month had to have destroyed her good will. Geranor had seduced a Maiden of Artemis, convincing her to break her vow of chastity and getting her with child. In Artemis' eyes, there was no greater crime, and Broteas was responsible for bringing the man to Arcadia in the first place. Moreover, the goddess' justice remained incomplete: though the faithless maiden had been executed, Geranor escaped. Surely it was Artemis' wrath that had caused the death of King Stymphalus at the Olympic Games. Broteas had accompanied the Arcadian delegation to Pisa; keeping out of Pelops' sight and avoiding the Thebans, he sought to find at last some way to recover the golden mastiff of Rhea. But after King Stymphalus' murder, anyone associated with Arcadia was suspect in Pisa.

He could not return to Arcadia, not with the king dead. Where else could he go? The rest of the southern peninsula remained under Pelops' influence – even if that influence was weakened by Pelops' murderous actions and the Tiresias' curse, Pisa had the largest, best-trained army and the strongest network of trade connections.

In truth, he wished to return to Lydia. Though Geranor himself had prompted these thoughts – and Broteas remained suspicious of them, given Geranor's offense against the goddess – Broteas yearned to see the land of his birth once more. He wanted to see what sort of man his son had become. He wanted to see his mother if she still lived; he even wanted to see his wife. But he was not sure whether going to Lydia was wise. His father might kill him for returning without Rhea's golden mastiff.

Broteas hoped that the Oracle of Delphi would tell him what to do.

"Greetings, fellow traveler!" shouted a man's voice behind him.

Broteas halted, shifting the heavy pack that contained the gold and jewels he had amassed in Arcadia, and turned to look: a short fellow with long arms was coming quickly up the path. The man pushed back his broad-brimmed straw hat, making his face visible – one of the ugliest faces Broteas had ever seen, but lit with a wide grin.

"On your way to Delphi?" the fellow called out.

Broteas grunted. "That I am."

"Good," the other man said brightly. "We'll journey together, then." Drawing near, he offered his hand. "I'm called Kallias."

Broteas' lips twitched as he clasped the fellow's hand. "Your mother must have loved you." The name Kallias meant beautiful, but this fellow – with his round face, overlong upper lip, small eyes, and long arms – looked like a monkey one might see as a seafarer's pet.

"Oh, she did, she did," Kallias said, taking no offense. "But it's not the name my parents gave me. I chose it for myself." He dropped Broteas' hand and together they started up the slope; the younger man slowed his steps to match Broteas' own limping pace. "Seeking advice from the Oracle, are you?"

"Yes," said Broteas. "Aren't you?"

"Actually, no," said Kallias. "I'm an artist – a sculptor. I've just returned from Egypt, where I did my apprenticeship. They know all about working stone, those Egyptians. Now I'm off to seek my fortune. I'd think Delphi could use a good sculptor, wouldn't you?"

"Why not?" Broteas said, not sure whether to believe the fellow's tale. He could have invented an Egyptian apprenticeship as easily as he had invented the name Kallias. "Tell me about Egypt," he said. "I've traveled far myself, but never to the land of pharaohs."

Kallias was happy to oblige, and his stories made the walk less tedious. As they passed a grove of gnarled old olive trees, Kallias described the pyramids – triangular buildings large as mountains that served as tombs for the ancient kings – and sang the praises of the Great Sphinx of Giza, the largest carving in the world. When they refreshed themselves at a spring, he told of the broad river Nile, explaining that in Egypt the men did the laundry instead of the women, because the river teemed with dangerous beasts: snakes, crocodiles, and hippopotami. Each type of monster seemed to have its own god in the Egyptian pantheon, and Kallias knew several stories about each. Broteas found the tales so entertaining that he stopped caring whether his companion spoke the truth.

Then they reached the point at which the trail switched back and at last holy Delphi was visible: a verdant hollow in the flank of Mount Parnassus, with rugged mountain peaks towering above. The white limestone of the temple was dazzling in the midday sun; surrounding it were several more modest buildings and, down the slope, a small agora. A pair of eagles wheeled high overhead, borne aloft on the mountain breeze. It was a scene of such beauty that it robbed Broteas of breath.

Kallias let out a long sigh. "You can see why it's called the center of the earth, can't you?" he said in subdued, reverent tones. But his lively manner soon returned. Clapping Broteas on the shoulder, he said: "I've been talking too much, haven't I? I always do. Here we are, nearly at our destination – and I don't even know your name!"

"I am Prince Broteas of Lydia," he answered, giving his real name for the first time in more than twelve years. It felt strange to his tongue, but the holy precinct of Delphi was no place for lies. The gods would not answer his question unless he gave his true name.

Kallias' eyes widened. "A prince!" He dropped his hand from Broteas' shoulder. "My lord prince, please excuse my familiarity. And a prince of wealthy Lydia, at that—"

Broteas could tell that the younger man was preparing to pitch his services. Hoping to forestall this, he growled: "I've not been in Lydia for a long while." He planted his walking-stick firmly on the path and resumed the journey towards the shrine.

Kallias scurried to catch up. "But you're a son of the great King Tantalus?"

"Yes," Broteas admitted, answering this and Kallias' other questions as briefly as he could. Fortunately it was easy to divert the man into telling a story of his own. The mention of Tantalus led naturally to Pelops; Kallias had attended Pelops' games as a boy, and it was the temples of Pisa, in fact, that first inspired his love of art. Broteas let the man ramble on about how he had befriended an Egyptian merchant, and wangled a trip to Egypt by agreeing to work as a stevedore; it was far better than talking about his younger brother Pelops, or trying to explain his own obscure and inglorious life. Then, as they entered the immediate vicinity of the temple, many sights distracted Kallias: the purity of the temple's lines, the liquid quality of the light, the perfect valley that housed the shrine.

At the temple, an acolyte brought the high priest Aeacus to meet them. He was a fair-haired man with a peaceful countenance. Broteas knew that Aeacus was also the king of Aegina, but so devoted to the gods that he preferred to spend his time in Delphi. To Broteas' astonishment, the white-robed man immediately said: "Prince Broteas of Lydia. We have a message for you."

Broteas blinked. "A message from the gods?"

Aeacus lifted a golden eyebrow. "Not exactly – although of course nothing happens without the gods' consent." He clasped his hands behind his back. "In this case, Prince Broteas, we have a message from your father, King Tantalus."

"So he still lives," said Broteas.

"He was living this spring, certainly; and though most had given you up for dead, he hoped you were still alive as well. He had some thought you would come to consult the Oracle." Aeacus glanced at the sculptor standing beside Broteas. "Do you wish to hear the message now?"

Broteas shrugged; he no longer had anything to hide. "Please."

"King Tantalus orders you to return home. Immediately, for he is growing old, and needs to see you before he dies. He asked that these words be repeated exactly: 'Only you, Broteas, can restore what has been lost.' That is all."

Nodding, Broteas said: "I understand his meaning. But I still wish to consult the Oracle."

"Of course," said Aeacus. "Tomorrow is the month's seventh day; the Pythia will speak. At dawn tomorrow you and your companion must be purified in the sacred spring of Castalia, and make an offering to Apollo. Goats are preferred; they are available in the agora. If you cannot afford a goat you may make an offering commensurate with your wealth."

"Thank you," Broteas said. "Where may I find lodging for the night?"

"In the temple guest-house," Aeacus said. "My acolyte will show you the way."

Broteas turned to follow the acolyte; but Kallias remained. "Most holy priest," Kallias began, "I'm not here to consult the Oracle. I'm a sculptor, you see, and..."

Leaving Kallias to promote his services, Broteas claimed his guest quarters, arranged to provide an unblemished goat for the sacrifice, and enjoyed a simple meal and a good night's sleep; at dawn he and the other suppliants went to bathe in the cool waters of the Castalian spring east of Apollo's temple. Then, dressed in a fresh tunic and sandals, his head bare, he followed the white-garbed acolytes up to the precinct of the Oracle. Sweet-smelling incense burned in the altar-flame at the center of the forecourt; the other priests swept the tiles with sprigs of bay and laurel while Aeacus scattered drops of water from the sacred spring. When this was done, Aeacus came forward to explain the order of the ritual events. Broteas, as the most prominent petitioner, would go first; the other men would draw lots to decide their turn. Each man's sacrifice would be offered to Apollo; if accepted, he would then be permitted to enter the sanctuary and pose his question to the Pythia.

The instructions complete, the priests sang to Apollo; the hymn was elegant in its simplicity. The morning was fresh, the air sparkling with light: such a day as surely pleased Apollo most. If Broteas were ever to receive clear direction from the god, it had to be on this perfect morning.

After the hymn, one acolyte led forward Broteas' goat and another sprinkled the beast with water from a golden shaker. Broteas was relieved to see the goat quivering from the hooves up: this meant Apollo accepted the sacrifice. Aeacus withdrew a knife from a basket of flowers and slit the beast's throat, and soon the offering burned upon the altar.

"Come with me," Aeacus said, beckoning Broteas forward.

Broteas followed the chief priest of Apollo; they passed between the whitewashed columns of the temple portico and into the shadowed interior. At the back of the building was a small structure, like a temple within a temple, inside which were stairs leading down into the earth. Broteas followed Aeacus into a low-ceilinged room, largely underground. It was cool, scented by a sweet but unfamiliar fragrance. A single lamp burned, revealing a thin curtain of translucent linen: beyond the curtain was the Pythia.

She was a slender maiden garbed in a long white tunic. She sat, slumped, atop a tall bronze tripod. Her bare feet dangled far above the ground. In one hand she held a branch of laurel; in the other a shallow dish. Humming softly, the Pythia did not look up as Broteas entered: she seemed to be in a trance.

"Remain here, while I pass within," said Aeacus. "You may ask the Oracle a single question." He drew the curtain and stepped inside to stand by the Pythia's tripod.

Broteas drew a deep breath. He had spent many days formulating his words, but now – in this sacred space – he feared his choice inadequate. But this was not the time to improvise.

"Holy one," he said, "should I return to Lydia now, even though I cannot bring what my father desires?"

The maiden sighed; the laurel branch in her hand trembled. Then she uttered something that Broteas could not understand.

But Aeacus nodded sagely and turned to Broteas. "The Divine Apollo gives you this answer: In Lydia, beauty begets beauty."

Broteas frowned. "I don't understand."

"You shall in time, if that is the will of the gods," said the priest.

The Pythia resumed her humming. Broteas remained where he was; he was not permitted a second question, but he hoped the Pythia might offer him some clue to the god's meaning.

"You may go," Aeacus said.

Well, *that* was clear enough. The god had dismissed him.

Broteas climbed back up the limestone stairs, his bad leg aching. Such a long journey, to be rewarded with a riddle! Broteas limped the length of the temple and headed out into the daylight, feeling no need to remain for the rest of the ceremony. He ambled on, pondering the words: *In Lydia, beauty begets beauty.*

The Pythia's answer seemed like a rejection – not just of his request, but of his entire existence. He had never been handsome. Instead, beauty – that sure sign of the gods' favor – had been bestowed liberally on others. His father Tantalus was famed for his godlike looks; his brother Pelops was no less handsome. Broteas' wife Euryanassa had been Lydia's loveliest maiden when he married her; their son, Young Tantalus, fortunately took after his mother. Broteas' sister Niobe was no great beauty, but she had never been especially ugly – and her children were the most glorious princes and princesses in all Hellas.

"Would you care to share my lunch, my lord prince?"

Broteas looked up to see that his steps had brought him back to the Castalian spring. In the shady green glade was the sculptor Kallias, eating a meal of bread, cheese, and olives.

Here was a man, Broteas thought, who might understand his dilemma: a man even uglier than Broteas himself, who had nonetheless made the creation of beauty his trade.

Kallias squinted up at Broteas. "Is something wrong?"

Broteas sat down beside Kallias and accepted a hunk of bread. He took a bite and then cupped his hand to take a drink of spring water. Finally he spoke: "I've had a confusing answer from the oracle. My question should have been answered with yes or no, but instead I was told: 'In Lydia, beauty begets beauty.' "

Kallias scratched his head. "My lord prince, I don't know that anyone could understand the answer without first understanding the question."

"That's not your concern," Broteas said sharply. He was not prepared to reveal that he had failed in the mission his father had given him – or that his father might kill him for that failure.

"I beg your pardon, my lord prince."

For a moment the two ate in silence; Broteas noted that the olives were excellent.

Then Kallias lifted a finger. "Perhaps the gods mean for me to do some work for you? That could be it, you know! Before I left Egypt, I asked a wise woman where I should seek work: she said I should go to Delphi. I thought the priests here must need a sculptor to adorn their temple – but they've told me they don't. So then why did the gods send me here? To meet you, my lord prince!" He smiled, dusting bread-crumbs from his hands. "My name means beauty – and, trust me, my work is beautiful. 'In Lydia, beauty begets beauty.' That could be it, eh, my lord prince? Can I make something for you in Lydia?"

"I don't—" Broteas began, automatically rejecting the sculptor's eager offer, but then broke off, considering. He looked down at the ripples in the spring, wishing he could see the will of the gods in the moving liquid. Could a sculpture dedicated to Rhea make amends for the stolen icon?

Broteas spoke. "What if – what if I said I needed an image of a goddess, one that could never be stolen. Could you do that?"

"Of course, my lord prince," Kallias answered promptly.

"How?" Broteas challenged. "Even the largest carving can still be moved."

Kallias gestured back at the rock face behind them, and the bulk of Parnassus beyond. "Not if we carve the image into a mountain. It's a technique most suitable for honoring a deity – the image can be as large as you like. The Egyptians are masters of this method – and I, if I may say so, was an excellent student. The image of the goddess remains part of the mountain. And no one can steal a whole mountain!"

Broteas was stunned. Of course! This must be the meaning of the oracle. The gods had not abandoned him after all!

He reached for Kallias' calloused hand and shook it firmly. "Brilliant!" he exclaimed. "We'll leave for Lydia tomorrow."

The sculptor grinned, his joy so infectious that it momentarily masked his ugliness. "Tomorrow it is! Tell me what you have in mind, my lord prince. Is there a suitable mountain near your palace?"

Broteas looked around, comparing the craggy face of Parnassus to his memory of the slopes of Mount Sipylus. He tried to describe its terrain to the sculptor; Kallias packed up the remains of their lunch and led them out of the glade, so they could better see the form of the surrounding peaks, and together they inspected rock faces and discussed possibilities. Broteas had not felt this confident, this elated, in years.

They talked until the sun dipped towards the western slopes; finally they headed back in the direction of the sanctuary. As they reached Delphi's main road they heard someone calling out: "Make way! Make way for my lord king!"

A long-legged youth jogged up from the west. "Make way!" he shouted again, gesturing for Broteas and Kallias to step aside. He ran past them, in the direction of the temple; but Broteas had no intention of stepping aside. He was Prince Broteas of Lydia; Apollo's Oracle had given him leave to go home and reclaim his heritage. And Lydia was far more important and powerful than any Hellene cities.

Then a chariot, drawn by two smoke-gray horses, came around the bend – and Broteas' jaw dropped when he saw the driver.

"Pelops!"

§ 8.03

Pelops reined his horses to a halt. "Who dares address me so?"

Behind him, Pelops heard Atreus stopping his chariot; but, fascinated by the pair of ill-favored men who stood before him, Pelops did not look back. He studied the elder of the two: a balding fellow, with a gray beard that failed to conceal his pockmarked skin. There was something familiar about his eyes…

"*Broteas*?" he gasped. "I thought you were dead!"

Broteas shaded his eyes against the setting sun. "Not yet."

No, thought Pelops, not a ghost. He did not share Myrtilus' insubstantiality; the ghost was always difficult to see with the sun's rays coming down at such a slanting angle. "I've heard our father is looking for you," he said, continuing to stare. Broteas seemed healthy enough; his hairy shoulders boasted plenty of muscle, though his skin had the texture of old leather, and deep lines fanned out from the corners of his eyes. Pelops asked: "Where have you been all this time?"

"I'm not going to answer that," said Broteas, crossing his arms.

Annoyance tightened Pelops' throat. Even after so many years, his older brother knew exactly how to irritate him. Broteas had never shown him the respect his accomplishments deserved. He refused to acknowledge Pelops' superior chariot skills, despite Pelops' defeating him soundly. He scoffed at the idea that the knowledge Pelops had gained during his years in the Hittite court would prove advantageous. He showed no compunction about publicly insulting Pelops – indeed, he had gotten Pelops banished from Athens, and the damage to his relations with that city had taken years to mend.

Behind him, Atreus jumped down from his chariot; he strode forward to confront Broteas. "Show respect to the king," he said, his hand dropping to the hilt of the dagger at his belt.

Broteas' mouth twisted. "He's not *my* king. He's my younger brother. And from what I've heard, he's offended the gods. That's not so respectable."

The youth Nikippes, jogging back down towards them, said: "My lord king, my lord princes: remember that Delphi is sacred to the gods. There must be no conflict here."

Pelops nodded, glad for Nikippes' reminder. He had brought the young man as much for his levelheaded demeanor as for his swift feet. Like Atreus, Nikippes had helped prevent Pelops from committing any further transgression after he threw the knife that killed Stymphalus. Pelops hoped that bringing these two with him would help placate the gods.

"You're right, Nikippes." Pelops jumped down from his chariot and handed the reins to the youth. Trying to put the best face on things, he said: "I shouldn't let my surprise get the better of me. It *must* be an auspicious sign to meet one's brother at Delphi." He held out his hand; looking startled, Broteas took it. "Who's your companion?" Pelops asked.

"Kallias," Broteas said, quickly disengaging his hand. "A sculptor."

A snort of laughter escaped Atreus; Pelops frowned at him, though he understood the sentiment – for a man so hideous, the name was absurd. He turned back to the sculptor. "Greetings," he said, with a nod. "Shall we proceed to the temple together?"

Broteas shrugged, and fell in beside Pelops; the rest followed, with Nikippes leading Pelops' animals. Pelops noted that his brother walked with a limp; his calf was scarred. "What happened to your leg?"

"An accident, many years ago," Broteas replied. "How's your shoulder?"

"I manage," said Pelops, imitating his brother's terseness. As they crossed the small agora, he wondered how he could get Broteas to divulge where he had been the last dozen years. Then he was distracted by the appearance of Aeacus, the high priest, crowned in laurel, at the entrance to Apollo's temple.

"Greetings, King Pelops," said the priest.

"Greetings, Aeacus," Pelops called. He gestured to his companions. "Prince Atreus. The noble Nikippes, son of Okyllus."

The priest did not descend the stairs, nor did he smile. "King Pelops, the Pythia has retired for the day. And before you enter the temple you must be cleansed of blood-guilt."

Pelops frowned. "I understand."

Myrtilus emerged from the shadow of the temple. "I told you to ride faster," he said. "Now you've missed your chance. The Oracle speaks only on the seventh day of the month."

With a tiny shake of his head, Pelops told the ghost to be silent. Then he addressed the priest. "What purification ritual is required? How long does it take?"

Aeacus frowned and followed the direction of Pelops' glance.

"Do you think he sees me?" whispered Myrtilus, drawing nearer. "Ah, how I would love for someone else to see me!"

Pelops hoped not: if Aeacus saw Myrtilus, the high priest would understand just how badly Pelops was cursed.

The priest leveled a piercing look at Pelops. "It's not lengthy. You must bathe in the Castalian spring, and make the proper offering." Clasping his hands behind his back, he continued: "Normally, no further oracles would be given until next month. But under the circumstances, I believe the god will make an exception."

"I would be most grateful," Pelops said. He needed the god's pardon, but had no desire to wait in Delphi for a whole month. Was this willingness to see him immediately a sign that the gods would forgive him?

"Or maybe Apollo wants your polluted soul to leave his holy premises sooner," suggested Myrtilus.

The ghost's interpretation was all too plausible. Even the Tiresias had turned away from him.

"Come," said the priest, descending the stairs. "My servants will show your men where to stable the horses. Meanwhile, you and your party may refresh yourselves at the guest house." He led them towards an adjacent structure; they passed through a hallway to an open-air courtyard, where other petitioners were already seated. As Aeacus departed, servants entered to wash the men's feet, and then others brought an evening meal. The repast was simple but delicious: hard aged cheese, fresh bread, fragrant olives in spiced oil, and an excellent wine infused with herbs. As the stars came out, the well-trained servants unobtrusively lit more lamps – and, whether it was the crisp mountain air or the sanctity of Delphi, Pelops realized that Myrtilus had vanished.

Feeling better than he had in years, Pelops listened to the pilgrims discuss the Olympic Games just past. To his relief they did not discuss how the festival had ended, and those who had attended praised the spectacle. "Everyone hopes the games will continue in the future, my lord king," said the short, ugly sculptor.

"I'm glad they're appreciated," Pelops said. Since taking the throne in Pisa he had held eight festivals, all in all – so many years of honoring the gods! Surely they would forgive him.

A trader from Corinth who had posed his question to the oracle that morning said: "The Thebans were splendid this year!" He went on to detail their many victories.

As the Corinthian described Phaedimus' triumph in archery, Pelops turned to Broteas. "He's talking about Niobe's sons," he said. "Our nephews."

Broteas lowered his wine cup and nodded. "Talented young men."

"Yes." Pelops caught his brother's gaze and repeated the question he had posed earlier: "Where have you been all this time?"

"In the wilderness," he said. "Seeking the favor of Lady Artemis."

"For twelve years?" Pelops asked. Broteas had always been an ardent hunter, but this seemed extreme.

"No, of course not." Broteas scratched his jaw, as if weighing his words, and then said: "Father tried to kill you, once."

Pelops glanced around the courtyard. The petitioners were discussing the Olympic chariot races; no one was listening to the two of them. "Yes," he said. "What of it?"

"Before I left Lydia," Broteas said, "I suspected that he meant to kill me. It seemed prudent to stay away."

"Ah." Pelops nodded. "I understand. And now what?"

"My time dedicated to Artemis is finished. So I sought the advice of her brother Apollo to learn whether returning to Lydia is wise. Our father, if he's still alive—"

Pelops became aware of someone hovering unnervingly close; he twisted around to see the ugly sculptor standing over him. "What are you doing? This is a private conversation!"

"A thousand pardons, my lord king," said the man, his eyes round. "I was simply struck by your ears—"

"What are you talking about?" Pelops said. "Are you mad?"

The little man laughed. "Perhaps after a fashion, my lord king – some say all artists are mad. As a sculptor I am fascinated by form and pattern; and, you see, your ears and those of your brother and son share the same unusual shape. Ears are difficult to carve well, and many sculptors overlook them; but I seek perfection in my craft, and so, when presented with such a perfect example of form to study I simply could not resist—"

"He *is* mad," Atreus declared.

Kallias shrugged, smiling. "But, my lord prince, if you would oblige me just for a moment, I can show your father exactly what I mean. Would you come here for a moment? And you, my lord prince Broteas, would you stand?" He arranged Broteas and Atreus in single file, displaying their left profiles, and pointed to Atreus' ear. "Look here, my lord king. Do you see? The curves of the ear are identical. Notice how each man's ear goes straight into his neck, instead of forming the lobe that you see, for example, on this fellow's ear," he said, pointing at Nikippes.

Puzzled, Pelops frowned. "Is this some form of augury?"

"Oh, no, my lord king, not as far as I know. Just an artist's observation. It's quite useful for me to observe the patterns of similarity that run in families. There's quite a resemblance between Prince Atreus and his uncle Broteas, of course, and the three of you share the same ears. Far more men have lobed ears than attached, you know – it's rather a distinctive feature."

Pelops realized that there *was* a strong resemblance between Broteas and Atreus. Their stocky build, the lines of their nose and jaw – even the shape of their fingers. And their ears... In all the years since Atreus' birth, Pelops had never been able to detect any trait that identified Atreus as his son. But, of course, a man never got a good look at his own ears. And unless they were particularly large, or somehow deformed, who even noticed them? But, reaching up to touch his own ear, Pelops felt that the bottom of his ear joined his neck in just the same way as Broteas and Atreus, exactly as the sculptor had said.

Broteas guffawed and reached for his wine. "Ears! Well, Kallias, I suppose the best sculptors pay attention to such trivialities."

Atreus, however, seemed to realize the matter was not trivial. He stepped closer and caught Pelops' gaze. "It appears, *Father*, that Delphi is full of answers – as everyone says."

"Perhaps." Pelops had mistrusted Atreus' paternity for so long that the removal of doubt was hard to fathom – especially as he had not come to Delphi seeking an answer to that question.

Atreus folded his arms. "What more do you want?" he asked, his voice bitter.

A fair question. What more could he want, than an answer at Delphi? Even if Atreus' paternity had not been *Pelops'* reason for the pilgrimage, it was certainly the question nearest *Atreus'* heart.

He set a hand on Atreus' broad shoulder. "For now, only a night's sleep, Son," he said, placing the faintest emphasis on the last word. "It's late."

Atreus' expression softened; he uncrossed his arms. "Good night, Father."

At first Pelops doubted he would sleep: his mind was churning with wonder. He had come to Delphi to resolve the situation he had created by killing Stymphalus – but instead, so far, he had encountered the brother long thought dead; escaped the shade of Myrtilus, at least for one night; and confirmed that Atreus was his son after all. He was not sure whether to be pleased by this last development: Atreus had both good qualities and bad. He was a brave soldier, but not always clever. A hard worker, and a hard drinker. He lacked finesse; his methods could be savage. On the other hand, despite a visit to Hippodamia, Atreus had served him loyally over the last twelve years. Pelops felt his heart warm toward the man whom he now knew was his oldest son.

Then there was Broteas – obviously sent by the gods so that they would meet in a place of sanctuary, a place where they must set aside old conflicts. Many years ago Pelops had thought of returning to Lydia to take the throne for himself; perhaps this meeting with Broteas was an omen that he should follow a different course.

And – he had come here to free himself of the blood-guilt associated with Stymphalus, but would Delphi finally rid him of Myrtilus?

When morning came Pelops realized how soundly he had slept; storms had rolled in during the night, but he had never heard them. Perhaps the torrential rains washed away some of Delphi's magic, for after the initial ceremony of purification, Pelops' encounter with the Pythia felt anticlimactic. The priest interpreted her humming mumbles to mean that Pelops must stay at Delphi another seven days, bathing in the sacred springs each day to cleanse himself of all pollution. He must pay a blood-price to Stymphalus' family in Arcadia, and offer rich gifts to Zeus, since it was the Thunderer's law he had broken, and to Delphi itself. According to Aeacus, Apollo also instructed Pelops to settle any other outstanding debts.

As the rains slackened, that afternoon, Pelops considered this. Because of the weather – and there was no surer sign of Zeus' intervention than thunderstorms – Broteas had not yet left. And Broteas believed Pelops had stolen Rhea's golden mastiff from Lydia. Of course, this was not true; the golden dog had *asked* to be taken west to Hellas. Pelops had no intention of returning the sacred mastiff to Lydia, but he could help even the scales with Broteas by burying his old grudges, and abandoning his ambitions towards the Lydian throne. To ensure the good will of the gods, and ensure that he could truthfully say to the Tiresias that he had been generous in paying his debts, he offered his heavy golden arm-rings and his cloak pin to Broteas – all the gold he had with him except the royal signet-ring and the narrow circlet crown he wore when traveling.

"The Oracle told you to do this?" Broteas asked, his voice suspicious as he turned the glittering objects in his hands.

"So I believe," Pelops said.

Broteas set the gold on the table beside his cot. "There can be no payment. The mastiff cannot be bought."

"Nor can it go where it does not belong. Its place is Pisa."

Broteas glanced out the guest-room's small window; the storms had cleared, and sunset stained the last clouds vivid shades of orange and red. "Perhaps," he said at last. "I tried to take it, you know."

Pelops nodded. "That leg injury: you got it at Rhea's temple."

Sitting down on the edge of his bed, Broteas said, "Yes. That wasn't my only attempt, of course. I tried to work through others; Niobe and her husband Amphion refused to help. I sought access other ways, and always failed." He looked up at Pelops. "I came to think the gods had turned their face from me. But now – now that I've encountered the Oracle, I see they had other plans."

Pelops would never have expected to hear his brother admit this – but they were experienced men now, both of them, with more wisdom than the callow boys who had raced in Lydia so long ago. "You understand that the mastiff belongs in Pisa?"

"So it seems." Broteas touched one of the golden arm-rings. "But this will help me ensure that Rhea is honored appropriately in Lydia."

After seeing his brother off the next morning, accompanied by the sculptor Kallias, Pelops remained for the prescribed remaining days of purifying rituals. As he restored himself to the good favor of Zeus and Apollo, he grew confident that he could regain the trust of Apollo's handmaiden, the Tiresias. When not occupied with ritual, he spent time with Atreus, seeking to establish the sort of relationship a king should have with his eldest son. Through all this time, he was never troubled by the charioteer's ghost, and he hoped that the rituals had purged this curse from him as well.

This hope shattered three days into the homeward journey. That evening at dusk, Myrtilus emerged from the forest and approached the campfire.

Pelops started at the sight of the ghost; Myrtilus laughed. "You didn't really think I was gone forever, did you?" he said. "You only asked how to rid yourself of *Stymphalus'* blood-guilt. What a shame each man is only permitted one question of the Oracle! But, then, even after all these years you still can't admit you murdered me."

Rising and stretching to conceal his discomfiture from Atreus and Nikippes, Pelops thought: *I refuse to let you goad me.*

"Oh, that's all right," Myrtilus responded. "Amphion and Niobe can take care of that."

What's that supposed to mean? Pelops asked silently. But the ghost did not answer.

§ 8.04

Niobe rubbed her neck with both hands as they approached the last gate; the ornate wig weighed heavy on her head. About a month after the worst of her fever last spring, she had started losing her hair – it fell out in appalling great clumps whenever she combed it, and each morning her pillow was covered with loose strands until she was virtually bald. Nimble-fingered Philomela had made her four beautiful wigs so that she could appear in public; and at night, though her husband kissed her and told her that she would always be beautiful to him, she wore a scarf tied around her head. Her hair was growing back now, but wispy, scant, and white: the feature that had been her one true beauty was gone, and Apollo's healers could offer her no treatment except prayer. So far the god had not been disposed to help.

She dismissed these thoughts, determined not to allow vanity, aches, or weariness to distract her. This day was *so* important to Amphion: the city walls were complete!

It had rained hard the day before, another of the intermittent downpours indicating that summer was nearing its end. Puddles still muddied the streets, forcing Niobe to step carefully when she descended from her sedan chair. But nothing could dampen Amphion's pleasure in the day. Catching sight of his face, she forgot her fatigue and was swept up in his joy. Her beloved Amphion had achieved more than any Theban king – more even than Cadmus! To protect his city, Amphion had moved a mountain of stone. And all the people of Thebes, and many emissaries from other cities, had turned out for the day's consecration ceremony.

Amphion had chosen to name the seven magnificent gates for their seven daughters. Upon hearing the king's decision, Niobe's sister-in-law Thebe pouted: she had wanted the largest gate to be named for her son Idmon. But Amphion pointed out that his nephew, like his sons, would go out into the world and glorify their own names with great deeds and achievements – an argument which Thebe could hardly dispute. Still Thebe frowned, and all through the day's ceremonies Niobe suspected that her sister-in-law was struggling to devise some way of turning the situation to Idmon's advantage.

The people of Thebes were enjoying the day: it was like a new festival, one celebrating the princesses of Thebes and the accomplishments of their father. And why, Niobe asked herself, shouldn't they be celebrated? She decided to speak to Amphion later about making this an annual festival. Her lovely daughters deserved no less! Besides, the girls reveled in the attention. At each gate, the princess for whom the gate was named was announced by the royal herald, and roundly cheered by the crowd; then the girl, wearing her best gown and a wreath of laurel, poured libations of wine and olive oil at the post of each massive oaken door and asked the gods for their blessing. The procession's path was admittedly awkward, as Theban streets did not always connect conveniently. They had to retrace their steps more than once, but the people did not seem to mind. Many brought wine of their own – not to mention crisp apples, dried figs and plump raisins: the procession became a sort of moveable feast making its way through the city, and at each gate the people were merrier than the last.

They had to make a few adjustments to the ritual. As Chloris was still with the Maidens of Artemis, Niobe took her place at the first gate. And little Phthia, for whom the last gate was named, was only three years old – so Niobe held the child's hand and made sure she did not pull the laurel wreath from her head while Thebe poured the libations and offered the prayers on her behalf.

When Thebe was finished, Amphion came forward. He looked so distinguished in his kilt of white linen and his purple-dyed cloak, a crown of laurel resting on his head, that the sight of him took Niobe's breath away. She was the most fortunate woman in Hellas, to have such a husband and such beautiful children! What other woman had such a magnificent family?

"Gods of Olympus," Amphion said, his rich voice echoing over the crowd, "accept our offerings, and give us your blessing! Grant all friends of Thebes safe passage to our city – and keep all enemies far outside these walls, for this generation and for future generations!" He lifted his arms towards the sky, and the people answered with a deafening roar.

Amphion smiled and lowered his arms. "Now let feasting begin in earnest!" At his gesture, servants appeared bearing amphorae of wine, and the people cheered again. Flute-girls moved through the crowd piping sweet melodies; yet more servants passed around skewers of grilled beef and baskets of fresh-baked bread.

Zethos pounded Amphion joyfully on the back. "It's hard to believe it's done, Brother! Now what will we do with our time?" Other men, including her sons, crowded round, shouting praise to the king.

Niobe stepped aside to let the men enjoy their camaraderie, and beckoned for a nurse to take charge of little Phthia. Her mouth watering, she moved towards the fresh bread, but she was intercepted by an envoy from Pisa: Okyllus, with his son Nikippes. They greeted her with respectful bows. "A most memorable day, my lady queen," Okyllus said. "A remarkable achievement for Thebes."

His tone seemed to imply that Thebes was not prone to great achievements. But Okyllus' attitude was mitigated by the congratulatory gifts he had brought from Pelops: ingots of copper and precious tin from the western trade, as well as dried fish, which was a treat for the people of Thebes, who had less access to the sea than most cities in Hellas. Yesterday, Nikippes had told Niobe about Pelops' visit to Delphi, and explained how he had encountered their long-absent brother Broteas at that sacred place. Niobe suspected that the Oracle had instructed Pelops to be generous: otherwise she could not understand why Pelops was suddenly sending gifts to Thebes instead of insisting on the reverse.

"Seven is an auspicious number, my lady queen," remarked the lanky youth, "even more so since the number of your daughters exactly matches the number of gates."

Niobe acknowledged the compliment by inclining her head. The boy shared his father's supercilious manner, but he was young – perhaps he would grow out of it.

"Your daughters are lovely," said Okyllus. "Especially Cleodoxa and Eudoxa. Have you yet decided whether they will marry their cousins Atreus and Thyestes? King Pelops is anxious for an answer, my lady queen."

Niobe swallowed her morsel of bread. "You must discuss this with my husband."

The tall, slender envoy smiled, but the expression did not reach his eyes. "My lady queen, King Amphion told me that I must address the subject to you."

"Did he?" Niobe glanced over at the group of men surrounding Amphion, wondering why her husband had not mentioned this to her. Of course, Amphion was still angry with Pelops for having threatened him with a blade at the Games – and who could blame him? She turned back to the Pisatans. "There's no hurry. The twins are only twelve."

Okyllus shrugged. "And next year they will be thirteen – and the year after that, fourteen – an ideal age for marriage! Time passes quickly, my lady queen: such an important decision should not be postponed."

Niobe rubbed her nose, frowning. "*Sixteen* is the proper age for marriage, Okyllus."

"Many marry younger, my lady queen. I beg you to consider your daughters' welfare. What could be better than to marry the sons of King Pelops?"

Young Nikippes broke in. "May I inquire, my lady queen, after the health of your eldest daughter? Princess Chloris' victory in the first footrace for girls is the subject of many songs."

Niobe was grateful to the youth for changing the subject. "She's well, thank you. Her service to Artemis finishes next year." She noticed that her youngest son, Ismenus, had wandered away from his nurse, apparently fascinated by the donkeys that had carted the wine to the gate. "Ismenus!" she shouted. The child did not turn; alarmed, she darted towards him.

Okyllus remained at her elbow as people stepped aside for their queen. "What are Princess Chloris' plans once her service to Artemis is complete?" he asked.

"I don't know," snapped Niobe. "She's had at least one offer of marriage, but the decision is up to her." The Pisatan faded back as she pulled her four-year-old son away from the donkeys' hooves. Ismenus wailed, but Niobe ignored his protests and sternly told the boy's flustered nurse to get him something to eat.

Nearby, Ogygia was chatting with her cousin Idmon. "It's so crowded," the girl complained. She put a hand to her head to adjust her laurel wreath and then fluffed her curling black hair. "Aren't there supposed to be jugglers? I can't see *anything*."

"Let's go up on the wall," Idmon said. "We'll see much better from up there."

Niobe stepped over to them. "Ogygia, you will *not* climb the wall. It's not safe."

"Oh, *Mother!"* Ogygia protested with a stamp of her foot.

"Why not, Aunt Niobe?" asked Idmon, squaring his shoulders. "I've done it hundreds of times. Thousands of times!"

Ignoring the boy's exaggeration, Niobe said: "Because it rained yesterday. The stones could be slippery. Besides, Ogygia, you're in your best skirts and I don't want you ruining them."

Thebe stormed over. "Are you telling *my* son what to do?"

"Thebe," Niobe began, "you know how hard it rained—"

With a toss of her hennaed hair, Thebe turned to her son: "Of course you can go up on the wall."

Ogygia appealed to Niobe. "Mother, please?"

"No – I said no! You'll stay here with me."

Idmon stuck out his tongue at his cousin, then triumphantly darted through the crowd towards the nearest stairway, meant to provide access for soldiers who would stand guard along the top of the wall. He ran up the steep, narrow stairs so easily that Niobe felt foolish. Perhaps she *was* being overprotective. She had had her share of adventures as a girl: sailing from Lydia to Hellas, learning to swim in the ocean – even escaping from the previous rulers of Thebes by climbing down a rope from a high window. If her daughters had an audacious streak, that was only natural.

Thebe nudged Niobe and pointed at her son. "Look how handsome he is!"

With his chestnut curls and bright blue eyes, Idmon *was* a handsome boy – and he adored attention. People turned to look at him; he waved from above, grinning broadly. Some of the Theban boys – and no few of the girls – shouted his name. He bowed in acknowledgement, flourishing his crimson cape. "Watch this!" he cried, and then leapt high in the air, landing with arms and legs outstretched. Those watching applauded, and more turned to see. A flute-girl started a bouncy tune, and then another joined her song; the people clapped in time to the music while Idmon strutted back and forth in time with the beat. Then he leapt again, landing precariously on one foot. Niobe gasped, but the grinning boy held his arms wide and bowed. The applause grew louder.

"Handsome *and* graceful," Thebe said, preening.

"I could do that," Ogygia muttered.

Niobe gripped the girl's shoulder. "Do all the jumping you like," she said, "but do it here on the ground."

Idmon leapt and landed on the other foot; then he jumped and twisted in midair, so that he faced away from the city. He wiggled his rear at the crowd, and the onlookers laughed. Glancing over his shoulder, he jumped and spun again, coming down on just one foot – but this time as he landed, his sandal skidded across the stones.

The people gasped, and Niobe's fingers dug into her daughter's flesh as she watched the boy's foot slide over the edge. It seemed to happen so slowly: she saw the utter disbelief in his blue eyes, saw his arms flail in the air as he tried to regain his balance, his cloak billowing out behind him – but he had leaned over too far. He spun like a leaf in the breeze as he fell, shouting, and landed headfirst on the cobbled street with a horrible crunching sound.

The crowd went absolutely silent.

Then Thebe shrieked, "No!" and ran over to her son's motionless form.

"Idmon!" bellowed Zethos, pushing people out of his way.

With a sickening lurch of her stomach, Niobe realized that there was no helping the boy. Idmon's neck was twisted unnaturally; a pool of blood, brighter in color than his tunic, was spreading beside his head. His eyes stared unblinking at the sky.

Ogygia let out a high, wordless wail.

"Idmon," sobbed Thebe, falling to her knees beside him. She clutched the boy's body to her chest. His head lolled back, smearing her arm with blood. "Oh, my son!"

"Fetch a healer!" Zethos shouted. "We need a healer!"

Amphion approached and touched his brother's arm. "No healer can help him, Zethos. He's dead."

Zethos brushed Amphion away like some annoying insect. "There must be a healer here!" he shouted, scanning the crowd. "I need a healer!"

"Idmon!" cried Ogygia. She tried to run over to the body, but Niobe stopped her. Sobbing, Ogygia buried her face against Niobe's side, moaning the name of her beloved cousin.

Cleodoxa and Eudoxa, their dark eyes round with shock, ventured closer to the scene; they moved uncertainly, as if the ground beneath their feet had become unsteady. Niobe led their weeping sister towards them. "Take care of her," she told the twins. "Keep her with you." Ogygia needed to be comforted and restrained; and it would give the older girls something to do.

A healer finally pushed through the crowd; the man knelt beside Thebe and her son, then shook his head in sorrow. "I'm sorry, my lady," he told Thebe. "Besides the injury to his head, he has broken his neck. No mortal can heal him."

"No!" Thebe screamed, convulsing with sobs. "No!"

Niobe went to her sister-in-law and said, gently, "Thebe—"

Thebe turned on her with a face like a Gorgon, her tear-reddened eyes ringed with smeared kohl. "Get away from me!" she raged. "You always wanted him dead!"

Niobe drew back. She had not expected the grief-stricken woman to be reasonable, but this was too much – especially before the entire city. Coldly she said: "*I* warned him not to climb the wall because the stones might be slick. But *you* insisted that he go up anyway."

Thebe gasped, and then her ferocious expression crumpled. "Oh, sweet Leto," she moaned, rocking the dead boy in her arms. "My fault," she said, pressing her cheek against his blood-matted hair. "My fault, my fault. Oh, my Idmon, forgive me!"

Amphion touched his brother's arm again; this time, instead of shaking him off, Zethos covered Amphion's fingers with his own large hand. Hoarsely he said: "Amphion, see to my son's body." Then he knelt beside his wife. Plying his great strength with gentleness, he pulled her away from the corpse and lifted her in his arms. She pressed her face against his neck, weeping. His own face wet with tears, Zethos turned towards the palace. The shocked citizens of Thebes moved aside to let him pass.

Amphion removed his purple-dyed cloak and placed it on the ground beside Idmon's body, then moved his nephew to the center of the cloak. He called forth Alphenor, Phaedimus, Damasichthon, and Ilioneus and then had the four oldest princes each take a corner of the cloak. Then he led them away, walking slowly up the road toward the palace, following the bereaved parents.

Niobe pressed both hands to her face and took a deep, shuddering breath. How could the gods allow such a thing to happen? Today was supposed to be a day of joy! They had completed strong walls to protect the city, offered prayers and libations at each of the seven gates – this should have been a day for Thebes to celebrate forever!

The crowd began ebbing away; faces which had been filled with elation now looked anxious. "A terrible omen," she heard someone say. "The walls must be cursed," said another.

No, Niobe thought angrily. It was just Idmon being foolish – and Thebe, as usual, defending her reckless son's every deed. The two of them had ruined the triumph Amphion had earned with years of backbreaking labor. And despite all Amphion had done to honor the gods – all his songs, all his unfailingly pious devotion, all the sacrifices he had offered – those gods had let it happen.

§ 8.05

Landing on the Lydian shore, the sculptor at his side, Broteas found himself in a place both familiar and foreign. The early autumn breeze held the scents of fish and spices that he remembered; the curve of the harbor and the shape of the hills had not changed. Yet the ships and the huts near the shore were all different – and nearly everyone around him was a stranger.

A darkly tanned man with a short gray beard and a fringe of gray hair walked through the bustle of workmen and merchants. "Can I help you, my lord?" he asked. "Someone in particular you're expecting to meet? Or perhaps I can arrange for a runner to go ahead to the city for you."

"Yes," Broteas said, examining the man's face. He felt he should recognize him. "A runner to the palace." He untied his waist-pouch and withdrew a scarab carved in turquoise. "I'll give you this in payment."

The fellow squinted at the jewel in Broteas' palm and nodded. "I'll find a boy to carry your message. To the palace, you say?"

Broteas closed his hand on the scarab. "That's right. Inform the king that his son Broteas has returned."

At those words, heads turned to stare; several dockworkers came closer. The harbormaster laughed, showing gaps in his teeth. "Prince Broteas! That's a good one. He's been dead for years!"

His braying laughter brought back the name. "Not exactly," Broteas said. He held his fist before the man's face, displaying the signet ring his father the king had given him long ago. Its lapis face was carved with a mastiff, the dog's image detailed with gilt. "You were deputy harbormaster when I left – back when we both had more hair. Tydeus, isn't it?"

The harbormaster gaped. "Uranus' balls! It *is* you! Look, men!" he shouted, his gesture inviting the other dockworkers and even the soldiers at the guard-post to join the small crowd that had begun to gather. "Prince Broteas has returned!"

Broteas sent the runner on his way before he consented to answer any questions; even then he said only that he had been in Hellas, and that his companion was a talented sculptor whose work Lydia would soon admire. The captain of the harbor guard insisted that Broteas take his own chariot for the journey to the palace; Broteas agreed, leaving Kallias to follow with a mule for their baggage. Still, once out of sight of the harbor Broteas slowed the two bay mares from a trot to a walk. He wanted to be sure his message reached the palace well before he did: King Tantalus was an old man now, and might need time to prepare. Besides, he wanted to look around him.

Lydia was apparently prospering; the grapes were plentiful on the vines, and the olive trees were heavy with fruit. Closer in to the city, workmen harvesting apples turned to watch him pass; a few, perhaps taking him for one of the king's soldiers, called out: "Long live King Tantalus!"

News of his arrival had spread through the city, if not yet to the orchard workmen. Curious onlookers lined the road to the palace; many shouted his name, but Broteas heard astonishment and uncertainty mixed with the welcome. The royal guard seemed wary; after he surrendered the reins to his chariot horses, two armed men led him into the palace, while a third followed behind as if he might decide to bolt.

The palace was mostly as he remembered; though some of the wall-paintings had faded and others had been changed altogether, the faint fragrance of cedarwood was a reminder of his youth. But there were far more soldiers on duty than before. Each major crossing in the corridors was manned by two spearmen, and when Broteas reached the royal antechamber his escort insisted on confiscating both his sword and his obsidian knife. When he objected, the elderly herald said: "My lord prince, it's the king's orders. Even Young Tantalus disarms before entering the king's presence."

His son! A wave of longing to see the boy – a man by now – flooded through him. "My son – is he in with the king now? And – my wife?"

The herald shook his head. "No, my lord prince. The king insisted that he and the queen receive you alone." Brushing some lint from Broteas' cloak, he continued: "Now, my lord prince, before you go in there are some things you should know. Though he won't admit it, your father the king is hard of hearing. Be sure to speak loudly and slowly, and stand so that he can see your mouth moving. He gets quite angry when he thinks people are mumbling."

"I understand."

"The queen's hearing is not so bad," the man continued, "but her eyes have gone milky these past few years; she can see very little nowadays."

"That must be hard for her," Broteas said. "Mother always enjoyed her weaving."

"Yes, the queen's weaving days are long past," said the herald. "But that's as the gods would have it. Come, now, we mustn't keep the king waiting." He gestured to the guards; the heavy doors creaked on their pivot-poles as the men swung them open.

"Prince Broteas, my lord king," shouted the herald.

Broteas walked into the audience chamber: a much smaller room than the palace megaron and with far more comfortable furniture. He was followed by the three soldiers who had escorted him through the palace; four more were inside the chamber, two standing at attention on each side of the royal couple. Broteas appraised his father. King Tantalus was certainly too old to serve as the model for a wall-painting of Zeus, as he once could have done; but he still looked commanding and regal, his silver hair abundant beneath the golden circlet crown. Queen Dione appeared far older than her husband; her face was wrinkled, her body frail, and as the herald had warned her eyes were cloudy with age.

She extended an unsteady hand. "Broteas, is it really you? Come closer, my son."

"Yes, Mother," Broteas replied, crossing the room to his mother and clasping her hand. "It's me."

She reached for his face with trembling fingers. "Broteas! Oh, my son! I knew they were wrong to say you had died! Praise Mother Rhea, you've returned at last!"

"Enough," King Tantalus snapped. "Wife, you can talk to him later. Broteas, show me the prize you have recovered!"

A chill ran through Broteas' gut; nevertheless he pulled away from his mother, and turned to face his father. He dared not show weakness. "I do not have it, Father."

"What!" Tantalus slammed a fist against the arm of his chair. "How *dare* you return without it? Be gone, and don't return to Lydia until you have it!"

Broteas knew he had to make his case quickly. "Wait, Father – I have something better."

"Better?" bellowed the king. "Nonsense! Guards, take him away!"

The soldiers standing behind Broteas grabbed his elbows; he pulled against them, shouting, "Hear me out, Father!"

Her voice quavering, Dione said, "Broteas? What's going on?"

"Take him away!" roared King Tantalus. "I'll have his head for coming back empty-handed!"

The soldiers pulled him toward the door. Broteas struggled, but with his bad leg he could not resist their strength. "I went to Delphi!" he shouted. "Father, I've been to Delphi!"

"Broteas?" screamed the queen. "Broteas!"

Curse his mother for interrupting when he was trying to make himself heard! He shouted louder: "Father, the Oracle spoke to me – the Oracle of Delphi!"

"Wait," commanded the king. The soldiers paused, and the king said: "Delphi, you say?"

Broteas glared at the guards and they released his arms. He limped back to stand before his father. Speaking slowly and clearly, he explained what had happened at Delphi. He told of meeting Kallias, then how he had asked the oracle whether to return to Lydia; he related the oracle's words and explained their meaning. When the tale was finished, the king remained silent for a long while.

"The Oracle of Delphi is never false," he said at last. "But what you suggest is costly."

"I will cover the expense myself," Broteas said. "I have brought back wealth enough for the materials and the workmen."

King Tantalus nodded – and actually looked impressed. Broteas had already decided not to reveal that his brother had given him much of this wealth. Mention of Pelops might well enrage King Tantalus – and even if it did not, why should he share the credit? The Oracle had directed Pelops to give the gold to him.

"You have my permission," said the king. "Leave now. You can speak with your mother later."

Queen Dione did not object; Broteas bowed and followed the soldiers out. He retrieved his weapons from the guards in the anteroom; he instructed the herald to find a room for the sculptor, and arrange for Broteas' baggage to be brought to his own rooms. After confirming that his family still lived in his old quarters, he went to see his wife.

The rooms were the same, though the furnishings had changed. His wife and son welcomed him back with the appropriate words – but his wife seemed uneasy, and his son was a stranger. Receiving warning of his arrival, Euryanassa had arranged for a bath and a private meal. Their conversation during dinner was awkward, punctuated by long silences. Young Tantalus was no longer a youth but a man past thirty, well used to recognition as the king's heir; summoning a deferential attitude was obviously a struggle. Euryanassa remained an attractive woman – but in the manner of motherly Demeter, with no trace of Aphrodite's spark remaining. When Broteas went to her bed that night she submitted silently, unresponsive beneath his thrusting hips.

He rose early the next morning. Leaving Euryanassa slumbering on the bed's far side, he pulled on a tunic and fastened his belt, then went out to the terrace with its view of Mount Sipylus. He took a seat and bade the servants bring his morning meal; a serving-girl brought him bread, cheese, and figs and poured him a goblet of watered wine. When he asked for meat she raised her eyebrows, then bowed and hurried off to see to it. As he waited, watching the shadows of fluffy white clouds move across the landscape, Broteas contemplated the situation in which the Fates had placed him. He had left a country where he could never be more than a guest – and yet where he felt completely at home; now, he had returned to the land of his birth and found himself less welcome than any guest. His own parents had offered him no hospitality. There was no banquet to celebrate his return, no formal announcement from the king. His wife and son treated him like an interloper. Even the accents sounded strange.

The girl finally returned with a platter of cold sliced meat. Setting it on the table, she said, "You've a visitor, my lord prince. One of the king's men wishes to speak with you."

Broteas blinked. Perhaps he had misjudged – perhaps his father wanted to arrange for a celebration after all? "Bring the fellow here," he told the girl, then took a bite of meat. It was tasty, though different from what he had become accustomed to in Arcadia.

Hearing footsteps on the terrace, he swallowed his food and took a sip of wine – then when he turned to see his visitor, he was hard pressed not to spray the liquid across the table. "Geranor!"

Geranor wore saffron yellow, the color of palace officials; the border of his cloak and tunic displayed a pattern of stylized mastiffs. Inclining his head, he said: "Yes, my lord prince."

Broteas slammed down his goblet. "You should be dead!" he hissed. "You seduced a Maiden of Artemis!"

"And *you* could have saved her life," Geranor replied, his eyes narrowing.

"Saved her? Artemis' justice was done in her case, Geranor, which is more than I can say of you."

Geranor pursed his lips, then said: "I thought you might have this reaction. That's why I came to you at once." Without waiting for Broteas' permission, he sat in the second chair. Lowering his voice, he continued, "Don't you see, my lord prince, it was the will of the gods that I escape and return to Lydia – how else could I be here?"

With a conscious effort, Broteas willed his muscles to relax. It *would* have been easy for the gods to arrange Geranor's death: capture at the hands of the Maidens, discovery by King Stymphalus' men, an accident at sea… perhaps they did have a purpose for the man in Lydia. Setting aside for the moment his outrage at Geranor's crime, he said, "King Tantalus sent a message to me at Delphi: did you tell him that I was alive?"

A wry smile touched Geranor's face; he reached out to take a fig from the bowl; a ruby ring – surely a present from King Tantalus – gleamed on his thumb. "No, my lord prince. Actually it would have been much more convenient for me if you'd stayed in Arcadia. It's what I expected you to do." He bit into the fig.

"I might have," Broteas said, infuriated by the man's impudence. "But somehow Pelops learned the secret of the man-wolves of Arcadia; in his fury he killed King Stymphalus."

"That's a shame," Geranor said, chewing the last of the fig. "I always liked Stymphalus. But again, that's as the Fates would have it."

"What *did* you tell my father about me?"

"That we'd separated some time ago, and that I had no idea whether you were alive and dead. All perfectly true." He plucked another fig from the bowl. "Since he didn't ask me exactly how long a time ago, there was no need to go into that." He held the fig out, gesturing with it as a scribe might gesture with a stylus. "My lord prince, over the last many years we've both done things – and failed to do things – that would best be forgotten. Don't you agree?"

Broteas leaned back and crossed his arms, resisting the urge to draw the dagger at his belt. It felt wrong to let Geranor escape punishment for his crime – but if he slew a man in King Tantalus' service, he would infuriate his volatile father. He could first reveal Geranor's crime, but then Geranor might speak of Broteas' failure to retrieve the golden mastiff: the man could claim Broteas never really tried to recover the icon after that first abortive attempt. Such an accusation would be very difficult to disprove, and would surely enrage King Tantalus. Geranor could even describe the dozens of man-wolf raids Broteas had organized over the years – and while these deeds were considered heroic in Arcadia, in Lydia they would seem ridiculous, undignified, and unworthy of the crown prince.

He let out a long breath. "Agreed."

"Good." Geranor tossed the fig into the air and then caught it with an overhand snatching motion. "We've worked well together over the years, my lord prince. No reason that can't continue."

Broteas grunted.

"So, my lord prince, how may I be of assistance? The king has put me at your disposal. I understand you're planning a monument to Rhea."

"Yes." Broteas got to his feet, observing that Geranor had at least the courtesy to do likewise. "I want to speak with the sculptor Kallias this afternoon. This morning I would like to visit my mother. Make arrangements for both meetings."

Geranor bowed, just a fraction shallower than he should have done. "Very well, my lord prince."

§ 8.06

The morning of the funeral, Idmon's linen-swathed body was carried out into the agora. Zethos, his graying beard close-cropped in mourning, wept openly. Thebe's wails of lamentation were as loud as any of her servants' cries; she was so consumed by grief that she barely noticed the people paying their respects. Most of Thebes turned out to mourn him; maids offered fragrant herbs or late-blooming aster, and Idmon's many friends among the sons of the Spartoi lay gifts such as arrows, strigils of bronze and ivory, game-boards, and daggers beside the bier. As the sun neared its zenith, so many locks of hair – cut by friends, relatives, and other citizens – had been tied into the mourning-wreath that they completely covered the ivy-twined branches of pine. Amphion could tell that the flute-girls, too, were upset; their rhythm was off, and they could not hold the notes steady as they played the dirge.

Niobe touched his arm. "They're drinking too much," she whispered, gesturing at Zethos and Thebe. "Both of them."

"It dulls their sorrow," he replied.

"But deepens it," she whispered back. "Look at Thebe. In two days she's aged twenty years."

Niobe was right: with her face bare of cosmetics and twisted with grief, Thebe looked like a crazed old woman. At least his brother maintained some semblance of control.

Amphion glanced up at the sun and then tucked his lyre beneath his arm. "It's time," he said. Niobe set her hand on his other elbow and they slowly descended the steps; their children followed. The bearers lifted Idmon's bier to their shoulders; servants brought the mule-cart with the grave goods Zethos and Thebe had provided for their son and loaded the other offerings onto it. The black ram to be sacrificed at the grave was led along behind.

Preceded by an honor guard of soldiers bearing spears and tall ox-hide shields, the funeral procession passed through the city and out the Cleodoxa Gate towards the royal tomb, a vaulted structure carved into the side of the hill. The oaken doors stood open for the first time since the death of Amphion's mother, Antiope; a priest and his acolyte waited beside the altar, and the boy came forward to fetch the sacrificial ram. The white-robed priest raised his hands, and the crowd – seeking footing on the slope – gradually fell silent.

Amphion heard Ogygia sniffle behind him. Poor child, she had adored her cousin; since the accident Amphion and Niobe had sought to comfort her, to no avail. Glancing back at her, Amphion's throat tightened in sympathy; her tears reminded him of how he had felt when his mother died. He wished he could help his daughter understand that life would go on, but he knew that only time would ease her grief.

The priest sprinkled meal on the ram's forehead, and then raised the axe high; the blow was clean. As the priest and his acolyte prepared the carcass for the altar, Amphion walked forward and set his lyre against his hip. His first chord was a bright one, befitting Idmon's bold cheerfulness; only after that did sorrowful notes enter. Amphion praised the boy's spirited nature, weaving in echoes of other stories familiar to his Thebans: Icarus, whose adventurous spirit led him to fly too near the sun, and Phaethon, too young to control the golden steeds of his father Apollo. A bright and handsome boy, untimely lost, always to be remembered. As he sang, Amphion felt his brother's gaze upon him; he saw Zethos' lips tremble. He did not think that the music even reached Thebe; her tear-swollen eyes remained fixed on the body of her son.

When the song was done, the priest lit the altar-fire; smoke billowed up into the clear autumn sky. Ravens circled far above. The final prayer was sung, then the bearers carried Idmon's corpse into the shadows of the tomb. Amphion, Niobe, Zethos, and Thebe followed into the cool, damp darkness and watched the servants lower the bier into the shaft dug in the tomb's floor. The grave-goods were placed around Idmon's linen-wrapped body: first jars of food, wine, and olive oil to sustain him in the Underworld, then the gifts from his friends and family, and finally the offerings from the people of Thebes – herbs and flowers, a model chariot with a two-horse team, a red-painted toy ship, a terracotta dog with movable legs and tail.

The procession back into the city was somber. At some funeral feasts, men could reminisce about a fallen comrade, or tell favorite stories about an aged father. But no solace could be found in the death of a child. The public banquet in the agora was subdued, and in the palace megaron no one had much to say. Conversation was sporadic, dropping off into awkward silences; it was during just such a sudden lull that Amphion heard Menoeceus saying, "...the worst sort of omen. It proves the gods want Cadmus' line to rule Thebes. Not foreign blood."

Niobe had warned him that this talk was circulating in the city; it needed to be silenced immediately. Amphion rose to his feet. "I hear you, Menoeceus."

The red-haired man flushed. "My lord king! I—"

"You what?" Amphion strode over to where Menoeceus stood with a half-dozen listeners. "Let me finish that thought for you. You speak this way because your children *might* be descended from Cadmus. *If* the stories your late wife's family told were true. But did Cadmus' line really serve Thebes so well? King Labdacus – and King Pentheus before him – were torn apart by the citizens!"

Menoeceus swallowed. "At times a death is needed to cleanse the city," he said, awkwardly.

"Then why call Idmon's death a bad omen?" Amphion retorted. "Perhaps the gods required his sacrifice in order to consecrate the walls." Niobe had suggested exactly this argument, and it was likely to carry weight in Thebes – a city where people remembered the ancient traditions, when the royal family had been sometimes called upon to offer one of their own to the gods.

It might even be the truth. Who knew the minds of the deathless ones?

"Perhaps," Menoeceus said, looking uneasy.

"How dare you!" cried Thebe, leaping from her chair. She rushed over looking ready to pounce, but Zethos stopped her and pulled her away to the side of the room.

Amphion turned back to Menoeceus. "And your talk of foreign blood will stop *now*. I was born in Thebes. My mother was Theban. My uncle, who ruled Thebes for decades, named me his heir, and the citizens acclaimed me as their king." He allowed his gaze to sweep over all the Spartoi, and then return to Menoeceus. "Every man here has sworn loyalty to me. Do your oaths *mean* anything?"

"Of course, my lord king." Menoeceus bowed stiffly; then he met Amphion's gaze, an insolent gleam in his eye. "May I ask how much we are sending to the queen's brother this year?"

Resisting the urge to glance at Niobe, or at Pelops' envoy, Amphion folded his arms across his chest. "You may not."

Menoeceus spread his hands wide. "Forgive me, my lord king. But as your chief record-keeper I have a fair idea."

Amphion clenched his teeth, drawing in and releasing a carefully controlled breath. When he had sufficiently mastered his anger, he said: "Walk with me, Menoeceus." He turned on his heel and left the megaron.

Outside in the corridor, he shortened his stride so that the younger man could catch up. When Menoeceus reached his side, he said in a low voice: "For your information, I am not sending *any* of this year's surplus to King Pelops."

Menoeceus stopped in his tracks. "But – my lord king, you've been setting aside the usual quantities for shipment."

Pleased to have caught him off guard, Amphion nodded. "We will be shipping it. But not to Pisa."

"Then where?"

"Other cities – other uses, to safeguard Thebes. But you will not mention this to anyone until after Okyllus and his son depart. Do you understand? Do I have your word?"

"Yes, my lord king," said the red-headed man.

"I am your king, Menoeceus. You will not question my actions again."

"No, my lord king."

To his wife, however, Amphion owed full disclosure. Now that Menoeceus had precipitated it, he needed to have the conversation with Niobe that he had long postponed. He returned to the megaron and told her that he wished to retire. Leaving the younger children to the servants, and Zethos and Thebe to their wine, they went to their private rooms. Amphion set aside his crown and changed into an old woolen robe while Niobe's maid placed the queen's wig on its stand and wrapped Niobe's head in a soft scarf. Then Amphion dismissed the servants, settled into bed next to his wife, and explained his plans.

When he was done, Niobe frowned – but said nothing.

He felt compelled by her silence to repeat some of his arguments. "Niobe, you heard Menoeceus tonight. You know he's not the only one who's tired of sending so much to Pisa." He reached for her hand. "Your brother supported us in becoming king and queen of Thebes, but it's time to strengthen our alliances with others. Philomela could take some gifts to Athens; she hasn't visited her family for a while, and she can help us there. And we should consider marriage links with other cities. Your nephew Tantalus in Lydia needs a wife, and we have many daughters. And for our younger sons – there's a princess in Sicyon not yet betrothed, and the king of Mycenae has a daughter, too. Even the king of Sparta has told me he'd consider a betrothal for his daughter, young as she is."

Niobe pulled her hand away and pushed herself up to sit straighter against the bed pillows. "What about Atreus and Thyestes? Pelops wants the twins to marry them."

"Atreus is a brute and Thyestes a skirt chaser. Do *you* want the twins married to them?"

She looked away. "No," she finally admitted. "But they're Pelops' sons."

"Niobe, last time I was in Pisa your brother tried to kill me."

The lamplight revealed distress in her dark eyes. "He missed, Amphion. Maybe he wasn't—"

"Don't try to excuse him," Amphion said, growing angry. "I'm only alive because I jumped out of the way. Niobe, your father tried to kill Pelops. Pelops tried to kill me. We don't want our children at his mercy."

"I know," she whispered, leaning against his shoulder, and Amphion's irritation melted away. "He's not the boy I grew up with any more. And that's why I'm afraid. If we turn against him – if he *thinks* we've turned against him – he'll retaliate."

He stroked her cheek. "That's why we gave Thebes walls. The city's better protected than ever. And now that Pelops has angered the gods, we should establish other alliances for our children."

Amphion had reason on his side. The murder of Stymphalus had revealed weaknesses in Pelops' hold on his allies. Even if he had received absolution at Delphi, the Tiresias' words showed that the gods did not have infinite patience with Pisa's king. Pelops' position was weaker than it had been in years, while Thebes was prosperous and strong. And the children – from Alphenor and Chloris to little Ismenus and Phthia – their children were admired everywhere.

Soon after Pelops' envoys departed, Philomela left for Athens with a cartload of royal gifts, while Naucles took messages and goods to Mycenae, Sicyon, Argos and Pylos. But Niobe's worries persisted. Though she acknowledged that the other kingdoms were responding well to their overtures, and took interest in the betrothals being considered for their children, Amphion never felt that she approved of what he was doing.

Adding to Amphion's concerns, that winter the Maenad cult grew especially troublesome. After Idmon's death Thebe became the wine-god's most devoted adherent, increasing the cult's popularity. She and the other Maenads went out night after night, downing countless cups of unwatered wine and dancing naked in the moonlight despite the cold, having drunken sex with anyone and everyone. Their wild orgies were often destructive. One night they rampaged through a field of winter wheat, crushing the tender young plants with their dancing. A few evenings later, they descended on an olive orchard, and damaged many valuable old trees. On a third occasion they set upon one of Thebes' prize bulls; several of the Maenads were expert knife throwers. Having slain the beast they ate some of the meat raw and paraded around the hillside with the beast's phallus and testicles lashed to a thyrsus staff.

The old cowherd was in tears when he showed the rotting carcass to Amphion. "My lord king, can't you stop these women?"

Amphion patted the shoulder of the old man, whom he had known since his youth. "Dionysus is powerful in Thebes," he said. "King Pentheus and King Labdacus both paid with their lives for interfering with the Maenads."

"But – my stud bull! What'll they do next?"

Amphion told Thebe how upset the old cowherd was, and tried to get her to understand the consequences of the Maenads' destruction. She was nursing a hangover; he left thinking she had heard nothing. But apparently she had heard enough. On their next outing, the Maenads went to the old man's cottage; they demanded that he come out and dance with them. It seemed they were trying to make amends. But he refused. At this point, the reports Amphion received grew confused and conflicted – but at any rate, apparently some of the revelers decided setting the man's home on fire would force him to come out and join their ecstatic dance. Instead the old cowherd stayed in his burning cottage – whether out of stubbornness or anger, or because he was overwhelmed by the smoke – and died in the blaze.

The next day Amphion found Zethos sitting on his balcony, staring towards the hills. There was a half-empty jug of wine beside him, and a cup in his hand. His beard was unkempt; his tunic looked as though he had slept in it.

Amphion began abruptly: "Where's your wife?"

Zethos turned slowly, blinking his reddened eyes like a sleepy bull. "Thebe? I don't know." He drained his wine cup and reached for the jug.

Amphion slapped his hand away from the wine-jar. "I've had enough, Zethos. Thebes has had enough. You're Master of the Herds – the Maenads murdered one of *your* men! Make your wife stop, or *I* will stop her!"

Zethos hung his head. "I can't talk to her."

"By the gods, you can! You will!"

"I've tried, Amphion! Don't you think I've tried? But she's gone. She doesn't hear me. My Thebe died with our son." Dropping the wine-cup, he buried his face in his huge hands and wept.

Torn between his anger at his sister-in-law and his love for his brother, Amphion did not know what to say. Zethos had adored Thebe from the moment he first saw her; to lose her, as well as his son, had broken him and Amphion could not help. So Amphion prayed to Apollo for assistance, and discussed the situation with Niobe. She recommended slipping calming herbs into Thebe's food and drink, but that was impossible, for most of the herb gatherers were Maenads or friendly with them.

Perhaps Apollo heard his prayers. A few nights later the Maenads tried to kill a wild boar in the woods; Thebe was gored and trampled, and died on the spot. The boar charged a second woman, who died the following day of her wounds. These deaths shocked the Maenads out of their wanton destruction. After Thebe was interred beside her son, the rowdiest of the Maenads departed from Thebes; the rest of the city resumed a normal life.

All except Zethos.

With Thebe's death, Amphion's concern turned towards his brother. Zethos spent his days sitting outside the royal tomb, even in the harshest winter rains. He poured libations of wine for the dead, and talked to their shades. Amphion hoped that as spring rolled round, the new season would cheer his sorrowing twin. Helping to birth the year's calves would give Zethos something to do, and remind him that life continued all around him.

But one morning Pelorus and Damasichthon brought sad news to the palace: Zethos had been discovered dead at the tomb. Though there was no sign of injury or wound, he was clutching his chest. Amphion felt sure his brother had died of a broken heart.

They buried Zethos beside his wife and son, and once more Amphion mourned at the gravesite. Zethos had been such a central part of his life! Memories of their boyhood flooded over him: Zethos killing a snake and their planting the teeth in hopes of growing soldiers like Cadmus; herding cows across the hills with their foster-father; Zethos encouraging him to play his homemade lyre. Then, when they were young men, doing battle in Sicyon; rescuing Niobe and Thebe from captivity in the palace; wresting control of Thebes from the cruel Dirke. And of course, there was the years-long project of the walls: without Zethos' great strength and his persistent encouragement, they would have never been built.

Through the haze of his sorrow Amphion felt his wife's hand on his elbow; she pulled him away, and they turned back to the city. The procession was a large one, for Zethos had been widely loved. How quickly the Fates could clip the threads of an entire family! Wiping his eyes, Amphion thanked the gods that he had many children, healthy and strong. Though his grief for Zethos remained heavy, he knew his children's youthful spirit, their plans and accomplishments, would eventually elevate his downcast mood.

As they passed through the Cleodoxa Gate, Niobe asked: "Are you all right, Husband?"

"Not yet," said Amphion. "But I will be."

NINE: CHAINS OF HADES

§ 9.01

Hippodamia's breasts ached. The pain had started in her right breast the previous year, sometime in the fall. At first she thought it was nothing – just one more symptom of age – but over time the discomfort grew, until the lumps and the swelling in her armpit could not be ignored. Her breasts had once fired Pelops' passion, but he had banished her to this miserable place. They had fed her children – the children who had abandoned her. And now the breasts *themselves* turned against her: misshapen, the skin scaling, the nipples dry and cracking.

She did her best to hide her affliction from Iopa and Ekhinos; she did not need to give those ignorant peasants one more reason to believe her cursed. But as the pain spread to other parts of her body, she could not hide her difficulty in walking. They knew she had trouble sleeping. And now her right arm was swollen and tender.

It was not worth the trouble to get out of bed. Summer was closing in, the days already scorching hot – at least in the cave it was cooler. And the wine was stored at the back of the cave; if she stayed inside, the servants could bring her a cup more quickly when the pain grew too strong. Wine helped her sleep, made the waking hours almost bearable.

She pushed herself up to a sitting position, grimacing at the pain. "Iopa," she called, "bread and wine! No water."

Iopa, who was sweeping the entrance, leaned her broom against the wall. "Yes, my lady queen." She ducked into the shadowy storage area, returning with a two-handled cup and a piece of unleavened bread.

Hippodamia dipped the stale bread into the wine to soften it, then chewed slowly. She had no appetite, but if she did not eat she would have no strength at all. She helped it down with a gulp of the thick, sweet wine.

Ekhinos hurried in from outside. "There's a boat, my lady queen!" he exclaimed. "A boat, headed for our shore!"

Hippodamia squinted up at him. "Are you sure?"

"Yes, my lady queen. It'll be here soon."

She put down the cup. It was probably only a fisherman, but she should do her best to look like a queen. "Fetch my good cloak," she told Iopa, "and then comb my hair. Quickly!"

Ekhinos went back out to direct the boat. Iopa fetched the cloak and the comb while Hippodamia exchanged her nightgown for a clean, if ragged, garment. Once her hair was in order she wrapped the crimson cloak, left behind by her son Atreus, around her arms and shoulders. No matter the day's heat, she would not let any visitor see her swollen arm and misshapen breasts.

This done, she walked to the mouth of the cave and stepped outside. The sunlight dazzled her eyes; when her vision cleared she could see a small craft landing on the sandy section of the beach. Several men disembarked. Two were rowers, another two seemed to be soldiers – but the last, she could tell even from this distance, was Pelops. She stared, dumbfounded, while he paused to speak with his men and Ekhinos. The jeweled clasp of the ivory armor covering his shoulder sparkled in the sun; his cream-colored kilt set off his tanned skin.

Hippodamia would not humble herself by going to him: let him come to her!

Pelops had gained a little weight over the years but still seemed fit, striding easily along the shore; though his beard had plenty of gray, his hair was thick and mostly dark. He exuded confidence and vitality – whereas she was now a disease-riddled old woman.

She waited at the mouth of the cave, watching his approach, until he was so near that he blocked the light.

"Hippodamia," he said.

"Husband."

He seated himself on the wooden bench where Ekhinos sat in the evenings to mend his fishing nets. "Leave us," he told Iopa.

"Yes, my lord king," the peasant whispered. She dropped her knee in an awkward curtsey, then made her way across the rocks toward the sand to her husband.

Hippodamia faced her husband. "Why are you here?"

"I want to talk to you," he said.

She shrugged, and lowered herself onto Iopa's stool.

Pelops placed his hands on his knees. Now that they were close, she saw deep lines in his face: horizontal furrows carved across his forehead and two vertical lines between his dark eyebrows. Still, he remained a good-looking man.

"You deserve this much, Hippodamia: Atreus *is* my son."

"Of course he is!" she snapped. Then, curious, she asked: "Since you wouldn't take my word for it, what convinced you?"

"I learned it at Delphi."

"At *Delphi*?" She had always told Pelops that Atreus was his – but she had never been sure herself. It was a tremendous relief to have confirmation from the gods. Hippodamia found she could breathe a little easier; even the ache in her breast subsided. Maybe her luck was changing at last!

Pelops nodded. "Yes."

After so long – so very long! Tears filled Hippodamia's eyes; she blinked them away, determined to show her husband no weakness. "How is he?" she asked once she was sure her voice would not quaver. "And how are my other children?"

He explained that he was arranging for Atreus and Thyestes to marry the twin daughters of his sister Niobe. Though Hippodamia had never liked Niobe, the alliance sounded suitable – and if the girls took after their mother, they would certainly be fruitful. There were no definite plans for the younger boys as yet; as to the girls, Eurydike was still queen of Mycenae, Nikippe had borne a boy to her husband, and Astydamia was now Queen of Tiryns. Pelops even gave her news of the children she had borne to her father, Sicyon and Alkippe. Then he began telling her about his nephews, Niobe's sons, and how well they had performed in last year's games.

She had listened intently while Pelops spoke of her children and grandchildren, but her attention wandered when he moved on to others. Leaning forward, she interrupted: "Pelops – now that you know Atreus is yours, let me come home."

"No."

She wanted to be strong, but this flat refusal brought back the tears. "Please," she whispered. "I've been here so long."

"You're still alive," he said. "And Chrysippus is dead."

Hippodamia wiped her cheeks with a trembling hand, cursing the tears – and then decided that weeping might be the best thing she could do. Pelops needed to see contrition, remorse – so she let the tears fall freely as she prepared her next words. "Husband, Chrysippus was a fine young man. I could see that you preferred him to our sons – to *my* sons." She met his gaze. "What I did, I did to protect them."

"I understand," Pelops said. "But I don't forgive you."

With a sickening certainty, she realized that she would never leave this cursed spot.

Her husband opened a pouch hanging from his belt. "I brought you something." He held up a small purple vial; it shone, translucent, in the sunlight.

"What is it?" Amethyst was extremely precious, found only where the vine-god Dionysus had spilled wine from his cup.

"You're suffering," he said. "This will end it."

Hippodamia was not surprised that Pelops had been receiving reports on her all these years: likely, Ekhinos sent word of his observations each time he fetched supplies, and her increased wine consumption had surely been noted. But this was something she had not expected. "You mean it will kill me. That's why you've come – to kill me!"

His expression did not change. "It's time, Hippodamia. End your agony. My healers say that this potion is painless."

Rage swelled within her. Pelops had tormented her for so long – she would not absolve him of her death by becoming her own executioner! Ignoring the pain in her hips, she leapt to her feet and knocked the vial from his hand. "Never!"

Pelops stood and retrieved the small container from where it had landed, then offered it to her again. "Be sensible. You're facing a painful death."

She pointed to the dagger he wore at his waist. "If you want me dead, let the blood be on your hands! I won't do it for you!" As those words left her lips it occurred to her that he could have killed her, or had her killed, at any time during her long banishment. What had changed?

A woman. This had to be about a woman.

Peering into his dark eyes, she saw a glimmer of shame; he looked away, tucking the vial back into his belt-pouch. A hint of color crept into his tanned cheeks.

"Who is she?" Hippodamia asked. "Who is it you want to marry?"

Her husband remained silent. When he had fastened the flap of the belt-pouch he looked out over the water instead of facing her directly, and she knew that she was right.

"Who?" Hippodamia insisted. "Tell me who she is!"

He folded his arms across his chest. "Chloris," he said. "The eldest daughter of Niobe and Amphion."

The world spun around her. It was one thing to know Pelops wanted her dead so that he could put someone else in her rightful place. It was another thing to hear the woman named – a woman more than twenty years younger than herself.

"She's your *niece!*"

Pelops shrugged. "Men often marry their nieces. Thebes is growing in power; I need to strengthen my ties with Amphion and his sons."

The laugh that left Hippodamia's lips was bitter. "But she must be well past twenty! What's wrong with her, that she's not yet married?"

"She's been serving with the Maidens of Artemis," Pelops replied. "But her time will be finished in a few months. And she's even more beautiful than she was when she won the first footrace for girls at the games."

"I will not kill myself so you can put that girl on *my* throne!"

"As you wish," he said. "It's your choice to suffer." He turned and started back over the rocks.

He would really do it. He would leave her here to die in agony, with only miserable servants for company. There was no hesitation in his movement, no turning back.

"Wait!" she screamed, the last of her pride dissolving. "Take me with you! Let me see my children again before I die: *then* I'll take the poison! You can have her – just let me see my children!"

He turned and shook his head; with the sun behind him, his face was in shadow and she could not read his expression. "Why should I trust you?"

Was there a touch of sadness in his voice, a hint of regret?

She stumbled after him, calling out: "If you don't take me, I'll last long enough to ruin your plans! I'm stronger than you think, Pelops! I've survived all these years in this gods-forsaken spot!"

He kept walking as if he did not hear her.

She tripped and fell to her knees, pain shooting through her bones. "You can't marry Chloris while I live! She'll finish her time with the Maidens of Artemis and marry some other man!"

Pelops motioned to his men. With their swords his soldiers barred her from approaching the boat; then, after Pelops had climbed aboard, they waded in afterwards. Hippodamia's shouted entreaties and curses had no effect. The rowers settled their oars into place and began to pull against the waves. Soon the small boat was gone.

Spent, trembling with frustration, Hippodamia shuffled back to the cave. She collapsed onto her cot, sobbing hoarsely, until fatigue overtook her and she slept. She woke only when Iopa shook her shoulder.

"Don't touch me," Hippodamia hissed.

"My apologies, my lady queen," Iopa said, bowing. "Do you want some wine? Some supper?"

It was already night; the patch of sky she could see from her bed was deep blue in color, and the sea an inky black. Her arm and breast throbbed, portending more severe pain to come soon.

"Wine," she commanded. "Without water."

Iopa nodded and soon returned with a cup; Hippodamia sat up and drank. As the wine warmed her, the scent of meat rose to Hippodamia's nostrils. "Did you butcher one of the goats?"

"Yes, my lady queen," said Ekhinos, standing behind his wife. "We thought you might like a change. Especially today…"

"Do you want some stew?" asked Iopa.

There was concern in their voices: they of all people knew what she had suffered. She had never thought that she would take comfort in the pity of a pair of unwashed peasants, and yet their attempt to ease her misery was her only consolation. "Yes," she said, accepting a bowl from Iopa. The goat meat had been simmered in wine, with onions, beans, and celery; she drank a bit of broth and it whetted her appetite. She ate as she had not eaten for months, emptying the bowl.

Outside the stars were brilliant over the sea; moths fluttered in circles around the lamp beside her cot. Hippodamia sipped her wine, watching them, and the pain in her bones abated. Iopa and Ekhinos sat just outside the cave, where she and Pelops had sat that afternoon.

Pelops. Gods curse him.

She tried to put him out of her mind.

Her stomach gurgled uncomfortably. She had not eaten meat in so long – she was unaccustomed to it. She should not have eaten so much. She lay back against her cushion, rubbing her aching forehead. As the constellations entered and exited the patch of sky visible from her cot, the stabbing pains in her belly grew worse. Her mouth watered, even though she was no longer hungry.

Iopa and Ekhinos edged into the cave.

The nausea grew worse. Hippodamia leaned over the side of her cot and retched. In the lamplight, the vomit on the cave's earthen floor showed dark streaks of blood. Coughing, gasping, she stared at her servants in horror and fear.

"You – you've poisoned me!"

Hippodamia spat and retched again, hoping that she might purge the toxin.

"King Pelops told us he would try to persuade you to accept something gentler," Ekhinos said. "But you refused."

Her belly was in flames, searing with pain.

"We had no choice, my lady queen," Iopa said. "It was the king's command."

Convulsions wracked her body and she soiled herself, adding humiliation to her torment.

Iopa and Ekhinos started packing, taking everything of value from the cave.

Her agony lasted through the night. As the light of dawn touched the sky, Hippodamia felt death coming for her. Iopa and Ekhinos departed, leaving her alone.

As the morning wore on, she grew weaker. But even after she could no longer turn her head to look at the Great Sea, even after she could no longer move at all, she could still mutter curses. She cursed Ekhinos and Iopa for poisoning her, for abandoning her. She cursed Chloris for tempting her husband. She cursed Niobe for having given birth to the wretched creature.

And with her last bitter breath she cursed Pelops.

§ 9.02

Death after a long illness: that was true enough, and that was the news Pelops sent to Hippodamia's family and his allies. Her body was not brought back to Pisa, but Pelops held a service, with prayers and libations of oil and wine on an empty grave. For the most part Hippodamia's children showed little grief – understandable, when their mother had been so long absent. Atreus drank too much at the funeral feast, and for several nights after; but that was all.

Relieved to have the matter resolved at last, Pelops received condolences from the neighboring kingdoms. To his annoyance, none of the kings with eligible daughters proposed a match – but that made little practical difference; months before, he had concluded that his niece Chloris was the perfect choice. The Maidens of Artemis had visited Pisa in early spring, just after Pelops received word from Hippodamia's servant-guards that her health had deteriorated significantly. Then, like a sign from the gods, Chloris told him that her time with the cult was nearly finished. She was both beautiful and intelligent: a woman with knowledge of the kingdoms of Hellas, a woman with whom he could discuss important matters as he had with Niobe. He *must* marry a virgin, of course – the years of doubting Atreus' paternity made that clear – but he did not want some flighty child he would be forced to humor and cajole. It did not matter if Chloris' most fertile years were past: he had other sons. Chloris was exactly what he needed.

Pelops sent Okyllus to Thebes to press the twins' betrothal to Atreus and Thyestes, and to discuss Chloris becoming Pisa's queen once her service to Artemis was done. But Amphion and Niobe replied that they would make no alliance for their eldest daughter without her consent; moreover, Cleodoxa and Eudoxa would not wed before the customary age of sixteen, so the marriages Pelops sought for his sons had to wait.

"They don't need to *marry* yet," Pelops argued. "Betrothal would be sufficient."

Okyllus spread his hands. "I suggested that, my lord king, but Amphion and your sister explained that their daughters were still too young to make that decision." Indicating his son Nikippes, he continued: "Both of us made discreet inquiries around Thebes, my lord king, and it appears that there have been many offers for the hands of the princesses. Some of the offers are very – ah – generous, my lord king. One might even call them extravagant."

Pelops slammed his fist on the table. "Amphion's a fool!"

"As you say, my lord king," said Okyllus, dropping his gaze. Nikippes also lowered his head.

Pelops rose and paced the length of the room. Why had he ever put that singing cowherd on Thebes' throne?

The ghost of Myrtilus, walking by his side, smirked. "Because he was sleeping with your sister. And lately she hasn't been talking sense into him, has she?"

Pausing before the window, Pelops wiped sweat from his forehead. But there was no breeze to be had, nothing to ease the summer heat. The city's streets were almost empty; a single merchant trudged past the palace, leading a laden mule whose hooves kicked up a cloud of chalky dust.

"Of course," the ghost added, "it doesn't help that you tried to kill Amphion last year. That tends to annoy people."

I didn't harm him, Pelops retorted silently.

"It would have been simpler if you'd killed him," Myrtilus said. "His sons aren't experienced enough to make trouble."

Pelops closed his eyes. Ever since Niobe's illness, his influence over Thebes had waned. Amphion had sent only a token gift last year – while making overtures to Athens, Sparta, Pylos and Lydia. Pelops needed to regain the upper hand.

He turned back around. "What do you suggest, Okyllus?"

"They haven't rejected your offer for the twins," he answered, his voice placating. "And I'm sure you can persuade Princess Chloris."

Pelops acknowledged this with a grunt.

"You're the most powerful man in Hellas," Nikippes added. "If you want her, how could she refuse?"

Pelops studied the gangly youth. "Well, then, Nikippes – are you ready for an errand of your own?"

The young man pulled back his shoulders and lifted his chin. "Of course, my lord king!"

"Go to Arcadia and find out when the Maidens of Artemis will next return. Find out exactly when my niece's service will be done."

Nikippes proved diligent in this task. Accordingly, late in summer, Pelops took the reins of his chariot and began the journey east to Arcadia – ostensibly to verify that Arcadia's man-wolves had stopped raiding their neighbors' flocks. A squad of soldiers marched alongside; Okyllus and young Nikippes, dapper in the yellow cloak Pelops had given him to reward his service, drove their chariots behind him, and servants followed with mule-carts containing provisions and gifts. The new king, eldest son of Stymphalus' sister, was only a child; Pelops had ensured that the regent was the man among the Arcadian nobility best disposed to Pisa, and most amenable to bribes.

The regent welcomed Pelops and his delegation effusively, and arranged a banquet the evening of their arrival. The palace at Tegea was modest, with crude, crumbling wall-paintings and meanly furnished rooms; during the banquet, Pelops recalled his youthful expectations of the barbarous western lands of Hellas. Though Arcadia failed to meet even those dismal standards, he praised the roast mutton and turnips, and pretended to enjoy the wine.

After the boy king was escorted to bed, Pelops set a hand on the Regent's shoulder. "A fine meal, my friend!" He slipped loose a silver wrist-cuff set with agates and offered it to the man. "Accept my thanks for your hospitality, and this trinket in token of our alliance."

The regent took the jewel and smiled slyly. "I'm honored, my lord king Pelops."

Pelops took another swig of the harsh wine. "Along the journey here, I noticed how thick Arcadia's forests are. Pisa could use more timber for our ships and building projects."

The Arcadian's eyes narrowed. "No doubt. What would you offer in trade?"

"You'd like to graze your sheep and goats in the western lowlands, wouldn't you?" Pelops asked. "That could be arranged. Of course, your herdsmen would need to keep the animals away from the crops."

The regent turned the silver cuff in his fingers; the engraved vine pattern that twisted between the stones caught the light. "Yes... I don't have enough workmen for the logging, though." There was a hint of reluctance in his voice, but Pelops sensed it was feigned.

"Leave that to me." Pelops was pleased: not only did he now have a rich source of timber, but as his loggers worked their way through Arcadian forests, some of them would build houses for themselves, and Pisa's influence would naturally grow. "Of course, you will still send one of every four yearling sheep and goats to Pisa." This was the Arcadian recompense to Pisa for the years of raids.

His host lifted his wine-cup. "Of course!"

Before the evening ended Pelops also arranged to obtain an animal from the Arcadian flocks to give to the Maidens of Artemis. The path to their sanctuary was too rugged for chariots, so the next morning he ventured forth on foot, with a few soldiers and servants and a local man to lead the dun-colored ewe. Soon they were in Arcadia's wild hills, fit only for herdsmen and hunters: craggy slopes clustered with trees and brush, here and there small streams and verdant glades. They neared the Maidens' campsite while the morning was still cool and fresh.

Pelops held up a hand; his party paused at the edge of the clearing. About a dozen sun-browned women dressed in undyed tunics could be seen in the glade. All but one wore their hair tied back; the exception was Chloris. She sat on a spotted deerskin draped over a rock, her dark tresses cascading in waves down to the small of her back, her lap filled with summer blossoms. The other maidens were gathering the flowers, which Chloris was braiding into a crown. As Pelops watched, a woman with a streak of gray in her hair tucked a bloom behind Chloris' ear and kissed her cheek. Touching the woman's hand, Chloris smiled – and Pelops' breath caught in his throat. By Aphrodite, she was more beautiful than he remembered!

"I hope you brought along a pomegranate," said Myrtilus' ghost. "That's the only way old Hades could keep *his* niece Persephone, by tricking her into eating its seeds."

Pelops waved this comment away as if shooing an insect – but the old story was on his mind. Persephone had been picking flowers with her companions when the Lord of the Underworld kidnapped her.

I'm not planning to abduct her, he told himself. *She'll marry me willingly.*

He entered the clearing. Several of the maidens paused what they were doing; others gasped and pointed, obviously recognizing him. Chloris, looking up, called out: "Uncle Pelops!" She set aside the half-made wreath of flowers and stood, blossoms falling from her lap.

Pelops walked towards her, holding out his hands. Chloris came to greet him, but the older woman with the crescent-shaped silver buckle on her belt was just behind her. "My lord king," she said, "we are honored by your presence, but we are preparing for a ceremony. Men are not permitted."

Chloris released Pelops' hands. "Selene, the ceremony—"

"I understand, priestess," Pelops interrupted. "I have no wish to offend the goddess. In fact, I've brought an offering." He gestured towards the ewe; as the shepherd led the animal forward, Pelops addressed Chloris. "Niece, does the ceremony mark your last day of service?"

Her dark eyebrows lifted. "How did you know?"

"It's my business to know things great and small," Pelops said. "In addition to my gift for the goddess, I've brought one for you – just in case you want to resume more formal clothing once your service is finished."

He snapped his fingers. The two maidservants of his party brought forward the large wicker basket and set it before Chloris. Removing its lid, they pulled out a set of skirts with flounces dyed in brilliant colors and a jacket decorated with golden rondels. This provoked a reaction every bit as good as Pelops had hoped: the younger maidens pushed forward to see, sighing over the rich blues and reds of the fabric and exclaiming over the gold-studded leather sandals. But the senior priestess, Selene, ordered the garments returned to the basket.

"Chloris," she said, "your time of service does not finish until tomorrow. And the rest of you don't need to worry about such things for years!"

The maidens stepped back, but they glanced at Chloris with envious eyes. Selene snapped her fingers and pointed; one of the younger maidens took the ewe's lead rope and led it away.

"I'll go now, my dear," Pelops said. "Will you join me at the palace in Tegea tomorrow?"

"Yes, Uncle," Chloris replied. "Thank you."

Pelops turned to go, not looking back as he led his party out of the glade. "A pity we can't stay to watch," Myrtilus said wistfully. "I wonder what they do in their ceremonies..."

Though Pelops had no desire to incur the wrath of Artemis, he was curious as well. Visions of Chloris remained with him through the rest of the day and into the night. She was perfect, absolutely perfect! Surely the gods had kept him yoked to Hippodamia for so long to ensure he would not wed another until her time with the Maidens was complete. He envisioned Chloris' bright eyes, her lithe arms and legs, her slender waist. What delicious pleasure it would be to slip the huntress tunic from her shoulders and admire her beauty unimpeded: her curves would be firm and supple beneath his hands—

Myrtilus coughed. "What if she doesn't come to meet you?" he asked, his indistinct form remaining just beyond the lamp's yellow glow.

"She'll come," Pelops growled.

The charioteer's shade sat down in a chair and clasped his hands behind his neck. "She might. To see her *uncle.* An old man with a crippled shoulder."

"Shut up," Pelops said turning away.

But even after Myrtilus fell silent, Pelops could not sleep. His shoulder *was* bothering him. The bed in the guest-room was uncomfortable, its wool-stuffed mattress hard and lumpy. Throwing off the sheets in disgust, Pelops shouted for his masseur and a cup of spiced wine. Finally he slept. Early the next day, he told the regent that he would meet his niece privately in the courtyard garden. He had the servants prepare a special meal and went to wait in the garden, wishing it looked more suitable to welcome the future queen of Pisa. But Chloris had been in the wilderness for so many years – perhaps even this modest space, with its wooden benches and leaning wicker trellis, would seem refined. Besides, he would soon transport her to Pisa, where he could shower her with comfort and elegance.

Chloris arrived in the afternoon, dressed in the clothing he had given her. Though her skin, bare of cosmetics, was not the milky white dictated by fashion, she was tall and slim and moved with grace. Her waist was narrow, her small breasts perfectly shaped; her thick, dark hair was twined with crimson ribbons. He tried not to stare too obviously as he offered her a cushioned seat and a cup of honeyed wine. She sat, the line of her back straight but not rigid, and accepted the goblet with a long-fingered hand.

"What a feast!" she said, looking at the table.

The Arcadians had supplied him with the best delicacies they could provide. The first course consisted of cheese-stuffed mushroom caps, fresh bread, and a small bowl of pickled octopus paste. Pelops dipped a piece of bread into the paste and handed it to her.

"Thank you, Uncle," she said, nibbling at it delicately.

"How long have you been with the Maidens of Artemis?"

Standing under the vine-covered trellis, Myrtilus objected: "A foolish question – she *knows* you know the answer, or you wouldn't be here."

Chloris glanced briefly over her shoulder and frowned. "Thirteen years, Uncle."

Could she see the ghost too, or did she simply wonder what *he* saw?

Myrtilus laughed. "You don't want her to think that you're mad, do you? But you *are* mad, old friend."

Pelops refused to let the ghost distract him. Focusing on Chloris' lovely gray eyes, he said: "You've led an unusual life."

"I suppose," she said. Her voice was sweet, with a hint of music in it. "I've met queens and goatherds, and traveled from sandy Pylos to the wilds of Thrace." Then she grinned. "One thing I can tell you, Uncle: your games are spoken of everywhere!"

The servants brought in a platter of goat-meat skewers and a dish of peas boiled with mint; for a time they talked about the games, and then the conversation turned to hunting. Chloris appeared to enjoy the meal, eating heartily. When the sweets arrived – almond-stuffed dates, which Pelops had brought with him, and hazelnut cakes from the palace kitchen – she seemed delighted with both options, and took one of each.

Pelops offered her more wine. "What are your plans now?"

"I'll return to Thebes," she replied promptly. "The regent here is to give me an escort."

Leaning forward, Pelops said: "I want to suggest another possibility."

Chloris observed him intently. "Yes, Uncle?"

"My wife died a few months ago, after a long illness. It's time for me to marry again. I can think of no one I'd rather have as my queen than you, Chloris."

"But—"

"My dear," he continued, giving her no chance to object, "men often marry their nieces. You know the first marriage of your grandmother Antiope was to her uncle Lycus."

"That worked out well, didn't it?" Myrtilus chortled.

"Chloris," Pelops continued, steadfastly ignoring the ghost, "you're not a child just leaving her mother's home. It would not suit you to wed some callow prince. And I have no patience for an empty-headed girl. I'd value your insights, as I always valued your mother's. At my side you'd truly be a queen."

Chloris blushed beneath her tan; she looked down, and Pelops wondered if her hesitance was simple modesty. She had lived apart from men since she was a girl; perhaps it was difficult for her to contemplate a man's embrace.

He reached out and slowly lifted her chin. Gently he asked: "What is it?"

She blinked. "I – well, I've just never thought about it," she whispered.

He moved his fingers along the curve of her jaw. "Never?" he asked, letting a teasing note creep into his voice. "Don't you find me attractive?"

She pulled away, looking down at her knees. "Those of us in service to Artemis avoid such thoughts." Her long, slender fingers wove together, the knuckles whitening. "One of the other maidens – she broke her vows. We had to kill her."

After Hippodamia's sordid history, Chloris' virginity was refreshing. Pelops began to reach forward, and then realized he should not touch her again just yet. "But your vows are complete, Chloris. It's time for you to take a husband."

"You should not be asking her," snapped the ghost. "You should simply take her!"

Is that how you tamed horses, by force? was Pelops' unspoken retort. *The apple wins them over, not the stick!*

Unclasping her hands, Chloris smoothed the flounce of her skirt across her knees. "I – I should like to consult my parents."

It was like coaxing a butterfly to land on his hand. "My dear, I've already consulted them. You know they will say that their daughters should choose for themselves."

"I know, Uncle – it's just that it's so sudden. I need some time to get used to the idea, that's all."

He reached for her hand, and lifted it to his lips. Then he turned her hand over and kissed her open palm. Chloris gave a little gasp; he perceived that she was trembling. She was *truly* inexperienced in the ways of men – and that excited him.

"I understand," he said, certain that this would win her over more thoroughly than any further argument. "Sleep on it, my dear, and we'll speak more tomorrow." He released her hand, gratified that her fingers rested on his just a trifle longer than necessary.

She took her leave and he watched her go, the graceful sway of her hips rousing an intensity of passion that Pelops had not experienced in years.

"We should make her promise *now,*" said Myrtilus.

"Tomorrow," Pelops said. He still felt the warm lines her fingers had traced across his hand.

§ 9.03

Sleep eluded Chloris. She remained restless, uneasy; her stomach churned. She burped, tasting again the evening's dinner. She had only eaten a bit of the octopus paste, which she loathed, to be polite – and she regretted even that small bite. She rose and poured a cup of water to rinse away the flavor, then lay back down.

But the bed was too soft, the woolen blanket too warm. The enclosed room seemed stuffy; she missed the cool breeze of the night air on her skin.

She felt as if she stood before a forked path, each direction obscured by overhanging branches. Which one should she take?

It had never occurred to her that Uncle Pelops would want her for a wife. Though Queen Hippodamia had been banished for years, he had still been married. Actually, she had not given the idea of marriage very much thought. When she heard that King Neleus of Pylos was a widower, the possibility of wedding him crossed her mind; she remembered his kindly face and good nature. But as the end of her service to Artemis neared, Chloris dreamed most of returning to Thebes: listening to her father's music, helping her mother to weave, laughing with her brothers and sisters. She had forgotten the long skirts and tight jacket that noblewomen wore, and that people would expect a woman her age to find a husband at once…

Chloris rolled from her side onto her back, trying and failing to find a comfortable position. Briefly she considered pulling the blanket down to make a pallet on the floor, but the idea seemed too ridiculous.

Her uncle was wealthy and powerful: the founder of the Olympic Games, he was famous throughout Hellas. Handsome, too, for a man of his years. This was the sort of opportunity that most maidens would grasp without hesitation. And yet not everything about Pelops was positive. Last year he had murdered King Stymphalus of Arcadia – a guest under his own roof! And some said he might have killed her father too, if others had not stopped him.

Of course, Stymphalus had provoked him, pushing him further than any man – especially a king – could bear. Pelops had been purified of the crime at Delphi. And maybe he had never meant to threaten her father: stories often grew in the telling and retelling. Pelops would hardly seek to marry her if there was enmity with her father – would he?

She sat up in the bed, hugging her knees to her chest. While Pelops had seemed perfectly pleasant in the courtyard – not at all like a man who would try to kill her father – his manner had seemed odd. Something looming, like the shadow of a thundercloud.

But she could be just imagining it. Most likely he felt awkward, as did she. Despite all his experience and poise, how often had the man proposed marriage?

She shivered, as she had shivered when he kissed her hand.

Chloris lay back down, trying to calm her racing thoughts. She recalled that her mother had always been fond of Pelops. And what he had said about wanting a queen upon whose insights he could rely – that had its appeal. Perhaps the union would be for the best.

And yet – why did he come to Arcadia just as her service to Artemis was ending, instead of meeting her in Thebes? Why did he put this question to her before she had any chance to become accustomed to life away from the Maidens? He could have offered to accompany her to Thebes; he could have made his proposal after they had gotten to know one another. Only a merchant trying to rid himself of bad merchandise pushed the buyer to decide immediately.

She pounded the pillow with her fist, trying to force it into some comfortable shape, and finally tossed it onto the floor. Uncle Pelops *had* told her to take time to think, instead of insisting on an answer there and then. Perhaps he would have considered it dishonest to take her to Thebes without first voicing the thought in his mind.

At long last she slept; but her slumber was fitful and brief. Finally, hoping that fresh air would clear her mind, she pulled on her well-worn tunic and sandals, girded on her knife belt, and slipped past the guard drowsing at the palace door. The night was nearly finished. Although dawn's fingers had not touched the horizon, the morning star glittered in the eastern sky.

She stopped in the center of the empty agora, staring up at the moon. "Artemis," she whispered, "help me. Show me what to do." But the goddess remained silent.

Chloris walked through the sleeping town until she was surrounded by familiar woods. She considered visiting the Maidens; perhaps Selene could advise her. But since Batia's death there had been a gulf between them. Instead she headed south, and soon the sky began to grow light.

Just as dawn was changing the color of the sky over the eastern hills she reached a spring. She stopped and cupped her hands into the dark water. As she slaked her thirst she heard goats bleating, and a woman urging the animals along.

"Morning, my lady," called the woman. "Your pardon, just bringing my little ones here for a drink."

"Go ahead," Chloris said, moving aside.

The gray-haired woman used her staff to urge forward a straggling beast. Once all her goats were lapping at the stream, she turned to Chloris. "You're nobility, ain't you? I can tell."

"How?" asked Chloris. "Have you worked in the palace?" That seemed unlikely. Usually, only attractive peasants were given work in palaces or the houses of the wealthy, unless they had special skills such as healing or midwifery. A woman with those skills would not be herding goats.

"Not exactly," said the woman, her grin revealing gaps in her teeth. "But I waited on Queen Hippodamia in her banishment. Years and years, I did."

"Really?" Chloris looked at her more sharply.

"You don't believe me?" The peasant's voice grew indignant.

"I didn't say that." If the woman was lying, then she was mad and there was no point in arguing with her – but if she told the truth, Chloris might learn something useful from this chance meeting. "What was Queen Hippodamia like?"

"Difficult," she said, looking pleased to have Chloris' interest. "There was no satisfying that one! She didn't like being in the cave: too dark, too damp. Didn't want to come outside: too hot, and the sun might burn her skin. Didn't like the food no matter what I cooked, didn't like the clothes she had. Didn't like this and didn't like that." She shook her head. "I guess it was hard on her, after living in the palace. But then she shouldn't have killed that boy, eh?"

Chloris shrugged and nodded in agreement. Aunt Hippodamia's crime *had* been terrible; if she had not been queen of Pisa she would have been executed rather than banished. "I heard that she fell ill," she said.

The peasant patted the back of one of her goats. "That's right. She would have died sooner or later, but I guess not soon enough for her husband." She gave a snort of laughter. "Had to give her a little shove into the ferryman's boat."

"What?" Chloris exclaimed, not sure that she had heard right.

"Oh, don't you know it, my lady. That man gets what he wants, King Pelops does, and I heard he wants to marry again." Leaning on her staff, she continued: "He visited the queen a few months ago, and she died that very night. My husband and me, we were lucky we didn't drink from the jug of wine he brought."

Her words landed like a blow; Chloris swayed.

"...I heard he didn't even bring her body back," the peasant was saying. "I would have thought he'd send his men to get her, give her the kind of burial a queen's supposed to have—" The spate of words paused. "Are you all right, my lady?"

Leaning against a tree to keep her balance, Chloris stared at the old woman, wondering if she were a goddess in disguise. She had asked Artemis for help – and the goddess had answered. These things sometimes happened in the songs her father had taught her.

"Grandmother," she said, carefully polite – even if she were only what she seemed, Chloris was in her debt: "you must not speak of such things. King Pelops is here – here in Arcadia!"

"What? But—"

"If what you say is true," Chloris continued, "then he did not hesitate to kill his wife. What's your life worth if he learns you're telling these tales?"

The woman fell abruptly silent. Fear twisted her homely features as she considered the repercussions. "Oh, my lady – I never thought – oh, you're right!"

In her heart Chloris had known the story was true; the woman's alarm confirmed it. "We'll say no more of this, Grandmother. You won't mention it to anyone, ever again – and tell your husband not to speak of it either. And you will forget that you ever spoke to me."

"Yes, my lady," she said, nodding rapidly. "I'll fetch my husband and we'll hide in the hills. Thank you, my lady." She herded her goats away, driving them as quickly as she could.

Chloris waited until she could no longer hear the goats' bleating. She spent one more moment wondering whether she had been visited by a goddess in disguise, then decided it did not matter. Pelops had poisoned his first wife when she became inconvenient. There was no reason he would not poison his second once her usefulness was done.

She could never marry Pelops. But she could not risk telling him that; he had a reputation for anger. He had almost killed her father! And Chloris recalled how strangely he had behaved all those years ago, outside Apollo's temple in Thebes. She had told him then she was not frightened of him – but she was.

It was still early; she had time if she hurried. She ran back to the palace, rushing to her room. She glanced around, her heart pounding like the hooves of a fleeing stag. What could she take that would arouse no suspicion? The gold-spangled jacket – if she rolled it up small, it would fit into her game bag, and the gold could prove useful. Her waterskin, of course. She slung the game bag over her shoulder and then her quiver, shifting the quiver to conceal the fact that the game bag was not quite empty. She filled the waterskin from the pitcher on the side table and tied it to her belt. Then, grasping her bow, she hurried out.

Near the main door she encountered one of her uncle's men: a lanky youth with a clean-shaven chin. Nikippes was his name, she remembered.

He stepped in front of her, blocking her way. "My lady princess! Where are you going so early?"

"Hunting," Chloris said simply.

"*Alone*, my lady?" he asked, his voice full of disapproval.

"Of course," she said, as imperiously as she could. "Tell my uncle Pelops that I wish to speak with him over the evening meal." With these words she strode forward; Nikippes gave ground, and then she was past him and back out in the sunlight.

Quelling her panic, she maintained a leisurely pace across the agora, heading north until she reached the edge of town and continuing some distance further, until she was sure no one was following her. When she reached a creek, she removed her sandals and walked upstream far enough that her scent would be lost. Then she dried her feet and put her sandals back on. She rearranged her gear for running: securing the waterskin against her quiver, then crossing the quiver-strap and the one attached to her game bag over one another so that everything rested snugly against her torso and the straps met between her breasts. She started for Tiryns, the nearest harbor city, moving at a long, loping pace she could maintain for most of the day.

At Tiryns she would find a ship to take her on towards Thebes.

§ 9.04

Myrtilus perched on the foot of the bed as Pelops' manservant helped him dress for the evening meal. "My, aren't you cheerful!" the charioteer's ghost observed. "You haven't been in such a good mood since Chrysippus' mother was alive."

Poor Danais, thought Pelops. He had loved her. But Chloris was a far better match. Danais had been a commoner; he could never have made her his queen – Chloris was true nobility.

"Which kilt would you prefer, my lord king?" asked his servant. "The blue, or the red?"

Pelops surveyed them. "The red."

"The more passionate color, eh?" asked Myrtilus. "I wonder if Chloris is dressing with such care. She doesn't seem to pay too much attention to clothes. Not like Hippodamia."

Pelops let his valet wrap the kilt around his waist and buckle his gold-studded belt. Chloris was nothing like Hippodamia, thank the gods! But the shade's comment reminded Pelops he had received, as yet, no reaction to his latest gift. "Fetch Nikippes at once," he ordered a servant.

"At once, my lord king."

Glancing out the window at the orange-stained sky of sunset, Pelops opened a vial of scented oil; he rubbed some between his palms and then ran his fingers through his hair and beard. He hoped the fragrance of coriander and sandalwood would appeal to Chloris as it had to Danais.

As his manservant fastened the final strap of Pelops' ivory shoulder-piece, Nikippes entered the room and bowed.

"Nikippes! How does Princess Chloris like the necklace?" It was the work of his best artisan, a golden pendant formed in the shape of a honeybee.

"I—" The youth hesitated. "I don't know, my lord king."

Pelops' brows lowered. "What do you mean, you don't know? She must have had *some* reaction."

"Princess Chloris has not yet returned, my lord king."

Taking a step towards him, Pelops said: "You told me she planned to dine with me this evening!"

The slender youth spread his hands. "That's what she said, my lord king. I thought she'd return by mid-afternoon at the latest."

Pelops' throat tightened. "If she went hunting alone, she may be hurt!" Why had she insisted on going by herself? Yes, Chloris was an experienced huntress, but Arcadia had its share of wolves, bears, and other dangerous beasts – even lions! "I'll speak to the regent. We should send out search parties."

"Yes, my lord king. I'll fetch him."

Pelops spoke to the regent, and several groups went to search in the dusk; he also sent Nikippes' father Okyllus to speak with the Maidens of Artemis. Their leader, Selene, came to the palace well after dark. "She didn't visit our camp today, my lord king," she said. "But Chloris knows the forests of Arcadia. I doubt she's in danger." Nonetheless, she agreed for the Maidens to join the hunt for the missing princess at sunrise.

He scarcely slept. Chloris could have fallen into a ravine, broken a leg; she could have been bitten by a poisonous snake. Some lawless brigand could have accosted her.

"She could already be dead," said Myrtilus, who was standing by the window.

"*Is* she?" asked Pelops, speaking aloud into the darkness.

"How should I know?" the ghost retorted. "I'm here with you, not down in the Underworld!"

When dawn came Pelops told himself that the daylight would help the Arcadians find her; but he could not escape the gnawing fear that Chloris was hurt, badly hurt. He waited in the palace courtyard, watching the sun creep towards its zenith, but no word came. Then Myrtilus suggested something even more appalling.

"What if she's run away?" The ghost leaned an insubstantial shoulder against the ramshackle trellis. "Her mother ran from you once."

"Why would she do that?" Pelops whispered, rubbing his temples. "I didn't threaten her; I didn't force her."

"And she didn't agree to marry you, either."

"She was about to – she just needed a little more time!" Pelops hissed. "She's injured, that's all! It's probably just a sprained ankle—"

"My lord king?"

Pelops started at the female voice – but it was only Selene, accompanied by another Maiden of Artemis.

"Have you learned something, my lord king?" asked Selene.

He shook his head quickly. "No."

"But I heard you say—"

"Never mind that!" Pelops snapped. "What can you tell me?"

Selene hooked her thumbs into her leather belt, calling attention to the crescent-shaped silver buckle, badge of her office as Artemis' high priestess. "Nothing, my lord king," she said simply.

The other maiden, a stocky woman a touch of gray in her hair, said: "She was always the best runner among us – both for speed and distance."

"*They* think she's run away," said Myrtilus.

"What kind of huntresses are you if you can't track her down?" Pelops asked angrily. "She may be dying! She needs your help!"

"As you say, my lord king," Selene answered stiffly. "We shall keep searching."

Pelops paced in the courtyard, drinking unwatered wine to calm his nerves. The afternoon shadows lengthened bit by bit. If Chloris were injured, why hadn't she been found? The Maidens were peerless in their tracking skills.

"She knows as much as they do," Myrtilus pointed out. "That means she knows how *not* to be tracked. She's run away."

Pelops dropped his wine-cup and lunged toward the charioteer, but of course there was no body for his hands to grasp, no neck to strangle. "Curse you, you bastard!" he raged.

"No, old friend," said the ghost, melting through his fingers, "it is *I* who have cursed *you*!"

His bad shoulder throbbing, Pelops bent to retrieve his cup. With shaking hands he poured himself more wine. When he was down to the lees, Okyllus ushered a peasant into the garden.

"My lord king, this farmer has something to tell you." Okyllus nudged the peasant's elbow. "Tell my lord king what you saw."

The man pulled off his broad-brimmed straw hat and held it before him. "I thought I'd seen Lady Artemis, till the soldiers came asking about it," the man said. "Artemis herself, running through my field – think of that! But she looked like the goddess: tall, beautiful, with a bow over one shoulder and a quiver full of arrows."

"What color was her hair?" asked Pelops.

"Dark, my lord king." The man shifted his weight. "Dark and curling, bound up with a red ribbon."

"And when was this?"

"Yesterday, my lord king. Early afternoon."

"She must have been injured later," Pelops said. "Which way was she headed?"

"East, my lord king. Going Tiryns way."

"Could you tell if she had had a successful hunt? Or did she seem to be tracking anything?"

"I – ah, my lord king," Okyllus interjected, "it's not likely she was hunting – not if she meant to return for the evening meal. This man's fields are some distance from Tegea."

"Takes me most of the day to walk into town," agreed the farmer.

"No!" Pelops burst out.

Okyllus glanced at Pelops, then told the farmer: "You may go." The Arcadian departed hastily.

"She's planning to board ship at Tiryns and sail away," said Myrtilus.

"But *why*?" asked Pelops, his disbelief turning to anger.

"I beg your pardon, my lord king?" asked Okyllus.

Pelops realized he had spoken aloud. "Why would she lie to me?"

"My lord king, I have no idea." The Pisatan noble hesitated. "Perhaps after so many years in the wild, the prospect of remaining inside..."

Pelops paced back and forth in the courtyard, then clenched his fists. "Ready the chariots. We're going after her."

"After her, my lord king? Not back to Pisa?"

"You heard me!"

The nobleman bowed. "Yes, my lord king. But it's almost nightfall, and the local roads are no better than goat tracks. We could break a wheel, or injure one of the horses—"

"Then see to it they're ready at first light!" Pelops roared.

"At first light, my lord king. Your men and your horses will be ready." Okyllus turned on his heel and strode out.

A fly landed on Pelops' leg; he slapped it, crushing it to a paste and then flicking aside the debris. How dare she – how *dare* she defy him like this?

"Your predecessor would kill her," Myrtilus said. "Put her head on a spear outside the palace."

Pelops whipped the dagger from his belt and threw; it passed through the charioteer's shade and struck a tree hilt-first, then bounced to the ground.

"For such impudence, Zeus would strike a woman with a lightning bolt. Burn her to a crisp."

"Shut up!" Pelops stalked past the ghost and retrieved his knife. It *would* be satisfying to watch Chloris suffer. Almost as satisfying as it would be to have her open her legs to him.

"She's probably in love with someone else," said Myrtilus.

If that were true, he *would* kill her. But he'd take his pleasure first.

"If you catch her," the ghost said. "But you won't. She's fleet of foot; she's had two days' head start. Chances are she's already aboard an outbound ship."

Pelops left at dawn with a party of six, two men in each chariot, leaving the rest of his party to follow afterward at a quick march. But the ghost was right. By the time he reached the stout-walled port city, Chloris had sailed – and the day's journey had transformed Pelops' rage from the boiling heat of Thermopylae's springs to something as hard and cold as the ice on Mount Sipylus in winter. He managed to be affectionate with his daughter Astydamia and civil with her husband, the king of Tiryns. Even when Pelops learned that his son-in-law had approached Amphion and Niobe about betrothing one of their twin girls to his younger brother – *and they were considering it* – he kept his manner polite and his voice even, hiding his fury at his brother-in-law's deception, his sister's betrayal, and the terrible insult their daughter had dealt him. He suffered his host's speculation about Thebes' new walls, and scoffed at the rumor that they could be as sturdy as Tiryns' massive fortifications. And with each bit of news about Thebes, each scrap of information about the overtures Amphion had made in the region, Pelops' heart hardened.

Towards the end of the evening, Pelops' host mentioned that the Tiresias was in Tiryns, visiting the local Temple of Apollo – and Pelops discovered that his anger towards the seer had evaporated. Though she had humiliated him at the Games, unlike Chloris the Tiresias had been justified in her actions. Stymphalus, despite his great crime, had been a guest: Pelops had violated the sacred duty Zeus demanded, and the prophetess had been right to call him out. But he had atoned for that transgression. Now he needed to repair his relationship with the Tiresias. She was still the handmaiden to the gods, and more than ever he needed the gods on his side.

Early the next morning he sent Nikippes to Apollo's temple to tell the seer he wished to speak with her. Then he went up to the roof garden to take his breakfast. There, from the top of the fortress palace within the fortress city, he looked out over the harbor: round-bellied merchant vessels and long, narrow ships of war floated at anchor.

"Your power is being challenged," said Myrtilus. He pointed north, towards Thebes. In the bright sun the ghost was barely visible, but his voice was clear.

"I know," Pelops growled, spreading soft cheese on a piece of bread.

"What are you going to do about it?"

"I'm thinking."

If Thebes were on the coast, like Tiryns, a surprise attack from the sea would be possible. But the city where his treacherous sister and her lyre-plucking husband ruled – this city to which Chloris had surely fled – lay so far inland that an invading army would be detected well before it reached its target. Pelops had the best fighting force in all of Hellas; before Thebes became a walled city he could have taken it easily. But the walls changed everything. Gods curse his sister and that traitor she had married! They had been planning this defection for years.

"Someone's coming," Myrtilus remarked.

Nikippes, probably, here to tell him when to expect the Tiresias. Pelops set aside his plate and cup – and, to his surprise, saw the prophetess herself, accompanied by her thickset manservant.

"Tiresias," he said. Then, noting how slowly she moved, he asked, "Are you well?"

Leaning on her staff, she turned her blindfolded face in his direction. "Well enough," she snapped.

This was beginning poorly. Pelops rose, pulling out a chair. "It's kind of you to come see me so early."

"Not especially," she said, panting. Her servant assisted her into the seat; she rested the cornel-wood staff across her knees. "I do as the gods bid me."

Pelops resumed his own seat and waved the manservant away. He bowed and withdrew to the far side of the roof garden.

"Tiresias," Pelops said, striving to set a better tone, "I regret the circumstances of our last encounter. You were right: I should not have killed King Stymphalus. I've done my best to atone for that."

Her thin, colorless lips drew into a tight line. "Yes," she said. "I know you went to Delphi. The gods have forgiven you."

Her expression, masked by the black linen blindfold, was even more difficult than usual to read. If the gods had forgiven him, why did she still sound so angry? Had she taken his killing of Stymphalus *personally*, for some reason? That made no sense.

"And now fate must take its course," she murmured, her voice barely audible. "Even I cannot delay that any longer."

What fate had she been trying to delay? "Tiresias, I don't understand—"

"*I* understand," she interrupted, bitterness in her tone, "that you came to Tiryns seeking your pretty niece, Chloris." Her gnarled hands gripped her staff.

Something in her manner caused Pelops to reassess the seer's mood. Perhaps she was not angry with him – perhaps she was angry *for* him, given how

Chloris had insulted him, how Niobe and Amphion had betrayed him.

"I did," he said cautiously.

"They say she's very beautiful. Even my servant Dolichus praises her loveliness." There was jealousy, harsh jealousy, in the old woman's voice. "It's hard to be rejected by one so young and beautiful."

Her words evoked a memory of a conversation they had shared many years ago, when Pelops was newly arrived in Hellas. The Tiresias had been a little older than Chloris was now – and *he* had been young and beautiful. He had confided in her his deepest desire: to rule an empire, to make a name for himself that would live for a hundred generations. And then she had touched his face, her small fingers leaving a tingling in their wake like a lover's caress.

Myrtilus' ghost appeared behind the seer's gray-robed shoulder. "You know what to say, don't you, old friend? She's the Tiresias, but she's also a woman."

Pelops nodded at the ghost. He said: "It's not her looks that interested me. Oh, your manservant might find her attractive. But all those years in the sun have left Chloris as brown as any peasant."

Her expression softened, as if what he said pleased her. "Then why...?"

"Why did I wish to marry her? Thebes has become powerful."

"Power," said the Tiresias. "I should have realized..."

"She *should* have realized," the ghost said, "but she didn't. She may speak for the gods, but she's weakening. After all, you can see me now."

That was true. Usually the aura of the Tiresias was so strong that it banished the ghost. Was she ill? Was she losing her abilities? In the last two years she had aged significantly.

"Tiresias," Pelops said, "Thebes is turning against me. I can no longer rely on my sister."

"Niobe," muttered the old woman sourly. "She never gave her heart to the gods."

Pelops ignored this comment about his sister, and continued: "Now that walls surround the city, my options are limited. I could lay siege to Thebes..." he paused, struck by a new thought. Perhaps he could convince the Tiresias and her servant to open one of the gates, and allow his men into the city!

She shook her head. "You must not harm Thebes. That is not what the gods intend. You do not want to start a war."

That was as clear a directive as he could ask. Her voice had resumed its conviction; even Myrtilus took a few steps back. And yet Pelops did *want* to go to battle.

"I'm from Thebes, you know," the Tiresias continued. "In Thebes, traditions matter."

"What does *that* mean?" said Myrtilus, his voice faint.

Pelops wondered the same thing. "Which traditions do you mean, Tiresias?"

"Theban traditions." There was weariness in her voice – or was she sad? "I did not want such sweet music to end... but I am growing old; the gods will not let me delay any further." She tapped her staff on the tiles. "You'll understand soon, Pelops. The answer has been with you all along."

She tilted her head, and though Pelops knew the eye sockets behind the blindfold were empty, he felt as though the Tiresias was looking directly at him. Under her sightless gaze, plans began forming in his mind like clouds taking shape in the sky. He *did* have the answer.

§ 9.05

The last of the hay had been scythed and laid out to dry. Amphion arranged a celebratory feast: the common people enjoyed fresh bread, cheese, and beef in the agora while the well-born gathered in the megaron to hear his new song.

The composition had played in his head for a long time; but the construction of the walls left him no time to develop and polish the piece as it deserved. Now, after so many years, he could indulge once more in long hours immersed in music, and delegate the day-to-day responsibilities of running Thebes to his son Alphenor. What a wonderful, refreshing change!

The Spartoi seated themselves around the hearth, and his children took their places to join him in the song. Niobe caught his gaze and lifted her cup in salute, her dark eyes sparkling. His new composition was already one of her favorites, and she was eager for its first public performance. Even Philomela, who usually avoided large gatherings, had come to listen.

Amphion settled the lyre against his hip and drew his fingers across the strings; then Prince Alphenor began to sing. Arpeggios wove around the prince's strong voice as he told of King Sisyphus, founder of Corinth, a man so clever that he sometimes bested the gods.

The children's chorus came next, describing Sisyphus' prosperous flocks. But in time the king's flocks shrank, while those of his neighbor Autolycus grew. Could Autolycus be stealing from him? Yet King Sisyphus could never catch the thief in action – and whenever he lost a white sheep, it was a black sheep that appeared in his neighbor's fold. Conversely, when Sisyphus lost a dark animal, his neighbor's new beast was white.

Now Autolycus was a wily man, a son of the trickster god Hermes: but King Sisyphus would not be outdone. Spying on his neighbor, he discovered that Hermes had given his son a magical rod that changed the color of the stolen sheep, so that they were hidden in plain view! Sisyphus devised a way to expose the theft. He marked the hooves of his sheep, proving they had been taken from him even though the color of their fleece had changed. With this evidence of his neighbor's guilt, King Sisyphus punished Autolycus by seizing half of Autolycus' flocks in addition to reclaiming the stolen animals.

Ilioneus sang the part of Hermes, complaining to Almighty Zeus: "What right has he to punish my son? This man thinks himself above the gods!"

Amphion's voice now joined the song. Conveying Zeus' amusement, his lyrics told Hermes not to take himself so seriously. For at this time Zeus had another all-consuming interest: a lovely water-nymph, daughter of a river god.

When Sisyphus learned that Zeus had abducted the nymph, he went to the angry father and said: "If you give me a freshwater spring within my citadel, I'll tell you where to find your daughter." So the river god gave Sisyphus a sparkling spring atop the Akrocorinth – and then, following Sisyphus' clues, found his daughter and snatched her from Zeus' arms.

Thwarted in his love-making, Zeus' amusement changed to fury. "Who is this mortal, to interfere with the gods? He must learn that he is only a man – and suffer the fate of all mortals! Hades, Brother, take this man to the Underworld!"

When Hades arrived at his palace, King Sisyphus was surprised: the God of the Underworld never fetched the dying himself. "This is a great honor!" Sisyphus said, offering Hades his own throne. "Surely there's no hurry for us to go: after all, I'll be your guest for eternity. Why not enjoy a change of scene?"

Damasichthon assumed the basso role of Hades. Flattered by Sisyphus' eager attention – so unlike the horror and fear most mortals showed – the god of the Underworld accepted a goblet of wine. Put at ease, Hades showed King Sisyphus the golden chain intended for him; Damasichthon produced a ribbon shot through with thread-of-gold to represent the chain.

"How cunning!" exclaimed Alphenor, singing the part of the sly king. "How does it work?" Hades let Sisyphus inspect the chain – and in a trice the king had bound the Lord of the Dead to his throne.

The guests in the megaron laughed and clapped as Alphenor wound the ribbon around his brother. Damasichthon's face portrayed helpless anger; the others danced around him, singing the chorus. Death itself, they sang, ceased: the Fates' knife sliced no life-threads, and fallen soldiers – no matter how dire their wounds – returned to their cook fires for rations. The war-god Ares, infuriated by this interference, sped to Corinth; he freed Hades and dispatched Sisyphus to the Underworld.

In the deep notes of the Lord of the Dead, Damasichthon described Sisyphus' punishment. He was compelled to push a massive boulder to the top of a cliff – but each time he neared the summit the boulder slipped from his grasp and rolled back down, so that Sisyphus had to begin his task anew. The last verse of the song was Alphenor's; and though he showed the pathos of Sisyphus' suffering, the mischief-making nature of the ancient king shone through to the last note.

There was applause, and the princes and princesses took their bow; Amphion grinned at Niobe's praise. Alphenor and Phaedimus released Damasichthon from the loops of ribbon while Amphion stood and stretched his arms. Walking around the room, he head a few guests compare Sisyphus' travails to the task of building Thebes' walls; but *that*, at least, was a task with an end.

Distracted by this thought, Amphion nearly collided with a tall, ruddy-haired nobleman. "Menoeceus!" he said. "What did you think of the song?"

"Beautiful melodies, my lord king," the man answered – but there was hesitation in his voice.

"Come, now, my friend," Amphion said, "A musician must hear criticism as well as praise if he is to improve. Something didn't please you. What was it?"

"My lord king…" The nobleman hesitated, then continued in a lower voice. "The verses come close to mocking the gods. Should this song be taught to children?"

Amphion shrugged. "That's how the myth goes, Menoeceus. And in the end, Sisyphus *is* punished for his deeds."

Menoeceus nodded. "True, true…"

The man was rigid in his views; knowing they would never fully agree on the best way to honor the gods, Amphion changed the subject. "I see you've have brought your children tonight."

The man's face lit with pride. "Yes," he said, "the youngest descendants of Cadmus: my boy Creon, and my daughter Jocasta."

"Your daughter's a very pretty girl." Jocasta was slender, with glossy dark curls and a broad, charming smile. "How old is she now?"

"The same age as your twin girls," Menoeceus said, his voice flat. "She was born the same day."

"Was she?"

"Yes." Menoeceus looked across the room at his daughter. "The midwife was called from my wife's childbed to attend the queen. My wife died that night."

Amphion's breath caught in his throat. No wonder Menoeceus was always so stiff-necked with him! Not only did he believe that his children deserved to inherit Cadmus' throne, he must feel that Niobe had caused his wife's death.

"Menoeceus," he said softly, "I never knew this. But we're all in the hands of the Fates."

The nobleman nodded. Certainly a pious man like Menoeceus – years ago he had moved his family to what was now the Eudoxa Gate in order to be closer to Apollo's temple – had made this argument to himself. But this information did explain the awkwardness in their relationship that Amphion had never fathomed.

Perhaps it presented an opportunity as well: one that would heal the breach and benefit both of them while increasing the city's stability.

Setting a hand on the younger man's elbow, Amphion drew him aside. "Jocasta seems a fine girl," he said. "If she's the same age as our twins, then she'll be fourteen next spring: not too young for a betrothal. What about marrying her to Alphenor?"

Menoeceus' ruddy eyebrows went up. "Interesting." Amphion could tell that in fact the man was enthused by the idea, though he was trying to hide it. "I would need to be sure that the gods approved."

"Of course." Amphion would need to persuade Alphenor – and, perhaps more importantly, Niobe. But the Sown Man had a point: if Amphion could publicly establish the gods' blessing on the marriage, his Theban dynasty would be firmly established, his line linked to that of Cadmus. He patted Menoeceus' shoulder. "Think about it, my friend. Pray for guidance, and I'll do the same."

With these words he drifted away from Menoeceus and joined the crowd of young people at the front of the megaron. Accepting praise for his song, he reminded his listeners that the princes and princesses had done most of the singing; when he found an opportunity, he drew Niobe and Alphenor away from the group. Once they were away from others, he suggested the idea of betrothing Alphenor and Jocasta.

Niobe wrinkled her nose. "I don't know," she said, frowning in the girl's direction.

Alphenor rubbed his smooth-shaven chin, and studied Jocasta with more interest. Her brother Creon appeared to have made some joke; Jocasta laughed, and soon the other youngsters were giggling with her.

Amphion slipped an arm around Niobe's shoulders. "My dear, no maiden will be good enough for your firstborn son," he teased, "but there are advantages to this alliance. Given the political tensions, it would be best for Alphenor to take a Theban bride."

"There are other well-born girls of marriageable age," argued Niobe. "What about Rhodia or Pinelopi? Even Melanthe – we shouldn't automatically assume that Menoeceus' daughter should be the one. Should we reward the man for being such a thorn in your side?"

"This could remove the thorn once and for all," he said. "And transform it into a tree that bears useful fruit."

Niobe shrugged slightly; though she did not like Menoeceus, she could surely see the benefit.

Amphion turned to Alphenor. "What do *you* say, my boy?"

The prince laughed and hooked his thumbs into his wide leather belt. "Well, for looks, I'd choose Jocasta or Melanthe." He coughed slightly and assumed a more solemn mien. "In all seriousness, I know there's much more to this than picking a pretty girl. We should do what's best for Thebes."

Amphion looked down at his wife, but she was distracted by some commotion at the doors to the megaron. Abruptly Niobe's jaw dropped; she gasped, "She's back!" and darted towards the entrance.

And then Amphion, too, spotted the tall young woman entering the room. "Chloris!" he shouted, rushing forward. He and his wife embraced their eldest daughter, Niobe weeping with joy; after that Chloris' brothers and sisters and Philomela swarmed around, and Amphion stepped back to let them hug her too. The initial surprise past, Amphion looked more closely at this eldest daughter. Chloris wore an old, tattered tunic; her hair was bedraggled and her quiver almost empty of arrows. She was thinner than ever, and there were lines of fatigue and worry in her suntanned face.

"You look like you ran the whole way!" Tantalus said.

Chloris ruffled her brother's hair, but she did not quite smile. "I did, almost."

"Why?" asked Amphion, sensing trouble. "What's happened?"

Chloris hesitated. "I'd rather discuss it with you and Mother in private."

Amphion told Alphenor to assume the duties of host for the remainder of the banquet, and to keep his brothers, especially Damasichthon, from drinking too much. Then he and Niobe ushered Chloris up to their private rooms. Ogygia and Neaira wanted to follow, but Niobe instructed them to wait.

In the royal rooms, Niobe told her servants to draw a warm bath, and to bring food and drink; while the bath-girls filled the tub, Chloris thirstily downed a cup of barley water. From her chair, she glanced around the room as if real predators might lurk in the wall-paintings.

"Chloris," Amphion urged, "tell us what's wrong."

"Whatever it is, we're here for you." Niobe reached out to squeeze her daughter's hand. Her short, plump, white fingers could not have been more different from Chloris' lean, tanned hand – and yet there was a similarity between the two women: the self-confidence with which each held herself, the assured tones in which each woman spoke.

Though Amphion was sure that Chloris was hungry – she looked far too thin – she ignored the tray of cheese and fruit, instead launching into her tale. She explained that Pelops had come to see her in Arcadia, proposing marriage. Unsure what to do, she delayed making a decision. Rising before dawn, she prayed to Artemis for help – only to learn in a most unexpected manner that Pelops had killed his first wife.

Niobe broke in, objecting: "Chloris, why do you believe this stranger?"

"Why would she invent such a story?" Chloris shook her head. "I had just asked the goddess for help, Mother. That woman was her messenger – maybe even the goddess herself, in disguise." She looked from Niobe to Amphion, and he saw a spark of fear in her gray eyes. "He killed the king of Arcadia. He tried to kill you, Father. And he killed his first wife… I couldn't marry him. I *couldn't.*" She pressed her lips together, toying with a piece of bread. "But I'm sure I've angered him, and I may have endangered you by coming here. I could go north – I've journeyed with the Maidens as far as Thrace. I know the hidden pathways—"

"Thrace!" Niobe interrupted, her voice full of horror – and Amphion recalled that Thrace was where Philomela had been so brutally abused. "Absolutely not! You're my daughter, and you're safe right here in my home! This is just a misunderstanding. I can handle Pelops."

Chloris answered with an exhausted smile. "I hope so, Mother."

Amphion touched his daughter's arm. "Chloris, you must be tired. Go take your bath – the servants will bring your food to you. You can share Ogygia's room tonight."

"Thank you, Father. That sounds wonderful." Chloris rose and kissed each of her parents, then headed off to the bath trailed by servants carrying a tray of food and a jug of wine.

When she had gone, Amphion dismissed the rest of the servants; Niobe sank back against the couch cushions. "Hippodamia poisoned… I can't believe it," she said weakly.

"You can't believe it, or you don't *want* to believe it?" Amphion asked. "You know it's true. It's more surprising that he let Hippodamia live so long. After all, she killed his son."

"Then – then perhaps it's not so bad." Niobe sounded as if she were trying to convince herself. "She *was* a murderess."

"Niobe, Pelops is *dangerous.*" He knew Niobe still had difficulty accepting her brother's misdeeds. "He may have slain Stymphalus in the heat of the moment, but he killed his wife in cold blood."

She said nothing.

Amphion continued: "He'll be furious with Chloris. With us."

"I know."

"Sometimes… sometimes I think your brother is mad, Niobe."

Her lips trembled. "Yes. Amphion, there's something I never told you about Pelops. I promised him I wouldn't. But now—"

"What is it?"

Niobe hesitated, adjusting her wig. Finally she spoke, her voice low and anxious – and Amphion learned that Pelops was haunted by the ghost of a man he had killed thirty years before.

"You're telling me the man is *cursed*!" Amphion could barely restrain his anger: Niobe should never have kept this from him. "Cursed! We were planning to marry the twins to his sons!"

"I know." Tears sparkled in her eyes. "I'm sorry, Amphion. I should have told you. But I gave my word…"

Her distress cooled his temper. Slipping an arm around her shoulders, he said: "It's all right, my dear. We never agreed to the betrothals. Don't cry – it's all right."

"Oh, Amphion," she said, leaning her head against his chest. "Why has it come to this?"

He stroked her shoulder, considering, and could find only one thing to say. "It's as the Fates would have it." And as he breathed in her jasmine-and-sandalwood perfume, for an instant he was a young man again: a cowherd turned musician, who dared to take a princess in his arms.

§ 9.06

"Husband, it's splendid," said Euryanassa. "Absolutely splendid!"

Broteas basked in the warmth of his wife's smile – the warmest smile she had given him since his return to Lydia more than a year ago.

The people gathered for the dedication of the new monument to Rhea craned back their necks to gaze up at the massive carving; with the ceremony concluded they spoke in reverent, admiring tones. The sacrifices had gone well, the smoke from the burnt offering rising to the skies in a straight column that confirmed the gods' approval. It was a satisfying culmination to months of work.

Bringing the monument into being had not been easy. With the sculptor Kallias, Broteas spent days hiking around Mount Sipylus last fall; finally they selected this high north-facing cliff east of the city. Taking into account the terrain and the contours of the bluff, Kallias then sketched out a design. Broteas secured his father's permission to begin work – and the king insisted that the monument must be complete within a year. Hearing this, Kallias threw up his large hands in despair. "Not possible, my lord prince!" he cried. "Not possible!" But Broteas convinced him that what the gods ordained was always possible, and he found a group of Hittite stone carvers to assist his Lydian artisans with the work.

Every few days, Geranor visited the worksite to assess the progress for his reports to King Tantalus, and every time Broteas had tangible advancement to show. First it was the increasing depth of the shrine, chipped painstakingly into the rock; then the arched roof taking shape, and then the image of the goddess herself. Though the two groups of laborers frequently argued – the Hittites insisted that Cybele, rather than Rhea, was the goddess' true name, which offended the Lydians – the project moved forward. Broteas did what he could to help: he hammered a chisel into the rock when there was coarse work to be done, helped cart away debris when the skilled sculptors were refining the forms. He pushed the men to toil in all weather, whether rain or sweltering sun: coughing against the rock-dust when the winds blew, harassed by biting flies when the air was still. One especially fierce thunderstorm that spring struck fear into the men's hearts; Broteas led both crews in a prayer to Zeus Thunderer, reminding the storm-god that their project honored his beloved mother. Lightning struck close by, blasting a pine to smoking splinters, but none of the men were injured and the project escaped unscathed. Zeus' high priest – a cousin of Broteas' wife Euryanassa – interpreted the event as an indication of Zeus' approval.

Gradually the common folk, who had questioned his sanity when he began the carving, began to speak of Broteas as bold and brilliant. Soldiers he had commanded more than a decade ago in the battles with Troy made a point of renewing their acquaintance. And even the well-born of Lydia could not contain their curiosity: many journeyed east from the city to look, and returned full of praise.

Now, Mother Rhea towered far above them. More than four times life size, she was seated on a massive throne, her skirts cascading down to her ankles. Her garments were painted in bright red and yellow, her skin creamy white, her braided hair night-black. She cupped her nurturing breasts in her hands as she gazed down upon her worshippers.

"Magnificent, Father," said Young Tantalus, peering up at the goddess.

His son's praise pleased him, but Broteas was more interested in the opinion of his father. Although others had come before, today was the first time for King Tantalus to see for himself what had been accomplished. The king was increasingly frail: even though he rode in a sedan chair like Queen Dione, the journey had been taxing for him. Geranor hovered beside him like a solicitous nursemaid. The king had been silent throughout the dedication ceremony, and his expression remained sour. But, surely, he found no fault with the work!

Unable to bear the suspense any longer, Broteas said: "Father – tell me what you think."

"Hmph," the old man grunted. "It will do." He barely looked at Broteas or the carving.

"Why isn't your father better pleased?" whispered Kallias, anxiety twisting his ugly features.

"Later," Broteas muttered. Raising his voice to be sure his father would hear each word, he said: "My lord king, no one will ever steal *this* icon from Lydia."

"I suppose not," the king answered, sounding petulant.

Though Queen Dione's age-clouded eyes could not see the results of Broteas' work, she spoke in his defense. "Everyone tells me how beautiful the goddess' image is, Son – they say even the Hittite Empire has nothing to surpass it. This will be the most famous place in all of Lydia!"

"Perhaps," said the king, still dissatisfied. "But what about when winter comes? The goddess will be cold, here on the north side of Mount Sipylus!"

"It was the best site for carving, Father," Broteas explained.

"Our offering-fires will keep her warm, my lord king," Geranor added in a loud voice.

Much to Broteas' annoyance, the king seemed mollified. "You're right, Geranor. Such a clever fellow!" He nodded slyly. "Extra sacrifices, yes. They'll come out of *your* allotment, Broteas."

"Yes, Father," Broteas said, bowing to hide his disgust. It was a colossal injustice – Geranor had seduced a Maiden of Artemis, but instead of paying for this sacrilege with his life, he had become the king of Lydia's closest confidant. Even Queen Dione seemed taken with him. Broteas hated to see his mother so deceived, but he thought it unwise to tell her the truth. She was forgetful, these days, and could not be trusted to hold her tongue – and if Geranor knew Broteas had revealed his secret, he would take revenge.

"It's time to go," said the king. "Geranor, tell the bearers that the queen and I will return to the palace now."

Geranor gave instructions to the slaves who carried the two gilded sedan chairs – somewhat ridiculous, Broteas thought, since the king could easily have done this himself. But lately the king did very little for himself, while Geranor did almost everything.

Broteas' son shouted a command to the guards escorting the royal family and soon the procession was underway. Young Tantalus led with the first squadron of guards, the royal couple carried just after; Broteas and his wife followed a short distance behind. As they made their way down the path, a vaguely familiar fellow threaded his way through the crowd to approach Broteas. Bowing with a flourish of his crimson and gold cloak, he introduced himself as Captain Naucles, an emissary from King Amphion and Queen Niobe. "I will carry news of this glorious achievement to your sister, my lord prince. She will certainly be impressed."

Broteas doubted Niobe's reaction; he had never been her favorite brother. And in comparison with Pelops and even Amphion, with his walls – Broteas had achieved little. Still, Broteas accepted the messenger's compliment and inquired after his sister and her family. The sea captain related that they were well, conveying news of young nieces and nephews that Broteas barely knew. With all the talk of Thebes, Euryanassa grew restless and excused herself to go join one of her sisters.

He knew his wife was sensitive about the fact they had only one child; he should have cut the conversation short earlier. Irritated, Broteas asked: "Do you have anything particular to say to me?"

"Yes, my lord prince." Captain Naucles lifted his hand to scratch his chin; his golden signet-ring caught the autumn sunlight. "Your son, Prince Tantalus, is still unwed, correct? And Thebes has many beautiful princesses."

Broteas used his walking stick to steady himself as they negotiated a steep section of the path. "I'm surprised that you're bringing this matter to me. My father is king. Only he can agree to a new alliance."

The sea captain lowered his voice. "Of course I'll consult him, my lord prince. But your father is old and not in the best health. *You* will surely be king by the time the match is consummated."

How poor was his father's health? Seeing King Tantalus nearly every day, it was hard for Broteas to tell. To the Theban he said: "I'll discuss the question with my son."

"Thank you, my lord prince." Captain Naucles bowed and then slowed his pace to fall back in the procession.

Broteas continued down the path, noticing the changing colors of the tree leaves and the bright berries on some of the bushes, and animal footprints in the dirt. Hunting. He had not been hunting for more than a year, and now that the statue was finally finished...

"The soldiers say they haven't seen anything so magnificent since the great walls of Troy."

The words came from Geranor, who fell into step beside him.

"My hope," Broteas responded, "is that it pleases the goddess."

"Of course." Geranor shrugged. "But surely it must please *you,* my lord prince, when the high priest of Zeus declares the Lord of Heaven and Earth gratified by the attention to his mother. And now even foreign envoys seek you out."

His eyes narrowing, Broteas said: "The man brought a message from my sister." Was Geranor trying to trap him into some ill-advised statement that he could repeat to the king?

"To be sure. But I hear what the people are saying, my lord prince. They are turning to you as the next king of Lydia."

If so, it was long overdue. He was six years past fifty! His father should have recognized him as heir long ago. But even with King Tantalus' power on the wane it would not do to voice such a thought. "My father is not a young man," was all he said, focusing his attention on the path, which was rocky and uneven along this stretch.

"Very true." Geranor moved closer; his tone grew unctuous. "My lord prince, we spent many years in one another's company. Can't we let bygones be bygones?"

Broteas swallowed back disgust. He was not sure whether Geranor spoke as the king's spy probing his loyalty or simply as a man seeking advantage with the next king – and he did not care. "A mortal offense against Artemis cannot be so easily dismissed."

Geranor's expression grew as rigid as a mask. "Excuse me for troubling you with my presence, my lord prince." He lengthened his stride, leaving Broteas behind, and remained close by the king's sedan chair the rest of the way back to the palace.

There was no banquet that evening; after the day's exertions, King Tantalus did not have had the energy for a long night. Instead, Euryanassa arranged for a family dinner on the terrace adjoining their rooms.

The evening breeze was pleasant; Broteas savored flatfish poached in Chian wine with fennel seeds and thyme, while he and his son planned a hunting trip for the next day. His wife and son praised Rhea's new monument, and related various conversations they had shared. All signs indicated that the people of Lydia, and the visitors from other kingdoms, were extremely impressed with Broteas' accomplishment and his piety.

As he sopped up the last of the sauce with a piece of bread, Broteas told Euryanassa and Young Tantalus of the marriage offer from Thebes. "Niobe's daughters are all beautiful, Son. They have their father's gift of song, and I'm sure their mother has schooled them in history as well as loom-work. Any of them would make you a good wife."

"It would make Queen Dione happy," Euryanassa added. "She'd love to have one of Niobe's children in the palace."

Young Tantalus leaned back in his chair. "The merchants who sail the western routes all say that Thebes' power is on the rise. In fact, these days I hear Thebes mentioned more often than Athens or even Pisa."

"It would be an excellent alliance," Broteas said.

"Then I'll ask Grandfather to approve the betrothal." The handsome young man rose to his feet, stretching. "I'll see if he can receive me now."

After Young Tantalus left, Euryanassa protested: "Why must we ask your father about everything? Isn't it time for him to step down? He's an old man. You and Young Tantalus do all the real work."

Broteas shook his head. "Father will never step down."

"But now's the perfect time," Euryanassa urged. "People know the old man's best years are past. They want *you* as Lydia's king."

Broteas set his cup aside and limped over to the balustrade, looking outward. The sky was deep indigo, shading overhead to black; in the houses below the palace, lamplight glimmered in courtyard spaces and through slatted window-shutters.

"His health is failing," Broteas answered. "The Fates will cut his life-thread soon enough. We don't have long to wait." He reached down and rubbed his scarred calf; the Egyptian liniment had helped, but what he really needed was exercise. Tomorrow's hunt would do him good. He sent a servant down to the stables with orders to have a pair of chariots ready in the morning.

Shortly after sunrise Broteas arrived at the stables; he strung his bow, checked the arrows in his quiver, and inspected his chariot and horse-team. But even once he had finished these tasks, Young Tantalus was nowhere to be seen. Had the young man overslept? Or simply forgotten? But before he could dispatch a messenger to his son's rooms, one of the king's servants came running up.

The man bowed and reported: "My lord prince Broteas, your son sends his regrets." Breathing hard, he continued, "The king sent him to meet with an important shipment at the harbor."

Annoying; but of course King Tantalus could not make the trip to the harbor himself. Broteas acknowledged the message with a disappointed nod, and lifted his hand to dismiss the man. But the servant, who had regained his wind, added:

"Both your son and the king wish you a successful hunt, my lord prince. The king says that he has a particular craving for venison."

"For *venison?*" Broteas could not imagine his aged father chewing such a tough meat.

The messenger smoothed his rumpled tunic. "Yes, my lord prince. He requested it specifically."

Presumably the palace kitchens had a recipe for making venison juicy and tender. Stew, perhaps. Broteas shrugged. "Tell my father that I will do my utmost to satisfy him."

The messenger bowed, and at Broteas' signal took his leave. Broteas called for two of the servants most experienced at the hunt to man the second chariot. Well, he thought, the day was not a complete loss. He had hoped to spend time with his son – but he *did* want to stretch his legs, and of course if the king wanted venison then the king must have venison. There would be other days to chase game with Young Tantalus.

The hunting party set out as the day's heat was rising; it was clear and bright, with only a few wisps of cloud overhead. The chariots made good time through the town and fields and soon neared the woods. When they passed the fork in the path that led to Artemis' shrine, Broteas whispered a prayer to the goddess, asking for her assistance in the chase. Once they were approaching the best hunting grounds, Broteas had his charioteer hold the glossy black horses to a slow pace so that he could search for signs of game. Before long he saw what he wanted: fresh hoof prints, a few broken twigs. He ordered the party to stop; leaving his charioteer to tend the two teams of horses and watch the vehicles, Broteas and the others headed into the forest, following the game trail.

Artemis, it seemed, was with him; a few red deer lingered at the base of a nearby bluff, and his party crept close without alarming them. Silently Broteas indicated a young doe at the edge of the herd, one that might provide his father with a relatively tender meal. His men nodded; all three drew back their arrows and let fly. Broteas' missile neatly pierced the animal's throat, and the other two arrows struck the chest and flank. The rest of the herd scattered in panic, but their chosen quarry took only a few steps before crumpling.

"Blessed Artemis," Broteas said, triumphant. After so many years of neglect, the gods were finally smiling on him. He had scrupulously honored them all his days – but, then, the deathless ones could not be expected to understand the brevity of a mortal's life. He was grateful for their favor now. "Let's gut this carcass and be on our way." The morning was less than half gone by the time they had field-dressed the animal and carried it out to the chariot-path.

To Broteas' astonishment, King Tantalus himself waited beside the two chariots.

Seated in his richly decorated sedan chair, gowned in purple-dipped robes, he gestured to the burden carried by Broteas' men. "A fine animal! You *are* a talented hunter, Broteas."

Setting aside his bewilderment, Broteas bowed and then answered in a voice loud enough for the king to hear: "I'm glad you're pleased, Father." He wiped sweat from his forehead, assessing the assembled retinue. In addition to the chair-bearers there were twice the usual contingent of guards; and for some reason the aged priestess of Artemis was there as well, looking as though her face would crack into pieces if she smiled. And, standing beside the royal chair, was his former companion Geranor.

"It's been a while since I hunted," remarked the king. "I'll have to go again soon."

Broteas had no reply to this nonsense; his father could barely totter across the megaron.

King Tantalus aimed a gnarled finger at Broteas, looking as angry as if Broteas had uttered his thoughts aloud. "You don't think I'll hunt again, do you? I know you're looking forward to my death!"

Broteas' stomach lurched. A gasp arose from the soldiers and bearers; Geranor reached out, as if he wanted to restrain the king, but of course he could not touch the royal person. Only the priestess of Artemis, her face as wrinkled as a raisin, remained impassive.

"No, my lord king, of course not!" Broteas objected loudly. "Why, you could live another hundred years!"

King Tantalus' rheumy gaze darted back and forth; then his lips curved into a crooked smile. "Ha! No need to flatter me, Son. It's only natural that an ambitious man wants to be king." The members of his retinue relaxed visibly. "Here, Son, you must be thirsty after your hunt." King Tantalus held out his own waterskin, its surface decorated with swirls of golden paint. "Have some of this."

Broteas hesitated, uneasy at his father's shifting demeanor.

Tantalus' thin white eyebrows came down. "I'm offering you a great honor!" he snapped. "To drink from my own waterskin!"

Broteas bowed. "Too great an honor, Father. It seems – inappropriate."

"Don't be ridiculous. If *I* offer you a gift, by definition it's appropriate."

"Still—"

"Do you mistrust me, Son?" The king tilted his head to one side, and the jewels in his crown flashed with the movement. He gave a short, unpleasant laugh, like a crow screeching. "Only a man with a guilty conscience fears punishment without any accusation of wrongdoing!"

Glancing at the soldiers, Broteas had no choice. He stepped forward, took the waterskin from his father, and untied the jeweled laces holding the stopper in place.

"Have no fear," Tantalus continued. "By my holy father Zeus, I swear that this beverage will not kill you." He laughed again.

Broteas drank; the liquid was honey-sweet, and more refreshing than he had expected. Swallowing, he tried to return the waterskin to his father.

The old man shook his head. "Finish it, my son. You have caught the venison I asked for – the least I can do is quench your thirst!"

Perhaps, Broteas decided, it was better to drink all of it. If the dose were miscalculated, he might purge himself of poison before fatal damage was done. If not, the full dose should bring a quicker death. And of course there was always the possibility that the beverage was only what his father claimed – a harmless refreshment.

Broteas drank the container dry.

His father accepted the empty waterskin, saying, "Now, tell me about your hunt. A fine young doe you've got there. How did you take her down?"

This question surprised Broteas; his father generally preferred to talk, not to listen. But he related how he and his men had found the first hoof-prints, how they tracked the herd, selected their quarry, and made the kill. The king prompted him with a question now and again, as if he really did mean to go hunting himself; but soon Broteas' description was complete. "Very straightforward, my lord king," he concluded.

"Artemis must have wanted you to succeed quickly today," said his father. "Eh, Geranor?"

"Prince Broteas has always had a bond with Lady Artemis." Geranor spoke smoothly, but his voice was guarded. He watched Broteas intently, as if waiting for something.

"Yes," Broteas said, not sure what was expected of him now. "I owe thanks to the goddess. May we offer her a portion from the quarry?"

Apparently Broteas had said the correct thing: the old king smiled broadly, revealing a gap left by a missing tooth on one side of his mouth. "Excellent, my son. Let's go to her shrine now. Geranor, you drive my son's chariot." He clapped his hands, and his bearers hoisted up the carrying-poles.

Broteas waited for Geranor to trade places with his usual charioteer and then climbed up behind him. Dealing with his father exhausted him; though he was not pleased to share a chariot-car with Geranor, he was content to let someone else control the horses. They moved forward at a walk, following behind the king's ornate chair; the men with the doe's carcass brought up the rear.

As they progressed slowly towards Artemis' shrine, Broteas realized that the morning's excursion had fatigued him more than he could have guessed. He leaned heavily against the chariot-rails, and discovered he was still thirsty, his tongue dry and swollen in his mouth. He reached for his own waterskin but fumbled with the laces, spilling as much as he drank. Geranor glanced at him with an odd expression.

Broteas' fingers were tingling; he could not manage to close his waterskin, and then it slipped from his hands. His toes, his feet, were numb.

"What—" he tried to say, but speech was difficult.

The king's sedan chair slowed, falling back until it moved side-by-side with Broteas' chariot; Artemis' wizened priestess walked alongside.

"Is something wrong?" asked King Tantalus.

"You swore," gasped Broteas, hearing the words slur past thickened lips. "You swore it would not harm me..."

"No, Son." The old man's eyes were malicious. "I said it would not *kill* you. You will die another way."

"No," Broteas moaned. His thighs were weakening; only Geranor's arm, reaching back to circle his waist, kept him upright. He wanted to slap away the offensive touch, to leap down from the chariot and run, but his limbs refused to obey.

"Wolfsbane," Geranor said quietly. "Appropriate, isn't it, after our time in Arcadia?"

Horror welled up in Broteas' chest.

"The poison immobilizes the limbs and the tongue," Geranor continued. "But the mind remains clear."

Broteas heard the sound of the horses' hooves, the sound of his own heartbeat. His heart was not racing – the rhythm remained slow and steady, as if his spirit had always expected this unjust fate.

The old priestess shook her fist at him. "You committed a crime against my mistress," she wheezed. "It's time for you to pay the price!"

No, he longed to cry out, *no!* He had always honored Artemis! But he could not form the words – only a thin croak escaped his throat.

"I had to tell them," Geranor said. His voice was gentle, almost apologetic. "It was my duty to the goddess. You seduced a Maiden of Artemis, got her with child."

No! he raged silently. *It wasn't me! It was him!* Yet all he managed was a pathetic, strangled noise.

"Abomination!" said the priestess. "We cannot allow such pollution in Lydia!"

I have always honored you, Artemis! Broteas thought, hoping that the goddess would take pity on him. *Geranor – Lady Artemis, you know it was Geranor!*

A large crowd was already gathered at Artemis' shrine – and before the altar, a pyre was piled high. King Tantalus called his bearers to a halt; Geranor reined in the horses. The aged priestess moved ahead and began addressing the people.

Broteas could move nothing but his eyes now. He looked at his father's face and saw it filled with malevolent glee.

"You thought you could take over," hissed King Tantalus. "I know what you've been doing. Sweet-talking Lydia's leading men, collecting new friends among the soldiers, tricking the priests into thinking you were a pious man. Negotiating with foreign cities!"

But I am your son, Broteas pleaded silently. *I am no threat to you!*

The priestess of Artemis droned on in the background; King Tantalus ignored her. "Your brother Pelops was ambitious, too. I couldn't tolerate that. But he had the sense to leave. And look at what he's accomplished: his own kingdom in the west! I'm proud of *him.* But you, my ugly son – when I sent you to retrieve the mastiff, you spent your time stealing sheep." He nodded. "Yes, your friend Geranor's told me all about that, too. *He* respects his king."

Geranor's steadying hand remained on his torso, a traitorous embrace. Broteas glared at him, putting all of his fury and hatred into this mute expression.

Beside the pyre, the priestess had finished her recitation. "Bring forth the criminal!" she cried.

King Tantalus lifted his hand. "They're ready for you now. Good-bye, Son."

A pair of men dragged him down from the chariot, pulled him forward. His feet scraped limply across the ground; he could not struggle, could not object when people called him vile names, accused him of abomination. Women spat at him, and he could not wipe the spittle from his beard. Then his captors lay him on the pyre; the dry wood pressed into the tingling-numb flesh of his arms, back and legs.

The bearers carried forward the king's sedan chair so that Tantalus could address the assembly. "People of Lydia: my son, Broteas, is guilty of a terrible crime. He violated a Maiden of Artemis." This was answered with hisses and jeers; but the king silenced the crowd with a sharp gesture. "For this he must die. But we should also acknowledge that he goes to his death willingly. He is bound by no rope; he is not gagged. He knows the punishment, and is prepared to accept it."

Broteas' heartbeat felt strangely sluggish – probably an effect of the herbs his father had given him. He did not feel panicked. He was going to die, and the true criminal would go on living, but Lady Artemis was not deceived. He took comfort in that: the gods knew he was innocent.

"Light the pyre!" commanded the king.

The aged priestess of Artemis lit the kindling with a torch: first to the left of him, then to the right, and finally she tossed the blazing torch at his feet.

Distantly, Broteas wondered whether his father even believed Geranor's story or if it was only a convenient excuse. As the shouts of the crowd rose with the flames, Broteas heard the echo of Niobe's voice, warning him that their father was dangerous.

The flames crept closer, licking at the flesh of his fingers and toes; the hair on his legs, arms, and chest burst into flame – and then his kilt blazed up, bright as a lamp wick. The agony was shockingly intense, worse than anything he had ever known.

And he could not even scream.

§ 9.07

His challenger, Vassos, proved a more capable wrestler than Laius had expected. Laius lost the first point when his opponent surprised him with a quick twist that landed him on the ground; he won the second by lifting the younger man and forcing his back to touch the sand. This brought a cheer from the men watching the match, who began to make noisy wagers on one or the other. Laius was larger and stronger, but Vassos – one of Atreus' well-trained soldiers – did not tire easily. With a great effort he brought Vassos down a second time, but then the soldier took advantage of Laius' growing fatigue and quickly toppled him. The next grapple endured for some time, neither man making any progress; finally Laius managed to gain a bit of leverage, wedged his ankle behind his opponent's foot, and both men thumped to the ground. The onlookers shouted boisterously.

"The last point goes to Laius!" called Thyestes, who was judging the contest.

Laius rolled away from his opponent and lay on his back, breathing hard. He was not sure that he *had* won – his knee might have hit the ground before Vassos' shoulder – but Thyestes was the arbiter. Why challenge a victory?

"Here comes the king," Thyestes warned. Laius struggled to rise as King Pelops strode through the columns of the gymnasium courtyard. The knot of loincloth-clad exercisers made way for their king, bowing as he passed.

"Who won?" asked the king.

"Laius," Thyestes answered.

"Vassos performed well, my lord king," panted Laius, gesturing at the younger man. "The match was close."

"Well done, Laius," said Pelops. "Come, I want to speak with you."

Laius brushed sand from his arms and legs, clasped Vassos' hand briefly, and then stepped out of the wrestling-pit. Warily he tried to assess the king's mood: since Princess Chloris' rejection last summer, King Pelops had been volatile. At first he spent much of his time in the armory, throwing knives at the wall; after that he had taken to drilling the army incessantly, keeping close company with Atreus – as Thyestes, sulking, complained to no end. The king's judgments had grown harsh; during the winter a woman accused of poisoning her husband was lashed to death, and two sons arguing over the disposition of their father's estate were both dispossessed and banished from Pisa.

"Laius, is my son Thyestes a good judge of wrestling?"

Laius swallowed. Was this a trick question – had Pelops seen his knee touch the sand? But he dared not criticize the prince, especially not after he had accepted the win. "I – I think so, my lord king," he replied uncertainly.

Pelops grunted. "He had better be," he said, turning from Laius to his handsome son. "From now on, Thyestes, you're in charge of the Games."

Laius gaped. The games were *his* responsibility – they had been for years! And they were his only source of true prestige in Pisa.

"Thank you, Father," Thyestes said, grinning broadly. "You can rely on me."

"Congratulations," Laius said, trying to quell his bitterness and wondering how he had offended the king.

A smile played on Pelops' lips. "Come with me, Laius; we'll get you scraped down. The rest of you, stay behind – I wish to speak with Laius in private."

Laius walked beside the king to the bathhouse. Though the springtime sun was warm, he felt that dark clouds hovered over him. "My lord king, if I've done a poor job with any of the Games…"

The king shook his head. "You've done well, Laius. But this position belongs to one of my sons. Atreus has the army; Thyestes should have the Games."

They ducked into the shadows of the bathhouse; Laius shed his loincloth, reflecting dispiritedly that competence might be useful, but kinship was more important. A servant came over with a flask of oil and a strigil; he poured a stream of oil across Laius' shoulders and began scraping down his back and arms.

Pelops took a seat on a stone bench at the side of the room. "Laius, have you had any dreams lately?"

Laius glanced over, puzzled. "Not that I recall, my lord king."

"Are you sure?"

King Pelops was watching him, intently – as if he *wanted* Laius to remember a dream. "Two nights ago I woke up troubled," Laius said cautiously. "But I couldn't remember the dream clearly." He had attributed the uneasy feeling to too many cups of wine and a spring thunderstorm.

"Think, Laius. Could it have been a dream about Thebes?"

As a child, Laius had many nightmares about Thebes. He preferred not to remember that place. But he said: "It's possible, my lord king."

"I thought so," said the king. "I dreamed of Thebes last night – and the gods told me it was the same dream that they sent you."

Laius twisted, bumping the bath attendant with his elbow. "The same dream?"

Pelops nodded. "They told me that you would not remember your dream right away, which is why they sent the vision to me as well. Laius, the gods need you to return to Thebes."

Laius' stomach lurched. *Thebes?* "But—"

"You're a descendant of Cadmus," said the king. "You'll be needed there."

By Theban tradition, the descendants of Cadmus were the royal house. King Amphion was the first exception to that rule for many generations – but then, King Amphion was married to Pelops' sister Niobe. This seemed hazardous ground to tread. "I don't understand, my lord king."

"We cannot always understand the gods' will," said King Pelops. "But my dream was quite clear – I imagine you'll recall the vision yourself better, before long. You must go to Thebes."

The strigil scraped down Laius' spine, making him shudder. "What about King Amphion and Queen Niobe?"

Anger flashed across King Pelops' face. Not only was there the matter of Princess Chloris, but Laius knew that Theban tribute had dwindled. Furthermore, rumor had it that Amphion had decided against Atreus and Thyestes as sons-in-law and was choosing different husbands for his twin daughters.

Pelops' features assumed an expression of hard piety. "We must all obey the gods, Laius. My brother's example shows what happens to those who defy their will."

The year's first merchant-ships from the east had brought news of Prince Broteas' death the previous autumn: having offended Artemis, he threw himself upon a pyre and was burned to death. Pelops was right; he dared not defy the gods.

"But what should I do once I get there?"

The king spread his hands. "I don't know; the gods have not revealed everything to me. But the Tiresias is in Thebes. Perhaps she can guide you once you arrive."

Laius still felt uneasy. "Nerissa—"

"Take her with you," the king interrupted. "And your sons, of course. I'll send some men with you, a full contingent of soldiers commanded by Nikippes. He's a clever young man: I want you to listen closely to him, Laius."

As the servant oiled the backs of his thighs, Laius summoned his courage and nodded agreement. He had no choice: the gods – and the king to whom he had sworn loyalty – had made their wishes clear. He must return to the city he had avoided for thirty years.

TEN: TEARS IN THE TAPESTRY

§ 10.01

The spring rains had stopped; Thebes had a fine day for the ceremony. Yet Niobe woke with a splitting headache, full of misgivings at the arrangements she and Amphion had made.

But a queen could not shirk her responsibilities. The day would have to proceed as planned, never mind the pounding behind her forehead or how her heavy wig made it worse. The megaron had to be prepared to receive all their guests, the children dressed in their finest, and Niobe needed to simply endure the wig and the cosmetics and all the rest.

She tried to divert herself by listening to her daughters' chatter. The twins – who had so long been the eldest girls in the palace – dominated the conversation. They first speculated about their upcoming betrothals to King Neleus of Pylos and to their cousin, Prince Tantalus of Lydia; then when they had exhausted that topic, they turned to fussing over pretty Astycratia, wheedling the maids to arrange her glossy chestnut curls in a style too elaborate for a ten-year-old.

"Girls, let your sister be," Niobe chided. "She doesn't need all that."

In unison Eudoxa and Cleodoxa objected: "But, Mother—"

"Ouch!" Niobe glared up at her hairdresser, who had jabbed her with a pin. "Be careful!"

As the woman muttered an apology, Ogygia stepped closer and asked: "Why are you so cross, Mother?"

Chloris, kneeling beside little Phthia, looked up. "She's losing one of her children."

"I'm not losing Alphenor," Niobe snapped. "He's staying right here in Thebes."

"But he'll soon be married," said Chloris. "And when a man marries, he turns to his wife instead of his parents. Isn't that what's bothering you, Mother?"

Niobe set her jaw and did not answer. Although having Chloris back was wonderful – she was a great help, especially on hectic days like this – sometimes she was a little *too* insightful.

"I wish Aunt Philomela was here today," said Eudoxa.

"So do I," Niobe said. "But you know she's needed in Athens. Her brother is ill."

"I'm sure she'd love to see you all dressed so beautifully," Chloris said, smoothing a fold of Phthia's sky-blue gown and then rising to her feet. She held out her hand to Neaira, who had been waiting quietly at the side of the room. "You look wonderful, all of you."

And they did, Niobe thought with pride. Seven lovely daughters, six of them flush with youth – and for all that Chloris was in her late twenties, her beauty was still celebrated. A year of palace life had restored her sun-browned complexion to a creamy tone, and though – like Niobe – she shunned the heavy flounced skirts of Hellene fashion, even the most traditional Theban matrons agreed that her flowing gowns complimented her figure. The sons of the Spartoi composed odes to her sparkling gray eyes, likening her to Athena; these compliments Chloris accepted with grace, but there was no flirtation in her manner. Niobe's eldest daughter displayed little interest in marriage – and, having rejected Pelops, that was probably for the best.

Efficiently, gently, Chloris helped Niobe shepherd the girls towards the megaron. They walked along the colonnaded hall, passing through bands of sunlight and shadow; servants drew aside to make room. As they rounded the corner, Niobe saw Theora. Niobe no longer needed the midwife's services for herself, but it occurred to her that Theora might assist in the birth of a grandchild before long.

She noticed the lines of worry on the woman's face. "Is something wrong, Theora?"

Theora smiled wryly. "It's nothing, my lady queen. I'm just nervous for my daughter." Her voice dropping to a whisper, she continued: "She doesn't have a chance of being selected. My family's not as wealthy as many among the Spartoi. Menoeceus gives far more to Apollo's temple than we do."

Her head pounding, Niobe pursed her lips; she feared that Theora was right. If it were up to her, she would choose the midwife's daughter Rhodia for her daughter-in-law. Rhodia was calm and sensible, like her mother, and though she was not a great beauty she would make a good wife. But Amphion had insisted on a different method for selecting Alphenor's bride, one that none could dispute. "The king believes this is best for Thebes," was all she could say.

"Yes, my lady queen," Theora said, bowing.

"Come, Mother," Chloris said. "They're waiting for us."

Niobe led her daughters into the megaron. The room overflowed with guests: most of the Theban nobility were there, along with envoys and ambassadors from several other cities. Her husband occupied his throne; their seven sons surrounded him, all resplendent in festival garb, all tanned and handsome.

As Niobe drew near, she heard Damasichthon talking eagerly about the feast. Sipylus was petting one of his dogs; Niobe told him not to let the animal get hair on his best kilt. Then she went to her eldest son and took his hand. His hair had already lost the curl that the palace servants had tried to impose; it was like hers in her youth, heavy and straight.

"Are you ready?" she asked.

Alphenor answered with a serenity that he had certainly inherited from his father and not from her. "Yes, Mother."

Niobe glanced around the crowded room, feeling the pressure behind her forehead swell. "Well? Where is she – the one who will determine your fate?"

Her husband answered. "The Tiresias is resting in a guest chamber. She's not so young anymore; she wanted to lie down before the ceremony."

Irritated, Niobe released her son's hand. Despite her aching head, *she* was not resting in her room. Still, the information presented an opportunity. "If she doesn't have the strength for this, then—"

"She'll come when we need her," Amphion broke in. "Take your throne, my dear. The young ladies will arrive soon."

The four young women were now making their procession through Thebes, allowing all the city's residents to see them. Meanwhile Niobe and her husband accepted greetings and gifts from the members of the Spartoi, and from various foreign envoys. From Sicyon there were matching pairs of leather house-slippers for the bride- and groom-to-be; Orchomenos' rulers provided two amphorae of sweet wine, and from Corinth there were round-bellied pots painted with winged horses and filled with almonds and walnuts. Pelops' envoy Okyllus presented a large jar of pickled octopus paste.

"Pelops knows I don't like octopus," Niobe muttered sourly.

"Neither do I," said Chloris mildly, standing nearby. "But everyone else will enjoy it."

Amphion reached over to squeeze Niobe's hand. "Here they come."

Those in the megaron applauded as the young maidens made their way forward, each carrying a gift of flowers for the queen. First was Theora's daughter, Rhodia. She looked pretty with her chestnut curls and bright-dyed skirts, but her hands shook as she held out her bouquet to Niobe.

The second maiden showed no trepidation whatsoever. The amber-skinned daughter of Naucles' business partner Euxenos by a long-dead Egyptian wife, Melanthe held her head high and walked with a sinuous motion that emphasized her curves. Her manner, even as she offered her armful of blooms to Niobe, suggested that with her striking looks she deserved to be queen even though she was not fully Theban.

Menoeceus' daughter Jocasta was the third maiden. Niobe drummed her fingers against the arm of her throne. If this girl became her daughter-in-law, Niobe would have to overcome her distaste for the father. Besides, Jocasta *was* a lovely girl – absolutely radiant, in fact, when she smiled.

Last came poor Pinelopi, whose heavy cosmetics could not hide the imperfections of her complexion. Though her family was powerful, it was hard to imagine this unattractive girl at Alphenor's side.

Catching herself in this thought, Niobe shook her head. *She* should not be criticizing Pinelopi's looks – she herself had never been beautiful, and yet somehow Amphion had fallen in love with her. Niobe rested a hand on her husband's forearm, remembering those long-ago days.

Four chairs had been arranged before the royal dais; each maiden took a seat. Amphion addressed the assembly, and then the Tiresias entered the room. Though she had earlier claimed fatigue, she did not lean on her manservant for support; she walked forward with sure steps, her cornel-wood staff tapping against the floor.

Amphion said: "Tiresias, you honor us with your presence."

To Niobe's annoyance, the old woman made no reply. When Amphion offered her refreshment, she declined his hospitality without even using his royal title. Amphion smiled tolerantly, but Niobe was indignant at the woman's impudence.

"Begin with her," the seer said abruptly, pointing her staff at Pinelopi. Her manservant led the girl forward. Pinelopi dropped to her knees without grace; the rondels sewn to her skirts clattered against the floor. The room hushed, waiting to hear what the Tiresias might say. But after the blind prophetess put her hand on the girl's face, she withdrew it immediately, announcing: "This creature is of no consequence."

The crowd gasped. Niobe watched in anger as Pinelopi stumbled back to her seat. How dare the Tiresias dismiss a girl's whole life with such heartless words!

Next Rhodia was summoned forward – only to be told that she would never have children.

Niobe could not prevent a hiss of rage from escaping between her teeth. Two girls' lives had just been ruined, utterly ruined! They would never be able to make a good marriage, either of them. How could Amphion have thought it would be a good idea to put the fates of innocent maidens in the hand of this – this viper? She glared at him; but he, like everyone else, was fixated on the Tiresias.

Amber-skinned Melanthe walked forward confidently, vitality in her every move; but Niobe held her breath, fearing more ill-omened words. This time the Tiresias cast doubt on the girl's paternity.

Melanthe did not react like the first two girls: rather than wilting, she looked as furious as Niobe felt. Niobe glanced over at the girl's father, a sunburned man whose solid, thickset bulk was topped by a shock of sand-colored hair; since Naucles was traveling, Euxenos stood alone. As much to himself as to anyone nearby, he said: "It's not true!"

The megaron buzzed with scandalized whispers; Niobe gripped the arms of her throne in helpless rage. Giving the Tiresias charge of this ceremony was like yoking a wild bull to a plow; they were powerless to stop it, and could only let the thing run its course. Three lives now, destroyed.

Some among the crowd were saying openly that Jocasta must be the Tiresias' choice, and Menoeceus himself looked smug and triumphant. What casual indifference to those other three maidens! But however lavish his offerings, he might find his confidence misplaced: what if the hateful old woman cursed his daughter too? She might announce that there would be *no* bride for Alphenor – completely undermining Amphion's rule! Glancing at her husband and her eldest son, Niobe saw that both seemed anxious.

"Silence!" the Tiresias barked. "The last remains. I must read her future." She leveled her staff at Jocasta. Despite being youngest of the four girls, Jocasta rose from her seat with a semblance of dignity and knelt before the prophetess.

Again Niobe found herself holding her breath. But this time the pronouncement was favorable. The Tiresias declared Jocasta "born to wear the crown" – surely delighting Menoeceus, who maintained his late wife and therefore his children were descended from Cadmus. Perhaps, Niobe thought angrily, he had suggested the phrase to the Handmaiden of Apollo.

The room erupted into cheers; Alphenor looked happy and relieved, and Amphion exchanged a grin with Menoeceus. Though the threat to her husband's rule was averted, Niobe's rage continued to swell. If Menoeceus had bought the Tiresias' favor, so be it: but why hadn't the other maidens been rejected more kindly – in ways that did not ruin their lives forever?

Concealing her fury, Niobe said: "It *appears* that we have found the next queen of Thebes." But she did not want the decision to rest entirely with the seer. "Come here, Jocasta."

The girl came forward and complied with Niobe's instruction to kneel. Niobe rose from her throne. Walking a circle around the maiden, she struggled to master her emotions. Jocasta seemed shocked, overwhelmed; she was probably ignorant of her father's machinations. What had been said to the other young women was not her fault. And she *was* a lovely girl.

"What do you think, Husband?" Niobe asked.

"My dear, if *you* have no objections…"

Niobe faced her son, whose wife this would be. "Alphenor?"

He reached his hand down to Jocasta, and helped her to her feet. "She's quite acceptable," he said, smiling.

"Acceptable indeed!" declared Amphion. "Now we must celebrate," he said, reaching for his lyre. In honor of the Tiresias, he sang a ballad about Apollo. The haunting beauty of his music stilled the megaron; when it was done, the servants brought out food and wine.

The throbbing in Niobe's head, which had lessened slightly during the song, returned full force with the cacophony of the milling crowd. Her husband's music did not make up for the damage done to three blameless maidens. Though no one else seemed to notice, Niobe saw how Theora led her weeping daughter away. Pinelopi's family remained: the mother seemed to be trying to coax her daughter to eat. At one side of the room Euxenos was arguing with the girl who might not be his child after all.

Jocasta, on the other hand, was surrounded by well-wishers, receiving congratulations from Niobe's twin daughters. Did the girl have any understanding of what had just taken place?

Descending from her throne, Niobe pushed her way over to Jocasta and grasped the maiden's wrist. Such large, blue eyes! "Come with me," Niobe said, heading for her private chambers.

When the door had closed behind them Niobe took a seat on her couch and gestured for Jocasta to sit as well. She studied the girl, remembering that Jocasta's mother was dead. Her father would no doubt encourage her to believe the Tiresias' words. What had happened was not this young woman's fault – but Niobe did not want her to trust the blind prophetess too far. What should she tell her?

Trying to ignore her headache, Niobe began with a statement designed to probe the girl's perspective. "So *you* are to be queen of Thebes."

Jocasta hesitated. "The prophecy may not be fulfilled for years."

"Prophecy!" The word was bitter in Niobe's mouth. *This* girl had benefitted from the crone's words – but the other three would be branded for the rest of their lives. And the predictions might not even come true! Certainly the Tiresias' prophecy about her, made in Athens so many years ago, had never been fulfilled. But she still recalled her humiliation when the prophetess proclaimed that Niobe – then a young girl herself – might bring a curse upon her husband's children.

Niobe waved a hand to dismiss the girl's gullibility. "Random words uttered by a blind beggar. Listen, child, prophecy is not achievement. If you become queen, you can't rely on prophecy. It may taste sweet as honey now, but it can quickly sour. Think of what she said to those other young women!" Niobe searched the girl's face. "Do you really think it was a true prophecy? Or did your father bribe the Tiresias to say those words?"

Jocasta's eyes widened, as if such an idea had never occurred to her. Niobe shook her head. If this girl was to be her daughter-in-law, such innocence had to be dispelled. Niobe decided to confront the matter directly. She ordered her servants to fetch the Tiresias and then took a cup of wine, hoping it would soothe her pounding head. Soon the old woman arrived, entering without her manservant.

"Tiresias," said Niobe. "I want you to answer a few questions."

"The trance is finished," said the seer, leaning on her staff. "I am not prepared to answer questions about the future."

"But my questions are not about the future; I seek answers about the past. *Without* your rhymes and riddles." Niobe turned her cup slowly in her fingers. "Did Menoeceus offer you gifts so that you would give his daughter the best foretelling?"

It took some pressing, but the Tiresias finally described the precious family heirloom Menoeceus had given her, and young Jocasta gaped like a fish pulled from the water. Upon further inquiry, the old prophetess detailed the gifts she had received from the fathers of the other maidens – nothing as valuable as Menoeceus' donation.

"You see, Jocasta," Niobe said. "A prophecy can be bought – as can many things."

"Apollo's favor is not for sale," interjected the Tiresias.

"Perhaps not Apollo's favor, but certainly the favor of his servant," Niobe said impatiently. "And what should we care for Apollo? What has Apollo done for Thebes?"

"Apollo is the city's protector," said the Tiresias.

"Amphion is the true protector of Thebes!" snapped Niobe, tired of credit for her husband's deeds being meted out to others. "Amphion cobbled the streets and widened the agora. He built the walls and their seven strong gates. It's my husband we should be grateful for – not some remote god who never shows his face!"

The old woman frowned. "You tread dangerous ground."

"Who should I fear?" asked Niobe. Words poured out of her; words she had repressed, it seemed, for a lifetime. "Why should we honor those who do nothing for us? Amphion has made Thebes what it is, I tell you – *he* is the greatest king this city has ever known! And despite what you once said of me, *I* am its greatest queen – the mother of Thebes. Fourteen children, all living. Your precious Leto has only two. Who should Thebes honor more?"

The Tiresias pointed at Niobe with her wooden staff. "You have insulted me, my god, and now his holy mother. You will know nothing but sorrow for the rest of your life!"

"I thought your trance was finished!" Niobe retorted, but a chill ran down her back.

"I speak as the god directs," said the Tiresias. Stepping forward, she said:

Niobe, great queen, your hubris offends.
Apollo has seen: his vengeance he sends.
His mother you mock, his might you defame:
He will hunt down your flock and ruin your name.

"Enough!" Niobe cried, throwing her cup at the Tiresias – she missed, but some of the wine splashed across the seer's robes. "Get her out of here!" Niobe ordered. A pair of servants escorted the blindfolded woman from the room.

Niobe tried to calm herself, but the Tiresias' malevolence left her shaking. Why did her husband put so much faith in this monster of a prophetess – and in the gods' benevolence? The gods were not kind! Her brother Broteas had been forced to throw himself into a fire to atone for some offense against Artemis, so Naucles had told her: *Broteas,* who had honored Artemis all his life! The gods were capricious, cruel; it was best to keep one's distance.

She forced herself to confront those who had heard the Tiresias' screed: the servants and her son's betrothed. "You will not speak of what you have heard," she ordered. Though all of them nodded, Niobe was sure that rumors would get out eventually. Rubbing her forehead, she wished she had not let her temper get the best of her. But done was done.

Then she looked at Jocasta. "So you want to be queen? As queen you must deal with insults, ingratitude, and enemies who would push you off your throne to take your place." Even her sister-in-law Thebe had plotted against her! "Are you my enemy, Jocasta?"

The girl answered in a soft voice. "No, Queen Niobe. I'm not your enemy."

Niobe took a deep breath and gazed at her future daughter-in-law. "Perhaps not," Niobe said. "Jocasta, you have my permission to wed my son Alphenor – if that's what you still want. Consider it carefully." She desperately wanted to be alone. "You may go."

"Thank you, my lady queen," said Jocasta. She rose, genuflected prettily, then left the room.

Niobe sagged back against the cushions. She had the servants bring a damp cloth for her brow; they complied warily, as if she might strike them – or as if the Tiresias' words might taint them. She remained on her couch until her eldest daughter came to fetch her.

"Mother, people are wondering where you are," said Chloris.

"Is the Tiresias in the megaron?" Niobe was ashamed of her outburst – and troubled, despite everything, by what the Tiresias had said.

"No. She left the palace."

Good, thought Niobe, setting the cloth aside and struggling to her feet. Her daughter beside her, she returned to the megaron. Damasichthon and Ilioneus had started a drinking game in one corner with their friend Pelorus and several other young men; Tantalus was strumming a song on his lyre, and elegant Phaedimus seemed to be flirting with Melanthe. Niobe went to her husband, who was speaking with their eldest son.

"Where's the bride-to-be?" she asked.

"Jocasta and her family have gone home," Amphion said. "I think the girl was overwhelmed by the day's events."

"You didn't frighten her, did you, Mother?" asked Alphenor.

Niobe affected indignation. "Do you think *I* could frighten anyone?"

"You terrify us all," her eldest son said with a playful wink. "Excuse me, Mother – if I don't take some food, my brothers will have devoured everything."

"We've set the wedding for five days from now," Amphion told her. "Is that all right?"

"Of course," Niobe said. "If that suits Alphenor and Jocasta."

"You look tired, my dear," Amphion said, taking her hand and squeezing it. "Sit down, and I'll have the servants bring you a tray."

Niobe nodded and let Amphion help her to her throne; then he went to speak with the priest and priestess who would perform the wedding ceremony. Leaning back against the cushions, she glanced around the megaron. The drinking-game was in full swing; Cleodoxa and Astycratia were singing along with their brother Tantalus, while a group of guests clapped in time to the music. Thebes was a happy and prosperous city, and would remain so; the Tiresias was just a spiteful old harpy. And she herself had said the trance was over: her vicious words would have no effect. This was *Niobe's* megaron; this was *her* palace, *her* beloved children. One of Sipylus' dogs yipped at little Ismenus; he was holding out a morsel of food, encouraging the dog to do some trick. She saw Ilioneus pinch the bottom of a passing servant-girl, who jumped and then smiled. Neaira was eating with her youngest sister Phthia, who had also set a plate and cup before her cloth doll. Even Ogygia was smiling, helping herself to some food.

And then it struck her. Niobe had seen all this before, in her dreams. Not once but twice – and both times, something terrible had been about to happen.

"No!" she cried out, and all eyes turned towards her.

Amphion strode over to her. "What is it, my dear?"

But she didn't know. She couldn't even speak – she sat frozen in place, unable to move, unable to breathe.

And then Damasichthon cried out in pain. "Gods!" he gasped, doubling over. Ilioneus steadied his brother as he sank to his knees.

"Damasichthon!" shrieked Niobe. She climbed down from her throne and rushed to her son. "What's wrong?"

His breath came quick and shallow, whistling between clenched teeth. "It hurts – hurts."

Niobe knelt beside her son. "Is there a healer here?" she cried, looking around the room in desperation. "We need a healer!"

But her youngest, Phthia, reached her first. "Mama – I don't feel good."

"Darling, I'm busy," Niobe said. "Your brother's sick."

"I'm sick too," wailed Phthia, coughing, and something in her voice made Niobe turn.

Phthia was coughing up blood.

§ 10.02

"Do something!" Amphion ordered the healer.

His smallest daughter and his largest son lay on the floor at the side of the megaron. Damasichthon was obviously in pain, but little Phthia's condition was even more terrifying. Moaning, she clutched a cloth doll to her chest; blood dribbled from her mouth.

The healer's voice trembled. "My lord king, I don't know what's wrong with her!"

The five-year-old vomited up more blood.

"My baby!" wailed Niobe. She wiped the child's face with the hem of her gown. "Phthia, darling, Mama's here!"

Only moments ago the megaron had been a festive place, crowded with people laughing, talking, enjoying the feast. Now the guests wore frightened expressions and spoke in horrified, hushed voices.

Damasichthon was shivering; Amphion heard his teeth chatter. He whipped off his cloak and handed it to Ilioneus, who draped the garment over Damasichthon like a blanket and then set a hand on his brother's sweat-beaded forehead.

"Do something," Amphion repeated, his voice harsh and hoarse with anguish.

"Bring me some water," the healer told a servant. As she hurried to comply, the man squatted down beside Damasichthon. "My lord prince, have you drunk much today?"

"No," Damasichthon whispered. "Just three cups."

"And the wine was well-watered," said Ilioneus.

"Then it must the same malady afflicting the princess." Worry etched deep lines into the healer's aged face. The maidservant returned with a cup of water; loosing a belt-pouch from his waist, Apollo's servant reached inside and withdrew several small cloth packets tied with colored thread. He untied one and shook some of its contents into the cup. He stirred the water with his finger, then held the cup to Damasichthon's mouth. "Drink this, my lord prince."

Ilioneus helped his brother to drink; Amphion looked on, not believing what he saw. Damasichthon was so strong – how could he fall ill so suddenly?

The healer turned to Phthia. "Here, little princess," he said. "Not too much, just a swallow." Niobe supported the child, who managed to swallow some of the medicine. Amphion watched intently for any sign of improvement.

"Mama… Papa… it hurts…"

It was Neaira who had spoken this time: Neaira, the quiet one, who never complained. Terror clutched Amphion's heart with a grip cold as ice. Trying to hide his fear, he dropped to one knee and pulled her close. "What's wrong, darling?"

She sagged against his arm; her young face distorted with pain, and then she retched. Her vomit splashed across the tiles. When the heaving stopped she sobbed: "Papa, I'm so sorry…"

"No!" Niobe screamed, her cry echoing round the room. "No, not my baby!"

Little Phthia lay limp in his wife's arms, her face paler than ivory beneath the streaks of drying blood: Amphion realized she was dead.

"It's a curse!" shrieked a middle-aged serving woman. "Queen Niobe insulted the gods, and the Tiresias cursed her!"

In the shocked hush that followed this accusation, Amphion sought his wife's gaze, desperate to know the truth; but Niobe was lost in grief, keening over their youngest daughter.

Prince Alphenor broke the silence. "How dare you!" he said, striding toward the servant who had made the charge. His face was dark with fury, his fist clenched. "My mother has done more for Thebes than any woman!" But before he reached his mother's accuser, he came to a sudden halt, clutching his belly. "By the gods!" he gasped.

"See!" cried the woman, pointing at Alphenor. "A curse! The queen insulted Leto, the mother of Apollo and Artemis! This is their curse!"

Panicked babble filled the room. "Plague!" cried some, and "Blasphemy!" "The queen's a foreigner – she brought this curse upon Thebes!" People edged away from the royal family.

"Run," shouted Okyllus, the Pisatan envoy, "or we'll be struck down too!" Those near the exit scrambled towards the door.

"Guards, stop them!" bellowed Amphion. "This is no curse! I've served Apollo all my life. There's a murderer in the palace! This is poison!"

"We've all eaten from the same banquet!" cried one of the Spartoi. "Why are only *your* children struck down?"

Could it be a curse? Amphion wondered, appalled. He looked over at his wife, remembering that her brother Broteas – despite his long devotion to Artemis – had been condemned by the goddess and sacrificed on her altar in Lydia. *Had* Niobe brought a curse upon them?

But the guards fled their posts; the room emptied quickly. Soon most of the servants were gone – but Amphion did not care. Sipylus had collapsed; a dog licked his face, but he only moaned. The twins huddled together in a corner, their arms wrapped around each other. Ilioneus, who had taken the cushion from Amphion's throne to put beneath Damasichthon's head, was now pale and sweating himself. Tantalus' lyre lay abandoned near the hearth; he was helping his sister Astycratia to sit down, and the girl had a hand pressed to her mouth. Alphenor lay on a bench, tended by his sister Chloris; little Ismenus and his sister Ogygia were there too, assisting their eldest brother. And over the horrendous scene washed Niobe's echoing cries of lament.

"How can I help, my lord king?"

Amphion glanced up to see Pelorus at his side. "Are you well?" he asked tersely.

Pelorus cast a worried glance at the princes who had been his friends since their boyhood. "I believe so, my lord king."

"Then run to the Temple of Apollo," Amphion said, wrenching a ring from his finger. "Give this to the god in my name as an offering. Plead with him to spare me and mine – those that still live—" His voice cracked as he looked at Phthia's tiny form, lying before the hearth. Amphion realized tears were running down his face and into his beard; he held Neaira closer, feeling the precious rhythm of her heartbeat, worried by the sound of her labored breath. "Remind Apollo of all I have done for him – and then bring the healers back with you. Hurry!"

The night was more terrible than any song of woe Amphion had ever learned. One by one his children faltered and weakened; in fear the remaining servants refused to touch them. A few, those who had served Amphion for years, brought blankets, water and wine. The priests of Apollo did not come; with the help of the single healer who had been there from the start, Amphion, Niobe and those children who still had some strength did what little they could to make the fallen more comfortable. Soon every cushion in the megaron was placed under his children's shuddering bodies; Niobe removed her wig to make a pillow for one of the twins.

Neaira was the second to die, about halfway through the night. She went so quietly that only Amphion realized her soft breathing had stopped. After that it was Damasichthon.

Pelorus returned just after dawn, alone; in a sorrowful voice he explained that the temple healers refused to tend the princes and princesses, maintaining that they were cursed by the gods. When runners arrived seeking aid for Pinelopi and her family, and then for Euxenos, who had also been stricken, healers were sent to them; but the priests refused to go to the palace. Pelorus had pleaded with them, offering every argument he could think of – and then, failing to convince them, he spent the night before the image of the god, begging for the lives of the royal family.

But the young man's prayers went unanswered. By noon Ilioneus, Phaedimus, and Ogygia were gone. Little Ismenus slipped away not long after. When Sipylus died, his dogs howled loudly; Pelorus dragged the animals away from his body and out of the megaron.

As the mournful baying receded into the distance, Amphion heard his son Tantalus whisper: "I'm afraid, Father."

Amphion nodded, tears welling up again even after he thought his eyes could make no more. "I know, Son. So am I."

"Would you play a song for me?"

Amphion retrieved his lyre and sat beside the boy. Amphion's throat was too choked with grief for him to sing, and his fingers trembled, but somehow he found the strength to pluck the strings: Tantalus had music to soothe him as he sighed his last. When the youth's spirit had flown, Amphion set the lyre aside and buried his face in his hands.

"My fault," sobbed Niobe, stumbling over to him. "My fault, my fault... I said terrible things to the Tiresias."

Amphion looked up, anger and sorrow warring in his heart. "Then it's true, what the servant said."

Niobe nodded, clutching at her thin white hair with both hands. "My fault – oh, my children, forgive me!"

"Ask the gods for forgiveness," he told her. "Perhaps they will listen."

Niobe fell to her knees beside the hearth, her hands reaching up into the afternoon sunlight as she implored Apollo and Artemis to let the rest of her children live. But the gods were stony-hearted: even as she prayed, Cleodoxa and Eudoxa died. Chloris put her hands over the girls' eyelids, closing them; then Niobe broke off her prayers and sobbed, beating the tiles with her fists. "Apollo, Artemis – spare them!" she screamed. "Take me instead!"

There was nothing Amphion could say to her. He shuffled over to Chloris, and looked down at the faces of his twin daughters. "At least now they will never be separated," he said. "And Ogygia has rejoined Idmon."

Chloris' eyes were red with weeping. "Father, why am I untouched by this?"

Amphion crouched to kiss Eudoxa's soft cheek; it was still warm. He kissed Cleodoxa as well, then helped Chloris to her feet. "I don't know," he said, wrapping his eldest daughter in his arms and making a silent prayer of thanks that she had so far been spared. He rested his face against her hair. "You served Artemis loyally for many years. That could be the reason."

"Excuse me, my lord king." Pelorus, unshaven, stood at the entrance to the death-filled room. "There's something you must know. The people are gathering in the agora. They're saying that Thebes is cursed – that this is the city's punishment for crowning a king not descended from Cadmus."

Amphion, his ears ringing with sorrow, found it difficult to understand the young man's words.

"No," wailed Niobe – but not in answer to the news from the agora. She had crawled over to where Astycratia lay. "No, my beauty, stay with me! Don't leave me, darling, don't leave me!"

But another child had died. Young Astycratia, who had promised to be as radiantly lovely as her grandmother Antiope, was gone.

Amphion squeezed Chloris tighter, then released her and walked over to face Pelorus. "Go on."

The young man swallowed. "They say it was hubris to think of wedding your son to the line of Cadmus. They're threatening to storm the palace – they say those responsible for this curse upon Thebes must be destroyed."

"What!" exclaimed Chloris, blanching. "Have they forgotten their oaths of loyalty?"

Amphion exhaled slowly. "And have you forgotten Theban history, Chloris? The people of Thebes have turned on their kings before."

"Father," groaned Alphenor, "Father I—"

Amphion went to where the young man lay. His firstborn – and his last living son. "I'm here, Alphenor."

"I'm sorry," Alphenor said, his eyes unfocused – or perhaps focused on something Amphion could not see. "I don't want to die…"

Amphion clasped his son's hand tight. "No, Son! Stay with me – stay with me!"

But the dark brows drew together; Alphenor's eyes narrowed into a squint. "So bright, Father. I never thought it would be so bright—"

Then the hand in Amphion's relaxed, and he knew that his son was gone.

Dry-eyed, Amphion stood. The ringing in his ears had stopped; he could hear the mob gathering outside. He glanced around the room. A few loyal servants remained, and one contingent of guards. And Pelorus, who had been almost like another son.

"Pelorus, have you strength for one more errand?"

"Anything, my lord king," he said, his voice thick.

"Have the royal bearers take a pair of curtained litters down to the house of Menoeceus. Go with them, and take some of the guards with you. Bring back Menoeceus and his daughter. The mob should let them pass."

"Yes, my lord king." He bowed and departed.

Amphion ordered his last few soldiers to barricade the palace doors until Pelorus returned. "Tell the people in the agora that I'll be out to address them later." He hoped this promise would keep them from forcing their way inside.

Once they had gone the room was quiet as the tomb it had become. The healer, obviously exhausted, shuffled forward. "My lord king, there's nothing more that I can do."

"More? You've done nothing!" Amphion snapped.

"No physic can counter the will of the gods."

Amphion looked around at the bodies of his children. Niobe crawled, weeping, from one to the next; Chloris was trying to calm her, but without success. "Then give my wife something to ease her despair," Amphion said. "She can't bear this."

"Yes, my lord king." The man reached for his herb pouch.

Amphion pressed his hands to his mouth. For so long Niobe had been his mainstay, his rock – his heart. But now she could not lend him her strength; she had nothing left to give.

"Chloris," he said. His daughter came to him, wiping her eyes and nose. "We have no time to grieve."

Chloris nodded solemnly, and took a shuddering breath.

Amphion pulled the remaining rings from his fingers and slipped loose his golden arm-ring. Looking for a container, he saw a basket of bread on a table; he dumped out the stale rolls, then dropped the gold into the basket. "You'll need this. And we must gather all the other jewels." He knelt beside the nearest of the bodies: Ogygia. He stripped the bracelets from her cold arms and removed her rings. "You're the last of our line, Chloris. You must marry and have children, if you can."

"Yes, Father."

"Your sisters Cleodoxa and Eudoxa—" his voice broke; he paused, dropping the last of Ogygia's rings into the basket, and then struggled on: "your sisters were betrothed to Prince Tantalus of Lydia and King Neleus of Pylos. I'm sure that either man would accept you as a wife."

Chloris considered a moment. "I've never met Tantalus of Lydia," she said. "But I know King Neleus – he's a good man. And he already has a son; he'll be less disappointed if I'm barren."

Amphion moved over to Phaedimus' body. "Your mother always liked Neleus." Phaedimus' signet ring and golden neck-chain went into the basket. "It might be better to avoid your mother's family."

Chloris took the jewels from Astycratia's earlobes. "What will *you* do, Father?"

"Distract the crowd, so that you and your mother can escape."

"How? To go out to that mob means death!"

Amphion nodded. Then he went over to the bodies of the twins and pulled the silver combs from their hair.

"Father, you can't!"

"They want a blood sacrifice," he answered. "That's what they'll have."

Sparing him further argument, Pelorus arrived, leading two curtained litters into the megaron. The bearers lowered their burdens; Menoeceus and Jocasta emerged. Amphion then explained his intentions. At first Menoeceus objected – but young Jocasta stepped forward, passionately advocating in favor of Amphion's request. His daughter's words softened Menoeceus' heart, and soon he relented. Menoeceus was an upright man; having given his word, he would treat Amphion's loved ones with respect.

Amphion guided Niobe into the litter that she would share with Jocasta. "Good-bye, my beloved wife," he said, squatting beside the litter and kissing her, then taking her hand. But she was so stricken with grief, so sedated by the potion that the healer had given her, that he was not sure she understood him.

Her dark eyes met his. "Amphion," she whispered, "it's my fault."

He was not sure of that: there might be other, far guiltier parties. But there was no time for discussion. "I love you, Niobe. I have always loved you. Remember that."

Amphion then turned to Chloris, who sat beside Menoeceus in the second litter. Menoeceus looked pointedly away.

Handing Chloris the basket of jewelry, Amphion said: "This will serve as your dowry. Remember you are still niece to King Pelops and the granddaughter of King Tantalus. You have powerful connections."

"Yes, Father."

"Be well, child. Take care of your mother. And if you see Naucles, remind him of his oath."

"Captain Naucles' oath?"

"He'll know what I mean." He touched her face. "Remember always that your father loved you." His voice cracking, he continued: "Think sometimes of your brothers and sisters. Live well."

Her reply was soft and sad. "Father, I will."

He drew the litter-curtains shut. "Pelorus, take them out the side door and guide them to safety. I'll go out the main entrance and distract the crowd."

"No," said Pelorus.

Amphion stared. "What do you mean, no?"

"The guards will protect them, my lord king," the young man said. "Let me stay with you."

"There's no need for you to risk your life," Amphion objected.

"My lord king, I don't intend to die. But I do intend to make sure that your wife and child reach safety."

Amphion nodded. Pelorus was a sly one, always thinking on many levels. What a useful official he would have been to Alphenor, if had his son lived! If, if, if – there was no time for ifs, no time for wondering what might have been. With a last order to the captain of the guard Amphion headed out towards the main palace doors, Pelorus close behind. He listened keenly, ignoring the noise of the mob outside calling down curses on him; he waited instead for the faint creak of the side door.

It came. He said to the soldiers: "Now."

The guards pushed the doors open, and Amphion stepped outside. It took a moment for the crowd to realize that their chosen victim had appeared; in that small space of time Amphion gazed out over the agora, washed in the warm glow of the setting sun. He remembered festivals and sacrifices, judgments and celebrations – the agora was the heart of the city, this city he had given so much. Here he had won Thebes; here his reign would end.

A man's voice boomed above the mob: "There he is!"

"My daughter is dead!" screamed a woman. "You've brought a curse upon Thebes!"

"Thebans!" called out Pelorus. The mob hesitated, many faces turning to look.

Amphion glanced back and saw the young man had drawn his dagger; the blade was aimed at him. Yes, a clever one, Pelorus – his ploy might give the crowd pause, gain a little time for Niobe and Chloris. It might even let Pelorus survive the night.

"Your king is here," Pelorus shouted. "He is ready—"

"Not my king!" interrupted someone at the base of the steps. "He's not of Cadmus' line!" yelled another.

Amphion lifted his hands. "Hear me, Thebans!" But they shouted him down; then a stone sailed in his direction, landing only a handspan short. He did his best not to flinch. "I have served you for nearly thirty years!"

"Thirty years too many!" was the answering shout, and the crowd bellowed its agreement.

"Get him!" yelled another.

The mob, emboldened, surged up the steps. Pelorus disappeared from view; Amphion hoped the young man would escape, but he could spare no more thought for that. He must stay alive a little while longer, that was all. He must give his wife and daughter all the time that his life would buy. When the first stone struck him, the pain came almost as a surprise – after all the grief he had endured, it was strange to think he could still feel physical pain. More stones followed, hitting his ribs, his legs. Fists landed blows; hands scrabbled at him, scratching, tearing. Something smashed against his head; he staggered and fell. Sandaled feet kicked his back, his jaw. He tasted blood.

The world began to grow dim; the sound of screaming and curses started to fade. The kicks and blows still rained upon him but each new agony grew more muffled, more distant.

Niobe, he thought. *Niobe, my beloved – may the gods keep you and Chloris safe!*

The agora whirled around him: spinning, tilting, spiraling away to a great distance. Although night was falling, he was pulled toward a brilliant light. In the midst of the light stood a glowing form – was that Hermes, with a lyre? Then Amphion was surrounded by music, glorious music.

§ 10.03

Unlike most of the leading Thebans, Menoeceus lived far from the palace – his house was beyond the tanners' quarter, just inside the city walls near the Eudoxa Gate. Chloris counted this a blessing: if they managed to pass through the crowds undetected and reach Menoeceus' home, she and her mother could escape the city in the pre-dawn hours.

She heard the side door of the palace creak open; well-trained, the bearers kept to a steady pace, and the soldiers seemed to be preventing anyone from jostling the litter. Then, at a distance, she heard the unruly crowd erupt with new and violent intensity – Chloris closed her eyes, trying not to think about what was happening to her father. The basket of jewelry, taken from the lifeless bodies of her brothers and sisters, was heavy in her lap.

Gradually the noise of the mob faded, and then she heard only the footfalls of the litter-bearers and the guards. Menoeceus, close beside her in the dim enclosure, murmured a prayer to Apollo.

Then, from beyond the curtains a shout broke the quiet: "Who goes there?"

The litter jolted to a halt. She heard the sound of running feet, people approaching their party: if only she could look outside and see what was happening! There were confused yells, and someone said: "Destroy them! Kill the blasphemers!"

The captain of the guard shouted, "Back away, you! This is lord Menoeceus and his daughter Jocasta! Let us pass!"

A hubbub followed, and then a woman said, "They went up to the palace to see the curse for themselves, remember?"

"Lord Menoeceus is a pious one," someone added. "No sacrilege from him!"

Chloris glanced at the man beside her, his eyes closed in prayer.

"And the Tiresias blessed his daughter Jocasta—"

"That's right," growled the soldier. "So get out of their way!" He shouted an order to his men, and the litter resumed its swaying forward motion, heading downhill. Chloris released her long-pent breath, thankful that the gods had spared her and her mother once again.

But, if what had killed her brothers and sister *was* a curse, why had she – and her mother, the purported target of the gods' wrath – been spared? And Pelorus said that a few others – Pinelopi, Euxenos – had also been struck down. What motive did Apollo and Artemis have to harm them?

When they reached Menoeceus' home, Chloris learned that his son Creon had also fallen ill. Did that mean the gods were angry with the line of Cadmus, too? After the Tiresias' proclamation about Jocasta, that appeared unlikely. Of course, Creon still lived – and a healer reported that his condition seemed to be improving. But if the gods were not angry with Cadmus' descendants it made no sense for Creon to have been affected at all.

Chloris had no answers. But answers were not important just then: her mother needed her. Menoeceus' servants prepared a guest room for them, and the healer tending to Creon offered Niobe a sleeping draught. Chloris held her close, listening to her mother mumble the names of her brothers and sisters, one after the other, until the medication finally took effect. Only then did Chloris allow herself to slumber. Her sleep was mercifully dreamless, but brief; she woke before dawn and went to find some of her father's men in Menoeceus' sitting room.

They confirmed that the people of Thebes had killed her father. Creon was recovering; seeing the relief of his father and his sister, Chloris tried to be thankful that they had been spared the terrible loss she and her mother suffered. It was hard not to resent their good fortune – but Menoeceus and his daughter had risked their own lives to help. They gave Chloris and her mother fresh clothing to replace the garments stained with blood and vomit, and provided food and drink for their onward journey.

"You have been generous, Menoeceus," she said. "You've risked yourself to take us in. If I can ever repay you, I will."

The red-haired man nodded. "I'll take you as far as the Temple of Apollo."

Chloris roused her mother, and helped her into the litter. At the Temple of Apollo they left the litters behind, since they would only attract attention; the king's soldiers tried to insist on accompanying them, but Chloris refused. She did not know these men well, did not know if they could be trusted not to let the truth of their identities slip. Perhaps in time they would come to believe in the curse, and covet the gold she carried. "No one will recognize the queen," she said. "She never appeared in public without her wig. And I can defend myself if necessary." She rested her hand on the dagger belted at her waist.

They said farewell to Menoeceus just as the sun was rising, and continued their slow progress towards the coast. Her father had told Chloris to find Naucles; if he was not at the harbor, one of his ships might be. And if not – well, she had gold enough to buy passage to Pylos. She would have to invent some tale to maintain their anonymity.

The sun climbed higher in a clear blue sky; Chloris adjusted her straw hat, and then noticed that her mother's had fallen back between her shoulder blades, dangling from its string. She settled the hat back on her mother's head as if tending a child – and then the memory of little Phthia holding her doll came back with an intensity that tightened her throat. An innocent child – Artemis was the protector of little children! Surely the goddess had not taken vengeance on a five-year-old girl!

"My feet hurt," said Niobe.

Chloris guided her mother over to a rock; she dropped the traveling-bag she carried and helped her mother to sit. "It's not so far, Mother. Remember, you walked all the way from Pisa to Sicyon, and then from the coast to Thebes."

Niobe shook her head. "That was a long time ago."

Chloris used some water to clean her mother's blistered feet and then bandaged them with strips of cloth torn from the hem of Niobe's gown – it was too long to walk in easily anyway. But Chloris knew her mother's feet would get worse before they improved. Perhaps, she thought, the pain would distract her from her sorrow.

Their progress, already slow, dropped to a snail's pace. Glancing at the sky, Chloris doubted they would reach the harbor before nightfall. As they trudged along the road – a road which her father had helped widen and make smooth, and yet his ungrateful subjects had killed him! – Chloris recalled what she knew of the terrain, and considered the best locations to camp for the night.

Then she heard a cart approaching from behind. Pulling her mother to the side of the road, she looked to see who was coming. She considered pleading with the traveler for assistance – but might her mother say something to give them away?

The cart was pulled by two horses: the animals signaled wealth. One of the Spartoi, perhaps? Chloris peered back, squinting against the sun – and then she recognized the driver. Waving her hand in a wide arc, she shouted: "Naucles! Captain Naucles!"

The weathered sea-captain pulled his horses to a stop. "Praise Poseidon, I found you!" He leapt down, tossing her the reins, and went to help her mother into the cart.

Soon they were on their way again, with her mother resting against a rolled-up blanket in the back of the cart and Chloris seated beside Naucles on the driver's bench. "How did you find us?"

"I meant to be in Thebes days ago," he said. "In time for the ceremony to select Prince Alphenor's bride. But it was just one of those trips: the winds were wrong, and then my cart broke a wheel on the way into town. I didn't get home until late last night. My wife told me what had happened to the king – but no one knew what had happened to your mother. Finally I found one of the royal litter-bearers; he knew me, knew he could trust me with the truth."

"Thank you," Chloris whispered, her eyes filling with tears. "Thank you for coming after us."

"I had to," Naucles said. He squinted off into the distance, his lips pressed together. Then he continued: "I was in love with your mother, once. A long, long time ago. She didn't love me – your father was the only man for her, from the moment she met him – but she was always kind."

He glanced back over his shoulder; Chloris saw that her mother had pulled the broad brim of her hat over her eyes. Perhaps she slept.

"Saved my life once, your mother did," Naucles said. "I was bitten by a snake, and she got me to the healers."

"You saved her life, too," said Chloris. "You rescued her from drowning. And you helped her escape from Uncle Pelops when he refused to let her marry Father. Mother told me the stories."

Naucles scratched his gray-streaked beard. "After your parents married and your father became king of Thebes, he had me swear that I'd take care of her if ever he couldn't." He smiled wryly. "I'm sure most people thought he was just being generous, showing me a mark of favor. But he knew I'd die to keep that oath."

Chloris nodded. "Father remembered."

"Of course." Naucles wiped his eyes with the back of one hand. "He was a good man, my lady princess."

"The best," Chloris said. She took a sip from her waterskin, considering this fact; it kindled anger in her heart – anger against the gods' injustice, against the Fates. "So why did this happen? Why did the gods do this to him?"

The captain's graying eyebrows lifted. "Well, Princess – I heard about what your mother said. She has a sharp tongue, sometimes. And she never liked the Tiresias."

His explanation did not make sense to her. "If Apollo and Artemis are so angry with my mother, then why did they let her live?"

Naucles drove on a while in silence. Finally he said: "Living without her children, without her husband – that'll hurt her worse than dying."

"Yes." Chloris looked at the woods they were passing; she struggled to reconcile what had happened with all she knew of Artemis and her twin. Artemis could be harsh, that she knew well: the death of Batia had seared the lesson into her mind. But she had done the goddess' bidding nonetheless – she had *always* served Artemis faithfully, even if, at the end of her service, she had begun to question the goddess' harsh judgments. "So I'm meant to suffer, too?"

"You were a Maiden of Artemis. Maybe she wanted to spare you."

A bitter laugh escaped her. "The gods let Mother live to hurt her, and they let me live to spare me? The same thing is both a blessing and a curse?"

"You sound like your mother," said Naucles. "She always asked inconvenient questions."

"Sometimes they need to be asked," Chloris said. She looked back at her mother. Yes, she was definitely asleep, praise the gods – whatever gods deserved to be praised.

Naucles pulled the reins to steer his horses away from a rut in the road. "Something else you should know. As I left the city this morning, I passed a group of soldiers headed towards Thebes."

"Soldiers! What soldiers?"

"Not an invasion force, nothing like that. I'd have gone back for my wife and daughter!" He brushed a fly away from his arm, then continued: "No, it just looked like the escort of someone important. They were Pisatans – wearing your uncle's colors."

§ 10.04

"You're king here now," said Okyllus.

Laius looked uneasily around the Theban megaron. The brightly colored frescoes, with their scenes of fantastic creatures and beautiful maidens, were vaguely familiar; but the room seemed smaller – and never had he imagined it strewn with the bodies of dead children. His soldiers were now removing the corpses – to where, he did not know. King Amphion's body – what was left of it – had been out in the agora. His soldiers were cleaning that up as well.

When his traveling party had drawn near the city, Laius sent Nikippes and two other runners ahead to announce his arrival – and he was greeted by crowds of cheering citizens. "Welcome back!" they shouted, and, "The curse is over!" But the cry he heard most often was: "Long live King Laius!"

That's who he was now. King Laius.

Drawing a deep breath, he pulled back his shoulders and looked at Okyllus. "Pelops' dream was right," he said with a shiver of awe. *This* was how it felt to be a man touched by the gods. A man for whom the Fates had a plan.

Amphion might have been a good man – but he should never have claimed the throne of Thebes. That was reserved for the line of Cadmus.

Nerissa, their son Gogos in her arms, crossed the megaron to join him. "How do you feel?"

Of everyone in the room, only Nerissa knew about the nightmares that had haunted him since childhood: nightmares that relived the night his father Labdacus was torn limb from limb in the Theban agora – the same way that King Amphion had died last night. But his father had offended Dionysus – and Amphion's family had offended Apollo, Artemis, and their beloved mother Leto.

On the other hand, the gods had given King Pelops the vision that sent Laius to Thebes; they wanted him here, now, at this crucial moment in the city's history. It was their divine will that he become king of Thebes. He would simply have to be careful not to offend any of the deathless ones.

"I'm fine," he assured Nerissa.

"Fine?" said lanky Nikippes, laughing. "Fine? My lord king, this should be the happiest day of your life!"

"You've reclaimed what is rightfully yours," added Nikippes' father Okyllus, who had left for Thebes as King Pelops' envoy several days before the dream-portent. "You should never have been asked to relinquish your claim – you were a child, not a man. Your decision was not binding."

A child. Laius watched a pair of soldiers carry away the last corpse, the body of one of the twin girls. Yes, he had been a child, about the age of Amphion's youngest son. He looked at his own young son Gogos – and then heard the voice of his elder son, Polydorus. "Father, you should try out the throne!"

Polydorus looked so elated, so excited – Laius could not help but grin. "All right," he said. After all, he would have to do it sooner or later. He walked across the tiles, trying to ignore the dark stains and the vomit. He stepped up onto the small dais, turned and sat on the marble chair. Its polished surface was cool against the skin of his thighs. No thunder shook the earth; there was no flash of lightning, no ill omen of any sort. The sunlight streamed in unalloyed.

Nerissa smiled up at him. "It suits you, Laius."

To his surprise, he found that it did suit him. Sitting on this massive throne, raised above the onlookers below – well, it made him *feel* like a king. Even the circlet on his head – one that had belonged to Amphion, retrieved by one of

Nikippes' soldiers – was starting to seem natural.

Okyllus came closer. "The common people of Thebes are ready to accept you," he said. "We've seen proof of that. Now you need to solidify your power with the ruling class – what they call the Spartoi. And I know exactly how to do that, my lord king."

"How?" asked Laius.

"You must marry Jocasta, the daughter of Menoeceus."

Laius opened his mouth to protest; before he could say anything, Polydorus exclaimed: "Father can't marry anyone! What about Mother?"

"Your father and your mother never wed," Okyllus told him. "The king is free to marry. And he must marry Jocasta."

Nerissa had turned away, but Laius could tell from the tense line of her neck that she was listening to every word. "I'd rather not," he said.

Okyllus fingered his cloak-pin; it was cast in the shape of a horse's head, the royal symbol of Pisa. "But you will," he said coldly. "The girl's father Menoeceus is one of Thebes' leading men – and her mother was descended from Cadmus, like yourself. If you don't marry the girl, Menoeceus will claim the throne for his children."

Laius shifted uncomfortably on the hard throne. "But—"

"The Tiresias herself proclaimed that Jocasta would be the next queen of Thebes. I heard the prophecy, and so did all the nobles of Thebes."

An alternative occurred to Laius. "She could marry Polydorus – then she can still be Thebes' next queen. I just won't marry."

"The son of a peasant, as heir to the throne? The Spartoi will never accept that!" Okyllus' face darkened. "The king will expect *you* to marry Jocasta."

That was plain enough. Laius might be *a* king, but Pelops remained *the* king. Pelops' soldiers had marched with him through Thebes. He would hold the Theban throne only at King Pelops' pleasure. And Okyllus was right – Pelops would be furious if he did not marry the girl the Tiresias had named as the city's next queen. Pelops might even declare that Laius was defying the gods.

The thought sent a chill down his back.

Polydorus stood with both fists clenched, looking ready to smash something; Nikippes edged away, appearing to investigate a lyre propped against the rim of the hearth. But Nerissa turned back to face the throne; she held little Gogos' hand, waiting to hear what Laius would say.

Okyllus kept talking. "Nerissa and your sons can remain with you, but you must make this alliance." He made a placating gesture. "It won't be a hardship. I saw the girl: she's beautiful. And quite young – she won't make any trouble."

Laius sought Nerissa's gaze; she gave a sad, almost imperceptible, nod, and he relaxed.

"Very well," he said, as if making an unforced decision. "Let's meet this Jocasta."

§ 10.05

The cart jolted to a stop; Niobe opened her eyes and stared up at the dusky

sky. There was salt in the air, and the sound of waves hitting rocks: the sea, they were near the sea. But Thebes lay inland… she supposed she should wonder where she was, but it didn't matter. Her children were dead – all dead, all but Chloris. Phthia, Neaira, Damasichthon: dead, all dead. Chloris was the only thread that bound her to the world of the living. Chloris, and her beloved Amphion…

"Where's my husband?" she asked, sitting up. "Where's—"

"Mother," said Chloris, climbing down beside her. "Don't you remember?"

"Where is he?" cried Niobe. "We can't leave him!"

Tears shone in Chloris' gray eyes – eyes so like her father's. "I told you before, Mother. He's dead."

"But he didn't fall ill! He was strong all through the night—"

A man bent over her. "He's dead, my lady queen. King Amphion is dead."

The man's voice and face were familiar. Naucles. Captain Naucles. Naucles would never lie to her, no more than Chloris would. So it must be true – oh, vicious gods, it was true! Amphion, dead… She buried her face in her hands. "My fault," she moaned. "My fault, my fault."

Chloris' strong arm slipped around her shoulders. "Let's go, Mother. Captain Naucles has a cottage near the shore. He'll give us something to eat."

Stiff, aching, Niobe allowed herself to be helped down from the cart; Naucles and Chloris steadied her, kept her from falling. Loose sand shifted beneath her feet; shifting as the world had shifted, nothing constant, nothing to be trusted. They passed from the fading sunlight into shadow, and then she was seated on a padded couch, with Chloris pressing a warm cup into her hands. "Drink, Mother. It will do you good."

Niobe looked up, saw the concern in Amphion's eyes – no, not Amphion, Amphion was dead. Chloris, her precious daughter – her only daughter now. Slowly she drank, tasting herbs and honey in the mixture, thickened with bread crumbs and egg.

"We'll set sail in the morning, Mother," Chloris said.

"Sail? To where?" asked Niobe.

"To Pylos, my lady queen," Naucles said. "It should be an easy journey. The winds are with us."

"We swam there once," Niobe said to Naucles. "I remember."

Naucles nodded, but his bearded, sun-weathered face remained sad. "Yes, my lady queen. That we did."

"And I'll marry King Neleus, if he'll have me," Chloris said.

Niobe remembered Neleus as a student in Pisa: an eager youth with lank hair and ears like jug handles. He always thought about the lesson, no matter what subject she had been teaching. He had been supposed to marry one of the twins, but of course they were dead. "I'm sure he will. But I don't want to go to Pylos – I want to go home."

She saw both Naucles and Chloris hesitate. "We can't return to Thebes, Mother," Chloris said.

"My lady queen, they'd kill you," Naucles warned. "Just as they killed King Amphion."

Anger surged within Niobe's breast, dispelling the thick cloud of grief. "Thebes," she spat, disgusted by the word. "Barbarians!" She felt ill; the scent of the mixture in her cup sickened her, and she pushed it away. Amphion had given his life to save her and Chloris – that meant she *had* to live, if she could. And she had to protect Chloris, too. "No, I need to go *home.* To Lydia."

"Mother, what are you talking about? King Neleus will give you a home in Pylos."

"He'd try, perhaps." Niobe's lips twisted bitterly. "But I can't go there."

"But—" Chloris stared at her mother with limpid gray eyes. "Do you want me to marry my cousin Tantalus, instead of King Neleus?"

"No!" The word burst so sharply out of Niobe that both Chloris and Naucles looked shocked. Niobe struggled to express herself. "Daughter, don't you see? This is my fault – *my* fault! The gods have cursed *me*, Chloris. Their wrath will follow me. I can't bring that on you – or on your children!"

Both Chloris and Naucles gasped at this but she could tell that they saw that she was not wholly mad, that her argument had merit. Before the evening was out Naucles agreed to have one of his ships convey Princess Chloris to Pylos; he, to fulfill his oath, would personally accompany Niobe to Lydia.

The days of the eastward sea journey blended one into the next. Naucles' men avoided her, making the sign against the evil eye whenever they walked past; she did not care. Each morning, each night, Niobe thought of her lost children, her beloved husband, and her tears mingled with the salt spray until she could not tell one from the other. The mournful creaking of the deck-planks blended with her lamentations like the strains of a funeral dirge.

After a passage of days, Naucles brought his ship safely to shore in the Lydian port. He arranged a mule-cart for the journey to the palace; as they proceeded along the Hermos River, Niobe watched the countryside creep slowly past, trying to remember how it had looked when she left more than thirty years before. The fields were green with growing barley; it seemed that the thatch-roofed farmhouses along the main road into the city were more numerous than before. But the spring tulips showed the same bright colors she had known as a girl, and the shape of Mount Sipylus in the distance was unchanged.

Sipylus. She had named a son for this mountain: had his shade found peace in the Underworld? She hoped there would be dogs better tempered than three-headed Kerberos to keep him company. But, knowing Sipylus, he would even tame Hades' guard-dog. A tear rolled down Niobe's cheek, and she did not wipe it away.

The well-tended roadway led them to the city's main gate. Two guards in the saffron-yellow and purple of Lydia, young men of twenty or so, demanded to know their business. Naucles answered: "I am Captain Naucles, a merchant of Thebes. The king knows my wares; I've been here before."

One of the guards scratched his jaw. "I remember you. Who's the old lady? Your mother?"

"This is Queen Niobe!" Naucles declared, indignant. "Niobe, queen of Thebes, daughter of King Tantalus!"

"Don't look like a queen," muttered the second guard.

Niobe glanced down at herself, realizing how she must appear: no jewelry at all, face bare of makeup, her thin white hair pulled back in a single plait, her sandals and gown unadorned.

"Do you want to face King Tantalus' fury? Then continue to insult his daughter!"

The men laughed. "The old man doesn't scare anyone these days," said one.

"His grandson is regent now," the other added.

"Then this woman is the regent's aunt!"

The guards exchanged a glance, shrugging. "If you say so," said the taller one. He waved them through with his spear. "They'll still search you before you see the regent, Grandmother. Just so you know."

The palace steward had better manners than the guards at the gate, but as they walked through corridors Niobe had known as a girl he confirmed this fact: all who desired an audience with the regent must submit to a search. A matronly servant took Niobe to a curtained side room and verified that she carried no weapons before she was taken to the megaron.

Regent Tantalus sat on a chair of polished ebony placed before the tall, vacant throne. As Naucles, his own body search completed, joined her in the audience hall, Niobe watched her nephew conclude a conversation with two men wearing the curl-toed boots of Hittites. The regent reminded Niobe of her brother Pelops as a young man: he was neither so tall nor so handsome, and lacked the injury to his shoulder – but something in his gesture, as he beckoned Naucles forward, seemed familiar.

The regent listened to Naucles' explanation, then turned to Niobe. "Family obligations are not to be taken lightly," he said. "But neither are my obligations to the kingdom. Did you bring this curse with you?"

A middle-aged woman standing near the throne objected. "Tantalus! How can you speak that way to your aunt?"

The regent frowned. "Mother—"

Niobe peered at the woman. She was tall and slender, with silver hair pulled back severely from her face. "Euryanassa?"

"You didn't recognize me, did you?" Arms outstretched, Euryanassa walked forward to embrace her. "And I might not have recognized you – but I remember your voice." Releasing Niobe, she looked up at her son. "Of *course* the king's daughter is welcome in Lydia." She clasped Niobe's hand, smiling. "There's someone else who wants to hear your voice, Niobe. Come with me."

Niobe let Broteas' widow lead her through corridors that grew more familiar with each step. Yes, that was the fresco she had liked as a child, with the blue monkeys capering among the crocus blooms – and there was the courtyard where her mother had spent warm evenings. The stairs to the women's quarters were steeper than she recalled; she was short of breath by the time they reached the second floor. Two plump servants admitted them to the royal women's wing, each touching the back of a hand to his forehead in respect.

"Here we are," said Euryanassa, pushing open a door. "Mother Dione, are you awake?"

Niobe remained near the doorway, transfixed with recognition. The richly patterned rugs – the wall painting that showed Athena at her loom – the wooden screen carved with jasmine flowers and twisting vines—

"Who is it?" The voice from the bed, fretful and weak, brought Niobe back to the present.

Euryanassa beckoned her forward, whispering: "She's nearly blind, and doesn't hear very well. But I think she'll understand you."

Niobe went to the bedside. "Mother?"

"Who calls me Mother?" said the toothless old woman, frowning. "I have no children. All my children are gone!"

Niobe's breath caught in her throat; the tears which came so easily to her, these days, spilled from her eyes. "No, Mother," she said, speaking slowly and clearly. "Not all of them. I'm here. Niobe."

The invalid's milky eyes shifted back and forth, as if trying to penetrate a fog. "Niobe? Niobe – yes, child, I dream of you often." The faded lips quivered. "But you always vanish like dew when the sun comes up..."

Niobe took her mother's hand; it felt brittle as a bundle of twigs. "I'm here, Mother. This time, I'm really here." She prodded her mother's memory: "Do you remember when you first taught me to spin? It was a rainy day, and the wool was dyed bright red. It took me all afternoon before I could keep the thread from breaking. What a lumpy, uneven thread I made – but I was so proud of it!"

"Oh – oh, Niobe…"

Niobe continued: "Do you remember when we wove that tapestry of Rhea giving her husband a stone to swallow?"

"My baby!" cried the old woman. "Niobe—"

"Yes, Mother. I'm here."

The cold fingers clutched Niobe's. "I knew you wouldn't forget," Dione said, her voice a mere whisper. "I knew you wouldn't forget your mother…"

The breath sighed from the old woman's lungs – and then she sagged back against the pillows, and her hand went limp.

Niobe started, horrified. "No – no!" she cried. "I *am* cursed!"

But Euryanassa gripped her arm. "Niobe, whatever else has happened, *this* death is not a curse." She continued: "She was very old, and her strength was failing. Think what happiness you gave her, returning in time to say goodbye!"

The warmth in her sister-in-law's words touched Niobe's heart and she allowed Euryanassa to embrace her. Niobe had never felt close to her other sisters-in-law; Hippodamia had had a cruel streak, while Thebe had been jealous and competitive. But in Broteas' widow, she detected no resentment – only comfort, and welcome. "Thank you," Niobe said, drawing back. "Thank you for your kindness. Thank you for taking care of her, all these years."

"It was my duty." Euryanassa patted Niobe's arm. "I must tell my son that his grandmother has died. But of course you want to see your father." She summoned a servant, who led Niobe to the king's well-guarded suite.

Niobe knew that her father had presided over Broteas' self-immolation less than a year before – and so his condition was more shocking than her mother's had been. A dank smell of urine filled his rooms, even though the window-shutters were open to the afternoon breeze. King Tantalus was skeletally thin: loose folds of jaundiced skin hung slack from his scrawny arms. Seated on a padded chair, attended by several healers, he did not seem to notice Niobe's presence even when the servant announced her.

She walked forward uncertainly. "Hello, Father," she said in a loud voice.

The old man finally looked in her direction. "Who are you?" he asked, peering at her. Then he turned to the white-robed apprentice at his right. "And where's my drink? I'm thirsty."

The man lifted a silver cup to the king's lips and helped him to drink. Once Tantalus waved the cup away she tried again, even louder. "I'm Niobe." When he showed no sign of recognition she added, practically shouting: "Your daughter."

He scratched at his thinning white beard. "Daughter?" he asked. "Niobe, yes, Niobe. About time you came – you need to have a word with your brother! Ungrateful, oath-breaking wretch – thinks he should be in charge."

Niobe wondered what brother he meant – and then realized her father had confused his grandson with one of his sons.

"Where's Geranor?" asked the king.

"Dead, my lord king," shouted the young healer.

Niobe bent down to the apprentice with the cup. "Who's Geranor?"

"A man who used to serve the king," the man explained in a low voice. "He died in a hunting accident shortly after the regent took control. We've told King Tantalus this before, but he always forgets."

The king slapped the palm of his hand against his knee twice, then paused, frowning. He struck his knee a third time and turned back to the young healer. "Curse you, I said I'm thirsty! Where's my cup?"

Niobe frowned; he had just finished drinking. The white-robed apprentice held out the silver cup to a servant, who filled it with water; Tantalus drank like a peasant who had been working the fields. Despite the young man's assistance, some of the liquid dribbled down the front of the king's tunic. The servant blotted the king's face with a cloth. Tantalus permitted this for a moment, then slapped the man away. "Enough! Bring my dinner. It's dinner time, and you haven't even brought me lunch. I should execute the lot of you – impale you on pikes in the agora! It'd serve you right. It's treason, starving your king!"

"Yes, my lord king. Your meal's coming, my lord king."

"Ha. That's what you always say." With a bony finger, Tantalus poked the young apprentice in the ribs. "I want to piss. Help me up."

The young man and the servant helped the old man to his feet; with their assistance he shuffled off to a corner of a room concealed by a carved wooden screen.

Niobe turned to another healer, a plump fellow with a long oiled beard. "Why don't you give him enough to eat and drink?" she asked. It horrified her to think that the regent might be starving his grandfather.

The man moved closer to her and said, "My lady, he eats and drinks constantly. But he cannot retain the memory of it." He glanced back at the screened-off corner, where there was a sound of liquid splashing. "And his body cannot retain the nourishment. It passes right through him. His water is sweet: flies would drink of his urine as readily as honey. Once the patient's condition reaches this point, his thirst and hunger never cease."

"There's no hope of recovery, then?"

"I have never seen one in King Tantalus' condition return to health." He shrugged. "But of course he has been a great favorite of the gods. Perhaps they will choose to heal him."

Her father came back to his seat and the servants began to feed him the meal, first softening the bread in the soup. He downed two cups of water and called for a third, still complaining of thirst. When she could get his attention, Niobe tried to tell her father that his wife had died; but he peered at her quizzically. "Who are you, woman? Who admitted you to the king's rooms?"

"I'm Niobe, Father," she repeated. "Your daughter."

"My daughter sailed west years ago." He accepted a spoonful of soup from one of his servants. When he had swallowed, he said, "Go back to your mistress, woman. Tell her to get that son of mine under control! He thinks he can run this kingdom – I've got a lesson to teach him!" He shook a finger at her menacingly.

Realizing she could not make him understand, Niobe took her leave. Euryanassa was waiting for her in the corridor and showed her to a guest room.

Niobe's nephew presided over Queen Dione's funeral three days later; the king was unable to attend. While Dione's passing was noted as the end of an era, the occasion was not very sad; the people of Lydia knew that she had long been ailing. For Niobe, the ceremony was bittersweet. She regretted that she had not had more time with her mother, but it was a comfort to have been able to say goodbye: a return to the natural order of things, to be a child burying a parent rather than a parent witnessing the untimely deaths of her children. Children whose funerals she could not even attend – had the ungrateful Thebans even buried them properly? The thought tore at her heart. Telling loyal Naucles that she needed to be alone, she wandered away from the royal tomb up into the foothills of Mount Sipylus, seeking privacy for her pain.

Soon, at her urging, Captain Naucles left Lydia to return to his own family. After his departure Niobe often walked through the countryside; exhausting herself during the day was the only thing that allowed her to sleep at night. Outside the city she was free of the whispered comments, the pointed fingers, the looks of fear mingled with curiosity, pity and scorn. On the slopes of Mount Sipylus there was no need to hide her sorrow; she could let the tears fall freely. Walking higher up the mountainside paths took her above the worst of the summer heat; occasionally she lingered near the massive carving of Rhea, thinking of the terrible price her brother Broteas had paid for offending the gods. But at least he had been allowed to die – while Niobe was forced to continue through the ever-present pain. It was her fault that her children had died; she owed them, and Amphion, her suffering as some tiny measure of recompense.

There was a special place, on the slopes above the city, where she often rested; day after day, her feet took her to the little stream in the shadow of the cliffs. It was as though the mountain wept with her: Mount Sipylus, after all, was sacred to Mother Rhea – and Rhea had also lost her children. Learning of her preference for this spot, Regent Tantalus built a cottage for Niobe nearby, so that she might stay there as long as she wished; Euryanassa assigned a maidservant to take care of the dwelling and to see to Niobe's needs.

Every day Niobe sat in the shadow of the pines beside the flowing water, remembering her husband and children. With each tear, Niobe whispered the name of a child: Alphenor, her eldest – his father's right hand! Beautiful Astycratia, with enormous eyes and rich chestnut curls. Large-hearted Damasichthon, sweeping her off her feet in a great bear-hug. Ilioneus, who once slipped a lizard into his aunt's jewelry-box, sending her shrieking from the room – and yet even Thebe had laughed after she recovered from the fright. Talented Cleodoxa, creating poetry beside her father, while Eudoxa worked the loom with her mother. Ismenus, her brave boy, announcing that he would defend her from giants and monsters. Her champion archer, Phaedimus. Neaira, who rose early to watch the dawn. Sipylus, who could train his dogs to do anything. Ogygia, who invented stories about the wall-paintings. Tantalus, who Amphion had been sure would surpass him with the lyre. The littlest, Phthia: Niobe could still see her chubby arms stretching upwards, begging to be lifted onto her father's shoulders.

Each time Niobe thought of Chloris, she paused in her weeping: then she pleaded with the gods – she who had rarely sought the gods' help – to forgive her offending words and to take no vengeance on this last daughter.

The Lydians knew, of course, that Niobe mourned for her dead children. A few ascended the slope to gawk or to sneer, but Niobe ignored them until one late-summer day, just as the sun was reaching its zenith, a woman of thirty years or so approached her and dropped to one knee.

Niobe asked bitterly: "Are you here to mock my sorrow?"

"Oh, no, my lady," whispered the woman. Niobe looked closer and saw that the woman's eyelids were red and swollen. "I brought you a gift." She held out a basket and lifted its lid to reveal a loaf of freshly baked bread.

Ashamed of her accusation, Niobe accepted the basket. "I thank you," she said. "But why bring me anything?"

"My son—" the woman choked on the word. After a moment she continued: "He was only nine years old, my lady – only nine! He died two days ago, of a scorpion bite."

"I'm sorry," Niobe whispered, holding out her hand.

The woman sat down on a rock beside Niobe. Haltingly the woman spoke: how her son had loved to throw stones, by hand or with a sling, and what a good shot he was. "He sometimes brought me a hare for the dinner-pot. And him only nine, my lady! What a hunter he would have been!" Niobe listened until the sun was low in the sky, and the woman rose to go home, saying: "Thank you, my lady. You've helped ease my heart today."

From that day forward others who had lost loved ones climbed Mount Sipylus to mourn with Niobe, knowing they need not grieve alone.

§ 10.06

Pelops dismissed the ambassador from Sicyon and turned to his herald for the next item of business. "A messenger just arrived from Thebes, my lord king."

"Very well," Pelops said, after a moment. "Show him in."

The herald admitted Nikippes, who bowed before Pelops' throne. "So," Pelops asked, "has my nephew Alphenor taken a wife?"

"Prince Alphenor is dead, my lord king."

At these words the crowded megaron fell silent.

"He and twelve of his brothers and sisters, all dead in a single night. Felled by arrows of Apollo and Artemis, they say." Horrified whispers arose from the listeners, but Nikippes continued: "King Amphion is dead as well. The Thebans decided he was cursed. When he went out to address them, the people tore him apart. Laius and I arrived in the city shortly after these events transpired; Laius has been installed as king of Thebes."

Atreus and Thyestes, standing beside the throne, looked at him with the same shocked expression worn by all the others in the megaron. His sons needed his guidance, but Pelops did not know how to react. His mouth had gone dry; his heartbeat felt oddly frantic, like the struggles of a trapped hare.

Myrtilus' ghost appeared beside him. "Your sister," he urged. "What about your sister?"

"Niobe?" Pelops asked.

"My lord king, it appears that your sister escaped the city with Princess Chloris. But no one knows where they went."

So – of all the children, *Chloris* had survived. Chloris! Why her?

Pain shot through his bad shoulder; Pelops fought the urge to wince. "And Okyllus, your father? Did he witness this – this catastrophe?"

"Yes, my lord king, but he suffered no ill consequence." Nikippes bowed again. "My father plans to return to Pisa once King Laius has strengthened his claim to the Theban throne by marrying Jocasta, daughter of Menoeceus. In the meantime, I bring gifts from King Laius." He passed a clay tablet to the herald, who began to read the itemized list aloud.

Myrtilus leaned close. "The wealth of Thebes – at your disposal once more."

As the herald's recitation continued, Thyestes edged nearer to the throne. His dark eyes fixed on Pelops. "Amazing," he whispered. "This must be the meaning of your dream, Father!"

Atreus folded well-muscled arms across his chest. "I *am* amazed."

The ghost whispered in Pelops' ear: "Your eldest son is suspicious."

A frown crossed Thyestes' face. "But, Father, we were to wed Cleodoxa and Eudoxa—"

"No, we weren't," Atreus said quickly. "Amphion was betrothing them to King Neleus of Pylos and Prince Tantalus of Lydia. Besides, finding brides won't be a problem now. The sons died too."

"Enough!" Pelops barked sharply. Silence fell; his sons and subjects and the foreign envoys looked at him warily, as if trying to gauge his mood. "I must consider the news of this tragedy in private," he said, descending from his throne. "Nikippes, my sons will review the inventory with you." The floor seemed unsteady as he crossed the room; ignoring the curious looks he received, he left the room and started down the corridor that led to his chambers.

Myrtilus had slipped ahead and was waiting for him in the hallway, studying an octopus painted on the wall. Pelops walked resolutely past, continuing to his rooms. An inventory of recent hauls of fish awaited him, neatly tallied on the waxen surfaces of several folding tablets. He walked past them. Feeling ill, he went to the window for a breath of fresh air: the olive trees were in bloom, perfuming the breeze. Pelops looked northeast, in the direction of Thebes, where the terrible event had happened.

"How many died?" asked the ghost from a shadowed corner. "Your brother-in-law, Amphion; seven of your nephews, six nieces. Do you even remember their names?"

No, Pelops thought. *Their names don't matter.* He turned away from the window and snapped his fingers for a servant. "A jar of wine," he ordered. "And a woman to rub my shoulder."

Pelops drank heavily that night. After the woman had massaged his shoulder and taken care of his other needs, he dismissed her and lay awake. Why, he wondered, was he so affected by what had happened? He had been expecting something of the sort. He drained another cup of wine and slept at last.

Shortly after midnight, he was awakened by music – a chorus of voices, singing in harmony. He turned on his side, peering into the shadows cast by the lamp that burned behind a fretted bronze screen. Where were the voices coming from? He must have been dreaming. But then why could he still hear the song?

"You're not dreaming, old friend," said Myrtilus, moving out of the gray gloom. "Look who I found!"

It was a chorus of ghosts.

Pelops clutched his sheets, surveying the insubstantial forms that surrounded him. Some of the spirits were those of well-muscled young men, some were slender echoes of feminine beauty – some had the shape of young children. And all of them were singing.

"Stop it!" Pelops ordered.

Then Amphion emerged from the shadows, carrying a lyre as insubstantial as his form. "You silenced our voices, Brother – now you will hear them the rest of your life."

"No," said Pelops, rising from the bed. Uneasy, he glanced down at his unprotected nakedness, the faded scars on his bad shoulder – but how could a man be shamed before the dead? "Go to the Underworld where you belong!"

"No, Uncle Pelops," chanted his dead nephews and nieces in perfect harmony as Amphion plucked his ghostly lyre.

The music continued throughout the night, and throughout the following day. It was beautiful; Amphion had been the most talented musician in all Hellas. But it never stopped. The shades of the dead had no need to rest; they did not pause to eat or drink. Their voices never grew tired or hoarse. They sang as Pelops adjudicated his peasants' disputes in the morning; they accompanied him out to the training-ground and chanted while he reviewed the troops; they followed him back to the palace, crowding into his study and continuing their song as he reviewed the plans for a colony to be founded by one of his younger sons. They refused his demands, requests, and – eventually – pleas for them to stop.

In desperation, Pelops appealed to Myrtilus: "How can I get some peace?"

"Why do you deserve that, old friend?" Myrtilus asked.

The voices sang on: some deep and rich, others sweet and clear as flutes. Wavering, indistinct shapes of handsome young men, nubile maidens, and beautiful children danced around him, dizzying, moving in time to the chords of Amphion's ghostly lyre.

"You were right," Pelops whispered to the charioteer, watching the multitude of youthful ghosts. "I *don't* even know their names."

The charioteer shrugged. "Maybe that's the problem."

An Egyptian healer had once told Pelops that knowing someone's name gave one power over him, living or dead. But even after he learned the names of his dead nieces and nephews and ordered each of them personally to go to Hades, the ghostly chorus continued. He could barely sleep; the music kept him awake. Putting his hands over his ears was no use. Pelops called for other musicians in an attempt to drown them out, but the resulting cacophony was even worse. No matter what he did – whether he closed his eyes or kept them open, whether he lay in bed or walked the corridors of the palace, whether he sought company or solitude – Amphion and his children remained with him: singing, always singing.

The summer solstice came and went, and the dead continued their song. Shortly afterwards, word arrived that Niobe had gone to Lydia, but without her surviving daughter. King Tantalus was said to be an invalid, rumored to be descending into dementia; Broteas' son now ruled as regent. Of Chloris there was still no news.

"I'm sorry, my lord king," Nikippes said as he concluded his report. "I'm sure we'll discover your niece's whereabouts soon."

"Perhaps her ship went down," suggested Myrtilus.

"Don't you know?" Pelops exploded. "Doesn't anyone know?"

Nikippes frowned. "My lord king, I—"

The volume of the ghostly song increased, maddeningly. "Stop it!" Pelops barked. Nikippes fell silent, but the ghosts sang on. Surely his dead nieces and nephews, his dead brother-in-law must know what had happened to Chloris – and yet they told him nothing useful, no more than Myrtilus ever had.

Nikippes shifted uneasily, staring at him. Everyone in the megaron stared at him.

Myrtilus laughed. "You'll soon be as mad as your father, my friend."

A ghost-niece moved closer and sang: "Why did you kill me, Uncle Pelops?"

How could his sanity survive this torment? He could not sleep, or eat, or think.

"No mortal can help you," said Myrtilus.

If mortals could not help him, then he would turn to immortals. He would pray to the gods – make atonement – perhaps go back to Delphi. With an effort, Pelops focused on Nikippes. "The Tiresias," he said. "Isn't she expected in Pisa?"

"Any day, my lord king," said the young nobleman.

"Bring her to me as soon as she arrives," Pelops said. In the meantime, he would beg the gods directly. He called for his chariot, but the horses were skittish and he did not trust himself to control them. Leaving behind his confused grooms, he went to the sacred district of Olympia on foot, tormented by the ghosts at every step. Hestia was a kind and gentle goddess: perhaps she would help him. Pelops told his guards to station themselves outside her sanctuary, but the ghostly choir followed him into the inner sanctum. Even when he commanded the priestess and her acolytes to leave so that he could pray alone, the shades remained with him.

"Here, too?" he asked. "Is nothing sacred?"

"Here, too," they sang, and repeated back to him: "Is nothing sacred?"

Pelops knelt beside the hearth flame and raised his arms. "Hestia, hear me!" he prayed, hoping his words would carry over the chorus. "I come to your hearth seeking peace – please, remind your brothers and sisters how much I have done for you! Grant me mercy!"

He repeated this prayer, and again a third time; then a different voice spoke over the harmonies of the song. "Father!"

Glancing up, Pelops saw a tall youth striding towards him. His luminous eyes were the color of amber; his hair rivaled the shining gold of the sun. The other ghosts stepped back to give him room.

Pelops leapt to his feet, arms outstretched. "Chrysippus!"

But his son was form without substance; Pelops' hands passed through the wavering shape. Chrysippus shook his head. "You cannot touch me, Father."

Pelops let his arms fall to his sides. It was a joy to see Chrysippus again – and yet they were still separated by the bleak gulf of death. "I've missed you so much! Why have you never come before?"

"I came to remind you what it's like to lose a child. Do you remember, Father?"

"Of course," Pelops said, his throat tightening. "The pain – it never leaves me. I mourn you every day, Chrysippus."

"How many children did your sister lose, Father?"

Before Pelops could answer, Chrysippus shimmered and vanished.

"Come back!" Pelops called. "Chrysippus, come back!"

But his son was gone. As Pelops fell to his knees, moaning at the pain of losing Chrysippus anew, Amphion's ghostly chorus crowded round, starting their pitiless song once more. He had asked the gods for mercy, and instead they redoubled his agony.

It was not until late in the day that Pelops mastered himself sufficiently to appear before his men and return to the palace. That night, Atreus came to his rooms with word that Chloris had married King Neleus of Pylos.

"What do you want to do, Father?" Atreus asked.

Amphion and his children were dancing a slow circle around his couch; Myrtilus, leaning against the painted wall, tapped his foot in time to the beat. Pelops found it difficult to concentrate. "Do?"

"About Chloris and Neleus."

Pelops looked into the eyes of his eldest son. Atreus, at least, understood the fury he still felt towards Chloris.

The chorus stopped their circling. "Let her live," pleaded Amphion's ghost. The dead children chanted: "Let her live!"

Atreus leaned over and touched his elbow. "Father?"

"I'll think about it," Pelops said – an answer that served both the living and the dead. He sent his son away, then took the golden mastiff out of its sealed chest. He carried it with him to his bed, hoping that the icon might protect him as the original mastiff had protected the infant Zeus. "Rhea, have mercy," he whispered, closing his eyes and trying to shut his ears. In time he slept.

The next day, Nikippes and Okyllus accompanied the Tiresias into the megaron. "Laius has finally consummated his marriage with Menoeceus' daughter," Okyllus reported. "But he did not seem happy about it afterwards."

The Tiresias shrugged.

"Well," Thyestes observed, scratching his nose, "Laius was always fond of Nerissa."

Pelops was indifferent to Laius, Nerissa and the new queen of Thebes. He studied the Tiresias, and then rose to his feet. "Prophetess, I would speak with you. Will you join me in my study?"

She inclined her head in assent; leaning on her manservant, she followed Pelops through the hallways. Once she had taken her seat in the study she told the bald fellow to wait outside. When the oaken door creaked shut she leaned forward, resting her blindfolded face in her frail hands; she seemed thinner and smaller than ever, more a blind old woman than the Handmaiden of Apollo – and her presence did not dispel the shades of the dead. Yet somehow her vulnerability encouraged Pelops: he had not meant to tell her the whole truth, but the words spilled forth. He told her everything about the ghosts and their endless song – even how Chrysippus had appeared to him and had then vanished.

"Ah, Pelops," the old woman said. "We were young once, weren't we?"

He glanced around at the singing ghosts, wondering if any of them comprehended her cryptic comment. "That's true, Tiresias, but I don't understand."

"Young, and foolish." The faded lips curved into a smile. "But the folly of youth is never fully overcome, is it? Your sister Niobe never learned to hold her tongue. The ambitious prince from Lydia never learned to keep his bargains."

Pelops swallowed. "I tried," he said, hearing the weakness of his own words. "I acted only when there was no other choice…"

Her gray head tilted. "You and your sister are not the only ones with failings, Pelops. I knew things would come to this, eventually – and yet for years I sought to delay the inevitable. I did not want to stop such beautiful music. So I avoided Thebes, even though it was my home." She slumped against the cushioned chair. "The next time I go to Thebes will be my last. Another will become the Voice of Apollo."

The ghosts circled the room like a flock of vultures waiting for an injured animal to die, their harmonies eerie and foreboding. "Tiresias," Pelops whispered, "I can't bear this torment. How can I be free?"

The old woman sighed. "What do *you* think you should do, Pelops?"

Pelops glanced up at his brother-in-law. How did one negotiate with a ghost? What could he offer those who were dead? "I should spare Chloris," he said, though it pained him to think she would escape his revenge.

Amphion's ghost smiled, and Chloris' siblings nodded agreement.

"More than that: I should wish her and her husband Neleus well."

The seer reached up to adjust her blindfold, as if the fabric chafed her skin. "Apollo and Artemis can be cruel with their arrows. Too cruel. But their mother Leto is sweet and merciful..." The prophetess gripped her staff in silence for several breaths, and then said: "Chloris' son shall be granted a long life. The years cut from her brothers and sisters will be added to his life-thread."

For a moment bitter envy seized Pelops' heart: *he* should have been the one to sire Chloris' son! But the choir of ghosts reminded him that he had many other sons, all but one still living.

"As the gods will it," Pelops said, dispelling his jealous anger. He gazed at the ghosts of Amphion and his children and said: "I swear by Zeus Thunderer, neither I nor my sons will do anything to harm Chloris and her children. To seal this pledge, I'll send Neleus a gift of gold."

Apparently satisfied by this, Amphion and his children faded away; only his old companion Myrtilus remained. When the last echoes of the ghostly chorus ceased, the silence was startling.

"Over the years you've done much to honor the gods," said the Tiresias, her voice sounding strangely loud. "Your temples, your games – these please the residents of Olympia. Because of this, Apollo and Artemis will shoulder the blame. Your role in the tragedy at Thebes will not be recognized."

Pelops felt as if a yoke had slipped from his shoulders. No need for another trip to Delphi? No necessity for further atonement, no need to face the shame...

"Pelops," she continued, "You've done what you needed to do to achieve greatness. Not all such deeds are pleasant." With the aid of her staff, the frail old prophetess climbed to her feet and headed unerringly towards the door. She rapped on its wooden surface and called to her manservant; he pulled the door open for her. The Tiresias paused on the threshold, turning her blindfolded face back to Pelops. "Your name will be spoken for a hundred generations. The land itself will bear your name."

When she had gone, the charioteer's ghost clapped his hands together triumphantly. Myrtilus crowed: "If you're remembered, Pelops, then I'll be remembered too!"

§ 10.07

At harvest time the Tiresias came to Pylos. Chloris did not want to see her, not after the devastation her words had called down upon her brothers and sisters; but although she was a queen – or rather *because* she was a queen – she could not publicly shun the Voice of Apollo. Neleus had recently announced that she was with child, so she even had to allow the old woman to tell her baby's future. She stiffened with terror as the Tiresias reached out to touch her abdomen.

The seer lifted her hand; her colorless lips pressed together, and her jaw worked from side to side.

Chloris clutched her husband's arm, fearing that she might faint.

"Your son will be known as the wisest man of his generation," the Tiresias finally declared. "His life-thread will be sturdy and uncommonly long."

Chloris swallowed hard, scarcely able to believe that disaster had been averted. Meanwhile the people of Pylos cheered, calling out her name and that of her husband.

"Tiresias, we rejoice at your words," said Neleus, smiling broadly. He lifted Chloris' hand and kissed it. "A son, my dear – both healthy and clever!"

The Tiresias nodded. "Let's go, Dolichus," she told her servant. "My work here is done."

Chloris watched her shuffle away, hoping never to see the prophetess again. Given the brevity of the Tiresias' stay in Pylos, she had the impression that the old woman was just as uncomfortable around her.

Neleus pulled her arm through his. "You see, Chloris, the gods are smiling on us. You've brought no curse into our marriage."

When she had arrived in Pylos months ago, Chloris had been nervous about how King Neleus would receive her – especially since he had been betrothed to one of her sisters. If not for the promise to her father that she would marry and have children, she might have run off into the woods and rejoined the Maidens of Artemis. But wholehearted devotion to the goddess who had slain her sisters would have been difficult to achieve – and she had to keep her word to her father.

Chloris had approached Neleus as a petitioner, without revealing her true identity to the people of Pylos: that way if the king decided she was cursed, no fear of the curse would linger in the hearts of his subjects. But despite everything Neleus had welcomed her. He listened with sympathy to her sad tale, reminding Chloris of how he had once comforted her years ago. Then, too, Artemis had been cruel; then, too, an innocent child had died. But Neleus had not put his first wife away; he had not called her barrenness a curse, and eventually she had given him a son. He was as kind and thoughtful with Chloris as he had been with his late wife. Though she still grieved for her fallen brothers and sisters, with Neleus at her side she felt safe.

They walked through the crowd, stopping occasionally to admire the bounty of the harvest. The year had been good: the crops of barley and wheat were plentiful, the grapes sweet and juicy. Most important of all, the flax was abundant. The plants had been threshed for their seeds to make oil, and now the stalks were soaking in earthenware tubs and in the region's ponds and streams to make the fiber ready to work. The people of Pylos were cheerful, sharing their good wishes for Chloris' pregnancy. A young girl offered her a bouquet of late roses; she accepted them with thanks.

"The people are happy with you, Chloris," her husband said. "As am I."

"I'm grateful to hear it," she said, lowering her head to inhale the scent of the blossoms. She knew what he wanted to hear – but she would not lie to her husband, and so far she had not been able to tell him that *she* was happy.

"Mother!" Neleus' son by his first wife came running up. "We've set up a target – will you come watch me shoot?"

Neleus grinned. "He knows you're better at archery than I, my dear."

"All right." Chloris followed the eight-year-old to the edge of the agora, where several bundles of hay had been stacked against the wall of one of the granaries. The spotted skin of a fawn had been lashed to the hay-stalks to make a target. Boys and girls had gathered around with bows in hand and quivers slung over their backs. As Chloris approached, a boy with downy cheeks let fly. There was strength in his shot, but his aim was high, and his arrow sailed over the target.

"Here," she said, walking forward to adjust the boy's stance. "Hold your arm this way. See?" She pulled an arrow from his quiver and offered it to him, appraised the way he tucked the shaft against the string and drew back to shoot. "Good," she said. "Now try again!"

This time the shot struck the target, though still above the center.

"Thank you, my lady queen!" shouted the boy.

"I told you Mother would help!" crowed Neleus' son. "You wouldn't believe how good a shot she is. Mother, show them!"

Resting a hand on the boy's shoulder, she said, "Not today, dear. I must think of the child I'm carrying. But let me watch you and your friends." The afternoon passed quickly, Chloris offering advice and encouragement.

At dusk, they returned to the palace. The boy went to wash before dinner but a servant told her that Neleus was waiting for her in the courtyard. "Chloris," Neleus said, coming to greet her, "Captain Naucles arrived while you were teaching archery – and he's brought someone with him I'm sure you'll want to see."

Chloris welcomed Naucles warmly: he often carried messages from Lydia. But who had come with him? A veiled woman stood in the shadows, far too tall to be Chloris' mother. Who might this be – perhaps a former Maiden of Artemis?

Then the woman stepped into the torchlight.

"Philomela!"

Chloris ran to greet her mother's friend; as they embraced both women wept.

"My route brought me to Athens," Naucles explained, "and Princess Philomela told me she wanted to visit you. Even without words, she makes her meaning plain."

"I'm grateful to you both," Chloris said, wiping her nose with the back of her hand. The people of Pylos had been kind to her – none more so than her new husband and his son – but no one here shared her memories of her family.

Philomela was a reassuring, comforting presence. And she knew, too, what it was to suffer. "Stay with us for a while, Philomela. Please, stay as our guest."

Philomela nodded, brushing away one of Chloris' tears.

"You're welcome in our home for as long as you wish," said Neleus.

The sea captain grinned. "Princess Philomela is probably the best weaver in all Hellas! Who knows what magic she can work with Pylian flax?"

They settled Philomela in a chamber near Chloris' rooms; and as the weather cooled Chloris spent her days in the weaving room. With this woman who could speak no words in reply, she could unburden her heart and talk about the tragedy in Thebes.

"Philomela," she said one sunny morning, "everyone says that living on after her children had died was Mother's punishment – but that I was spared because of my devotion to Artemis. But what if—" she stopped, her throat tightening. She took a deep breath, and dropped her voice to a whisper. "What if it was the other way around? What if someone wanted to spare my mother and make *me* suffer?" She set her hands on her swelling belly. "I can't stop asking myself that. If the same thing can be both a blessing and a curse, who is to say which of us is being punished?"

Philomela, her distaff tucked beneath her arm, caught up her whirling spindle. Her blue eyes were attentive above her veil.

"Maybe I'm being foolish," said Chloris, sniffing back tears. "It doesn't make sense. The Tiresias herself came to Pylos and blessed my unborn child. That's hardly a curse."

Setting her distaff and spindle aside, Philomela held up a finger, indicating that she had a thought she wanted to share. She went over to a chest which she had brought with her from Athens and opened the lid on its leather hinges. She pulled out a woolen tapestry and unrolled it, draping it over the surface of a work table.

"Oh, Philomela," said Chloris, stunned by the colors and the delicate detail of the work. "This is beautiful! We must show Neleus." She sent a servant to ask her husband to join them; then, clasping Philomela's hand, she bent over the multicolored cloth.

When Neleus arrived he was equally appreciative. "This is magnificent, Princess. The people and the cattle look so lifelike! This tells of life in Thebes, doesn't it?"

Philomela nodded.

"This is my family," said Chloris, running her finger along the top band of the tapestry. "Here's my father singing, along with my brothers and sisters – and here's Mother, listening to the song." She moved down to the next band. "Here are my brothers, winning prizes at the Olympic Games. And this is me winning the footrace, then joining the Maidens of Artemis. Here's Mother, at a festival in Thebes – one for Athena and Hephaestus, I think. Philomela is beside her: see the veil she's wearing? They must be telling a story to the children."

Coming closer, Philomela nodded again, her blue eyes bright.

"And this is Father and Uncle Zethos building the walls – and this must be the death of my cousin Idmon. And here..." Chloris broke off, trying to understand the meaning of Philomela's last few scenes.

King Neleus drew his finger along the tapestry, frowning. He dismissed the servants from the room, and then said quietly: "Princess, are you saying that King Pelops is responsible for – for what happened in Thebes?"

The mute woman nodded.

"My uncle?" whispered Chloris, feeling weak. Neleus was at her side, then, his strong arm around her; he helped her over to a chair. "Why, Philomela? Because I wouldn't marry him?"

Neleus knelt beside her. "It's more than that, Chloris. You and your brothers and sisters were too talented," he said. "Thebes was growing too powerful – and your father was making allies of his own. You refused to marry Pelops; your sisters rejected Atreus and Thyestes. Your brothers threatened the prospects for Pelops' sons. Pelops must have feared Hellas would become the domain of Amphion's sons. Now it will belong to the sons of Pelops."

"Are you sure this is true, Philomela?" asked Chloris. "How could you know?"

Philomela made a gesture that Chloris did not understand, then shook her head. She pointed at the tapestry – at a scene showing Pelops dropping something into a jar. The object was depicted by a glittering bead of jet.

His brow furrowing, Neleus said, "Poison?"

Philomela nodded vigorously.

"How did you learn of this, Princess?" Neleus asked.

Philomela looked from Neleus to Chloris, her eyes pools of helpless frustration. Finally she shrugged, and pointed again at the tapestry.

Struck by a flash of realization, Chloris whispered: "He poisoned his first wife. He poisoned Hippodamia. Her servant told me. When I learned that, I knew I could never marry him."

"Even though Hippodamia was no danger to him," Neleus said darkly. "She'd been banished for years. If he did not shrink from poisoning her, he would not hesitate to do the same against a growing threat to his family's power."

Chloris got to her feet; her husband steadied her as she went to look again at Philomela's woven story. The jar, the jar into which Pelops was dropping the ominous bead of poison... she had thought the pattern Philomela had crafted was a flower painted on the side of the jar, but no...

"He poisoned the octopus paste," she said. "He knows Mother loathes it, but he didn't realize that I hate it too. That's why we didn't fall ill!"

Philomela gave a wordless cry and nodded.

Neleus' face hardened. "It's not safe to display this tapestry," he said. "King Pelops has proved his ruthlessness. He laid the blame for these deaths on your mother, and on Apollo and Artemis: he doesn't want his hand in the crime known."

"But—" Chloris stared at her husband. "But Philomela displayed the tapestry showing what King Tereus did to her! The truth should be known!"

Taking her hands, Neleus said: "That was different. King Tereus was far away; Thrace could not threaten Athens or Thebes. But Pelops is our neighbor –

the most powerful man in the region. This tapestry will have to stay in its chest until it's safe to bring it out."

"That may be *years!"*

"It may be never. But – given what the Tiresias told you at the harvest festival, and the gold necklace he sent as a wedding gift – if we don't provoke him, we should be safe."

Chloris opened her mouth to protest again – and then she stopped, for she felt the strangest sensation.

"What is it, my dear?" asked Neleus.

"The baby," she said, with wonder. "I felt him kick inside me. I felt him kick!"

He placed a gentle hand on her belly, and then grinned. "I feel him too!"

Philomela clapped, and Chloris felt herself smile – and then guilt overwhelmed her. How could she feel happiness, when there had been so much death? She gazed at the floor.

But Neleus lifted her chin with his hand, forcing her to look at him. "My darling, smiling is allowed."

"But my brothers and my sisters – my father—"

"For *their* sake, my dear. Do you think they would be pleased, when you meet them in the Underworld, to learn that you spent the rest of your years in mourning?"

It was a point of view she had never considered. "No," she admitted.

"Then don't! Take joy in being queen, in being a mother and a stepmother. Take joy in me, your husband – and in your friend, Philomela."

Chloris embraced him. "You're right, Neleus. Thank you." Releasing her husband, she turned to Philomela. "Thank you."

Neleus rolled up the tapestry. "We'll store this away for now. Someday, when it's safe to let the truth be known, we'll take it out again." He handed the rolled cloth to Philomela, who tucked it away and closed the chest.

"Now," said Neleus, "why don't you two work on something new?" He kissed Chloris before he left, and the tingling warmth in her lips reminded Chloris how grateful she was – how *glad* she was – that she had married him.

Philomela brought several skeins of thread over to the work table and began to lay them out, displaying their many varied colors in the autumn sunlight. There were threads of ochre, white, and blue; threads dyed in precious eastern purple, threads stained with the bright yellow of saffron. Threads of crimson and midnight black; threads worked with slender bits of gleaming metal – gold, bronze, and silver.

Chloris picked up a thread of bronze; it sparkled in the light. "Well, Philomela – what shall we weave next?"

AUTHORS' NOTE

As always, we begin this authors' note with a spoiler warning – in this case, for the entire Niobe trilogy spanning *Children of Tantalus: Niobe & Pelops, The Road to Thebes: Niobe & Amphion, and Arrows of Artemis: Niobe & Chloris.* In what follows, we assume that you have read all three novels.

Several years after finishing the first edition of this novel, we decided to issue a new edition in response to comments from readers. We heard that you would find a character list and family tree diagram helpful – and that standardizing the spelling (as opposed to sticking with transliterations from Greek) would make it easier to read. And so we also take this opportunity to share with you some thoughts about the story, the setting, and the characters.

Arrows of Artemis continues the stories of the children of Tantalus – Pelops, Niobe, and to a lesser extent, Broteas – until the deaths of Niobe's children (traditionally called the Niobids). The myths say that the children were slaughtered by the deities Apollo and Artemis. But while we love writing about Greek gods, we do not actually believe in them; we think someone else – a mortal – must have killed Niobe's children. The question then becomes: who has escaped accusation of mass murder for millennia?

The first novel we wrote in the Tapestry of Bronze series was *Jocasta: The Mother-Wife of Oedipus*. While doing the research for *Jocasta*, we examined many myths and myth fragments, and determined that Pelops was probably responsible for the deaths of the Niobids. We believe he had motive, means, and opportunity – and a personality consistent with committing this crime.

Let's first look at motive: what reason could Pelops have had to murder his nieces and nephews? Unfortunately nephews, nieces, and sometimes even sons have been killed throughout history in order to clear dynasties for the ambitious. Both Pelops and Niobe produced large numbers of children; the region may have not been able to support so many potential kings and queens.

And the children of Niobe and Amphion were probably more capable than the children of Pelops and Hippodamia. We know that Chloris won the footrace of the first girls' games, so she was physically fit. Though raised in poverty, Amphion became a powerful king; he was also a gifted musician. He loved his brother Zethos, and there is no hint of rivalry or animosity in their legend. Perhaps we are ascribing too many good qualities to Amphion, but it seems to us that he must have been vigorous, intelligent, and emotionally stable; he could have passed on these qualities to his children. Pelops was certainly charming and capable, but he and his wife Hippodamia – both abused by their fathers – performed very dark deeds. Pelops murdered a guest at one of the Olympic Games, and Hippodamia killed her stepson. Both Pelops and Hippodamia were associated with the murder of the charioteer Myrtilus – perhaps excusable if Myrtilus was trying to rape Hippodamia – but according to the stories they broke faith with an important ally.

Of Amphion and Niobe's children, only Chloris survived, and she became the mother of Nestor: he is not mentioned in *Arrows of Artemis* but gained a reputation for wisdom. On the other hand, several descendants of Pelops and

Hippodamia were responsible for horrific acts. (See *Clytemnestra: The Mother's Blade* for more on the sons and grandsons of Pelops as well as a little about Nestor.)

Pelops and Amphion must originally have had a strong alliance. But over time Thebes' status increased. The construction of the walls might give Pelops concern about the loyalty of Amphion and Niobe; and he probably feared that their many children would surpass his own. Although the princes and princesses other than Chloris died, as did Amphion, Niobe did not. Did Pelops spare his sister in particular? And is it significant that she chose, afterwards, to return to Lydia rather than to go live with her brother?

While we invented the event that triggered the mass murder, Chloris' rejection of Pelops is not implausible. Marriages between uncles and nieces was common, and after the exile and death of Hippodamia it seems reasonable that Pelops would seek a new wife.

So, how did the Niobids actually die? The arrows of Apollo were supposed to be gold, and the arrows of Artemis silver – but other myths say the arrows were invisible. Apollo was often blamed for the unexpected deaths of men (not just the Niobids), while Artemis held responsible for the unexpected deaths of women. Poison, administered one way or another, seems likely. Being a powerful king, he could have found such means; as Niobe's brother, he or his agents would have opportunity. Afterwards Pelops could easily spread a story about the gods that was convenient to him – even blaming Niobe by claiming she had insulted the gods. Having returned to Lydia, she could not contradict him. And Pelops was already known for inventing or at least retelling tales about the gods, such as his death and resurrection in *Children of Tantalus.*

The king who followed Niobe and Amphion was Laius, who had lived with Pelops since childhood. Laius could not have taken the throne of Thebes without Pelops' support. Of course, Laius also had motive to murder the children of Amphion and Niobe, so he is another possible suspect in the deaths of the Niobids. However, given what we have gleaned from the myths about the personalities of the two men, we believe that Pelops was the perpetrator and Laius the pawn.

The goddess Artemis is said to have hunted with a band of virginal female friends; in our telling, this became the itinerant band of devotees known as the Maidens of Artemis. We made Chloris one of their number for several reasons. If Niobe had fourteen children – seven sons and seven daughters – we needed a reason that the daughters, especially, would not be married and gone from Thebes at the time of the murders. We solved this problem by making most of the daughters younger, and creating a reason for Chloris not to marry early. This also gave us the opportunity to further develop the cult of Artemis, which is important in other Tapestry of Bronze novels.

Niobe returns to Lydia, to her father's palace. Her father King Tantalus, is both old and ill. The myths say this particular Tantalus was punished after death for his misdeeds, by being forced to stand in a river that retreated when he bent down to drink and under a fruit tree with branches that rose out of reach when he tried to eat. We represented this myth by giving him Type 1 diabetes, which can make sufferers perpetually hungry and thirsty no matter how much they eat and drink.

Niobe never recovered from the deaths of most of her children, but was said to spend her time weeping on Mount Sipylus, until the gods took pity on her and turned her into a rock. The rock can still be seen if you travel today to Manisa, Turkey, or more easily if you visit our website (on the *Arrows of Artemis* page), with Victoria kneeling before it. The statue ascribed to Broteas is a few miles down the road from the Niobe rock; carved into the cliff, it can be glimpsed from the parking lot of a picnic area dedicated to Cybele. Given the steepness of the slope, the scree and the thorn bushes, it's extremely hard to reach; hence, no photo is offered.

Discovering this unsolved (indeed, largely undetected) mass murder in the myths – and realizing that so many clues pointed to Pelops – we felt compelled to tell the tale. Poor Niobe, blamed for the deaths of her children through the millennia, when they were certainly murdered by someone else! This seemed cruel insult heaped upon terrible injury, and we wanted to correct the record – or at least call it into question. Interestingly, in the myths, Apollo and Artemis realize that they overreacted by murdering the Niobids, and express regret. Though they could not bring the Niobids back to life, they awarded a very long life thread to Chloris' son Nestor in recompense.

Thank you for joining our exploration of the lives and deaths of these characters, and perusing our theory about the most likely murderer. We hope you will enjoy the other novels in the Tapestry of Bronze series; to learn more, please visit our website www.tapestryofbronze.com.

Thanks for reading!

Victoria Grossack & Alice Underwood

CAST OF CHARACTERS

MORTALS

Actaeon. A legendary hunter, killed by Artemis for spying on her bath.

Aeacus. King of the island of Aegina, which was named for his late mother Aegina, Thebe's sister; he is also a priest, so devoted to the gods that he prefers to spend his time in Delphi.

Aegina. Deceased sister of Thebe, mother of Aeacus.

Aeolius. A wealthy sea captain and friend of Pelops.

Alcathous. A younger son of Pelops and Hippodamia.

Alexandros. An alias used by Prince Broteas of Lydia.

Alkippe. Princess of Pisa, daughter of Oenomaus by his daughter Hippodamia.

Alphenor. Eldest son of Amphion and Niobe.

Amphion. King of Thebes, known for his musical ability and for building the city walls.

Antiope. Queen of Sicyon, wife of Epopeus, niece and ex-wife of Regent Lycus of Thebes; mother of Amphion and Zethos.

Anyte. A Maiden of Artemis.

Arachne. A mortal woman who, legend has it, offended Athena by claiming she could weave better than the goddess.

Astycratia. Daughter of Amphion and Niobe; one of the gates is named for her.

Astydamia. Daughter of Pelops and Hippodamia and Queen of Tiryns.

Atreus. Eldest son of King Pelops of Pisa. Brother and rival of Thyestes.

Batia. A Maiden of Artemis.

Broteas. Prince of Lydia, son of Tantalus and Dione, elder brother of Pelops and Niobe.

Butes. Prince of Athens; brother of Erechtheus, Procne and Philomela.

Cadmus. Legendary founder of Thebes.

Callisto. A legendary follower of Artemis, killed for breaking her vow of chastity.

Chabrias. A Theban soldier.

Chaerilis. A Theban soldier, uncle of Chabrias.

Chloris. Eldest daughter of Amphion and Niobe; one of the gates is named for her.

Chrysippus. Son of King Pelops of Pisa by his mistress Danais.

Cleodoxa. A daughter of Amphion and Niobe; one of the gates is named for her.

Copreus. A younger son of Pelops and Hippodamia.

Creon. Son of Menoeceus; brother of Jocasta.

Damasichthon. A son of Amphion and Niobe.

Danais. Pelops' mistress, died giving birth to their son Chrysippus.

Dione. Queen of Lydia, wife of Tantalus, mother of Broteas, Pelops and Niobe.

Dirke. Now deceased, she was wife of Regent Lycus of Thebes. The spring outside the Ogygia Gate is named for her as it is where she died.

Dolichus. Servant of the Tiresias.
Dysponteus. Prince of Pisa, son of Oenomaus and Evarete.
Ekhinos. A peasant who serves Hippodamia in exile.
Electryon. King of Mycenae; husband of Eurydike.
Epopeus. King of Sicyon, husband of Antiope, father of Lamedon.
Erechtheus. King of Athens; brother of Butes, Procne and Philomela.
Eudoxa. A daughter of Amphion and Niobe; one of the gates is named for her.
Europa. Mortal princess seduced by Zeus in the form of a white bull; she gave her name to Europe.
Euryanassa. Wife of Prince Broteas of Lydia.
Eurydike. A daughter of Pelops and Hippodamia, sister of Atreus and Thyestes. Queen of Mycenae, wife of King Electryon.
Euxenos. Naucles' business partner; father of Melanthe.
Evarete. Former queen of Pisa; mother of Hippodamia.
Exarchos. Pisatan steward who formerly served as a herald.
Geranor. A Lydian soldier in service to Prince Broteas.
Gogos. Younger son of Laius by Nerissa
Hippodamia. Daughter of King Oenomaus of Pisa; wife of Pelops.
Hippodamus. Prince of Pisa; son of Oenomaus by his daughter Hippodamia.
Idmon. Son of Zethos and Thebe; he was named for the foster-father of Zethos and Amphion..
Ilioneus. A son of Amphion and Niobe.
Iopa. A peasant woman who serves Hippodamia in exile.
Ismenus. A son of Amphion and Niobe.
Jocasta. A noble Theban girl; daughter of Menoeceus and sister of Creon.
Kallias. A sculptor.
Labdacus. Former king of Thebes who was killed by the Theban people; father of Laius.
Laius. A prince of Thebes; son of Labdacus.
Lamedon. Son of King Epopeus of Sicyon.
Letreus. A younger son of King Pelops of Pisa.
Lycus. Now deceased; served as regent of Thebes.
Melanthe. A Theban girl, daughter of Euxenos.
Menoeceus. A Theban nobleman, father of Creon and Jocasta.
Myrtilus. Charioteer for King Oenomaus, now a ghost haunting Pelops.
Naucles. A wealthy trader; old friend of Queen Niobe.
Neleus. King of Pylos.
Nerissa. Sister of Danais, mistress of Laius.
Nikippe. Daughter of Pelops and Hippodamia
Nikippes. A young Pisatan of noble birth.
Niobe. Queen of Thebes; sister of Pelops, wife of Amphion, mother of fourteen children.
Oenomaus. Former king of Pisa, father of Hippodamia; slain by Pelops.
Ogygia. A daughter of Amphion and Niobe; one of the gates is named for her.
Okyllus. A Pisatan nobleman.

Pelops. King of Pisa, husband of Hippodamia, son of Tantalus and Dione, brother of Broteas and Niobe.
Pelorus. A young Theban nobleman.
Pentheus. King of Thebes in the time of Dionysus.
Perseus. The legendary founder of Mycenae; son of Zeus by the mortal Danaë.
Phaedimus. A son of Amphion and Niobe.
Philomela. A princess of Athens, sister of Erechtheus and Butes.
Phokos. One-armed Theban nobleman.
Phthia. A daughter of Amphion and Niobe; one of the gates is named for her.
Pittheus. A younger son of Pelops and Hippodamia.
Polydorus. Elder son of Laius and Nerissa
Polyxo. Herb woman of Pisa, mother of Danais and Nerissa.
Rhodia. A well-born Theban girl; daughter of a midwife.
Selene. A Maiden of Artemis.
Sipylus. A son of Amphion and Niobe.
Spartoi. Nobles of Thebes, also known as "Sown Men."
Stymphalus. King of Arcadia.
Tantalus (1). King of Lydia; father of Pelops and Niobe. Sometimes called "Old Tantalus."
Tantalus (2). A son of Amphion and Niobe.
Tantalus (3). Son of Broteas and Euryanassa.
Tereus. King of Thrace.
Thebe. Wife of Zethos.
Theora. A Theban midwife.
Thyestes. Second son of King Pelops of Pisa. Brother and rival of Atreus.
Tiresias. Title given to an important Hellene seer; considered the Voice of Apollo and a servant of Athena.
Vassos. A friend of Laius.
Wave. One of Pelops' horses, given to him by Aeolius.
Wind. One of Pelops' horses, given to him by Aeolius.
Zethos. Fraternal twin brother of Amphion; husband of Thebe and father of Idmon. Master of the Herds.
Zeuxippe. Queen of Sicyon, daughter of Lamedon.

DEITIES

Aphrodite. Olympian, goddess of love. Married to Hephaestus; lover of Ares, by whom she has a daughter, Harmonia. Patron of Corinth.
Apollo. Olympian, god of light (the sun), prophecy, music, healing and plague. Twin brother of Artemis.
Ares. Olympian, god of war. Lover of Aphrodite, father of Harmonia.
Artemis. Olympian, goddess of the hunt and childbirth and associated with the moon. Twin sister of Apollo.
Athena. Olympian, goddess of wisdom, war and weaving. Patron of Athens.
Clotho. One of the three Fates, the youngest, who collects the material for life

threads and spins it.

Cronus. Once ruler of the Titans (a generation of gods); husband of Rhea, and father of Zeus, Hades, Poseidon, Hestia, Demeter and Hera.

Demeter. Olympian, goddess of the harvest. Mother of Persephone.

Dionysus. Olympian, god of wine. Son of Zeus by Semele, a daughter of Cadmus and Harmonia.

Eos. Goddess of the dawn.

Eros. Son of Aphrodite; god of lust.

Hades. God of the Underworld.

Hephaestus. Olympian, god of crafts and the forge. Married to Aphrodite.

Hera. Olympian, goddess of marriage. Patron of Argos.

Hermes. Olympian, god of lies, thieves, messengers; guides the newly dead to Hades.

Hestia. Goddess of the hearth, she gave up her throne in Olympus to tend the central fire.

Leto. Mother of Apollo and Artemis.

Persephone. Daughter to Demeter and Zeus; wife of Hades.

Poseidon. Olympian, god of the sea, horses and earthquakes.

Prometheus. A god known for giving fire to mankind.

Rhea. Wife of Cronus, mother of Zeus, Hera, Hestia, Hades, Poseidon and Demeter. In order to save her son from her husband's wrath, she had to hide Zeus in a remote cave, protected by a mastiff guard-dog.

Uranus. Former ruler of the gods. Father of Cronus, castrated and deposed by him.

Zeus. Olympian; king of the gods. God of oaths and hospitality (xenia).

FAMILY TREE

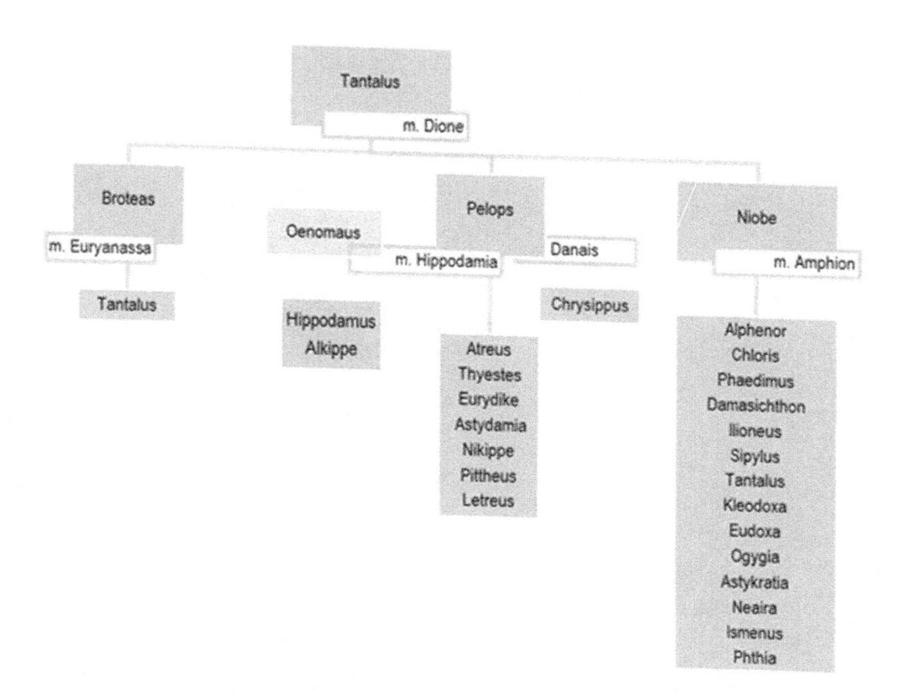
Tantalus
m. Dione
Broteas
m. Euryanassa
Tantalus
Oenomaus
Hippodamus
Alkippe
Pelops
m. Hippodamia
Danais
Chrysippus
Atreus
Thyestes
Eurydike
Astydamia
Nikippe
Pittheus
Letreus
Niobe
m. Amphion
Alphenor
Chloris
Phaedimus
Damasichthon
Ilioneus
Sipylus
Tantalus
Kleodoxa
Eudoxa
Ogygia
Astykratia
Neaira
Ismenus
Phthia

Made in the USA
Monee, IL
11 May 2021

68206714R00216